CW00537811

PRAISE

"*The Sister Knot* is a moving, thorough, and entrancing novel about how two orphaned young Berlin women become each other's family during and after the Holocaust."
SIMONE YEHUDA, CONTRIBUTING AUTHOR OF *THE ONES WHO REMEMBER: SECOND-GENERATION VOICES OF THE HOLOCAUST* AND PLAYWRIGHT

"a rich exploration of how individuals can emerge from challenging beginnings, finding strength and comfort in each other, despite the different paths their lives take... beautifully written and emotionally charged."
DEEPAK SINGH, AUTHOR OF *YAAD MOHALLA*

"Liane follows a difficult path that includes an out-of-wedlock child and jail. Her close friend, Frima is adopted into a loving family looking for a traditional daughter to bring them joy and grandchildren... The arc of their story will remain with readers long after the last page."
BETH KIRSCHNER, AUTHOR OF *COPPER DIVIDE*

"What a painting of the intense, complex, difficult and joyful rhythms and layers of women's relationships to one another."
RUSTY ALLEN, AUTHOR OF *ELLA'S WAR*

ABOUT THE AUTHOR

Ann writes novels, stories, memoir, poems, and essays. Her awards include a Pushcart Prize nomination for creative nonfiction, the Walter Sullivan prize in fiction, an Editors' Choice selection by Historical Novel Review, and St. Lawrence Book Award Finalist nomination. Ann's fiction credits include the novels *One the Shore, Tazia and Gemma, A Brain. A Heart. The Nerve., The Great Stork Derby,* and *One Person's Loss.* And short stories in *North American Review, Sewanee Review, PRISM International, Ascent, The Long Story,* and elsewhere. In addition to writing, she has a doctorate in developmental psychology, a Master of Fine Arts in fiber, and certification as an end-of-life doula.

asewovenwords.com

The SISTER KNOT

ANN S. EPSTEIN

www.vineleavespress.com

The Sister Knot
Copyright © 2024 Ann S. Epstein

All rights reserved.
Print Edition
ISBN: 978-3-98832-057-5
Published by Vine Leaves Press 2024

No parts of this publication may be reproduced, stored in a retrieval system, or transmitted in any form or by any means, electronic, mechanical, photocopying, recording, or otherwise, without the prior written permission of the copyright owner.

This book is sold subject to the condition that it shall not, by way of trade or otherwise, be lent, resold, hired out, or otherwise circulated without the publisher's prior consent in any form of binding or cover other than that in which it is published and without a similar condition including this condition being imposed on the subsequent purchaser. Under no circumstances may any part of this book be photocopied for resale.

This is a work of fiction. Any similarity between the characters and situations within its pages and places or persons, living or dead, is unintentional and coincidental.

Cover design by Jessica Bell
Interior design by Amie McCracken

To the women who sustain one another with love and friendship

CONTENTS

PART ONE:
LIANE (1946)

CHAPTER 1

The mildewed hallways reeked of garlic and piss as we climbed to the sixth-floor apartment that would be our home until, hopefully, they found each of us a better one. A sign on the door, in large blue letters framed by sunflowers, read "Oyf Haskhole" in Yiddish.

"Camp Beginning," the chaperone translated, giving us our first English lesson. For Frima, me, and four other children, it was the beginning of a new life after the Nazis had failed to end ours. They'd succeeded with our parents, which made us orphans, a label I scorned. It implied we were helpless and depended on adults. Frima and I had taken care of ourselves on the streets of Berlin for the past five years. We were resourceful enough to avoid the extermination camps which would have killed us too.

The six of us were a typical assortment of war children, although we were all Jewish. At Kloster Indersdorf, the institute for displaced youth near Dachau where we'd lived briefly before coming here, children came from many countries and every religion. War doesn't discriminate. We six were chosen because a Jewish-American agency sponsored us. Our group included a boy and a girl between three and five, who'd been too young to know their ages or parents' names when they were hidden. The Institute had named them Mendel and Berta. They looked like a miniature old man and woman but were quiet and would be adopted easily if prospective families didn't object to their thumb-sucking and bed-wetting. Two older boys, Salomon and Reuven, were in their mid-teens, a couple of years older than Frima and me. Their attitude was that because they'd suffered, the world owed them a living. I knew we had to go out and earn it.

We'd walked the few blocks to Oyf Haskhole after descending the stairs from a train that ran high above the ground. Miss Stone, the dumpling-shaped woman with springy gray curls in charge of us, called it "the elevated." As we rattled along the tracks, I looked into the upper-story windows of the buildings we passed and wondered if the tenants had learned to blot out the sound of the trains at night. Frima and I had done that at the Institute, only there, instead of trains, we shut our ears to the nightmare screams of children who had survived the camps.

There were almost as many signs labeling things here as we'd grown up with in Germany. The one at the station platform said "Fordham Road" and the street we turned onto was called "Morris Avenue." Frima and I would have to learn English quickly to get around the Bronx as readily as we'd navigated Berlin. As far as my eyes could see, there were few landmarks to help us. All the buildings looked identical to ours: dirty red brick, three to six floors tall, many with street-level store fronts. On either side of our entrance was a butcher and a fish store. Neither smelled too fresh but women in summer dresses, carrying satchels, passed through their doors.

I could feel our neighbors' eyes staring at us through their peepholes when we passed their doors, as if we were the Gestapo coming to round them up. For a moment, everything seemed backward. Before Miss Stone herded us into our apartment, 6F, one of the boys asked about an unmarked door next to it. She told him that it opened onto a staircase that led up to the roof. He asked if people tried to escape there. "That's where we hang the wash," she explained. Another child worried about where we'd dry our laundry in winter if there was snow on the roof. "Don't concern yourselves," said Miss Stone. "All you children will be gone by then." She no doubt meant well, but I didn't believe her. Promises were as empty as unfilled stomachs.

We'd barely stepped inside and set down our own satchels when shouting erupted in the hallway. When our chaperone opened the door, a rotten cabbage sailed through and bounced off the wall before she closed it. The door was made of thick metal, but it couldn't blot out the angry words our neighbors were chanting. We didn't have to speak English to understand them. "Child psychopaths," they screamed. "Their minds and bodies are diseased."

"They'll infect the families who adopt them."

"They'll infect our entire country."

"Death to vermin."

Insects, rats, or subhumans. *Untermenschen* was what Nazis called Jews in Germany. We hadn't been warned that many Americans felt the same way, but it didn't surprise me. Nastiness lives everywhere, sometimes hiding behind a nice front. It was too soon to tell about Miss Stone or the people who'd paid our way here, but I knew better than to let down my guard.

Miss Stone pointed to the kitchen. We instinctively huddled under the table but were told it wasn't necessary here. Instead we stood, still in a tight group. The chaperone picked up the telephone next to the sink and explained she was calling the building's super, Anoush Kasparian.

"Hello, Mr. Kasparian? This is Shirley Stone, the caseworker from the National Refugee Service. There's a disturbance on the sixth floor. I'd appreciate your assistance."

I assumed the authorities here were on the side of the mob, the same as in Germany. So I was surprised when, two minutes later, I heard the super berating the people in the hall. "Amot! Shame on you. You sought refuge in America when you fled your homelands, just like I fled Armenia after the Turks butchered us. T'voghnel! Leave these poor children in peace."

The shouting continued but soon after Mr. Kasparian threatened to evict everyone, the grumbling died down and we heard their footsteps retreating. Miss Stone looked through the peephole and opened the door to a small but wiry man with a bristly mustache holding a big hammer in one hand and a crowbar in the other. He put them behind his back as he bowed to her and smiled gently at us. The super told our caseworker to call him if there was any further trouble and before he left, he addressed us directly, "Be good, children. Prove them wrong."

Miss Stone showed us our bedrooms, boys in one and girls in the other, at opposite ends of the hall. She slept in the living room on a foldout couch, which she closed during the day. Each bedroom had a three-drawer dresser and a shared closet, more than enough space since we had so few things to unpack. We each had our own night-stand though, which held a lamp and an illustrated book. Berta's was *The Margaret Tarrant Nursery Rhyme Book*; Frima's was *Grimm's Fairy Tales*; mine was *Hans Christian Anderson's Fairy Tales*. The drawings in Frima's were dark and ugly; mine were bright and pretty. We traded books. It was easier than switching beds.

When our caseworker came in to make sure we were settled, she said that when we were adopted we'd each have so many clothes and shoes that we could fill an entire dresser and closet of our own. I waited for her to say we'd have our own bookcases too. Instead, she looked at the object I'd placed beside my book and wrinkled her nose. "What's that piece of trash?"

"It's not trash," I said. "It's sculpture." I'd begun assembling small statues soon after I landed on the street. It satisfied my need to put back together what I'd lost, although the works were as vague and abstract as what I sought to recapture. At first, I found wood and metal scraps in old buildings abandoned before the war. As children, we knew little about Germany's failing economy but saw beggars pore through garbage bins. We never expected to scrounge ourselves someday. Once the war heated up, I collected the defective parts piled outside muni-tions plants before they were loaded onto trains to be melted down and remade. Later still, it was easy to find splintered wood, twisted iron, and other odds and ends in the rubble left by Allied bombs.

At first, Frima couldn't understand my interest in "trash" either but she was curious about how I made the sculptures. I stole a rasp to file down sharp metal scraps, and for jagged wood, I snuck into a carpen-ter's shop to take sheets of sandpaper; I figured he wouldn't miss one or two. Sometimes just rubbing two scraps together was enough to smooth their edges. Meanwhile, our edges were getting rougher. The biggest problem was attaching the parts. I tried to cook up glue from the bones of dead fish on the riverbank, but that took water and heat, things we needed for ourselves. Ditto strips of leather or rubber, which we stuffed inside the soles of our holey shoes. Eventually, I settled on wire, which was easy to find outside the factories and inside the wreckage.

Before long, Frima started to bring me things that she found on her own foraging trips. Watching me work was as much a distraction for her as making the sculptures was for me. Her best "find" was two slender rods with metal bands around the middle that made them look as though they were embracing. I mounted them on a chunk of wood for balance and added thin curly wires streaming down from the top of one rod and short, thick bolts sticking straight out from the other. Frima named it *Sisters*. That's the sculpture that was on my nightstand.

"This isn't art. It's trash," Miss Stone repeated. She asked if I had more, but before I could answer, she dumped the ten inside my satchel onto my bed. "Down the incinerator they go."

Frima grabbed the woman's arm. "Who are you to say what art is? And which of our belongings we can keep? These are Liane's. If you take them, that's stealing."

Miss Stone stared at Frima's iron grip until Frima let go and replaced it with an iron stare. The caseworker's face softened but her voice was still firm. "It's a small apartment for seven people. There's not much room as it is and we need to fill it with beautiful things. Liane can keep one." The lady wasn't a pushover. I had to give her that. Miss Stone told me to choose. I told Frima to choose for me. Of course, she picked *Sisters*.

Although the apartment was crowded, it was spacious compared to the places we'd holed up in the last five years. Sometimes I pinched my elbow to convince myself I was really here. The kitchen table was big enough to seat everyone. The bathroom, though small, was a luxury. Miss Stone vowed to find bigger and better homes for all of us. "The more of you I get adopted, the more donations NRS will receive to bring others." She said it typically took six weeks to place younger children and up to three months for older ones. Boys were harder than girls, but I knew Frima and I wouldn't be easy. Adoptive parents preferred children who were hidden to those who'd survived the camps or lived on the streets. They thought trauma made them bitter and tough; they were right. But we didn't care. Frima and I didn't want to be adopted. As she told me the night we left Germany, "Liane, we are all the family the other needs."

CHAPTER 2

We hadn't known each other when we were little. Frima's elementary school was in a wealthier neighborhood. But on the street, we grew closer than sisters. At first, we blended in with the other kids without arousing suspicion. There was so much poverty in Germany at the start of the war that their families, most of them not Jewish, had turned them out to fend for themselves. Later, as the war dragged on and Berlin was bombed, there were plenty of real orphans in the streets.

Frima and I met one night when we both sought shelter in an abandoned warehouse. When it was reclaimed as a munitions factory, we hid in the underbrush at the river's edge. If a member of the Gestapo stood on the banks to smoke, we escaped discovery by submerging ourselves in the water. Sometimes we hid in the nearby forests, but it was hard to find food there. In the city, bakers pitched stale loaves of bread behind their shops. Potatoes, which we dug up overnight in gardens, were as valuable as diamonds. Now and then we got lucky and found a carrot or an egg in the garbage. If we split up to search, we shared whatever we found. We lapped up water from puddles. Winter was harsh and food was scarcer, but the clean, fresh snow quenched our thirst.

As we got older and our bodies filled out, Frima and I began selling ourselves in exchange for something to eat and clothes, baubles, or a tube of lipstick to make us more desirable. We stopped hiding in the forest after that. It made us too dirty to attract men and besides, there were plenty of bombed-out buildings to sleep in by then. SS officers were the best customers because they had more money than soldiers. Many were not much older than us, and we preferred younger men who seemed sweeter, or at least safer, than older ones. A few even worried about us getting pregnant, but we assured them it was all "taken care of." We didn't admit we hadn't started getting periods yet in case it made us sound like babies. Frima and I soon learned how to flirt by batting an eye, licking our lips, or revealing more leg. It didn't take much to draw men's attention, and then we let them use their imaginations. Some liked us to say we were virgins. Others, that of all the lovers we'd had, they were the best. We told them whatever they wanted to hear.

Our lives at Oyf Haskhole were very different. Miss Stone wanted us to feel well cared for but not so comfortable that we'd regret leaving when the time came. She was strategic; I admired that. We adhered to a strict routine. The day began with a thorough washing, after which the caseworker checked us for lice and signs of infection in the deep sores that refused to heal. Miss Stone wasn't squeamish. I gave her credit for that too. Then we ate breakfast, beginning with Rice Krispies. Their snap, crackle, and pop was the rare thing that brought a smile to the wan faces of little Mendel and Berta. Miss Stone also fed us fried eggs, bread with butter and jam, and tall glasses of milk with Bosco chocolate syrup. She made us use knives and forks; the younger children had never learned how, and the older ones had forgotten. Mendel and Berta had to be constantly reassured there was plenty to eat, and even then, Miss Stone would find bread hidden under their mattresses. She worried about rats.

Next came English lessons. Miss Stone spoke to us in German with a few English words mixed in, gradually reversing their proportions. We learned the words for food, clothes, soap, and other common objects, practicing things we'd need to know when school began, like counting. Then we'd go to Zunder's Grocery Store one block over to try out what we'd learned. On the way, we passed the seltzer man and another selling produce from a horse-drawn cart. His celery looked as wilted as his horse. I wondered how Frima and I would have survived if the only customers available to us in Berlin were as pathetic as the men surrounding our camp in the Bronx.

One day, coming home from Zunder's, we walked by some boys playing stickball in the schoolyard. Salomon and Reuven climbed the fence to watch and asked Miss Stone if they could join them. "We'll whip their backsides," they said, although they used a cruder word. She told them they weren't ready to play with American children yet, though she'd get them ready by fall. Salomon jumped down inches from Miss Stone, which startled her, while Reuven wiped his nose and sneered, but neither said anything. I wondered if they'd try to get away from this camp the same way they'd escaped Arbeitsdorf, but none of us knew how to survive on our own here. Yet.

Lunch was cottage cheese and fruit, and more milk to strengthen our bones. After the meal, Miss Stone gave us each a dime to buy ice cream from the Good Humor or Bungalow Bar truck or sent us in pairs (older and younger, or boy and girl, but never the two older boys together) to Sis's Candy Store where we would get eight-cent egg creams and two-cent salted pretzel rods. Our treats were followed by a quiet "digestion period" in our bedrooms. Supposedly this was necessary because our stomachs were still delicate after years of starvation, but Frima and I suspected Miss Stone didn't want us to hear her making telephone calls in the kitchen, trying to find us homes. On days when Berta napped, we crept down the hallway to eavesdrop.

The third week of camp, we overheard "... a thirteen-year-old girl ... Quickly becoming proficient in English ... If so, it's not obvious ... Mature in some way, immature in others ... Oh yes, very healthy and putting on weight with the good food she's fed here ... Would you like to meet her? ... I understand. Take your time to look over the papers and then we'll set up a time."

Not knowing which of us Miss Stone was talking about, we tiptoed back to our room and sat under the open window. Frima clutched my hand and whispered, "We should have said we were sisters so they'd be forced to take us together." I said it wouldn't help. We'd met children at the Institute who'd been separated from their siblings and had no idea what happened to them. Besides, we looked nothing alike. No one would take us for sisters, let alone twins.

"Suppose the people on the phone want to meet you ... or me?" I asked.

"I swear I'll act so horribly that no one will want to adopt me," Frima said. I promised to do the same. Then we each bit the calloused pad on our index fingers until we drew blood and pressed our fingers together. We got back on our own beds quickly because we never knew when Miss Stone would come around to rouse us. A short rest period could mean she'd had a bad day and didn't want to listen to more rejections, or she'd had a good day and knocked off early after a success. A long rest could mean she refused to give up or was on a roll. That day was a short one.

Digestion and hand-and-face washing over, we'd troop off to Bryan or Devoe Park to try out our English with American children. Despite coaxing, Berta and Mendel were too shy and hid inside the wooden playhouse where they built tiny beds with twigs and spoke German to each other. The older boys walked up the slide or climbed up the monkey bars and rained down pebbles they'd stashed in their pockets, aggravating parents. Miss Stone spent a lot of time apologizing for their behavior, but I never saw a mother's hostile expression melt into understanding.

Frima and I sat on the swings practicing English with each other, out of Miss Stone's earshot. We took turns pretending to be glamorous women and smitten men. A conversation might go like this: "Hey doll, how'd you like to see a movie?"

"What does it cost, big boy?"

"Just the price of your hand on my arm, beautiful."

"Sold. One ticket and away we go."

When we tired of our game, we'd watch the people sitting on benches, eating paper cones of salted French fries slathered in ketchup. No matter how much food Miss Stone fed us, we were always hungry.

Sometimes at the park, I'd spot broken toy parts in the sandbox, wheel spokes on the bike path, or rusted bolts underneath the bench slats. I soon began to collect these; it was like an addiction I couldn't break. But, like an addict, I was afraid of being found out. I worried that Miss Stone would check inside my satchel so Frima volunteered to hide my finds in hers. She told me, "After I accused her of stealing from you, Miss Stone won't risk being accused of spying on me."

Late afternoon, we'd trudge back to the apartment for more lessons followed by dinner, an unvarying menu of meat, vegetables, and potatoes, except for Friday nights when Miss Stone lit Shabbas candles and we drank tiny glasses of watered-down wine and ate challah. I thought that observing Jewish rituals was senseless. Why practice a religion that wiped out our families and almost did away with us? I did enjoy the wine though and would have snuck a full-strength gulp if Miss Stone hadn't kept the bottle locked inside a cabinet. German soldiers never bought drinks for Frima and me. I guess they figured it was a waste of money when they could get what they wanted from us for the price of a sausage. Our fixation was reining in hunger, not getting drunk.

After dinner, everyone helped with the dishes and then it was story time. We didn't listen to Miss Stone tell us stories. Rather, she listened to ours. She said it was important for us to "get it all out" to heal our minds along with our bodies. We sat in a tight circle, "to feel protected," she said, and she never interrupted us. Berta couldn't remember the names of the Catholic family that took her in, but she talked about being hidden inside a trunk full of smelly blankets when the SS knocked on their door. Mendel slept in a barn, behind straw bales, and the farmer who hid him threatened that if Mendel didn't muck out the stables clean enough, he'd turn him in. Salomon and Reuven recounted the hard labor, meager rations, and random shootings at the work camp where the Nazis sent them. After two years, they escaped inside a coal car. They blackened their bodies and waited until nightfall so they would blend in with the darkness.

Frima and I spoke about hiding in root cellars and bombed-out buildings, scavenging in garbage dumps, and stealing cigarettes from sleeping drunks to trade for food. Miss Stone loved to hear about our constant hunger, knowing she could fill our bellies now. We told her whatever she wanted to hear, but neither of us spoke about the men who also filled us up.

When story time was over, Miss Stone did paperwork while we listened to the radio and read books from the traveling library. Sometimes I worked on my sculptures in the bedroom while Frima, her satchel open, alerted me to the caseworker's footsteps. Then it was lights out. We older kids didn't mind going to bed at the same time as the younger ones. Sleeping in a safe place was another luxury we'd never tire of. Frima and I lay on our pillows, clutching the single items we'd each rescued from childhood. Hers was a doll, Sugar, with a nearly-bald head and a faded dress torn off below its belly. Mine was a matted stuffed bear, minus one button eye, who I'd named Ittel Rosa as a toddler. I think it was after a friend, but I no longer remembered her or her family. I barely remembered my own.

Here's what I do remember: Loud knocking up and down the hallway, my mother hiding me in a crawl space under the floor. Before she put a rug over the loose boards, she handed me Ittel Rosa and said if I got scared and wanted to cry, to hug my bear. I buried my mouth in her fuzzy belly, and when, after two days, I crept out, I held her in front of me for protection. Now I used her to protect me from nightmares. She couldn't prevent them, but by holding her I could get back to sleep. Frima needed Sugar for the same reason. Frima's bad dreams were about real fears, like getting caught stealing or searching for food that disappeared just as she reached for it. It's hard to say what my nightmares were about. They were more abstract, like my sculptures.

On our third night of camp, Miss Stone told me and Frima that we'd have to give up sleeping with our bear and doll before we could be adopted. She wasn't being mean, she explained, but new families didn't want reminders of our old families. That's why she didn't even buy toys for Mendel and Berta, saving that privilege for their adoptive parents.

"Let go of your past and look to the future," Miss Stone urged. When I clung to Ittel Rosa and Frima clutched Sugar, the caseworker tried to reassure us, "When you're ready, that is." She didn't understand that being in a new country and living with strangers only strengthened our urge to hold onto those old connections.

Our routine was unvarying except for when Miss Stone took us on field trips to the public library, Bronx Zoo, or other places she said would show us life in our new country. Everyone was excited about seeing a baseball game at Yankee Stadium. We rode the elevated in the opposite direction from the one we'd traveled our first day here. This time, I wondered if the people in the apartments we passed looked out their windows at us. Mendel and Berta ran up and down the center aisle of the car, ignoring Miss Stone's pleas to sit still. They found it exhilarating to ride a train that was headed to a good place from which they would safely return. Salomon and Reuven also relished being on a train where they weren't crammed together with dead bodies held upright by live ones.

It was close to sundown when we got home, stuffed with hot dogs and Cracker Jacks and eager to collapse on our soft beds. Nevertheless, Reuven paused outside the apartment door and traced the letters on the sign. "Miss Stone," he asked, "why do you call this place a camp?"

"Because here you breathe fresh air and eat good food every day. The intention is to give the word camp the happy connotation it deserves."

Reuven snorted. "It's the other way around. Memories of the concentration camp blot out whatever you try to substitute." As we filed inside, he muttered to Salomon, "Sometimes I want to break free of this place too." Nothing against Miss Stone, but so did I.

CHAPTER 3

In mid-summer, Anoush knocked on the door and told Miss Stone that he had a surprise for the older kids. We followed him to the basement where he led us to a ping-pong table another tenant had left behind. He handed us a box filled with paddles and white plastic balls, showed us how to hit the balls over the net, and explained how to score the game. Miss Stone came down briefly to see what we were doing and pronounced it an "acceptable" way to release our anger.

When she left, Salomon said to me, "We'll let you girls win. One point for every kiss." Reuven pointed his paddle at Frima's breasts. "Two for showing us your titties."

We'd give them nothing. They had nothing of value to give us. I brandished my paddle. Frima and I took our places on one side of the table, the boys swaggered to other, and we matched them hit for hit, slice for slice, slam for slam. By the time we finished playing, half the balls were cracked and the net was ripped in three places. We'd stopped keeping score.

The game was diverting. We didn't have to think or talk about where we'd been or might be going. But after a week I was bored. Frima had begun to let the boys win every volley, so I knew she was too. One afternoon we got off the swings in the park and approached two Jewish-looking girls about our age, making sure Miss Stone saw us. Later, when we told her we'd made friends with them, that they were sisters, and had invited us to their house the next day, it sounded plausible. Miss Stone picked out the nicest clothes she could find for us to wear. We assured her the girls had given us thorough directions and we could find our way there without her.

The older boys trailed us downstairs. "Where are you really going?" Salomon asked. We told him it was none of his business and that if he breathed a word to Miss Stone, we'd tell her about the coins he and Reuven filched from someone's storage bin. It was one thing to play ping pong with them in the privacy of the basement, but we had no intention of being seen with them in public. We didn't associate with Jewish boys on the streets of Berlin either. If they ever got picked up, being circumcised would have marked them as Jews. We'd be tagged along with them and either shot on the spot or packed onto trains. On our own, Frima and I could pass for Catholics or Lutherans. No one bothered to ask our last names. She was no longer a Gersten and I stopped being an Asher.

Germans, at least those who believed the party line, were convinced that all Jews had large noses, dark eyes, and kinky black hair. Frima's wavy red hair, green eyes, and straight nose got by without a second look. My frizzy brown curls were passable; my hazel eyes unremarkable. Only the slight bump in my nose sometimes got noticed. Once an SS officer asked me whether there were Jews in my family. He claimed to be an anthropologist and said my ears and profile struck him as Semitic. I looked offended and walked away, outwardly calm but quaking inside. I went straight to a store that sold religious articles and stole two big crosses for Frima and me to wear.

After ditching Salomon and Reuven, we headed east on Fordham Road. All we saw were more apartments and neighborhood stores, but the wide thoroughfare promised something more interesting ahead. We'd have taken a street car if we'd had the nickel fare, only we didn't have any money. Yet. Wilting under the summer sun, we were on the verge of turning back when the apartments grew sparser and the stores taller, with large overhead signs. We walked toward the one that said "Uptown—it's Alexander's" and came to an intersection with the Grand Concourse. Grand it was, broader than Berlin's boulevards, lined with stores, restaurants, and movie theaters. Frima and I knew we'd struck gold.

Some of the movie houses were grimy, like the seedy places where cheaper men took us back home, but Loew's Paradise loomed like a palace. When the big clock over the entrance struck 2:00, a mechanical knight rode forth to slay a fire-breathing dragon. Frima and I pretended to study the movie posters out front while giving the eye to the prospects who walked by. It wasn't long before two young men in uniform invited us to "see the show." Frima and I winked at each other, pleased we hadn't lost our knack for picking up suitors, what we called "freier" in German.

Inside, we were awed by the lobby's marble pillars and goldfish pond. The men led us up the carpeted stairs, lined with tapestries, and ushered us to the last row of the balcony. Overhead, the ceiling glittered with jeweled constellations, which gave us something pretty to look at while they did their business. No one pretended to watch the movie. We all left in the middle of a reel. "Money or food?" my freier asked when we were back on the sidewalk.

"Both," I answered.

We headed further east, stopping at Accessories Galore, where Frima and I each chose a scarf. I was drawn to a gold bracelet, but that would have been hard to explain to Miss Stone. More believable was that our new friends had given us their old scarves, especially if we wrinkled them on the way home. Our next destination was Jahn's Ice Cream Parlor, decorated like the Gay Nineties with stained glass Coca-Cola light fixtures and booths with red leather cushions. The men treated us to sundaes. You could hardly see the ice cream under the whipped cream, hot fudge sauce, nuts, and sprinkles. Frima's soldier challenged mine to eat a kitchen sink, twenty scoops in a basin-size bowl. If you ate the whole thing by yourself, Jahn's gave you another for free. My "date" didn't want to try, but Salomon or Reuven could have done it with room to spare.

When we left Jahn's, the men asked if Frima and I wanted them to escort us home and sighed with relief when we declined. They gave us each a dollar and fifty cents and took off down the hill. We turned uphill, running, skipping, and panting along Fordham Road until we were back at Morris Avenue. Miss Stone admired our scarves and offered to iron them. She asked if we were hungry but we said our friends had treated us to ice cream. Our caseworker was pleased that our visit had been a success. We delighted her further by saying we'd been invited to come back.

She also claimed credit for herself. "My lessons are paying off. I'll find you new homes before you know it." She hesitated. "Do you suppose your friends'...?"

I was terrified she'd ask us to get their telephone number so she could inquire whether their parents were interested in adoption. Scarier was the dreamy look on Frima's face. "I expect their family has its fill of girls," I said. Miss Stone slipped a meatloaf into the oven and said not to worry, there were plenty of childless couples or parents with sons who'd appreciate a daughter.

After that, Frima and I visited our friends twice a week. We would have gone more but it didn't seem realistic that their family would invite us that often. Thankfully, those two girls never returned to the park. On our second excursion, we lingered in the theater lobby to stare at the marble fountain with a sculpture of a child on a dolphin. We imagined ourselves leading magical lives, riding sea creatures across an endless ocean. The third time, when the men were done, we persuaded them to pay and leave us at Loew's to watch the movie. This arrangement satisfied everyone and we used it from then on. Frima adored the film *Margie*, a romance about a mother who tells her teenage daughter about having to choose between three suitors for the homecoming dance. She dreamed herself into the role of the daughter. I preferred *Two Sisters From Boston*, in which a pair of rich socialites thumb their noses at society to sing in low-class dives. When the more prudish sister joined the gutsier one, it reminded me of how I'd had to persuade Frima to sell her body on the streets. We joked that as a redhead, she should have been the more fiery one, but mousy me turned out to be the rebel. Even though I liked that movie more than Frima did, we both applauded when the two sisters stood together against everyone else's disapproval.

After leaving Loew's, Frima and I raced giddily from store to store. Alexander's sold nice clothes at discounted prices, with bins for slightly defective garments. We bought these, telling Miss Stone they were hand-me-downs from our friends and soon invented friends for our friends. Miss Stone was happy that more people had accepted us and wanted to help. Even American Jews had been reluctant at first, afraid our bad reputation would tarnish theirs. A month into our subterfuge, our caseworker announced that to reciprocate their kindness, she'd make brownies and chocolate chip cookies for us to bring next time. The whole apartment turned as hot as the oven where she baked them. Frima and I slipped the goodies to Salomon and Reuven to continue buying their silence. They ate half and sold the rest on the playground. We were all enterprising.

Our favorite store was Woolworth's, also called the "five and ten." All the merchandise was displayed on the counter so we could steal things with ease—jewelry, makeup, candy. After some of our customers offered us cigarettes, Frima and I began to buy or shoplift these ourselves. We thought that smoking made us look more alluring, like the stars in the movies we devoured.

One day when we got home, we ran into Anoush downstairs. He smelled the smoke on our breath. His expression was more disappointed than disapproving. He pleaded. "Don't prove the neighbors right. Show them you're good girls, worthy of good homes. You are still young. I was already too old for school when I came here, but you can get an education. Do better than me, not be stuck in a basement." The super swiped at his eyes with a big, dirty handkerchief.

I didn't care what impression I made, but Frima grabbed my hand and dragged me to Sis's, where we stole a pack of Peppermint Life Savers and crunched them in our mouths on the way back. Miss Stone told us to tell our friends to please not fill up our stomachs with candy.

***

A week later, our caseworker was jubilant when Frima and I entered the apartment. She'd found a home for Berta with an older childless couple, and another family, who had a girl and wanted a boy, were interested in Mendel. "Now I can turn my full attention to finding families for you older children," Miss Stone said. Then a frown crossed her face as she explained that she was under pressure. The refugee program was expanding and NRS had bought a closed YMCA building in another part of the Bronx. Thirty new children would arrive by the end of summer, in time to enroll for the start of school. "I intend to find homes for you before then," Miss Stone promised. "I'll regard it as my failure if any of you move with me to the Y."

Frima crossed her fingers behind her back. I didn't know if she was hiding them from the caseworker or me. Salomon and Reuven shrugged. It made no difference to them. Wherever they lived, they'd claim it as their turf and defend it. I was upset, however. I'd learned how to navigate this neighborhood and find my way to a more enticing one. I had no idea where the Y was or whether Frima and I could get to another area as promising as the one we'd discovered.

Miss Stone, seeing my worried face, mistook it for discouragement. She followed Frima and me to our room and sat next to us on my bed, promising again that she'd find us each a home. Then she leaned over to embrace us. "Ugh!" She pulled back. The scent of the twenty-five cent bottles of perfume we'd swiped from Woolworth's an hour ago had hit her nostrils.

Frima and I rubbed our necks, but we couldn't disguise this smell as easily as the cigarette smoke. I giggled like the teenage daughter in the movie Frima liked and told Miss Stone that our friends' mother had let us try on her dresses and high heels and use her cosmetics.

Miss Stone didn't buy my story. I'd never seen her get angry, but she hissed. "I don't know where or how you got this cheap stuff, but I'm sure your friends' mother buys a more expensive brand." She snatched Frima's Sugar and my Ittel Rosa. "If you two are ready to wear perfume, you're ready to get rid of these." Then she, and our childhood toys, were out the door.

For the first time since being left alone, I let myself cry, pressing my fists into my cheeks and my forehead into my pillow. Frima sat beside me, dry-eyed, hands open in her lap.

Early next morning, before anyone else was awake, I crept downstairs to retrieve Sugar and Ittel Rosa from the trash bin. As I scurried to the stairwell, Anoush came out of his basement apartment to carry the garbage to the curb. Hugging our toys to my chest, I lied. "Last night, Frima and I decided we were too old for these. But we couldn't sleep, so I'm taking them back."

He nodded. "I kept a toy fire engine for years before giving it to a little boy whose family came to America with less than I did. It had a ladder that slid up and down. I still miss it." He patted my bear. "Some day, you'll give this to your own child. A bright ending to a dark past."

I smiled and hurried upstairs, then crawled into Frima's bed. We used to startle at the slightest noise, but now Frima slept soundly. I jostled her awake. She stretched and raised her eyebrows when I put my finger to my lips. Then I held up my bear and withdrew her doll from under my blouse. "They were on top of yesterday's newspapers, so they didn't get any new stains." I made Sugar dance a sort of shimmy.

Frima thrust the doll away. "Throw it back in the trash. I don't want it anymore."

I was stunned. I tried to sweet-talk her. "But Ittel Rosa will be lonely without Sugar."

"We'll be lonely if all we have is each other and a stupid old doll and stuffed bear." Frima took Ittel Rosa from my arms and wrapped me in hers. "We can keep getting food and clothes on the street, but it's risky. And temporary. If Miss Stone finds us homes, we'll get all we need to eat and wear forever. From a family."

"Two families," I reminded her. "One for you and one for me."

Frima hugged me tighter. "We'll refuse to be separated. Miss Stone has to find us a place together. Or two homes very close to each other."

The laugh that came out of my mouth tasted bitter. "Do you really trust our caseworker, or some strangers you've never met, to take better care of us than we do ourselves?"

Frima reminded me of what Mr. Kasparian had said the day he smelled cigarettes on our breath. "We can do better."

"Don't believe him," I said. "He's a dirty old man who thinks we'll give him sex in return for helping us get adopted." Frima winced. I snuggled with Ittel Rosa in my own bed until Miss Stone called us to breakfast. Frima left the room first. I put Ittel Rosa in my satchel along with Sugar. Frima might change her mind the next time soldiers' boots marched through her dreams.

CHAPTER 4

It was three days before Frima and I could reasonably claim another visit with our friends. Miss Stone told us to ask their mother to call her at lunch time, just to check in, but I knew she was checking up on us. I said the mother usually went shopping while we ate, but Miss Stone said, "No call, no more visits." I reassured Frima when we got downstairs that we had all day to think of an excuse for the missed call. We'd had years of practice making up excuses.

"I'm not worried about that," said Frima, but she walked fast, something she does when she's upset. Maybe she was still bothered by what I'd said about Anoush.

We wandered around Woolworth's, pocketing lipstick to put on when we crossed the street to Loew's Paradise for the one o'clock matinee. At noon, a mother with two small girls approached the lunch counter. Despite the heat, she wore black. A war widow. The woman lifted her daughters onto the stools and ordered two orange sodas, counting coins from a worn change purse. The older girl sipped slowly. The younger gulped, spilling half the drink down her dress.

"Mama," she cried. "Want more soda."

"I'm sorry sweetheart. I can only afford one apiece." The little girl continued to sob until her sister gave her what was left of hers. The child drank it but remained distraught as the mother led her daughters out of the store, leaving her change purse on the counter.

I scooped up the purse, which held fifteen dollars in bills and change, and slipped it into my pocket, shivering with excitement. Frima and I regularly took things from stores but we'd never stolen money from a person. It was an unspoken rule that I no longer saw a reason to obey.

Frima looked aghast. "That poor mother needs every penny to take care of her children."

"We need that money to take care of ourselves."

Frima held out her hand. I reluctantly gave her the purse. She raced out of the store just as the light on Grand Concourse changed to green and returned it to the mother. I saw the momentary panic in the woman's eyes as she considered what might have happened, followed by relief at what actually did. I couldn't hear, but I saw her deliver effusive thanks. She offered a bill to Frima who waved it away and dashed back into Woolworth's. I wished she'd accepted it. A dollar would have bought us ten round trips on the streetcar, enough to get us through the summer.

We didn't say anything as we made our way to Loew's and stood outside the theater. No men approached us, perhaps sensing the tension. By late afternoon, with heat radiating from the pavement, we were both ready to go home. I dreaded the walk, which would seem longer than usual given our silence. "Let's sneak onto the streetcar through the rear door," I suggested, "and bypass the fare." Frima looked skeptical. I cajoled. "Consider it practice for when we hop buses and trains to far-off destinations. We'll travel across America, just the two of us."

An approaching streetcar was a block away. "What if we get caught?" Frima asked.

"So what? We know how to evade the police. Besides, the penalty in this country isn't death. At worst, they'll send us to a juvenile home from which we can escape."

Frima shook her head and continued to walk west. I passed up a ride on the streetcar and caught up, matching her rapid pace. At the next corner, she slowed and took my hand, a gesture of forgiveness. At heart, Frima was the better person. She deserved a better life.

***

When we got to Oyf Haskhole, Miss Stone fluttered around the living room, straightening slip covers. She spoke breathlessly. "A couple. Interested in adopting a teenage girl. They'll be here after dinner." Apparently, in her excitement, she'd forgotten about the telephone call. I was relieved. I'd been so distracted after my tiff with Frima that I'd forgotten to think up an excuse.

Miss Stone filled a crystal bowl with rainbow-colored sucking candies. "First impressions carry the day. Or, in this case, the evening. I picked out a nice cotton skirt and blouse for you to wear and bought a pair of ruffled anklets." Her eyes were on the candy bowl so I couldn't see who "you" referred to. She handed me a dustcloth and pointed at the coffee table and lamp stand.

"But, Miss Stone..." I began.

"Wash your hair before dinner, dear, so it dries in those natural waves you were blessed with. Liane, would you polish her shoes?" Miss Stone hugged Frima. "Remember to cross your ankles when you sit down."

I dusted the furniture. Frima filled the bathtub. While she washed, I helped cook dinner— boiled chicken and string beans. A box of bakery cookies, tied with string, sat on the counter. I wondered if they were for only Frima and our guests or if the rest of us would get to share them. At meal time, I wasn't hungry, and Frima stared at her plate. I kicked her under the table as a signal to eat. I needed time to figure out what to do and I didn't want to arouse any suspicion.

After dinner, the boys did the dishes. Frima headed to the bedroom, Miss Stone pulled me aside. "Isn't this exciting?" she whispered, reminding me to help "spruce up" my friend.

Frima was already dressed when I entered our room and closed the door. "I'm not leaving you," she said, but her eyes gleamed as she looked in the mirror to brush her hair with long, firm strokes. She tossed her head and golden red waves framed her face and grazed her shoulders.

I sat on the floor and buffed her Mary Janes until they were bright enough to reflect the gleam in her eyes. "Go," I said, buttoning my mouth before I begged her to stay.

Frima knelt beside me and repeated what she'd often said. "You're all the family I need."

I buckled the shoes onto her feet and we stood up. "Well, I don't need you anymore. It was different in Berlin, when we helped each other survive, but here you'll only hold me back. I'm tired of carrying you along. I want to be free and go places you're afraid of." I sneered. "You don't even have the guts to sneak onto a streetcar."

Miss Stone called from the living room. "Frima, come meet Mr. and Mrs. Oberlander."

"You look nice." I stood behind Frima while she took a last peek in the mirror. Her eyes shone with pleasure; her mouth was pinched with pain. I nudged her out the door.

With Berta gone, the bedroom was all mine. I crawled under the covers with Ittel Rosa and blotted out the sounds in the next room, the trick I'd perfected at Kloster Indersdorf. The old lessons were still valuable. Here I was learning new ones; their worth remained to be seen.

PART TWO: FRIMA (1946–1947)

CHAPTER 5

They told Frima to call them Father and Mother, but she was afraid to jinx the adoption before it was final. Mr. and Mrs. Oberlander sounded too formal, so she opted for their first names, Otto and Greta, while privately practicing the last name that would someday be hers too. The Oberlanders had come here two decades ago, but their relatives, who'd stayed behind in Austria, had all been killed by the Nazis. Otto and Greta had chosen to adopt a teenager because she would give them grandchildren a decade or more sooner than a younger orphan.

Meanwhile, they wanted Frima to have a happy American childhood. By now, they were Americanized themselves. Their six-room apartment had a mahogany dining room set, slip covers on the love seats, bookshelves with *The World Book Encyclopedia* and *Shakespeare's Complete Works*, and *Life* and *National Geographic* fanned out on the coffee table. Greta ordered *Seventeen* for Frima. A Baldwin piano sat beneath the windows opposite a record cabinet. Frima liked to lie on a love seat and imagine herself dancing to songs like "Whatta Ya Gonna Do?" As Otto insisted, she slid each record back into its jacket before she put the next one on the turntable.

Frima had her own bedroom and bathroom. The Oberlanders' room was the largest. Greta called the third bedroom her sewing room, although she shopped at Bloomingdale's for Frima's clothes: pleated skirts, pointy-collared blouses, loafers. Otto gave Frima his "daddy shirts" to wear with jeans, and Greta gave her a locket. Frima gazed at the photo of the three of them when she practiced her new name. This ample wardrobe was matched by the lavish bedroom. Otto owned a furniture store that was thriving in the post-war boom. The "top of the line" rosewood set had twin beds covered with ruffled spreads and stuffed animals. The fanciest piece was a mirrored triple dresser. Frima moved aside the makeup tray from Greta and put *Sisters* in the center.

On the day before she'd left Oyf Haskhole, Miss Stone had given her a leather bag with a nightgown and change of underwear. Frima was allowed to pack only the book of fairy tales. The caseworker said that from now on, her parents would buy her everything. That night, when Miss Stone called "lights out," Liane took "Sisters" off her own night stand and put it in Frima's bag.

"Are you sure?" Frima asked. "It's your favorite sculpture. Also your best."

"It's your favorite too. And you found the parts."

"Promise me you'll make more."

Liane smiled. "I couldn't stop even if I wanted to."

Hearing Miss Stone's footsteps, Frima returned *Sisters* to Liane's night stand. "All set for tomorrow?" the caseworker asked. She hugged Frima, switched off their lamps, and left.

Liane, her face unreadable in the dark, sounded cross. "Why did you ...?"

Frima tiptoed to Liane's bed and slid in beside her. "Suppose Miss Stone checks to make sure I haven't taken anything else 'old' with me? I'll pack it just before I leave in the morning."

When Mrs. Oberlander saw *Sisters*, she tentatively said that it looked out of place on the dresser. Mr. Oberlander was direct. "A filthy old hunk of wood doesn't belong on fine furniture."

"It *is* old," said Frima. "And I found it in a pile of dirt. It stays where it is."

Greta wrung her hands. "Perhaps it's okay to hold onto one little piece of the past. Otto?"

He grunted. "For the rest of the summer. But when school starts, it goes."

"No." Frima moved *Sisters* closer to the front of the dresser. "Liane made this and she's a permanent part of me. The sculpture lives where I do." Mrs. Oberlander motioned her husband to follow her out. Frima sat on her bed, looking at *Sisters*. Because of the mirror, she could see it from the back. In fact, it was visible wherever she sat or stood. She and Liane were inseparable. But not the same.

Liane's father had died when she was three, his lungs damaged in the First World War, and her mother raised her alone by keeping house for well-off families. Frima's family had been comfortable. Her father was an accountant, her mother a homemaker, and her brother David, five years older than Liane, was a top student until the Nazis barred Jews from public schools. On the street, the girls became equals in poverty but were often at odds about what they were willing to do to survive. At first, while Frima didn't mind going through trash bins, only Liane was willing to steal. "I wasn't raised that way," Frima said.

"Neither was I," Liane had retorted. "But our parents would want us to do whatever was necessary." Frima soon gave in, as long as they followed an unspoken rule not to steal from people. When they got older, Frima didn't want men to touch her, let alone do more. Liane had repeated that their parents would understand and forgive them. Once again, Frima had been persuaded. On one matter, though, they'd never agreed. Liane smiled when SS officers praised Hitler or cursed Jews in hopes they'd give her more money. Frima couldn't risk arguing with them but remained stone-faced. She felt she'd shown more integrity than Liane.

Nowadays, recalling their differences eased Frima's longing when she missed Liane. Yet she instinctively reached for her whenever she had nightmares of them fleeing hand-in-hand from a nighttime bombing raid. But the only thing on her bed to grab was a grinning stuffed monkey or fuzzy tiger. Neither brought comfort. Awake and trembling, Frima wished she still had Sugar.

CHAPTER 6

"Just a few more things," Greta said on their last shopping expedition before school started. "A few" turned out to be four sweater sets and a green velvet dress for the High Holy Days, which were next month. It was still August though, and overheated after trying on the heavy clothes, Frima sagged against the counter while the sales clerk rang up their purchases.

Her spirits lifted at the sight of the rhinestone charm bracelet on a twirling display stand. "Greta, look. Isn't this pretty?" The diamond-like gems cast rainbows on the wall.

"I'm afraid it's rather..." Mrs. Oberlander eyed the clerk. "Gaudy." Frima understood that Greta meant "cheap" but didn't want to offend the woman who worked at the high-priced store.

The saleslady pointed to a rack of ID bracelets. "Girls engrave the names of friends or a boyfriend on these. If you purchase five or more, we engrave them for free."

Greta nodded her approval. "Frima? I'd rather buy you five or ten of these."

Frima only needed one, engraved "Liane." "No thanks. The locket's enough, after all."

"Perhaps you'll change your mind once school begins." While Greta paid, Frima slipped the charm bracelet into her pocket. At home, she hid it in a pair of boots at the back of her closet.

"When can I see Liane?" Frima watched the Shabbas candles flicker in front of the open window.

"We don't think it's a good idea," said Greta. "Too many bad reminders."

"You have to make a clean break with the past." Otto began to eat his soup.

Greta smiled. "Should we walk to the library tomorrow? They can issue you a temporary card until your name changes."

"I'd rather wait." Frima pushed aside her uneaten soup. "I want to see Liane."

Mr. Oberlander's face turned red. His wife touched his arm. "Let's discuss this Sunday," she said, "when Shabbas is over. We'll call Miss Stone. I'm sure she'll agree with us."

On Saturday, Frima nibbled breakfast and skipped lunch and dinner. She stayed in her room, leafing through magazines. On Sunday morning, the Oberlanders called Miss Stone from their bedroom with the door closed. As soon as Frima heard them dial the last number, she raced to the kitchen and picked up the wall extension.

Otto did most of the talking. "Unfortunately, Frima can be quite stubborn when it comes to Liane and won't take no for an answer," he concluded.

"So," Greta said, "we'd like your advice on how to make her let go of the idea."

Miss Stone was silent for so long Frima thought the connection was broken. At last she said, "I agree with Frima." She told the Oberlanders about Anna Freud's research with war orphans who'd lived together in England before being sent to America for adoption. "Children who grow up without adults form strong attachments to one another, and although they can eventually bond with grownups, they'll never be as close with them as they are to their peers."

Mrs. Oberlander gasped. "You mean Frima will always care more about Liane than us?"

"Frima wants and needs the love of parents. But orphaned children also benefit from their bonds with one another. They develop a strong sense of fairness. What goes for one, goes for all. Contrary to stereotypes, those adopted into good homes, like yours, don't become maladjusted. They grow up to have happy families of their own." The caseworker took a deep breath. "I don't think there's a risk if Frima remains friends with Liane."

"There's a risk establishing our parental authority," said Otto. "Children go astray without firm rules. Especially if they've seen the worst of human nature, like Frima has."

Miss Stone hesitated again. "Freud's orphans expected adults to respect *their* rules. If not, they responded with aggression, verbal and physical." Frima covered her mouth so they wouldn't hear her breathing. "It's your decision," Miss Stone ended. "Call me if you have more questions."

As soon as she heard both phones click, Frima hurried back to her room. Half an hour later, Otto and Greta appeared in her doorway. Frima looked at them expectantly. Greta sat on the bed opposite hers and said, "Miss Stone told us about the latest research on children like you."

Otto stood in front of the dresser, blocking Frima's view of *Sisters*. "As we feared, it's risky to let you see Liane. So your mother and I will abide by our original decision."

Greta crossed to Frima's bed and put an arm around her. "You have a new family now. When you start school, you'll make new friends. Your father and I want what's best for you."

"You're not my parents. Yet."

Otto sat on the other side of Frima. His eyes pleaded. "The war is over. We can't erase the past but your mother and I want you to have a wonderful life from now on. Let's not fight."

Greta stood. "Brunch? Your father bought bagels this morning. We have herring in cream sauce, smoked whitefish, tomatoes, fresh corn on the cob. And Stühmer's donuts."

Frima lay down and turned her back on them. "You can eat without me."

Two days later, she still hadn't eaten. Mrs. Oberlander was frantic. Despite the heat, she cooked and baked Frima's favorites. On Tuesday night, while the Oberlanders ate in the dining room, Frima strained to hear their conversation from her bedroom.

Greta begged Otto. "We don't have a choice."

"If we don't stick to the rules now, we're setting ourselves up for trouble later."

"Miss Stone said orphans get angry when grownups don't follow *their* rules."

"She also said orphans stay closer to each other than to adults. If we don't let Frima see Liane, they can't remain close."

"Otto, Frima's new clothes are already hanging on her. If the agency sees she's losing weight, they'll hold up the adoption or, God forbid, deny it."

Frima heard nothing after that, not even the clinking of silverware. At bedtime, the Oberlanders again appeared in her doorway.

"We've decided to let you see Liane," Greta said.

Frima suspected Miss Stone's warning, as much as her own hunger strike, had helped sway their decision. She silently thanked the caseworker for taking her side.

"You can invite Liane here," said Otto.

"We don't want you to go back there."

"One visit."

"And then?" Frima asked.

'We'll see," the Oberlanders said in unison.

Frima drank a glass of chocolate milk and ate two donuts before going to bed. She slept soundly. On Wednesday morning, with Mrs. Oberlander beside her in the kitchen, Frima called Oyf Haskhole. Miss Stone put Liane on but stayed by the phone "to make arrangements."

"Hi, Liane. How are you?"

"Fine. You?"

"I'm good, but I miss you. Greta and Otto said you could visit. I have my own room."

"I have my own room too. Now." Liane's laugh was half amused, half bitter.

"I even have my own bathroom." Frima felt her cheeks flush. Why was she bragging?

"There's a lock on ours. Good enough for me."

"When can you come? The Oberlanders will send a cab to bring you and take you back."

"I know how to ride the bus." Liane coughed. "But I'm not coming."

Frima looked at Greta. Her arms were crossed and a tiny smile played on her lips. Frima grinned. "Would you feel more comfortable if I visited you at Oyf Haskhole?" she asked Liane.

"Sounds good to me. I'll check."

Miss Stone got on the line and asked Frima to give the receiver to Mrs. Oberlander. After the caseworker reassured her that she would be there the whole time, the women agreed that Greta would drop off Frima at two o'clock the following afternoon and return for her at four. They handed the phones back to the girls to say goodbye. Then Frima passed Greta the phone to hang up. The tiny smile on her mother-to-be's lips had been replaced by a gaping mouth.

***

Greta waited in the taxi until Miss Stone waved from the window that Frima had arrived upstairs. The caseworker quizzed Frima about her "new life" and Frima, remembering how she and Liane used to tell the caseworker what she wanted to hear, answered that the Oberlanders were lavishing her with food, clothes, and affection. Satisfied that Frima was happy and settling into her new home, Miss Stone released her and Liane to go to the girls' bedroom. The boys blocked them halfway down the dim hallway. Reuven spun Frima around. "If it isn't Her Royal Highness, Queen Frima. Where'd you snatch the glad rags?"

Frima flicked his fingers off her arm. "I don't have to steal anymore. I bat my eyelashes at my daddy and sweet talk my momma, and they buy me classy clothes." Frima had worn jeans, a blouse with blue corn-flowers, and saddle shoes but ditched the daddy shirt. Why rub it in?

Salomon tilted his head back and looked her up and down. "Not a queen, Reuven. More like a princess." He blushed. "You look nice, Frima."

Liane tugged Frima toward her bedroom. Passing the boys' room, Frima saw Mendel napping on his old bed. "Why is he here?" she asked.

"The Bedels brought him back. He barely talked and continued to wet the bed. Since the adoption had already gone through, there was a ruckus about his last name. Because his original surname wasn't known, the court just gave him the name Mannlich, German for "'male.'"

"Poor Mendel Mannlich," said Frima.

"I don't think he cares. Miss Stone was more upset. So was Anoush. The dirty old super's taken the kid under his wing and brings him along on jobs. Mendel seems happier around tools than people. I think Anoush would adopt him but only married couples are allowed to."

"How's Berta doing?"

"Okay, I guess. Her adoption also went through and the parents haven't returned her. Yet. Miss Stone wants to place the rest of us by the end of summer when the lease on the apartment is up. Then she'll take charge of the big orphan camp that used to be a YMCA. If they let her."

"Why wouldn't they?" Frima couldn't imagine what the agency would have against her.

"Because her record here is terrible. All she has to show for her efforts is Berta and you. Assuming the Oberlanders don't change their minds and give you back." Liane winked. "Miss Stone did find one older couple interested in adopting a teenager. She sent Mendel to Anoush's and made dinner for the rest of us. Meatloaf, mashed potatoes, string beans, and apple pie from the bakery. They were nice people. He was a pharmacist and she was a teacher."

Frima leaned forward. A lot had gone on since she'd left. "What happened?"

Liane snorted. "Salomon cracked his knuckles and Reuven wiped his nose on his sleeve."

"And you?"

"I took a second helping, talked with my mouth full, and then took thirds. On the way out, they told Miss Stone they couldn't afford to keep me. If only they knew how cheap I came."

"In that case, you'll like your present." Frima reached into her pocket and dangled the charm bracelet.

Liane snatched it and fastened the clasp around her wrist. The glass beads sparkled. "I adore it, but I can't believe your mother bought it for you."

"She didn't," said Frima.

"I have a present for you too." Liane pulled her satchel from under the bed and gently put Sugar in Frima's hands. "I almost gave her to you when you left, together with *Sisters*, but I was afraid you'd tell me to throw her out again." Liane took out Ittel Rosa and held the bear on her lap. "But in Berlin, you eventually saw things my way so I saved your doll just in case."

"I'm glad you did." Frima made Sugar kiss Ittel Rosa and held her close. "But I didn't always come around to your way of thinking."

Liane took in Frima's clothes and shoes. "You may be even less willing now."

"Who knows? Maybe someday you'll see things *my* way." Frima put her arm around Liane, even though she doubted it. Liane returned the hug. Frima knew her friend doubted it too.

CHAPTER 7

Frima wanted to see Liane again but not at Oyf Haskhole, and Liane still refused to come to the Oberlanders. Miss Stone offered to take them both to the Museum of Modern Art, an idea that met with Greta's approval.

"What time should I bring Frima home, Mrs. Oberlander?" Miss Stone asked when she came to get her.

"By five. Dinner is at five thirty sharp. Otto is very punctual. Please, call me Greta."

"I'm Shirley. Five o'clock is perfect. The superintendent is keeping an eye on the boys and I'll get back to Oyf Haskole in plenty of time to relieve him and get dinner on the table. Regular meals are so important for children who never knew when, or if, they'd get another. Frima is filling out beautifully."

Frima blushed and hurried outside, where Liane was waiting. With Miss Stone beside them, they barely spoke on the subway to the museum. Once there, Frima found the brash colors, meandering lines, and frantic swirls unsettling. She was relieved when Miss Stone led them to an exhibit titled "Eleven Europeans in America," with paintings of real things until she saw that they were also weird. Melting objects. People hovering in space. A wall plaque next to a Marc Chagall read: "Surrealism uses symbols to express imaginative dreams and visions, free from conscious rational control." Miss Stone added, "'Sur' is French for on, or on top of. Chagall's painting makes you feel as though you're floating above reality, on top of what's actually there."

Frima equated dreams with nightmares. Why put them on canvas? She looked to Liane for confirmation, but Liane's body swayed above her toes as if she too were about to take flight. Frima turned away from the disturbing images. She felt the color drain from her face. Miss Stone led her to a bench. "I'm sorry. I didn't mean to bring up bad memories. What would you rather see?"

"Liane's the artist," Frima answered. "Ask her."

"Sculpture." Liane headed for the door.

Frima and Miss Stone followed. By the time they caught up, Liane stood before a free-standing piece, painted black, that looked like pieces of charred wood assembled in an intricate puzzle. The work was as unreal as Liane's but massive and solid. Liane read the card aloud:

Untitled
Louise Nevelson, b. 1899
Russian Jew, emigrated to U.S. early 20th century
Studied at Art Students League of New York
Materials: Found wood, oil paint
Artist's statement: For years, my son and I walked through the streets gathering wood to burn in our fireplace to stay warm. The fuel we gathered later became the fuel for my art.

Frima turned to Miss Stone. "If Louise Nevelson's artwork can make it into the Museum of Modern Art, there's no reason Liane can't be famous someday too."

The caseworker pointed to the card's fourth line. "Nevelson trained as an artist. If you want your work to be accepted in a museum, you might first consider going to art school too."

Liane snorted. "You mean make myself acceptable to a family who'll pay for me to go."

"It would certainly improve your chances."

"I'll take my own chances," Liane said. "It's Frima's turn to choose where we go next."

"Photography," Frima decided. "*Life* magazine says it's the art medium of the future."

"Tea first," said Miss Stone, "before it's too late and spoils Frima's appetite for dinner."

"We both get enough food," said Liane. "I'm hungry for more art."

The caseworker bit her lip. "Do you want Mrs. Oberlander to get upset and refuse to let you girls see each other again?"

Liane snatched the brochure from Miss Stone. "Photography, one floor up."

Frima watched the caseworker's face fall. She and Miss Stone were on the same side. Frima took the brochure from Liane. "Coffee shop, one floor down."

CHAPTER 8

"Adoptions are rarely contested and with no surviving family, Frima's case is straightforward. We've reviewed the questions you'll each be asked. Your hearing's at ten thirty. I'll meet you in the waiting room at ten fifteen." David Abner, their attorney, was a few years out of law school, with crinkly eyes and a soothing voice. When he'd heard Frima's story, he told them his last name was originally Abrams, but with strict Jewish quotas to get into law school, he'd changed it to Abner.

When their case was called, the clerk confirmed that Frima was over twelve, then made them swear that what they were about to say was the truth and nothing but the truth. The judge said the court would take their testimony and asked the attorney to proceed. Speaking softly but confidently, David Abner asked Otto to state his name, his wife's, and the child's. Otto's voice shook. It was a bit steadier when he stated when he and Greta were married, their address, and the size of their apartment. Mr. Abner smiled. "You're doing fine, Mr. Oberlander. Now, please tell the court about your job." Otto's voice grew strongest as he described the furniture store.

"Are there other members in your immediate family besides your wife and yourself?"

"No, sir. We have no children. That's why we're so eager to make Frima ours."

Next, the lawyer asked Otto where Frima was born and how she came to the States. He turned to the judge. "Your Honor, normally counsel would present papers from Frima's parents agreeing to terminate their rights, but they were killed in a concentration camp. There are no other surviving family members, so we ask the court to declare the child eligible for adoption."

The judge leaned down and spoke to Frima. "I'm sorry about your parents, but you're lucky to have found new ones and a new life in this country." He told the attorney to proceed.

David Abner now addressed Greta. "Mrs. Oberlander, you have heard your husband's responses. If you were asked the same questions, would your answers be substantially the same?"

"Yes, sir." Greta fidgeted. "May I add something?" The lawyer nodded. "My husband and I will give Frima many advantages. She can put the past behind her and enjoy a bright future."

Then, as Frima had been told to expect, the judge asked if she wished to be adopted by the Oberlanders. Following Mr. Abner's instructions, she answered simply, "Yes, your Honor."

"It is the finding of this court that the adoption is appropriate, in the child's best interest, and hereby approved." The judge pounded the gavel. "Congratulations Mister, Missus, and Frima Oberlander." He gave the lawyer permission to take a photograph of the new family. Otto and Greta stood on either side of Frima, arms wrapped around her shoulders, their heads pressed against hers. Frima felt as if she were floating above the picture. Now she understood surrealism.

"Time to celebrate," Otto declared as soon as they stepped outside. "Lunch at Ratner's Delicatessen, with cheesecake all around for dessert." He headed toward the subway.

Greta stopped him. "First I want to hear the magic words."

Otto looked puzzled but Frima knew what she meant. "Mother. Father." She kissed them each on the cheek and smiled. But inside she asked herself, "Will you be all the family I need?"

***

Frima's bedroom felt like home that night. As she huddled under the covers with Sugar, she chanted all the things that were hers now, never again to be taken away: shelter, food, clothes, and two loving parents. Yet something was missing. For the past five years, home had included Liane. Frima didn't want to go back to where Liane lived now or return with her to the streets. She wanted to bring Liane here. She waited a couple of weeks until the newness of the adoption had lost some of its luster before asking her parents if she could invite Liane for a sleepover.

"I'm not ready to share you," Greta admitted.

"I want to show off you and Daddy so Liane can see what she's missing."

Greta sighed. "I'll have to get used to sharing you when school starts. I'll ask your father at dinner." Otto agreed, provided Liane came on a Sunday, when he was home. If she was going to continue being Frima's friend, he wanted to get to know her. Liane could come for brunch and spend the night. Frima assumed Miss Stone would say okay. The problem was convincing Liane.

"You can't stay away forever, Liane. This is where I live now."

"We can see one other without a chaperone. I'll meet you on Fordham Road. Mommy and Daddy—or whatever you call them—will give you bus fare. You won't have to sneak a ride."

"If you come here, I'll take you to better stores than Alexander's." Frima lowered her voice. "The clothes are nicer and it's easier to shoplift. They don't watch you as closely."

Frima heard Liane's charm bracelet jangle. "Where do I say I got the fancy clothes?"

"Tell Miss Stone they're presents from me. Or from my mother."

"She likes to believe the best about people, but she isn't that dumb or gullible."

"We'll invite Miss Stone to brunch too. Mom will act nice to make a good impression."

"On me or the caseworker?"

"When Miss Stone sees how nice my mother is, she'll believe your new clothes were a gift from her." Frima paused. "But you have to act nice back to make it believable."

Liane said she'd dress respectably. "And don't worry. I won't wear the charm bracelet."

On Sunday, Greta shopped at the appetizing store and baked marmorgugelhupf, swirling extra chocolate into the Austrian marble bundt cake. She offered Liane the bagel tray and asked Otto to pass the cream cheese and lox to their guest. Liane took a stalk of celery. Greta reddened and turned to the caseworker. "My daughter is continuing to fill out well, if I do say so myself."

Miss Stone smiled. "Frima is developing into a young woman." Frima blushed. Liane crunched her celery. Miss Stone asked Frima which high school she planned to enroll in.

"Walton. I'm nervous because it's so big. Six thousand students, the biggest girls' high school in the world according to the booklet they sent. But my mother says it's very prestigious."

"I'm sure Miss Stone is familiar with its reputation," said Greta. "Graduates attend top colleges, even the Ivy League. If Otto's business continues to do well, we can afford the tuition."

Otto plunked the bagel tray in front of Liane. "Which high school are you going to?"

She shrugged and looked at Miss Stone. "Evander Childs? Roosevelt? Morris? Depends on where I'm living this fall."

"Wouldn't it be great if you went to Walton too?" Frima asked.

Liane snapped what remained of her celery stalk in two.

Greta began to clear the table. "Time for coffee and cake. Girls, milk or cocoa?"

"Coffee for me too," said Liane.

Mrs. Oberlander almost dropped the bowl of capers. "I think not," said Miss Stone.

Frima helped carry the dishes to the kitchen. Her mother's lips betrayed a faint smile.

When they returned to the dining room with the coffee service and cake platter, Otto was lighting a cigar. Liane eyed the ashtray. Frima prayed she wouldn't pull out a cigarette. Liane winked at her and took a bite of cake. "Mrs. Oberlander. This is the best marble cake I ever had." She ate another bite. "Thank you for all the trouble you've gone to. I'm sorry I didn't eat more. I guess I was nervous about meeting Frima's parents." Greta beamed. Even Otto smiled at Liane.

Clever Liane had salvaged things at the last minute by buttering up Greta and Otto. Relief flooded Frima. The fantasy of her parents adopting her sister had survived brunch.

***

Mrs. Oberlander sent Miss Stone home with leftovers. Frima offered to do the dishes with Liane, but her mother said that sleepovers were for fun not chores. Seeing Liane's surprise, Frima told her, "Mothers are less strict than caseworkers. They're free to break the rules."

"How far is yours willing to go?"

"What do you mean?"

Liane circled Frima's room, looking in the closet, opening drawers, picking up *Sisters*. "Are there any rules your mother's strict about?"

"Being on time for dinner, with a healthy appetite. Both my parents are unbendable."

Liane studied their reflections in the mirror. "You said there were good stores nearby."

"They're closed on Sunday. But we can go to Franz Sigel Park. It's only a few blocks."

Otto peeled a couple of bills from his money roll and told the girls to buy themselves ice cream. "No later than three o'clock," he said, "so you're hungry again by dinner time. Mother is making schnitzel." He smiled at Liane. "By then, you should be relaxed enough to eat."

Frima and Liane sat on a shady bench near the park's playground. Liane took a pack of cigarettes from her pocket and they both smoked. A Good Humor cart pulled up to the park's entrance. Liane licked the air provocatively. "Do you want to humor the Good Humor Man?"

"Not hungry," said Frima. She pointed to the candy store across the street. "Besides, we need the money my father gave us to buy mints before we go home."

Liane released a slow stream of smoke. "We could steal them."

Two boys about their age walked up. Nice looking kids in crisp jeans and short-sleeved cotton shirts. One with brown hair, the other a redhead. "That's our bench," they said.

"Ours." Liane pointed to the names Daisy and Diana scratched in the wood. "That's us."

"You girls look too good to vandalize a bench," said the brown-haired boy.

Frima tossed her curls. "Who told you we were good? In fact, we're quite bad."

"Prove it," said the redhead, whose hair was a shade darker than hers.

Liane grabbed Frima's hand. The boys ran after them to the candy store. While the boys distracted the owner with questions about his comic books, Frima and Liane stuffed their pockets with Almond Joy, Bazooka Bubble Gum, and Dots. Returning to the park, they found a patch of grass far from the playground. Brown Hair asked which one was Daisy and which was Diana.

"You choose," answered Frima. "What are your names?"

"Bob and Bill," said Red Hair. "You choose who's who."

The four of them systematically ate their way through the two dozen candy bars. "I wish you'd stolen chocolate cigarettes," said Brown Hair. "They're my favorite." His eyes bugged out when Liane offered them real ones. The boys looked at each other, then shook their heads.

Liane put them away. "Suit yourself. I'm not gonna waste them on a couple of babies."

"We're not babies," Red Hair whined.

"Prove it," said Frima. She and Liane lay back and gazed at the sky while Bob and Bill felt them up. The boys joked that on the first day of school, they'd brag about having gotten to second base this summer. Frima squeezed Liane's hand to stifle a giggle. How young and naïve these boys were. She wondered if she'd feel a lot older than the girls at Walton.

After a while, she and Liane nodded off. It was after six o'clock when they woke up. Bob and Bill were gone. So was the money Otto had given Frima. Liane laughed. "At least they were grown-up enough to steal a couple of bucks. I guess they figured they could get away with it."

Frima didn't think it was funny. "We won't get away with being late for dinner."

Her father was pacing in the living room when Frima and Liane walked in. Her mother stood in the kitchen doorway, scowling.

"Daddy. Mommy. I'm sorry we're late. It's been so long since Liane and I yakked that we lost track of time. Can we help set the table?"

"It was set an hour ago. I hope the veal isn't dried out. You two change and wash up."

"Pronto," Otto barked and took his seat at the head of the table.

"Frima, if Liane didn't pack a dinner dress, I'll find one of yours that will fit her." Greta followed them into Frima's bedroom and searched in the closet while the girls undressed. Seeing Liane's jeans tossed on the bed, she folded them. Two candy wrappers fell out of the pocket. Before Frima could throw her jeans in the hamper, her mother pulled three wrappers from hers.

Mrs. Oberlander told them to put their clothes back on, then marched them into the dining room, clutching the wrappers in both fists. "Not only are they late," she said to her husband, "I doubt they're hungry after eating this chazzerai. I'll call Miss Stone to pick up Liane right now."

Frima felt a sharp pang low in her abdomen and ran toward her bathroom.

"It's no wonder you have a stomach ache after eating all that garbage," Otto called after her. "Go. Do your business. We'll talk when you're done."

The pain wasn't like ordinary cramps. Yanking down her jeans, Frima sat on the toilet and doubled over when another pang stabbed her. Only when it passed, and she lifted her head, did she see the blood stain on her underpants. "Mommy," she yelled.

Greta's frown turned into a broad grin. She gently slapped Frima's cheeks "to make the blood flow and give you the children I couldn't have." When she went for supplies, Frima overheard her tell Otto, "our dream of having grandchildren is going to come true." Minutes later, Greta returned with clean underpants, a sanitary belt, and Kotex. Frima followed her back to the dining room, where Otto hugged her and poured three glasses of schnapps. "Prost!"

"Where's Liane?" asked Frima. In all the hubbub, she'd forgotten her friend was there. Apparently, so had her parents.

"She must have gone to your room," said Greta. "It's too late to call Miss Stone now."

"I'll drop Liane off on my way to work in the morning," said Otto. He downed the rest of his schnapps. "You understand, Frima, that there'll be no more sleepovers with that girl. We won't forbid you to see her. You're growing up and beginning to make your own choices. But your mother and I trust that from now on you'll make wiser ones."

***

Frima knocked on her door before entering. Liane lay on the second twin bed, holding Ittel Rosa. She must have brought the bear in her overnight bag. Sugar, as usual, waited amid the stuffed animals on Frima's pillow. Liane sat up. "That was exciting." Frima didn't detect sarcasm.

"Are you jealous?"

"Are you kidding? Being able to get pregnant would put the kibosh on my adventures. I give poor Miss Stone enough reason to worry as it is."

"You'll get your period soon enough, once she's done fattening you up." Frima examined herself in the mirror. "Good thing Bob and Bill turned out to be babies after all."

"Now you have to be careful you don't make your own babies. Until you get married."

"I'm in no rush. Neither are my parents. First, high school, then college." Frima plopped down on Liane's bed with the latest issue of

Seventeen and opened it to a photo of "The Best Wallet to Take to College." Liane flipped back to the cover, which featured a woman in a red beret and black and white checked dress. She had Liane's dark coloring but with straighter hair.

"That's a cute outfit," Frima said. "It would look good on you."

"It's prissy. And a beret would pop right off my frizzy head. I'll create my own style."

"I'm sure you will. You're an artist."

Liane tossed the magazine on the floor. "I'm bored."

"I'm too excited to sleep." Frima was also sad. This could be the last time the girls spent the night together. As soon as she heard the Oberlanders go to bed, she beckoned Liane to the living room where, with the volume on low, she played the original Broadway albums of *Annie Get Your Gun* and *Showboat*. Then she put on Bing Crosby and Frank Sinatra.

Liane wrinkled her nose. "I can't believe you listen to this mushy stuff."

"They're Greta's favorites but I like the romantic songs too."

"It's a little late for that, don't you think? Romance is supposed to come before sex." Liane fluttered her lashes. "Unless you plan to erase the past and pretend you're a girl?"

"Too late. I'm already a woman. I never thought I'd become one before you."

Liane sniffed. "It's not the only thing you'll become before me."

"You're still our leader." Frima's stomach hurt. She was finally tired. She put the records back in their jackets and walked to her bedroom. Liane followed.

CHAPTER 9

On the first day of high school, Frima stood against the wall of Walton's assembly hall watching thousands of girls reunite after summer vacation. It had been years since she'd gone to school but she remembered enough to recognize the "in crowd" when three girls walked toward her and the rest parted like the Red Sea. Joan, a tiny brunette with reflective black eyes, led the pack. She appraised Frima the way soldiers used to, taking in her looks and pliability. If one man didn't like her, there were plenty of others. But in high school, there was only one popular clique.

Joan asked her name. Frima stumbled. It was the first time she'd said "Oberlander" in public. "Berlin," she replied to the next question, remembering the rotten cabbage that had greeted the orphans at Oyf Haskhole. "My family was killed there. This summer, I was adopted by an American couple."

Joan left to confer with her group. When she returned, she put her arm around Frima. "I can't imagine what I'd do if I lost my family. Even my pain-in-the-butt little brother."

"The brother I lost was older. I looked up to him but now I have no one to..."

"The Periwinkle Girls will be your new guides." Joan introduced Dorothy and Marilyn. "You'll also meet the boys at Dewitt Clinton, our brother school. Won't they find Frima's accent charming?" The Periwinkles chorused "Yes." They linked arms, Joan and Frima in the middle, and marched to the front row. A tall woman with stiff posture but a soft face waited on stage for the chatter to die down. "For those who are new here, I'm Marion Heffernan, your principal. The school year begins with the world at peace, our joy tinged with sadness for those lost fighting for freedom. This morning, I introduce a student who lost more than most. Her entire family was wiped out. Miss Frima Oberlander is eager to start her life again. I trust you will welcome her."

The principal smiled at Frima. Joan squeezed her hand. Mrs. Heffernan reminded them that Walton held learning sacred and they were all expected to adhere to its principle of respect for one another. "Discover your greatness because you can change the world. Learn your lessons but also pursue a passion for the arts: dancing, painting, music. Expand your wings; the sky is the limit. Women's role in the war proved this holds true for us, not just men. The future is yours."

Frima felt self-conscious entering her classes, but after a brief greeting, everyone turned to their lessons. Still, she was relieved when the lunch bell rang. She sat with the Periwinkles, named for the small blue flower that was Walton's emblem. Each Periwinkle wore at least one item of that color. Principal Heffernan stopped by their table and told Frima, "I know the war interrupted your education. I'm happy to tutor you until you feel confident proceeding on your own." She then addressed Joan. "Miss Dubiki. I see you and your friends have also taken Frima under your wing."

"We saw she was special even before your speech. We'll tutor her too." Joan assigned the others biology, algebra, geography, and French. She herself took English "since literature shapes our ideas about life." Mrs. Heffernan said Frima was in good hands and continued her rounds.

When school let out, Frima accompanied her new friends to Barton's Soda Shop. Walton was in a part of the Bronx she and Liane hadn't explored. Like the area near Alexander's, Jerome Avenue had lots of stores but was more like Oyf Haskhole's poor immigrant neighborhood than the Grand Concourse where Frima lived now. Joan and Dorothy lived within walking distance; Marilyn took a bus to school. Money wasn't the criterion for Periwinkle membership. Looks mattered, but not as much as intelligence and ambition. Walton, more than their neighborhood schools, would fulfill their parents' aspirations for them, the same ones the Oberlanders held for Frima. She swore she'd make her dead parents, Abraham and Mirla Gersten, proud too.

***

By November, Frima had several blue outfits with matching hair barrettes. She was keeping up in all her classes, thanks to her twice-weekly sessions with Mrs. Heffernan and peer tutoring by the Periwinkles. Once her parents were confident she'd do well academically, they urged her to sign up for extracurricular activities. "Grades alone won't get you into a top-notch college," her father told her as they relaxed in the living room on a chilly evening. "Especially given the strict quotas for Jews, who are accused of being 'grinds.' You have to show you're well-rounded."

Mrs. Heffernan had talked about developing a passion for the arts. "I like music," Frima told her parents.

Greta moved to the piano bench. "My sister Leonie studied piano in Vienna before Jews were banned from the conservatory. Her last letter said her piano was confiscated so she could no longer practice. Not long after, she was herded on a train to Mauthausen. It would bring me such joy, Frima, if you took up the piano." She slid down the bench to make room.

Frima stayed on the love seat. "Any instrument except piano." Greta and Otto stared. "I studied it as a little girl. One day, when I came home from a lesson, my parents and brother were gone. Our neighbors, who were Catholic, said all the Jews had been rounded up. They took me in for a couple of days but were afraid of getting caught. So when it was dark, they packed up some food and sent me on my way. The wife crossed herself when her husband shooed me out." Frima took a deep breath. "Any instrument except piano," she repeated.

Otto and Greta sat on either side of her. Listening to their synchronized breathing, Frima had an idea. "How about a woodwind?"

"If that's what you want." Greta's voice was strained. Otto nodded.

"I could study clarinet and audition for Walton's ensemble band. They've won citywide competitions." Her father thought that would look excellent on Frima's college application. Her mother said she'd find a clarinet teacher tomorrow.

"How about some clarinet music now?" Otto put Benny Goodman's *1938 Carnegie Hall Jazz Concert* on the record player. The big band's swinging rhythms urged them to get up and dance, but the three Oberlanders sat quietly and stared at their feet.

CHAPTER 10

On a Saturday evening, an hour after the season's first snowfall ended, the curbs were already slush puddles, and the snow as gray as the sky. Otto was working late during the pre-holiday rush; Greta was in her sewing room embroidering a new challah cover for Chanukah. Frima finished practicing the clarinet and went into the empty kitchen to call Oyf Haskhole.

"Long time, no talk, no see," she said when Miss Stone put Liane on the line. "Things have been busy."

"Same here." Liane told Frima that moving to the old YMCA, which had been pushed back from Labor Day, was finally about to happen. The new facility would house 130 war orphans. "Mendel is going, although I doubt he'll get a second chance at adoption."

"Poor little Mendel."

"Poor Miss Stone. Suppose she ends up with a hundred and twenty-nine additional bedwetters."

"I take it you're not going with Miss Stone and Mendel?" Frima asked.

"I'm moving to a group home, still in the Bronx, but north of here."

Frima asked about Reuven and Salomon.

"Also group homes, but not with me or one other. Miss Stone says they'll do better apart. I think she has higher hopes for Salomon, just like she did for you."

Because I had higher hopes for myself, Frima thought. She asked Liane about school. In the end, Frima had been relieved when Liane hadn't signed up for Walton. Liane said she'd already started at the school near the group home, Evander Childs, which Otto had called a place for losers. But Frima knew Liane was smart. "You'll do well there," she told her. "Good luck."

"You're the lucky one," Liane snapped. Then she softened. "Let's get together. It's too cold to hang around outside, but we could go back to that museum. Day after Thanksgiving?"

That was Joan's birthday; the Periwinkles were going ice skating at Central Park. Frima told Liane she was busy.

"What about the first weekend in December?"

Frima had band rehearsal and the Winter Wonderland dance with the Clinton boys. She suggested the following weekend.

"I'm going back to Oyf Haskhole then to help Miss Stone pack up." After an awkward silence, Liane added, "We'll figure out something, eventually."

"We always do." Then, not knowing what else to say, Frima repeated, "Good luck."

***

On the fourth night of Chanukah, Frima got four ID bracelets engraved with her name and each of the three other Periwinkles. Although they talked about dating, especially after a junior named James asked Joan to go steady, their sights were set on college. "Forget boys. We need girl talk."

Joan slipped her arm through Frima's. "It's time for a slumber party. Will your parents let you have one at your house?"

Frima said she'd ask. Despite the Liane disaster, they were enthusiastic.

Greta proposed a Saturday night through Sunday lunch. Otto approved. The store would be closed, and he wanted to meet Frima's new friends. They settled on the following weekend. After devouring schnitzel and cake, the Periwinkles went to Frima's room and put on their frilly PJs. Then they dumped their makeup cases on the dresser and spread out in a line in front of the mirror. "What's this funny-looking thing?" Joan dangled *Sisters* as if it were contaminated.

"From my ... other family," said Frima.

Joan carefully set it back down. Then the Periwinkles tried on one another's eyeshadow and lipstick and rolled one another's hair. They checked Frima's closet, unzipped her sweater bags, and drooled over her jewelry box. To think that a year ago she was a scrawny orphan with one threadbare dress and shoes held together with twine. Liane was right. Frima was lucky.

Greta knocked on the door. "Telephone, dear. It sounds like Liane. Shall I say you're busy and will get back to her another time?" Frima hesitated but decided to take the call. She followed her mother into the kitchen. To give Frima privacy, Greta joined Otto in the living room, where Bing Crosby's *Hawaiian Songs, Volume One* spun on the record player.

"I called to give you my new phone number," Liane said. Frima wrote it on the notepad beside the phone. "I cried on moving day. I'm not sure who was more surprised, me or Miss Stone. The woman did her best. We didn't make it easy. Well, you did, most of the time. And as far as I know, Berta is doing okay. But Miss Stone doesn't have much to show for the rest of us. I don't know why the agency is letting her run the bigger place unless it's because no one else wants the job. My new group home is more like the apartment. Six of us, except all girls and all in high school. I'm next-to-youngest. The oldest is seventeen. Next year, she'll be on her own."

Liane rambled on. Frima was sorry she'd taken the call. "Miss Stone should do better in the new camp. She'll have help."

"We call the woman in charge of us here The Warden. Not to her face, but I'm sure she knows. She's no dummy. Unlike my classmates. Most are in the commercial program. Except the Jewish kids, who are in the college program."

"Do you consider yourself Jewish?"

"No. You?"

Frima shrugged as if Liane could see her. "There are Jewish girls at Walton, but I'm not part of their crowd."

"My crowd at Evander is the 'juvies.' I learn more from them than my teachers." Frima strained to hear her own friends, but Bing Crosby drowned them out. Liane continued. "The art teacher lets me hang around the studio and use the materials, but I mostly bring in stuff I've scavenged. He promised to include my artwork in the student show this spring. I'll invite you."

The record ended. In the silence, while her father put on the second volume, Frima heard laughter in her bedroom. She tried in vain to catch what the Periwinkles found funny. "That's nice," she told Liane, although she'd already forgotten the last thing Liane said.

"You're quiet. Did I interrupt your wild Monopoly game with Mommy and Daddy?"

"No. I just have a couple of friends over for the night."

"Must be rather tame then."

Frima heard Liane strike a match and inhale. "I'll call you tomorrow afternoon when my friends are gone and I have more time to talk."

Liane exhaled. "Sunday afternoon is chore time here."

"Tomorrow night then."

"It's my turn and Betty's to cook dinner."

"Betty?" For the first time in their conversation, Frima paid attention.

"My roommate. She's a sophomore."

"Another orphan?"

"No. Her mom can't take care of her. She doesn't know where her dad is. She ran away from home a lot. So, after her mom's last binge, the court decided Betty was better off here."

Frima shuddered. "I'll call you after you finish eating dinner and washing the dishes."

Liane took another drag on her cigarette. "You can try but Betty and I usually go to the movies. The Warden gives us a weekly allowance." Frima didn't ask how much, sure hers was a lot more. Liane laughed. "Of course, it doesn't cover all my expenses. I have to supplement it."

"Can you get away with it there?"

"Despite her title, The Warden keeps an eye on us less than Miss Stone did. As long as we avoid the cops and don't bother her, she doesn't care." Liane snickered. "Time for story hour with cocoa and popcorn at Ye Olde Grouppe Home. Enjoy your happy new life. Bye."

Liane hung up before Frima could return the goodbye or agree on a callback time. Upset, she returned to her bedroom but was soon caught up in the Periwinkles' chatter. At ten, Greta gave them hot chocolate and peppermint sticks. Then they danced to *Jitterbug Jamboree*. It was midnight when Frima and Joan each tumbled into a bed, the others on mounds of floor pillows.

Frima dreamed of a Gestapo roundup, bodies packed like sardines in an airless cattle car, then standing in a selection line. Before being assigned to the group on the right or the left, she bolted awake. Her pounding heart thumped above her friends' rhythmic breathing. Frima reached under the pillow for Sugar, pressed the doll to her heaving chest, and held on for dear life.

PART THREE:
LIANE (1947–1951)

CHAPTER 11

Betty and I smoked, waiting for the drag race to start. Behind us were our Juvie friends and a few vets old enough to buy us beer. In two lines, five cars each, the drivers hunched over the wheels of their Ford and Mercury hot rods, revving their flathead V8 engines. Betty blew a perfect smoke ring.

"I wish the damned race would start," she muttered. "I'm thirsty." It was hard to hear above the noise of the engines, but since booze was never far from Betty's mind, I could guess what she'd said. "Louise is the flag girl again?" She spat as Louise walked past us to the corner.

Flag girls were pretty and stacked and usually sophomores or juniors. Freshmen like me were still proving ourselves, while seniors who weren't knocked up or engaged were considered old maids.

I teased Betty. "Jealous, Miss Nowak?" My roommate was a stacked sophomore with a Polack's blonde hair and blue eyes. Only on second look did you see they were slightly crossed.

"I'm too fucking fat to be chosen flag girl. But you got a good chance next year."

"No thanks. I'd rather watch the race without worrying about when to drop the flag."

"No kidding. Last year a flag girl argued with the judge. Told him he was blind."

"What happened?"

"He gave her a black eye." Betty laughed. "She looked pretty ugly for a while. But even when her eye healed, you better believe she was never picked to be flag girl again."

"Tough tits." I'd picked up Betty's slang. If only I could learn to blow smoke rings too.

We were outside Evander Childs, on Gun Hill Road. The whole square block was taken up by our high school, a three-story yellow stone building fronted by three huge wooden doors. I was never sure if the wrought-iron fence was to keep neighborhood bums out or trap students inside. Gun Hill Road was four lanes, the main drag across the North Bronx. Uphill, heading west, was where the Revolutionary Army kept the cannons they fired at the British. The hot rods sounded like cannons thanks to special mufflers that magnified the roar of the exhaust. Each race started at the west end of the street as soon as the light on the east corner turned green. The rule was that rodders had to wait until traffic had cleared, but it was often broken. It was expected that other cars would get out of the way, even if their drivers had to pull onto the sidewalk.

The first two races went off without a hitch. Traffic was thin right after school let out. By the third race, it was heavier. The racers faced downhill for maximum speed and a faster getaway if the cops showed up. Sure enough, the race had just started when we heard the sirens. Betty and I ditched our cigarettes and joined the Juvies sitting innocently at the top of the school steps. Others headed for the athletic field. The hot rods peeled around the corner, three turning left and three right. The cops nearly crashed into each other deciding which way to go.

Fifteen minutes later, a scout gave the all clear. Those of us on the steps joined the others behind the bleachers, where we smoked and got buzzed on booze. A few older guys were gang members. The school was neutral territory, so turf rumbles were rare. But I was nervous about their zip guns, which they'd made in shop class with elastic bands and door latches. The guns themselves didn't scare me. In Berlin, I considered them simply another article of clothing. Here the danger was less that a zip gun would intentionally kill someone than accidentally blow up.

"What's buzzin', cuzzin'?" An older guy, a rodder in the third race, sat down next to me.

"Nada," I said. I thought better of trying to blow a smoke ring. Not cool if I flubbed it.

He asked for a fag. I bummed one from Betty and handed it to him. He inhaled half in a single drag, then said he'd trained as a mechanic in the war and built the fastest rod ever. I was skeptical but didn't dare say so. He dressed like a gang member: Garrison belt, brass buckle, and pointed shoes with metal cleats that could kick a man to death and shred his flesh in the process.

He placed my hand on his crotch. "Canceled race got me all hot and bothered. Need me a dame to cool me down." He stood and tugged me by the wrist toward his car.

My toes gripped the soles of my sneakers. "Six bucks," I said, all calm and collected.

"You're cracking me up." He looked incredulous.

I freed my hand and held out my palm. "I'm serious. Pay or the answer is no."

He sneered. "Baby. You're chicken."

I got up and stuck my face in his. "I got more moxie than you, buster."

"I oughta give you a knuckle sandwich." He pulled back his fist. I waited for the punch, but he hitched his belt, stomped off to his hot rod, and peeled off down the hill.

I stood there trembling until Betty pulled me back down beside her. "That was a gas," she said. "Now let's get the hell out of here before Mr. Shithead changes his mind and comes back."

We headed to the projects a couple of blocks away and sat on a stoop. Betty had brought a couple of beers. I'd had enough, so she drank both. She smiled at me. She had good teeth and under the booze and fags, she smelled like caraway seeds. I had a flash of my mother baking rye bread, slicing off the heel for me, and spreading on a thick layer of plum jam. I didn't remember much about my mother but smells sometimes triggered memories. My shaking finally stopped.

Betty handed me a cigarette and said it was time to practice. I made a small 'O' with my lips, put the tip of my tongue behind my bottom teeth, and pushed the smoke with the middle of my tongue. Out came a steady stream. She told me to tap the side of my cheek. The smoke came out in gusts. Better, but still no hole. "Damn, this is too hard." I started trembling again.

Betty hugged me. "Should we skip the races for a while in case that guy comes back?"

"Good idea. They're fun but kind of pointless." I caught Betty's expectant look. "As pointless as frosting an armchair," I said.

"As pointless as polishing a candle," she answered.

It was a game we played whenever one of us was frustrated or down. I finally relaxed. "It felt good to stand up to that jerk," I said.

"I bet. I wish I'd had the courage to do that when I was younger." The first week we met, Betty told me she'd been raped by her mother's boyfriend and later her foster father before being sent to the group home. Her story wasn't unusual. She assumed mine was similar or that, like most other juvies, I'd had sex with guys my age without having it forced on me. Whatever the reason, when it came to not being a virgin, I wasn't the odd one out.

None knew my real story, however. That afternoon, relieved but rattled, I decided to trust Betty. I told her about selling my body for food or money, a pair of warm shoes, even baubles and trinkets that sparkled through my layers of grime. "Anything to survive, plus a bit more."

Betty listened in silence. "In the end, we're not so different," she said when I'd emptied myself out. She slid closer and intertwined her nail-bitten fingers in mine. "We're sisters."

I didn't say I'd never been as powerless as her, that at eight I'd taken matters into my own hands. Nor did I tell her I already had the only sister I wanted. "Cousins at the very least," I said.

***

It was dark by the time Betty and I reached the two-story, brown-shingled row house we called home. The Warden, whose real name was Cecilia Zettici, barely glanced up from the armchair where she sat listening to *Famous Jury Trials* on the beat-up *Philco*. Not until the commercial break did she follow Betty and me to the eat-in kitchen. She was about fifty, a widow whose husband had been gassed in the first war, like my dad, and died of lung disease ten years ago. Built like Betty but dark like me, she had a large mole in the middle of her forehead. A target.

She pointed to the franks and beans and half-pot of coffee on the stove. "Leftovers if you're hungry." Meals here weren't up to Oyf Haskhole's standards. The Warden used to buy milk but stopped when it soured because no one other than me drank it. I didn't crave Miss Stone's food, but I did miss the feeling of cold white milk gliding down my throat.

"You cut it awfully close to curfew, girls." The Warden lit the burner under the coffee pot. "Nine on weekdays, eleven on weekends," she reminded us, "three hours earlier on nights it's your turn to cook or clean up." As long as we weren't truants, we could do whatever we wanted between school and curfew. Ditto on weekends, provided we got home on our own and not in a cop car.

I lifted the lid to sniff the franks and beans. Betty sniffed too. We pinched our noses. The Warden took the lid from me and started to put it back on the pot. Then she sniffed the beer on our breaths. "If you girls want to drink, that's your business. I won't try to stop you."

"Good," said Betty. "That would be as pointless as frying a radio."

"But don't you *ever* bring booze into this house. My one unbreakable rule." The agency that ran the homes, United Neighborhood Houses, did unannounced inspections. If they found liquor here, they'd cancel The Warden's contract and she'd be out on the street. "Without a high school diploma, I won't find a job that pays this well and puts a roof over my head. Got it?" She poured the rest of the coffee into her cup and headed for her tiny bedroom across the hall.

I rummaged in the cupboard for peanut butter. Betty toasted four slices of bread. We washed down our sandwiches by diluting the last of the orange juice, rinsed our dishes, and headed for the stairs. With the radio off, you could hear the steps creak. On the second floor were three rooms for six girls. Because the building was boxed between two other row houses, the only windows were at the front, where you could stare at the street awash in slush or cracking under the heat, and the back, which looked out on a yard with shriveled tomato plants. We often stood in line for a turn in the small bathroom. A cabinet under the sink held boxes of Kotex and sanitary belts. No one said congratulations the first time I got my period. Like everyone else, I took what I needed and told The Warden when we were down to one box so she could buy more.

Betty and I sat on our beds. The corduroy spreads were worn but the mattresses were surprisingly firm. Betty lit a cigarette, passed it to me, and took one for herself. "At least The Warden didn't say to be careful and give us that 'it's a dangerous world out there' crap."

"No need to. Everyone here has learned how to handle themselves." I fiddled with the bolts and wooden scraps I'd found behind the bleachers, picturing a sculpture with a sharp sliver slicing the metal between base and tip. "Why do grownups tell children to beware of strangers?"

Betty hugged her knees. "It's the people you know who are more dangerous."

I nodded. "When friends and neighbors turn on you, they do the most damage. Warnings against strangers are as pointless as ..."

Betty finished. "Painting potato chips."

***

I didn't mind not going to drag races after school. It gave me more time in the art studio. Art was the only class I liked. Betty was in the secretarial track; I opted for the academic one. Not that I figured on going to college, but why learn to take dictation from a man when I was already a savvy businesswoman? Still, algebra was boring and ancient history as decrepit as the old guy who taught it. English was useless too. I learned it by speaking it and had no patience for reading.

Mr. Archer, the art teacher, made his subject come alive by encouraging the class to get inside the heads of the artists. He let us call him

Thomas and pinned up artsy backlit photos of his family in the studio. Barely thirty, he'd gotten married and been hired within two months of coming home from the war. He and his wife Mary had a baby named Lily, their "Easter flower."

The first week of classes, he'd taken us to look at the mural in the school's entryway, a history of civilization, and said, "The palette and imagery say mankind advances from being downtrodden by oppression to being lifted up by decency and equality. Art expresses those same ideals." Not always, I thought. Nazi art roused people to kill millions. I liked the Abstract Expressionists, whose work was about individual attitudes and beliefs, not society's. Jackson Pollock's drip paintings bubbled up from inside him and splattered onto the canvas. Yet I knew from my own pieces how much calculation was behind making something look spontaneous.

Mr. Archer teased me. "So you like Pollock because he's a nihilist?"

"Whatever that means, Thomas, the answer is yes."

"He's a rebel. He has no tolerance for convention. Or other people. The sole aim of his work is to communicate his own thoughts and feelings, whether the viewer shares them or not."

"I happen to share his," I said.

"And they are?"

"Anger. Rage. Fuck the world."

"Maybe also relief at having survived? Even gratitude to a higher power?"

I shook my head. I had only myself to thank. Mr. Archer encouraged me to try painting and other media, but I always came back to sculpture. A week before Christmas, he showed me photos of Louise Nevelson's recent work. She'd begun using bits of stone, bronze, and terra cotta. I pored over the photos and told him, "If I had the moolah, I'd buy one."

"They're cheap. Critics hated her last show. She hasn't worked with found objects since."

"Fuck the critics. Let them flap their lips but I'm going to give weirder materials a try."

"That proves you're a nihilist, Liane."

Over the break, I returned to Oyf Haskhole to salvage odds and ends that Miss Stone had discarded before moving. Anoush also gave me stuff—cup handles, umbrella spokes, lamp harps—left behind by former tenants. I asked why *he* saved broken parts.

"You never know when they'll come in handy to fix other broken things." Anoush stroked the shiny objects before handing them to me. "Use these to make something whole."

In January, I brought a carton full of new sculptures to school. Mr. Archer called them extraordinary and said I could use the studio every day until the janitor kicked me out. He promised he'd find money in the budget to raid local scrap yards and buy me fasteners and bases. "You have talent, Liane. I want your work to be the center of the annual student show in May."

"No thanks, Thomas. Just a regular place in the show is fine with me."

"Jackson Pollock isn't opposed to getting rich and famous. What gives?"

I couldn't explain. But I did tell him to get me more materials and to talk to the janitor.

"Have you flipped your wig?" Betty asked when I said I'd refused to star in the show.

"Street life teaches you that it's better to fade into the background than draw attention."

Betty snorted. "Bullshit. You called attention to yourself to pick up men. Here's a chance to stand out for your artwork instead of your body."

The next day I told Mr. Archer I'd changed my mind. He gave me a key and spoke to the janitor. The studio became my candy store and I didn't have to steal anything. Each new material I tried was like tasting a new flavor. I made off-center stone piles that Mr. Archer said reminded him of trail markers, perfect symbols for high school students finding their way. My gear-like metal sculptures of polished brass and shiny aluminum were the closest I came to using color, but I balanced them with rusty iron cogs. I still loved weathered wood, but now I had fresh maple, oak, and mahogany, whose shades and grains I overlapped in horizontal slabs or spiky towers.

By May, I had over sixty pieces. Mr. Archer told me to pick out my ten favorites for the show. I thought of Jewish parents forced to choose which children to save. I longed to ask Frima for help but hadn't invited her because I cringed to think of her meeting Betty and the other Juvies. Frima would chatter about the sock hop, the Juvies about crashing a party. I especially didn't want Frima thinking Walton was a much better school than Evander, even though it was.

Turnout for the show was huge. All the faculty and lots of students came. Even the New York City Board of Education sent someone. Most exciting was that Mr. Archer had invited his former professors, artist friends, and others he knew in what he called "the art world" to opening night. A tall, skinny man, whom he introduced as his college mentor, pulled me aside.

"Miss Asher. Liane, if I may? Mr. Archer did not mislead me about your talent. Which art schools are you considering?" He listed Cooper Union, the Art Students League, and Pratt. "My colleagues and I are founding a new School of Visual Arts, which should be established by the time you graduate. I would be glad to append a personal recommendation to your application."

"Thank you but I prefer the school of life."

Feeling an elbow in my back, I spun around to see Betty. She poked me towards a corner. "You nearly blew a chance to star in the art show. Don't make the same mistake about college."

"How am I supposed to pay for it?"

"A scholarship? Get a job as an artist's assistant?"

"Evander students don't win scholarships. And starving artists spend what little they have on paint. And food. Not on hiring lackeys." I could have added that dreaming of college was as pointless as sashaying up to an SS officer and asking him and his wife to adopt me. Instead, I said nothing. The Juvies got a vicarious thrill from my success. Why spoil it? We had little else going for us. Maybe dreams weren't so bad after all. Frima and I had nightmares, but our good dreams kept us alive.

***

The day I helped Mr. Archer take down the show, I went drinking with the Juvies after school. For once, I matched Betty beer for beer. By the time we stumbled home and crawled upstairs, I was totally buzzed. I decided to call Frima. We hadn't talked in months.

"Liane. Perfect timing. We just finished dinner. Are you okay? You sound a little fuzzy."

"Bad connection. I'll tell The Warden to call the phone company. How are you?"

"Terrific. Last night was the citywide high school band concert. Walton took first place. The bandleader said my clarinet playing clinched it. Did you see the photo in the *Post*?"

We didn't get the paper, so Frima described her performance and the applause. I wanted to upchuck. Instead, I swallowed and told her, "I was the sensation of Evander's art show and even got offered a scholarship after I graduate."

"I knew you'd go places with your sculpture." I heard Frima swallow too. "You said you'd invite me to the show."

"You didn't invite me to the band concert." There was silence on both ends of the line. "So what are you doing this summer?" I finally asked.

"I'm going to be a CIT—counselor in training—at Camp Boiberik. Daddy says it will look good on my college application. How about you?"

"Betty and I got jobs scooping custard—soft-serve ice cream—at the Carvel two blocks from here. No fare, no need to sneak on the bus. The Warden says if I work my way up to shift manager, it will look good on my corporate executive application." I felt bad as soon as I said it. "Seriously, stop by with a friend. The store's latest gimmick is 'buy one, get one free.'"

"Sounds like a good deal," Frima said. "We should get together."

"Fine by me. I have plenty of time between now and the end of school. You?"

"Hold on while I check the calendar." A minute later, Frima was back on the phone. "I have another band concert and then the annual Walton-Clinton dance in June."

"How about after school's out?" This was sounding like when I called Frima last winter.

Frima groaned. "I leave for camp two days later. But there are two weeks between when camp ends and school starts."

"You mean the end of August?"

"Yes." Frima sounded triumphant. "So it's a date? I'll put it on the kitchen calendar."

"Me too," I said. "My calendar's hanging over the hole in the bedroom wall."

Chapter 12

Carvel's manager bought me and Betty beer as long as we showed up on time, took breaks on the clock, and didn't give him or customers any lip. It wasn't easy when heat made people irritable, but the promise of a cold beer helped us hold our tongues. One July day, when it hit the mid-90s and Betty and I were as sweaty as the beer cans, even the shade alongside the stand offered no relief. We decided to drink back at home, where we'd chipped in to buy a small fan for our room.

I found an old burlap sack to hide the goods and we waited until The Warden would be tuned into *Famous Jury Trials* so we could sneak past her. With the fan on high, we didn't hear her coming up the stairs. "I bought two more boxes of Kotex," she said and opened our door at the same time. It was too late to hide the beers in our hands or the empties on the dresser.

She told Betty to pour what was left down the toilet and throw the cans in the trash bin three houses down. "Then drag your ass to the kitchen and scrub every damn pot til it shines like the queen's silver. You're on cleanup duty the rest of the month." Betty took one last sip and scuttled off to dispose of the evidence. Then The Warden shoved my clothes into my suitcase and began dumping my art stuff into the burlap bag. "As for you, Liane, you're out of here for good."

I took over the packing before she crushed anything. "Why are you being harder on me?"

"Because Betty hasn't given me trouble for four years. I trust her to keep her nose clean another two until she's eighteen and gone. You're too damn clever for your own good. You've been here less than a year and nearly got me fired already. I won't trust you for three more."

"It's because you and Betty are Catholic and I'm Jewish."

The Warden shook her head. "It's because you remind me of me and I hate to see you waste your life like I wasted mine. A kick in the ass like this might straighten you out."

"Bullshit. You want to make your own life easier." I wrapped Ittel Rosa in a sweatshirt and shut my suitcase. "Where am I supposed to go?"

"Back to that camp. The social worker can figure out how to deal with you."

"It's closed and I don't have the new address."

"The superintendent at the old building will know where they moved. I'll call him now." The Warden turned to go. "You can stay tonight. I won't throw you out on the street at this hour, although I'm sure you could handle it. But I want you gone by noon tomorrow."

I was the first one up the next morning, long before my eleven o'clock shift. There was no way Miss Stone would take me back. By the time I finished a bowl of dry cereal and my third cup of coffee, I had a plan. I'd volunteer to work the late shift, which the manager had trouble filling and hated to get stuck with himself, if he let me sleep in the back of the store. Not only would I close up at night, I'd open in the morning so he could come in later. I'd find a park to nap in during the day. Betty could sneak me food from the home when she came in for her shift and let me in to shower and do laundry on Sunday mornings when The Warden went to church.

At eight o'clock the doorbell rang. "Anoush. What are you doing here?"

"I come to rescue you," he said.

I was about to tell him I had no intention of moving in with a dirty old man like him when The Warden appeared, pinning up her hair. "Mr. Kasparian. What are you doing here?"

"I come to persuade you to let Liane stay." I don't know if his response surprised me or The Warden more. Anoush continued. "I see this young lady when she come here. Terrible what happen to her and the other children. They have right to be angry and do bad in the world. Some do. But Liane smart. She learn English quick, soon speak better than me." He smiled. "She also take good care of her friend. And she figure out how this country work."

I wondered how much Anoush knew about me and Frima. Surely he didn't think telling The Warden that I'd become a talented thief and pick-up girl would convince her to let me stay?

"Liane take things from my work area. Bent nails, pieces wire, broken faucets. Not worth anything, so I wonder why. One day, I fix sink while Miss Stone and children out. I check see if other rooms need fixing and see statue Liane make with things she take. I go museum on my day off, is free, so I know is real art. If Liane live yet another place, go yet another school, she give up. You and me, Mrs. Zetticci, too late for us. But we should no give up on Liane."

I looked from one to the other. Mr. Kasparian extended his hand. Mrs. Zetticci shook it. He put on his hat and left. She went to the kitchen and reheated the coffee. I went upstairs and quietly, so as not to wake Betty, unpacked my suitcase and the burlap bag. Then, cradling Ittel Rosa, I crawled into bed until it was time to leave for my shift.

***

A week before school started, Betty and I saw *The Red Shoes* at Loew's Paradise. I hadn't been to that theater since Frima and I fought over the woman's change purse, the same day Frima met the couple who adopted her. The movie was gruesome—the ballerina leaps off a balcony that turns into a station platform with an oncoming train—but I liked that she chose her art over love. I was explaining the magical ending to Betty when we ran into Frima and a friend in the lobby.

Frima blushed and stammered. "Hi, Liane. I was going to call you. This is Joan. She goes to Walton with me." They wore matching light blue shirt-and-shorts sets and white sandals. I introduced Betty. We had on our usual rags, but in July we'd splurged on sneakers, which were comfortable for standing and serving custard all day.

"I can't believe it's still this hot so late in the summer," said Joan. "Why don't we all go to Jahn's for ice cream?" She turned to Frima. "I bet you've never been there." Frima said she'd only heard about it and it sounded like fun. I rolled my eyes and smirked at her.

We sat in a red leather booth, me and Betty across from Frima and Joan. On the jukebox, Patti Page sang "Confess." We all ordered sundaes, but Joan and Frima asked the waitress to hold the chocolate fudge. They didn't dare drip syrup on their blouses. When Joan pointed out the kitchen sink on the menu, Frima exclaimed, "I can't believe one person could eat twenty scoops of ice cream." Betty said she could but would rather spend the money on twenty beers.

I grinned at Frima. "Which of us said Reuven or Salomon could eat a kitchen sink by himself the last time we were at Jahn's?"

Joan asked who Reuven and Salomon were. I said they lived with us at Oyf Haskhole before Frima's adoption. Puzzled, Joan turned to Frima. "So you *were* here before? With them?"

I decided to "rescue" Frima from another lie. "She was here with me. And our freiers."

"What are freiers?" By now, Joan looked totally confused.

Frima kicked me under the table. I saw dread in her eyes, a feeling I understood. I also saw pleading, which irked me. Frima answered Joan quickly. "It's a German word. It means sponsors. I forgot that two people from the organization that brought us to America took us here one afternoon. Once a month, they'd check up on the six of us and treat us to a special outing."

Joan patted Frima's wrist. "I'm not surprised you forgot. This country must have been overwhelming when you first got here, especially after everything you'd been through."

Our sundaes arrived. I waited until we'd all eaten a few bites. Then I said, "The freiers sponsored us, all right. And treated us to more than ice cream. Of course, we treated them back."

Joan's eyes narrowed. "Meaning what?"

I licked my spoon, letting my tongue linger on the cold metal. "That Frima may not be as innocent as she seems. Remember, I've known her longer, and better, than you."

"Liar!" Joan thrust her face across the table, inches from mine.

"Don't you call my friend a liar." Betty flipped nuts down the collar of Joan's shirt.

Joan grabbed Betty's spoon, filled it with chocolate sauce, and flicked it at Betty's t-shirt. Poor stacked Betty, it landed on her left boob, leaving a shit-colored stain over the nipple. Soon the four of us were hurling whipped cream at one another. The manager kicked us out.

We stood dazed on the sidewalk. Betty lit a fag, shivering in the heat. "Lucky he didn't call the cops to break up the fight. I can't get in trouble with The Warden again."

"Relax. Mrs. Zetticci has rules about beer, not ice cream." I lit two cigarettes and offered one to Frima. Joan informed me that Frima didn't smoke. Frima accepted the cigarette, took a drag, and smiled at me. I blew a perfect smoke ring at her, my first ever. "Hey, Betty. Look at that," I said. The ring hung in the still air, long enough for Betty to bump it with one of hers.

Joan filled her lungs with clear air. Her voice quavered. "Suppose Jahn's reports me and Frima to Walton? Our outfits are a dead give-away that we're students there."

Frima told Joan, "Not everyone knows periwinkle stands for the pride of Walton High."

Betty announced she was going home.

"I've had enough for one day too," said Joan. "Let's go, Frima."

"I think I'll hang out with Liane for a while." Frima looked uphill, toward the stores on the Grand Concourse. "We haven't seen each other for a long time."

"Suit yourself." Joan tossed her head, then took off in the opposite direction from Betty.

Frima's eyes followed her, then looked down at her spattered clothes. "You could have ruined my reputation. At Walton, it matters. A lot."

I examined her blouse and my t-shirt. "It's only whipped cream. No chocolate. Your reputation is not indelibly stained." I waited until Frima smiled. "Alexander's, for old time's sake? We'll wash up in the ladies' room. I could use new clothes to start the new school year."

Frima hooked her arm in mine. "Me too. It's boring wearing light blue all the time."

CHAPTER 13

Things were cool again between Frima and me after we swiped some stuff at Alexander's. Frima told the Oberlanders she'd bought hers with allowance money, and Mrs. Zetticci didn't notice what I wore. Frima was still too busy to see me much during sophomore year. I didn't expect her to invite me to a sleepover to meet her friends; she didn't ask to hang out with me and my crowd. Periwinkles and Juvies lived by different rules, and Frima and I inhabited separate camps now. It was enough that we'd managed, so far, to still find common ground.

So we didn't visit, but we did call each other every couple of months. We stuck to safe, neutral subjects—how her classes were going; my latest art project. Once, when Walton let out early for parent-teacher conferences, she took the bus to Evander to see what I was up to in the studio. She liked the broken crockery pieces, although *Sisters* would always be her favorite. I was glad Betty and the other Juvies were gone the day she came by. It spared us both the awkward introductions and mutual disapproval. I would have been okay introducing her to Mr. Archer, though.

The next summer, Frima returned to Camp Boiberik, promoted to junior counselor, while Betty and I went back to scooping soft serve at Carvel. Betty would graduate in a year, and the manager and her typing teacher promised to line her up with a secretarial job. "Work will be harder than going to school," Betty said. "I can only drink from Friday to Sunday night if I want to show up sober on Monday morning." I told her she could do it, but my hopes weren't high.

A couple of weeks before school reopened, Betty came back from a drag race gnawing her nails. I hadn't been to a race since last year, opting instead to go home after my shift, where I could sculpt while I had our room to myself. Betty said she'd heard that the Board of Education was cutting high school budgets and giving that money to elementary schools gearing up for the baby boomers who'd be starting kindergarten in a year or two. "They're shutting down extras like gym and shop and secretarial classes," she moaned, "just when I need them to get a decent job."

"What about music and art?" I asked. Betty made a slashing motion across her throat.

I panicked. I needed studio time and materials to survive. Things weren't as drastic as we feared; the principal announced those subjects would be scaled back, not eliminated. Even so, I was afraid Mr. Archer wouldn't give me special treatment anymore. I'd have to share what little there was with the other students. Unless, that is, I made myself special in another way.

On the second day of classes, I put on the slinky, peach-colored dress I'd stolen from Alexander's a year ago. I'd never had an occasion to wear it. I got to school early and cornered Mr. Archer in his office. His desk was covered with photos of his wife and daughter. I sidled up to him. "If you continue to let me use the studio and extra materials, I'll return the favor."

Mr. Archer moved his briefcase between us. "What exactly are you offering, Liane?"

"I'm more grown up than you give me credit for, Thomas. I'm not a child. War ages you."

He gave me a pitying look. "I saw my share of orphans at the DP camps after VE Day. War doesn't make you an adult. It makes you a broken child."

I wanted to break him, to stab his heart with the sharpest metal scrap he'd salvaged for me. I panicked, thinking I'd killed myself instead. "I suppose now you'll cut me off."

"On the contrary. I intend to keep nurturing your talent. I have faith in you as an artist and I believe art has the power to heal." He handed me the key to the cabinet where he'd stored the art materials he'd bought with this year's budget and said he'd already spoken to the janitor. Then he told me he needed to prepare for his first class. Eyes down, I headed for the door.

"Oh, and Liane." I faced him. "From now on, it's best if you address me as Mr. Archer."

***

The day before Christmas Break, I was in the studio getting my last "fix" before school closed for ten days. Mr. Archer was there too, putting things in order for when students returned in January. I heard high heels clicking down the hall, accompanied by unsteady steps. Seconds later, a little girl burst into the room, squealed "Daddy," and flung herself into my teacher's arms. His wife raced in after her and gave him a big smooch before noticing me.

"Oops, I didn't mean to embarrass you," she said and extended her hand. "I'm Mary and you must be Liane. Thomas has told me so much about you. It's about time we finally met." I felt a pair of arms around my knees. Mary laughed. "Sorry, that's Lily. I'll call her off if you want."

Aside from the crabby crowds at the ice cream stand, the last time I'd had any real contact with kids that age was with Berta and Mendel. It was bittersweet to see a happy, normal child. "No, it's fine," I said. "She's cute." It was true. Lily had her father's floppy brown hair, her mother's wide-set green eyes, and her own unique dimples.

Mary asked her husband if he was ready to go. When he answered, "Affirmative," she turned to me. "Can we give you a lift? It's no trouble and it's beginning to snow. I'd feel better knowing you got home safely than letting you take the bus."

Before I could decline, Mr. Archer scooped up Lily and ushered all of us to the car, which was full of Juicy Fruit wrappers, empty Junior Mint boxes, and sticky baby stuff. I imagined raiding trash bins to make a sculpture dedicated to the modern American family's garbage.

Mr. and Mrs. Archer sat up front; Lily leaned against me in the back. Her parents took turns improvising verses to "The Twelve Days of Christmas," substituting "Mommy" or "Daddy" for "My true love" and prompting Lily to fill in the presents she wanted. "Dolly," she said nearly every time.

"What do you want Santa to bring you, Liane?" Mary asked.

"Garbage," I answered. "Interesting garbage."

CHAPTER 14

Second semester of junior year flew by, and Mr. Archer gave my work prominence again in the spring art show. I returned to Carvel for the summer. Betty's replacement was a sweet fourteen-year-old kid, barely old enough to get a work permit. We did our jobs and stayed out of each other's hair. I smoked alone during breaks and scouted the neighborhood for junk.

Mrs. Zetticci had thrown Betty a graduation party, complete with a store-bought cake. My hardened roommate, now former roommate, was touched that The Warden had paid for the cake out of her own pocket. Betty had gotten a job as a secretary at a plumbing supply company. With post-war construction still going strong, her position was secure, provided Betty didn't screw up. She'd gone on a three-day binge after commencement but sobered up in time to move out of the group home and report to work the following week. I was keeping my digits crossed for her.

Senior year classes loomed as boring as ever, except for world history, which began with a unit on World War Two. I'd seen the war at street level but now, from a safer position, I was ready for the big picture. Instead, the teacher mostly bragged about how American soldiers and citizens had sacrificed to lead the Allies to victory.

I raised my hand. "Excuse me, but the Allies bombed Berlin while people like me were struggling to survive there. They killed innocent children and grownups who hated the Nazis."

"The generals had no choice, Liane. If we hadn't dropped those bombs, Hitler would have killed even more people. Not only in Germany and the rest of Europe, but all around the globe. That madman's goal was world domination. Ours was global democracy."

I stood. "As far as I'm concerned, propaganda like 'America is the greatest country on earth' is no different than Hitler's German nationalism." I heard several gasps. The teacher took a menacing step toward me, then pointed a shaking finger at the door. I left and never went back.

***

Mid-year, others in my academic track applied to college. Betty, during one of her sober phone calls, told me I should apply too. "Sitting at a desk beats standing behind a counter," she said, "but not by much. You're still taking orders."

I said it was pointless to even think about going to art school.

"As pointless as ..." she began.

"Hope," I snapped. Betty must have given up hoping some of my star status would rub off on her because she didn't call me again for a long time.

Mrs. Zetticci also urged me to go on. When the agency still hadn't sent a new girl after a month, she let me set up a workshop in Betty's half of the room. I'd come home from the studio, snarf down dinner, then head upstairs to stack, twist, sand, file, glue, and nail. Sometimes I'd turn on the radio, which Betty had snuck out of Woolworth's by pretending she was pregnant, and dance around to look at my sculptures from different angles. Once Mrs. Zetticci caught me shimmying to Doris Day singing "Bewitched." She asked if I'd turned in the forms for college yet. I told her it would take more than hocus-pocus for me to apply, let alone get in. Unlike Betty, Mrs. Zetticci kept on bugging me, but I think she was genuinely doing it for my sake, not hers.

Of course, Mr. Archer told me I absolutely had to go to art school, that it would be a crime not to use my God-given talent. The awkwardness between us had long since evaporated, and even though he took new students under his wing each year, I was the only one who had a key to the cabinet and was allowed to use the studio after hours. He'd already written a letter of recommendation for me and said he'd remind his old professor of his promise to write one as well. I said I'd let him know. Not that my plans had changed, but I hated to disappoint him too.

Frima was the most insistent. She visited me again at Evander one afternoon and said she was applying to three of the "Seven Sister" colleges. I stacked some stones I'd found near the athletic field and told her, "I doubt our sisterhood can scale an ivy-covered wall."

She laughed. "I can't picture you at Barnard, Vassar, or Bryn Mawr either, but you belong in art school."

"Impossible. I don't have a rich daddy to pay my tuition."

"Then go to Hunter. It's free."

I dismantled the pile of stones and began lashing together plastic tubes using frayed twine and leather strips. "Hunter is a regular college, not an art school."

Frima leaned against the counter and watched me work. "You can major in art."

"Then I'd have to take all those other boring classes. It would drive me bonkers."

Frima threw up her hands. "You're already nuts. It's a good thing I still love you."

I tightened the twine and said I loved her too. "Now shoo. School closes in an hour and I want to finish this piece."

***

The day before graduation, I turned in my key to Mr. Archer. He said to let him know when—not if—I changed my mind about school and told me, "I expect to see your work featured in *Arts & Architecture* someday." He gave me his copy of the latest issue, June 1951. The cover showed a grid filled with odd shapes and squiggly lines. The work was two-dimensional, but it reminded me of the materials I used to build my sculptures. I told him that wherever I ended up, I'd find a place to make art and I'd pin the magazine cover over my workspace for inspiration.

He made me promise to visit, then hugged me goodbye. It was the kind of hug I imagined a father giving his daughter. I ran down the stairs, past the mural, and out the middle door. I hadn't expected to feel any regrets about leaving Evander, but as I turned around and looked back, I decided it wasn't such a bad school after all. Mr. Archer had pushed me and my art had grown more than if I'd depended solely on the kinds of trash I first used ten years ago. He also helped me understand that what I couldn't express in words, I could say with my hands.

The end of school also meant my stay at the group home was over. I told Mrs. Zetticci I didn't want a graduation party, but she still bought a cake for everyone to share. A couple of the girls gave me cards. Even Betty mailed one that said, "Congratulations and best wishes on your next adventure!" Underneath she'd written, "Find the point."

I decided to spend one more summer at Carvel, but Mrs. Zetticci wanted to make sure I was set up after it closed for the season. She got me a year-round counter job at a pizza parlor owned by her cousin Jim. He was branching out into spaghetti and lasagna and adding tables to serve sit-down meals. If I stayed on as a waitress, I could earn tips. Without a better offer, I said yes. Mrs. Zetticci also took it upon herself to prepare me for "life on the outside."

"You make it sound like I'm getting out of prison." I smiled. "I used to call you The Warden behind your back."

"What? You think I don't know?" She made me sit across from her at the table and said she was going to give me a lesson on how to manage my money.

"What? You think I don't know?" I echoed her.

"Do you know how to save?"

I cut myself a slice of cake. "Enough for food and rent, I don't need more."

"What about art materials? Your teacher's been supplying you the past four years."

"Getting what I need on my own has never stopped me before. I'll be fine. Don't worry."

But as I lay in bed that night, the last one Ittel Rosa and I would spend in the group home, I worried. Since leaving Berlin, I'd grown soft. I'd have to toughen up again.

PART FOUR:
FRIMA (1951–1955)

CHAPTER 15

"Tomorrow's when you should start applying to colleges." Otto put Stan Kenton on the turntable. Greta, lying on the couch, nodded. Earlier they'd danced to the *Arthur Murray Party* on their new television, a Chanukah present to themselves. In forty-five minutes, it would be 1951.

Frima sat on the floor, leafing through magazines. "Joan finished Hunter's application in an hour."

"Public institutions don't expect much." Greta put her feet down.

"The Seven Sisters are more demanding." Otto joined Greta on the couch.

Frima looked up at them. "Hunter's teacher certification program is one of the best."

"You never told me you wanted to be a teacher." Greta sounded hurt.

"Yes, I did. After a lady spoke at an assembly about the shortage. All the children born after the war are entering school."

"The Sister Colleges train teachers. A degree from one of them is more prestigious." Otto tapped his feet. Frima couldn't tell if he was keeping time to the music or growing impatient.

"Daddy's right," said Greta. "You'll have your choice of the top jobs after you graduate."

"I have to get in first. The guidance counselor said that last year only two Jews were admitted to Barnard, and their fathers give lots of money to its brother school, Columbia."

Otto planted his feet in the thick carpet. "Your academic record is excellent. Ditto your extracurricular activities. You'll stand out from the other Jewish applicants."

"Even if I got accepted, I doubt I'd be welcomed. I just want to fit in, like at Walton."

"Almost midnight," said Otto. He put on a Guy Lombardo record and counted down from ten. When he got to zero, the three of them waltzed around the coffee table. "To our daughter's success." He and Greta raised flutes of champagne, Frima ginger ale. She forced the fizzy liquid past the lump in her throat. Hours later, she lay as awake and alert as the nights she and Liane had sheltered during bombing raids. She propped Sugar on her stomach and asked what to do.

In a confident voice, she made the doll answer. "You have nothing to lose by applying. You can always turn them down if they say yes."

Frima sighed. "I won't get in anyway."

The doll bobbed its head emphatically. "If anyone can, it's you. Think of the other times you had doubts and managed to surprise yourself."

"I had a reason then. What's my reason now?"

"To honor your parents."

"My birth parents or my adoptive ones?"

"Both. Now go to sleep. We need our beauty rest."

***

Joan also urged Frima to apply. "Your father can afford the tuition. And money opens doors."

"A crack, and only if you're a very rich Jew. He doesn't have that much."

"Then prove your value a different way." Joan snapped her fingers. "Tell them you're a war orphan who survived on wit and grit. Convince them you'll do their school proud."

"You think it will work?"

"It impressed Principal Heffernan," Joan answered, "in a school of six thousand girls."

Frima applied to Vassar, Barnard, and Bryn Mawr. And Hunter for safety. Her essay read:

My parents and older brother were killed by the Nazis when I was eight. For five years, on the streets of Berlin, I survived by scavenging food and clothes from garbage bins. Occasional acts of kindness from strangers also saved me and kept alive my hopes for humanity. After the war, a refugee agency brought me to America where I was adopted by loving parents and was fortunate to attend one of New York City's top public high schools for girls. These blessings and benefits instilled a deep patriotism in me. I hope to further avail myself of such opportunities and contribute to the country that gave me a second chance. I believe the institution of higher learning that will best enable me to fulfill that dream is _____ College.

In late January, Frima called Liane. "I mailed the applications. It's out of my hands now."

"Don't worry. You're a shoo-in."

"I'm also Jewish, remember? So I wrote about why my background was an asset." Frima read her essay to Liane.

"Telling them was a good idea."

"Actually, it was Joan's."

After a pause, Liane said, "You left out the juicy parts. Was that Joan's idea too."

"She knows nothing about that. Promise you won't rat me out like you almost did before."

"I promise. Sometimes I get jealous, but I hope you get in. You deserve better than me."

"When I was adopted, you said you were glad to see me go because I'd hold you back, not because you wanted me to get ahead."

"I say a lot of things."

"So I shouldn't believe you?"

"I didn't say that."

Frima gripped the phone. "What should I believe?"

"You're smart. Figure it out yourself." Liane hung up.

***

Vassar and Bryn Mawr sent form letters within a week, stamped "Applicant does not meet the college's requirements." But another letter arrived a month later, on cream-colored stationery: "The Barnard Admissions Committee is impressed by your school records and unusual essay. We are interested in learning more about you. Please call our office to schedule an interview."

The interviewer, Mr. Richards, was silver-haired and as tall as Otto but half as wide. He wore a pinstripe suit and gold cufflinks. Frima wore the tweed suit and silk blouse Greta had bought her to make a good impression. Mr. Richards served tea. "Your essay mentions acts of kindness."

"Yes. Once a woman caught me digging potatoes in her garden. I was afraid she'd turn me into the Gestapo. Instead, she brought me a cup of soup and a loaf of bread. Others offered gloves or shoes, whatever they could spare, given that they didn't have much themselves."

"Did they ask for anything in return?"

"No. I had nothing to give them."

"Perhaps you had to steal? Or do other things you're not proud of?" The interviewer pressed his fingers to his lips. Sunlight streamed in the window. His cufflinks gleamed.

Frima squirmed. Was his look suggestive or was she remembering the appraising eyes of soldiers? "Most memories are so painful that I buried them. I'd rather hold onto the good ones."

Mr. Richards stood to signal the end of the interview. He said decisions would be made by mid-April and thanked Frima for her time. As she would tell Sugar that night, "He was polite but noncommittal, as only the rich can afford to be, because they don't have to beg."

***

Principal Heffernan reminded seniors to continue studying after mailing their applications since admissions were contingent on final grades. Frima did so gladly. Along with band commitments, maintaining her grades was a good excuse to decline dates. Nevertheless, the Periwinkles expected her to attend Clinton's football games and dances. As determined as they were to go to college, boys were still on their minds. Frima couldn't explain her aversion to them. Liane alone would understand, but Frima had been too busy to see her in months. She gratefully accepted Liane's invitation to Evander's final student exhibit. Liane's work had changed. She told Frima that after seeing huge metal sculptures at the 9th Street Art Show, she'd scaled down the ideas to her smaller work. Frima squinted at "Page," a slab carved with lines of letter-like squiggles. "I feel like I should be able to read what it says."

"That's the point. It's like a secret you keep trying to crack, but ..."

"The artist isn't telling," Frima finished. She and Liane shared a smile. "Where will you show your work after you graduate?" she asked.

"I don't care, as long as I can make it."

"I envy you. Simply doing isn't enough for me. I want recognition."

Liane's chewed an already bitten fingernail. "Is that what finally persuaded you to have sex, wanting soldiers to say you were pretty?"

"God, no. I felt as ugly as the garbage we fished out of the trash."

"How do you feel now?"

Frima examined her polished nails and tossed her wavy red hair. "I'm noticed for being pretty but I've been chaste for five years. I've almost convinced myself that I'm a virgin."

Liane snorted. "You can reinvent yourself in lots of ways, but not that one."

***

Admissions letters arrived during spring break. Marilyn was off to Catholic, all-girls Marymount Manhattan College. She'd marry her fiancé Frank after sophomore year; the Periwinkles predicted she'd be pregnant and leave before finishing her junior year. Dorothy was in the first class of girls admitted to City College. Joan was going to Hunter's Downtown campus. They turned to Frima, who read aloud:

"Barnard College is impressed by your courage in overcoming challenging circumstances. We trust you will return this recognition through outstanding scholarship, admirable community service, and an exemplary life that brings honor to yourself and our institution."

"I told you your essay would win them over." Joan was proud of her. They all were. Frima pledged that despite attending a Sister College, she'd remain loyal to Walton's Periwinkles. That night, as she tucked Barnard's letter beneath the *Sisters* sculpture, Frima also promised, "and I'll always remain loyal to my first, and forever, sister."

***

Fifteen hundred girls, in periwinkle blue caps and gowns, watched their parents fill Walton's assembly hall. Otto and Greta sat in the first row of guests. Principal Heffernan spoke. "Four years ago I urged you to think big, words you have taken to heart. Today is commencement, which means 'beginning.' I have faith that you will continue to bring honor to your parents and this school." She called Frima up to give the valedictorian's speech.

"Our achievements would not be possible without the guidance, inspiration, and support of parents, teachers, and peers who believed in us when we doubted ourselves. Walton prepared us to be leaders. Be humble but don't let humility stop you from aiming high. Remember where you came from and bring others along with you. Don't give up when life is hard. You have the tools to make it better: love of family and friends, a positive attitude, and determination."

The applause was sustained. Frima returned to her seat until one by one, students were called up alphabetically for their diplomas. When Principal Heffernan got to G, Frima imagined accepting one for Frima Gersten, to be delivered via angel to Abraham and Mirla. Thirty minutes later, she claimed Frima Oberlander's diploma and waved it at Otto and Greta.

After the recessional, Otto drove them to Le Pavillon. The restaurant's paneled interior was dark, but the crystal chandeliers, linen tablecloths, and gleaming silverware dazzled their eyes. The waiter extolled nouvelle cuisine and said he'd be back with complimentary gin cocktails for Otto and Greta and a special creation for the young lady. They studied the menu until the waiter returned with their drinks and addressed Otto. "Monsieur, may I recommend our feature du jour, filet de sole bonne femme?" Otto said they'd all have that and accepted the suggested Sauvignon Blanc to accompany the dish. "Magnifique." The waiter bowed and swept off.

Frima sipped something pink and sweet. "What did you order for us, Daddy?"

"I have no idea," he admitted. "I was too embarrassed to ask."

By the time the food came, they were more relaxed. They tried to guess what was in their dish. "Fish," said Greta, which reduced them to giggles.

"Onion and mushrooms," said Otto.

Greta slapped his arm. "You can see those. Ditto the cream sauce. Guess by taste."

Frima nibbled. "Lemon?" She sniffed. "And something winey."

She put down her fork. It tasted awful. Her parents hardly touched their entrees either. The waiter brought their salads at the end of the meal. "Is the food not to your liking, monsieur?"

"No, no. It is excellent. My daughter graduated today. We're all too excited to eat."

"She's going to Barnard," Greta said.

"Ah." The waiter presented Otto with the check inside a leather folder and left.

Frima peered over her father's shoulder. Thirty dollars for food, ten more for drinks, plus a tip. A lot for a meal too strange to eat. Barnard students ate in places like this all the time. Her parents believed that Frima had joined their ranks, and by extension, so had they. But she knew that although the Admissions Office had accepted her, she'd still be an outsider among her peers.

CHAPTER 16

Before she left for her last summer at Camp Boiberick, Frima completed a stack of registration forms. Greta pushed aside the residence hall application. "You'll live at home and commute."

Otto agreed. Frima assumed the dorm was too costly. Her parents were comfortable, but Barnard's tuition was still a stretch. "No. I can afford it," Otto said. "Mommy will explain."

"The other girls in your class have lived with their parents for eighteen years," Greta said. You've been with us for four. Surely it isn't too much to ask for four more before you're gone?"

"Living here is more than I dreamed of. Still, I was looking forward to being on my own."

Greta dabbed her eyes. "I guess it's natural for a young woman to test her independence."

"I've had my independence. I wanted to exercise it under better circumstances." Frima saw the grief in her parents' eyes. "Suppose I lived in the dorm but came home on weekends?"

"Oh, yes." Greta's sigh filled the room. "Otto?" He nodded and blinked.

It meant fewer social activities with classmates, but Frima didn't expect many invitations. She could see Joan on weekends. Liane too, although those were her busiest days at the pizza parlor. Besides, what would they talk about? Frima would say, "I'm taking history, calculus, and nineteenth-century literature."

"I'm taking orders for spaghetti and lasagna," Liane would reply.

The week she returned from camp, Frima received a packet from Brooks Residence Hall with photos of the elegant stone dormitory and standard room furnishings, which Otto declared too plain. It also contained a letter saying Frima's roommate would be Elizabeth Lee Stanton, from Montgomery, Alabama, a graduate of St. Timothy's School. Frima pictured a rich Southern belle. She wondered what Elizabeth would make of the letter describing her.

On moving-in day, Frima and the Oberlanders arrived mid-afternoon. "Welcome, Class of 1955" signs were festooned with white and blue streamers, almost the same blue as Walton's periwinkle. In Frima's room, the bed closer to the window was made up, so she assumed Elizabeth had claimed it, although five monogrammed suitcases were strewn on the bed left for Frima. She was pondering what to do when a petite blonde bounced in, wearing a fur-collared dress despite the early September heat and swinging a cowhide drawstring pocketbook.

Greta extended her hand. "You must be Elizabeth. We're Frima's parents. I'm sure you two girls will become good friends."

"Friends call me Bitsy." She stared at the hand. "My parents dropped me off early this morning. They're headed home. Daddy is arguing a case before the Alabama Supreme Court tomorrow. He's in line for a judgeship." She threw her pocketbook on her own bed. Frima took that as a signal that she could begin removing Bitsy's luggage from hers.

"Don't touch." Bitsy reddened. "Your fingerprints may smudge the leather." Frima and her parents looked at one another. So, Bitsy didn't want a "dirty Jew" contaminating her things.

***

In October, Frima invited Joan for lunch and a campus tour. Frima usually sat alone in the dining hall and having company made her nostalgic for Walton. Joan said little at first, awed by the linen napkins and heavy silverware, but soon they were trading stories about classes and teachers.

Joan was taking honors English. "The professor is short and pudgy and wears a bow tie. And get this, my English prof has a German accent."

"Probably a refugee from the Nazis," Frima said.

Joan blanched. "I never thought of that." She took two lumps of sugar using the silver tongs. "Fancy. Hunter students are smart, like Walton's. It feels like home. How about you?"

Frima stood. "I'm ready to walk off lunch." She led Joan past Barnard's ivy-covered halls, inside the music building's practice rooms, through the art studios, and into the natatorium. Then they crossed the avenue to Columbia's Low Memorial Library and strolled along College Walk. Male students in tweed jackets, their scarves whipped by the wind, hurried past.

Frima didn't glance at them but Joan stared. "Lucky you. Hunter's like a convent."

"Miss Modern. I thought you weren't interested."

"Not in the guys from Dewitt Clinton, or should I say Dimwit Clinton? They didn't exactly share Walton's academic reputation."

'Whereas the young men at Columbia are smarter?"

"Also richer." Joan linked arms with Frima. "But you're just as stand-offish as you were in high school. It's time you loosened up, Miss Frima Oberlander."

"I'm looser than you think."

"Aha. A woman of mystery. Men find that attractive."

"And women?"

Joan glanced at her sideways. "Women prefer friends who open up. Spill your guts."

Frima pulled her coat tighter. "I'll save that for when you give me a tour of Hunter." They scheduled a date for Thanksgiving week. Frima hoped that by then, Joan would have forgotten her promise to open up.

Six weeks later, they met outside the 68th and Lexington IRT station. Although Hunter was older than Barnard, most of its buildings were constructed during the Depression and not very interesting to look at. "Except for one," Joan said, "which you'll appreciate." They walked to the Eleanor Roosevelt House, which the former first lady had bequeathed to the college.

"Eleanor cares more about the Jews than Franklin ever did," Frima said.

"More about women and the poor too. She's always been ahead of her time." Joan looked at her watch. "Time to go. I'm meeting friends for dinner. Let's get together again soon."

Frima walked to a nearby café and ordered hot chocolate. Sitting by herself in a booth for four, she was overwhelmed by loneliness. It was past time to call Liane.

***

"Lasagna's on the house." Liane tucked the order pad in her apron pocket and led Frima to a Formica-topped table at the back of Jim's Pizzeria and Italian Eatery. The other tables were empty. A lone customer ate a slice of pizza and nursed a Coke at the counter.

"Here you go Toots. Fresh pan for you and your friend, Red." Jim put two steaming plates on the shelf of the pass-through. "Free seconds if you want. Wednesday night. Gonna be slow."

Liane brought their food and fetched silverware at the waitresses' station. Frima spread a paper napkin from the table dispenser across her lap, cut her lasagna with a knife and fork, took a bite, and closed her eyes. "Heavenly. Residence hall food is bland, although mercifully it's not kosher. My parents would never mix meat and milk."

Liane forked off a big wedge oozing meat and cheese. "What's on the menu tonight?"

"Turkey fricassee. They're still serving leftovers from the night before people went home for Thanksgiving. My roommate Bitsy took the train to Alabama a day early. It was nice to have the room to myself. The quiet felt less lonely than the silence when she's there."

"Bitsy? Holy crap. What a puny name." Liane took another forkful. "I never got used to sleeping alone after you and Berta were adopted or Betty graduated. My roommates now leave me alone to work."

"I'm glad you're still making art. Will you invite me to a 'show' in your room?"

"I barely have enough space to make work, let alone exhibit it."

"So where do you keep your finished pieces?"

"In a carton, in my closet." Liane picked at the rest of her lasagna. "Tell me about you."

Frima cleaned her plate while she talked about her English Literature and French classes.

"My favorite is history. It's a year-long survey course, beginning with ancient civilization. I'm not sure how I'll deal with the war when we get to it next semester."

"If it's like my high school class, expect lots of rah, rah, America. What about music?"

"Barnard doesn't have a band, so no clarinet. I don't mind. Classes keep me busy enough."

"Dating?"

Frima laughed. "Jews are off limits to Columbia men. Besides, I'm not interested. You?"

"Nope. Waitressing and art keep me busy." Liane whispered, "Although, I do find time to give some customers a little extra service. If Jim found out he'd fire me, but it's hard to get by on my salary and tips. I have to buy supplies I can't find on the street. Mr. Archer spoiled me."

"You have your diploma. Why not find a better job?"

"I like the night shift. Daylight's better for scavenging and sculpting anyway. I'm not cut out to work nine to five."

Frima agreed. "You could get a job at a nicer restaurant."

"Yeah. If I can pronounce the names of the dishes on the menu."

"It doesn't have to be a fancy French restaurant." Frima couldn't see Liane at Le Pavillon, but why not something in between that and Jim's? "An Italian restaurant with tablecloths or a steak house? You can pronounce sirloin and baked potato."

"Too high class for me. I'm not an Oberlander. I'm still a dirty, slutty street urchin."

"Cut the self-pity, Liane. Why must things be one extreme or the other?"

A crowd of twelve came through the door, bringing a rush of cold air. Jim pushed two tables together and motioned Liane to take their orders. "Gotta get back to work," she told Frima. "I hope they want Chianti. The tips add up after three bottles."

While Frima put on her coat, Liane brought her a loaf of garlic bread, still warm and pungent in its foil wrapper. "To stink up your dorm room. It'll force Miss Itsy Bitsy to sleep in the lounge and you'll have the room to yourself again until the air clears."

They hugged, the garlic bread between them. "If all the windows were propped open for a week, my roommate's nose would still be stuck in the air." Frima kissed Liane's cheek. While yours, she thought sadly, will remain stuck in the gutter.

***

"I swear, if I look at one more irregular verb my eyes will cross." Bitsy broke the silence, more intense than usual since they were studying for finals. Frima suggested they quiz one another. Bitsy scoffed. "You speak French with a German accent. I can't understand a word you say."

Suit your Southern-accented self, Frima thought. She'd requested a roommate change for the second semester but was told she'd have to wait until sophomore year. Bitsy swiveled in her desk chair to face Frima. "What are you wearing to tonight's Midnight Breakfast?" The twice-a-year event, on the night before finals week, was a Barnard tradition. This semester's theme was "An American in Paris." Board trustees would serve the students croissants, Eggs Benedict, and crepes. Some girls wore pajamas and robes, others got dolled up as if for an all-night ball.

An ivory satin gown and mink wrap lay on Bitsy's bed. Frima pointed to the cotton PJs and plaid flannel bathrobe she herself had on. Bitsy gaped. "Mon Dieu! Not that ratty old thing!" From her closet, Bitsy pulled a burgundy velvet, gilt-embroidered, Chinese robe. "It's too long for me but it'll fit you." It did, except that Frima's pajama bottoms hung an inch below the hem.

Bitsy got on her knees to pin them up. "There. Now you look respectable."

Frima admired herself in the mirror. Had Bitsy really knelt at her feet?

After passing through a door decorated like the Arc de Triomphe, the students entered the candle-lit dining room and were handed calligraphy place cards with assigned seats. Frima didn't have to worry about who'd sit with her. In fact, since her table mates didn't know one another either, she could join their conversation. Dressed in Bitsy's robe, she felt like one of them. Yet an occasional pinprick in her shins reminded her that after exams and Christmas break, during which others skied, ate ham, and exchanged expensive gifts, she'd again be on her own.

CHAPTER 17

"What's that racket?" Otto demanded.

"Rock 'n' Roll, Daddy. It's what everyone listens to in the dorm."

Otto reminded Frima she was in her parents' house for the summer. "You can play Tony Bennett and Nat King Cole, but not that awful noise."

"The generation before yours said the same thing about jazz." Frima lowered the volume but let the record continue to spin.

Greta shut it off. "What's gotten into you? Show your father some respect."

"You insisted I live at home when I'm not in school. It's my house too."

Otto and Frima glared at each other. Greta wrung her hands. "What if Frima confined that music to her bedroom?"

"You're treating me like a prisoner." As lonely as Frima had been at school, her parents' roomy apartment felt crowded. To escape, she got a sales job at Bergdorf Goodman. It was boring, but she liked window shopping on Fifth Avenue during lunch. In July, she bought *Anne Frank: The Diary of a Young Girl* at Scribner's, then sat on a bench in Central Park to read Eleanor Roosevelt's introduction: "*By turns thoughtful, moving, and amusing, her account offers a fascinating commentary on human courage and frailty and a compelling self-portrait of a sensitive and spirited young woman whose promise was tragically cut short.*" Frima thought of everything Otto and Greta had given her. The rest of the summer, if her self-pity resurfaced, she remembered Mrs. Roosevelt's words and appreciated her good fortune. She took it as a sign that she was a real grownup now, not the one she'd merely played at being five years ago.

Due to a mix-up, Frima and Bitsy were assigned to the same room as sophomores. Frima would have to wait another year to move unless she proved extenuating circumstances. But what could she claim: "My roommate hates me because I'm a Jew?" It was easier to leave things as they were. By now, she and Bitsy were used to mutual avoidance. However, Anne Frank's diary had convinced Frima not to remain silent. The Student Government Association usually addressed issues like curfew but occasionally got involved in national elections and America's role as the leader of the free world. Frima would bring a pressing issue before them.

She pored over news reports in the library, then got on the agenda at the next meeting. Her topic was "The Plight of the Lost Children." Frima began, "Now is time to leave girlish matters behind and earn our title as the 'Women of Barnard.' Today I draw your attention to those whose childhood was lost to the war, the hundreds of thousands of orphaned or displaced youngsters who never got to play. Most live at state-run institutions in appalling conditions." Despite her painful memories, she'd read that Kloster Indersdorf was one of the better places.

"Many of you are aware that I'm a Jew. Some know that I'm also a war orphan. Yet, I am speaking not only of Jewish children but those from all religions and countries, including where your families originated. A letter to *The New York Times* warns that children in Soviet-occupied territories 'will be taught hatred for the ideals we hold dear and militarized for a Communist conquest of the world.'" Two students in the front row raised their hands to their mouths. "Being alarmed is not enough. We must act. I propose the Barnard student body do three things. First, petition Congress to make foreign aid contingent on humane conditions for these children. Second, help bring more of them to this country so they grow up in a democracy. Third, send letters to the United Nations Relief and Rehabilitation Administration explaining our concerns and proposals, with heart-wrenching photos of the squalid institutions and suffering children."

A dozen girls signed onto the Lost Children campaign, half from Delta Gamma. Dolly, a senior, told Frima that DG stood for "Do Good" and the sorority supported charitable causes. Dolly's father worked for the Department of State and knew high-level UNRRA staff. "He'll make sure our letters don't end up in the slush pile." Sure enough, two weeks later, Frima got a reply from a dignitary who encouraged the group to continue writing and said he'd forward their mail to other officials. Frima had hoped for more, but the DGs were pleased. Dolly even hugged her. Too bad Bitsy wasn't there to witness it. They invited Frima to the DG house to write a second letter. "Come for afternoon tea," Dolly said. Too bad Otto and Greta couldn't see that.

Frima brought more articles from the *Times*. The others had scoured the *Herald Tribune*. Their scholarship and commitment reminded Frima of the Periwinkles, and for the first time at Barnard, she felt accepted. She looked around the solarium, warmed by late-afternoon sunshine streaming through leaded glass windows. "How do you get to join DG?"

Dolly explained. "After a month of getting to know those we invite to pledge, the chapter votes on who we want to join. We send our recommendations to the national office and girls who are approved attend an initiation, where they're pinned with DG's Golden Anchor Badge."

Frima pictured herself being pinned. "Is anyone ever not approved?"

"Not in our chapter. We'd never recommend anyone unsuitable. DG is a private club."

Frima felt a chill. "Private club" was code for "No Jews allowed."

CHAPTER 18

"Help me decide." Frima pleaded on a midnight call to Joan. The deadline to declare a major was two weeks away. The choice seemed obvious. History was her favorite subject. "But as much as I love the past, I long to shape the future." Frima sighed. "I know I sound crazy."

Joan clucked. "Is that any way for a Walton Periwinkle to talk?"

Frima lay down in the dorm corridor, uncoiling the telephone cord hanging from the wall outlet. "Pep talk, Dr. Freud. Bitte." Joan was majoring in English with a minor in psychology.

"My diagnosis iss neurotic ambivalence. Ve must resolve these opposing forces."

Frima giggled.

"Seriously, didn't you want to be a teacher?" Joan asked. Frima acknowledged she did. "Teach high school history. Students love learning about pyramids and mummies, and you can slip in modern history so they don't repeat their parents' mistakes. Teens will lap that up too."

"Adolescence is too late to change them. They're already cynics." Frima was an exception, for reasons she couldn't explain. A legacy from her birth parents? The Oberlanders' kindness?

"Then teach elementary school," Joan suggested. "Young children are more malleable."

"Unless they've been irreversibly traumatized." Like Mendel. Yet Berta was okay. "So the solution is to major in education and teach children not to hate others based on looks or beliefs."

"Noble vork," Joan said. "Your analysis iss completed."

Frima said to send her the bill. "The funny thing is, I told my parents that since I wanted to be a teacher, I could go to Hunter instead of setting my sights on Barnard."

"And they said?"

"A Sister School would open more doors."

"More than for our immigrant parents," Joan added. "Thank God we were born smart."

Frima crept to her room, where Bitsy slept soundly. Reuven and Salomon were smart; it didn't help them. Ditto Liane. But Liane was also talented. Maybe that would be her door opener.

**

Frima immersed herself in pedagogy courses that fall. In the spring, she was assigned to student teach fourth grade at P.S. 92, a public school in Harlem. The teacher was a gray-haired Jewish woman, Mrs. Gewirtz. Most of the staff was white. Frima did the prescribed reading, math, and geography lessons. Mrs. Gewirtz, observing at the back of room, nodded encouragingly. When it was time to create her own lesson plan, Frima proposed one on tolerance. Mrs. Gewirtz smiled quizzically but gave Frima free rein. The autonomy felt good after years of following orders.

Frima wanted to really engage the children. They often sang, unprompted, at recess, so she borrowed Otto's recording of Frank Sinatra singing "The House I Live In" and began, "Today we're going to learn about democracy, a big word. The song we'll listen to asks, 'What is America to me?'" The children sat on the floor in a semi-circle as Sinatra sang about people he met on the street and at work, in small towns and big cities. Frima replayed the third verse: "The children in the playground / The faces that I see / All races and religions / That's America to me."

"Did you like the song?" she asked. Thirty heads nodded. "What is the man saying?"

A small girl with scabbed knees raised her hand. "He likes the house where he lives."

The boy next to her, who had a perpetually runny nose, added, "It's close to stores."

"Yes, but he's not only talking about where he lives. What is he telling us about how we should *all* live in America?"

The darkest-skinned boy spoke next. "Be nice to people no matter what color they are."

Frima was delighted, but then a lighter-skinned girl said, "I ain't gotta be nice to you. You too dark." Frima waited for the boy to defend himself. Instead, he rubbed his arm as if wiping off the color. Before Frima could think what to say, the children were out of their seats, making fun of one another's skin and hair, shouting that they were dumb or smelled bad. Amid the pushing and shoving, the record player got bumped. Frima heard the needle scratch Otto's record.

Mrs. Gewirtz smacked a ruler on the blackboard. The children quieted down and were sent back to their seats. "We don't call one another names or use nasty words here. You're all beautiful in God's eyes. Anyone speaking like that again will be sent to the principal's office. Now, arms crossed on desks, heads down, and eyes closed for ten minutes."

Later, in the teachers' lounge, Mrs. Gewirtz told Frima not to blame herself. Even her own lesson plans sometimes went awry, and she'd been teaching for thirty years. "These children have been brought up to not like themselves or anyone who looks like them. It's not their fault either."

Nevertheless, Frima was angry at them for defying her. Her head knew they were victims of discrimination as much as she was, but her heart couldn't summon any sympathy. Would that prevent her from being a good teacher? A good mother? Despite the love lavished on her by the Oberlanders, Frima was still a "lost child" herself. A lost child doomed to be a lost adult.

CHAPTER 19

Frima's confidence recovered the following fall, when she student-taught in Queens. Along with new houses for veterans and their families came new schools. Frima's students had fathers who were heroes and mothers who baked cookies. They were verbal and well-behaved. Her advanced methods courses were also going well. She anticipated a problem-free last year at Barnard.

Then the Brooklyn Thrill Killers hit the news. That summer, four Jewish teenage boys had killed two men, drowning one and beating the other, and tortured several others. Frima received antisemitic calls, letters in the mail, and messages tacked to and slipped under her door. "Too bad Hitler missed a few," "My brother died because FDR sent him to fight for the Jews," and "Barnard Thrill Killers are coming to get YOU." Bitsy complained that she felt threatened—any harm intended for Frima could hurt her—and was moved to a new room. Frima, in greater danger, asked to be moved too, but was told Bitsy had been given the only one available.

Living without Bitsy should have brought relief, but being alone magnified Frima's fear. Dorm staff put a stop to the notes but couldn't prevent the calls and letters, some stamped with swastikas. Frima was told she'd graduate in a wheelchair or not at all. Most frightening were the silent calls and empty envelopes. She thought of phoning her parents, but they'd be as powerless as her. Besides, telling them her Jewishness was being used against her might sound like saying "I told you so." She was tempted to quit school altogether, but that would hurt them more. Two weeks after Bitsy moved out, Frima finally requested protection from Barnard's chief of security.

"What did you have in mind?" he asked.

"Isn't it your job to figure out what will make me safe?"

He smirked. "A daytime guard to walk you to and from classes? A nighttime guard outside your door? A food tester to make sure your meals aren't poisoned?"

Frima stared at her lap.

"The college thinks it best not to call attention to the matter. Things will die down." He stood. Frima understood the matter was closed.

She agreed about not standing out, though, and considered giving up the Lost Children campaign, but without her, it would fizzle. When a month passed with no attacks, and the calls and letters waned, Frima relaxed a little, but her loneliness persisted. Liane would understand how targeted and isolated she felt. Frima called; Liane invited her to the restaurant.

"I'd prefer a more private place to talk." Frima whispered.

Liane cooed. "Ooh. You've got secrets to spill?"

"No. Just paranoia to unload."

"How about Loew's Paradise, for old time's sake? We can sit at the back of the balcony."

Frima suggested Jahn's. "A booth next to someone loudly slurping a kitchen sink."

They met that Sunday afternoon before Liane's evening shift. When their sundaes arrived, with extra whipped cream and chocolate syrup, Frima unloaded. "I can't escape the Jewish Thrill Killers. Even girls who used to be friendly keep their distance. They claim it's for their own safety." Frima laughed bitterly. "A psychiatrist blamed the boys' violence on comic books."

"Bullshit. Trauma leads to that kind of rage. Did you read what one defendant said? 'If you wanted to fit in, you had to kill.' That's why Germans went along with massacring Jews."

"All the same, Anne Frank proved turning against others isn't inevitable. I let go of my anger. Sometimes." She'd even felt a little sympathy for Bitsy's fear. "Can you let go of yours?"

"Mine's always there, but art helps me release it. Better to torture materials than people." Liane twisted strips of her napkin into a chain. "What do you do when you can't let it go?"

"I bury it thinking of the good things that have happened to me since Berlin."

"And that works?" Liane asked.

"It's all I have." Yet it wasn't enough. Frima's good fortune depended on others. Liane's art was wholly her own. So why wasn't Liane using it to open doors? "You can take your life into your own hands," she told her. "Check out scholarships. Call that teacher you liked and ask if his artist friends need an assistant. It would be an apprenticeship, like my student teaching."

Liane aimed a gooey spoonful at Frima. "Lay off me and take care of yourself. I'm happy doing what I am. Can you say the same?" Frima watched with relief as Liane popped the spoon into her mouth. But she had no answer to Liane's question.

***

Frima's final student teaching assignment was in the Bronx, at an elementary school that served the children of working-class immigrants. Eventually, they'd attend Liane's old high school. In May, she assembled her certification portfolio, including an essay that said, "I learned the importance of teachers in the lives of children, especially when home cannot meet their basic needs." After passing the exam, she applied to several public schools and two private schools. She assumed they'd no more accept a Jewish teacher than a Jewish student, but Otto and Greta argued that Barnard had admitted her. Yes, Frima thought, then relegated her to the margins.

She was ready to leave Barnard on commencement day. She watched the Oberlanders enter the auditorium, looking as proud as the other parents. For graduation, they'd given her a set of suitcases, which

Frima could have used the last four years when she was going back and forth between the dorm and their apartment. Now she was getting an apartment with Joan and two other new teachers from Hunter. "You can still use them to come home on weekends," said Otto.

"Until you're married," Greta said. And give us grandchildren, was understood.

After the ceremony, Frima met them on the lawn. Greta hugged her. Otto kissed her on both cheeks, a charming holdover from his Austrian upbringing. "Time for a photo," he said. Frima looked around for someone to take it. Bitsy stood two yards away. Frima thrust the Brownie into her hands. Startled, Bitsy instinctively snapped a picture, but as she handed the camera back to Frima, she furtively wiped her hands in the folds of her graduation gown. Frima smiled to herself. Life was precarious, but for the moment, she'd savor this small victory.

PART FIVE:
LIANE (1956–1960)

Chapter 20

The lock was flimsy but it was all I could afford. "You stashing drugs?" the woman across the hall had asked when I put it on my bedroom door.

"None of your beeswax," I told her. I'd rather she and my other housemates think I was dealing than hiding scraps and artwork. Not that they were nosy, but befriending them was as pointless as stewing a knee sock. I missed Betty. Some nights, I drank a bottle of Chianti myself. I disliked the buzz, but it filed the edges off my loneliness.

I'd moved into the apartment in the same low-rent neighborhood as my old high school two months ago. Another waitress, one of the many who passed through Jim's Pizzeria and Italian Eatery, had offered me her room when she left. It wasn't a bad deal. Rent and utilities were four hundred a month, split five ways. I could manage my share if tips were decent. If not, my "office" behind Jim's dumpster made up the shortfall with change to spare.

My housemates and I shared a living room with a stained couch and sagging armchairs, tiny bathroom, and galley kitchen. At Jim's, I ate a late lunch or dinner for free, depending on my shift, and dunked stale Italian bread in my coffee for breakfast. Of the three bedrooms, mine was the smallest but I had it to myself. In addition to a single bed and dresser, a salvaged table served as a workbench. Above it, I'd pinned the five-year-old cover of *Arts & Architecture* from Mr. Archer. The room's best feature was a big closet that held my waitress uniforms and only dress, leaving space for my art stuff, which I stored in cartons that once held tomatoes and Parmesan cheese.

As I bundled up to go to work, I welcomed the quiet. Christmas was over, but the carols my housemates had blared on their radios rang in my head. Jim's was one mile west up Gun Hill Road, a climb I didn't mind unless it was pouring or freezing, in which case I took the bus. But I'd rather spend the fifteen-cent fare at the hardware store midway between my apartment and the restaurant, where I checked the discount bin for defective items: half-grooved screws, unspooled wires. The more damaged, the more interesting. The last two weeks, however, I'd eyed a new soldering iron which, at $1.25, was beyond my ten-cent limit. It would take lots of "office hours" to earn that kind of dough. And while I wasn't above pocketing an occasional item—more for the thrill than the thrift—this one would poke another hole in my moth-eaten coat.

"Veal Parmesan and shrimp scampi top of the menu tonight," Jim hollered as soon as I walked in. "Family with four kids in booth three, two tables in back need bussing ASAP, and cheese shakers gotta be refilled before the late crowd arrives."

"Anything else, Il Duce?" I muttered as I pinned my name label above my pocket. I really wasn't annoyed though. Jim was a good boss, fair and hard-working himself. He'd improved the restaurant since I'd started waitressing there. It was a family place now with white table-cloths, grown-up entrees, and children's meals. Jim's lasagna was still the best in the Bronx. My job hadn't changed, but the pricier menu brought bigger tips. I charged my special clientele more too.

I was cleaning up the wreckage at booth three after the bleary-eyed parents and cranky kids left when a biker, a restaurant regular and semi-regular special of mine, sauntered in. The guy sometimes gave staff a hard time, especially after a third glass of Chianti, complaining the spaghetti sauce was cold or we'd stinted on the meatballs. Jim always gave in; he didn't want any trouble. The biker's nickname was Knuckles; brass knuckles bulged through the pocket of his leather pants. He knew my real name, pinned above my left breast, which he often stared at.

"To hell with a glass, bring me a jug of Chianti." Knuckles sprawled in a booth for six. I would have asked him to move to a smaller table, but Jim was watching, ready to step in on the customer's behalf. Besides, I was thinking about that soldering iron.

"Sure thing. You want to hear tonight's specials?"

"Only if you're on the menu, Dollface." Knuckles reached into his pocket. I couldn't tell if he was rubbing his brass knuckles or himself.

"I'll bring you the shrimp, half a dozen extra on the house." I spoke loud enough for Jim to hear. My boss smiled. Then I whispered. "My break's in an hour. Meet in the usual place?"

At nine, I waved at Jim and exited through the rear kitchen door. Another waitress gave me an I-know-what-you're-up-to look, but I wasn't worried about gossip or word getting back to Jim. Neither she nor the others would report me because Jim would be deaf to their complaints. I was his favorite waitress, the only one who stayed while the rest came and went like the flu.

Knuckles was leaning against the dumpster, hugging himself and stomping his feet. "Fuck, it's too damn cold out here. What say you invite me back to your pad when you're done working for the night?" He pulled me towards him and tried to wrap me in his jacket.

I squirmed away. "Sorry, no can do."

"Come on, baby. My ardor's gonna freeze up, not to mention my dick. I've been giving it to you good for what, half a year now, and you ain't never asked me up to your place."

"I share a room with two other girls. One has a baby. They won't go for it."

"Bullshit. The kid'll sleep through it, and your friends can join the fun. I'll pay 'em too."

"No means no. Next time, come in the spring." I turned and headed toward the back door.

"Coming for you now, baby." Knuckles yanked me from behind and spun me around. He raised his brass knuckles, the look on his face so cocky, I figured I could catch him off guard. Quickly, I grabbed the brass knuckles, tossed them in the dumpster, and started to run. But Knuckles caught me again and punched me, hard, in the right eye. I screamed.

Jim flew out the kitchen door. Putting me behind him, he told Knuckles, "Set foot in this place again, I call the cops." The biker took a step toward the dumpster, then apparently deciding not to dive for his trashed hardware, left. Jim went inside and came out with a hunk of ribeye steak. "You gotta be more careful who you go out with," he told me as he taped the meat over my bruise. "I don't want my number one waitress getting beat up no more." He walked me down the alley to the street, where he hailed a cab and paid the driver to take me home.

I understood that he hadn't called the cops or taken me back inside to avoid a scene. That was fine with me.

"You're gonna have a heck of a shiner," Jim said as he closed the taxi door. I didn't mind that either. I was more upset that I wouldn't be able to buy that soldering iron.

***

My bruise was still purplish-yellow when Frima called the following week. "Sorry I've been out of touch," she said. "My first year teaching, I'm struggling to stay one step ahead of the students, even if they're only third graders."

"Eight-year-olds know a lot. We did," I said.

"Too much," Frima added. "I'm at P.S. 94, the last place I student taught. The kids will go to Evander, or Walton, or Clinton unless they pass the exams for Science or Stuyvesant. Most of their parents barely speak English, but they want the best for their children."

"You'll see to it that they make it." My eye throbbed when I smiled into the receiver.

"Are you still working at Jim's? My school isn't far. I could stop by for an early dinner after class lets out, or come to your apartment if it's nearby. I still dream about that lasagna."

"Yeah, I'm at Jim's but working double shifts the next two weeks. Customers are sick of Christmas leftovers at home." I was lying, but I didn't want Frima to see my shiner and two weeks bought enough time for the bruise to fade. Nor did I want her to see the dump where I lived or come to the restaurant. Jim might tell her to look after me or fix me up with a nice guy. "How about your place?" I suggested. "Friday after next?"

"Come for dinner. Sixish." Frima laughed. "Unlike my father, I'm not a stickler for time."

The path to her apartment complex was shoveled and I pictured the courtyard between the four units filled with flowers in summer. A paneled elevator took me upstairs where a carpeted hallway led to a brass doorknocker. Frima opened the door before I could check out its sound.

We hugged for a long time. Frima hung my coat in a closet already jammed with coats, boots, and shoes. Then she gave me a tour: a large bedroom she shared with Joan, a second for the other two teachers, a small den with a television and bookshelves, a spotless bathroom, and a big kitchen with a stocked pantry and racks of cookware. I figured the rent was twice what I paid.

"It'll just be the two of us for dinner. Barbara and Shirley are visiting family and Joan has a date, but she'll join us for a quick drink first. She'll be home any..."

A key clicked in the lock and Joan bustled in. She gave the hanger with my coat a shove to make room for hers. Frima led the way to the living room where she and I sat on the couch across from a hutch filled with knickknacks. Joan walked over to a bar on wheels. "Frima and I enjoy a highball before dinner." She handed Frima a Whiskey Sour and mixed herself a Tom Collins. "What can I offer you, Liane?"

"You have any beer or plain red wine?"

"Vermouth. Dry or sweet?" Joan wrinkled her nose at the latter. Clearly it was less classy.

So although I would have preferred dry, I asked for sweet. It was syrupy, but I slugged it back and asked for another. I didn't feel like smoking either but I lit up so I could dirty the porcelain ashtray on the coffee table.

Joan plopped down in the armchair to Frima's right, took off her pumps, and put her feet on an embroidered hassock. "Whew, I'm bushed. I love my job but as any teacher will tell you, it's a relief when Friday rolls around." Her toe nudged Frima's foot. "N'est-ce pas?"

Frima smiled at Joan, raised her eyebrows at me, and tucked her foot under her skirt.

Joan set her drink on a coaster. "I teach English at Walton, as I'm sure Frima mentioned."

I put my sticky glass on the polished coffee table. "No. Why would she?"

Joan nudged a coaster toward me. "And Frima is shaping younger minds. Our lives have such purpose." She sighed and sipped her drink. "What are you up to these days, Liane?"

"Tending to kids' bellies while you take care of their minds."

"I vaguely recall Frima saying you worked at an Italian restaurant." Joan smirked. "Been to Jahn's lately?" She looked at her watch. "Time for me to get ready."

Frima and I made small talk while Joan changed. Her date arrived at 7:30 sharp. He shook hands with me, promised Frima not to keep Joan out past midnight, and bid us "adieu."

"Très pleasant cocktail hour," I said. Frima grinned and poked me in the ribs. I followed her to the kitchen, poured the remains of my second vermouth in the sink, and sat at the table while she made dinner. "Broiled lamb chops, baked potatoes, string beans. I'm no cook. By the time Greta tried to teach me, it was too late. Luckily, my roommates are more talented. We take turns cooking and doing chores." Frima indicated the lists attached to the fridge with magnets.

I opened cabinets and pulled odd-looking utensils out of drawers. I motioned toward the living room with my cigarette. "Très bourgeois. The kind of stuff Otto would buy."

"He did actually, but Joan and I chose it."

"Your friend boasted that your lives had purpose. It sounds noble enough." I exhaled out the side of my mouth. "But what's the point if there's no passion behind it?"

Frima took out the potatoes and slammed the oven door. "You're jealous."

She was right—half right—but I'd never admit it.

"And you're stubborn as hell." Frima forked the lamb chops onto two plates.

"Agreed. But my stubbornness kept me alive. You too. N'est-ce pas?"

Frima sat down and spread a linen napkin in her lap. "Touché. But fifteen years later, you still look undernourished. Now, be a good girl and eat your lamb chop."

I did. The food was simpler than Jim's fancy new fare. But it tasted good, maybe better. And Frima had made it for me.

CHAPTER 21

WASHINGTON'S BIRTHDAY SALE. EVERYTHING 10% OFF. I saw the sign in the hardware store window on my way to work. Two hours into my shift, a Continental Mark II parked outside the restaurant and the driver walked in. His thick, silver hair was combed in a pompadour, a soft woolen top coat hung on his broad shoulders, and his polished boots squeaked on the black and white tiled floor. When he took off his leather gloves, I saw he wasn't wearing a wedding ring.

I opened the top two buttons on my uniform and straightened my name label before I brought him a menu. "You're a new face here. Would you like to hear about Jim's specials?"

"Just the ones you recommend, Liane."

"Chicken Cacciatore. Perfect to warm your belly on a cold night. With Jim's secret herbs and plenty of wine in a zesty sauce. And my favorite, Osso Buco. The tenderest veal shanks your tongue ever had the pleasure of rolling around in your mouth." I licked my lips.

"The Osso Buco it is. I believe a glass of Barolo would be rich enough to stand up to it."

I smiled and turned slowly, giving him a lingering view of my ass as I wiggled toward the kitchen. During the meal, I refilled his wine glass on the house and brought him a complimentary plate of cannoli and torcetti for dessert

"Does Jim treat every new customer this well? If word gets around, he'll lose money."

"Not everyone. He leaves it to my discretion who gets special treatment." I considered batting my eyelashes, but a man his age might find it too little girlish. Before handing him the check, I wrote on the back: "If you'd like another special tonight, I recommend you take me for a ride after my shift ends. I'll wait for you behind the restaurant at eleven. – L"

I was disappointed when he didn't leave a bigger tip but figured I'd collect plenty from him later. After I'd cleared the last table and refilled the salt shakers, I smoothed my hair and applied a fresh coat of Tomato Red lipstick. Then, fantasizing a regular source of extra income, I stepped through the kitchen door. My sugar daddy was waiting in the icy moonlight. Fingers tingling, I walked toward him, but my heart stopped when Jim emerged from the dumpster's shadow. "Liane, I don't believe you've been formally introduced. Meet my Uncle Matteo."

"The young lady's informal introduction was sufficient to tell me who—and what—she is. I trust you'll take care of her, James?"

Jim nodded and hugged his uncle goodbye. He waited until the older man disappeared down the alley before he turned back to me. "This restaurant exists because my uncle gave me the money to open it ten years ago. He trusted me. I thought I could trust you. My uncle wants me to fire you. I'm tempted but you're the best waitress I've ever had. You don't quit, you show up on time, and you talk customers into ordering the most expensive items on the menu. Six waitresses I got, but you're responsible for half my profits."

I wanted a drink. Even sickly sweet vermouth would do. "You've been a decent boss."

Jim handed me a cigarette. "I know your life ain't been easy. So I'm giving you another chance. But you gotta mend your ways. No more playing hooker with the customers."

I watched steam from my breath mingle with the cigarette smoke. I was tempted too. I had a steady job, a cheap place to live close by, and just enough time and space to make art. If the restaurant continued to do well, my salary and tips would increase. Anoush had persuaded Mrs. Zetticci to give me a second chance. Jim was willing to do it on his own.

I crushed the half-smoked cigarette under my heel. "Thanks but no thanks. I quit." I was done depending on nice men to rescue me. Bastards like Knuckles made more sense to me. The image of Jim's open jaw lingered as I walked down the alley to Gun Hill Road. This time there would be no taxi ride home. But just like my earlier failure to score, I could forget about buying that soldering iron.

CHAPTER 22

My next job, at a men's shirt factory, lasted less than a week. As deft as my hands were sculpting metal, they were clumsy sewing on buttons. By Thursday my fingertips were too sore to grasp a bolt or twist a wire. Neither the foreman nor I were sorry to bid each other farewell. My housemates offered to cover my rent for a while and told me to help myself to their dry cereal and canned soup. What I couldn't mooch from them, I filched at the A&P.

The following Friday, I climbed the steps of Evander as classes let out. Mr. Archer, about to leave, put down his briefcase and flashed a big grin when I appeared in his doorway. "Liane, what a treat. What have you been up to? Any photos or work to show me?"

I turned my pockets inside out to show him they were empty, but I was glad he'd assumed I'd stuck with my art. "Still making sculptures, Mr. Archer, but I'm between jobs and in a spot." Five years had passed since graduation, but standing in the studio, it felt like yesterday. "Could you recommend me for a janitor's job? Give me a key to the supply cabinets and let me work in here after I finished cleaning? I wouldn't take anything home except what I used in my pieces."

Mr. Archer had stopped smiling. "I can't do that. It's against the rules for employees to take school supplies for their personal use. No matter how noble or creative the motivation."

"They wouldn't know that it wasn't a student who used those materials."

"I'm sorry, Liane. I could lose my job." He turned around the pictures on his desk so I could see his family. In addition to Lily, he and Mrs. Archer now had a little boy.

I lit a cigarette and took a drag to steady my hands. "Understood," I said.

"But that's not the only reason I'm saying 'no.' If I help you slink back here, you'll continue on the same losing path. I'd rather help you go to art school. It's not too late. In fact, your life would make you an interesting candidate to an admissions or scholarship committee."

My hands shook even more. "I'm an artist, not an interesting subject in a psychology experiment. Besides, studying at a la-di-da art school would smooth away the rough edges that make my work mine. You used to tell me to follow my own path. Now you want me to take the same one you did. I'll find a way without your help."

I left before Mr. Archer could see my tears, which froze on my cheeks during the short walk home. I clomped up the stairs and tore the magazine cover he'd given me off the wall. But I didn't crumple it or pitch it in the trash. I slipped it between two pieces of cardboard and slid it under my bed. Then I plopped on the ratty mattress. The bedframe's rusty coils made a satisfying creak. I was my own person now, an adult who'd outgrown my old teacher.

***

I ended up working for the New York City Transit Authority. The first year, I stocked candy and collected coins in subway vending machines, only I didn't like being "invisible" to commuters. The second year, I sold tokens so I could banter with them. Some people thought working in a tiny underground booth was claustrophobic, but it reminded me of the tight spots where Frima and I sought safety in Berlin. I often took a night shift and had the apartment to myself all day to make art. Also, guys who rode the subway at two in the morning weren't rushing to work or home to their families, so I picked up extra business. It's not that hard for two people to cram into a booth, slip sight unseen below the window, and find enough room to screw. I didn't have to take off my clothes, so if a customer rapped on the window, I could pop up, sell them a token, and disappear again to finish my business. Plus, no other TA employees were around to gossip.

One day, covering for a coworker with a sick kid, I worked a double shift from midnight through morning rush hour to the end of the midday surge. By the time I resurfaced aboveground, I was woozy from lack of sleep and a July heat wave. The apartment would be a hotbox too, but at least I'd get some shut-eye. My latest sculpture— a mountain of nicked washers cascading like tears—could wait until tomorrow. With everyone at work, the silence in the building wasn't surprising. Yet as I dragged myself up the stairs, my Berlin instincts told me something was off. Added to the usual garbage, the grungy halls were strewn with busted kitchen utensils and torn clothing. I recognized my housemate's flannel shirt. Three buttons had been missing forever, no one else could possibly want it, but it had belonged to her old boyfriend and she slept with it, same as I cuddled Ittel Rosa at night. Heart thumping, I took the last flight two steps at a time.

The lock on the apartment door was broken. It was sturdier than the one on my bedroom, so the odds were a hundred to one against my stuff being spared. Yet I made myself walk into every other room first, prolonging the flimsy hope. The few items worth something—a radio, the toaster, every bottle in the medicine cabinet—were gone. Otherwise, drawers and closets hung open, their contents dumped on the floor. A stack of towels had been repeatedly stabbed.

I kept my eyes down as I walked toward my room, looking up only when I reached the threshold and saw my mangled lock. Nothing was missing, but the thief or thieves, pissed at finding nothing of value, had destroyed everything. My sculptures were crushed or dismembered. Wood scraps, shoved in a pile, were charred after a half-assed attempt to burn them. An empty matchbook from Lucky's, the corner candy store and popular hangout, was useless as evidence. Metal pieces, already deformed when I salvaged them, were further dented. My own hammer, lying beside them, was more worthless evidence. Only Ittel Rosa, hidden beneath my pillow, was untouched. I loved her imperfections and couldn't have handled strangers adding more.

Surveying my wrecked art, I felt more violated than when men had used my body. Then it had been my choice, albeit a desperate one, and I was no more damaged after we'd finished than when we'd started. You could even say I was enriched with money, food, or whatever currency we'd agreed on. As I sat on my mattress, I held what was left up to the daylight and turned it this way and that. The added pits and twists in the metal made the pieces more interesting. Ditto the blackened edges of the wood. My mind and hands began to reassemble them into new sculptures. I looked under the bed. The sheets of cardboard were where I'd left them. I slid the unwrinkled magazine cover out from between them and rehung it over my workbench.

I'd just finished pounding in the tack when a policeman appeared in my doorway, his brow dripping with sweat. The building superintendent had called the cops. "I guess I wasn't supposed to touch anything until you guys investigated," I said, climbing down from the table.

"Don't worry about it. This is the twenty-eighth reported robbery in the neighborhood this month. Mostly we're trying to figure out if they were done by gangs or individuals. Sometimes we can apprehend gangs or rings, but hoods working alone or in pairs, we ain't likely to catch."

I smiled to myself. I knew what he was talking about.

By the time the cop poked around and left, it was three in the afternoon. I napped on the unmade bed for a couple of hours until my housemates came home from work. Then I endured their shrieking and crying until I had to leave for my regular nighttime shift. We commiserated with one another, but they'd never understand what really bothered me about the whole mess.

The next few months passed by in a blur of frenzied work and sex. I screwed to blot out loneliness more than to make money. But as long as I had the dough, I paid for whatever I got from the discount bin at the hardware store. I'd learned how it felt to be robbed. Not that I kidded myself that I'd never steal again. But until almost the end of the year, I was a reformed woman.

CHAPTER 23

I stopped patting myself on the back and kicked myself in the ass when I missed my period. It wasn't the first time. I'd often skimped on food to buy art supplies, lost weight, and then stopped menstruating. But after a month of gorging on toasted cheese sandwiches, ice cream, and donuts, I knew I was pregnant when my period still hadn't come. What I didn't know was who knocked me up. The possibilities were numberless and nameless.

I stopped eating again. Not because I was nauseous. Compared to the other tortures my body had been through, being pregnant was a piece of cake. Maybe I wanted to starve the thing. Or atone for my stupidity. More than once, I started to call Mrs. Zetticci, or Anoush, or even Betty for advice. But they'd all be disappointed in me and I was already disgusted with myself. Still, even though I wasn't showing yet, I couldn't keep my condition a complete secret. My housemates noticed I hadn't replenished my supply of sanitary pads in our shared bathroom cabinet.

"You pregnant?" one asked point blank. I admitted I was. "What you gonna do about it?" I admitted I didn't know.

She told me two of the other girls could give me the name of the guy who'd done their abortions. "I gave my mistake to my older married sister. Kid thinks I'm his aunt."

"Will you tell him when he's older?"

"I'll worry about it when the time comes." She shrugged. "But I can tell you that none of us wants a baby crying and shitting up this place. You keep it, you're gonna have to move."

I told her that one way or the other, I'd take care of things. No one asked about the baby's father. Whether they didn't care, respected my privacy, or didn't want a reminder of their own damned stupidity, I was glad to be left alone. By them. But I still needed to talk to someone.

In the end, I phoned Frima, who wouldn't look down on me because then she'd have to look down on herself. We met at Reservoir Oval, a park near her school, where forsythia bushes were starting to bud. I didn't say anything. Frima waited patiently, matching my stride. After two laps, I steered us to a bench. "I fucked up. Or got fucked up. Or fucked over. Fuck. Fuck. Fuck."

"You're pregnant," she said.

"Thanks for telling me." I wanted a cigarette, but smoking was the one thing that made my stomach heave.

"What do you want to do?"

"I don't know."

"Joan's brother has the name of a doctor in New Jersey."

I kicked a small mound of matted leaves, blackened hangovers from last fall. "Keep Joan out of this. If I want to get rid of it, my housemates or Betty know where I can get an abortion."

"Those guys are butchers. The one in Jersey is a real M.D."

"It doesn't matter. I can't imagine getting an abortion. Not after what the Nazis did."

Frima squeezed my hand, a tacit agreement that we needn't say more about that option. She fiddled with the latch on her purse. "If you decide to keep the baby, I'll help you financially."

I laughed so loudly that the white-haired ladies on the next bench turned in our direction. Lowering my voice, but not by much, I said, "How, with Daddy's money?"

"You can move in with us."

"Joan and the others would love that. Your *Good Housekeeping* apartment would become a dirty, smelly mess cluttered with diapers, drool, and sticky toys plus my artsy playthings."

Frima stared up at the still-bare redbud trees. "Do you want me to just butt out?"

I plaited her curls as if they were coiled strands of wire. "I know you're trying to help. But I've gotten myself in an impossible situation, and it's up to me to figure a way out."

***

I used my free subway pass to take the train to the Salvation Army Home for Unwed Mothers in Queens. A classified ad at the back of *The Post* said it was "a quiet place for girls and young women to reflect on their future." The home was an old house with big rooms, each with four to six beds. "You'll bunk with Mary, Patricia, and Carol," the social worker, Mrs. Gordon, said.

"I haven't decided whether to move in," I told her. "I'm just checking the place out."

Mrs. Gordon took me to their room anyway. "The girls will tell you about our services. I've got to make some calls. Come to my office for tea in an hour."

They really were girls. At twenty-seven, I was nearly twice as old as the youngest. Their beds were army cots that reminded me of my brief stay at Kloster Indersdorf, but while the Institute had a chaotic warmth, this place was as spare of feelings as it was of furnishings. Each cot came with a nightstand and foot locker. The donated maternity clothes belonged to the home and stayed there, save for whatever dress a resident was wearing on the day of her departure.

At first, all they talked about was how they got there. "Me and my boyfriend only had sex three times. My bad luck, I got knocked up."

"I didn't know you could get pregnant with your panties on."

"Only difference between me and them what pretend to be virgins is I got caught." It was important to the girls that I not think of them as sluts. I made no such claim for myself.

"What's it like to live here?" I finally asked. "What did Mrs. Gordon mean by services?"

"They feed us okay. Milk at every meal." I smiled, thinking of Miss Stone.

"Boring. Nothing to do but 'think about your mistakes, dear, and be grateful we'll give you a new start.'" The girl who spoke could have been a ventriloquist doing a Mrs. Gordon act.

"So what's next for each of you?"

"Adoption."

"Adoption."

"Adoption."

"That's it?" Maybe it came out like an accusation because two of the girls drew back.

The third pleaded. "I had no control. My mom and dad brought me here. It's like being in a skidding car. All you can do is skid until it stops. Nobody asked what I wanted. I was going to have the baby, they were going to take it, and then I was going to go home and get on with my life like nothing happened. If I chose to keep my baby, I'd be disowned or dishonor my parents."

No one to disown me, I thought, or for me to dishonor. Not that I felt free, but I'd already decided that I could feed myself, keep working, and make art by living where I was. No rules to follow but my own. These girls had to be kept out of sight. Once their babies were born, without parental support, adoption was their only choice. They were too young to manage on their own. But that wasn't the case at my age, nor frankly had it been since I was a lot younger than them.

After wishing them good luck, I headed downstairs to Mrs. Gordon's office, where tea, a pitcher of milk and a tray of Oreos and Nilla Wafers, were waiting. There were no comfortable chairs; we sat on either side of her desk. "I take it the girls were helpful? Gone astray, alas, but good-hearted nevertheless. They're making the right decision for their babies."

"I can understand deciding to have the baby, but why is adoption the only right decision? Why shouldn't I keep a child who already belongs to me?"

"Because a single woman is in no position to be a mother. To be blunt, you're unfit. Financially and emotionally, you can't provide as well as a stable married couple."

"I have a steady job. And who's to say I won't love my child as much as, if not more than, a husband and wife?"

"If you really love your baby, then you'll give it up for adoption. Think it over. You'll see I'm right." Mrs. Gordon handed me a brochure and circled her number at the bottom.

I knew I'd never call, but I thought about her words on the long ride home. Raising a child could give my life as much purpose as making art, if not more. I passed the stop where Frima had lived with the Oberlanders and remembered the night they came to Oyf Haskhole to meet her. I'd pushed my "sister" away so she could have a better life. Surely I owed my child the same. I didn't want to try to raise it and fail, only to admit it when the child was older and unadoptable. Like me. Mrs. Gordon was right. The only reasonable option was to give up my newborn baby.

***

"I thought you'd never pick up." Frima sounded relieved and annoyed. My gut had told me it was she who'd been phoning at all hours the past week, which is why I hadn't answered.

"My shift keeps changing. Since I sleep at odd hours, I turned off the ringer."

"A crazy schedule can't be good for the baby." Her tone softened. "How are you feeling?"

"Fine."

"Any movement yet?"

"Yeah."

"What about seeing a doctor? The one in New Jersey who Joan's brother knows is also a regular OB/GYN. Or find your own doctor. I'll pay if you need help."

"No thanks." I pressed my lips together to stop from crying, "Help."

"Okay, Mumblemouth. At least tell me, in a complete sentence, what you plan to do."

I promised Frima that I'd get enough sleep and watch my diet.

"That's not what I meant," she said, "and you know it."

So I repeated what I'd told her the last time we went to Jahn's. "Lay off me and take care of yourself."

She cursed and hung up.

True to my promise, I kept to a regular schedule. I drank milk and ate fruits and vegetables every day, and even bought cheap cuts of meat three times a week. My job, sitting on a stool, was made for pregnancy. I moved the stool farther back as my stomach swelled and made a piss pot with a funnel, a flexible tube, and an empty wine jug to pee in between breaks. In my sixth month, I registered with an adoption agency. All I had to do was sign the papers after the child was born. They would take care of everything else.

I was leaving for a Monday night shift when I went into labor. It began with a slow leak followed by contractions that weren't too painful but soon grew close together. I called Anoush. "I'm having a baby," I said. "I need help getting to the hospital." He didn't ask questions, just said he'd be there in a cab right away to get me. Between contractions, I tossed a nightgown and a change of clothes into a small suitcase. When I heard the cab driver honk, I added Ittel Rosa.

Anoush told the cabby to go to Montefiore, half a mile up Gun Hill Road. I'd forgotten it was Halloween until we passed knots of noisy kids wearing costumes and masks. I was relieved to enter the quiet hospital, then jarred again when the staff who greeted me at the registration desk were also in costume. Thankfully, they'd dispensed with the masks. Anoush threw a quarter in the Trick or Treat for UNICEF box on the counter. "I'm her father," he said. I stared at him before I realized they wouldn't let him stay with me otherwise. We looked nothing alike, but to the blonde woman behind the desk, our frizzy dark hair was enough to make us appear related. Either that or the fake wart on her nose made her as giddy and loose as a kid. She wrote my name and "Mother's Father" as the accompanying person, then shooed us through the swinging doors.

A nurse pointed Anoush to the "pacing area" and led me to a labor room. "First baby? It'll take hours," she said. Less than four hours later, my baby was born. The nurse immediately took it from me and headed for the door.

"I want to see it," I told her.

"That's a bad idea. Besides, the parents are waiting in the nursery to see their child."

"I haven't signed the adoption papers yet. Until I do, I'm still the parent."

I must have been yelling because Anoush suddenly appeared. With a menacing look, he told the nurse to give me the baby. She glared but handed it over. Anoush half-pushed her toward the doorway, then turned his back on me and my child to block her view and give us privacy.

I unwrapped the blanket and touched my daughter's perfect fingers and toes. Her eyes were closed and her squishy nose looked like any newborn's, so there was no clue who her father was. Not that I'd remember him anyway. But the tangle of dark curls was mine. "Sarah, after your grandmother," I whispered, knowing she'd soon be renamed by her new mother and father.

After five minutes, the nurse fetched a doctor, who shoved Anoush aside and took Sarah away. I was on my own and free again. I'd acted responsibly as an adult, just as I had looked out for Frima as a child. And yet a question snagged me like a wayward wire: Had I done enough?

Tired of questions and decisions, I fell asleep. When I awoke, Anoush was at my side in a six-bed ward. A devout Christian, he told me that it was All Saints Day, a feast day to remember saints and martyrs. "God will remember that you sacrificed your daughter for her own good, just as He sacrificed His son for the good of all humanity." His eyes held sorrow but no judgment.

The social worker bustled in with the adoption papers; I signed the forms without reading them. A new nurse gave me instructions on how to stop the flow and ease the pain when my milk came in. An orderly brought me a breakfast tray. Anoush urged me to eat. "I'll send Mendel to your apartment later with food. What should he bring?"

"Anything but milk," I said. I couldn't imagine being hungry again. But with coworkers subbing for me the rest of the week, I'd be bored. "Ask him to pick up the latest issue of *Arts & Architecture* magazine. And send me a tube of glue if you have a spare in the basement."

Anoush patted my arm. "Good. You are still making the art. I will buy you two tubes."

While he went to hail a cab, I packed my suitcase. The orderly stripped the bed. I felt him stare at my back as I tottered to the lobby, where other new moms sat in wheelchairs, tended by nurses, waiting for their nervous husbands to bring the family car to the hospital entrance. They clutched their bundled newborns to their breasts. Before long, a cab pulled up. Anoush calmly held the door open. I stepped outside, cradling Ittel Rosa, half-naked and threadbare, in my arms.

PART SIX:
FRIMA (1961–1968)

CHAPTER 24

"Play with Junior while I get a diaper." Joan brushed the hair from her flushed face and shuffled to the boys' bedroom. "Thank God he's nearly potty trained."

From the couch, Frima watched the toddler bang blocks together. His big brother zoomed past with a toy airplane, knocking her on the knees and toppling the little one. She cringed.

Joan spread a towel on the rug. She told the squalling two-year-old to pipe down and her five-year-old to slow down. "Guess what? I'm going back to work!"

"That's wonderful, Joan. Will you teach English again at Walton?"

"No. I've been gone five years. My job's been filled, and I'm ready for a change. I'll be the executive secretary for a client of Paul's with a lighting company." Paul March, Joan's husband, was an accountant.

"Paul's okay with you working?"

"Not at first. But my folks can watch the kids. And I was going crazy at home." Joan lowered her voice. "Paul even called me a cranky bitch. He apologized but felt so guilty that he agreed I could work. Richard, my boss, is his friend as well as a client. Paul trusts him."

"I'm happy for you, and your folks will be happy spoiling the kids." Otto and Greta were still waiting for Frima to get married and give them grandchildren.

As if mind-reading, Joan asked, "What about you? Twenty-eight and still an old maid."

Frima shrugged. "I'm still seeing Marty."

"For three years, and it's going nowhere."

"Marty's good to me. Besides, I can't see myself at home with little kids either."

"Why not? You're with kids all day in the classroom. It's easier to take care of a couple of your own than thirty who belong to others."

Frima looked at Joan's sons, who had neither quieted nor slowed down. With her third-graders, Frima was in control. She folded her hands. "In my case, I'm not so sure that's true."

***

Marty, an assistant principal at Frima's school, was divorced. His children lived with his ex-wife two subway stops away. He picked up Isaac, seven, and Rachel, eleven, on Sunday mornings and brought them to his apartment. Frima came over in the afternoons. Her relationship with the kids was easy. Marty's attitude was, "They already have a good mother. They don't need another."

In nice weather, they hiked or picnicked at Van Cortland Park. On wet or chilly days, they stayed inside. Marty and Frima sat on the couch, she leaning against his softening middle, while the children played Monopoly on the rug. When they squabbled, Frima was happy to let him play peacemaker. At the end of one visit, as Marty helped his kids put on their jackets and boots, Isaac asked, "How come Frima stays overnight and we never do?"

Rachel rolled her eyes. "Don't you know anything, dummy?"

Marty explained that their mother wanted them home since tomorrow was a school day.

"Rachel and I could come on Saturday sometimes," Isaac offered.

"I'll ask your mother," Marty answered.

Frima hoped their mother would say no. The children waved goodbye to her. Marty said he'd be back in a jiff. While he was gone, she washed the dishes and looked at the kids' drawings and photos on the fridge. In three years, she and Marty had never taken a picture together.

They'd met on a committee to help the school's Puerto Rican immigrant children learn English. Marty, twelve years older than Frima, had gotten involved because his Russian-born parents had told him of their struggles on the Lower East Side. When he asked why Frima cared, she'd spoken of her years in Berlin. "People were hostile to us here too. But I got lucky. I was adopted and loved. So I'm repaying a debt to the next generation of displaced children."

She and Marty developed an easy rapport, conducting home visits and co-tutoring. She watched him deal with troublesome children whose families were going through a rough time. Marty never blamed the children or their parents. He was as patient with them as he was with his own kids. When they began dating, Marty was equally straightforward with her. He told her about his divorce and was honest about not wanting more kids. "The split was amicable. We married young and grew apart. Simple as that. We didn't want to file for divorce on the grounds of cruelty, adultery, or abandonment, which would have hurt Rachel and Isaac. So we claimed 'constructive abandonment,' meaning we had to swear that we hadn't had sex for a year."

"Was it true?" Frima had asked.

"For eleven months, but the last month, knowing our marriage would end soon, we did it for old time's sake." Marty chuckled. "Are you going to turn me in for lying to the judge?"

Frima grinned. "No. I won't report you. Or your former wife." After a pause, she'd asked, "What was the sex like?"

"I thought it would be exciting because it was forbidden, but coming together just made me sad that our family was coming apart."

After she and Marty had been dating for several months, the question of sex between them inevitably arose. Frima would have to tell him the truth that no one other than Liane knew. Marty made it easier by saying, "Whatever you did to survive on the street, I won't judge you."

A floodgate opened. Frima told him about prostituting herself to soldiers, seeking out SS officers who were better able to pay her or procure food. "I slept with the enemy."

Marty held her face gently between his hands. "You did what you had to, to stay alive."

Frima admitted that the habit of exchanging sex for money or goods hadn't ended until after her adoption. She hung her head. Marty lifted her chin. "We don't shake off childhood even under the best circumstances. My kids get lots of love, but I know the divorce will leave scars."

Wiping away tears, Frima told Marty, "That was fourteen years ago. I haven't had sex with anyone since. I think I'm ready now." Only she wasn't. Their first time, she was so tense that it hurt when Marty tried to enter her. Lying on a warm, clean mattress, her back remembered cold, rubble-strewn ground or cramped, grimy cinema seats. Marty withdrew and held her, saying he would wait. After that they took it one step at a time, cuddling, stroking, lying naked together. A couple of months later, Frima again announced that she was ready. This time, she was. The next night, back in her own bed, Frima held Sugar and cried about being lucky again. She looked at *Sisters* and hoped that someday, soon, Liane would finally meet with good luck too.

Tonight, as she dried the dishes, Frima moistened in anticipation of Marty's return. They held hands as they walked to his bedroom, made leisurely love, and spooned as they drifted off to sleep. Frima thought that their sex wasn't exciting either, but the realization didn't make her sad. It made her feel content and normal. Rather than coming apart, sex with Marty had healed her.

***

"Did you enjoy the assembly?" Marty asked Frima's parents. He and his children and she and her parents stood at the back of the P.S. 94 auditorium after the winter talent show.

"Yes, Mr. Fleischer." Greta stared past him at the departing families. Otto scowled. They addressed Marty by his last name, even though Frima had brought him to Shabbas dinner last year. Greta hadn't thanked Marty when he complimented her cooking; Otto hadn't talked about furniture. Tonight they'd barely nodded when he'd introduced his kids. Isaac and Rachel tugged Marty toward the exit. He bade Frima and her parents goodbye and followed his children out.

Frima went home with her parents, wedged between them in the back seat of the taxi. No one spoke until they arrived at the Oberlanders' apartment, where Otto put on *Time Further Out*, the latest Dave Brubeck album, and Greta asked Frima to carry the serving dishes to the dining room. "My arthritis has been acting up and the auditorium was chilly." Otto, stooped and moving slowly, walked to the head of the table. Frima may have imagined the tremor in his hand as he passed their plates, but his hair was definitely grayer. Greta's had turned completely gray a couple of years ago and she hadn't dyed it. "Who do I need to look younger for?" she'd asked.

"You remember the Steins?" Otto handed Frima a matchbook with "Mazel Tov Danny" in gilt lettering on the cover. "Their youngest grandson had his bar mitzvah two weeks ago."

"Lovely affair." Greta's eyes were sad above her smile. "Chopped liver sculpted like a Torah scroll. Roast beef. And two bands, one for the grownups and another for the kids."

Otto chuckled. "I still can't abide rock and roll, but I got a kick watching Danny and his friends do The Twist."

Frima grinned. "Daddy, you're getting soft-hearted."

Her father sighed. "I'm getting old. So is your mother."

Greta was nearly seventy. Otto had passed it. They didn't have a young grandchild let alone one old enough to dance The Twist at his bar mitzvah. Frima resolved to break up with Marty for their sake as well as the memory of her parents. She'd tell Marty on Saturday. He'd be hurt, but his kids would be there on Sunday to cushion the pain, just as they had after his divorce.

Marty paled when Frima told him. "Why? We go so well together."

"Yes. As far as we go." Frima squirmed as she watched his shoulders heave.

When Marty finally spoke again, he was puzzled. "Is it because you want children?"

"I ..." Frima didn't want to lie. Not to Marty.

"We can get married. That would make you Rachel and Isaac's stepmother."

Frima shook her head. "My parents ..."

"Don't want to be step-grandparents." Marty bent to blow his nose.

Frima noticed the gray at his temples. "Without you, I don't think I could have ..."

"Taken the next step." Marty sighed. "Next steps get harder as you get older. Take it now, while you're young." He kissed the top of Frima's head. "With my blessing."

Frima let herself out. She'd tell the Oberlanders next Friday, at Shabbas dinner.

CHAPTER 25

"Bob's a dreamboat," Joan told Frima. Robert Horner was a friend of Joan's cousin. The men had met at City College, then Bob got a scholarship to NYU's law school, specializing in corporate tax law. "If Bob had been Catholic, not Jewish," said Joan, "I would have married him myself."

Frima changed her dress three times before their first date. Her roommates talked her into the plain black sheath. Bob was taking her to dinner and a Broadway show called *Come Blow Your Horn.* He arrived promptly at five. Nearly six feet tall, curly brown hair, hazel eyes, and a relaxed smile as he chatted with Frima and her friends. When it was time to go, Bob helped Frima put on her coat. As he turned his back to open the door, her roommates gave Frima a thumbs up.

Over steaks, they talked about themselves. Bob described himself as middle class. "My dad owns a small printing company. My brother works for him and will take over when Dad retires. I was the first to go to college, then law school. It's not medical school, but my folks are proud." Bob blushed, which Frima found endearing. "Tell me about you," he said.

"Joan already told you I was orphaned in Berlin and survived on the streets during the war. That's all you need to know about my past. I don't dwell on it. So many good things have happened since." Frima spoke of being adopted by the Oberlanders, then by the Periwinkles. "After that, I was fortunate to graduate from Barnard. Now I teach elementary school."

Bob raised his wine glass. "To teaching, the most noble profession. My mom taught for a couple of years before leaving to raise my brother and me."

"Did she go back when you were older?"

"No. By then my father didn't want her to. He liked having her around to take care of him. Now that my brother and his wife have two kids, she's busy with the grandchildren. Mom jokes she's just a homebody, but she sells herself short. She's really a wonderful homemaker."

After the show, Bob and Frima had coffee at a diner and talked about the show, which put the playboy lifestyle under a microscope. "Like any red-blooded American boy, I fooled around in college, but now I'm ready to settle down." Bob put his hand over Frima's. "You?"

Frima felt a tingle from her fingertips to the pointed toes of her high heels. She smiled at Bob. Later, in bed, she told Sugar. "I feel half my age, like a teenager having her first crush."

They saw each other every Saturday night and soon added Fridays along with weeknight calls. When he picked her up, Bob courted her roommates with flowers to win their approval as well as hers. After three months, he invited her to dinner at his parents' house, then introduced her to his brother's family. Frima took him to Shabbas at the Oberlanders. Otto showed Bob the furniture in every room; Greta plied him with second helpings and sent him home with leftovers.

One night, when they'd been dating half a year, they saw the film *The Miracle Worker*. Frima expected they'd go out for coffee afterwards as usual, but Bob asked if they could go back to her apartment. Instead of his familiar, easy grin, his smile was anxious. "Sure," said Frima. "Although all my roommates are out for the evening. They'll be disappointed to miss you." She wondered if he'd ask her for sex, but he divided women into nice and naughty, and his chaste kisses indicated he put her in the first group. All the same, he *was* a red-blooded American male.

Sitting on the couch, as Frima reached to pour them coffee, Bob took her hand and put a blue velvet box in her palm. Inside was an engagement ring with a small diamond. "Marry me, Frima. You're the miracle in *my* life."

Frima didn't take the ring out of the box.

Bob got down on one knee. She couldn't help laughing. "My law practice is doing well. I can afford an apartment in Riverdale, but I don't want to move in alone. I love you. Please say yes. It will make our parents happy. It will make me happy. And I promise to make you happy."

Frima wasn't surprised by the proposal, but she hadn't expected it so soon. She suspected Bob had prearranged with her roommates to be gone so they could be alone. "You already make me happy, Bob. But I'm not ready to say yes. Can I have some time?"

He struggled to his feet and got back on the couch. "July Fourth isn't far off. Tell me in time for the fireworks." Frima handed him the box. Bob took out the ring and held the diamond up to the light. They watched it sparkle. "Keep it while you decide," he told her.

Frima stowed it in a drawer. When her roommates came home, they eyed her expectantly but she said nothing. She needed to talk to someone, but who? Not her parents. Joan was hardly objective. She hesitated to call Liane. Why stir up her friend's pain? But in the end, there was no one else to turn to. Liane alone wouldn't assume that "yes" was inevitable.

They took another walk around Reservoir Oval, where the yellow forsythia blossoms had given way to green leaves. "This time, I'm the one with the problem." Just as Frima had known that Liane was pregnant, Liane guessed Bob had proposed. "My parents aren't getting younger."

"They're not the only ones." Liane traced an imaginary line down Frima's cheek. "What's holding you back?"

"I'm not in a rush." Frima scooped up the last fallen petals. "Bob's my first real romance. I'm still enjoying feeling like a teenager."

Liane shook her head. "Bob's a grown man. And face it, you're a woman. Neither of us are kids. We lost our chance and there's no going back. Are you afraid?"

"No. Just uneasy. Bob's not as low-key as Marty. He's a man on the rise, impatient to have a family. It's normal. Bob's normal. I'm the hang-up."

"Will he be good to you?" Liane's voice was stern.

"Very," answered Frima. "He already gives me nice things without my having to pay him in advance. He makes me feel special."

"You are special and deserve to be treated that way. Marry him, with my blessing." Liane gave a mock bow. "Not that you always listened to me, but in matters of life and death, you did."

Frima took a deep breath. "And you were right."

***

In late June, Frima accepted Bob's proposal. Joan threw an engagement party. She'd recently had her third child, a girl, and told Frima, "You and Bob better get married soon so you can catch up with Paul and me." Otto promised to furnish their apartment. Greta gave Frima the silver candlesticks that had belonged to her mother in Austria.

"But Mommy," Frima had protested, "*you* light these every Shabbas."

"I want you to use them now," Greta said. "Someday, you'll pass them to your daughter."

They planned a traditional Jewish wedding. Frima would have preferred a simpler affair but went along to please Bob and their parents. The day of the wedding, in late November, it poured. Greta reassured her. "In Jewish tradition, rain is good luck—a desert people's sign the crops will grow." Frima smiled bravely. She'd survived much worse. This marriage would work.

Before the ceremony, Bob signed the ketubah. The marriage contract committed him to provide Frima with food, clothing, and marital relations. His parents walked him down the aisle, where he waited under the chuppah, an embroidered shawl that had also been Greta's wedding canopy. As Otto and Greta escorted Frima down the aisle, she scanned the guests. Bob's side was full with three generations of family, his friends from high school through law school, coworkers, and clients. On Frima's side sat her parents, Otto's senior employees, the Periwinkles, her roommates, and a few co-teachers. She wondered where Liane was and if she'd come at all.

Under the chuppah, Frima circled Bob three times to represent the virtues of marriage: righteousness, justice, and loving kindness. He slipped the ring on her finger. They each drank from the cup of wine. Then came the moment when Bob stomped on the wine glass and everyone shouted "Mazel Tov." The rabbi explained that breaking the glass signified that even moments of joy must be tempered with the remembrance of sorrow. For thousands of years, that sorrow was the destruction of the Second Temple. In modern times, it was a reminder of the Holocaust. Breaking tradition, Frima stomped on the shattered glass too. "Never forget," she told herself.

After the ceremony, Frima and Bob retreated to the rabbi's study for yichud, a time when they could be alone. In ancient times, this period of seclusion may have been when the marriage was consummated. That barbaric tradition was long abandoned, but their wedding night still lay ahead. To explain why there was no blood on the sheets, Frima would tell Bob her hymen was probably broken when her body was shaken and injured during the war. She'd already made it clear that she didn't like to dwell on the pain of the past; it was unlikely he'd push her tonight.

When the newlyweds emerged twenty minutes later, the eating and dancing commenced. All the guests, even the non-Jews, joined in the hora. Otto and Greta danced to a jazz number they'd practiced for weeks. Frima's marriage had rejuvenated them. When it was time for the bride and her father to dance, Otto led Frima in a fox trot. Finally, the bride and groom danced together. Bob was an energetic dancer, if not as skillful as her father. At last, exhausted, Frima took her seat at the head table and scanned the crowd. Still no Liane.

She arrived as the cart with the wedding cake was wheeled out. Guests, their eyes on the seven-tiered fantasy, oohed and aahed. Frima, her eyes on Liane, saw her stumble to the bar and guzzle champagne as people toasted the bride and groom. Joan said she'd known Bob and Frima for fifteen years. "Who knew, when I met them, that I'd bring them together? Bob is everything a woman could want: smart, kind, successful, good-looking. Frima is all that, but also a survivor of inhuman hardship who maintained faith in human goodness. I wish them nothing but goodness."

Everyone started to eat their cake but stopped when Liane tottered to the head table and raised her empty glass. "I don't know Bob, but I've known Frima longer and better than anyone." Frima closed her eyes, wishing she could plug her ears. Liane continued. "Bob, you married a rare gem, cut and polished by the forces of nature. May you sculpt an extraordinary life together."

Frima, in tears, embraced her. Otto and Greta focused on their plates; Bob's parents eyed Liane with curiosity. Joan went to the ladies' room. Liane took Joan's seat. Bob's arm circled Frima. "So, my new wife, who is this lifelong friend of yours who I've never met?"

"The one responsible for the survival Joan spoke of. Without Liane, I wouldn't be here."

Liane began to eat Joan's cake. "Promise me you'll be good to Frima, Mr. Horner. Not just that ketubah crap. You must be as patient and forgiving with her as you'd be with a child."

Bob blinked but raised his right hand. "You have my oath. Frima deserves the best."

"Damn right." Smirking slightly, Liane handed Frima an unwrapped cardboard box, six inches square. "Your wedding gift." Frima anticipated a light and intricate sculpture. Instead, its thick, heavy strips of dull metal were twisted in a serpentine coil. Bob raised his eyebrows. He'd never agree to display it. Nor did Frima want to. While *Sisters* would keep its place of honor on her dresser, she'd stow *Knot*, a clumsy insult aimed at marriage, at the back of her closet.

CHAPTER 26

A year later, Frima gave birth to David, named for her brother. She felt a sense of satisfaction when he was placed in her arms, but not the thrill that books and magazines led women to expect. How had her birth mother felt after her children were born? Had Mirla experienced that flood of emotions? And what about Greta, who would never know the rush of giving birth? Was the moment when an adoption judge pronounced a childless woman a mother marked by its own special elation?

From the day they brought him home, David was a colicky baby. Greta swaddled her grandson during the day; Bob bottle-fed and walked his son at night. For all of his professional haste, her husband was more patient with their child than Frima was. Her lack of maternal instinct haunted Frima. But who could she ask for advice? Not Greta, who'd never raised a baby. Nor Liane, which would be useless, if not cruel. Joan recommended Benjamin Spock's *Common Sense Book of Baby and Child Care*. "Trust your instincts; you know more than you think you do. Your natural loving care for your child is what's most important." Loving care did not come naturally to Frima. She didn't feel like a mother. Or know if she wanted to be one.

Two years later, Lisa was born. Named for Bob's grandmother, she was an easier baby. Yet Frima felt equally distant. Her parents, of course, were ecstatic. Greta knit blankets and took care of her grandchildren every day. Otto came on Sundays, furnished the nursery, and ordered toys from F.A.O. Schwarz. Between the Oberlanders, Bob's parents, and the attentions of Bob himself, David and Lisa seemed not to notice Frima's emotional absence. While they played, she sat in an armchair and read history or wrote letters to Congress about educational inequality.

But her husband noticed. One Saturday, as he sprawled on the rug with the children and a pile of blocks, he frowned up at Frima. "Join us. The city we're building needs a woman's touch."

She kept her place with her finger. "In a minute, when I finish this chapter."

Five minutes later, David said, "Ding. Time's up, Mom."

Frima stood. "I have to start dinner."

Lisa held up two blocks. "Please, Mommy. Help me make a school. You're a teacher."

"I *was* a teacher." Frima patted the kids on her way to the kitchen. "Maybe after dinner."

But after they ate, she washed the dishes while Bob bathed the children, read to them, and tucked them in. Later, when he and Frima were in bed, he asked, "What's wrong with you?"

"I didn't want dinner to be late. You know how cranky the kids get when they're hungry."

"That's not what I mean and you know it. A wall of fog separates you from them. No, a wall of stone. I don't understand. You used to be so concerned about your students, you still worry about poor and immigrant kids, and yet you're aloof with your own. It's crazy."

Frima didn't disagree. Perhaps she should have told Bob about her past after all, not the sex, but what it meant to grow up without parents. "Do you remember what you swore to Liane?"

"That I'd be good to you."

"That you would treat me with the same care and patience you would treat a child."

"Children eventually grow up. You're in your mid-thirties."

"I can still change. Give me time."

Bob rolled over and turned out the light. "I'll try. But I can't speak for David and Lisa."

***

When David started kindergarten, and Lisa was a chatterbox with a vocabulary almost as big as his, Frima found them more interesting. She enjoyed teaching them. Bob stopped criticizing her until one evening, after the kids were in bed, he said it was time to enroll David in Hebrew school. Riverdale Reform Temple had a preschool Sunday class, so they could sign up Lisa too.

Frima stiffened. "I'm not sure I want them to go to religious school."

"Nonsense." Bob paused. "Would you rather they go to a conservative synagogue?"

"No, that would be even worse."

"What would we tell our parents? They're committed to our people's survival in the wake of the Holocaust. So am I. I assumed you, of all people, felt the same way."

"I suppose we should have had this discussion before we got married."

"We're having it now." Bob leaned forward and tapped his foot, slowly and loudly.

"I've never denied my religion," Frima said. "I just didn't care whether or not I practiced it. Now I've decided that doing so would be hypocritical."

"You light Shabbas candles on Friday, with your mother's candlesticks."

"For her sake. Not God's. Certainly not my own."

"Then why not agree to send our children to religious school for her sake? And mine?"

"Because I don't want David and Lisa marked. Why should they go through what I did?"

Bob looked at Frima in disbelief. "This isn't Germany or the 1930s."

"Antisemitism is never out of date. I endured it at Barnard. I'm thinking of my children."

"You're thinking of yourself." Bob stood. "I'm enrolling the kids. I'll drive them there and back every week. They'll be out of your hair for a few hours. *That* should make you happy."

Hours later, when he was snoring, Frima snuck Sugar into bed. "I'm a bad mother and a bad wife," she confessed. Moonlight illuminated the sculpture on her dresser. Frima hadn't called Liane in months. "I'm a bad sister too." Sugar offered no absolution.

***

The following year, David's first-grade class was assigned to write about their parents when they were their age. Since Bob would be home late, he asked Frima. "I don't remember," she told him. "And I can't ask my mother because she died when I was only two years older than you."

"Why can't you ask Bubbe Greta?" Lisa asked, curious, and sat next to her brother at the table.

"Mom was older than me when Bubbe Greta and Zayde Otto adopted her." David gnawed his eraser. "Try, Mom. I have to turn in something tomorrow."

Frima told him about her brother. "Your Uncle David, who you're named for, was the fastest runner in his class. He won every race and kept his medals in a special box."

Her son looked skeptical. "For real? You're not just making that up?"

"Aren't you fast?" David said he was tops in his class too. "See?" said Frima. "You take after your uncle." She helped him write his report, teaching him medaillen, the German word for medals. She found some blue ribbon in her sewing basket to pin to his paper.

When David left to put the report in his school bag, Lisa stayed at the table. "Mommy, what did little *girls* do in Germany?"

"They played with dolls, just like you and your friends."

Lisa fingered a remnant of David's ribbon. "I wish I had one of those dolls."

Frima told her to close her eyes, then walked unsteadily to her bedroom. She took Sugar from her nightstand drawer and brought it back to the kitchen. "You can look now." Frima handed Lisa the doll. "She was mine when I was your age. For real."

"Yuck. She's ratty." Lisa threw down the doll and ran to her room. Frima, more relieved than hurt, brushed Sugar off.

"You're still mine. I promise not to give you up for adoption again."

CHAPTER 27

"David, can you put this away?" As Frima handed him the Cheerios, she saw his tongue poking a bulge in his cheek. "What's in your mouth?"

"Nothing." He clamped his jaws shut.

Frima pried them apart. Chewing gum. She found the rest of the Juicy Fruit pack in his pocket. "Where did you get this?" David stared at the floor. "The checkout line at the A&P?"

"Uh-huh. I took it while you and Lisa were unloading the cart."

"You *stole* it! You know better. Go to your room while I decide what to do with you."

"Are you going to tell Dad?"

"No. I'll handle this." Bob would be too lenient. Last week, when Lisa denied breaking a porcelain doll she'd been warned not to play with, Bob said it was no big deal even though the figurine was a gift from his mother. Lisa still hadn't admitted her guilt and ought to be punished too.

Frima dug out Spock. His baby advice hadn't helped; maybe what he said about older children's moral development would. *"Don't think of them as cheaters and liars. It's normal to want and take what doesn't belong to them, and try to avoid the consequences."* Frima and Liane had been forced to steal and lie. Her kids got whatever they needed. And more. She slammed the book shut.

"David, Lisa. Come to the living room. Now." Her children stood close together, facing her. "Lisa, you're grounded the rest of the month. No television or playing with friends." Lisa's lower lip quivered. "David, the same. But since you're older, you also have to wash the dishes."

Her son eyed her with disgust. "Aw, Mom. Washing dishes is for girls."

"One more word and I'll wash your mouth out with soap."

David glared. That night, she made him rewash the plates when they were still greasy. The rest of month, he cleaned them thoroughly, stomped to his room, and left the next morning without eating breakfast. Frima, who wrote letters on behalf of hungry children and saw feeding her own as a mother's minimal obligation, was rattled. You can starve a child but not force him to eat. She had no sympathy for a son who refused her food. Frima doubled David's penalty.

***

"You have to try these cinnamon buns." Joan shoved old newspapers off the coffee table to make room for the platter. "A bakery opened near the office. Richard brings in a box every morning."

"Richard?" Frima took a bite. The roll was sweet, yet spicy, and buttery.

"My boss, remember?"

"Oh, right. Paul's friend. You've worked for him for seven years already."

Joan absentmindedly ran her finger along the dusty tabletop. "Only now Paul wants me to quit. He says I'm neglecting the house and our children."

"To which you say ...?"

"No way. I went to work because being home alone with the kids drove me crazy. With our youngest in first grade, I'll go crazy here alone, period. I still shop, cook, and do the laundry. If Paul wants a cleaner house, he can hire a maid. Or do it himself. Or pay the boys to clean."

Frima smiled to herself. "Cleaning is girls' work."

"Show me the law that says so." Joan ate a second bun. She'd put on weight lately. "Men dictate what women should or shouldn't do. Well, I have news for them. Times are changing."

"You sound like a libber." Frima grinned. "You always were a modern woman."

"I *am* a libber." Joan's dark eyes sparkled. "I've joined a women's consciousness-raising group. We meet on Wednesdays. You should come and hear the stories. Some husbands are more controlling than Paul, even abusive. Compared to them, he rates above average as a 'good guy.'"

"I expect Bob does too. So why should I get riled up? Frankly, if Paul isn't that bad, why are you going? It'll only make you unhappier with him."

"I'm already pretty unhappy."

"Because he wants you to quit your job?"

"Because he wants me at his beck and call."

"Well, Paul loves you. He needs you."

"He needs a maid. I want more." Joan looked over her shoulder as if someone might be listening. "I'm having an affair with Richard." Frima said nothing but felt a disapproving frown form on her lips. Joan sat back. "Don't be so quick to judge. Come to the next CR meeting."

The following Wednesday, Frima sat with Joan in a circle of twelve women who took turns talking about husbands or boyfriends who criticized their weight, told them what to wear, or satisfied only themselves in bed. More sympathetic in Frima's mind were the women who were paid less than men doing the same job. Most worrisome were those who'd been called stupid cunts or beaten. Two had been raped. They stayed with their partners because they had no income of their own and often abased themselves to save their lives. Their stories made Frima think of how she and Liane had not just surrendered their bodies but flattered men's egos. Even Greta, happily married, stooped to cajoling Otto, who still usually refused to see things her way.

When it was her turn to talk, Frima skipped her past but described her marriage. "My husband's basically good to me, but there's no question he's the man of the house." She told them how Bob had overruled her on the children's religious education. "It may sound like a small thing, but he ignored my wishes and worse, he violated my principles.

My son, who's still in elementary school, is already disrespecting me. I dread what will happen when he becomes a teenager."

"It's not a small thing at all," a woman said. "Men's attitudes are passed down from one generation to the next. If women don't stop that, our mistreatment will never end. Sexism is like racism, antisemitism or any other 'ism.'" That was the argument Frima understood best of all.

***

A few days later, Frima arranged to meet Liane when Liane got off work, clerking at a store that sold crystals, beaded jewelry, and roll-your-own supplies. They went to a nearby coffee house. Frima hadn't planned to talk about her kids, thinking it would be too painful for Liane, but Liane asked to see their pictures. "David looks like you," she said, "red hair, green eyes, a deceptively sweet smile. Does Lisa take after Bob? I don't remember what your husband looks like."

"Lisa has his dark good looks and innate sense of fairness. She also inherited Bob's even temper. Except when it flares. And she can be stubborn."

"Call it persistence. Good for her."

"Good for a girl or woman. A challenge if she's your daughter. What are you up to?"

"Selling crap. You saw where I work." Liane waved vaguely in the store's direction.

"I meant your art."

Liane grew more animated. "I'm still using wood and metal but adding damaged beads and crystals that the store throws out." She whispered. "I'm also not above ruining a perfect specimen that I want, telling the owner it was dropped by a customer who was stoned or tripping."

"Do you ever get stoned?"

"Sure. I'm stoned now." Liane fluttered her lashes. "You?"

"No. If I got caught, Bob could lose his law license. What about taking LSD?"

Liane shook her head. "I'm afraid of a bad trip. Too many demons waiting to haunt me."

"I've read that acid frees your creativity."

"Mine's already free. I don't need anything artificial to unleash it." Liane grinned.

Frima grinned back. "I'm glad your work is going well. Do you sell it at the shop?"

"It's not that kind of place. Roll your own, craft your own. I make art not tchotchkes."

"What about exhibiting your work?"

Liane dumped five packets of sugar into her now-cold coffee. "A gallery opened down the street last year. I brought in a few pieces. The owner said he wasn't interested."

"Hmph. I bet all the artists he exhibits are men."

Liane shrugged. "I never noticed."

Frima told Liane about the CR group, leaving out Joan. "The movement was made for you. There must be groups for female artists."

"Women's lib is garbage. As fake as the new-age crap I sell."

Acidic coffee backed up Frima's throat. She said Liane was close-minded, the antithesis of an artist. "Either you like being oppressed, or you're too chicken to do anything about it. You lack the guts to show your work. You bought the Nazi's message that you weren't good enough."

"While you think you're better. How many times do I have to tell you to worry about yourself? If you're so unhappy, change your own fucking life. Don't try to change mine." Liane shoved her chair back and stormed out. Frima gave her five minutes to disappear then left too.

***

"Strawberry cupcakes with *pink* icing. You have to make them yourself because the bakery ones only come in chocolate and vanilla." Lisa described the birthday cupcakes she intended to bring to preschool tomorrow. Frima said they'd be ready when her daughter got home that afternoon.

Hours later, Lisa cautiously opened the box from Gruenebaum's. Inside were three dozen vanilla cupcakes with white icing, decorated with pink flowers. "You *bought* these," she wailed. "Other moms bake and go on class trips and sew costumes for the play. You never do anything."

"I read to you every night and help David with his homework. I cook for our family. There are children all over the world who are starving and have never owned a book."

"It's not fair. You promised."

"I didn't promise to bake, only that the cupcakes would be ready. Besides, these will taste better than anything I could make myself. Your classmates will love them."

"*I* hate them! I hate you!" Lisa dumped out the utensil drawer. Then, while Frima moved the bakery box to a high shelf, Lisa ran to the dining room, where silverware clattered to the floor. Frima pursued her but failed to stop Lisa from tossing her brother's clothes and her own from their drawers onto the carpet. She finally caught up with her daughter in the master bedroom.

Lisa headed for the dresser. Frima leaned against the drawers to block her from opening them "Enough. Put everything back and then sit on your hands at the table. Right this minute, or you're not bringing any cupcakes to school. And you won't have a birthday cake at home either."

Lisa backed off. But instead of leaving, she scooted around Frima, snatched *Sisters* off the top of the dresser, and threw it at the opposite wall, where it left a black mark and ricocheted onto the hardwood floor. Lisa, eyes big and mouth quivering, ran to her room.

Frima froze. After a few seconds, she slid to the floor and crawled to the sculpture. The metal bars that once embraced were bent askew, a hair-like coil had broken off. Frima wrapped the statue in a sweater and laid it in her nightstand drawer beside Sugar, who looked up at her. "Am I a bad mother, Sugar?"

"You're good to me," the doll answered.

"That's different. I'm not your mommy." But Frima was Lisa's mother, and David's, and ill-suited to the role. Not for the reasons other women spoke of—boredom, frustration at not having careers—but because she'd never learned how to mother anyone but herself.

Frima smoothed what was left of Sugar's hair. "What should I do about *Sisters*?"

"Ask Liane to fix it."

"I can't. Not after our fight."

The doll considered. "Then keep it as is to remind you that relationships are fragile."

Frima returned Sugar to the drawer and *Sisters* to her dresser. She rummaged at the back of her closet until she found *Knot*, Liane's wedding present. It was less ugly than she recalled but sturdier. At the reception, she'd seen it as a snide commentary about Frima "tying the knot" with Bob. Now she saw that the piece stood for the unbreakable bond between her and Liane. She'd display it after all. Not on the dresser but on her desk, a paperweight to anchor her heart.

"That's different. I'm not your grandma." But Frima was Liana's mother, and David's, and ill-suited to the role. Not for the reasons other women spoke of—boredom, frustration at not having careers—but because she'd never learned how to mother anyone but herself.

Frima smoothed what was left of Sugar's hair. "What should I do about Sissy?"

"Ask Liane to fix it."

"I can't. Not after our fight."

The doll considered. "Then keep it as is to remind you that relationships are fragile."

Frima returned Sugar to the drawer and sutures to her dresser. She rummaged at the back of her closet until she found it not, Liane's wedding present. It was less ugly than she recalled but sturdier. At the very least, she'd seen it as a smile companion piece to Frima. Tybur had knot, with luck, knew she saw that the piece stood for the uneven balance between her and Liane. She'd display it after all, she set on the dresser, not on her desk, a paperweight to anchor her heart.

PART SEVEN:
LIANE (1968–1972)

CHAPTER 28

Not that I'd admit it to Frima, but her comment about exhibiting my sculptures got me thinking. My closet was filling up, and if I sold a few pieces, I'd have space for new work and money to buy an assortment of materials and better tools. Getting into a gallery was unlikely, but all I needed to set up at a summer street fair was a folding table, price tags, and tissue paper to wrap what I sold. If the cops chased me away because I hadn't paid for a permit, I'd pack up and go then come back when they'd left. Same as we used to do when the fuzz broke up our high school road rallies.

A lot of art fair stuff was crap: knitted tea cozies, spindly beaded earrings, lopsided ceramic mugs. But now and then I'd meet a true artist, one who wove intricate geometric tapestries or painted multi-layered landscapes. My favorite was Matt, a sculptor of dense metal mazes, whose pieces were twenty times as big as mine. They rarely sold, though. People bought a few of my two-dollar items each week; Matt's cost at least thirty. But the poor sales didn't bother him. He made a good income as an electrician, wiring fancy new houses. Now and then, if a client bought one of his sculptures, Matt spent the money on more metal. "I like to work big," he said.

"I wish I could. Not as big as you, but pieces larger than I can fit in my hand. When I try, they teeter or fall apart." I laughed. "Duct tape works, but it looks like a first-grader made them."

Matt admired the way I wired and interlocked parts together. "Ingenious. Organic. But for heavier objects, you need a soldering iron."

"Tell me about it," I said. He took the comment literally. I was losing my sarcastic edge.

"Buy a good one, at least thirty watts, with several shapes and sizes of tips so you have the right one for a particular project." Matt pointed out examples in his own work. "Conical tips for precision soldering. Broad, flat chisel tips for soldering larger components."

I realized that I knew nothing about soldering irons. But I was more convinced than ever that I needed one. Once it was in my possession, I'd figure out how it worked.

***

A new hardware store near my subway stop was having a grand opening sale. Even marked down to $12.50, the top-of-line soldering iron Matt had recommended was too expensive for me. But among a crowd of customers at the sale, I could slip it, unnoticed, into my satchel.

The soldering iron was at the end of an aisle, facing away from the owner who stood at the cash register. When the customers near me were distracted, I took it from the shelf. But as I held it above my open bag, I heard a click and a whir, then saw the owner over my shoulder aiming a Polaroid camera at me. His wife, back at the counter, hit the alarm, automatically locking the door. Everyone froze. The cops arrived two minutes later. In a high-crime neighborhood like mine, they were never far away. The wife let them in while the owner continued to block my exit.

"You're under arrest," said the burlier officer.

"Don't you need a warrant?" I asked.

The cop held the photo under my nose. It was still developing, so it was blurry, but the expression on my emerging face already looked like someone caught in the act. "With probable cause, we're allowed to issue a warrant *after* we bring you to the station."

I extended my arms.

"No handcuffs. You're not resisting arrest," said the skinnier cop. "Just come with us to the patrol car."

The heavyset officer sat with me in the back and held up the now fully developed picture. I looked guilty as hell. When we got to the station, he completed the warrant and told me I was being booked on a preliminary charge of petty larceny. "Why only petty?" I asked.

The cop looked at me like I'd lost my mind.

"Because the soldering iron you stole was worth under a hundred bucks."

I wished I'd taken a dozen. Grand theft sounded a lot more respectable.

***

I thought I'd be twiddling my thumbs for days, but the women in the holding cell with me said New York City guaranteed a first appearance before the court within twenty-four hours of arrest. I was skeptical, but they were right. The judge announced the charge, saying "petty" with a seriousness that made me feel better. Then he recited my rights, including "You have the right to counsel. Are you hiring an attorney or should the court appoint a public defender?"

"If I could afford a lawyer, do you think I'd steal something worth twelve bucks?"

"I think, Miss Asher, that you should refrain from saying anything else that might bias the court against you. Bail is set at two hundred and fifty dollars. Report back here in four months."

"Why four months?" I added, "Your honor."

"To give you time to talk things over with the P.D. and collect additional evidence."

"What additional evidence? You have the Polaroid. Case closed." Investigating further seemed as pointless as ironing a teacup. Once again, the judge advised me to shut up and assigned Mitchell McDougal as my P.D. If the stereotype that Jews were the best lawyers was true, then I was up shit's creek. Still, I knew better than to mouth off about the long wait, Irish counsel, or high bail, which I had no way to pay. I'd be stuck in jail the whole time. The only person I knew with that much dough was Frima, who I was too ashamed to ask. I preferred to keep this latest fuck-up private.

That night, I wavered. Despite sharing a cell with five others, I hadn't felt so alone since I'd hidden under the floorboards when my mother was taken. Three decades later, it wasn't her I wanted but Ittel Rosa. I'd tell her I was scared. In Berlin, I'd made up my own rules. In jail, others made the rules. How would I survive the next four months, let alone a prison sentence?

In the morning, I made my allotted call. Anoush hadn't judged me for being pregnant. He wouldn't now. For reasons I couldn't fathom, he saw possibilities in me I couldn't see in myself.

"Anoush? Hi, it's Liane. I only have a couple of minutes to talk."

"You are in trouble?"

"Yes. Big trouble. Or petty trouble, depending on how you look at it. I'm in jail and I need two hundred and fifty dollars bail to get out. Is there any way you can help?"

"Hold on," he said. I heard a drawer open, metal clink, papers rustle. Two minutes were almost up by the time Anoush picked up the phone. "Yes. I can scrape together." I told him where I was and he said he had to make a couple of calls, then he'd come to the station house.

I was in the lunch line when a guard called my name and said to follow her. Anoush was signing a form at the desk while a clerk counted out wrinkled bills and stacks of coins. At last the clerk nodded, told me I was free to go, and reminded me not to travel outside the city and to show up for my court date. "Show up for your appointments with the P.D. too if you don't want your sweet little ass to rot in prison," he called from behind as Anoush ushered me to the door.

I swore to Anoush that I'd show up for my court date and that he'd get his money back. He said he wasn't worried. As soon as we were out on the street, Anoush asked if I was hungry. I nodded, not because I was but because I wasn't ready to be dropped off at my apartment and find myself alone again. Holding my elbow, Anoush steered me to a coffee shop on the corner.

"You order for both of us," I told him.

"I like cheeseburger." Anoush scratched his head. "But you no can eat?"

I smiled. It felt good to tighten a different set of muscles. "I can. I don't keep kosher."

Suddenly, I was starving. When our food came, I loaded mine with ketchup and mustard and requested extra pickles. Without asking if I wanted it, Anoush ordered me a double chocolate milkshake. "You need go shopping before I take you home?"

"No, I've only been gone one night." It felt like the whole four months.

Anoush insisted on riding the subway to my stop and seeing me to my door. "You call, you need something," he said. "Even you don't need something." He patted my arm and left. No questions. No advice. Calling him was the only smart thing I'd done for myself in a long time.

CHAPTER 29

Mitchell McDougal was a freckled stereotype of his name, so young I was tempted to call him "Mitchie." However, I called him "Mr. McDougal" since he alone could keep me out of prison. Sitting opposite him in a cubicle at the P.D. building, I nevertheless couldn't help asking how recently he'd earned his law degree. He reassured me he handled dozens of cases a week. Now, instead of fearing he was underqualified, I worried he was overworked.

"You have three choices, Miss Asher. You can plead guilty, not guilty, or stand mute, which the court treats as a not guilty plea. I advise you to plead guilty. The evidence—the photo—is irrefutable. And a judge is more likely to hand down a lighter sentence if you admit guilt."

"How much more likely?"

"I'm a lawyer, not an odds maker." Mr. McDougal looked at me sternly. "Judges consider other factors too. You have no record, which works in your favor. There are also extenuating circumstances in your background. I had a few minutes this morning to check your public high school records and saw that you're a war orphan, brought to this country as a teenager, then shuffled from one group home to another. Counsel can present that information at a defendant's misdemeanor arraignment. I'd like your permission to do so, plus any other details you can give me about that difficult period in your life that might sway the judge prior to sentencing."

"No. I knew perfectly well what I was doing when I lifted the soldering iron. Saying trauma made me do it denies my free will. I'm a hundred percent my own person."

The P.D. closed my folder. "You're making this harder for me and yourself. Will you at least permit me to talk about the damage done to war orphans in general?"

"You mean, not talk about me or my experience in particular?"

Mr. McDougal nodded. I said okay. Not that I liked being lumped in with the likes of Salomon and Reuven or Mendel and Berta, but I disliked being singled out for pity even more.

Fall was half over by the time I reappeared at the courthouse. I gulped the clear crisp air as I ascended the steps and told myself I was likely to exit a free woman, sentenced to nothing worse than probation. The P.D. did exactly what he said he would, then sat beside me at the back of the room while the judge deliberated. Ten minutes later, I was called to the bench.

"Miss Asher, I've considered multiple factors in reaching my decision. One is the lack of a prior record, another is the research presented by counsel. These work in your favor. That said, you survived and were brought to America, where you got a free education and opportunities not limited by your religion. I therefore sentence you to a year in prison, the maximum allowable, in hopes that you will use that time to appreciate your good fortune and think about your future."

He lowered the gavel. Mr. McDougal wished me luck and left to meet his next client. He didn't say he was sorry. He probably blamed me for refusing his advice. I didn't know who was at fault, but assigning blame was as pointless as buttering a calendar. Two guards marched me to a van which took me straight to prison. I wasn't allowed to go home and pack. I didn't care about my clothes, and my art supplies—wooden shards and metal scraps—would be seen as potential weapons. But my heart ached for Ittel Rosa, a winking bear of no use to anyone but me.

***

The New York Women's House of Detention was an Art Deco building I'd admired when I went to art fairs in Greenwich Village, unaware that it was a prison. No sign on the door announced it. I was even more surprised when I saw the artwork inside. A guard told me that the prison's first superintendent had commissioned the art as part of her campaign to uplift the women and treat them as individuals. I soon learned that this one-time place of beauty was now a shit hole of brutality. Prison life was as dehumanizing as Jewish life under the Nazis.

After being awakened at five, inmates were counted, a routine we endured ten times a day. Thirty minutes for breakfast, then off to mindless jobs preparing food, washing clothes, or pushing a mop. Lunch at noon, then back to work until three, when we were "free" to go to the library, exercise area, or commissary. The store sold sanitary pads—we were given only one a day—and basics like soap and toothpaste. They also sold groceries, which we used to cook "mac 'n' cheese" (dried noodles and Cheetos Puffs, heated in the snack's foil-lined bag) and "chocolate pudding" (crushed Cap'n Crunch and hot water). Miss Stone would have disapproved, but after a week of eating mess hall slop, she'd succumb too.

What passed for dinner was at six, then inmates could choose between religious services, counseling, or GED classes. I regretted having my high school diploma because without a goal to aim for here, I was bored. Instead, I went to the library to read trashy novels and psychology texts, the only books available. At eight, we were herded back to our cells until lights out at eleven. The others called those hours "family time," creating in-house families and reenacting familial squabbles. But a prison family held no attraction for me. I'd had no experience with a real one.

Our dehumanization went beyond tedium. Per diem pay was less than a half-dollar, and wages could only be spent in the commissary. In other words, the prison paid itself for our work. Moreover, prices were high. Visitors, permitted on weekends, could deposit money in your account, but no one came to see me. Nor did I have anything to trade on the black market. Some women sold their bodies to the guards—though many men simply forced themselves on inmates—

but my days of trading sex for goods were over. With every aspect of their lives controlled, the women acted like dependent children. I was grateful that without a childhood to revert to, I wasn't tempted to lower myself that way. But after I realized that my own prostitution was no different, I stopped judging them. We all did what we considered necessary to survive.

I neither formed alliances nor made enemies. The only time I got in trouble was when I worked the breakfast shift. Groggy and crabby when the guards woke me early, I fought them as they tried to snip my curls to fit underneath a hairnet. They beat me and, for good measure, shaved my head, which took four months to grow back. At least I saved on shampoo. After that, I lay low. Berlin had etched invisibility into my muscle memory. Still, the numbing routine wasn't all bad. Compared to the unpredictability of my life so far, it was comforting to know what would happen in the days, weeks, and months until my release. The only time I'd come close to having any structure was my stay at Oyf Haskhole. Nearly thirty years later, I finally appreciated what Miss Stone had done for me and the other orphans. And unlike prison, she fed us good food.

The mindless routine also gave me time to reflect on my future as the judge had urged. But I didn't need to think. I needed to make art. My hands itched to do something more useful than ladle oatmeal into bowls and fold laundry. One job I did look forward to was construction. The work was boring—building commissary shelves, repairing mess hall benches—but it gave me a chance to pilfer metal and wooden scraps. While others studied or played house at night, I'd create sculptures, then dismantle them and hide the pieces inside my mattress before the curfew count. None of the works survived more than a couple of hours. If I sensed the guards or my cellmates were getting suspicious, I'd return the stolen materials the next day.

One Sunday, five months into my sentence, I was told I had a visitor. Anoush sat in a corner on an orange vinyl chair, an empty one beside him, smiling as though awaiting a family member. While others held hands with husbands or boyfriends—no kissing allowed—or fed noisy kids from the vending machines, we inclined our heads together to hear each other.

"How did you find me?" I asked.

"Tracking you down not easy. Police no trust why I want see you, since we not related."

"I'm glad you kept at it, Anoush." I swallowed the lump in my throat.

Anoush wagged his finger at me. "You make me angry."

I sat back. Anoush had never scolded me before, not even for getting pregnant or arrested.

"Not because you get in trouble. Because you no call. You allowed make calls in jail?"

I grinned. "One a month. Twenty-five cents a minute. I spend my quarters on toothpaste."

Anoush promised to bring me a roll of coins. I told him he had to turn it in at the front desk, where it would be deposited in my account. Then he pulled a paper bag from a large pocket of his overalls. I looked at the guard as I took it. "It okay," he said, spreading his arms and legs. "They check me outside, make sure I not bring you anything dangerous."

I squished the bag and felt Ittel Rosa's limbs and button eye. I took her out and hugged her to my chest. When I'd arrived at prison without her, I told myself it was just as well, that the other women would jeer at me or worse. I soon learned that many had a falling-apart lovey of their own. I pressed Anoush's hand and set Ittel Rosa face forward on my lap so she could study her new surroundings. "This was the absolute best thing you could do for me."

"When I not hear from you after the court date, I send Mendel for your things before new renter throw them out. I save your clothes, art materials, and sculptures too."

"Mendel?" I thought of him as a little boy but realized he was nearing his mid-thirties.

Anoush said Miss Stone had let him take Mendel "off the books" when another adoption looked unlikely. Mendel had seemed fine until he dropped out in the middle of high school. Miss Stone and Anoush then persuaded him to enroll in the vocational ed program. "He do very well. Now he licensed mechanic and earn good living." Anoush looked like a proud father, which he sort of was. I wondered if Miss Stone thought of Mendel as one of her successes too.

The fluorescent lights blinked. Visiting hours were over. Anoush said he'd come again in two weeks. "Okay I bring Mendel? He a good example, you turn your life around when get out. You remember what I say long ago about proving the neighbors wrong? Still not too late."

That night, Ittel Rosa and I had our first talk in months. "Today was full of surprises. Seeing Anoush, being reunited with you. I didn't mind when Anoush scolded me, and I didn't even resent his advice. Somehow, it's easier to take it from him than from Frima."

The bear's matted coat looked ruffled. "What about from me?"

I smoothed her fur. "You've known me even longer than Frima. After all we've been through, how could I not trust you to give me sound advice?"

Ittel Rosa winked at me. "Then listen because I'm telling you it's time to call Frima."

***

The following weekend, Frima visited and brought six boxes of tampons. She cringed when the guard searched them. I said it was no big deal, you got used to being humiliated in prison. "We got used to being mistreated by the Nazis," she retorted. "That doesn't make it right."

Because being out of touch for long stretches was our pattern, Frima hadn't worried when months passed without hearing from me. Then, when I finally did call, she wasn't surprised I'd landed in prison. She was used to me fucking up, but at least she refrained from saying she hoped I'd learned my lesson. Instead, she told me to make a list of the other things I needed. Grateful, I let myself relax. It felt like old times when we were just two friends catching up. I asked to see photos of David and Lisa. Frima said Bob's law practice was doing well. She was bored, but between housework and driving the kids around, she didn't feel she could go back to work. "All in all, I have no right to complain," she finished. "What do you do with your time in this place?"

"Try not to go bonkers. Like you, I clean and cook. A woman's work is never done."

"Any art work?" Frima's skeptical voice told me she already knew the answer.

"The art of shelving books and folding jumpsuits." I snapped my fingers, so stiff from the damp air and harsh cleaning solutions, they couldn't handle art materials anyhow. "Which reminds me. Guess who I met in the prison library?" Of course, Frima had no idea. Besides me, who did she know who'd end up behind bars? "Moira Fromberg. Reuven's ex-wife."

"How'd you know he was her husband? I don't remember his last name if I ever knew it."

"Same here. But when she found out where I was from, we put two and two together. One day, Moira was reading a book about a woman who keeps on loving the man who beats her. She threw it in the trash when the librarian wasn't looking."

"What did she do when she saw that you were?"

"Started to fish it out but I told her I didn't care and wouldn't rat her out. That's when we started talking. She's in prison for stabbing Reuven in the stomach with a kitchen knife. He beat her like clockwork and she was afraid he'd kill her that time. She claimed self-defense but the court didn't see it that way. Moira got five years and lost custody of her kids."

Frima winced. "That's horrible, but I can't say I'm shocked. The seeds were there. Reuven was nastier than Salomon. Even Miss Stone was wary around him. Who knows why? Maybe Reuven had a rougher time in the camps. The guards could have singled him out."

"Men don't need that kind of history to be mean." I thought of the bikers I knew in high school and Knuckles at the restaurant. "They learn it at their daddy's knees."

"Exactly why I said you should join a consciousness-raising group."

I scoffed. "Thinking you'll change men by yakking with a bunch of women is as pointless as planting a sponge and expecting an apple tree to grow."

"We're building strength in numbers."

"A pack attracts attention, the negative kind. We're safer defending ourselves."

Frima looked sad. "Yeah. Ultimately, we're each alone."

I patted her arm. "We'll always have each other. And for the next seven months, I have the company of a house of women." I also had Anoush and Mendel, who took turns with Frima visiting me. Oddly, Mendel, who I knew least, was the one I most looked forward to seeing. He'd become a good person. All because a few caring people convinced him he could do better, and he chose to prove them right. Could I do the same? If I'd saved my money, I could have bought the soldering iron in a couple of months instead of spending a year in prison. Life on the streets hadn't taught me patience. There, you grabbed what you could before it was gone.

But I was no longer on the street. I was locked up in a place that, however badly, met my needs for food and shelter. I could do an about-face. I asked Frima to bring me hand lotion and did exercises to flex my fingers. The prison hired a new program director who let me teach a sculpture class. We couldn't use metal, wood, or sharp tools, but we had buckets of clay to mold and could fire our pieces in the kitchen's industrial oven. Mendel brought me art magazines and a book about glazes. Anoush acted like the proud father of two, a son and a daughter.

On the day I was released, Anoush and Mendel were waiting outside with a present and a card: "Congratulations on your freedom. Make it count, make it beautiful." Inside the box was a thirty-watt soldering iron. I couldn't wait to heat it up and fuse the scraps of my life together.

CHAPTER 30

Anoush's friend, a superintendent in a nearby building, found me a cheap studio apartment with enough room to set up a workspace. I hung Mr. Archer's magazine cover, which Mendel had retrieved, over a workbench that Anoush cobbled together. Mendel had rescued all my sculptures and scraps too. I applied to waitress at a fondue restaurant. After a year of prison food, the stuff people put in their mouths seemed no weirder than the crap that came out of them. I got up the nerve to ask my old boss for a reference.

I walked into Jim's Pizzeria and Italian Restaurant at closing time. His eyebrows shot up. Then he grinned, parked me at a table, and came back with a bottle of Chianti for the two of us and a big dish of lasagna for me. "To old times," he toasted. "Mangiare! Then tell me where you've been."

The first bite nearly made me groan aloud. Skipping the details, I told him I'd just finished a one-year prison sentence and was turning over a new leaf. "You were good to me, and I wasn't very kind in return. I have no right to ask, but I've applied for a waitressing job and wonder if you'd be willing to recommend me."

"I'd rather hire you to work for me again. The past is the past and in the last what—twelve, thirteen years?—I've still never had a waitress more dependable or better with the customers than you."

I looked around the restaurant, which had been redecorated. The china was thinner and the silverware heftier. I could make good money here and I couldn't ask for a fairer boss. "I'm bad at resisting temptation, but the answer is no thanks. I need a fresh start."

"I understand." Jim refilled our glasses. "To Liane's future. I'm happy to vouch for you."

First Anoush. Now Jim. My ideas about men were also in need of a fresh start.

My impression of Mendel continued to change too. A hard worker, he was also a patient teacher. I now owned a good soldering iron with no more idea how to use it than when I'd stolen one. Mendel started with the basics. First was using caution; the iron could be heated to 800 °F. The solder, a tin-copper alloy, came in two types, depending on the core or "flux" inside. Rosin core was for electrical work; acid core, which I'd use, was for plumbing and other metal work.

"Check and check," I said. "Just tell me how the damn thing works."

Mendel wouldn't be rushed. "You apply the solder to the tip." He explained how to choose which of the assorted flat and pointed tips to use based on the dimensions and location of the parts being joined. "You don't heat the solder itself. The iron heats the metal, then you apply the solder while continuing to heat the joint. As the solder melts, it dissolves oxidation. When you remove the heat, the solder cools, fusing the metal parts together." He demonstrated.

What Mendel hadn't told me was that the whole thing would smoke as the flux burned off. Black, noxious-smelling puffs. Standing in a one-room apartment in the Bronx, I was back in burned-out Berlin, choking on the fumes that followed an Allied bombing. My hand trembled. When it was my turn to try, I couldn't control the soldering iron. It was the first time that making art didn't come easily to me. The tears filling my eyes made it that much harder.

Mendel took the soldering iron and gave me a minute to compose myself. I sat on the bed, my back to him. When I returned to the workbench, he told me to take good care of the tips. "Use a brass sponge, the kind you'd buy to clean dishes. Otherwise, oxidation—rust—builds up and the tips won't accept the solder as readily."

"Wait. Are you saying you can't apply solder to a rusty surface?"

"Yes, exactly."

"Then fuck this. My work is all about using rusty metal." I unplugged the soldering iron.

Mendel touched my shoulder. "When I fix a car, if the usual repair doesn't work, I invent a new solution. Maybe you'll come up with new ideas for your sculptures."

"Fat chance," I snorted. Mendel smiled weakly and left. When the iron cooled, I cleaned the tip, then shoved everything in the back of my closet. I took down the magazine cover too.

***

Frima called a few days later. After years of not seeing each other for months, her alternate-week visits while I was in prison provoked a mutual promise to get together more often when I got out. Frima made sure we followed through. "Watching out for me?" I joked.

"Somebody has to. Anoush is a dear old man, but a womanly touch doesn't hurt."

"You mean a motherly touch? Sometimes you treat me like a daughter. How old is Lisa?"

"Seven." Frima's voice was guarded.

"So you're practicing how to keep me from going astray before she becomes a teenager?"

"I'm your sister. Period. Now, tell me what's going on with you."

I didn't push the mother thing, but I'd hit a nerve. While Frima didn't talk much about her children to spare me memories of giving up Sarah, I knew Frima well enough to hear what she wasn't saying. She was good at many things; motherhood wasn't one of them. Why would it be?

"I'm waitressing at a Hungarian restaurant," I told her.

"What about the Font of Fondue?"

"Could you work at a place with a name like that? After two days, I was ready to dip the snotty maître d' in melted cheese. Hungarian food is more to my liking. Ditto the owner."

"You're not messing around with the boss, are you?" Frima really did sound like a mom warning her wayward child.

I laughed. "Don't worry. Mr. Haydu's a nice guy but his only passion is cooking goulash. It's Mrs. Haydu who supervises the staff and her temper is as hot as the paprika in her husband's stew. She and I trade jibes about the customers. Same sense of humor. We get along fine."

"You'll be happy to know my cooking's improved." Frima sounded proud. "It had to since we entertain Bob's partners and clients. Come for lunch. Nothing too Frenchy, I promise."

"Come to *my* place. I'll feed *you*." Not counting prison, it was the first time I'd invited Frima to where I was living. After housemates, and cellmates, I missed having people around.

"You're not planning on serving one of your prison commissary specialties?"

"Nope. You'll get a proper, Hungarian meal. Courtesy of Goulash Garden."

The night before, Mrs. Haydu sent me home with a half-dozen take-out containers. Two kinds of soup: halászlé made with fish and meggy-leves made with cherries. Two main dishes: főzelék, a vegetable stew, and túrós csusza, pasta with cheese and bacon. After informing me that Bob and the kids kept kosher, Frima picked out all the bacon and gobbled it up first. Then we attacked the somlói galuska, three tiers of cake topped with whipped cream, chocolate, raisins, and walnuts, and finally slowed down over coffee and rétes, apple-filled pastries. I offered the leftovers to Frima, but she said Bob wouldn't let them inside the house, let alone everyone's stomachs.

We pushed away from the table and sat on the bed, Ittel Rosa propped between us. Frima stared at my empty workbench. "Where are you hiding your latest work? In the closet?" She poked around without waiting for my permission. "I recognize these pieces from before prison."

"I haven't had time to make anything new."

"Bullshit. You've been out two weeks. In the old days, you would have made art every minute you weren't at work or sleeping." She pulled out the soldering iron. "What's this?"

"Read the label on the box." I held Ittel Rosa in front of me, like a shield.

"Don't wink at me." Frima addressed the bear. "Why isn't Liane using this to make art?"

I answered for myself. "Because I'm too old to learn how to use it. I lost my chance along with my childhood. Making art requires an innocence that abandoned me in prison."

Frima returned to the bed, bringing the soldering iron with her. Gently, she wove her fingers through my hair, which had grown back wilder than ever. "Feeling sorry for yourself?"

"No. Just pissed." A tear fell on Ittel Rosa's head. I didn't know if I was angrier at my clumsy hands or at allowing myself to cry. I hadn't broken down when the hospital took Sarah or when the judge gave me the maximum sentence. "I don't know why I'm crying now," I admitted.

"Because art is the most important thing in your life. Without it, you're as good as dead."

"So I die. Who cares?"

"Me. Your parents. My parents. The Ashers and Gerstens went to their deaths hoping we'd make it out alive. They knew it wouldn't be easy, but they counted on us surviving. On wisdom replacing innocence. Just because we lose something or it's destroyed doesn't mean we can't get it back or repair it." Frima held my face in her hands. "Look at our friendship."

She was right. Frima and I had been through enough fire to oxidize our surfaces, yet we were as tightly fused as ever. I practiced with the iron until the smoke became a reassuring sign it was working. Joy flowed through me like solder when I realized I could let the metal re-rust *after* I'd joined the parts. By leaving the shiny solder visible, I could highlight the rusty areas. It was a breakthrough in my work. Mendel had been right too.

A month later, I invited Frima to lunch again. Thrilled by my cluttered workbench, she asked me to demonstrate my new technique. Then she pulled a small object, wrapped in a scarf, from her leather handbag and handed me the mangled *Sisters*.

"For fuck's sake, what happened?" I almost cried for the second time.

Frima told me about her fight with Lisa four years ago. "You and I were on the outs too, so I couldn't ask you to fix it. Somehow the time never seemed right, then you went to prison." She handed me the hair-like coil that had broken off. "I saved it."

"No wonder you wanted me to learn to solder." I smiled to show I was kidding because now Frima looked ready to cry. Then I bent *Sisters'* arms back into position so they embraced again and reattached the broken piece with solder so it was more secure than the original wiring.

"As beautiful as before." Frima cupped the sculpture in her hands. "As good as *Knot.*"

"I assumed you buried *Knot* the day after your wedding. You looked like you hated it."

Frima admitted that she did, at first. "I thought it was clunky and ugly. Later I came to see *Sisters* and *Knot* as equally beautiful. And now they're equally sturdy."

"Do you display them?" I hadn't seen Frima's married apartment; I tried to picture them.

"*Sisters* is on my dresser, like always. After Lisa damaged it, I wanted to put it in a drawer, but Sugar convinced me not to. She said fragility was a normal part of relationships."

I smiled. Frima talked to Sugar just like I talked to Ittel Rosa. And both answered back.

"After that I dug *Knot* out of my closet. I realized the sculpture says more about the bond between us than about me and Bob getting hitched." Frima re-wrapped *Sisters* and put it in her handbag. "*Knot* sits on my desk. I use it as a paperweight."

I frowned. "Paperweights hold things down."

Frima smiled. "They keep them from blowing away."

PART EIGHT:
FRIMA (1973–1978)

CHAPTER 31

The call came when Frima was leaving to pick up David and Lisa after school. "Mrs. Horner? This is Trudy, your father's secretary. I'm sorry to bother you, but he's apparently had a heart attack. He complained of chest pains then keeled over. An ambulance took him to New York Presbyterian Hospital. Your mother's on her way there now. She asked me to call you."

Frima hung up; she couldn't remember if she'd thanked Trudy. She called a friend to get the kids, left a message for Bob at work, and raced to the hospital. An ER nurse led her to a small room where Greta sat, hunched and moaning. A doctor followed her in. "A myocardial infarction, Mrs. Oberlander, a complete blockage of his coronary arteries. We did everything we could."

Greta's soft moan became a loud keen. "I told him, 'Otto, you're eighty. It's time to stop working. Last week, he complained the air was being squeezed out of him. I said to see a doctor. Did he listen? No! He lies down for half an hour, then goes to his store. Furniture, he sells." Her sentences ran into one another. She began to rock. "Aye, aye, aye. What's to become of me?"

The doctor looked to Frima for help. She held Greta's hands to stop them from churning. "Don't worry, Mother. I'll take good care of you. So will Bob and the children."

"The ambulance should have taken Otto to Mount Sinai, the Jewish hospital." Greta's sobs escalated until her breathing became ragged.

The doctor ordered a sedative and said they'd keep her in the hospital overnight. "Routine observation," he reassured Frima. After Greta was taken away, a social worker came in to ask the name of the funeral home that would pick up the body. Frima had no idea. She said she'd get back to them. Back at home, she called her parents' synagogue where, to her relief, a woman said the Chevra Kadisha, or Sacred Society, would handle everything from preparing the body to arranging the funeral to providing food during the week the family sat shiva. Her parents had already bought plots at Mount Hebron Cemetery.

The next morning, Frima brought her mother back to the Oberlanders' apartment. That afternoon, the Chevra Kadisha called to ask whether the family wanted Otto buried in a shroud or his own clothes. Although Greta was calmer and coherent now, Frima worried that asking would agitate her again. She figured her father would want to be buried in his best suit and also chose a top-of-the-line rosewood casket. Before the service, she and Greta viewed the body. Frima, who hadn't been allowed to see Otto in the hospital, said goodbye. He looked peaceful yet proud; she was glad she'd chosen the suit. Greta, unkempt, sobbed throughout the short ceremony.

Through the following week, Frima greeted their few guests—Bob and his family, the next-door neighbor, employees from the store. Joan promised to light a votive candle. Frima hadn't expected Liane to come but accepted her offer to get together when shiva ended. The entire seven days, Greta sagged in an armchair, where she remained at night, unwilling to sleep alone in the bed she and Otto had shared for nearly fifty years. Frima disliked having the Chevra Kadisha underfoot, but her mother seemed soothed by the constant murmur of prayers. The only prayer that comforted Frima was the Mourner's Kaddish. Not the words, which praised God with no mention of death, but the rhythm of the ancient Aramaic lines which repeated like a jazz riff.

***

Three months later, Bob, a tax lawyer, took care of selling Oberlander's Furniture and announced, "Your mother is financially set for life."

Frima, who visited Greta every day, groaned. "How long is that? She mopes around all day, alone in that huge apartment. She won't move to a smaller place closer to us because she refuses to get rid of a stick of furniture, which all came from my father's store."

"Give her time. It's only been a few months. Wouldn't you feel worse if Greta was one of those widows who dye their hair, shorten their skirts, and gallivant around town the minute their husbands are in the ground?" Bob pulled Frima to her feet and did an impromptu jitterbug.

She laughed at the incongruous image. "You're right. I need to let her grieve." But winter passed, spring arrived, and Greta was no different. If anything, her mother seemed to sink lower.

"Spring cleaning, Mom. Passover is next week." Frima, armed with a bucket of cleaning supplies, spoke cheerfully to cover her dismay at the moldy food and yellowed newspapers. She opened a can of tuna and sliced the tomato she'd brought. "Did you eat lunch?"

"I don't remember." Greta sat in the same armchair she'd occupied all through shiva. She smelled like she hadn't washed or changed clothes since Frima had bathed her earlier in the week.

"Join me then? I don't like to eat alone." Frima bit her tongue. Obviously, neither did her mother. Frima wasn't hungry but ate with gusto to encourage her. Greta took a bite, then stared into space. Frima gave up and tackled the kitchen. The refrigerator was filled with uneaten food. Although Greta had no appetite, she continued to cook Otto's favorites. Frima was relieved to see a pillow at one end of the couch, a sign her mother had stirred from her chair during the night.

Next Frima sorted through the unopened mail and scoured the tub. The landlord wanted to replace the old bathroom tiles but Greta wanted everything in the apartment left as-is. Finally, Frima set to work with the vacuum cleaner. When she turned it off, she was surprised to hear her mother speaking. "... the saxophonist. Not as good as Tommy Reed, but smooth enough for a local club." Greta laughed. "Yes, Dear, I thought we'd dance our feet off too."

Greta chatted with Otto, just like Frima did with Sugar! Frima had an idea. She put Glenn Miller's "In the Mood" on the turntable and extended her hand. Her mother smiled coquettishly and let Frima lead them in a lindy hop. Years dropped away as Greta, limp as a rag doll moments ago, danced with a spirit that Frima remembered from the early days of her adoption. When the song ended, Greta pulled more records out of the cabinet: Tommy Dorsey, Benny Goodman. She went into the bedroom and came out with Otto's bathrobe. With her nose buried in its folds, she continued to dance. She was as far away as she'd been at lunch, but her gaze was focused.

That night, Frima asked Sugar, "Did I do the right thing? She's living in the past, but at least she's living. If nothing else, the exercise may do her good and keep her alive."

Sugar nodded solemnly. "*You're* keeping her alive. You're a good daughter."

"Greta was a good mother. I wish I could say the same about myself."

CHAPTER 32

"I've made a decision." Frima had stayed up until Bob got home from a late-night meeting. David and Lisa were already in bed.

"Must be momentous if it couldn't wait until tomorrow." Bob poured two glasses of wine and suggested they sit on the couch, where he rested his feet in Frima's lap.

"I want to go back to work. Teaching."

Bob swung his feet to the floor. "We discussed this before we got married. I said no."

"And I accepted it thirteen years ago. But I don't want to end up like my mom. I need a life independent of being a wife and a mother. I miss being in the classroom, being useful."

"Nonsense. You take care of the house. I don't want to walk through the door at six to find you looking over homework instead of looking after me. I also need you to entertain my clients and their wives. So you're helping me with my work."

"And I'll continue to. But I miss helping children in the classroom."

Bob stood and put on his slippers. "Then try helping your own children for a change."

Frima gulped half her wine. "I cook and clean their rooms. I drive them to music lessons and doctor appointments and make sure they return library books." She ticked off more items.

"You're an efficient family secretary, but I'm talking about really being there for them. David's a year away from being a teenager. Kids his age can go off the rails. I can only do so much as his father. He's bound to go to battle with me. He needs a mother who's in his corner."

"What do you expect me to do? He holes up in his room, listening to music. Or he's off with his friends. He never answers my questions with more than a mumbled word. Or syllable."

"Because you never ask about what interests him. And Lisa? Don't get me started."

"You already started. By all means continue." Frima downed the rest of her wine.

"You and your daughter don't talk at all. Unless it's to shout."

"One way. She shouts at me. In her estimation, I can't do anything right."

"Because compared to her friends' mothers, you don't."

"Such as?"

"Whatever mothers and daughters do. Look at fashion magazines, try on makeup, talk about boys." Bob shrugged as if women should know that instinctively.

"Isn't she a little young for that?" Frima asked quietly. She wanted to shout, "Should I turn her into a little whore, like I was?" but the window for telling Bob about that had closed. "Our kids have lives outside the house now and need me less. I need to get out of the house too."

"If you want to help others, why not join the Sisterhood at shul? You're a good organizer. You ran that Campaign for Lost Children in college. They could use your expertise in their fundraising drives. The money goes to charity. That should satisfy your urge to be useful. Who knows? You might even decide to become active in our children's religious education after all."

"After I washed my hands of it years ago? That idea shows how little you know me."

"I could accept your refusal if I believed it was about religion. But it's because you don't want to be involved with your children, period." Bob stalked to the bedroom. Frima knew the only reason he didn't slam the door was for fear of waking the kids. Her husband would play the "good father" to the hilt to make her look like the "bad mother."

Not that he needed to. Frima wrote the role for herself.

***

Two years to the day after Otto's death, Frima let herself into the Oberlanders' apartment. "Mom, I brought you a Yahrzeit candle. We can say Kaddish together," she called from the foyer. Bing Crosby was crooning "I'll Never Smile Again" at high volume in the living room. Frima hung up her coat and left a bag of apples in the kitchen before going in. Greta, in a faded house dress, lay on the floor beside her chair. Frima ran to her, but Greta's arms were rigid; she must have died soon after Frima left yesterday. At eighty, Greta had died at the same age as Otto, but unlike his sudden death, she'd slipped away. She still listened to records, yet she hadn't danced in months.

Frima held Greta's stiff hand and waited for tears, an ache, tension, or release. But either she felt empty or was filled with such a mix of emotions that she couldn't differentiate them. The record ended. She let the needle return to the beginning and played it again. When Bing Crosby had finished, she listened to Glenn Miller, Tommy Dorsey, and every Broadway show album her parents owned. Had owned. Not until dark did she walk to the kitchen and start making calls.

The Chevra Kadisha again handled the funeral. Fewer people came to Greta's than Otto's. The store's old employees, save Trudy, were gone. Frima said the Mourner's Kaddish with even more fervor than she had for her father. Re-orphaned, she chanted it for all four parents. As long as she lived, Frima was supposed to recite the prayer on the anniversary of their deaths. Yet after today, she'd never say it again. Dayenu. Enough. She was done with Jewish rituals and death.

A week after Adath Israel's Sisterhood bundled her parents' clothes for charity, Frima asked Joan to meet her at the Oberlanders' apartment. She didn't want to be alone while she emptied shelves and drawers so the Hebrew Immigrant Aid Society could take the furniture. Joan offered to bring boxes for whatever Frima wanted to save.

"Just bring trash bags. I've already retrieved their valuables. Given my mother's neglect the last two years, mice have probably chewed whatever else is left."

Joan counted twenty photo albums arranged chronologically in the hutch: Bob and Frima's wedding, the grandchildren's birthdays. "Are you sure you don't want to keep these?"

"They're duplicates. I have the negatives." Frima dumped them, along with decades of knickknacks. From a desk drawer, Joan pulled out a large box labeled "Walton" and a smaller one marked "Barnard." She and Frima each carried one to the couch. The first held programs from every high school band concert; papers and exams, none graded lower than A; Frima's diploma, and her valedictorian certificate. Joan sighed. "Those were the best years of our lives."

"What about college?" Frima asked.

"I loved Hunter, but I didn't feel as special. Nothing came close to being a Periwinkle."

"Your college days still beat mine." Inside the other box, Frima found her bachelor's degree and the commendation for her work on the Lost Children Campaign. Nothing more.

"You've had a good life since then," Joan insisted. "A handsome, successful husband; two smart, wonderful children."

"That's them, not me. I feel like I let Principal Heffernan down. Walton graduates were supposed to change the world."

"I'm disappointed too," said Joan. "Marriage isn't what it was cracked up to be."

"Are you still having an affair with your boss?"

"No."

"Good." Frima squeezed Joan's arm. "I was afraid you'd get caught and be out a husband and a job. Even if marriage to Mark isn't what you expected, it's better than being divorced."

Joan squeezed back and grinned. "I'm having an affair with someone else."

Frima examined the award for her work with refugee children. "College wasn't all bad, I guess. I got a teaching degree and set off to make things better for my students. Past tense."

"Stop talking like you're already dead. You still have years of being a mother ahead of you. Your children will make you proud. And at some point, you can go back to teaching."

"Bob won't allow me to."

"Men! Don't listen to him. Or volunteer at your synagogue. Bob can't object to that."

"He doesn't, but I do." Frima put her degrees and awards back in their respective boxes, closed the lids, and reached for another trash bag.

Joan frowned. "At least keep those. David and Lisa might want them someday."

"I doubt it," said Frima. She swept the boxes into the gaping bags. "Dayenu. Enough."

***

"What happened to the high-achieving, impassioned young woman I used to be?" Frima asked Sugar that night. The children were sleeping at friends' houses, Bob was at a dinner meeting with a client, and she was home with only self-pity for company.

The doll spoke severely. "You faded like your mother, but you are *not* dead yet."

Frima left Sugar on the bed and wandered to the dresser, where she picked up *Sisters*. Liane had turned her life around when all seemed lost; could she? She walked to her desk and held *Knot*. Tonight its weight seemed unbearable. Frima crawled under the covers with the doll and both sculptures. She remembered the night, after a bombing raid, when she and Liane had together lifted massive charred timbers to crawl into an abandoned building to sleep. Tonight, the world pressed down on her like those fallen beams. It was a burden she would have to bear alone.

***

"Mom, Shabbas starts in twenty minutes. I can't find Bubbe's candlesticks." Lisa stood in the kitchen doorway.

Frima continued slicing a tomato. "I packed them up."

"I don't understand. We light the candles every Friday night. With Bubbe gone, isn't it more important than ever?"

"I only lit them to make your grandmother happy. She won't know the difference now."

Lisa's mouth dropped open. "I will. So will Daddy and David." Her face softened. "But if being reminded of your mother is too upsetting, we could buy new candlesticks."

Frima was touched by her daughter's sensitivity, a kinder side she wished Lisa would show her more often. All the same, she said truthfully, "No. I'm done with Shabbas and everything else Jewish. It's a lightning rod for pain."

"But you *are* Jewish. We all are."

Frima began slicing a green pepper. "Then you and your father and brother can light candles and say the blessings. I'll respect you. I just won't join you."

Lisa narrowed her eyes. "Respectful? Hah. You're being totally disrespectful. To your parents and the six million Jews who died in the Holocaust."

"Oh, please. Let's not go there."

"Okay. Let's just talk about your parents, then. Or, only your mother."

"I took care of her, every day, for the last two years."

Lisa stomped her foot. "A total sham. You're were as bad a daughter as you are a mother. The only one you care about is yourself."

"If I didn't take care of myself, I'd be dead. And you wouldn't exist."

"You should have died. A Jew who would keep our religion alive should have lived."

Frima gasped. "I'm not stopping you, but I won't pretend to believe in something I don't. Nor do I accept that I was a bad daughter. I loved and respected my parents in other ways."

"Like what?"

"By making something of myself. Getting a teaching degree. Fighting for poor children."

Lisa snickered. "You got a degree you don't use and wrote letters that changed nothing. You're a hollow shell. The Nazis killed you after all." Her lips quivered but her body was rigid.

Frima raised her hand to slap her daughter but lowered it when she realized she was still holding the knife. Her hand shook. "The candlesticks are in a shoe box on the shelf of the coat closet. You can light them. Daddy and David can recite the prayers over the wine and challah."

"And you?"

"I'll sit at the table. Silent. And when you three are done, I'll eat with you."

***

Dinner didn't go the way Frima said it would. She was questioned, not by Lisa who, perhaps sensing she'd gone too far, looked remorseful. Instead, her daughter nodded approvingly when her brother led the attack.

"Mom, why aren't you lighting the candles?" David asked as soon as his sister reached for the matches. "Lisa's not allowed to until after her bat mitzvah, which isn't for two years."

"Since when do you care about rules?" Frima shot back.

Bob reassured Lisa. "Nothing in scripture says you can't. It's just a tradition. Go ahead."

Lisa lit the candles, covered her eyes, and sang the blessing. Frima thought that would be the end of it, but after her family chorused "Amen," David's cross-examination resumed. "Don't you care about Zayde Otto and Bubbe Greta? Observing Shabbas is a way to remember them."

"Our son has a point," said Bob. "Every week, Jews say Kaddish at the end of Shabbas services. We commemorate death, not birth, to acknowledge the mark people make on the world."

Frima ignored her husband's lecture. "Of course I care about my parents," she told her son. "Not a day goes by when I don't think of the difference they made in my life."

Lisa finally spoke up. "You miss them because they were real parents. They did for me what you didn't. Bubbe baked my favorite birthday cake when you settled for store-bought. Zayde drove me to their house to practice piano because you wanted our house quiet while you read."

"They came to every Little League game," added David. "You didn't even ask the score."

"What about making a home and feeding you?" Frima filled their plates. "Protecting you from the world's cruelty?"

David sneered. "The law requires those. A good parent also shows love. Like Zayde and Bubbe showed us."

"Our children are grieving," said Bob. "Can't you understand their sense of loss?"

Frima threw down her napkin. "They have no idea what loss is. They grew up with four grandparents and two parents."

"Four grandparents and one parent," snarled David.

"You got that right," said Lisa.

Frima scraped their plates into the trash. Her family stared open-mouthed.

"Punishing your children by denying them food? You of all people should know better." Bob put on his jacket and handed David and Lisa theirs. "Come on, kids. We'll go to my folks' for the evening. They'll do double duty as your grandparents. I'll do double duty as your parent."

CHAPTER 33

Despite the September chill, Frima went for a walk to escape hearing Lisa practice her Torah portion. Bob was handling all the bat mitzvah arrangements. He'd made a large contribution to the synagogue, hired the caterer for the luncheon after the service, and rented a hall for the big party that night. Even with all the details out of her hands, Frima wanted more distance from the affair.

Since the fight two years earlier over the candlesticks, Lisa no longer called her a bad Jew but still said she was a bad mother. She complained that Frima never took her shopping. Then, when Frima did, she accused her of not knowing what kind of clothes her daughter liked. "You have no idea who I am. I might as well be motherless." Then there were battles over homework. Lisa nagged Frima to help her. Hoping for a truce, Frima set aside an hour every evening. But whether Lisa was careless, lazy, or simply not that bright, she wasn't as good a student as Frima had been. When she corrected her daughter or urged her to try harder, Lisa erupted. "Just because you're a perfectionist doesn't give you the right to demand it of me." She refused to show Frima any more work and instead asked her brother for help or, ostentatiously, turned to her father.

Chagrined, Frima called Joan. "Help! My daughter hates me."

"She used that word?"

"Yes. She also detests me and wishes she could trade me for one of her friend's mothers."

"Strong language," Joan acknowledged, then coaxed, "Is she *ever* nice to you?"

"Now and then she surprises me with her sweetness," Frima conceded. "She compliments my cooking or appears beside my desk with a cup of tea and toast slathered in jam." Frima sighed. "A minute later, she's complaining about something I did or didn't do. I can't predict which side will turn up or figure out how to make it be the nicer one." She didn't tell Joan that she'd asked Bob if he had any ideas or that his response had been, "Maybe if you showed that side of yourself more often, she'd show it to you." Advice that was truthful to give, painful to receive, beyond her to follow.

"It's gotten worse since Lisa started preparing for her bat mitzvah," Frima continued. "She doesn't say it, but I know she still holds it against me that I'm not observant. Religion is my curse. Again."

"All kids that age turn on their parents. Especially girls and their mothers. I was a real bitch, like every twelve-year-old girl with her mom."

"I wouldn't know," Frima whispered.

"God. Me and my big mouth." Joan tried again. "Lisa's mother-bashing is normal and has nothing to do with you or being Jewish. In ten or twenty years, she'll grow out of it."

Frima thanked Joan for the reassurance, but she wasn't convinced. She asked Sugar, "Am I a bad mother?"

"Honestly, yes."

"Do you have to be so honest?"

"If I don't tell you the truth, who will?"

"You sound like a mother." Frima couldn't help laughing.

"No. Just an old friend who cares about you."

Frima sighed. "You're right. I am a bad mother."

Sugar's eyes were sorrowful. "It's not your fault. How could you be a good one?"

"Greta was my mom long enough for me to learn from her."

"Early damage left too much scar tissue."

"So I'll never heal?" Frima lay Sugar's bald head against her heaving chest.

"Healing isn't your responsibility alone," the doll answered. "Joan was right. Lisa has to grow up. Hopefully, she'll come to understand what you went through and how you were hurt. Meanwhile, stay connected. You know Lisa is capable of kindness. Don't let go, even when she pushes you away."

Frima called Liane. Their visits had become less frequent again. Frima blamed herself. She was emotionally drained. "Can I invite you to Lisa's bat mitzvah? I could use the moral support."

"Save yourself the cost of a thirteen-cent stamp. I disrespectfully decline."

"I wish I could decline too." Frima sighed. "What's up with you these days?"

"Things are going well, actually. I sold several pieces at art fairs over the summer. Still no luck finding a gallery, though. I'm thinking of going back to school."

"Great. Which art program?"

"None. Social work."

"Huh? Where did that come from?"

"You know the expression: 'Set a thief to catch a thief?' I figure it takes a delinquent to know how another delinquent's mind works."

"Meaning you can help them be better thieves or turn them around?"

Liane laughed. "The latter, or something like that. The more damaged, the better."

Frima crossed Liane's name off the guest list and wished her good luck. "Get your degree quick. One of these days, juvenile court may add my daughter's name to your caseload."

***

Family members were called to the bima for aliyah, the honor of reciting prayers before Lisa's Torah reading. David, Bob, and Bob's parents avoided looking at Frima as they marched past her and mounted the small stage. The other guests stared with disapproval. Spared from pretending, Frima was nonetheless self-conscious and hurt sitting alone beneath them. Growing up, she'd been an outcast because she was Jewish. Now she was ostracized for not being Jewish enough.

On the bima, Lisa, wearing a blue velvet dress and her first high heels, looked radiant. Her Torah recitation was perfect, chanted in a sweet sing-song. *Genesis 24* acknowledges Rebecca as the leader of her generation. Lisa's sermon was about her own willingness to lead. "Torah commands us to safeguard the land. I will fight on the front lines to guarantee the future of our planet." Frima heard echoes of her own valedictorian address at Walton's commencement. She hoped that her daughter's passion, unlike hers, would not diminish.

CHAPTER 34

Frima heard the loud rap while preparing dinner. She thought Lisa had forgotten her key or Bob, arms loaded with tax briefs, couldn't reach his. David was at band practice and wouldn't be home from school for another hour. But when she answered the knock, Frima saw her son staring at the doormat and a policeman, gripping David's elbow, staring at her. His badge identified him as Officer Kupper. She didn't recognize the name but his face looked vaguely familiar. Small for a cop, yet wiry, his stern expression softened by warm brown eyes.

"Mrs. Horner? David's mother?" He nudged her son forward. Frima gulped and nodded. David still wouldn't look at her but the officer peered into her face. "Frima?"

Her mind raced. He was about a decade younger than her, too old to be a former student. "Oh my goodness. Salomon!" Between him and Reuven, Salomon was the nicer one who didn't tease her.

Officer Kupper rested his hand on David's shoulder. "I'm sorry to meet you again under these circumstances, but I've just arrested your son for breaking and entering, vandalism, and theft." David had jimmied open the door of an elderly woman's apartment, smashed a television and stereo, and pocketed jewelry estimated to be worth a thousand dollars.

"He didn't hurt her?" Frima thought of Greta, home alone and helpless after Otto died.

"No. Fortunately, she was out. But her daughter came by just as your son was leaving and caught him in the act. He ran. She called immediately with a good description and we picked him up a couple of blocks away. The old woman came home soon after. According to the daughter, her mother was quite upset—she has a heart condition—and is in the hospital for observation."

Frima motioned Salomon and David inside. "You're sure there hasn't been a mistake? My son's a good kid. Does well in school, plays clarinet, never gives us trouble." Unlike Lisa, David was quiet and kept his distance, which was fine with Frima.

Salomon pulled a plastic bag, marked NYPD, from his pocket. It held a pearl necklace, cameo brooch, rings, and earrings. "We found these in your son's backpack."

Frima led the way to the living room, where she collapsed on the couch. Officer Kupper remained standing. David, stone-faced and silent, stood against the wall. Frima addressed him. "I don't understand. You have everything you need: your own television and stereo, nice clothes, summer camp. ... " Her voice trailed off. She turned to Salomon. "What happens now?"

"There'll be an arraignment in juvenile court. He'll enter a plea. Depending on what he pleads, there'll be a trial or he'll be given a sentence at that point."

"Will he have to go to jail until the arraignment?" Frima thought of Liane.

"No. He's fifteen. Kids are only kept in detention if they're in danger or have no suitable home to go to. That doesn't apply in David's case."

Frima shook her head. She looked at David, then at Salomon. "I still don't understand."

"Life is full of surprises. Take me. I could have gone from juvenile delinquent to full-fledged criminal. Instead, I became a cop." Salomon approached David, his voice soft but urgent. "You grew up with lots of privileges, not least among them two parents. Your mother and I were much less fortunate. In my experience, kids who do what you did are angry. I don't know what you have to be angry about, but I suggest you focus on what you have to be grateful for."

David finally looked up. He nodded at Officer Kupper and glanced at his mother before turning away again. His slim, young body sagged. "Can I go to my room now?"

Frima said yes. She walked Salomon to the door and thanked him. "Maybe he'll listen to you more than to me. I've heard the last people teenagers listen to are their parents."

Salomon's badge glinted in the overhead hallway light. "You and I wouldn't know, but I hope your son is shaken up enough to listen to someone."

***

At dinner, Bob asked David flat out why he'd done it. David frowned and said there was no reason or excuse. When he didn't say more, Bob declared, "You're to come straight home from school from now on. No friends, phone calls, or television. One hour of radio or records Sunday afternoons. Your allowance will go toward legal fees."

"Okay." David's forehead smoothed. He appeared to welcome the punishment. Bob asked if Frima had anything to add. David turned to her expectantly. She didn't. Reuven had often done outrageous things to get a rise out of Miss Stone. Had her son been trying to get Frima's attention?

After the kids were in bed, Bob told Frima, "I'll handle David's case."

"You're a tax lawyer, not a criminal lawyer."

"Then I'll get one of my friends to do it. Several are defense attorneys."

"Who don't know the first thing about juvenile law." Frima crossed her arms. "You made the decisions about Lisa. Leave David to me."

Bob saluted. "About time you got involved."

The next morning, Frima checked the phone directory for David Abner. His name wasn't listed. The lawyer who'd handled her adoption would be in his sixties now, perhaps no longer in practice. Not ready to give up, she dug out her adoption papers and dialed his old law firm.

"Sorry, no David Abner. We do have a David Abrams. Shall I put you through to him?"

Frima said yes. She vaguely recalled he'd changed his name from Abrams to Abner to avoid antisemitism. "This is Frima Horner, calling about my son, David. Over thirty years ago, you handled my adoption by Otto and Greta Oberlander. You probably don't remember, but ... "

"I do actually. You were a war orphan in your teens. It was rare for children that old to be adopted." His voice matched Frima's memory: gentle and patient, yet straightforward and honest. She explained her son's arrest and asked if he'd be willing and available to take on the case.

"It's a good sign that he was released to your custody, but those are serious charges. I'll accept the case, provided you understand that I can't guarantee the outcome."

"I learned early in life that nothing is guaranteed. But sometimes things turn out well." Frima gave him her phone number. "Can I ask why you changed your name back to Abrams?"

"As I learned more about the Holocaust, I wanted to reclaim my Jewish heritage. If it's any reassurance, I've specialized in cases of delinquent children who were traumatized by the war or whose parents were. It didn't end with your generation. The effects can be passed down."

Frima attempted a chuckle. "Are you reassuring me or warning me?"

"Both. Your adoption worked out. For many, it didn't. Even for those who seemed to succeed, it's not uncommon to see problems in their children."

"Like my son?"

"Until I know more, I can't say what's behind his actions. But I am saying not to be hard on yourself. You've done the best you could."

Frima wished Bob were listening on an extension. Lisa too. And David.

Mr. Abrams explained the Department of Juvenile Justice would contact them to schedule an intake conference, not to discuss the pending case, but to gather basic information about David and the family. Meanwhile, the prosecutor would prepare a document with the formal charges.

"We already know those. The arresting officer told us."

"Those charges could change by the time the prosecutor's done. For better or worse."

Frima caught her breath.

The lawyer continued. "You'll be served formal paperwork in person or by certified mail. The system is only required to give you seventy-two-hours notice before you have to show up in juvenile court, so it's good that you contacted me right away. It gives us time to prepare. Can you, your husband, and your son come to my office tomorrow?"

"My son and I can." Frima faltered. "I don't know about my husband."

"Don't force it. A son's transgressions are harder on a father. Like daughters and mothers. As long as your husband goes along with us and holds his tongue before the judge, it'll be fine."

Over two long meetings, Frima watched David warm to the lawyer, who listened intently and questioned him about the details. His eyes followed the lawyer's pen as he wrote everything down. Now and then her son glanced at her, as if to say, "See. This is what it's like to be heard."

Mr. Abrams walked them through what would happen at the arraignment and how David should act. "This is his first chance to admit or deny the charges, that is, plead guilty or innocent. I advise a 'not guilty' plea." Frima asked why when Officer Kupper's evidence was so clear. "A not-guilty plea buys us time to do our own investigation and decide how to best move forward. The victim's lawyer will present the worst possible case against David. We can attempt to refute at least some of those charges. At the same time, we'll document his clean record up to now and, beyond that, his model behavior as a student and a member of your family's synagogue."

It wasn't *her* synagogue but Frima played along. The lawyer's final words were to David. "Don't excuse yourself or blame others. Act contrite. Demeanor counts as much as evidence. In juvenile cases, decisions often depend more on what lies ahead than what an offender has done."

**

Two months after David's "not guilty" plea, his case went to trial. The victim's lawyer spoke first. "Your Honor. The evidence is irrefutable. Further, the young man's actions have taken a grievous toll on my elderly client's physical and emotional health." He detailed her long hospital stay to undergo testing and observation, panic attacks upon returning home, and general mental distress. The tiny woman sat with her eyes cast down; her daughter glared at David.

Then David Abrams spoke. Frima put a protective arm around her son. Bob sat stiffly on his other side. "Your Honor. My client is not a 'young man.' The law defines him as a juvenile. The plaintiff was discharged from the hospital after a brief overnight stay. Medical records do not confirm a heart attack or other ailments. There is no documentation of panic attacks other than the testimony of her daughter, who is not credentialed to make a psychiatric diagnosis. That said, the defense does not dispute that the plaintiff experienced psychological distress." He closed by summarizing the defendant's otherwise exemplary behavior and his positive home environment.

David looked straight ahead during the proceedings, his narrow body convulsing with an occasional shiver. Frima believed his regret was genuine, not mere compliance with his lawyer's instructions. He walked stiffly when he was finally called to the bench. Frima reached for Bob across the gap that now lay between them. Her husband's hand enclosed hers and squeezed.

The judge pronounced David guilty. "As your attorney has informed you, the sentencing options are incarceration, probation, community service, counseling, and/or fines." He looked past David at Frima and Bob. "I can also order your parents to attend counseling." Frima stifled the urge to volunteer. The judge turned back to her son. "I'm assigning you two hundred hours of community service at a nursing home. While you didn't know that the apartment belonged to an elderly woman, behavior has unintended consequences for which you alone are accountable."

"I understand, Your Honor."

"Despite the magnitude of the damage and theft, I've opted for probation in the custody of your parents, not incarceration. Your home
offers a good environment, and since you have no prior offenses, there
is every reason to believe you can turn your life in a positive direction."
The judge straightened the papers on his desk and sat back. "Is there
anything you wish to say?"

"Thank you, Your Honor. I'm truly sorry for what I did." David looked
at the old woman, who squinted at him and looked away. Her daughter
stared ahead, stone-faced. David turned back to the judge. "I've learned
my lesson and I intend to be a model citizen from now on."

The judge declared a ten-minute recess. David remained at the
bench. Frima, Bob, and the attorney soon surrounded him. For the
first time since he was a little boy, her son allowed Frima to hug him.
Bob thanked the lawyer and left, ushering David in front of him.
Frima waited with David Abrams while he packed up his briefcase.
She wished she could hug him too.

"Thank you," she said. "You've saved my life twice. I hope I never
need your help again, but I can't express enough appreciation for how
much you've done for my son and our family."

"My pleasure. This work gives me the same satisfaction as retaking
my name. Seeking justice is another way to avenge the loss of our
people."

Frima thought about how Greta and Otto had turned her life in a
positive direction. They had proven it wasn't too late for her to become
a good daughter or them to learn to be parents. Her son was only a year
older than she was when they adopted her. It wasn't too late for him or
her. Becoming a better parent, to both her children, was how she could
pay them back with love.

***

David cautiously accepted Frima's attempts. He didn't initiate conversations but answered her questions in short sentences instead of
monosyllables. He was most receptive when she got out her high

school clarinet and they played jazz duets. Frima convinced Bob to relax the stereo restrictions and gave David her parents' old records, which she hadn't listened to since Greta died. Together they recreated the great solos of Benny Goodman, Artie Shaw, Woody Herman. No wonder her parents had loved this music. How hurt they must have been when Frima rejected it for rock 'n' roll. "Music appreciation evidently skips a generation, like cooking skills," she said.

Her son smiled. "I don't know about appreciation, Mom, but your playing is pretty chill."

Her daughter still pushed Frima away, blaming her for David getting into trouble. "FYI," Lisa said, "David agrees you never cared about us. You didn't even go through the motions."

Frima winced. "Your brother never said anything like that to me."

"That's the problem, Mother. Why would he bother?"

Frima didn't defend herself. At heart, she believed that Lisa was right.

PART NINE:
LIANE (1975–1980)

CHAPTER 35

"Did anyone ever tell you to go to college?" Mrs. Haydu asked me one night after Goulash Garden had closed. We were setting up for tomorrow.

"Half a dozen people, twenty-five years ago."

"I'm telling you now."

"A little late, don't you think? I'm forty-two."

Mrs. Haydu spread the last tablecloth and folded the napkins. "So? Our upstairs neighbor got her degree at sixty-five. She graduated together with her grandson."

I put out the silverware. "What would I do with a college education at my age?"

"Teach. I seen you handle those teenagers who come for lunch on Thursdays."

"The rowdy bunch?" I usually worked dinner shift, but a couple of weeks ago I'd covered midday for a sick waitress. Six high school kids had ordered three meals between them. They'd yelled at me to bring more bread. Entering customers, hearing them, had left. After a two-hour meal, the leader picked up an unused knife, said it hadn't been washed, and said he'd call the health department unless lunch was on the house. Without missing a beat, I said I'd report them to the truant officer unless they paid up or washed the dishes themselves. They paid. On their way out, I gave them extra mints and winked. "Next time, just say the authorities *should* be notified. Wait for the owner to offer to cancel the bill. An implied threat is always scarier than a real one."

"The other waitresses are afraid of those kids. They let my husband deal with them." Mrs. Haydu shook her head. "Not you. This Thursday, they ordered six meals, paid up, and even left a tip."

I smiled. "How much? I deserve a cut."

"Hah. Two dollars. You can ask Marianne for half." Mrs. Haydu called to Mr. Haydu in the back that it was time to go home. "Seriously, Liane. You'd be a good high school teacher."

"Too many rules. I'd break more than my students."

"What about social work?"

I joked to hide my interest. "There are easier ways to get rid of me."

"Not so fast. It will take you at least four years and you'll still have to work during that time. After you graduate, I'll be happy, and proud, to let you go."

"Thank you." I hoped those two words were enough to show I was grateful.

"On one condition," Mrs. Haydu added. "You have to come back once a month."

I followed the Haydus out the door. "To work?"

"No," said Mrs. Haydu. "To eat my husband's goulash. On the house."

***

At the library, I looked up schools of social work. New York University and Fordham University, both private, were too expensive. But Hunter, the public college where Frima had urged me to study art, had a Bachelor of Social Work program and decent financial aid. I sent for a brochure, which said that to be admitted, you had to already be enrolled with sixty out of 120 undergraduate credits completed. Students applied after sophomore year and spent the next two earning their BSW. All I had was a high school diploma. I made an appointment with an admissions counselor.

I was summoned by Reena Goldstein, a plump woman who greeted me with a warm smile. "I'll be honest," I began, sitting on the edge of my chair in her cluttered office.

Mrs. Goldstein smiled. "A good trait for an aspiring social worker."

I breathed easier, sat back, and told her my history: war orphan, group homes, high school diploma, unskilled jobs, a year in prison for petty larceny, law-abiding and hard-working since. "At my age, four years is a long time to spend in school before beginning a late-in-life career. Is there a way I can knock off some of those credits so I can start the social work program earlier?"

"How did you survive during the war?"

"Theft, prostitution, ingenuity." The truth popped out of my mouth without hesitation.

"Good instincts too, no doubt. You survived high school?"

"I got decent grades. Except for art, where I excelled." I felt my face redden. "I assume you'll need to verify that with a transcript."

"Ordinarily, that's a standard part of an application. But for older students, the admissions committee only needs proof you got your diploma. Unless there's a red flag, the rest of your record is irrelevant. You're not the same person you were then. We're interested in who you are now." Mrs. Goldstein described the requirements in detail then started to make some notes.

I tapped my foot on the scuffed linoleum. Mrs. Goldstein looked up from her notepad. "Don't worry. Your incarceration won't be held against you."

I held my foot still. Also, my breath.

"Here's what I can offer, subject to the approval of the committee, which hasn't overruled me yet. I'll waive thirty pre-admission credits. You can do half the remaining thirty credits this summer and half in the fall, during which you must pass the Introduction to Social Work gateway course with a grade of 'B' or better, complete a thirty-two-hour volunteer assignment, and obtain an overall GPA of at least 2.75. You can then apply to the social work program for the following spring. If you go to summer school again, you'll graduate with a BSW in just two years."

"What's the catch?"

Mrs. Goldstein laughed. "Wariness is another useful attribute for a social worker. Clients often try to put one over on you." She got serious. "There's no 'gotcha' but to get credits waived, you have to write two papers, one on your years as a street orphan, one on your year in prison."

"What kind of papers?" The last paper I'd written was a book review in Senior English.

"More than recounting what happened. Reflective papers about what you learned and, most importantly, how you'd apply those insights as a social worker." Mrs. Goldstein looked at me steadily. "You'll have to dig deep inside yourself. It's likely to be painful. Are you up to it?"

I closed my eyes. The images came easily. Then I checked my guts for the feelings that went with them. My stomach roiled; my breathing was labored. "Yes," I answered.

***

Being back in school wasn't as weird as I feared. Many students were older, like me, and from modest backgrounds. Keeping up with the assignments wasn't that hard either. Evening shifts left my days free to study. Unlike Evander, where attending classes was as pointless as stapling onion skins, I would use what I was learning. Even the course on social work theory. The teacher wrote THEORY and PRACTICE on the board. He circled the word THEORY. "Theory teaches you to understand where your clients are coming from. Bad neighborhoods, bad homes, bad schools. That doesn't mean they're bad kids, only kids who put on a bad boy or tough girl act." He circled PRACTICE. "So, you hang out with them, listen, get to know who they are. And you see that under the grown-up swagger, they're children, looking for the love and respect they don't get from parents and teachers. They think joining a gang will give them what they want."

"Doesn't it?" I asked. "Gangs become their family. They develop street smarts and defy teachers who call them stupid. Dealing also puts money in their pockets to buy food and clothes."

"The family model works at first. Kids are too naïve to realize street life eventually robs them of more than it gives them." The teacher spoke about his work in the South Bronx, where he grew up. "I know it's hard to delay gratification, to believe playing it clean will get them more in the end. That's where a social worker comes in. You give them instant positive markers along the way. You feed them, sometimes out of your own pocket, and let them experience success at a pickup basketball game. You organize a neighborhood softball team they can belong to."

I thrust harder, enjoying our duel. "Aren't you implicitly criticizing their older brothers and cousins, the heroes and kingpins who went a different way? They look up to those people."

"Not as much as you think. Kids are gullible but they're not dumb. They see that very few make it to the top. Most end up as the big guy's lackey. Past a certain age, they're washed up."

"Sounds like the rest of America." I thought of the jobs I'd had over the past thirty years: scooping ice cream, slinging subway tokens, filling napkin dispensers and water glasses.

"The point is, it doesn't have to be *their* America. Theory teaches you there are ways out. Not easy, but possible. Practice is how you turn the possible into the real, one client at a time."

I realized it was no longer my America either. What had taken me decades to achieve, I could help teens start to build now. School was teaching me I could make better choices without judging myself for having made bad ones, exactly what I hoped to do for my future clients.

At the end of the semester, I took a week off work and even set aside making art to write my two papers. By Sunday, I was a wreck on the outside: fingernails chewed to nubs, hair unwashed, clothes unchanged. But on the inside, I'd tried hard to go "deep," as Mrs. Goldstein had urged.

Life Lessons Learned on the Street

Five years as a war orphan in Berlin, beginning when I was eight, was not the childhood I'd wish on anyone, not even the daughter of the Nazi who marched my mother to her death. Objectively, I was a bad kid. A liar, a thief, a prostitute. Objectively, I was also a great kid. I survived. The same is true for troubled teens. Living on the street, or what was left of it after the same people who later saved me bombed it, taught me three lessons I can use as a social worker. Rely on yourself. Do what's necessary and don't judge your behavior harshly. Circumstances imposed by others drove you to do what you did. At the same time, take responsibility. Blaming others is as pointless as knitting with nails. Know who to turn to for help. The people with the least are most likely to share what they have. Trust those who have been where you are, myself being an obvious example. It took me decades to accept that some people cared about my welfare. If I'd recognized that earlier, my life might have been easier. I want to help teens get there sooner. Step outside yourself. Find something—an activity, a cause, a person—that takes you beyond self-absorption and gives you a reason to live. For me, it was making art and ensuring the survival of a friend who was like a sister. My clients will have to find their own motivation, but I can help them explore. I've learned that while not everything is possible, the improbable can come true.

Life Lessons Learned in Prison

In most ways, my year in prison was easier than my five during the war. I had food and shelter. I was there for a fixed amount of time and knew I'd emerge alive. Yet in other ways, it was harder. Being locked up was my own fault. I'd made dumb choices with predictable consequences. I had to face authority, not hide from it. Once I accepted that I was there, however, I went from making the best of it to making something good come out of it. Here is what I learned.

Keep your head down. Calling attention to yourself leads to the guillotine. Troubled teens act out in ways that put them in worse trouble. Some, girls more than boys, disappear and are overlooked. Learn when, where, and how it's okay to speak up for yourself. A social worker can help you figure that out. Embrace routine. Teens complain routine is boring, but when life is chaotic, order brings comfort and reassurance. Start by repeating one simple action each day—wash your face in the morning, say a prayer of thanks for a cigarette—then gradually add others. No matter how crazy their lives, teens can create structure and stability. Believe in the power to change. Don't look for a big break or a miracle. Take it one step at a time; give yourself credit for each move forward. You won't be a snail forever. You'll pick up speed. And then you'll be on your way.

I got an "A" on both papers. My GPA was 3.5. I filled out the three-part social work application. The first, labeled "résumé," asked for high school attended, year of graduation, and work history. I listed Jim's, the Transit Authority, and Goulash Gardens. Part two was the essay, "a personal statement about why you want to pursue a BSW, what makes you a suitable student, and why you want to enroll in the Care Coordination or Child Welfare track." The former was bureaucratic; the latter was where I could offer the most. Writing the essay was easy, using the words from my papers. I suspected Mrs. Goldstein had that in mind when she assigned them.

The final part of the application was the Field Work Experience Verification Letter from my volunteer work at a foster care agency. My supervisor let me read it before she submitted it. "Miss Asher showed an impressive capacity to empathize with our clients. She listened to their problems, acknowledged strengths, encouraged hope, and helped them obtain services that would improve their lives. I believe her abilities are rooted in her personal experiences. I trust she will apply that understanding during her studies and throughout her subsequent social work career."

Only two weeks after submitting the application and two weeks before the admissions committee was to make decisions, Mrs. Goldstein called me to her office. My heart sank. Maybe my prison record had disqualified me. Or the committee decided I should take those thirty credits after all. But she hugged me as soon as I walked in. "Congratulations. You've been accepted."

"Are you sure?" I asked. "It seems awfully quick."

"I expedited your application."

"Are you sure?" I repeated. "I haven't gotten the letter yet."

She held up her pen. "I'm signing it now. We're not supposed to say anything until five days after all the letters are posted. Promise you won't tell?"

I whooped. I danced. I promised. "I won't disappoint you," I said.

"You won't disappoint yourself," said Mrs. Goldstein.

That night, I told Mrs. Haydu and swore her to secrecy too. After we closed, the Haydus surprised me with a Dobos torte that Mr. Haydu had somehow found time to bake and a bottle of Hungarian Sopron champagne. Mrs. Haydu poured three glasses. "Today a waitress. Tomorrow a social worker." We ate the entire cake and drank the whole bottle. Heading home, my brain at once fuzzy and clear, I thought about the words I'd written for school: Turn to others for help, rely on yourself, and believe in your own power to change. I was my own best social worker.

***

Frima was excited for me too. We resumed biweekly calls, and I invited her to Goulash Gardens to celebrate. Mrs. Haydu, hearing Frima was a lifelong friend, brought us a feast that would have outdone the take-out meal I'd served her four years ago, except that the first time for something good is the best. Like the first for anything bad is the worst. Frima asked about my classes.

"I love them all, except one about the laws and policies that govern practice. By the time I graduate, a third of them will have changed. Learning the rules is as pointless as shuffling paper towels."

"Even if the laws have changed for the better, you're primed to disobey them."

"Are you suggesting I'm not good at obeying laws?"

"Not suggesting. Stating the obvious." Frima grinned, a mouthful of red and white food dribbling onto her chin. I laughed. We were as giddy as that night in Berlin when we'd found three loaves of barely burned bread in the baker's trash bin. "Is there a class you like best?"

"Social environments, the conditions that make kids get into trouble. The prof speaks from experience. He had a tough childhood: absent father, abusive mom who abandoned him for alcohol and drugs. I can put myself in his shoes, same as the kids he's teaching us how to help."

Frima put down her spoon. "Whoa. It's not the same. In your situation, your mother was forced to abandon you. In his case, and the ones you'll be handling, it was their choice."

"Not totally, or even mostly. His mom and the families I want to help are victims as much as ours were. I've come to see our childhoods differently. I thought we survived because we were cunning. Now I see we were also resourceful. We overcame forces seemingly beyond our control. What I hope to do is convince troubled teens that it's within their power to overcome them too."

We dug into dessert. Frima asked about my latest sculptures. I said I didn't have much time for art these days but intended to get back to it after graduation. "Right now, school is what keeps me going." Stuffed, I shoved away from the table. "I owe you an apology."

"Whatever for?"

"When we came to this country, I scorned your positive attitude. Only now can I fully appreciate how you took life into your own hands. Will you accept my belated admiration?"

Frima pushed the remains of dessert around on her plate. "Sometimes I think I've lost that ability. Lisa makes me feel powerless and hopeless."

I'd been learning how to help parents with rebellious teens. "Look at Lisa's behavior from her perspective. Get unstuck from your own position. If you react differently, she will too."

Frima hoisted her glass of ice water. I flinched, expecting her to throw it in my face. She lowered her arm but said between clenched teeth. "You're not my social worker, Liane. You're not anybody's social worker yet. And you're not a mother either!"

Dinner backed up and burned my throat. "Get the fuck out of here," I snarled.

Frima stood. "You don't have to order me. I'm leaving under my own power."

Mrs. Haydu watched her go, then raised her eyebrows at me. I shook my head. I didn't want to talk to her. But later that night, hurt and confused, I propped Ittel Rosa at the head of my bed. "Frima was wrong about my not being a mother. But was she right to get angry?"

My bear adopted a professorial tone. "Theory. First lesson: What angers people?"

"Feeling they've been wronged."

"Good answer. Frima has plenty to be aggrieved about."

"Yes, but there's more going on. She doesn't usually get that mad. That's my MO."

Ittel Rosa leaned against the headboard. "What else makes people angry?"

"Guilt!" Ittel Rosa nodded for me to go on. "Frima's angry because she never learned to be a mother. The aggrieved Frima deflects blame and cries, 'It's not my fault.' The guilty Frima blames herself. My parenting advice confirmed her guilt and wham, she blew up at me."

Professor Bear nodded. "Very good, Miss Asher. You've earned an 'A.' But continue. Why did you get so angry back?"

"My own guilt?"

"Explain, please," said Ittel Rosa.

I smiled. "Second lesson: Don't give unsolicited advice. I blame myself for blowing it."

"Excellent. I'll raise your grade to 'A+.'"

Class dismissed. I didn't want to be Frima's social worker. I just wanted to be her friend.

***

My final year of school, I did an intensive internship at a non-profit agency serving abused and neglected children. I'd learned not to judge their mothers; I'd come to forgive mine. Graduation was on a Sunday, August ninth. Hurricane Belle was approaching and my classmates prayed the storm would hold off until after the ceremony. If I'd been religious, I would have prayed for a reconciliation between me and Frima. I invited Mr. and Mrs. Haydu, who couldn't leave Goulash Gardens but sent me flowers and a card like proud parents. Anoush and Mendel did come and took me to lunch at an Armenian restaurant. They, along with the Haydus, were my family now.

The hurricane held off until after midnight, dumping nearly four inches of rain on the city. Meanwhile, I held back my own tears as I snuggled with Ittel Rosa, listening to the wind batter the trees. "Frima is my closest relative. She'd have been there if our friendship weren't battered." I told my beat-up bear that I felt powerless to mend it, like a sculpture crushed beyond repair.

"It's not consigned to the junkyard yet," she reassured me. "Give it time."

"How long?" I asked.

Ittel Rosa sheltered from the storm inside my arms. "You'll know when the time is right."

CHAPTER 36

I was nervous but confident about my job interview as a Child Protective Specialist with the city. The recommendation from my social environments professor said I was the least judgmental student he'd ever taught. I was hired on the spot. It also helped that the department was short-staffed. Hunter had prepared me well for my responsibilities: investigate allegations of abuse and neglect, assess child and family strengths and needs, connect them with other services, place children in imminent danger in foster care, and reunite families when possible. As part of those duties, I filed petitions and testified in family court. I kept records of everything.

I was on call twenty-four hours a day, but most of my evenings and weekends were free. Coworkers invited me to join them for drinks, movies, and ball games but stopped after the fourth time I turned them down. I was eager to get back to making art. Although I'd surprised myself by expressing what I'd learned in words, my feelings emerged best in my sculptures. The new works were gnarlier than before. More parts, more twists, figures that either hid or burst out of unexpected places. I began to think of my creations as small social environments.

Cases were rotated annually. At the beginning of my second year, I was assigned Susan Rebenstock Adler, a thirteen-year-old runaway and truant with bulimia. She was the only child of a single mother, the father having disappeared when she was two. Neglect was suspected. I arranged foster care with the goal of helping Susan return home. Then I delved into the file.

Father's name: Michael Adler
Father's history: Unknown; no contact information
Mother's maiden name: Berta Rebenstock
Mother's history: Age 32; war orphan; brought to U.S. at age three; last name unknown; adopted by Arnold and Mitzi Rebenstock; intermittent low-wage jobs; food stamps; briefly hospitalized for depression

Susan's mother was the girl from Oyf Haskhole, the first orphan adopted. Miss Stone had been thrilled. Things hadn't turned out so great for Berta after all. And Susan was paying the price.

Our first interview didn't turn out so great either, but I'd been trained to expect that. Susan sprawled on the armchair in my office and stared at the ceiling. She wore torn jeans and a t-shirt that said "Charles Manson for President." Like many bulimics, she was pudgy but not seriously overweight. I started with open-ended questions. "Why do you think you're here?" "What's going on?" Susan blew her greasy bangs off her forehead. I switched to closed-ended questions: "Are you feeling upset?" "Do you think it's hard for your mother to deal with your running away?" More silence, although Susan did give me a "you've got to be kidding" look. I brought her a coke from the vending machine—my dime—which she guzzled down. Then she closed her eyes. I thought she might be genuinely tired. Sleeping on the street isn't very restful.

She dozed off, then awoke disoriented and unguarded. I saw my opportunity. "I won't force you to talk with me, but these meetings are required. So, two suggestions. First, let's meet someplace other than my office. You say where. Second, I'll bring a cassette player. You bring your favorite tape. We can just listen to the music. Deal?" Susan nodded, scribbled the location of a McDonald's far from her home and school where she wouldn't be recognized, and bolted.

I wasn't sure if she'd show up the following week, but she was waiting at a table in the back. Susan shook her head when I offered to buy her something; bulimics were self-conscious about eating in public. She pulled Eric Clapton's *Slowhand* out of her backpack and I slipped it into the cassette player. "*If you want to hang out, you've gotta take her out, cocaine. If you want to get down, get down on the ground, cocaine. She don't lie, she don't lie, she don't lie, cocaine,*" Clapton sang.

"Cocaine is one of my two favorite songs," Susan said.

It was the first time she'd spoken to me. I stopped the tape. "Why?" I asked.

"I like how he repeats 'She don't lie.' Because my mother did." Susan told me to fast forward to "Lay Down Sally," her other favorite. "*Lay down, Sally, and rest you in my arms. Don't you think you want someone to talk to?*" Without prompting, she said, "The song's about a boy and girl, but all I want is someone who'll ask if I want to talk to them. Mostly my mother."

"I hope someday she will," I told her, "but I'm asking you now."

Susan drew imaginary circles on the tabletop. "Yeah, I guess you are."

I rewound the tape and handed it to her. "I'm listening. Talk."

Instead, Susan returned the cassette to her backpack and pulled out a tattered notebook on whose cover she'd written in neat purple ink, "My Journal." She flipped to a page in the middle and read. "*My mother hides her darkness under a bright, shiny exterior, like the surface of a lake that hides its secrets by reflecting the clear blue sky above, while meanwhile storm clouds build and strike when you least expect it. I'm out in the open with no place to run for shelter, except for food. But my shelter is temporary, and not very safe.*"

"You write beautifully," I told her. I meant it.

Susan's usually defiant expression turned shy. "You really think so?"

"Yes," I answered. "Keep writing. I'll buy you another notebook. And a new purple pen."

I thought of my theory teacher saying, "They're not bad kids. They act tough, but for all their grown-up swagger, they're children in search of love and respect." Susan's file had cited multiple problems. I asked, "What bothers you most about yourself? What do *you* want to fix?"

Without hesitation, she answered, "Eating and vomiting. And hating myself afterward."

"We'll start there," I told her. She agreed to keep a log of her feelings each time she binged and purged, and I said I'd make her a dental appointment since constant throwing up often damaged tooth enamel. "Let's make sure your smile is beautiful when you're ready to use it."

Susan slowly opened up. As we reviewed her bulimic episodes, I explained that eating was a way to gain control when she felt she had none while paradoxically making her feel out of control. To show she could take things into her own hands, we set short-term goals: Not binging for one day, two days, five days, a week. Her bulimia didn't disappear, but the incidents were less frequent. Susan held her head higher and her smile was beautiful indeed.

***

Once I'd connected with Susan, I scheduled a home visit with Berta. She had few memories of her short time at Oyf Haskhole, but our shared history made her more willing to talk to me than other parents whose custody of their children was at stake. The dingy two-bedroom apartment was in a grimy pre-war building, but the way Berta picked barely noticeable bits of lint off the carpet and upholstery suggested she'd made an effort to clean up before I came.

"I want Susan to come home," she said. "Please. Tell me what I have to do."

"First is what I have to do." I explained how I was treating Susan's eating disorder and added, "Food can be a problem for people who were deprived as children. Like we were. Without meaning to, we pass on that anxiety to our own kids. Susan is angry at you for not taking better care of her. Food is a way to get back at you."

Berta cracked her knuckles. "My daughter knows how to push my buttons."

I smiled. "Kids are good at that, especially daughters with their moms." Berta asked if I had a daughter. "Mmm," I said, my way of deflecting personal questions whose answers might raise doubts about my credibility. "But you can help Susan get better by not pushing back."

Berta sat forward and folded her hands in her lap. "How?"

I told Berta that the important thing was for Susan to feel she had control over her life. "Not that she's free to skip school or run away from her foster home, but she does have the right to decide what goes into her body. Don't make a big deal of how much or how little she eats."

Berta's sigh shook her frail body. I wondered when she'd last eaten a full meal.

"Giving up control isn't easy for any parent," I said softly. "But when you consider the control our parents had to give up—raising us—the challenge won't seem so insurmountable."

Berta leaned back and closed her eyes, reminding me of my first interview with Susan. Her mother wasn't sleeping well either. When she opened her eyes, I told Berta she also needed to take care of herself. I gave her a list of food and housing programs and recommended a counselor whose fees our agency covered. "It's never too late to lessen the effects of childhood trauma."

"Did therapy help you?"

Tempted to again say "Mmm," I answered honestly. "I never got counseling, but making art has always been my therapy. You need someone, or something, on your side. The only times in my life when I gave up were when art failed me. Going back to making art was my salvation."

Berta shook her head. "I don't have anything like that."

"Yes, you do," I said. "Your daughter. Getting Susan back and taking better care of her will save you. It will also save her."

***

Four months into working with Susan and Berta individually, it was time to see them together. I suggested we meet in my office, which was neutral territory, but they both wanted to meet at the apartment. It was the first time Susan had been back home. Still, they sat far apart, mother on the couch, daughter opposite in an armchair. I pulled up a straight chair in the middle. I knew better than to fuck up like I had with Frima. No lectures. These two had to listen to each other, not me.

I asked them to talk about the problem as they each saw it. Berta said she was angry when the school called to say that if Susan skipped one more day, she'd be suspended. At the end of her rope, she'd threatened to kick Susan out. Susan said she was ashamed to go to class wearing filthy clothes with ratty hair, where the other kids held their noses and called her Slutty Sue.

Berta studied her daughter's outfit, bought by her foster mom. "I can't remember the last time I washed your clothes. Or bought food or cleaned house. When you still lived here, that is."

"I do. It was three months before I left. I ran away before you kicked me out. I figured you wouldn't care." Susan wiped her eyes on the sleeve of her new jacket.

"I did care, but ..." After a few seconds, Berta regained her voice. "Miss Asher is helping me get back on my feet now. I want you to move back."

Susan regarded her mother warily. Berta looked at me. "Not yet," I told them. "But if you both continue to make progress for the next two months, I'll recommend terminating foster care. In the meantime, I'll authorize supervised visits."

"Supervised by you?" they asked simultaneously. I answered, "Yes."

Susan moved to the couch and sat beside Berta. Mother and daughter didn't take their eyes off each other until the hour was up and it was time for me to take Susan back to her foster home. She wrote something in her journal, tore out the page, folded it, and handed it to Berta.

I imagined that it contained three words.

**

Ittel Rosa had said I'd know when the time was right to call Frima. It was now. I told her about meeting Susan and making the connection with Berta. I worried about violating confidentiality, but my coworkers discussed cases with their families, and Frima was my sister. Again.

"I'm sorry I gave you advice about Lisa," I said. "I was out of line."

"I'm sorry I made that crack about your not being a mother. That was worse."

We forgave each other, another knot in our relationship untied or retied depending on how we chose to look at it. Frima wanted to know more about Berta and Susan. I told her what Susan had written in her journal about clouds.

"I assume the storm is inside me, yet I can't help blaming my daughter. She's so damned rigid. And righteous." Frima was on the verge of tears. "Maybe you should treat Lisa and me."

"We're too close and you're too rich to qualify for public services. But consider private counseling. Some problems are too complicated to handle alone."

Frima laughed. "You sound like me thirty years ago. We've switched roles."

"No, I've just caught up with you."

"You're still moving forward."

"I can't keep going without you beside me," I said.

"You draw strength saving me." Frima laughed ruefully. "Don't worry, you're not done yet."

CHAPTER 37

A year later, Berta and Susan were rotated off my caseload. Susan was back home, repeating eighth grade, and Berta still struggled with depression, but the prognosis for both of them was good. I was reviewing records for a new case when I came across the name of Miss Stone, who had treated the teenager's young mother and grandmother fifteen years ago. She'd since retired, but the agency gave me her phone number and she invited me to visit.

I wasn't prepared for the tiny, gray-haired woman who greeted me in a small apartment furnished with comfortable love seats and embroidered throw pillows. In my mind, she loomed large. But as soon as she greeted me, I recognized the business-like but warm tone from over thirty years ago. She served tea with lump sugar and milk.

"Still pushing milk?" I said.

Miss Stone laughed. "It was good for the children's bones. Good for an old lady's too."

"You took good care of us at Oyf Haskhole. What happened after you moved into the bigger space?"

"I was there six years. All told, we brought two hundred children here, placed about half of them for adoption, and two-thirds of those worked out. Not as successful as I'd hoped, but considering what would have happened to them in Eastern Europe after the Communists took over, they were still better off here, even in group homes." Her voice was questioning.

I reassured her the group home was fine. "We had a roof over our heads, food to eat, and a free education." I asked how she ended up working at the agency where I was now.

"I continued with the refugee agency as an administrator, but I missed working with children, so I joined the Bureau of Child Welfare, which is what your agency was originally called. Now that I'm retired, I do needlework when my arthritis permits. My eyes are still good, so I read. My niece drives down from Connecticut once a month to take me to lunch. It's a quiet life. I worried I'd be lonely, but it's a relief to no longer have to solve other people's problems."

"Now I'm solving them. But first I had to solve my own." I didn't mention my daughter, but I did tell Miss Stone about going to prison. She frowned but didn't say anything. I smiled. "Don't worry. I won't be offended if you say, 'I could have told you you'd come to no good.'"

She chuckled then. "Anyone could have told you that."

"Except Anoush. He never stopped believing in me. Just like he had faith in Mendel."

"Yes. That success story surprised me. Just like yours, Liane." Miss Stone squeezed my hand. "I'm happy for you. What about Frima? You two were so close. Are you still in touch?"

"Like sisters," I said, glad I could say that truthfully now that we'd made up again. "She graduated from Barnard, taught briefly, married a lawyer, and now has two children of her own."

"The couple who adopted her were lovely. Especially the mother. She would have been a good model for Frima."

I hadn't intended to say anything, but when I coughed, Miss Stone raised her eyebrows. Call it social worker instinct, but she knew I hadn't simply swallowed the wrong way. "I'm afraid mothering doesn't come easily to Frima," I admitted, "especially with her daughter."

Miss Stone sighed. "It's not uncommon. Survivors carry their trauma forever, often passing it along to the next generation. I wish I knew how the rest of you turned out."

"Not always the way you'd predict." I said Reuven was a wife batterer; Salomon a cop. Berta, like Frima, struggled with being a mother, only more so. We counted. Of the two she had high hopes for, Berta had failed and Frima was only a qualified success. Of the four predicted failures, only Reuven was a total loss, while Mendel, Salomon, and I had come out ahead.

Miss Stone traced the butterfly she'd embroidered on a throw pillow. "The prognosis in cases of domestic violence is grim. I doubt Reuven will flip to the success column. But I'm still hopeful that Frima will improve. She has a lot going for her, including her friendship with you."

***

Reassuring Miss Stone about my time in the group home made me wonder what had happened to Betty. I found a number in the telephone book. The woman who answered gave me another number, which led to a third, then a fourth, where I eventually reached her. Betty declined my offer to meet for coffee, saying she wasn't at her best right now. She'd recently moved into a shelter after being homeless, followed by rehab. "Maybe this time I'll get my life back on track."

I gave her my number. "Promise you'll call me when you do."

"*If* I do. Sometimes I think trying is as pointless as playing tiddly-winks with diamonds."

"Diamonds are valuable," I told Betty, "even if you're only squidging winks into a pot."

After I hung up, I got to thinking about when The Warden had come down harder on me than Betty because "You're too smart to end up like me." I couldn't tell Mrs. Zetticci I'd turned out okay—her great nephew had called a few years ago to tell me she died—but I wouldn't wait until it was too late to tell the other person, besides Anoush, who'd pushed me to succeed.

I flashed my Child Protective Services badge at Evander's security guard. Assuming I was there regarding a student's case, he let me in. I found Mr. Archer's name on the staff bulletin board and ran up to the art room, where he pointed a dripping paintbrush at me, grinned, and introduced me to his students as a former "star of the studio." After telling them to practice scumbling on their own, he led me to his office. It felt natural to hug each other, like old friends.

"I'm glad you're still teaching. I was afraid you'd retired."

"Five years to go before I leave school and go back to being a starving artist, albeit with a modest pension."

"Five years ago, I went back to school."

"In art?" Mr. Archer asked with the same excitement Frima had.

"No, in social work. But I still make art and the magazine cover you gave me still hangs above my workbench." I showed him two recent small, intricate sculptures, and we talked about how the soldering iron added complexity to my structures. He asked if I was selling my work.

"I did for a while at summer street fairs, but with a full-time job, that's no longer an option. And without connections, it's impossible to get into a gallery."

Mr. Archer studied my pieces again. "You know, Liane, in the decades since the war, art has shifted from Realism to Abstraction and Minimalism. Sculpture's been reduced to its most essential and fundamental features. Your style fits the art scene now better than it ever did."

"What good does that do me? I'm still a nobody, an outsider."

My old teacher grinned. "A retired college classmate opened a gallery in Soho. You never let me write a letter of recommendation for you to go to art school. If I make a phone call, will you go to see him?"

I accepted immediately.

Mr. Archer laughed. "In the old days, you would have refused. On principle. Have your principles changed?"

"In my teens, they were in draft form. With research and experience, I've revised them."

***

Jack Baldwin handed me an espresso as soon as I entered Explosion Gallery on Greene Street. "Tom recommends you highly," he said.

"I appreciate Mr. Archer calling you and your agreeing to see me, Mr. Baldwin."

"First names, please. Let's see what you got." He eyed the small satchel I'd brought.

I arranged half a dozen pieces on a large pedestal, where they looked dwarfed, but there was no other empty surface in the gallery. "I've always done small abstract work, using found natural materials," I told Jack. "Even now when I can afford to purchase more expensive supplies and make bigger work, I gravitate toward intimate pieces you can hold in your hand."

"Continuity in an artist is held in high esteem. By some. Others value constant change."

"Mr. Archer, I mean Tom, said the art world had changed and caught up with me."

"Actually, it's moved past you. Are you familiar with Claes Oldenburg and George Segal?" Jack lit a Gauloise and aimed it at the works in his gallery. "No one that famous here, of course, but you see their influence. Now tell me, Liane. Can *you* see your work fitting in here?"

I looked at the large, figurative sculptures made of plaster and plastic. At Jack, smoking a skinny French cigarette the world had also moved past. "No, I can't. Not because it's out of style. Critics didn't catch up with Louise Nevelson until ten years ago. Her work was too feminine for them." I looked at the exhibit tags. All the artists were men. "You can take your fake phalluses and shove them." I scooped up my sculptures, centered my espresso cup on the pedestal, and left.

Despite my bravado, I was ready to call it quits. I used to see making art as an end in itself, but now that I worked in a field where results mattered, where lives were at stake, I felt differently. I called Frima, the person who'd had faith in me the longest. "Pep talk, please."

"You make art to survive, not to make money," she reminded me.

She was right. Art was my salvation. "If I were religious, I'd thank God for the gift that keeps me alive." I paused. "What keeps you alive?"

Frima was quiet for so long that I was afraid mentioning religion had touched too raw a nerve. Finally, she murmured, "I don't know."

"How about this?" I asked. "You stay alive so you can keep on saving me."

PART TEN:
FRIMA (1985–1988)

CHAPTER 38

"What's this?" Bob held up an envelope from the New York State Teacher Certification Board.

"I've made a decision," Frima answered, echoing the words she'd said ten years ago.

Bob tossed the envelope back on the side table. "Here we go again."

"This time is different. Before, I accepted your refusal to allow me to teach again. Now, I'm going to do it."

"Why? Nothing has changed." Bob sorted through the rest of the mail.

"On the contrary. Our children are no longer at home." David was a senior at Stanford, majoring in engineering. Lisa, a sophomore at Barnard, was studying political science. Still daddy's girl, she barely acknowledged Frima when she visited their apartment. Yet, with mediocre grades and SAT scores, she'd shown no qualms about using her status as a "legacy student" of her mother's to get into Barnard.

"What about me?" Bob plopped on the couch and pouted.

"Teaching will still leave time for me to take care of you. Besides, you're a big boy. You can pop a dinner in the microwave."

"My mother never cooked a frozen or canned meal in her life."

"I'm not your mother." Frima carried the letter into the bedroom and called Joan.

"Bravo," said Joan. "It's about time you became a liberated woman. When do you start?"

"It's not that easy. Teachers have to complete a hundred and seventy-five hours of professional development every five years for their certification to remain valid. For a lapsed certification like mine to get revalidated, I have to pay a fee and complete all those hours."

"You haven't taught in twenty years, since you were pregnant with David. That's seven hundred hours!"

"Actually, only three hundred and fifty. They knock off five years each for raising my two children."

"It's still a lot."

"Yeah. But if I go full-time in the spring and summer semesters, I can start teaching in the fall. Several schools offer the required courses. I'm enrolling at Hunter College, your alma mater."

"Good choice," said Joan. "Take it from me, their teacher education is the best. If I ever decide to revalidate my certification, I'd go back there. I'm sure you'll ace the courses."

But for the first time, studying didn't come easily to Frima. The way literacy and math were taught had changed in the past two decades, and her mind couldn't connect the "why" to the "how." She called Liane, who'd also gone to Hunter. "You figured out the link between theory and practice in social work. Can you help my brain do the same in early elementary education?"

"I'd love to," said Liane. "But we've got two case workers on maternity leave and half a dozen pregnant teens freaking out. I haven't had time to solder a piece of metal in two months."

Frima couldn't admit her failure to Joan. One night, in desperation, she called David in California. It was three hours earlier there, and her son had just gotten back from the library.

"How on earth can I help you Mom? I'm an engineer."

"Isn't that what engineers do? Apply theory or basic science to practical problems?"

"Yeah," David conceded. "Give it a try. My brain is fried from studying circuits all night, but talking about how to teach little kids could be interesting."

Frima summarized her dilemma. Theorists were split between "open education," which gave children freedom to explore on their own, and "back to basics," which was more structured. The open approach appealed to her philosophically, but it could be a disaster for the poor and minority kids she'd be teaching. "They don't learn the basics at home. Their test scores are in the basement. Yet I don't want to stifle them. So what am I supposed to do in the classroom?"

David asked what Frima had done twenty years ago. She described how she'd combined methods, encouraging children to make connections between the information she imparted and their own lives. "There you go," he said. "Theory is a tool. One size won't fit every situation. Use what works, find better alternatives, or invent your own. That's what engineers do."

It sounded to Frima like a principle for survival. She recalled how Miss Stone had helped them learn English at Oyf Haskhole: structured vocabulary lessons in the apartment plus talking with shopkeepers and neighbors on the street to pick up syntax. Frima could adapt that technique with students for whom English was a second language, pairing them with native speakers.

"High five, Mom. You've engineered a testable plan."

It was getting late, even on the West Coast. Frima thanked her son for his help.

"All I did was let you talk. You connected the dots yourself," he replied.

But to Frima, their call had accomplished more. They'd spoken as equals, two students learning their craft. She was more comfortable in that role than she'd ever been as his mother.

"By the way, Mom. I've decided to apply to grad school for a master's degree, even a doctorate. You should consider getting a master's too, once you're back in the classroom."

"First I have to find my footing there." Frima didn't want to go further but was bolstered that her son thought her capable of juggling several roles. If only her husband did too.

***

"How's it going?" Liane asked a month later. "Sorry I didn't call sooner. I've been putting out fires. It's like being on Berlin's bomb response squad, except I'm on the side of the good guys."

Frima told her not to worry. "I turned to someone else for help."

"Joan?" Liane's jealousy hadn't abated in thirty years. Nor had Joan's toward Liane.

"My son." Frima hesitated. "I feel bad telling you. You can't call on your daughter."

"Neither can you," Liane snapped.

"Touché," said Frima. Again she hesitated. "Do you ever think about her?

"Yeah." Liane's tone was abrupt. "So you depended on a family member other than me?"

Frima treaded with caution. "How do you feel about that?"

"You sound like a social worker." Liane laughed. "Seriously, I feel mixed."

"Ditto," Frima admitted. "David said I should get a master's degree. Why don't you get one too? We can study together."

"An interesting idea. We're both proving it's never too late to learn."

"Do you think it's too late to unlearn?" Frima asked.

Liane took a long time to answer. "Yes," she finally said. "You can learn new lessons but you can't erase the old ones. The brain is a permanent chalkboard whose dust never fully settles."

CHAPTER 39

Frima loved being back in her old classroom at P.S. 94. She imagined it was how adults felt returning for a visit to their childhood homes. The old wooden desks were gone, but the Formica-topped tables that had replaced them were already beat up, as were the outdated second-grade texts. Other than their clothes and haircuts, however, the students looked much the same: Puerto Rican immigrants, with a growing number of Dominicans, Spanish being their first language. Frima was glad she'd included Spanish among her PD courses. As for the vociferous debate over whether the kids should be taught exclusively in English or bilingually, she opted for the latter. It was criminal to deprive them of their heritage. Maybe someday she'd relearn German.

A few children could count by rote; the rest not at all. A couple couldn't even differentiate between numbers and letters. Frima began the school year doing math lessons at the kindergarten level. "Today we're going to sort these blocks into two piles by color, rojo y azul, red and blue." She had the children work in teams, pairing counters with non-counters. "Who wants to tell us how many red blocks you have? Luis, your hand is up."

"One, two." Luis bit his lip. "One, two," he began again.

"Abnar, can you help him?"

"Sí, Mrs. Horner." Abnar, who came from a big family, counted to six.

It took a month for the whole class to count consistently to ten. Most important, their counting wasn't rote. They matched numbers one-to-one with objects. Frima let them count on their fingers when the principal, a back-to-basics woman, wasn't prowling the hallway and poking her head in the door. At the next standardized testing, the children's scores had risen to first-grade level. The principal was thrilled. "See," she said, "drill works." Frima merely smiled. She learned, at her students' age, that subterfuge had its time and place in the game of survival.

The class's literacy skills were worse. Second graders were expected to write multiple-paragraph compositions; some of hers were still learning letters and simple words. Her professor had said, "Children talk and write when they have something to say." She ditched the worksheets and asked her students to create their own picture books and read them aloud.

"*The Rat* by Mia Morales. Once upon a time, a rat big had very hungry. When los niños fall asleep, he ate the hot dogs. Then Mama came home and whacked him dead with a broom."

"The mother in your story was brave. She took good care of her children," said Frima.

"Sí. Y fuerte," added Mia.

"Yes. And strong too." Frima said Mia's story was good because it told who it was about, what happened, and had a happy ending. "You also used 'time' words like 'when' and 'then.'"

"'When' and 'then' rhyme," piped up Diego.

"Very good, Diego. What's another word for 'big' that rhymes with 'rat'?"

"Fat!" the class sang out.

Frima asked Mia to show everyone her pictures. Later, she'd explain that in English the word order was "big rat" and correct the verb "had" to "was." Frima knew from her own experience that Mia and her classmates would pick up grammar and syntax simply by speaking, reading, and writing more. Criticism took a back seat to encouraging their self-expression and confidence.

As the students' confidence grew, so did Frima's. David said "Way to go, Mom" when she called to tell him. She didn't expect Lisa to be interested, but it hurt that she couldn't share her work with her husband. The few times Frima had read Bob her students' compositions or mentioned their rising test scores, he'd responded, "Uh, huh. When will dinner be ready?"

***

"Frima! When did you come back to P.S. 94?" Marty Fleischer, the older divorced teacher Frima had dated two decades ago, appeared in the teacher's lounge one day to take Camila Ramos, the school's Parent Liaison, to lunch. He told Frima he and Camila had been seeing each other for ten years. "When you and I were together," he added, "Camila's position didn't even exist."

"A lot's changed, except the needs of students and families. I'm surprised to see you here. I thought you'd be retired by now."

"One more year to go. But I've been at another school the last five. Once a month I come by to have lunch at the Korean deli around the corner with Camila."

"I didn't know Koreans lived in this neighborhood. I don't have any in my class."

"They don't. They live in Bedford Park. But they own stores here. Like Hibiscus Garden, the Puerto Rican restaurant. Camila's convinced me life offers more than pastrami on rye."

"I've seen her with parents. She can be very persuasive." Frima admired her gentle force.

"Camila and I are a good team. Both divorced, kids all grown. No desire to get married or even share an apartment. Just comfortable growing old together."

"I'm happy for you. When I last saw your kids they were, what, eleven and seven?"

"Now Rachel's a teacher too, Isaac is in advertising, and they're parents themselves." Marty showed Frima photos of his grandchildren.

"Looks like they turned out fine."

"It wasn't a straight path." Marty described Rachel's struggle with depression and Isaac's with drugs. "But in the end, they both made me proud and happy for them. What about you?"

Frima told Marty about Bob, his work as a tax lawyer, and raising their children before returning to teaching. She was as open with Marty as he'd been with her when she described David's brush with law. She told him about Lisa going to Barnard, although she withheld the fact that their relationship was strained. "After Germany, I never expected to be a parent. Or to teach other children who have it rough. I'm one of the lucky ones." Saying this, Frima actually felt it.

"Today's kids have it rougher than the ones we taught two decades ago. I almost regret retiring." Marty grinned. "But not enough to change my mind. I'm ready for a new adventure."

Marty and Frima hugged goodbye. He invited her to join him and Camila for lunch next time. "Order tostones. Puerto Rican French fries, but with unripe plantains instead of potatoes."

"Deal," promised Frima. "I'll be adventurous too."

***

"Marty was so at ease with himself, he was easy to talk to." Frima, done reading her students' stories, snuggled in bed that night with Sugar. Bob was working late again.

The doll pouted. "What about me? Aren't I easy to talk to?"

"Of course you are. But Marty's the only friend I have who can look back on tough times with maturity. Seeing Marty, I know I made the right decision to let him go, marry Bob, and give Otto and Greta grandchildren."

"No regrets?"

Frima thought for a minute. "If I'd stayed with Marty, I wouldn't have had to stop teaching. I might have become a principal. On the other hand, I might have burned out. And I wouldn't have the satisfaction I do now, seeing the kids in my classroom grow. Or my own children."

"That hasn't been an unqualified success. Neither has your marriage."

"True. But, if Marty's kids and David could change course—hell, if Liane could turn her life around when she was almost forty—I can have hope for my husband and daughter."

"That depends on whether you're counting on them or yourself to make the change."

Frima tucked the doll away. Before she closed the nightstand drawer, she told her, "I take back what I said Sugar. You're more mature than I gave you credit for."

***

Frima had an urge to talk to Liane, always her chronological age but now, with a college degree and proper job, her peer in maturity too. She proposed they have lunch someplace other than the Hungarian restaurant. "Thirty years in New York, yet I've never been to the Lower East Side."

Liane tsked. "I've spent plenty of time in the Village, counting art fairs. And prison."

"I'm sure we'll find better places to eat." Frima thought of Marty. "Something more adventurous than bagels and knishes." It turned out to be easy. The area was no longer a Jewish enclave. The East Village was gentrified but the West Village was a hodgepodge of artists and new immigrant groups. They ate pork with chili peppers and lime at a Filipino cart, cooling their mouths afterward with Indian mango lassi. Then they meandered into storefront galleries.

"These are grungier than the gallery owned by my art teacher's friend," said Liane

"Could you show your work down here?" Frima asked casually, not wanting to push.

"Maybe. The sculptures aren't big, synthetic blobs like the ones at Explosion Gallery." Liane studied the labels. "Fuck. Everything's still made by men." She clomped out the door.

Frima followed. "Dessert?" she asked brightly. "To sweeten your sour mood?"

"Yes! Something girly. How about these?" Liane held up Bangladeshi pithas, biscuits each adorned with a unique sculptured design. They shared a half-dozen. Liane bought three more.

"Still hungry?" asked Frima. She'd barely finished her third.

"Not to eat. For inspiration. A series of cookie-size slabs, each topped with its own design of curled and interlaced wires." Liane's fingers were already bending the imaginary strands. They walked towards Tompkins Square Park. Frima asked if Liane was still putting out fires at work.

"It's gotten calmer since the city's finances recovered. We're fully staffed and fewer kids are going hungry. My latest case is typical. A mother kicked her daughter out for piercing her tongue. It *is* kind of disgusting. But what good is a rebellion if it doesn't gross out adults? Of course, piercing isn't the issue. In junior high, kids and parents simply stop talking."

"For my students, the breakdown comes earlier. Parents want their kids to learn English, but when they do, the kids no longer want to speak Spanish with their parents. Progress on one front creates problems on another. But the families we both work with are dealing with poverty."

"Yeah. I link them with other services. Much as I'd like to think of myself as a one-stop savior, these families need more than I can give them on my own."

"Still, when you consider where you and I came from, it's amazing we're helping others."

"If I were a capitalist," said Liane, "I'd say the refugee agency that brought us here got a good return on its investment."

Frima's high spirits suddenly evaporated. "The irony is that we're improving the lives of other families while mine is messed up and you have no family at all."

"Not in the conventional sense, but I have a great proxy family: the Haydus; Anoush and Mendel. Did I tell you Mendel got married? He just had a baby boy. I'm the godmother."

"Congratulations. Another return on investment."

"A boy will have more opportunities. Maybe someday, our daughters will too."

Frima stopped walking. Liane had said "our" daughters. Gingerly, Frima entered the door Liane had opened. "Do you think about your daughter often? Do you know her name?"

"Not her adoptive name. When she was born, I named her Sarah, for my mother, so that's how I think of her now. I try to picture her at twenty-seven."

"What do you see?"

Liane spoke with her hands. "Taller than me but with the same tangled dark hair." Her interlaced fingers were like a profusion of curls. "She's a painter, or a poet, who supports herself doing temp jobs. Sloppy in her personal habits but precise about what she creates. We visit every Sunday to critique our work. I give Sarah wine and cookies. She serves me whiskey and cake."

Frima steered them to a bench. "It sounds as though you and Sarah have a wonderful relationship. If only Lisa and I got along like that. Or things were smoother between me and Bob." She fished in her bag for a tissue. "Your invented family is better than my real one."

"I love them, but honestly, I wish I had a real family too." Liane drew Frima close. "My training focused on parents and kids, but a professor reminded us that relationships with siblings last the longest. Longer than with parents, spouses, or children. I'm glad I'm not an only child."

Frima wove her fingers through Liane's. "Me too."

CHAPTER 40

As if he'd heard her lament, Bob stopped complaining about Frima not taking care of him or the house. He even started cooking simple dinners once a week. "I'm a liberated man," he joked.

Frima was guardedly hopeful, but the fact that he was working more lately could explain why he noticed her absence less. Then Bob really surprised her by complimenting her hair or clothes and buying her flowers for no reason. "I feel like I'm being courted," she told Joan.

"Marriages are revived by a little competition. In your case, the competition is your job, not another man. Bob's making a play for your attention."

"It's working," said Frima. "I'm falling in love with my husband all over again." Otto and Greta had survived early financial setbacks, losing their families, childlessness, yet they'd come through these struggles stronger. Perhaps she and Bob would make it to old age together after all.

Two weeks before spring break, over dinner at a cozy neighborhood restaurant, Frima suggested they get away for a few days. "It will be like a second honeymoon." She slipped off her shoe and slid her foot up his trouser leg.

"I can't take off then. It's the middle of tax season."

"Of course. Selfish of me to forget." Frima pulled her foot away.

Bob fiddled with his wine glass. "But you work so hard the rest of the school year, you deserve to go someplace. By yourself. I'll be so busy,

I'll hardly notice you're gone." He grinned. "Besides, I know how to cook dinner now. Really, sweetheart, I'll be fine on my own."

"I won't." Frima wanted company. She couldn't invite Liane. School holidays were rough on the kids she worked with and mini vacations were hardly her style. "I could ask Joan. She'd love the idea. A girl's night out, only it would be for three days and three nights."

Her husband paled.

Frima teased. "Afraid Joan will fill my head with more women's lib rhetoric?"

Bob laughed. "Joan doesn't scare me. Sure, ask her."

Joan had to work too. Spring was high season for the lighting business; people itched to redecorate. So Frima booked herself a cabin at one of the remaining small resorts in the Catskills. She packed jeans and flannel shirts to hike the gentle trails and escapist novels: Danielle Steel's *A Perfect Stranger* and Stephen King's *Pet Sematary*. Sugar was swaddled inside her bathrobe. Reclining on the bus ride north, she thought how lucky she was to have a husband who trusted his wife to go off alone. Their reunion would be even more passionate than a second honeymoon.

The wood-paneled cabin, nestled in a valley, was spare but clean. Frima walked to the main house, called Bob from the lobby, and went to bed after dinner. Snuggled under the down comforter with Sugar, she slept soundly. After a hearty breakfast of oatmeal and muffins, she called her husband again, this time at his office, to tell him her hiking plans for the day. Bob's secretary said he'd phoned in with a head cold and was working from home. Frima called the apartment. When there was no answer, she figured he'd gone to the drugstore. So she had a second cup of coffee, sent picture postcards to him and the kids, then called again. Still no answer. Concerned, she dialed Joan to ask if she'd check on him during her lunch hour. Joan's office reported that she'd called in sick too. And there was no answer at Joan's house either.

Instead of a two-mile hike, Frima took two steps to the registration desk. The next bus back to the city left in an hour. Frima changed her ticket and canceled the rest of her reservation. Back at the cabin, she lost her breakfast and repacked. Unlike the relaxed ride up, the return trip was an anxious blur. Frima wasn't sure if the knot in her stomach was from worry or suspicion.

Standing in the hallway outside their apartment, Frima heard voices. She unlocked the door, which opened directly into the living room. Bob and Joan lay naked on the couch, a bottle of wine on the coffee table. Frima dropped her suitcase. Joan scrambled for her clothes—silk shirt, linen pants; Frima was still wearing hiking clothes—and bolted. Bob watched her leave. Only when Frima slammed the door behind Joan did he cover himself with his shirt, a birthday gift from Frima. His once-thick chest hair was thinning and turning gray. He waited for Frima to speak.

Her mind was blank, as numb as the first time she had sex. She could never remember where, who with, or even her exact age. Hearing her husband's heavy breathing, she came back to the moment. Joan's words replayed in her mind. "Were you trying to make me jealous?"

Bob blinked. "Are you?" He sounded curious.

"No. Just blind-sided."

His face fell. "I never meant to hurt you," he said.

Frima snorted. Her husband's words were as cliché as the romance novel she'd packed, still unread. "Is the affair retaliation for my going back to work?"

Bob shook his head. "It started before then."

Over twelve years ago, Joan had told Frima she was no longer having an affair with her boss, but with someone else. Had her husband and best friend been betraying her that long? Frima couldn't bear to know. Bob hadn't moved from the couch. "Since you're not sick," she told him, "go to the office. When you come home, go back to the couch and sleep there."

Frima had nothing more to say and nothing more she wished to hear. She carried her suitcase to the bedroom, unpacked Sugar, and crawled under the covers. "I wasn't the most affectionate wife in the world. Was Bob justified turning elsewhere?" she asked the doll.

"He knew what he was getting into when he married you."

"Not really. I held back details that might have made him more understanding. And Bob was right when he said I wasn't a good mother. All the same, he promised Liane at our wedding that he'd be patient and forgiving with me." Frima hissed. "But Joan has no excuse. For all her blather about sisterhood, screwing Bob is the least sisterly thing she could do."

Frima fetched *Sisters* from her dresser and *Knot* from her desk. With them on either side of her and Sugar on her chest, she lay in the darkening room and stared at the shadowed ceiling. Bob returned from work. Frima heard him moving around the kitchen, then settling on the couch for the night. When he left the next morning, Frima was still in bed, awake.

***

Although Frima could have sued for divorce on grounds of adultery, she and Bob agreed it would be less upsetting for their children to file on the basis of not having lived together for a year. She moved out; the Riverdale address mattered more to Bob. Frima found an inexpensive furnished apartment close to her school. She'd look for something nicer in a year.

Telling the kids would be harder than moving. Talking to her son would be easier than her daughter, so she phoned him first, early evening California time. Frima counted the rings. David picked up on the eighth.

"Hi, Mom. I'm studying for finals right now. Can it wait?"

"No. It's important."

"Okay, but keep it short."

"Your father and I are getting a divorce."

David was silent. Was he waiting for her to say more? At last, in a half-joking tone, he asked, "Is Dad having a middle-age crisis?"

"No, it started long ago."

"'It'?"

"Breaking his marriage vows." Frima heard her son gulp. "I'm sorry. I hadn't meant to tell you. It just popped out."

"Don't sweat it. I'm old enough to handle the truth and mature enough not to judge." He paused. "I was planning to come home for a couple of weeks after exams. Where should I stay?"

"Dad's staying in the apartment. I'm renting a small place near work."

"Then I'll split my time."

"That means a lot to me," said Frima. "Take the bedroom. I'll sleep on the couch. You're too big for it."

"You're too old. I'll bring my sleeping bag. One condition, though."

Frima tensed. Would he expect her to do his laundry? Keep kosher during his visit?

"No bad-mouthing Dad," her son said, his tone wary.

"Agreed," Frima didn't ask if he'd make the same demand of Bob. It was enough that he didn't say she'd brought this on herself. The call had taken ten minutes. "I'll let you get back to studying."

"One more thing," David said. Frima held her breath. "I'm sorry about the divorce, Mom. And I love you."

"That's two things, David. Thank you for both."

***

Frima girded herself for the call to Lisa. She remembered when a much-younger Lisa had surprised her with small acts of kindness or been solicitous of Frima's feelings after Greta died. She'd hoped that once she was past adolescence, Lisa would soften and once again show that side of herself. Instead, her daughter's resentment had hardened. Frima had no reason to expect any sympathy from her now. Nevertheless, she craved it. Even a dollop would soothe the pain.

She dialed Lisa's dorm room. Her daughter picked up right away. George Michael's *Faith* played in the background. "Have you spoken to your father yet?" Although Frima had talked to David, instinct told her that Bob had gotten to Lisa first.

"About the divorce? Yeah."

"He told you the reason?" Perhaps Bob had let the truth slip too, and Lisa, with her rigid sense of morality, would take Frima's side. On principle, if not emotion.

"Yeah. He had an affair with Joan."

Her daughter's voice was clipped. Why had Frima wished for the impossible? "Then you know I've moved out. Let me give you my number."

"Don't bother."

Frima gripped the telephone cord. "David will be here in two weeks. Would you feel more comfortable coming over to my apartment when he's here too?"

"No. I don't intend to visit you at all."

Frima willed herself not to cry. Or plead. "This isn't easy for me, making a new start after more than two decades of marriage. I hope you and I can make a new start too. Promise, I won't intrude on your relationship with your father. I just want you to let me be your mother."

"You can't separate the two. I'm long past needing the mother you never were. As for Dad, you drove him away too into the arms of your best friend."

"Joan is not my best friend. She never was and she certainly isn't now."

Lisa's voice was as hard as ever. "Well, if you're looking to make a friend of me, forget it. You made your bed. Lie in it. Alone."

George Michael singing "Please, please, please don't go away" were the last words Frima heard before her daughter hung up.

CHAPTER 41

Bob called several times, but it was months before Frima's hurt and anger abated enough to have a conversation. They met at a coffee shop on a Sunday afternoon, far from either apartment. Bob thanked her for coming; his hands shook as he stirred his coffee. "Ask me whatever you want."

"How long were you and Joan ... seeing each other?"

"Two years, beginning soon after Lisa left for college. It was before you went back to teaching, although it picked up then. You were so busy, you didn't notice."

"How did it start?"

"Joan." Bob sounded like a child telling his mother that a friend made him do it. "At first I turned her down, but she convinced me." He poured more sugar into his coffee, which he hadn't yet tasted. "It didn't take much persuading. You always kept your distance. It was easier for me to see how withdrawn you were with the kids. Once Lisa was gone, I realized I was lonely too."

"You were vulnerable. And Joan took advantage."

"She made me feel special. Told me you didn't appreciate what a great husband you had."

Frima would have laughed if her liberated friend hadn't lifted Bob by putting her down.

"The funny thing is, what began as my need for attention grew into me loving Joan. I saw I had more to give than you were open to receiving." Bob pushed away his cold, undrunk coffee. "Maybe my own mother set too high a standard of what to expect in a marriage, but that's what I grew up with and what I want for myself. Does that sound selfish?"

"Wanting to give is the opposite of selfish. Wanting a wife who can give is normal." Bob did deserve better. If she'd let him, he would have shown that same warmth to her. "My idea of male-female relationships is distorted. Perhaps I should have told you more about my early years in Berlin. It might have helped you understand me and even allowed me to heal."

"You had Otto and Greta. From everything I could see, they loved each other very much."

"By the time I was adopted, something inside me was already dead and decayed." Frima put her hand over Bob's, which had finally stopped shaking. "I never meant to hurt you." She repeated the line he'd said to her months ago. This time, the words didn't sound cliché.

***

The divorce, finalized exactly one year after Frima moved out, was uncomplicated. She was working, so alimony wasn't an issue. Nor, with David and Lisa over eighteen, was custody. Between her late parents and Bob's, their college tuition was covered. Bob bought out Frima's share of their apartment, which had gone co-op in 1982, so she was able to purchase her own—more modest than the one in Riverdale but still more upscale than the area around P.S. 94.

Frima went back to their old apartment once, to pack the rest of what she'd left behind. She'd only taken clothes, Liane's sculptures, and Sugar to her temporary place. Now she packed her history books, some kitchenware, and Greta's fancy serving pieces. She left the furniture for Bob, except for two items, both from Otto—the dresser where she kept *Sisters* and the desk where *Knot* sat. On a final walk-through, Frima found a box labeled "CANDLESTICKS" in the hall closet. She'd almost given them to Lisa when she turned twenty but decided to wait until she got married. Now she vowed never to let her daughter have them.

David came home to help her move. Although Frima had been living alone for a year, not until the divorce became official did it feel permanent. And strange. Other than the brief time after Bitsy moved out of their dorm room, Frima had lived with others: the Gerstens, Liane, the Oberlanders, fellow teachers, Bob and the children. In some ways, she liked being on her own. She had only herself to please. She could read or listen to jazz and talk openly to Sugar. Still, the place had a haunted quality. Bare rooms echoed with the sound of her own voice. Before she could fill them with furniture that she chose, she'd have to figure out who she was.

One Sunday morning near the end of the school year, Frima was drinking her third cup coffee and reading *The New York Times Book Review* when there was a knock on the door. She looked through the peephole and opened it.

"I didn't call," said Joan, "because I was afraid you'd hang up on me. Can we talk?"

Frima turned off the stereo, Ella quietly singing "In a Mellow Tone," and went back to the couch. She'd let Joan decide where, or if, to sit. Joan took an armchair but perched stiffly on the edge of the seat. Frima nodded at her. Joan could talk. It didn't mean Frima had to respond.

"I guess you heard Bob and I broke up," Joan began. Frima hadn't. "He wanted us to get married." Joan twisted her wedding ring and shrugged. "I'm Catholic. I won't get divorced."

Adultery was okay; divorce wasn't? Frima sniffed at the hypocrisy. "Why did you do it?"

Joan answered calmly as if she'd anticipated the question. "I used to listen to you talk about Bob in our CR group. You never appreciated what a good husband you had."

"You slept with Bob as an act of charity? At my expense? You're too pious to end your own marriage but not above destroying someone else's?" Frima snorted. "That's the most convoluted crap I've ever heard. No matter how you try to justify it, it was wrong."

"You're right." Joan stared at her hands, now folded in her lap. Her voice trembled. "I'm here to ask your forgiveness."

Frima stood over the armchair. "Do you remember my high school valedictorian speech?" Joan looked up at her hopefully. "I talked about not giving up when life got hard, how Walton prepared us to be leaders, and the importance of carrying the love of parents and friends as we moved forward. My life started out hard. I have bigger sins against me to forgive than your puny one. You're a burden, Joan. I'm not sure how I'll move forward, but I won't be carrying you with me."

A fresh cup of coffee in hand, Frima turned the music back on and resumed reading the newspaper. Halfway through the recording, when Ella was singing, "Just go your way, and laugh and play. There's joy unknown in a mellow tone," Joan finally rose and let herself out. She didn't beat a hasty retreat as she had that day over a year ago. Frima's tone wasn't mellow, but neither did she feel the rush of victory. Her heart and soul felt as empty as her apartment.

***

The finality of the divorce unleashed a flood of grief. Frima mourned the loss of the family she'd created with more intensity than the deaths of the families she been born and adopted into. Her attention often wandered in class. She met Liane at Reservoir Oval. "Help. I don't know who I am or who I'm supposed to be. I'm falling apart. Can you put me back together?"

"With a soldering iron or a glue gun?"

Frima smiled. It felt good. "Anything that will work." She waved at two of her students jumping rope. They'd soon be moving onto third grade. Her life was going backwards.

"Divorce isn't the end of the world. You've recovered from much worse."

"We both have. You more than me." The thought didn't make Frima feel better.

"An article I read said Holocaust survivors cope better with crises than other people. After getting through the worst, they know they have the skills to deal with whatever life throws them."

"They have faith, something I don't."

"Not faith!" Liane was adamant. "Many, if not most, lost it. Faith is fragile. It shatters."

"Ours never had a strong foundation to begin with." She and Liane never trusted that the building they'd slept in one night would be standing the next. "So if they don't have faith ...?"

"They have hope, for the future. Something specific to work toward. You and I survived because we had hope that we'd find the next meal, the next place to sleep. I have hope that the next piece of art I make will be good; that the next client I help will improve."

"What can I hope for?"

"That a troubled student will succeed. That you'll turn your condo into a haven, not just a refuge. I tell my clients it's their choice not mine. I also tell them to start small and concrete."

Frima wondered what next year's crop of second-graders would bring. All she had to do was make a difference in one life, then another. She could do that. "My place does need better lighting." Frima smirked. "I won't buy the fixtures from Joan's company."

"That's the spirit." Liane kissed Frima's cheek. They walked down the ramp that led to the park's gate and hugged goodbye. What Frima wished she could hope for was a reconciliation with her daughter, but that dream was as shattered as the faith she never had.

PART ELEVEN: LIANE (1985–1990)

CHAPTER 42

What I hadn't shared with Frima from that article was what Freud said after the Spanish flu took his daughter's life. "Some losses we never get over. And that is how it should be. It is the only way of perpetuating a love that we do not want to abandon." That's how I felt about the daughter I'd named Sarah, after my mother.

I filled the emptiness with a sculpture series I called "MothersandDaughters," closing the spaces between words and naming each piece by first initials: my mother and me (S&L), Frima's birth mom Mirla and Frima (M&F), Greta and Frima, Frima and Lisa, Berta and Susan. Last would be me and my daughter, reversing the initials of the first. I wanted the sculptures to have arm-like append-ages, reaching along tortuous paths until they ultimately joined, but no matter what I tried, the parts kept detaching. The series was a jumble of severed connections.

After a year, I'd completed a dozen. I filled a suitcase and took them to the West Village. Approaching galleries owned by men would have been as pointless as panning for gold in a bathtub, so I went to three founded by women. At the first, Paula Cooper held forth about ballsy artists like Carl Andre, Donald Judd, and Sol LeWitt for half an hour before she asked to see my work. "Why bother?" I retorted and left. It was the same at Mary Boone. All her clients were men and she'd decided to abandon minimalism in favor of conceptual art. "Not my bag," I told her and took mine to Barbara Gladstone's. "Do you show women artists?" I asked right away. Why waste more of my time?

Barbara's eyes glittered like the rhinestone earrings dangling from her wrinkled earlobes. "Yes! A young Iranian exile." She showed me two stark photographs. "Shirin is exotic. Dark skin, sleek hair, penetrating eyes. With a fascinating back story. The art world will love her."

I nudged my suitcase toward Barbara. She stared at it, then at my face and hair. "Tell me about your life," she said. Not "tell me about your work." If my art couldn't speak for itself, I wasn't interested. I took the subway home and shoved my unpacked suitcase in the closet. I left Frima a message. "Know any junk dealers who want to buy a shitload of metal, wood, and wire?"

My phone was ringing when I got home the next day. Frima was excited. "The sister of a woman I teach with shows her paintings at White Columns, a nonprofit art center in SoHo. The founders are men, but they exhibit work by women. They open at noon on Saturday. Go!"

"Where were your friend and her sister born?" I asked.

"Brooklyn, I think. Why?"

"It doesn't matter. Thanks for the tip."

On Saturday, at noon sharp, I introduced myself to the founders of White Columns. "Open the suitcase," said Jeffrey Lew immediately. "Yeah, let's see your work," said Gordon Matta-Clark. We were off to a good start. My fingers trembled as I undid the latches. They held each piece and asked about my materials and techniques. Jeffrey said it was fashionable to say that art wasn't about anything except itself: color, form, size. He pronounced that critique "crap."

"Yeah," Gordon echoed. "So what inspired these pieces?"

Without going into detail, I explained that fraught mother-daughter relationships were part of my history and work. Jeffrey declared, "What a fascinating theme. Should the labels list only the title and price or include a statement about the germ for the series and each piece?"

"Whoa, you said 'labels.' Does that mean you want to show my work?"

Gordon grinned. "Unless you prefer to keep it hidden in your suitcase."

"No, no. I'll write a general statement about the series, but not each piece. Even if they're anonymous, I worry about confidentiality." I smiled. "My social work training."

"Got it," said Gordon. He and Jeff began talking about pedestals and placement.

I looked around the cavernous loft, afraid the space would swallow up my tiny sculptures. "Big art can be read from a distance; mine you have to see up close."

Jeff sketched a set of small, intimate booths. "We'll build them with plywood." "And rig up spotlights," added Gordon. "Paint the walls white or leave them natural?" they asked me.

"Natural," I said. "Like my materials."

Jeff wrote that down then chewed his pencil. "The booths will also let people, especially women, view each work unobserved. That way, if it stirs up emotions, they can cry in private."

"That's so ... sensitive."

Gordon guffawed. "We're New Age Guys. But old-fashioned enough for contracts." We'd split sales fifty-fifty; White Columns would absorb all the other costs. Most galleries took sixty percent and charged artists for installation and publicity. My show would go up in two weeks.

I called Frima the moment I got home. "You saved me again."

"We keep saving each other."

"Let's make a suicide pact to die at the same time," I blurted out.

Frima didn't hesitate. "We'll remind each other when that time comes."

"Meanwhile, I owe you a thank-you feast at Goulash Garden."

***

My second year at the gallery, I thanked Frima for another reason. I was at her apartment, whose furnishings were still depressingly minimalist, when I told her that my consciousness had been raised. "It's about time," she said. "For an avant-garde artist, you're a decade behind. Try this." She gave me a mug of coffee. One thing she'd bought was an expensive Melita filter setup.

"Yum." I was used to instant and frankly I couldn't taste the difference but if I encouraged her, maybe she'd get interested in cooking. Anything, in addition to teaching, to take her mind off Lisa. "I'm more avant-garde than you know." I put a finger over my lips. "I joined the Guerilla Girls."

Frima poured me a refill. "Why? You're the original loner."

"I converted when the other women at White Columns said a Guerilla Girls' survey found female artists accounted for less than five percent of the work in museums, while only fifteen percent of nude paintings and statues depicted men. They called the survey a 'weenie count.'"

Frima spewed coffee, then asked to hear more.

"Two Gorilla Girls came to a meeting of our CR group. They wore gorilla masks and introduced themselves as Rosalba Carriera and Eleanor Coade. Not their real names; they took them from a seventeenth-century painter and an eighteenth-century sculptor. The masks and pseudonyms are to call attention to the issues not themselves. That's why I swore you to secrecy."

"I've kept ours for forty years. Anything more you can tell me, beyond the outrageous posters and public performances reported in the newspaper?"

"We mainly do background research, which I'm good at it. Social workers have a knack for uncovering what goes on behind the scenes."

"Are they making a difference?"

"A 'weenie' one. Some art buyers are betting that works by women will increased in value in the next decade. My sales figures are up ten percent. That means I can cut a half-day from my job to make art." I smirked. "Or trouble."

CHAPTER 43

"A woman, late twenties or so, was looking for you yesterday afternoon," the receptionist said. I'd come to work following a half-day sculpting and a long night pasting posters outside MOMA. She looked at her memo pad. "Sandra Rose?"

I didn't recognize the name. "What did she look like?"

The receptionist shrugged. "Ordinary, except for a navy skirt and blazer which you rarely see around here. And a manicure. Pale blue polish. No wedding ring. I said you'd be back today."

I still had no idea who it was. An early client who'd turned her life around and joined the establishment? A lawyer suing me for slandering a parent? The mystery woman waited a week before coming back. Between my current clients, art, and mischief-making, I'd forgotten about her by then. But when she walked into my office, her identity was clear. She was my daughter.

I was surprised I wasn't surprised. Perhaps I'd unconsciously suspected, or hoped, it was her. Or had prepared for this moment for twenty-eight years. I'd been right to picture Sarah, now Sandra, as taller than me; half right to see her hair as tangled, although hers was less frizzy and fairer than mine. Same hazel eyes but no tiny bump on her nose like the one that nearly betrayed me to the Gestapo. No feature either to indicate who, among my token-booth quickies, her father was. I said what I'd want to hear if I were her: "I'm glad you found me. How?"

"Lisa Horner, your friend Frima's daughter. We met in a study group at our synagogue on Jewish mother-daughter relationships. Lisa complained about having a distant mother ... " Sandra stopped. "Maybe I shouldn't be telling you this?"

"You're not telling me anything I don't already know."

Sandra looked at her nails. "Lisa's a nice person, but she had nothing nice to say about your friend."

"Fuck Lisa," I said. Sandra winced. "How did you make the connection to me?"

"When I said I didn't even know who my birth mother was, Lisa told me about her mom being a war orphan, and I knew that much about you from the adoption records. We put two and two together and I figured you were the friend Lisa's mother had survived with in Berlin."

"That doesn't explain how you got my name. Lisa doesn't talk to her mother. If she had, Frima would have told me." This drawn-out tale was beginning to annoy me. I didn't want to hear about Frima and her daughter Lisa; I wanted to hear about me and my daughter, Sandra. I still mourned the decision to give her up for adoption. Did she mourn the loss of me, her birth mother?

Sandra wouldn't be rushed, though. Maybe she needed to impress me with her smarts. "Names are sealed in adoption records but not in those kept by relief agencies. I got yours from the one that sponsored you and Frima. A few years ago, a reporter interviewed the case worker at the time to find out what she knew about the children she'd taken care of."

I figured that was Miss Stone, who'd died last year. Her niece had called to tell me.

"A notation beside your name said 'Social Worker.' I started with city welfare agencies; yours was the third I called." Sandra grinned and requested a glass of water. "May I sit?" she asked. I nodded. Her smile disappeared. "I didn't contact you right away. I waited a month before I showed up at your office. When you weren't here, it took a week to get up my courage again."

"Does your adoptive mother know you found me?"

"Yes."

"How does she feel about it?"

Sandra wiped the bottom of her glass before setting it on my desk. "She understands it's something I have to do. But she doesn't want to meet you."

"Good. I don't want to meet her. Or your father." My daughter didn't seem surprised.

"I dreamed about meeting you," she continued. "You were a fairy godmother, in a glittery dress, who waved a magic wand to fix broken toys or stop my friends from being mean."

I snorted. Sandra looked uncertain. "It's a lovely image," I said. "Go on."

"But inside, I was afraid I wouldn't like you, or you wouldn't like me. That my emotions would drown me. Friends say I'm too bottled up. That alone makes some people dislike me."

"My social worker self says that's your repressed anger. At being given up for adoption."

Sandra bit her lip. "Now that we have met, I worry my anger will drive you away."

"When you've dealt with hate, anger doesn't scare you." I reached across the desk. "I won't give you up again. I spent your lifetime dreaming about meeting you too. I even had a name for you, Sarah, for *my* mother. But I like Sandra. The names are close, but you're your own person."

Sandra's face relaxed a bit. "What should I call you? I already have a mom."

"How about Liane? That's my name."

Her face brightened. "How about 'Li?' It would be a name that no one but me calls you."

I didn't like it. My mother had named me Liane. Other than Ittel Rosa, my name was all I had left of my early life. But I didn't want to shut Sandra down when the door had just opened. "Let's give it a try."

She grinned wide enough for me to see a lifetime of good dental work. "My father?" she asked hesitantly. "The adoption papers said

'Unknown.' Do you have a name? Are you in touch? Anything that will help me find him?"

"He really is unknown," I said quietly.

"I don't understand."

I swallowed. "I was promiscuous. With a lot of nameless men. I had no idea who your father was, is. I doubt he'd remember me either. I'm sorry. I know this is hard to hear."

Sandra's voice was defiant. "I'll be fine." That was bullshit, but it wasn't my place to tell her. I wasn't her social worker. Besides, I admired her spunk. She sounded like me. She squared her shoulders and said, "The important thing is that I have you. How did you picture me, Li?"

The name really grated, but I let it pass. "I suppose all parents imagine children in their own image. I pictured your hair as darker and frizzier but otherwise you looked the way you do. Since I had lots of other jobs before I got my degree, I thought of you as being a temp worker."

"I write copy for Young and Rubicam Advertising. I was a business major in college."

"Don't worry. I still like you," I told her. "What you don't know about me is that I'm also a sculptor. So I imagined that on your own time, you did something artistic, like painting or ..."

Sandra bounced in her chair. "I write poetry!"

I bounced too.

"My parents were strict about school but encouraged outside interests. I took art classes, music lessons, and joined a children's theater group. When I showed an interest in writing, Mom bought me journals and a subscription to a kids' book-of-the-month club."

"I'm grateful for how they raised you. I never could have given you those advantages." I left unspoken the words, "That's why I gave you up," hoping Sandra would fill them in.

-"My parents gave me a good life. Yours must have been a lot rougher?"

"You already know some of the bumpy parts. Childhood in Berlin, adolescence in group homes, having you when I was a year younger than you are now. I'll save the rest until we know each other better. The important thing is that making art has been my salvation."

"Can I see your work?"

I pinched myself. I wasn't dreaming. "Come to my place? Sunday afternoon?" Sandra nodded. "Bring your poems," I said. "We'll share and I'll ply you with wine and cookies."

Before my daughter left, we exchanged an awkward hug. I was glad she was only a little bit taller than I was. I hoped, as we got to know each other better, she wouldn't look down on me.

***

Sandra and I visited every Sunday, alternating houses. She lived in a two-bedroom apartment on the Upper West Side. I'd imagined her as sloppy in her personal habits but precise in her creative work, like me. Sandra was particular about both. At my request, she served us whiskey and cake. The best part of my fantasy-come-true, however, was sharing our poetry and art.

At first, we were both nervous. I let Sandra go first; it seemed the motherly thing to do. She stood, like a kid in front of the classroom, and read me a poem she'd written two years ago.

Diagnosis

Seconds? my hostess asks.
Yes, I answer,
Aware even thirds will fail to fill me.
Tighter? the tailor inquires.
A touch, I say,
Knowing the skirt will still bag.
Inside a womb-hole
A mass grows.
One empties;
The ousted other becomes emptiness.
Odd. The X-ray technician points:
A mass? A hole?
Both, I propose.

Matter? Missing?
Entity? Enigma?
Find? Forget?
Diagnosis? Dilemma.

"Is that about me?" I asked when she finished.

Sandra stammered. "I wrote it after my then-fiancé called off our engagement, thinking of the babies we wouldn't have. But reading it now, the missing mother symbolism is obvious."

"Try to express the longing more abstractly. Play around with images of emptiness."

"I think this one's better, Li. It's still about maternity, but more metaphorical."

"Good." I patted the chair facing mine. "But sit so I can feel your breath when you read."

The Talipot Palm

I am old and very tall;
Twenty-five meters after eighty years of growth.
My time has come to bloom.
Only once am I allowed to burst forth
In clusters of creamy flowers
That yield yellow-green fruit
To seed twenty million like me.
Then I will desiccate and die.
The Buddha's words were inscribed on my palms.
I am a symbol of virility
To the men of the Andaman Islands.
Who are they
To steal my maternal identity?
But I shall have my revenge.
I will take my daughters with me
When I depart their earth.

I raised my glass of wine. "Wow! I love the emotional intensity, especially the anger."

Sandra beamed. "I may be 'buttoned up,' but the feelings flow when I write."

"That's *why* you write. It's why every creative person does what they do." I told her to be even more open. "Come at things slant, but be brave enough to attack head-on now and then."

Hypocritical advice, given how indirect my work was. I was glad MothersandDaughters was on display at White Columns, not in my apartment. I wasn't ready for Sandra to see the series. Instead, I showed her my pieces about the struggles of being poor. The materials were literally covered in dirt. I'd shown the "emptiness" of hunger with wooden chunks, representing food, lying just beyond the reach of wire arms emerging from the gaping holes of metal washers.

Sandra asked if she could hold them. I nodded. She lifted each one, admired its intricacy, and returned it to its exact place on the workbench. "The inspiration is from your own life?"

"A combination of my own memories and my clients' lives. Want to see how I make them?" I showed her the bins of raw materials, my soldering iron, and how I interlaced wires.

"The work is delicate, yet you confront heavy themes." Sandra promised to bring me old costume jewelry made of different metals with interesting stones. "Your technical proficiency is impressive, but you should experiment. Work bigger, let bigger feelings flow."

We laughed at the similarity of our advice to each other.

"Like mother, like daughter," she said. "Like artist, like poet," I rejoined. We concluded she was a seedling, and I the Talipot Palm.

I washed the dishes after Sandra left, as if she were judging my housekeeping. Propping Ittel Rosa on the counter, I told her, "I've always worked small, even after I learned to solder, so I'd be free to pack up and go."

Her skeptical eye regarded me. "You've had a stable job and lived here for a decade."

"My life still felt temporary. Motherhood hovered like a distant fantasy. Since becoming a mother for real, my life feels permanent. I could carry that feeling into my artwork."

"And Sandra can carry your reality into her poetry. What you can't say to each other directly, you can share through your work. But," Ittel Rosa warned me, "Sandra will push you."

"I don't mind. Except when she pushes my buttons." The bear's lone eye looked at me inquisitively. "By calling me 'Li.'" I left the rest of the dirty dishes in the sink.

***

Of course, I told Frima that Lisa had been the link that brought me and my daughter together, but neither Frima nor I suggested that she meet Sandra. It would have been painful for Frima, who hadn't spoken to Lisa since the divorce. I was wary too. Frima and I used to be jealous of each other's other friends; I didn't want competition between my closest friend and my daughter.

Early the following year, I asked Sandra if she still saw Lisa at synagogue. "I saw her last week," she answered. "A new study reported a big drop in observant Jews, so Sisterhood held a discussion about why we continued to practice our religion. I said knowing my extended birth family were Holocaust victims made Judaism's survival important. Lisa felt the same way."

"Many survivors don't," I said. "We won't even talk about it. But your generation does."

Sandra agreed. "Hardly any older people were at the meeting. Lisa told me her mother feels bitter about being a Jew. They're so far apart, their break is 'irreparable.' Lisa's word."

"If only I could solder them back together." I sliced the Zabar's coffee cake while Sandra poured cut-glass tumblers of whiskey. "Can you repair the rift? Persuade Lisa to be understanding?" I asked.

"I doubt it. Lisa strikes me as rigid and inflexible."

"What if you reminded Lisa that I gave you up for adoption but Frima never abandoned her? That might give her second thoughts about her mother."

Sandra slammed down her fork. "Li! Quit being hard on yourself. Giving me up was a selfless act, same as your mother's. If I criticize you to make Frima look better, I'd be lying."

"It beats letting Lisa hold onto a lie. Besides, deep down, don't you feel abandoned? I'm still angry at my mother, despite knowing her good intentions, and having done the same thing myself."

"I once felt that way, but not anymore. If you'd raised me while your life was a mess, we may have ended up like Frima and Lisa. Now we're free to create a less tangled relationship."

My daughter and I still had a lot to untangle, but she was right. Suppose I'd had to leave her in someone else's care the year I was locked up, which I still hadn't told her about. "What we're building is wonderful," I agreed. "There's only one thing that troubles me."

"Yes, Li?" Sandra gripped her tumbler.

I hastened to reassure her. "Nothing about you. But with Frima and me, whenever one of us found something, we'd share it. See if you can help Lisa and her mom share what we have."

"I'll try, although it hinges on Frima accepting Lisa's embrace of religion as much as Lisa understanding her mother's rejection of it. But I believe people *can* change." Sandra sipped her whiskey. "Do you think you'll ever get interested in Judaism?"

"Do you want me to?"

"It would give us another link. I also think it would be valuable to you."

I couldn't imagine how. "How?"

"For the same reason faith matters to me. Whenever I dwell on the meaningless slaughter of relatives I'll never know, religion saves me from nihilism."

"I could use a dose of that." I gulped half my drink. "I'll try. For your sake and mine but not at your conservative synagogue. I'll find my own more liberal path."

Sandra grinned. "Judaism is split into warring branches, but one trunk supports them all."

I clinked our glasses. "Amen."

***

I joined Ezrat Nashim, a Jewish feminist group that met for study, prayer, and social action. My tutor was Malka Simon, who told me their demands: women should be counted as members of a minyan, not be excluded from certain commandments, and have the right to act as witnesses and initiate divorce. "For this, the rabbis considered us radical," she said. Like the Guerilla Girls, I thought. More so, considering Jewish women were up against thousands of years of patriarchy.

Malka gave me things to read, including a feminist siddur, or prayer book, that referred to God as She, and an article in which the author wrote, "For the first time, I understood what it meant to be made in God's image." I didn't care whether God had boobs or balls, but I was pissed off at how women were treated in scripture: disinherited, considered "unclean," held responsible for their own rape. "How can you read this and still want to be a Jew?" I wailed.

"The Torah was written as dogma by men intent on preserving their power. Readers treat it as open to debate." Malka smiled. "Which Jews excel at."

I smiled too. While my journey would detour from my daughter's, this ancient book would return us to a common thoroughfare. Judaism also provided a path to tell Sandra about my stint in prison. As the High Holy Days neared, we discussed repentance and forgiveness. The time seemed right to confess that eight years after she was born, I served a year at the Women's House of Detention. I told her about stealing the soldering iron, skipped the sordid details of prison life, but said it was my wake-up call. "I began making art again. Now I build on that experience in my job."

Nervous, I waited for a reaction. Sandra poured wine and handed me the cookies. "The day we met, you said you had more to tell me about yourself when we knew each other better. I imagined it was much worse. I regret you had to go through that, Li, but to me, it's no big deal."

"So you forgive me for being a convicted criminal?"

"It was a minor crime. You repented, society forgave you, and so did God."

"And you?"

"I have no reason to forgive you. For that." Sandra nudged my wine-glass closer. "It's more than twenty years in the past. All I care about is us in the present and future."

I drank the entire glass and told her to read me her latest poem.

The following Sunday, taking a cheesecake out of Sandra's refrigerator, I saw a pan of leftover lasagna. "I thought you kept kosher."

"Torah says, 'Thou shalt not boil a kid in its mother's milk,' which could simply mean don't slaughter and cook it in front of her, not refrain from eating meat and milk together. I have no problem breaking rules that don't seem reasonable."

"Are there rules we absolutely can't break?"

"No working on Shabbat. The nature of work changes, not the explicit law forbidding it."

"I work on the Sabbath. I have to, for the sake of my clients. Even the rabbis agree that pikuach nefesh, saving a life, takes precedence over all other Jewish laws." I felt a little smug.

"Rescuing clients is okay. But it's wrong to catch up on paperwork."

"Even if it will save my own sanity?" I joked.

"No!" My daughter was vehement.

Sandra and I met on Sundays. She didn't have to know what I did on Saturdays. Still, I enjoyed our debates. Fighting about Torah was a safe way for her to air unacknowledged anger toward me. I was glad to avoid it too, but part of me itched to get it out in the open. So the day I blew up shouldn't have come as a surprise. My excuse was that a client had called at two that morning, whining about her foster mom. Her voice reminded me of Sandra's when she asked me to clean my bathroom before her next visit. But the real reason was my own undetonated bomb.

We were at her place. She held out a drawstring bag. "My mom's old costume jewelry, which I'll never wear. It's yours to turn into art, Li."

I didn't take the bag. "My name is Liane."

"You said I could call you 'Li.'"

"I said we'd give it a try. I tried and I hate it."

Sandra twisted the strings in her trembling fingers. "What do your clients call you?"

"The parents call me Miss Asher. The kids call me Liane."

"I don't want to be like one of your clients. I'm your daughter."

"Calling me Liane doesn't make you a client. That's what most other adults call me too."

Sandra tossed the jewelry bag on a chair. "Maybe I should stop calling you anything."

We didn't see or speak to each other for two weeks after that outburst. I usually waited for the other person to cave, but this time I made the call. "Sandra?"

"Li ... ane?" my daughter croaked.

"Call me Li."

She sobbed. "Are you sure?"

"Yes," I said. "That's my name. To you. For us."

Later I told Ittel Rosa, "That's what it means to be a mother. You let your child win."

***

The next Sunday, Sandra visited me. I scoured the bathroom, even the kitchen sink. She swung the drawstring bag to which she'd added outdated necklaces of her own. I told her to toss it in the bedroom, hoping that when she came out, she'd also compliment me for making the bed and picking up my clothes. Instead, she emerged carrying Ittel Rosa, who I'd propped on my pillow.

"What's this?" she asked, stroking what little remained of my bear's fur.

I told her the story of hiding with Ittel Rosa when my mother was taken away, of the bear being the only childhood possession I had when I came to America, and of continuing to talk to her ever since. "Does that sound crazy?"

"Not at all," my daughter answered. "I still have my stuffed bunny. Loopsy's floppy ears hear things I don't dare tell anyone else."

"Ittel Rosa's eye sees things no one else is privy to." I reached out for my bear.

Sandra held onto her. "Give Ittel Rosa to me? She can tell me the rest of your secrets."

"She can tell you whatever she wants, but I'm not parting with her yet. I promise, when I die, Ittel Rosa will be yours." Sometimes, I told myself, you can't let your child win.

CHAPTER 44

Jeffrey, at White Columns, handed me a business card embossed on linen paper. "A woman swept in here yesterday and left this for you." Gordon added, "Big hair, big caftan, big voice."

Miranda Falcon
Contemporary Art Agent
Making the Unknown, Known

"Her name is well known," Jeffrey said. "She scavenges in the grungy West Village, finds the 'next big thing,' and promotes the artists to trendy East Village galleries."

"Tell Liane Asher she simply *must* call me *ASAP*," Gordon imitated Miranda Falcon's Brooklyn-come-Paris voice. "I simply *adore* her work."

Two days passed. My office wasn't private and I wanted to call her from home on a day I was making art. Frankly, it also took that long to muster the courage. This could be my break, but Miranda sounded obnoxious and I had to suppress the instinct to blow her off.

"I've been anticipating your call. For three days." Miranda's voice was gently scolding.

"Sorry. I have another job that pays the bills and was waiting for an opportune moment."

She didn't ask about my other job. "Your sculptures augur the future. When the art world tires of 'big,' the pendulum will swing back to small, intimate pieces. I'm connected with avant-garde East Village galleries, places you've seen in the *Village Voice, Art News, Art in America.*"

I'd never read those magazines. "Very impressive." I hoped I sounded sincere.

Miranda's breathy voice continued. "I also peruse Japanese and European art magazines. They know what's going on before we do." She put me on hold while she checked her calendar. "Tomorrow. Two o'clock." She hung up without asking if that was convenient for me.

Tomorrow being Saturday—Shabbat—it was. Maybe I'd be blessed. Making art was my way of praying. Still, I was uneasy taking such a big step. I needed another pep talk ASAP.

"You still owe me dinner," Frima said when I called. "Is tonight at seven okay?"

"Yes," I answered. "How kind of you to ask."

Friday nights were busy at Goulash Gardens, but Mrs. Haydu ignored the waiting list and sat us at the first empty table. She hugged me. "Liane, we haven't seen you in long time."

"I've been busy seeing clients and sculpting."

"Her moment is about to arrive," Frima announced.

"Not so fast," I said. "I'm not sure I want it."

My old boss wagged her finger. "You weren't sure about going back to school either, but after I talked you into it, you were glad you did."

"True."

Mrs. Haydu turned to Frima. "You talk her into this one." She poured us each a free glass of golden Tokaji. "Get Liane to agree, and the rest of the bottle is on the house too."

I studied the menu and ordered for us. When I began to fiddle with the silverware, Frima moved mine to her side of the table and told me to stop avoiding the topic. "Isn't representation by a major gallery what you want? What"— she mouthed 'Guerilla Girls'—"is all about?"

"Yes. But I'm small stuff. Literally."

"That's a big load of crap. You underrate yourself and sabotage your chances of success." Frima drank the golden wine. "The Nazis told us we were worthless. Don't let the bastards win."

I drank too. "Is that why you're an activist at your school?"

"My daughter accused me of doing nothing with my life. I'm trying to prove her wrong."

"Have you heard from her?" I hadn't told Frima about asking Sandra to cajole Lisa.

"No. I leave messages, but she never calls back." Frima set her mouth. "I won't give up."

"Good," I said. "Activists never do."

"And I won't give up on you. Tomorrow, two o'clock, you will be at Miranda Falcon's office." Frima raised her empty glass toward Mrs. Haydu, who brought us the rest of the bottle.

***

"I'm considering several galleries," Miranda announced. Her assistant handed me a contract with Post-it Notes where I had to sign. "Civilian Warfare Studio on East 11th and The Fun Gallery on East 10th are the top contenders. Which do you think would best showcase your work?"

"Civilian Warfare," I said, simply because I liked the name.

Miranda phoned a week later. "You open in eight months at The Fun Gallery." She described it as a small downtown place that drew big uptown collectors and said that Patti Astor, the underground film star who founded it, "shaped artists' work without compromising their street credibility." I concluded that the Guerilla Girls would approve and called Frima.

She sounded upbeat when she said, "Hello?" Her voice faded when she heard it was me. I asked if she was okay. "I'm fine," she answered. "Just stupidly hoping it was Lisa. I left another message on her machine this morning." Frima sighed. "But that's old news. Tell me new news."

"My agent came through. My solo show debuts in November."

Frima whooped. "I'll order a case of champagne for the opening. Tell me more."

I said I would expand my MothersandDaughters series. "Not just the number of pieces; I'm going to make a couple of bigger ones too."

"Bravo," said Frima. "I have some new news too. The principal at P.S. 94 is retiring at the end of the school year, and she's recommending me to replace her."

"Congratulations! But I thought your methods were the opposite of hers."

"They are, but I don't let on. She just sees my class's rising test scores and thinks that if I'm principal, I'll achieve the same for the whole school. Which I can, *my* way."

It was my turn to whoop. "That's subversive."

"Seeing how the Guerilla Girls' tactics boosted your career convinced me to become subversive too."

I laughed. "What do you mean *become* subversive? You've had fifty years of practice."

***

I worked, or prayed, my ass off getting ready for the show. I made two pieces, twice the scale of my usual sculptures, with extra wood for added heft. In one, the mother figure loomed larger; in the other, the daughter overpowered the mother. Patti put them at either end of the long gallery to entice viewers to move between them. I thought they'd entice critics to spew absurd theories about reverse domination in the female progression from birth to death. If asked about their meaning, I'd smile serenely and say I preferred to "keep mum."

The Fun Gallery show also had nearly twice as many smaller pieces as I'd exhibited at White Columns. The new mother-daughter pairs, several of which were intact, drew on fictional characters in books and movies. Below the titles, Patti put labels that said "Inspiration: Book" or "Inspiration: Movie," urging viewers to guess their origins. I also redid the one of me and Sandra. While the size of L&S remained small and intimate, the links were sturdier.

The day before the show opened, while we finished setting up, Miranda Falcon hung a discreet "SOLD" sign under a work inspired by a client. Unlike White Columns, there were no price tags at the Fun Gallery. Not classy, I surmised, and asked my agent how much I'd be paid.

"After my commission and the gallery fee, you'll net a hundred dollars. You're still a nobody, so you come cheap until you become a somebody and are worth a lot more. That's what astute buyers are looking for." Her silver and turquoise bracelets clinked as she patted my arm. "But being chosen by a famous collector is invaluable to that upward trajectory."

"Who's the famous collector?"

Miranda tried, with limited success, to modulate her voice. "Michael Lynn."

I said I'd never heard of him.

My agent sighed loudly. "I'll enlighten you. A young showbiz lawyer with a good eye. He was an early buyer of work by Jean-Michel Basquiat, Cindy Sherman, and Julian Schnabel."

"Never heard of them either," I said although of course I had.

Miranda believed me though. "Oh, Liane. The Press will find your naïveté refreshing."

The following night, young men and women in black and white, with silver studs in their noses and lips—another "next big thing" according to Miranda—circulated bearing trays of crudités, cheese, and mini-croissants. The bar served Korbel Brut, courtesy of Frima. Guests who didn't know about arriving fashionably late began to come at eight. The first was Betty, my roommate from the group home, who I hadn't seen in nearly four decades. I barely recognized the gray-haired, sallow woman who'd been only a year ahead of me in school. "I'm so proud of you, Liane," she mumbled between missing teeth. "To think I knew you way back when."

"I'm honored you came," I told her. "But how did you know I was having a show?"

"The October *Evander Alumni News.* I subscribed the last time I got out of rehab. At my fortieth reunion, I met a woman from my typing class. We're helping each other stay clean."

I squeezed her bony shoulder. "That's great and far from pointless." Betty smiled with her mouth closed. "But how did my show get into the magazine?"

"I sent it in!" Mr. Archer, my art teacher, appeared at my side and hugged me. "I retired in 1987. In forty-two years of teaching, you stood out more than any other student." He'd come with his wife, grown daughter, and son-in-law. "I brought along a friend," he said with an impish grin.

"Congratulations, Miss Archer. Jack Baldwin from Explosion Gallery, remember?"

As if I needed a reminder of Mr. Archer's Gauloise-smoking friend who'd asked if I could see my puny wire works fitting in with the large plastic blobs he favored. "The name doesn't ring a bell. But thanks for coming. My work's already drawn the attention of one notable collector."

I excused myself to greet the other guests. Unfortunately, no Guerilla Girls could come without blowing their cover or mine. But my heart melted when Anoush, close to ninety and blind, was led in by Mendel, who'd also brought his wife and my godson. Under Patti's nervous eye, I let Anoush hold several pieces so he could "see" them with his hands. "They are as delicate and beautiful as you," he said. "Now the whole world will see what a good person you are."

I led him to the only chair. "I haven't lost my talent for being bad," I said.

Anoush laughed. "This too is good. Liane will always be Liane."

Mendel and his family surrounded Anoush in what looked like a three-generation portrait. "Let me know if you want any used auto parts," Mendel said. "I still hope that someday you'll make an automotive series." I described a few larger pieces I'd visualized that might lead me to take him up on the offer. He said I could call it the "Junk Series." I laughed and told him that all my work was junk, the "good kind." Miranda would have called it the "valuable kind."

My restaurant retinue walked in next. I smiled to see them being served. My old boss Jim joked that I should do a pasta series with wire in different thicknesses and shapes. The Haydus had no goulash-themed ideas but were skeptical about whether they could afford any sculpture. "I'll give you one gratis," I said. "If you hadn't pushed me and fed me, I wouldn't be here today."

The rest of my "family" showed up around half past eight. Sandra was first. With her hair swept up and long earrings dangling down, she wouldn't have been identifiable as my daughter unless you took time to study our faces. I introduced her to Miranda. "You never told me you had a daughter," she exclaimed. She'd never asked. Then I showed Sandra every piece in the show. She beamed when I led her to "L&S," its neatly soldered links gleaming under a spotlight.

I caught up with Frima who was sipping champagne and lingering in front of "M&F" and "G&F." She hurried past "F&L." We walked around the rest of the show arm in arm. "Scavenging in Berlin," I said, "I never imagined we'd be alive today, let alone at the opening of my exhibit."

Frima smiled. "The forces of fortune and talent were behind you, Liane."

"So were you, Sister."

Long after nine, the art world finally arrived. Except for Frima and a few colleagues from work, the other guests had left. Nevertheless, the gallery buzzed. My agent made the rounds. It was the first time I'd seen Miranda act subservient. She introduced me to Lucy Lippard, critic for *ARTnews*. Lucy gushed. "I love the unnamed book and movie labels. It's very 'post-happening.'"

I shoved a hunk of brie in my mouth. I was starving. "That was the gallery owner's idea. Frankly, I think it's dumb. Guessing the source turns art into a parlor game." John Perreault, the *Village Voice* art critic, gave me a thumbs up. Lucy glowered at both of us and stalked to the bar.

Miranda, uncharacteristically, whispered in my ear. "Brilliant, Liane. Controversy sells."

Frima, who'd overheard, pulled me aside. "Are you crazy, insulting a famous critic?" I told her my agent didn't appear to think so. Frowning, Frima surveyed the room. Her face relaxed. She raised her glass of champagne. "Tonight was a fitting celebration, Liane. Everyone who cares about you came."

"No one cares more than you. I wouldn't be here if you hadn't told me more times than I can count not to give up."

Frima grinned. "And when you screw up again, which you will, I'll tell you again."

PART TWELVE:
FRIMA (1995–2000)

CHAPTER 45

A couple of months into the new school year, Frima was already tired. She was worn out from securing more resources to boost test scores, training bilingual volunteers, and supervising enrichment classes for parents. "I'm losing my fighting spirit," she complained to Liane.

"Nonsense. Bodies weaken with age, not passions. Get more rest, coffee, and food."

But Frima had no appetite. Her fatigue persisted after Christmas break despite taking it easy. David had split his visit between her and Bob. He and Frima had gone to the movies and spent hours listening to the Oberlanders' jazz albums. He'd taken her out to dinner every night, so proud that his new engineering job let him pick up the tab that he didn't notice she hardly ate.

When school resumed, Frima dragged herself through winter semester and then spring. "I don't get it," she told Sugar after turning in one night at eight. "My efforts are finally paying off. With all the programs I've put in place, I'm working less. Yet I'm more exhausted."

"You're certainly spending more time in bed," said the doll. "I like the company, but you toss and turn so much, it disrupts my beauty rest."

"I can't find a comfortable position. My back hurts like I've been moving furniture when the sad truth is that I still haven't bought any." Her body was doing other strange things too. "My urine's dark. My skin and the whites of my eyes are yellowish. Weirdest of all ..."

Sugar completed the sentence: "You scratch yourself all the time. It drives me crazy."

"My skin itches."

"For an educated woman, you sure act stupid. When are you going to see your doctor?"

Frima made an appointment after school let out in June. The doctor looked at her chart and told her not to get alarmed. "You're sixty-three. A little underweight, but that's better than having the opposite problem. Your heart and lungs sound fine. That said, you had poor nutrition and no medical care as child. The effects can be delayed, cumulative, and not obvious at first. The jaundice does suggest an issue with your liver." He ordered tests for anemia and a urinary tract infection. When those tests revealed nothing, he referred her to a hepatologist.

His earliest appointment wasn't until after school started in the fall. The brusque young man ordered more blood tests, then sent her to an oncologist, Dr. Naomi Marx, a Jewish woman whose first opening was in the new year. Frima felt that she'd finally landed in capable hands.

The oncologist took a detailed account of Frima's symptoms and her medical and health history. Diabetes? Pancreatitis? Smoking? Alcohol consumption? Obesity?

No. No. No. An occasional glass of wine. Obviously no.

"Is there a family history of pancreatic, breast, colon, or ovarian cancer?"

"I don't know anything about my biological parents."

"Adopted?"

"In my teens. The rest of my family was wiped out in the Holocaust when I was eight. My parents would have been in their thirties. From the little I remember, they were healthy. I have no recollection of my grandparents or aunts and uncles."

Dr. Marx suspected pancreatic cancer but needed to rule out other possibilities and see how far whatever was wrong had progressed. She ordered tests to get a clearer internal picture. Frima, already weak, was nearly undone by the imaging procedures—endoscopic ultrasound with a biopsy, CT and MRI scans—plus more blood work. She groaned when the oncologist handed her the list of appointments and preps. "I've already been poked and bled to death. The tests turned up nothing. Unless the other doctors missed something."

Naomi Marx told her not to blame them or the lab. "The pancreas is hidden deep in the back of the abdomen so early images may miss a tumor. Even proteins shed by the tumor don't show up in the blood until the cancer is at a late stage."

"How many stages are there?"

"They're numbered from 0 to IV, the higher the number, the more advanced."

"What number am I?"

"I can't say until I see all the test results. It's unlikely that you're 0 or I. Let's hope you're not at IV, meaning the cancer has spread to other organs in your body." Dr. Marx told Frima to come back the following week when she'd be able to give her a diagnosis and review treatment options. A week later, she gave Frima a brochure and a list of hotlines she could call for support.

When Frima got home, she put the brochure, unread, beneath *Knot*, and crawled into bed holding *Sisters* and Sugar. There was only one person she wanted to talk to.

***

"You can visit me now," Frima told Liane. "I bought a new couch and a comfortable armchair."

"What prompted these extravagant purchases?"

"I'll tell you when you get here."

"Saturday morning? Coffee?"

"Irish coffee." Frima read the brochure. Liane would have questions and demand answers.

Liane sprawled on the flower-cushioned chair. Frima poured coffee, added whiskey, and sat upright on the pale green sofa. "Are we celebrating or drowning our sorrows?" Liane asked.

"I have pancreatic cancer," Frima said straight out. "Stage Two."

"Oh my God. Two out of how many?"

"Zero to four."

"That doesn't sound so bad?" Liane's voice quivered; the hand holding her coffee shook.

"It is. I'm late Stage II. The tumor is already three centimeters and the cancer's spread to a few nearby lymph nodes. Not to distant sites or other organs so far, as best the tests can detect."

"Bottom line?"

"The five-year survival rate is thirty percent."

"Shitty odds." Liane drank up and refilled her mug with pure whiskey. "Why so low?"

Frima repeated what Dr. Marx had told her. "By the time the symptoms get bad enough to see a doctor, the cancer is already advanced."

"Undetectable tumor, my ass. Sounds like a defense against malpractice claims."

"Stop. You're not being helpful."

"Sorry," Liane said. "Excavating the past is as pointless as storing toenail clippings in a safe deposit box. What's next?"

Frima described the treatment that lay ahead, depending on what they found and how she responded: surgery to remove all or part of her pancreas and affected lymph nodes, three to six months of chemotherapy, and five or six weeks of radiation. "I'll be wiped out. Pukey too."

"You should have bought a puke-colored couch." Liane sat beside Frima and stroked her hair. Aging had burnished the red to a gray-flecked bronze. "I suppose this will fall out?"

"It depends on which drug they use. My doctor will decide that after the surgery."

"Do you want me to come with you?"

"No. I don't want you to watch me being tortured. Just be on call."

"Deal. I can sleep on the couch. Just don't ask me to clean your house."

Frima laughed, faintly. "Deal."

Liane held Frima's face. "You beat the odds before. You can do it again."

"I'll try, but I'm so damned weary. What if my fighting days really are over?"

"Then I'll keep you alive, just like I did in Berlin."

Frima interlaced their fingers. "Remember our suicide pact after White Columns accepted your work? If I die, promise you won't kill yourself after all. I need to know you'll keep making art."

"I promise. But I won't turn your death into a sculpture." Liane sobbed. "Just please, please come out of this whole, not in scraps."

They closed their eyes. Hours later, when Frima awoke, Liane had gone. Frima was covered by a blanket with Sugar tucked beside her. *Sisters* and *Knot* sat on the armchair. The dream she'd just had flooded back. Frima was a guest in a mansion and couldn't find the way to her room, where Liane was waiting. Whichever staircase she tried was wrong. Suddenly, Liane appeared at the top of the last flight of steps and shouted down, "Where the hell have you been?"

CHAPTER 46

Frima was napping between chemo treatments when the phone rang. She figured it was Liane, checking to see if she was drinking enough water. Frima hated the question as much as she hated drinking water after training her body to go without it as a child. But she'd be able to reassure Liane she was doing well. She'd returned to work a few weeks after surgery and only reduced her schedule twenty percent, although the treatment's cumulative effects might cut that more after upcoming rounds. Seeing students restored her energy and resolve. Meanwhile, staff and volunteers took up the slack and didn't pepper her with questions or advice. Unlike the family members who visited her roommate in the hospital after surgery and thoughtlessly shared their own medical mishaps. Or the chemo clinic, which wasn't private and didn't even have curtains around each bed. Other patients told horror stories of what Frima could expect, including death.

Rolling over, Frima waited to see if the hyper-vibrating sensation, a state of total alertness that sometimes alternated with exhaustion, would return. All was calm. She examined the pillow for hair, but so far the drug cocktail Dr. Marx had chosen hadn't caused it to fall out. Not that Frima was vain, but her hair hid the patches of eczema that sprouted behind her ears. Nor had she experienced nausea, although swallowing was painful since she'd developed sores at the back of her throat. "Thrush," the doctor had said, a disease Frima had read about in Dr. Spock when the kids were babies. A prescription mouthwash, mixed with baking soda and salt, had helped.

"Hello?" Frima picked up the new extension beside the couch. With phones in the kitchen and bedroom too, she never had to go far to reach one. Liane suggested she add a fourth next to the toilet, but Frima was too embarrassed. "Big deal," Liane had replied. "I've heard you crap plenty of times."

"Mother? It's me. Lisa."

Frima sat up quickly. She gasped from the residual pain of the surgery plus the shock. All those times Liane had been on the line when Frima hoped it was Lisa; now it was the opposite. The brochure had listed "cognitive fog" as a side effect of chemo, and Frima occasionally forgot things or lost focus, but the voice she heard was clear. They'd last spoken when Lisa was in her mid-twenties; she was now thirty, yet her forthright tone was unmistakable. The confidence was missing, however. Lisa sounded as shaky as Frima felt. Frima took this as a good sign.

"I … It's wonderful to hear from you." Frima leaned back and rearranged her body to find a comfortable position. It took a few seconds. "Sorry. I'm just so surprised that you called."

"I surprised myself."

"Why the hell now?" Frima nearly screamed but held the words inside her aching body.

"Sandra, Liane's daughter, convinced me to phone you."

Frima's heart sank. Sandra must have told Lisa that she had cancer, and her daughter was calling out of pity or duty. Pity was the last thing Frima wanted, and Lisa's overdeveloped sense of morality was what had driven them apart in the first place. "What did Sandra say?"

"She said I should call you to make *her* mother happy." Lisa chuckled, a genuine laugh. "Seriously, Sandra invited me to her engagement party. Liane wasn't there. It was a tough call, but Sandra thought it best to keep Liane and the Roses separate." Not a word about cancer.

"I gather Liane and her daughter's adoptive parents aren't anxious to meet either."

"The problem is Sandra and Howard, her fiancé, plan to have kids. Soon. She's five years older than me. It will be awkward juggling grandparents on birthdays and holidays."

"I can see that." The Oberlanders and Horners had split time evenly. Juggling a third ball would have thrown them off balance. But what did that have to do with Lisa calling her? Now?

Lisa answered her unspoken question. "I'm serious about someone too. Barry Klein. He's CEO of a new media company. Sandra's dilemma got me thinking how wonderful Bubbe Greta was to me and David. I don't want to deprive my children of their mother's mother. I mean, you."

"I don't want to miss knowing them. I don't remember either of my grandmothers."

"A speaker at my synagogue said it was easier to be a grandparent than a parent. 'Love without the responsibility' he called it. You saw how Bubbe Greta took care of David and me. So maybe being a grandmother will come easier to you."

"My mother doted on you. Unfortunately, that allowed me to take a back seat." Frima took Sugar's advice, blaming herself, not her daughter.

Lisa didn't take any responsibility but offered, "Besides, David said you aren't such a bad person and I should give you another chance. No promises, but I'm willing to try."

"So am I. You were brave to call me. Can I call you next time?"

After two seconds, Lisa said, "Yes."

***

Frima phoned her a week later. She'd had another nightmare where she'd searched frantically for a phone and when she found one, couldn't remember the number to call. Lisa answered on the second ring. "I expected your machine," Frima said. "You've always been out before."

"Not always. I have Caller Display. When your name came up, I'd ignore the call."

"And today ..."

"I picked up as soon as I saw it was you."

A good start. "We have a lot to catch up on. I'd like to know more about your work."

"I'm a lawyer."

"David told me. He's proud of his little sister. You followed in your father's footsteps."

"Sort of." Lisa sounded annoyed. "Dad's a tax lawyer, he works behind the scenes. I discovered I have a flair for the courtroom. I'd love to become a prosecutor."

"I can picture you in a courtroom. Even at your bat mitzvah, you commanded the bima."

"You were there? I'd forgotten."

Not such a good start after all. "Of course I was. I'm not observant but I don't deny my religion. Being Jewish matters to you. I want to understand its importance in your life." Frima's daughter reminded her of the students whose walls would come down if you asked them about themselves. And listened to their answers.

"I never questioned being Jewish. I just was. Daddy made sure we practiced our religion. When you refused to join us, it was like you didn't want to be part of our family."

"I'll try to explain. For you, being Jewish meant belonging to a community that was warm and welcoming. All your experiences were positive. For me, my religion made me an outcast. Judaism killed my parents and my brother, and left me cold, hungry, and scared all the time."

"The Nazis did that!"

"I know. Objectively. But children see themselves the way the world sees them. Nazis said Jews were dirty, dumb, and less than human. To leave that self-image behind, I had to reject that part of my identity." Frima hadn't meant to talk about herself, but she felt Lisa listening.

"I'm beginning to understand, Mother. I was in college, studying the Holocaust, when I first thought about *choosing* to be Jewish. Later, at synagogue, we discussed the importance of carrying on our religion. Only a few older members took part, none of them survivors. They didn't want to talk about the horror. It's my generation who wants to bring it into the open."

"The lessons you pass on can help all victims of bigotry." Did Lisa see that Frima, in her own way, was using her experiences to save her students? They just didn't happen to be Jewish.

"From the little I know, Judaism is based on admirable values. I'm grateful your father made it a key part of your upbringing." Frima was suddenly tired. "I'd love to continue this discussion. And see you. Will you come to my apartment for dinner next Sunday? Kosher, I promise."

Lisa hesitated. "I'm not ready for that."

"What if we meet for coffee?"

"Mmm. I'd like to see you, but the idea of sitting face-to-face makes me uncomfortable."

Frima grasped for a third suggestion. "Can you take time away from your job to visit me at work? I'm a principal now and I can show you around the school." Not only would there be other people around, but it was an opportunity for Frima to show Lisa another side of herself.

"I can do it Wednesday morning." Lisa's quick response was reassuring. And fortuitous. Frima had more energy early in the day. Maybe Lisa would agree to go to lunch afterward.

"Hadran alach, Mother."

"Your answering machine message ends with that. I always wondered what it meant."

"It's Hebrew for 'We will return to you.' You recite it when you finish studying a Torah tract as a way of saying that even though you're moving on, you'll come back to it again. At my synagogue, we say it instead of 'Goodbye.' It's a hope and a prayer that the parting isn't final."

***

The bell starting classes rang at 8:30. Frima had suggested that Lisa come at 8:00 and shadow her through the morning. Lisa arrived at 7:59. The sight of her jolted Frima. In the five years since they'd seen each other, her daughter had matured from a recent college graduate into a professional young woman. Her hair, dark like Bob's, was short and styled to emphasize the green eyes she'd inherited from Frima. She'd slimmed down and wore a trim burgundy suit. Only the way Lisa avoided looking at her and fiddled with the clasp on her shoulder bag signaled that beneath her daughter's poise, she was as nervous as Frima.

Frima introduced her to the secretary. "Lucky girl," the woman said. "Seeing how patient Ms. Horner is with our students, some of whom would test a saint, I bet she was a great mom."

"Mmm." Lisa studied the bulletin board and its notices in English, Spanish, French, and several other languages and alphabets.

Frima explained that at least one staff member could interpret for families from diverse backgrounds. "Somehow the kids communicate with one another on their own." A mother came in and handed Frima a bag from the pharmacy. They conversed in Spanish while her son peeked out from behind his mother's skirt. Frima knelt. "Buenos días, Santiago. Te echamos de menos ayer. We missed you yesterday." The boy held out his foot so she could admire his sneakers.

"Gracias, Señora Horner. Eres muy amable."

The mother thanked Frima and turned to her son. "¿Listo?"

When he answered, "Sí!" they left for his classroom.

"Santiago's in kindergarten, shy but very bright. Mrs. Amador brought in his new asthma medicine. Come with me while I give it to the school nurse, Fabiola Etienne. She's from Haiti, around your age, but she's lived in the neighborhood since she was ten. The families trust her."

Fabiola made some notes on a whiteboard, then smiled at Lisa." So, what do you do?"

"I'm clerking at a law office."

"Your mother must be proud. A public defender?" Fabiola asked hopefully.

"Um. We're usually on the side of the plaintiff." Lisa squirmed.

"Your mother set up a pro bono legal clinic at the school to help families with tenants' rights and employer discrimination cases. Maybe you could volunteer there?"

Again Lisa stammered. "I'm kind of busy, but I'll think about it."

Undeterred, Fabiola continued. "We also have a free health clinic on Saturday mornings. If you have any friends with a medical background, we can use volunteers there too."

"Thanks for the information. Nice to meet you." Lisa sidled toward the door. Frima followed her out. "Good grief," said Lisa, "does she think all Jews are lawyers and doctors?"

Frima laughed. "Parents in this neighborhood haven't reached professional ranks. Yet. Hopefully, their kids will. For now, most volunteers at those clinics do happen to be Jewish."

"Well, the doctors I know don't work on Saturdays anyway. Where to next?"

Frima kept up with her daughter's brisk pace. "It doesn't feel good to be singled out for being Jewish, does it? Even as a backhanded compliment?" Lisa didn't answer, but glancing sideways, Frima saw her tuck the Jewish star she wore on a chain inside her blouse.

The rest of the morning was spent visiting classrooms. Teachers drew Lisa aside to tell her how much P.S. 94 had improved in the eight years since her mother became principal. At noon, Lisa accepted Frima's invitation to treat her to lunch. At last, they faced each other. To Frima's surprise, her daughter reached across the table and squeezed her hand. The food arrived. Although her appetite was still shaky, Frima forced herself to eat. Cancer had no place in the relationship they were slowly forging. That news could wait. "So, what do you think?" she asked.

"You really have made a difference in the children's lives." Lisa traced a line in the marbled Formica tabletop and looked up at Frima, tears in her eyes. "I wish you'd done the same for me."

"I wish I had too. I'm so very sorry."

Lisa continued to look directly at Frima. "I'm not ready to forgive you. Maybe I never will. But Judaism commands us to do Tikkun Olam, repair the world. It's the essence of being a good Jew. Ever since I was little, I rejected you for rejecting our religion. Today, you showed me there's more than one way to fulfill that commandment. In essence, Mother, you are a good Jew."

CHAPTER 47

It took twelve months of calls, lunches, and shopping trips before Lisa agreed to have dinner at Frima's. By then, Frima had completed the grueling treatments. The chemical cocktails had exited her body; her mind no longer faded in and out. Her appetite was better if not robust, while the lingering after-burn of radiation rarely flared. Dr. Marx prescribed medications for whatever wasn't yet back to its BC, Before Cancer, state. Most important, periodic scans came back clear.

Frima made roasted chicken, noodle pudding, and yeast rolls and chilled a bottle of wine. All signs of cancer were stowed away except for her current prescriptions, which were in the medicine cabinet. She trusted her rigidly principled daughter not to look inside.

They began with a tour of the apartment. Lisa picked up *Sisters* and *Knot*, asking only, "Liane's?" Frima nodded, relieved that her daughter had no memory of either from childhood, and invited her to help make the salad. While Frima sliced tomatoes, Lisa went to get the lettuce. She stopped in front of the refrigerator. "Cancer?"

On the door was Frima's schedule to check her blood sugar level and take medications to boost her appetite and relieve pain. How could she have forgotten to take it down?

"I recognized the names of the drugs," Lisa said. "My law school professor took them. We met at her home when she wasn't up to coming to class. She had ovarian cancer. You?"

"Pancreatic cancer."

"That's the worst!" Lisa's hand flew to her mouth. "God forgive me. It just came out."

"It's okay. I know. But so far I'm beating the odds. Even my doctor is surprised." Frima grinned. "Naomi Marx, a Jewish woman. You'd like her." She peeled a cucumber and handed Lisa a salad bowl. "Our reconciliation strengthened my determination to fight."

"We've been back in touch for a year. Why didn't you tell me? Would you have told me at all if I hadn't found out on my own?" Lisa ripped the lettuce and hurled it into the bowl.

"Eventually." Frima added the tomato and cucumber. Lisa got the wine. They carried the food to the table.

Lisa spoke first. "On second thought, I'm glad you didn't tell me or leave a phone message to get me to finally call you. If I had, it would have been out of duty, not chesed."

"Chesed?" Frima asked.

"Another Hebrew term. The closest translation is the compound word 'lovingkindness.'"

"It's a beautiful concept."

Lisa nodded. "Pure. Unforced."

"To a pure mother-daughter connection. Untainted by obligation." Frima raised her glass.

Lisa returned the toast. "Does David know?" she asked.

"Outside of my doctor and a few colleagues, the only other person who knows is Liane."

"Can I tell him?"

"No. I will. He should hear it from me."

"Can I tell Dad?"

"That's up to you and your brother. Your father and I have no unsettled business but he has a right to know whatever affects his children. I'm not being secretive. I just want privacy."

Lisa said she'd respect that. They began to eat. Frima asked how Barry was doing.

"He's great. His company just got a contract to develop educational software."

"Sounds interesting." Frima nibbled her chicken. "I'd like to meet him."

Lisa twirled the stem of her glass. "Not yet. When we began dating, I said some horrible things about you. I need to fix that." She blushed. "I guess I exaggerated to earn his sympathy."

The pang that hit Frima wasn't from her surgical scar or indigestion. She joked to mask the pain. "Even as a little girl, you had a flair for drama. No wonder you're good in court."

Her daughter blushed. "Since I visited your school, Mother, I'm considering becoming a public defender, not a prosecutor. Helping people wrongly accused seems more ... Jewish."

Frima smiled. "You can put your histrionics to work garnering sympathy for underdogs."

Lisa's eyes sparkled. "I never thought I'd say this, but it matters to me that you approve."

"It matters to me that you care."

After dinner, they listened to Otto and Greta's favorite albums. Frima told Lisa about the years after she was adopted. "It wasn't easy for any of us, and I tested them. Weaker people might have given up and sent me back to Oyf Haskhole. I don't have faith in God, but I grew up believing in the force of evil. Your grandparents taught me to believe in the force of good."

"I'm glad you all stuck it out so Otto and Greta could become my zayde and bubbe."

Long past Frima's usual bedtime, Lisa got her coat to leave. "I changed my mind again."

"You're going to be a prosecutor after all?"

"No." Lisa giggled like she had as a little girl and hugged her mother. "I'm ready for you to meet Barry. Come to my house for Shabbas dinner next Friday?"

"I'd love to. I'll bring a challah." Frima would bring something else too.

***

Meeting her daughter's boyfriend this late in life felt strange but less fraught than when Lisa was young and always angry. Frima hoped she and Barry Klein would like each other, of course, but she wasn't out to impress him. Or correct Lisa's exaggerations. Frima cared about two things: That Barry be good to Lisa, and that she and Lisa continue to build on their own relationship.

Lisa's apartment in the East Bronx was bigger than Frima's. She had the entire top floor of a two-story brick-row house. Barry, sitting on the couch, stood up when he and Frima were introduced. He was a couple of inches shorter than Lisa, wiry, with a wispy beard and alert eyes.

"It's a pleasure to meet you, Ms. Horner." Barry extended his hand.

A nice, polite Jewish boy, Frima thought, as she shook it. "Please, call me Frima."

"Frima. I've heard a lot about you."

Lisa, her eyes wide, froze like a frightened rabbit.

Frima suppressed a laugh. "I've heard incredible things about you, too. Tell me about the computer programs you're developing. Lisa did tell you I'm an elementary school principal?"

"Yes. In a neighborhood where a majority of the kids don't speak English at home. I happen to be working on a program for English Language Learners." Barry described a game that paired pictures with words in English and another language, followed by sentences where children filled in a missing word. They scored one point for using their home language, five for using English. "We're beta testing languages that use the Roman alphabet."

"Public schools are enrolling more children from Korea, Russia, and Arab countries too."

"I know. Our demographics team is on top of that. We're creating a phonetic version."

"Ah. Then they must also know that schools with a preponderance of immigrant children don't have computers. Or the money to buy them." Frima settled back in her chair.

"Um, I guess so."

Lisa chimed in. "His company's development department works with foundations to donate hardware to schools in underprivileged communities." Barry looked at her gratefully.

"Then tell your development people to also drum up money to train teachers to use the computers. Most of them don't even know how to turn one on, let alone use your programs."

"I'm sure they've thought of that." Barry's tone was confident now. "Soon computers will be used to teach everything. Not just literacy but math and science. Even art and music, how to draw or play an instrument. My field is going to take off." He flashed Frima a self-satisfied grin.

"Sounds exciting, but machines can't replace hands-on learning. Children learn English best by talking with adults and other kids who already speak it. They learn math by manipulating objects, science by observing nature, art by picking up a paintbrush, and music by plucking a guitar. I'm not against technology. I just don't see it as a panacea. Or worship it as a savior."

"I'm not saying computers are gods. But educators who think like you will become obsolete." Barry folded his arms.

"Perhaps you're right." Frima hoped she'd be dead by then. But Barry's unintentional rudeness reassured her. His cockiness was a sign that he was well-matched to butt heads with her daughter.

Lisa stood. "If you two will excuse me, I'm going to finish setting up for Shabbas."

"I'll help." Frima followed her to the dining room, where Lisa handed her one end of a white linen tablecloth that used to belong to Greta and grabbed the other. The cloth billowed like a sail in a gentle wind as they lifted it and lowered it on the table. Frima set out the napkins.

Lisa fetched silverware and glasses from the sideboard. "How are you feeling, Mother?"

"Encouraged. I went for blood tests this week. The two markers aren't totally accurate—you can get a false negative or false positive— but they can suggest whether you have pancreatic tumors. Dr. Marx was pleased that both markers were low. The last scan also came back clean."

"You look good. Have you gained more weight?"

"I've put on ten pounds in the year since you first called. The doctor wants me to add a few more, but I'm in the target range. And my appetite is good. I'm looking forward to dinner."

"I'm looking forward to feeding you. You're going to beat this."

"I'm a positive person," Frima said. "But also pragmatic. Beating the odds means living longer, not curing what's incurable. I want to live long enough to see you get married."

Lisa kissed Frima. "Did you tell David yet? I don't want to say anything until you do."

"Yes. I phoned him this week."

"What did he say?"

"Will you leave me Zayde and Bubbe's jazz albums if you join the angel band?"

"Mother! How horrible."

Frima chuckled. "No, that's just your brother. Sweet as kosher wine but not touchy-feely. He made light of it but his voice shook. I told him dying was not on my To-Do ASAP list."

"Don't add it."

"I'll do my best to delay it. I have lots of years to make up for."

Lisa put two pewter candlesticks on the table and asked Frima to fetch candles from the top drawer on the left in the kitchen. Frima returned with them and a cardboard box she'd hidden in her satchel. The lid was water-spotted, the corners dented. She handed the box to her daughter.

Lisa caught her breath, lifted the lid, and unwrapped two frayed towels. "Hadran alach," she whispered. "Bubbe Greta's mother's candlesticks have returned." She replaced her plain pewter ones with the ornate silver pair and asked Frima to insert the candles.

"From Austria to America, across an ocean and a century. You're the fourth-generation owner." Frima recalled the Yiddish-German expression, "Zei gezunt. Use it in good health."

"Yours as well as mine." Lisa's green eyes found her mother's. "Dinner," she called.

Barry came immediately. He and Frima stood on either side of Lisa as she lit the candles and recited the blessing. Frima remembered another tradition. On Friday nights, after saying "Amen," Otto would bless her. Just as years later, Bob would bless David and Lisa. In the warm glow of the Shabbas lights, Frima placed a hand on her daughter's head. "Follow your own light. If you're a good person, who cares about others, then I'll know I was a good mother after all."

PART THIRTEEN:
LIANE (2000–2003)

CHAPTER 48

"Hi, Li. I decided I *will* invite you to my wedding." Sandra crowed as if I should be happy.

I switched the receiver to my left ear, where my hearing wasn't as good. It was another small indignity of aging, like thick toenails. At least I didn't drool, pee myself, or discover I'd put my keys in the freezer. "What changed your mind?"

"I can't keep you and the Roses apart forever. I'd rather you meet and work out the jitters before Howard and I have children which, God willing, will be soon."

"I assume your parents agreed? After all, they're paying for this shindig."

Sandra huffed. "Howard and I are footing the bill ourselves. It's not like we're struggling twenty-somethings."

"Well, Ms. Late-Thirty-Something, I didn't get a regular paycheck until I was older than you. Even then, I couldn't have afforded a fancy wedding like yours, let alone a honeymoon in Cancun." I switched the phone back to my good ear. "Answer my question about your folks."

"To be honest, they weren't overjoyed. I gather you're not thrilled either. But they said that inviting you was the right thing to do. You'll come?"

"For you." I also liked Howard, the easy-going heir to Lowenthal's Home Furnishings, which he'd expanded into a chain of hardware stores. In fact, I got along with him better than with my daughter, who never ceased trying to reform me. My future son-in-law and I talked nuts and bolts. He gave me his outdated models and damaged goods, whose parts were perfect for the smaller pieces I'd gone back to making now that I had mild arthritis in my thumbs.

"Nice to meet you," I said as I shook Ittel Rosa's paw that night.

Her eye regarded me dolefully. "You've known me for sixty-seven years. Are you going batty?"

"No, I'm going to Sandra's wedding and rehearsing meeting the Roses."

In the next few weeks, I soothed my nerves by drinking alcohol and making a series of slabs with a solid pair of objects on one end, a jangly single object on the other, and a magnetic figure in the middle that pulled the other three toward it. I didn't need a social work degree to interpret the family tableaux. My agent placed them with EcoArt, a new gallery that specialized in work made of recycled materials. "Environmental art is the future," Miranda gushed. "You're a natural, Liane." I didn't care. I just wanted to get past the shiny new wedding.

***

Ittel Rosa was wary of the copper wire earrings I wore, approved the pale blue dress, and raised a nonexistent eyebrow at the tatty fringe of the antique embroidered shawl. I sat halfway back in the synagogue during the ceremony, where I could observe unnoticed. I tried to spot Lisa among the bridesmaids but they all looked identical in daffodil-colored gowns. Sandra wore a tailored, off-white, calf-length dress. Her hair was twisted atop her head with a tiara of lily of the valley and seed pearls. She read a short poem she'd written to Howard. The verses about building a home together were corny, but I liked the line, "I love you for not sanding off all my edges."

I skipped the receiving line, but at the reception, introductions were unavoidable. Sandra led her parents to the corner where I was standing and cleared her throat. "Mom, Dad, this is Liane Asher. Liane, Joseph and Sylvia Rose." My daughter was keeping their last name. I didn't blame her. It was prettier than Lowenthal, and likely better for her career. Sandra surveyed the big room packed with guests, murmured, "I'll leave you to get acquainted," and made her escape.

Joseph was medium height and weight, with gray-brown hair but rosy cheeks and a warm smile. Sylvia, in heels, was his height but rounder. She wore a silky, ankle-length lavender dress and amethyst earrings set in gold filigree. Disassembled, they could have been turned into an interesting sculpture. She looked me up and down. I'd missed a mud splotch on my navy flats. I raised my glass. "Mazel tov. Howard's a fine young man. The newlyweds are well-matched."

"Yes. It's quite a simcha," said Joseph. He grabbed a small knish off a passing tray.

"He's not so young," said Sylvia. "Neither is Sandra. We're praying our daughter and son-in-law give the two of us grandchildren soon."

Joseph turned red and snagged a stuffed mushroom. "We three will work out an equitable time-sharing arrangement when, God willing, we all become grandparents."

I snatched my third glass of wine, smiled at him, and told Sylvia, "I have no desire to be 'Bubbe,' so the title is yours, or you can share it with Howard's mother." I turned back to Joseph. "You're very kind but you get dibs on time with the little ones. You raised Sandra, I'm Liane-come-lately, and I don't know squat about handling children until they reach adolescence."

Excusing myself, I followed a server to the kitchen and exited out the back door to the alley. It made me nostalgic for my days waitressing at Jim's and Goulash Garden. When I got home, I told Ittel Rosa, "Sandra will be miffed if her parents tell her I was rude to them."

"You're jealous," the bear accused me.

"You're right. And I feel bad about misbehaving on Sandra's wedding day." I changed into jeans and headed for my workbench. "But not too bad."

**

"Come for coffee," said Frima. "I have two pieces of news to share."

"Did you buy more furniture?" I asked.

She laughed. "No. I spend most of my time on the couch."

That ruled out my second guess, which was that she'd taken up Chinese cooking. "What's the news?" I asked.

"I'll tell you when you get here."

The last time Frima pulled this, three years ago, was when she announced she had cancer. I said I'd be there the next morning.

Frima was upright, grinding coffee beans at the counter when I arrived. We sat at the table laid with ceramic mugs, woven placemats, and fringed napkins. "Ugh. Crate and Barrel?"

"Lisa bought them. Her decorating principles are as firm as her religious beliefs."

I laughed, "Our daughters are like identical twins raised apart. So, out with the two pieces of news. Should I listen with my good ear or my bad one?"

"First, I'm retiring at the end of the school year. I'd planned to wait until seventy but hanging on another two years isn't fair to the children and families. I'm not up to it."

"You're tired, that's all. We're both slowing down." I refused to believe there was more going on. After all, I had less energy for my job, although not for making art.

"The Superintendent was supportive. Between my savings and public school pension, I'm okay financially. What I dread is not having work I care about." Frima pulled at a thread in her placemat. "I supposed I could volunteer on one of the service committees I set up."

"That's the spirit. I can make it to seventy, then work full-time making art. I'll get a small pension from the City. Sandra offered to help. As if I couldn't take care of myself. The bitch."

Frima wagged her finger and grinned. "The district's throwing me a retirement party. Will you come?"

"I'll pass. I might say something crude and embarrass you. I assume Lisa will be there?"

"She's helping to organize it. After she gets back from her honeymoon in Hawaii. That's the other big announcement. Lisa and Barry are getting married at the end of May."

"I know. Big Mouth Sandra leaked the news. She's Lisa's Matron of Honor." I hesitated. "That means you and Sandra will meet for the first time." I'd kept them apart for a decade, not even introducing them at my gallery opening.

Frima's unconcerned "Yeah" was a relief. Her focus was on Lisa. "Being mother-of-the-bride on her big day is my chance to make up for failing her as a child. Bob and I will cooperate to make sure everything goes smoothly. The divorce was long ago. We're on good terms now."

"Thank goodness I didn't have to do anything for Sandra's wedding other than attend. But I'm happy for you."

Frima and I clinked coffee mugs. "We're happy for each other," she said.

"Don't tell Sandra," I whispered, "but to be honest, our sisterhood is more important to me than motherhood."

"Don't tell Lisa," Frima whispered back, "but to be honest, I feel the same way."

CHAPTER 49

The ringing stopped by the time I reached my apartment but started again five minutes after I let myself in. A telemarketer, I decided; time I got Caller ID. Yet a premonition made me answer.

"Don't tell Lisa," Frima said, "but I'm calling you first. The cancer has metastasized."

"Meaning?"

"Bits of tumor that weren't detected before have spread. I'm waiting for the results of a PET scan to know whether I'm Stage III or Stage IV."

"Meaning?"

Frima explained. In Stage III, the cancer was still confined to the pancreas but had spread to four or more nearby lymph nodes. By Stage IV, it had spread to other organs, usually the liver but also the lungs, bone, or brain. "Either way, it's too widespread for surgery. Even if it's only in one more organ, the assumption is that undetected cancer cells have already reached others."

"Nuts and bolts crossed you're Stage III."

"Both are death sentences. The only difference is the amount time I have left. The five-year survival rate for Stage III is three to twelve percent."

"And Stage IV?"

"You're already dead." Frima sounded matter-of-fact.

I wanted to hurl every piece of hardware on my workbench against the wall.

"I'll let you know as soon as I get the test results," Frima said.

"Call Lisa and warn her now," I said. "Don't let on that you told me first. And when you get the news from the doctor, call Lisa first for real. I'd rather you phone me, but Lisa will be pissed at you if she finds out. I'm okay playing second fiddle." My voice broke like a cracked violin.

Two days later, a Friday, Frima rang. "Late Stage III. Dr. Marx phoned as soon as she got the results. Her office was about to close, but she didn't want to wait until Monday to call me."

"Did you tell Lisa?"

"Yes, per your instructions. I actually apologized for calling her on the Sabbath."

"And she said?"

"'Don't talk nonsense, Mother. Caring for the sick is a mitzvah. I'm here to help. Barry is too.'" Frima sighed. "Thanks for ordering me to call Lisa first. I don't have the strength to lie."

"Don't waste what you have thanking me. What's next to keep you stalled at Stage III?"

Frima told me what she knew so far. Chemotherapy might shrink or slow tumor growth. She'd get a drug called Gemcitabine, either alone or in combination with others. Radiation or a nerve block could relieve pain; a stent would help keep a bile duct open. "None of these is a cure," she reminded me. "At best, they'll prolong my life and make me more comfortable."

"Odds were you'd die when you were eight. I'm betting you'll beat the odds again."

"It's not your decision, Liane."

"It's not God's either. She wouldn't do this!" I shouted. Frima was silent. I told her to get some rest. I crawled into bed too and consulted with Ittel Rosa. "Sisterhood is like 60-40 solder. It creates the strongest bond. But is my bond with Frima strong enough to withstand her death?"

"I don't know," my bear answered. "I've never lost anyone."

I bargained with the Holy One's female persona. "Please Shekinah, I'll give up Sandra if You let Frima live." I slipped into sleep, straining to hear Her answer.

***

I pounced when the phone rang. I'd finally signed up for caller ID so I knew it was Frima. She shared more about the chemo and radiation she'd undergo. "I had a scan to map the radiation. I start Monday, five days a week for six weeks, half an hour per session. Chemo is once a week every three weeks. Dr. Marx will evaluate my progress after the second or third round." Frima's voice was surprisingly strong. "I've been through both before. I know what to expect."

"Will you lose your hair this time?" I couldn't bear the thought of her bald. Or bony.

"It doesn't matter. It's been a long time since I cared about my looks."

"I want you to still care. You're my favorite work of art."

"In that case, I'll do my best to oblige," Frima said.

Her number popped up again the next afternoon. "Shitty day," she announced. "I went to a chemo class where they gave me a binder with my appointment schedule. I came home, took a nap, and when I woke, I couldn't find the binder. I must have left it in the lobby. The notebook gave me a sense of control and I couldn't even manage to keep it. I'm so depressed, I'm not even sure I want to start treatment." Frima sniffled. "I feel better now. Thanks for letting me vent."

I accepted her thanks. Not that I needed to hear it, but she needed to say it. "This fucking disease IS out of your control. Of course, you lost it when you lost the binder. But, as I tell my clients, eventually, through small steps, you can restore that sense of control."

"You're the one in control. Thanks again."

Her gratitude was becoming a burden. "You gave me a lot of pep talks over the years. Now I'm giving one to you. Don't surrender to cancer."

"Thank you." Frima giggled.

"I'll give you more than a pep talk," I said. "I'll retire early to nurse you back to health."

"What about your clients?"

"I have only one client now. You."

"I don't know, Liane. Lisa can take me to appointments. In fact, the clinic prefers that patients be accompanied by relatives."

"Lisa's more interested in sniffing out incompetence so she can file a malpractice suit."

"I do believe you're jealous at the thought of Lisa taking care of me."

"Bullshit." But Frima was onto a different truth. "I'm jealous that your relationship with Lisa is smoother than mine with Sandra."

"Sandra will take care of you one day. Not because you have some terminal illness but because she's your daughter. Period."

"Is that why she keeps trying to improve me? Because she loves me?"

"The nice thing about being sisters, unlike mothers and daughters, is that we don't try to improve each other." Frima's voice grew urgent. "You don't have to be jealous of Lisa. Nor I of Sandra. Our relation-ships with our daughters are a blip in time. Yours and mine stretches across our whole lives. Our daughters look toward the future. We look back at the past."

"Stop talking as if you—we—don't have a future too. I refuse to let you die!" I didn't care that I was yelling like a bully.

"You're in denial," Frima yelled back.

"Leave the social work jargon to me," I snapped. "I know you'll survive."

"Based on what? Faith?"

"Crap on faith." I softened my voice. "Remember I once told you that Holocaust survivors coped with stress better than other people? Not because they have faith, which is fragile. But because they had hope, something concrete that they could work toward?"

"I remember. We held on by working for the next meal or place to spend the night."

"I have hope that you'll make it and I'll do whatever it takes—feed you, rock you, make you laugh—to reach that goal."

"I used to be the optimistic dreamer. You were the practical realist. We've switched."

My voice caught. "Like I said. Whatever it takes."

"Only don't retire," Frima pleaded. "Lisa would be devastated if I chose you and not her to supervise my treatment. I don't need you to be my manager. I need your energy to keep me going and the distraction of working with your other clients energizes you."

"Not as much as making art."

"Then cut back on your job and use that time to make art."

That was an order I could accept.

***

Frima called most days with updates. Even when she was low, I forced myself to stay high. After the first chemo session, she had a port installed, which made the second easier. "The Benadryl in the cocktail put me to sleep and the time flew," she bragged. "I haven't started to vibrate yet."

I congratulated her. "You sound like your old self. My spunky partner in crime." Two days later, when the effects of chemo usually hit her, I called Frima. "How goes it?"

"No nausea, although my appetite's gone. I can't focus. I'm dead tired." Frima sounded faint. "I tell myself to stay strong for Lisa and David. I don't let on that sometimes I want to give up. You're the only one I can be open with. Let me know if it's too much. I'll understand."

"No you won't. And you don't have to. It's never been part of our deal. Besides, I've been through enough nightmares of my own to handle whatever darkness you throw at me."

Frima's chuckle was mirthless. "Sometimes the light goes out of me. I feel fractured."

"Ready for a Kabbalistic midrash?" I asked. "A mystic Jewish story?"

"From Lisa, no. From you, I'm listening."

"You know the phrase 'tikun olam?' It's often translated as 'healing the world.' The story goes that evil came into being when Creation fractured God's divine light. The image is of a shattered glass vessel. Our earthly task is to restore the vessel's wholeness through good deeds."

"I can barely drag my ass out of bed. How am I supposed to do good deeds?"

"A positive attitude can restore the wholeness of your mind as you restore the wholeness of your body. You don't need to lift a finger. Just lift your spirits."

Frima sighed. "I'll leave the lifting to you."

The next time Frima called, she was more upbeat. I didn't remember her first bout with cancer being such a roller coaster. Something more than the chemo cocktail was taking her for a ride. I started to make up and down arrows on my kitchen calendar every time we spoke.

"My energy's back," Frima announced. "I'm organizing and cleaning out my apartment."

She sounded like she was preparing to die. Even if she was ready to accept that, I wasn't. "If you find any good junk, save it for me," I joked. "What else is going on with you?"

"I'm tired of talking about me. Tell me about you."

Frima was all that mattered in my life, but I did my best to amuse her. Imitating my agent Miranda, I bellowed, "Fair Frima, you strike me as more discerning than your friend. Someone who reads *The Times*. Perchance you saw Pepe Karmel's piece about Friederich Petzel Gallery? As you know, connections must be *cultivated* prior to being *consummated*. Ergo, I've arranged a coffee date with Mr. Petzel this Wednesday at nine. Liane will join us at nine thirty."

"Will you?" Frima sounded like my cheerleader of yore.

"Yeah," I said. "I can pretend to be stricken with a stomach bug at ten if the pretension is too much to take." Frima laughed. I bet myself that Lisa didn't make her mother laugh like I did.

"Won't Miranda be angry if you leave?" The concern in Frima's voice was touching.

"I can never predict whether she'll be pleased or pissed when I'm pissy. But she tries hard to find new outlets for my work and leaves me free to experiment. If I were a big money-maker, like her other clients, she'd be less willing to let me take risks. The arrangement suits me."

"So does ours," Frima said.

When she called a couple of days later though, I marked a down arrow on the calendar as soon as she said my name. "I'll be right there," I told her.

A pot of coffee, cold, was on the counter. Frima sat upright and rigid on the couch in a gold-trimmed green plush robe that I didn't recognize. Probably from Lisa. Normally green set off Frima's red hair, but today the color emphasized her sallowness. She patted the seat beside her, which I took, but instead of turning toward me, she addressed the opposite wall.

"Dr. Marx called. The Gemcitabine isn't working. I'm officially Stage IV."

I swiveled her face toward mine. "Can anything more be done?"

"I'm eligible for an experimental treatment, Folfirinox. It combines four drugs and might help me live longer."

"When do you start?"

"I don't."

"You have to wait until the drug you're taking wears off?'

"No. I'm not going ahead with chemo at all. Folfirinox has more severe side effects." She ticked them off on her fingers: Bruising, bleeding, diarrhea, dizziness, swollen face and mouth.

I clapped my hands over my ears. "I've heard enough."

Frima lowered my hands. "I've *had* enough. I want the poison to leave my body, take drugs to manage the pain, and die in peace. As you would say, continuing is as pointless as ..."

"Cleaning your eyeglasses with a dirty diaper."

Frima kissed me on both cheeks. "Thank you for understanding. And accepting."

I understood. I didn't want to accept. But this decision was Frima's alone to make.

"I'm ready to go," she said. "I got a second chance to be a daughter and a mother. I did work I'm proud of. Most importantly, I saw you succeed as an artist. I had no reason to hope. The odds were against you and I couldn't change them. But I always believed in you. Call it faith."

"You made me have faith in myself," I said. "Have you told Lisa?"

Frima stood and made a fresh pot of coffee. "I called her before I phoned you. She said it wasn't my decision. It was God's and God expects us to do everything in our power before we accept death. I stopped talking at that point. I was out of words."

"Did Lisa finally shut up?"

"She said if I had nothing more to say to her, and since I wouldn't talk to a rabbi, I should speak to a psychologist or social worker. It wasn't healthy to bottle up my feelings like she had."

"For shit's sake. There's no comparison. Lisa has her fucking nerve laying that old crap on you when you've done everything, despite being sick, to make it up to her."

Frima chuckled. "Jewish guilt." We sat at the table. "My daughter was right about one thing though. Talking helps. I can't share my feelings with a stranger, but I can talk to you."

I dumped sugar in my cup. "I also happen to be a social worker."

"Who accepts me as I am."

"Who always has." I sipped the coffee. The sweetness nauseated me. "Only do me one favor? Sit with your decision a few days before making it final?" Frima agreed. She was being polite, trying to ease *my* pain. I felt guilty for even asking.

Frima stared into her mug. "A woman in the bed next to mine asked if I ever wondered, 'Why me?' I answered, 'No. If not me, then who?' I didn't say it to blow her off. I meant it."

I nodded. "We learned not to ask that question. There's no rational explanation for why the Nazis targeted us. We were Jews, period. No other reason was needed."

"Just like no reason is needed for why some people get cancer." Frima returned to the couch and lay down. "God has nothing to do with it."

"She fucking better not." I covered her hideous robe with a blanket, turned off the light, and let myself out.

CHAPTER 50

When Frima announced her decision to Dr. Marx, the oncologist told her that she'd be dead within six months, twelve if she defied expectations. Frima's days of defiance were over as were my years of denial.

She enjoyed a respite after her body cleared itself of Gemcitabine and before she needed heavy doses of pain medication. I suggested we use that time to take a nostalgia tour of the places that marked our arrival in America. "Unless you'd find that morbid?" I asked.

"It'd be fun," Frima replied. "Our new lives were about to begin. We were together."

"Fifty-six years later, we still are."

We started at the refugee agency's "orphan camp," today a rundown Bronx apartment building. The sooty brick needed pointing and a cracked concrete path led from the sidewalk to the entrance. Iron bars covered the first-floor windows; a few on the upper floors had dented air conditioning units. We climbed the crumbling front steps and stood on the stoop. The front door was now made of shatter-proof glass so residents could see who was coming and going.

I peered inside. "You need a key or someone to buzz you in."

Frima and I grinned at each other. We sat on the stoop as though we lived there. Soon, a woman with three young kids unlocked the door. While she was distracted ushering them inside, we slipped in and pretended to fetch our mail from the boxes in the lobby until they got on the elevator—a change from our walk-up days. When the empty car returned to the lobby, I held the door open for Frima, assuming we'd ride up to the sixth floor, where we had once really lived.

"I want to take the stairs," she said.

"Are you sure you're up to it?" I asked.

"The Gestapo isn't chasing us. We can stop at every landing if I need to catch my breath."

The only thing chasing us was time. I followed Frima so I wouldn't climb too fast for her. The hallway was deserted. We stood in front of the apartment door, remembering the welcoming blue letters framed by sunflowers: OYF HASKHOLE—CAMP BEGINNING.

"Pity we can't knock," said Frima. "The tenants might suspect intruders and shoot us."

"Back then, the neighbors saw as enemies, misfits, and potential law-breakers too."

"In the end though, most of us did all right." Frima smiled. "Even you." She leaned against the wall and accepted my suggestion that we ride back down. While she rested in the lobby, I took the stairs to the basement. Anoush's old apartment was now a storage area filled with half-stuffed couches, busted bedframes, and three-legged tables. Nothing worth salvaging.

Walking to the Grand Concourse was a trek so we took the bus. Frima insisted on paying both fares. After getting off, we strolled the short block to Loew's Paradise Theatre, now called the Paradise Theater. It was surrounded by scaffolding. A sign explained its history. The old movie house became a multiplex twenty years ago, closed in 1994, and stood empty for six years. A new owner began restorations three years ago to turn it into a film and concert venue.

Frima and I stood by the ticket booth where we used to lure customers. The Seth Thomas clock over the entrance was gone, but the theater's exterior was otherwise intact. The façade, recently sandblasted, glowed clean and warm in the late spring sunshine. I wondered aloud if the soldiers we'd lured, now impotent old men, savored memories of their times with us.

Frima shuddered. "I don't. Do you?"

I stepped back to look at the front of the huge marquee, whose letters spelled COM NG SOON. "I don't miss the fumbling sex in the balcony, but I do miss the victorious sense that they were poorer for the encounter and we were richer."

Frima shook her head. "I didn't feel richer. Remember my favorite film, *Margie*, about a mom and her teenage daughter? The only thing I felt was poor that I didn't have a mother."

"And then, like in the movies, you got a rich one." Frima's laugh made me feel wealthy.

We weren't allowed inside, where traces of the multiplex were being demolished. It was just as well; we wanted to preserve our memories, especially the marble fountain of a child riding a dolphin and the auditorium with stars twinkling on the ceiling. As we turned to go, I saw on the side of the marquee: GRAND REOPENING 2005. "We'll go," I told Frima. "My treat."

Frima shushed me. "That's two years too late. Let's enjoy today."

Two blocks north, we passed the corner where Alexander's Department Store once stood. Our place to steal clothes and costume jewelry was now a discount mini-mall. Our last stop would be Jahn's Ice Cream Parlor, where we'd gone with our pickups and introduced our high school friends to each other. I groaned. "Remember when Betty and Joan got into a hot fudge fight?"

"I wish I'd had a jar of hot fudge sauce the day I caught Joan with Bob. I should leave her one in my will."

"Shut the fuck up about your will. Enjoy today, remember?"

Frima wanted to walk downhill to Jahn's, now a Starbucks. Tiffany-style lamps and red leather booths had been replaced by wood and chrome. Customers pecked at laptops. "So much for ordering a kitchen sink," I said. We flicked milky froth from our Ventis at each other.

I sipped my coffee. The caffeine sobered me. "Everything changes or disappears."

Frima slid her cup across the table until it touched mine. "Our sisterhood is constant."

"I wish you were like Loew's," I said, "and could be restored to your former glory."

We finished drinking in silence. I hailed a cab. Frima fell asleep on the way home.

***

Three months later, in the middle of a heat wave, Frima was in the hospital. Although she was under hospice care, guests were restricted to family members and visiting hours. Hospice tried to administer her pain medications so she'd be most lucid during those times.

"I'm here to see Frima Horner," I told the sour-looking nurse at the reception desk.

She checked her logbook. "Her son and daughter are already in the room. You are?"

"Liane Asher."

"I don't see your name on the list of family members."

"I'm her sister."

"Asher is your married name?"

"No. She was adopted. I wasn't."

The nurse frowned. "Sorry. There's no Asher in Mrs. Horner's medical records either."

"Ask her children."

"We're supposed to minimize interruptions while patients are with their next of kin."

I crossed my arms. "No rush. I'll wait."

She stomped off. Moments later she returned. I smirked. "What did they say?"

"That you were their mother's sister. I asked if you were their aunt." The nurse scratched her ear. "They said no but reaffirmed you were Mrs. Horner's sister." She waved me down the hall. I thanked her. She shrugged. "No point making a fuss when the patient will soon be dead."

It was quiet inside Frima's room. All the whirring and beeping machines had been turned off. The only tube was the one delivering pain medication. Frima was asleep, breathing shallowly but evenly.

Lisa stood beside the bed; David, in a chair by the window, stood up when I walked in. They said they'd be in the family lounge and to let them know when I left.

I pulled the chair alongside the bed and stroked Frima's hair, which was fanned out on the pillow. When I saw the brush on the nightstand, I silently thanked Lisa for taking such good care of her. I interlaced my fingers with Frima's, whose nails were trimmed.

Frima's eyes fluttered open. "I was dreaming that you were arguing with a hearse driver, refusing to pay the fare."

"It was a limo. I was your date for the prom." I swiped a pink carnation from a vase, bit off most of the stem, and tucked the stub in the top buttonhole of Frima's pale green pajamas.

She raised and twisted her head to look at the flower. "Thank you. It's beautiful."

"Shall we dance?"

Frima's head flopped back. "I'm afraid I'll have to sit this one out. All the next ones too."

"You're leaving me again," I wailed. "I won't allow it."

"It was you who pushed me out the first time. When the Oberlanders came, you shoved me out the door. You said I was holding you back and you needed to be free of me."

"I lied. Because it was best for you. Nothing good comes of your leaving this time."

"I know. But if you hadn't said those cruel words back then, I might have stayed."

"Which would have been the end of us."

She squeezed my hand with surprising strength. "When I was child, I longed for a mother. When I grew up, I pined for my daughter. All I needed was a sister and I had you all along."

I squeezed back. "And I had you, tied to me tight as a knot."

We released hands. Frima folded hers on the blanket and closed her eyes. "Our daughters will carry on our sisterhood. Lisa promised me that she and Sandra would take care of you."

"I can take care of myself." I told Frima I'd be back. I didn't say when. Half of taking care of myself had been taking care of Frima. I had no idea how I'd do either without her.

CHAPTER 51

Lisa called me the morning that Frima died. In keeping with Jewish tradition, the funeral would be the next day at Lisa's synagogue, the same one my daughter attended. Their rabbi would lead services in the sanctuary and at the graveside, where Frima would lie next to the Oberlanders.

Frima's death didn't surprise me. The service did. "Your mom wanted a Jewish funeral?"

"She never said what she wanted."

I gripped the receiver. "Take it easy," Ittel Rosa cautioned. "Lisa's just lost her mother."

Tough shit I thought, and yelled, "Religion had nothing the fuck to do with who Frima was."

Lisa's voice was tight. "It's not your decision, Liane. It's our family's."

"I'm family too."

"You're my mother's sister, but you're not part of the family." Lisa told me what time the service started. "Sandra will be there. Do you need directions or will you come with her?"

"I'm not coming at all. I'll invent my own ritual." I slammed down the phone. It clanged with the finality of death.

***

The following Sunday, Sandra brought a copy of Frima's will. "Lisa asked me to tell you what was in it," she said. "She'll come around eventually, but she doesn't want to talk to you yet."

I tossed a cushion at the wall. "She'll be ready to talk to me before I'm ready to speak to her. What's in the will that could possibly concern me anyway?" Lisa was welcome to the ugly clothes and furniture she'd helped pick out and I'd never learn how to use the damn coffeemaker.

"David gets the record collection, if that's of interest. More important, she left *Sisters* to me and *Knot* to Lisa."

Without analyzing Frima's logic, I knew she'd made the right choice.

Sandra continued. "You get Sugar, to keep Ittel Rosa company."

My bear would be happy. I told Sandra, "I promised to leave Ittel Rosa to you. Now you'll also inherit Sugar. It's up to you whether to keep both or pass Sugar along to Lisa."

"Hopefully, that's a long way off." Sandra picked up the cushion and tucked it behind me. "Frima also left you this." From her tote, my daughter handed me a shoe box tied with twine and a card with my name on the envelope. She waited for me to open them, but I set them at the back of my workbench. I was no readier to lift the lid or read the note than I was to talk to Lisa.

I was ready to make a sculpture for Sandra and Lisa to share now, however. They hadn't yet earned the title *Sisters II* or *Knot Redux* so I settled on *The Next Generation.* It was a bit larger than the small pieces I'd gone back to making and fashioned from different materials: gold and silver wires, shiny but inexpensive gemstones whose flaws were hidden beneath a polished surface. I stopped after I'd laid everything out, unsure how to fasten the parts. I'd leave the work unfinished until I saw how Sandra and Lisa's relationship developed.

I was equally unsure how I'd develop. Frima and art had been the two pillars of my life. Sandra was important, but when I'd bargained to save Frima, I'd offered to give up my daughter, not my art. Now that one of the two pillars holding me up was gone, I was afraid I'd topple.

"Suppose you had to choose between Frima and art?" Ittel Rosa asked.

I'd survived without Frima since the day she was adopted, which I wouldn't have done without art. With Frima gone for good, my life might be shakier but I wouldn't collapse.

"We never fully comprehend death's finality," I told my bear. "We expect the dead to reappear. As a child, I expected my mother to come find me. When she didn't, I felt betrayed."

"You're no longer a child," Ittel Rosa pointed out. "You know better."

"Death is still hard to grasp, let alone accept. But I won't let myself feel betrayed by Frima. I know where to find her, and she'll never stop looking for me."

***

The trees were bare when I finally opened the note:

Dear Liane,

Make a new whole from these scraps.

Eternally, Frima.

I opened the shoe box and smiled. Inside were small, well-used objects. I'd been searching for a ritual to honor Frima. Now she'd given me what I needed.

First, I reaffirmed my vow not to make a sculpture commemorating her death. Closure wasn't what I sought. Freud was right when he said that some losses should remain. Then I laid out Frima's gifts on my workbench: kitchen utensils, a faucet, a house key, pliers, and wire cutters. Finding food, water, shelter, and the tools to make art had been the mission that kept us alive in the years after we met and created the bond that kept us together for the rest of our lives. Finally, I began an untitled work, assembled from scraps, forged into a new living shape. Such is the knotted art of sisterhood. Fragile yet solid. Rusted and shining. A work that lasts forever.

ACKNOWLEDGEMENTS

Like the two women in *The Sister Knot* who defy the forces that work against them, writing a book requires unwavering determination, a willingness to bend the rules, and a large dose of support. I could not have succeeded in creating this novel without all three.

I am grateful to those who offered unflagging encouragement as this book traveled from concept to completion. The "sisters" in my "Sunday Writers Group" offered commentary, course correction, and cheers to keep me on the path. For their guidance, I offer special thanks to Marty Calvert, Janet Gilsdorf, Cynthia Jalynski, and Danielle Lavaque-Monty. The novel began with the story "Orphan Camp" which was critiqued during workshops with the "sisters and brothers" in my "Saturday Writers Group." For their help, I am indebted to Lawrence Coates, Amy Gustine, Marni Hochman, Keith Hood, Danielle Lavaque-Manty, Paul Many, Cathy Mellett, Polly Rosenweig, and Sonja Srinivasan. To all the fellow writers with whom I hone my craft, may we continue to learn and grow, commiserate and celebrate, together.

The Sister Knot is the fifth novel I've published with Vine Leaves Press. Their faith in my writing is invaluable. Alana King green-lighted this book's selection and copy edited the manuscript. Melissa Slayton's keen insights about the narrative and her willingness to work with me made for a smooth and productive developmental edit. Amie McCracken designed the book's interior and shepherded it through production. Above all, I am in awe of Jessica Bell, who founded the press, designs the covers, and anchors our amazing international VLP community of authors and staff.

Although the "family" in this novel was born of necessity on the streets of Berlin during the Holocaust, I treasure the ties that were formed under less traumatic, but often trying times, in my own family. I'm thankful for the resilience derived from my genes and upbringing, notably my grandmothers Mindel Alsofrom and Lillie Savishinsky, my parents David and Kate Savishinsky, and my brother Joel Savishinsky. I would not be "me" without the family I created when I gave birth to my daughter Rebecca Epstein, and the family she created with my son-in-law Milton Dixon and my grandsons Oscar and Emmett Dixon-Epstein. They rejuvenate and sustain me.

Finally I must give a shout-out to the pioneers of the women's movement in the 1960s and 70s. Of all the social movements I joined in those decades, feminism was the most formative in my development and continues to motivate my activism today. Sisterhood is powerful!

Part One of *The Sister Knot* was adapted from the short story "Orphan Camp" (*Summerset Review*, Winter 2019).

VINE LEAVES PRESS

Enjoyed this book?
Go to *vineleavespress.com* to find more.
Subscribe to our newsletter:

The Man with the Pink Sombrero

DENNY DARKE

Papillon Publishing

Copyright © 2024 by Denny Darke

All Rights Reserved. No part of this publication may be reproduced, stored in a retrieval system, or transmitted in any form or any means – by electronic, mechanical, photocopying, recording or otherwise – without prior written permission.

The Man with the Pink Sombrero is a book of fiction. It's not real. Like a Disney movie or swimming breaststroke to Jupiter. The characters in this book are entirely fictional. Any resemblance to actual persons, living or dead, is entirely coincidental. Names, characters and incidents either are the product of the author's vivid imagination or are used fictitiously. The opinions expressed are those of the characters and should not be confused with the authors. However, *La Noche de Rábanos*, or the Night of the Radish, is an actual event that occurs on the 23rd of December each year. The participants in the radish carving contest usually emanate from Oaxaca and the neighbouring communities. Any religious or secular rationale for *La Noche de Rábanos* used in this publication is fictitious.

No portion of this book may be reproduced in any form without written permission from the publisher or author, except as permitted by Canadian and U.S. copyright law.

Denny Darke and *The Man with the Pink Sombrero*

"Wildly inappropriate, politically incorrect, insensitive, ridiculously offensive. I loved it."
—Gwendoline, 84, Cheltenham.

"The best book that I have EVER read."
—Jeremiah, San Francisco, aged 5.

"Someone in my congregation informed me that SOMBRERO was the work of the dark angel, and the author had, cleverly, written subliminal occultic messages throughout the book that could be understood when read backwards, much like the some of The Beatles records were *backmasked*. Apparently, SOMBRERO has been *bookmasked*. Unfortunately, I read the entire book back to front and found no evidence of this."
— Rev. Howard Jones, The Drink the Kool-Aid People's F'Tang F'Tang Tabernacle, Atlanta, Georgia.

"Wow! Darke is SO totally Dark. This dude writes with an acerbic twist. SOMBRERO is both salty and boujee—it makes you want to say, 'yaas I wish Jimmy was my bae.' Dude, it's so lit and cray enough to float my boat. So, sorry, not sorry if you don't think this bookie wookie is not the GOAT. Peace out, bruv!"
— A. Random-Bloke, THC & CBD Academy, Brixton.

"I loved the book; it made terrific fuel for my campfire. The trouble was that I lost my iPad, cell phone and Kindle with a 7″ display in the flames on the same day."
— Ron Staggasaurus, Florida.

"You need to read this book bigly."
— Dr. Augustus Wiseman, Professor of English at the University of Klingon, Wisconsin.

"I fink it's good, a bit like me mum's pies. Tooooo many big wurds for me and me famjam."

— Harry the Dog Jr. Isle of Dogs, London.

"The book verged on every kind of ridiculous hyperbole imaginable. I bet Darke isn't the author's real name. That said, I did like Maria Tortuga and would also meet her in real life. I have written a few articles and wonder if she would like to read them, with the view of publishing them in *Le Figarola?* If Jimmy still has "contacts" within *Coastal Life* Magazine, he can use my "Greensingles" dating site contact address. Fred's ex, Tonya, sounds like another person I'd want to date. I'm on Tinder under the tag name of 'Malcolm Eco Green Warrior.' Can you also ask Raul if his speech issue was healed temporarily when he visited Mella's house in the latter part of the book?"

— Malcolm Poskett, Stonehenge, UK.

"Darke's debut book is his best work yet!"
—J.W.H. Myers, Coastal Life Magazine.

"I'm really proud of my grandson. Any one messin' with my Denny will have me to answer to!"

— Charlotte Darke, aged 133

To the beautiful people of Mexico.

To Shelley, one of the kindest-hearted people I have ever known.

To my children.

ONE

To Move a Mountain

Señor Montannah Montana was a dedicated landowner who worked hard to cultivate his farm in Mexico. The first names of the Montanas were always mountain-inspired, reflecting their deep connection to nature. "Our extensive family line is reminiscent of a massive mountain range," Montannah would often assert. These included:

Montanakilamanjaroa,

Everestmontana,

Kaytwomontana,

Mountfujimontana,

Matterhornamontana.

Sometimes, every fifteenth Montana born would be given an amusing or more tongue-in-cheek name, like their great-uncle Montanafontanabanana.

Raul and Fred broke the mould, as the family could not go against a prophetic proclamation given to their mother, Guadalupe, before their birth. Some extended family members were relieved, as the Montanas were running out of mountain ranges to choose from.

Señor Montannah felt blessed when the Lopez family demanded he grow cannabis and coca plants for them, as the soil on his land was incredibly fertile. He was bored producing maize, coffee, sugar cane, beans, tomatoes, bananas, pineapples, mangoes, papayas, cacao, and avocados.

Not only was it exhausting, but it just wasn't boujee enough for his tastes. Montannah was overjoyed to participate in the 'Make Mexico Green and White Again' initiative, as he deeply revered the environment. He'd also rake in insane amounts of cash from selling drugs.

Cartel boss Armardo Lopez soon became terrific friends with the Montanas and swore Montannah's children would one day become his left and right hands. To drive the point home, he cut his own hands and made a blood covenant with Montannah, who did the same, swearing an oath his sons would serve Armardo until their last breath.

Subsequently, Armardo, the twins' godfather, was at their birth. His wife, Francisca, had been longstanding best friends—soulmates, really—with Guadalupe Montana. Guadalupe had exceptionally sharp, chiselled features; she was once told by a brave soul her face was like a sculpture made by a disgruntled artist who had been high on magic mushrooms. Francisca had reassured her pal she was a strikingly attractive woman with a strong, regal presence. The Lopezes were excited about the delivery; they wholeheartedly believed it heralded something special. A divine being, the Blessed Red Virgin, had visited Guadalupe and prophesied over her.

After the birth of the twins, the local newspaper, *Le Oaxaca Sol*, reported:

Good News: Oaxaca mother delivers twin baby boys.

The Bad News: One is enormous and the other tiny.

The newspaper's editor and the reporter disappeared the next day. The storyline was swiftly reprinted as:

Good News: Oaxaca mother gives birth to IDENTICAL twin boys.

Bad News: Family, friends and medical staff cannot differentiate between them.

According to the story, Mrs Montana claimed the Divine Entity accurately predicted her twin sons' names, Raul and Fred, and they would be impossible to tell apart. Divine revelation foretold the fame of the Montana boys throughout Mexico. She recounted the Red Virgin's vision depicted two wolves fiercely protecting the alpha of the pack from predators.

The editor of the highly respected and best-selling newspaper, *Le Figarola*, had heard about the non-identical/identical twin 180-degree turnaround by *Le Oaxaca Sol* and contacted the Montana family. He asked for an interview with Guadalupe Montana to clarify the perceived flippity-floppity of eye-witness accounts.

Initially, Mrs Montana was hesitant. However, the editor promised her front-page headlines and a free three-month advertising spot in the paper for her homemade products. Ultimately, he persuaded her of the value of adverts in *Le Figarola*, as they would expose her merchandise to the paper's vast daily readership.

Guadalupe's 'Lil Red Riding Hood extra strength CBD gummy bear edibles and Triple C cocaine-infused cookies proved to be her most successful domestic items, unbeknownst to the editor. He was horrified when he finally learned about the treats' secret ingredients. Drugs, advertised in his paper? He'd have to pay several drug-enforcing entities significant sums to avoid being imprisoned or sentenced to death.

Of course, where there were drugs, there was also crime. Fearing for his safety, the editor instead sent Maria Tortuga, an impassive Colombian and the most junior rookie of all his journalists, to the Montana's home. He had long wanted her gone; her precocity and hubris drove him nuts. If she were to unfortunately "disappear" like the reporter from *Le Oaxaca Sol*, he would be spared the indignity of forking out any severance pay by firing her, which he was on the verge of doing anyway.

The editor instructed Maria to wear a yellow top, a blue skirt, and a pair of knee-high red boots for a visit, symbolizing the Colombian flag. The editor told her the Montanas were wannabe Colombians who loved Colombia more than life, and they had essential business connections there. The truth was the Lopez and Montana families utterly loathed Colombians due to longstanding bad blood between cartels. Rumour had it, if Armardo Lopez entered politics and became president, he would obtain gravity bombs, short-range missiles, and artillery shells, all of which would be equipped with nuclear warheads from North Korea or Iran—and use them to nuke the shit out of Colombia.

Finally, as her *pièce de résistance*, the editor commanded Maria to drape herself in the Colombian flag and sing the Colombian national anthem, '*¡O, gloria inmarcesible!*' when meeting the Montanas. He gave her strict instructions to find out the veracity of *Le Oaxaca Sol's* article about the 'miracle' twins and lied on a stack of Bibles that *Le Figarola* would print verbatim whatever she discovered, and her name would become legendary in investigative journalism. He waved her away, hoping that was the last time he had to see the condescending and arrogant little shit.

⌁⌁⌁ ⌁⌁⌁

DURING HER PREGNANCY, Guadalupe refused to have amniotic tests. This was much to the chagrin of the doctors, as they feared she was in danger of losing Fred. An ultrasound revealed he had thick, dark hair in the womb. He was so hairy, in fact, the doctors were worried he might be a werewolf. Montannah Montana laughed when he saw the images, as he thought his son looked like Fred Flintstone. His name had been more prophetic than anyone could have guessed.

A reporter had been dispatched by Mexico's leading newspaper of integrity, *Le Figarola*, to interview Guadalupe about the miraculous events surrounding the twins' birth. Maria Tortuga was an attractive woman with delicate facial features, and shiny raven-coloured hair pulled back into a ponytail. Thanks to the cute freckles scattered across her nose, Maria appeared younger than her age. At a mere twenty-four years old, she had grand ambitions to become the *crème de la crème* in her profession.

Now living in Guadalajara, Maria found it difficult to disguise her melodic Colombian accent. She wanted to integrate and immerse herself in Mexican culture and was determined to sound more Mexican. Maria tried hard to develop a lisp when she spoke English so her *s's* became more like *th's,* which fooled no one, as most of the people she met only spoke Spanish. In her natural Colombian accent, Maria spoke slowly in a dulcet, singing tone. Spanish speakers from different countries loved her voice; however, hardcore, patriotic Mexicans tended to hate it. Her best friends and colleagues described Maria as young, attractive, aspiring, narcissistic, and annoying.

Arriving at the Montana's hacienda in her flashy Mustang car, Maria was determined to make an excellent first impression, so she complied with the instructions given to her by her boss and draped a Colombian flag over her trendy suit. She looked forward to meeting the pro-Colombian Montana family. Maria pushed open the half-ajar door of the large farmhouse, knocked, and walked straight in, where she saw the nursing mother fully engaged with two hungry babies suckling both breasts. Maria stood to attention, put her hand on her heart, and started to sing '*¡O, gloria inmarcesible!*' Aside from her *el tricolor nacional*, Maria was also dressed in a fetching yellow jacket, blue pants, and a pair of red Gucci knee-length boots, just as she'd been told.

Guadalupe's first instinct upon seeing this stranger wearing Colombian colours and singing the National Anthem of Colombia was to punch her right in the mouth. Instead, she took the higher ground and simply told her, "*Cierra la boca,*" or "Shut your mouth." Without being asked, Maria walked over to a chair, dusted off some biscuit crumbs, and sat beside the mother.

"You have some nerve, young lady!" snarled Guadalupe.

"Please call me Maria," said the reporter with a smile.

Guadalupe displayed her disdain by spitting a large loogie on Tortuga's feet. "We don't get on with your type, you Colombian devil."

Thankfully, Ms Tortuga wasn't offended, or if she was, she hid it well. Her stolid disposition made her well-suited for situations like this, when she was forced to get a story out of a hostile environment. Maria took a handkerchief from her jacket, wiped the spittle off her boots, and assumed Guadalupe struggled with postpartum phlegm issues. She took out her state-of-the-art dictation device, pressed record, and set it on her knee. Showing off her pearly-white teeth, she again smiled at Guadalupe, "Tell me about these wonderful twin boys."

Bearing in mind the deal she had struck with the newspaper, Guadalupe wiped her mouth and tried to make herself more at ease with the insensitive bitch. "Well, young lady, I feel incredibly blessed. My boys were born healthy, robust, and identical. They are every mother's dream."

Maria looked at the babes, and her characteristic composure faltered as she gasped in astonishment. Fred and Raul weren't even remotely similar, let alone identical. Raul, who stared at her without blinking, was a long, slender giant of a baby and was as bald as a coot. Fred, on the other hand, had a mop of black hair and was clearly a little person. Even as an infant, his limbs were noticeably smaller than average. The news that *Le Oaxaca* had reported them as identical twins shocked Maria.

"Yes, my identical twins, Raul and Fred, not only look like mirror images of each other, but when they are older they will be able to do anything the other sets his mind to. They are perfectly alike in looks and in abilities. A true miracle has occurred in the Montana family."

This caught Maria off-guard, but by now she had collected herself, and did no more than lift one of her beautifully sculptured eyebrows in surprise.

Guadalupe continued: "If my Raul became a champion pole vaulter or high-hurdler, Fred would follow in his brother's footsteps."

Ms Tortuga snickered. She had never met anyone living in more willful denial.

"Is something amusing to you?" asked Guadalupe angrily.

"No, ma'am," Maria lied. "So, let me clarify what you just said. If Raul grows up to be a tall, strapping, seven-foot basketball player—"

"He's a tall one, isn't he? Raul is such a vigorous nurser," interrupted the proud mother, gazing lovingly at him. "And so is his voracious brother," she finished, breaking into a grin as she turned her eyes to Fred, who was attached to her other breast.

Maria gave a sweet smile and continued her question. "If Raul can jump high above the hoop and slams the basketball through the net—"

"Sounds like my boy," chuckled Guadalupe.

Tortuga cleared her throat. "Mrs Montana, are you asserting that Fred Montana, who by all appearances will reach a full adult size of three to four feet, will be able to execute the same manoeuvre?"

"Of course. What are you getting at?"

"Err, Mrs Montana . . . did the paediatrician not tell you?"

"Tell me what?"

"Fred has a condition called achondroplasia."

Guadalupe furrowed her brow, pressed her lips together, and raised her chin in defiance.

The reporter stated in a matter-of-fact tone, "Despite Fred being a remarkably handsome boy—" She briefly halted, inhaled deeply, and summoned all the tact and diplomacy she could gather, "He'll be as big as Tyrion Lannister in *Game of Thrones*."

"Go to hell! You arrogant devil woman," yelled the infuriated mother. Maria Tortuga stopped the tape recording, picked up her notebook, and got up from her chair. Making the sign of the cross and snarling, the unhappy Guadalupe yelled at the reporter, "The Blessed Virgin herself had prophesied my boys would be identical twins. Who should I believe? A Divine Source or a Colombian paparazzi slut?" Then, hocking up another loogie, she again bid Maria good riddance.

It was then Ms Tortuga noticed Don Armardo Lopez standing in the shadows, listening to the conversation. His amber eyes bore down on her like a predator staring out from the dark, and as he stepped into the light, she saw that his face was contorted into a horrifying scowl. For the second time today, her composure failed her. She froze where she stood as her blood ran cold. Everyone in Mexico knew the leader of the terrifying Wolfpack Cartel. He walked towards her, each footstep resounding like a crack of thunder in Maria's ears.

"The boys look good, eh? It's absolutely impossible for me to tell them apart. They are my lovely godchildren, and Guadalupe is the dearest companion of my wife. She is in regular communication with the Red Lady. If Guadalupe likes something, it's safe to say we will too. What she despises, we loathe," he said while mimicking a throat-slashing gesture.

Maria's knees buckled beneath her as she trembled uncontrollably.

"Anyone who upsets our dear Guadalupe upsets us both. Whoever insults *her* insults my wife and me." Emboldened by his support, Guadalupe began flinging expletives at the reporter, sounding less like a mother nursing her children and more like an officer at a naval base. Don Armardo hushed and calmed her, and commanded Maria to sit back down. She hurried to obey. After Guadalupe fell silent, the cartel leader spoke in a voice as cold as Maria felt.

"Here's how the rest of this interview is going to go. You will do your job and report the truth *exactly* as it is told to you, and bring the story of my miracle godsons back to your editor. If you do this, you will live to write your drivel another day. If you do not, we will know, and we will wrap you in your Colombian flag and lay you to rest in a crocodile's belly. Or maybe we'll do it the old-fashioned way and stick you in a barrel of hydrofluoric acid. Everyone's all about being eco-friendly these days, but it can be such a pain. Sometimes you just want to get it done quick and easy, you know? Quick and easy for me, anyway. You, not so much."

Maria was now faced with a choice: her journalistic integrity or her life. With Don Armardo looming over her, staring at her the way a wolf might look at an injured rabbit, the choice was easy. She looked at the twin boys and their snarling mother and, rubbing her eyes, said, "I'm so sorry, my contact lenses must have fallen out." Retrieving eye drops from her purse, she applied the stinging fluid and blinked a dozen times. Her artificial smile widened as she looked back and forth at the suckling babies.

"It's glaringly apparent, Don Armardo Lopez, the boys are absolutely identical in every conceivable way!"

"And?"

Swallowing hard, she answered, "And Mrs Montana had a miraculous visitation from the Divine Red Entity, the Virgin of the Radish, who had accurately told her the boys' names would be Raul and Fred, breaking Montana's mountain range tradition for naming firstborn sons. The Divine Entity's name is so incredibly holy that if *Le Figarola* were ever to misuse it, a lightning bolt would fall from heaven and turn our office to ash."

"And?"

"*Le Figarola* will publish this account on the front page with the headline 'Multiple Sources Verify Birth of Miracle Montana Twins.'"

Guadalupe continued to snarl, even more wolflike than the Don. "Remember the three months of free advertising, too. Your worm of an editor promised."

Armardo, who had walked closer and was now hovering directly over the reporter, "Make it six months."

"Of course," muttered Tortuga, her voice shaking uncontrollably.

Armardo added, "Multiple source verification is good. You will include the names of the verifiers, including Pope Felix the Eighth, The President of The United States of America, and our national hero, Carlosus Sultana."

Maria's heart was racing, and she couldn't catch her breath. "B-b-b-b-but what if the Pope, the President, and Carlosus Sultana," Maria crossed herself several times after saying Sultana's name, "sue for defamation of—"

"They won't," Don Armardo replied, his voice dripping with confidence.

"Sir, forgive me for asking, but how can you be so sure?"

"The Pope and The President are both on my payroll."

Maria gasped, "And C-C-C-Carlosus Sultana? The same Carlosus Sultana who sang 'My three-legged friend,' or as sung and hopped throughout Columbia, '*Mi amigo de tres patas?*'"

"Yes, the very same Sultana. He is my dear friend, and his music . . . soothes me." As imperious as he sounded, with the threat he made earlier lurking behind his every word, Maria heard in his sincerity a chance to earn Don Armardo's goodwill, or at least keep him from killing her in a brutal fashion. She began to speak effusively of her admiration for Sultana, and of how the three-legged doggy song had a profound impact on her life. By the end of her story, Armardo's stern expression had melted away, and a small smile was playing at the corners of his mouth.

"Rupert, or Rupee, was the Weiner dog's name. I was the one who inspired him to write the song."

"Oh my gosh, Mr Lopez, how did you inspire one of the greatest Mexican songs of all time?"

"I had been hanging out with Carlosus and asked him when he would release his next record, as it had been a few years since his last hit. He told me he had put his songwriting on hiatus, as he was far too busy caring for his beloved Rupee. As I sat in his shrubbery, drinking a cup of hibiscus tea, his stumpy-legged sausage dog kept growling and snarling at me. Suddenly, he jumped up and scratched my hand with his long claws. I whipped out my garden secateurs, grabbed Rupee, and trimmed his nails. Unfortunately, I snipped off too much and removed his whole leg."

Maria gulped loudly.

"Carlosus was inspired by his dog's loss. My friend was also concerned *his* fingers might be next *unless* he wrote a new song for me. The rest is history. '*Tres Piernas,*' or 'Three Legs,' was released soon after. I believe it has sold over forty-million records."

"What happened to Rupee?"

"Rupee's still alive and kicking—well, not so much kicking as hobbling. The wretched dog was still yapping away the last time I visited Sultana a few months ago."

Two

The Journey

THE MORNING OF THEIR departure was hectic; the flight had been delayed a whole day, which meant the Myers family had to stay an extra night at the hotel. Jimmy and his young son Max went through Lucy's carefully packed suitcases to find their swimming gear, which resulted in a disordered heap of clothes and belongings being scattered around the hotel room. The hotel reception called first thing in the morning, reminding Jimmy the shuttle bus had arrived. The passengers were waiting and keen to leave the lobby. Jimmy and Lucy had forgotten the hour time difference between home and Calgary. Aware that missing the shuttle would result in further chaos and delay their journey, Jimmy haphazardly shoved everything into the suitcases as quickly as he could, much to Lucy's chagrin.

They dashed downstairs, checked out, and hopped onto the shuttle bus after putting their two large suitcases and hand luggage in the rear of the vehicle with Max's smallish bag. Halfway to the airport, Jimmy couldn't remember where he had put one of the two items where he kept their money and his important documents. He had decided to split them between a forest-green Lululemon belt bag and his expensive Burberry charcoal-coloured travel wallet. The latter held all nearly all the vacation cash and a spare credit card; he had not heeded Lucy's advice to give everything to her or put it in the two-litre Lululemon bag. Jimmy had insisted on holding their money, understanding she would be preoccupied with Max, who was experiencing his first trip abroad. Lucy took responsibility for their passports, insurance, and other essential documentation for the journey. Jimmy felt the bag draped over his chest, but when he patted the pockets of his cargo pants, he felt no sign of the wallet.

What had started as a relaxed, cursory check of all his pockets devolved into an aggressive, more frenzied pat down. Jimmy asked Lucy if she'd seen his Burberry wallet. She hadn't. He kept checking himself furiously; they had already gotten on the shuttle, and the prospect of asking the driver to stop and let them off was unappealing. It would be an awkward conversation, and going back to the hotel to check for the wallet would only put a damper on their vacation. So Jimmy did what all impatient, ill-prepared travellers do: he hoped he'd just misplaced his wallet and convinced himself it would turn up somewhere in their belongings.

When the shuttle bus finally arrived at the airport, Jimmy shoved his way through the crowd to be the first one off, picked up a cart, and put all their bags on it.

"Did you make a final check of the room? I was busy packing and I didn't get a chance," he asked Lucy as she disembarked to join him. She found him crouching by the contents of his green belt bag, which he had taken out and laid on the floor. He was scouring them intently and beckoned her down to help. He was so intent on finding his wallet he didn't even notice the indignation on her face.

"None of us got a chance! We all rushed out to catch the shuttle, remember? Just take a deep breath, put your things back, and keep going. You probably tossed your wallet in with the luggage by mistake," Lucy replied. Jimmy didn't respond. He was unusually quiet, his face ashen and his frown lines prominent. After looking over his things and determining his wallet was not among them, he did what Lucy said. He put his bag back on and he, Lucy, and Max took their luggage and hurried through the terminal.

The gate attendant made the final boarding call for their flight, and the passengers hurried to board the plane before the doors closed. Jimmy began to feel nauseous. He was lost in thought, retracing his steps in hopes of remembering where and when he'd last had his wallet.

"It'll turn up, honey. Let's enjoy the flight, eh?" Jimmy turned to see Lucy beside him, looking concerned. He gave her a halfhearted nod and tried his best to take her words to heart. During the flight, he ordered a glass of red wine and attempted to watch the in-flight entertainment. He flicked through the available options:

The Notebook
P.S. I Love You

Lost
Planes, Trains, and Automobiles
The Lost Boys
Dumb and Dumber
American Loser
The Jerk
An Idiot Abroad

The last one caught his attention; "an idiot abroad" is exactly what Jimmy felt like. His family had just set out on a three-month adventure, and already he might have lost his wallet. They hadn't even gotten to Mexico yet. He whispered a sarcastic and silent thank you to the universe for the in-flight entertainment's reminder they were going on vacation with only a few dollars just before the holiday season.

When the plane landed after the six-hour trip, Lucy was cheerfully playing with Max, telling him they were now in Mexico and talking to him with an exaggerated 'May-hee-coh' accent. Jimmy gazed at her and reminded himself of how lucky he was to have her in his life. She was a beautiful person, both inside and out. Jimmy knew full well he was married to a stunner, with her sparkling, emerald-green eyes, short, light brown hair, full lips, and well-proportioned body. She still had a cluster of freckles, which made her look younger than she was. Lucy spoke beautifully, each word rolling off her tongue with the musical lilt of her Welsh accent despite having lived in Canada for half her life. But what Jimmy loved most about his wife was her graciousness, kindness, and fabulous sense of humour. She was doing her best to keep his and Max's spirits up while, if the situation were reversed, he knew he would have accused her of misplacing the wallet.

Jimmy made a conscious decision to stop beating himself up over his blunder and think positive. As he anticipated his first cold cerveza on foreign soil, his thoughts drifted to the clinking of glasses, the chatter of locals in the background, and the feeling of a cool beverage in his hand with the sun beating down on him.

ARRIVING AT PUEBLO de Velásquez Airport, Jimmy saw the immigration queues stretched for miles. The crowds of tourists were corralled into lines that snaked through the area, resembling a ride at Disney World. The airport's air conditioning was not working, and the body heat from the multitude of visitors, crowded into never-ending queues, was not making the masses of new arrivals any more cheerful. Max was getting restless. Lucy stripped off as much as possible without being indecent, but her remaining sub-zero winter clothing still made her sweat profusely. Although the warmth and humidity were welcoming, they were causing her to overheat.

"That's Mexico for you!" moaned a fellow passenger in front of the Myers family, indicating the long lines. Some other travellers were pushing their way to the front of the long file of clammy, perspiring Canadians, aggressively declaring, "I'm a resident. Make way for a resident." To Jimmy, this sounded like code for, "Step aside, turd. I'm super-important and need to get to the front!" No one else knew whether they were or were not supposed to push to the front. However, these folks knew the ropes and decided to jump the queue. Jimmy looked at the much shorter line for 'Nationals,' 'Residents,' and 'Landed Immigrants,' and muttered to himself.

His thoughts drifted back to his missing wallet, and he cursed to himself periodically as he unconsciously patted his Lululemon bag. Already, he was back to beating himself up. He couldn't help it; he would've been stressed even without the missing wallet.

"Let it go, Jimmy. It's either in the checked baggage or we really have lost it, and either way it's too late to look."

"I *have* let it go," lied Jimmy. "I'm pissed off. I keep getting bumped into by these jerk-offs." Jimmy hardly muttered another word throughout the entire ninety-minute wait in the oppressively-hot airport with the insufferably-rude people. He was looking forward to being reunited with their baggage, getting to the condo, and going through their bags one item at a time.

Finally, they reached the immigration official's kiosk. Jimmy was sweating so much his wet shirt clung to his body. Garcia, a stern-looking immigration agent, began to question him.

"What sum of money have you brought into Mexico?"

"You won't believe this, but—"

"I don't want your life story; how much money did you bring into Mexico?"

"About thirty dollars." That was all Jimmy had left in the Lululemon bag.

"Thirty dollars? Are you an idiot?"

"No, as I was trying to explain—"

"That you are an idiot abroad?" Interrupted Agent Garcia. Jimmy frowned and nodded in agreement. He certainly was, but he didn't need to hear it from this snarky immigration agent.

"How long you stay in Mexico?"

"About three months."

"Ten dollars a month? You think we Mexicans are stupid?"

"Yes, to the latter," Jimmy said flippantly, still thinking about the 'idiot abroad' comment.

"You say I am stupid?"

"Umm, no, sorry."

Agent Garcia was tall and had a commanding presence—a solid-looking square jaw and stubbled face gave Garcia a no-nonsense appearance. He motioned for another agent to approach, and an equally stern-looking agent named Espinoza to approach, and they complied. This official wore their uniform with pride and professionalism. With short-cropped hair, the agent looked like a dead ringer for Demi Moore in G.I. Jane. The two officials spoke to each other in Spanish. Espinoza, with pursed lips, tutted, shook their head in disapproval, and folded their arms across their chest.

"So, you working here in Mexico?" asked Agent Garcia.

"No, sir, we are on vacation."

"You here for three months?" probed Garcia.

"Yes, sir," Jimmy said, relieved to be back on topic.

"And all you have is thirty dollars?"

"Yes."

"You here to sell drugs?"

"Absolutely not."

Agent Garcia turned to his colleague and said in English, "That's what they all say." Espinoza touched her chin and nodded in agreement. She was scrutinizing Jimmy as if he was a suspect in a crime.

"You sell your ass for money?" pressed Agent Garcia.

"*What*?"

"You sell your body for money in the *romántica quarter* of the city?"

"No! For goodness' sake, I'm with my wife and child."

"You sell *them* for money too?" Espinoza chimed in, indignant. Jimmy rolled his eyes and shook his head. Agent Garcia also shook his head and asked, "How does a family of three intend to survive in Mexico for three months with just thirty dollars to your name?"

"I lost our money on the way from Calgary to Mexico. I'm going to call my bank to send us more."

"That's what they all say," Espinoza muttered under her breath to her colleague.

"How you do this stupid thing?" Garcia snapped.

"I don't know, but I—"

"You think I'm stupid, but you are the stupid one," Garcia interrupted, clearly still sore over Jimmy's earlier comment.

"Yes, that's true," said Jimmy with a nod.

"So, you *do* think I'm stupid?"

Lucy had been listening to the conversation between Jimmy and the two officials, and she moved forward to speak on behalf of her husband.

"Please, Agent Garcia, we did lose our money. We have money in our bank at home and will ask them to wire us enough to live here for three months."

"Why do you choose to be with such a loser of a guy?" enquired a puzzled Agent Espinoza.

"Because we're married, and he's not a loser."

"He loses money, yes? Why be with him if he loses all the money?" Garcia added.

"Because I love him," Lucy said matter-of-factly. She turned to her husband and smiled. The two officers looked at each other, surprise written on both their faces. Their attention went back to Jimmy.

"How much did you lose?" Garcia asked.

Lucy sighed. "About five thousand."

"We talk to him, not you," barked Agent Espinoza. Lucy held up her hands in a gesture of apology.

Garcia asked Jimmy once again, "So, you lose five thousand?"

"Yes, I can't find it. It may have been stolen; it may be in our luggage."

"It could be up your *culo peludo*. You look there? You sat on it, and it got lost in the jungle, yes?" sniggered Espinoza.

"*Culo peludo*? What does that mean?" Jimmy asked, although he had enough context to make a guess.

"My colleague, Agent Espinoza, thinks you have a hairy ass. Maybe you lost your wallet up there and didn't realize . . . and you might have hidden narcotics up there too!"

"What?"

"Maybe your ass is so hairy that you think we couldn't find any wallets, money laundering equipment, weapons of mass destruction, or other contraband if we looked up there," said Garcia, who looked at Jimmy with a furrowed brow.

"My ass isn't hairy," gasped Jimmy. Then the officers turned away from him and began talking loudly in Spanish amongst themselves. Jimmy asked Lucy what they were saying.

Lucy sniggered. "*He* said something like, 'Do you think this foreigner is a lying shit?' *She* replied, 'Yes, his donkey face suggests he's a drug mule and has half a ton of heroin up his arse.'"

"I don't have a hairy ass," Jimmy remonstrated, at a complete loss as to what else to say. Whatever he said, these agents would just misinterpret it. Lucy, however, had had enough.

"*¡No señor! Él es un buen hombre,*" she blurted out. They both looked at Lucy, let out a dismissive sound, and continued their conversation.

"What did you say, Luce?"

"I said you were a good man."

"Please tell them I don't have a hairy ass. I had it waxed before we came."

Lucy sighed.

Before she could say anything else, Agent Garcia whipped his head around and stared directly into Jimmy's eyes. "You are sweating like a suckling pig who is about to be spit-roasted . . . just look at yourself, sweaty little piggy. You not only sell your ass at the *Malecon,* but you might have five kilos of cocaine or heroin up there too."

"Or a meth lab," added Espinoza.

"Oh, come on, guys! It's humid here, and we've been overheating. I have nothing up my ass."

"*¡Culo de burro!*" Garcia shouted indignantly.

"Donkey's arse," Lucy interpreted helpfully.

"No, he is a *culo peludo,*" stated Garcia, who picked up Jimmy's passport, opened it, and read out, "Hameee Eellungtun Orashow Myuurs."

"*¿Qué clase de nombre es* Horacio? Wellington?" said Espinoza. She chuckled and looked at Jimmy. "*¡Su nombre es estupido gringo!*" Garcia joined her, both officers began laughing heartily.

"What are you saying? What's so funny?" Jimmy asked in utter confusion.

Lucy translated, "They think your middle name is the most stupid gringo name they have ever heard." Jimmy scowled, but said nothing. At this point, he was convinced the best way to make his case was stay quiet.

Finally, Agent Garcia said, "Listen here, I stamp your passport, but only because your wife has an honest face."

"Thank you, sir," said Lucy; then, turning towards Agent Espinoza, she said with a kind smile, "And thank you, Ma'am."

Agent Espinoza looked at Jimmy, "You, I no trust. I do not want to see you in the *romántica quarter* of town selling drugs or your gringo *culo peludo*, do you *comprender?*"

Jimmy went scarlet but said nothing. He looked down at his son, as if realizing for the first time that Max had heard everything.

"Welcome to Mexico!" Agent Garcia said with a broad grin as he stamped all three passports.

Jimmy's face was so red it looked like he had already been sunburnt. Being utterly humiliated in front of his wife and son was quite possibly the worst way he could have started this vacation. However, Lucy found it hilarious, as did Max, who was laughing as much as his mom.

"What's a hairy arse, Mamma?"

"It's a hairy *ass*—a horse-like creature with long ears that makes a braying sound." Max frowned and looked confused.

"Never mind, sweetie. I'll explain later."

They made their way to the large baggage collection terminal and collected their luggage from the carousel. They were relieved to find all three cases were present. They walked off with all their luggage, and came to an extensive line of people waiting to pass through customs. Jimmy thought the entry into Mexico would never end. He also hoped the rude and inappropriate immigration officials hadn't flagged him and he wouldn't have to endure a body cavity search. Thankfully, the three of them were able to negotiate customs without incident; they passed the dozens of time-share workers and finally entered the busy arrivals section of the terminal.

The arrivals exit was a chaotic mess of people, signs, and posters. Every hotel and travel agency had a representative holding up a sign with either a name or company logo scrawled on it. Much to Lucy's relief, Jimmy had prepaid for a cab when he made the booking. He was glad too; this way, they wouldn't have to figure out how to get out of here. The last thing he needed was another embarrassing interaction.

"Okay, we're looking for a guy named Juan," he said, scanning the roiling crowd. As he did so, he took a quick picture of himself and Lucy and sent it to the holiday company in the hopes they would recognize them and could help with their money troubles.

"Do you think he'll be holding a welcome sign?"

"Maybe. I don't know."

"I wonder what it'll say? 'Mr Hairy Arse?' Or maybe just 'Gringo Drug Mule?'" Lucy leaned close to him as she spoke so Max wouldn't hear, but Jimmy still covered his ears as he stared daggers at his chuckling wife.

"Not funny," he muttered. She kept smiling; evidently, she disagreed. Jimmy, who had just about had it with jokes at his expense, marched ahead of her and Max with two of the suitcases. They hurried after him, Max pulling his small, fluorescent blue *PAW Patrol* case.

Juan, the cab driver, was standing at the back of the throng of people. He was waving and wearing a huge smile. He had a white button-down shirt with barely-perceptible sweat stains around the armpits, and black slacks.

"Hey! Mr Jimmy Myers? Over here!"

The Myers family was finally on their way to Los Piñata.

THREE

The Oversharing Cab Driver

OUTSIDE THE AIRPORT, JIMMY was still recovering from the emotional abuse he'd suffered. Karma was a bitch. He messed up the beginning of their vacation by losing the darn wallet, all because he hadn't listened to his wife, and the universe had delivered swift retribution in the form of the immigration agents from hell. Still, he knew he had to stop playing the victim card and move on. There was a whole three months of vacation ahead, and he couldn't blame the agents for being suspicious; arriving in a foreign country with thirty bucks and expecting to live there for nearly three months, it was little wonder the officers had interrogated him. He took a deep breath, looked up at the blue sky, and felt the sun's warmth. *Life is pretty good right now, all things considered.*

Juan, the cab driver, was from Chihuahua and spoke English well. He placed the Myers' bags into the rear of his black sedan and asked if they wanted to stop at a grocery store on the way to their destination, a resort called the White House, or *La Casa Blanca*. Juan mentioned a huge supermarket on the highway, ten minutes from Pueblo de Velásquez Airport. He said it was the perfect spot to buy alcohol and gather supplies before reaching Los Piñata. With the holiday season in full swing, he worried nearby stores might either be low on goods or closed for a few days. Lucy still had her credit card and knew that few places in the small town used them. She thanked Juan for his advice and agreed they should quickly stop at the grocery store.

Once there, Jimmy reminded Lucy to buy some 'essentials,' like rum, tequila, wine, gin, and stacks of beer. Lucy rolled her eyes, took Max's hand, and disappeared into the store. He saw an opportunity to search their bags again, hoping to find his missing wallet. Juan, however, was a chatterbox, and he didn't notice his passenger was preoccupied and struggling to answer his questions. Soon Juan began talking about his lineage, though how he'd reached the subject Jimmy had absolutely no idea. As he delved deeper into his Ancestry.com research, he became more animated, gesturing wildly to emphasize his points. It seemed like Juan was talking about 8,000 years of his family line, and he wouldn't stop yakety-yakking. If Jimmy was going to get his ear talked off while looking for the wallet, he could at least learn something useful. He attempted to change the subject by asking about Los Piñata; Juan was happy to oblige.

"Señor, Los Piñata is a wonderful place. The locals are friendly, and they appreciate the gringo dollar."

Jimmy asked about day trips, local artisans, and the best places to eat and drink. He also asked if Los Piñata was safe, as Mexico had a sketchy reputation for violence, kidnappings, and corruption.

"Is it safe, amigo? Well, it's safe for gringos."

"What do you mean?"

"The locals must watch what they do. People who upset the cartel tend to go missing, if you know what I mean."

"Cartel?"

"*Si*, there are several cartels in Mexico. The cartel controlling our area is the most violent, called *El Cártel Manada de Lobos*, or The Wolfpack Cartel." For the first time since Juan started talking to him, Jimmy turned his attention away from his search. If by some stroke of misfortune he ran afoul of the cartel, he'd lose more than his wallet.

"Why is it safe for us but not for you? My family will be here for three months. Won't we run into this . . . Wolfpack Cartel?"

"Mr Myers, you will not see them because you're a gringo. The cartel does not want to upset gringos because of tourism. Tourism is perfect for business, and what is good for business is good for the cartel. You see, *El Cártel Manada de Lobos* tax the merchants' takings."

"They can do that?"

"*Si. El Cártel Manada de Lobos* is very influential, you see. They have so many connections that they are like another branch of the government. We must pay

Federal Taxes, cartel taxes, or both. Those who don't pay taxes to anybody get taken away and their bodies end up in *El Río Cocodrilo.*"

"What is *El Río Cocodrilo?*" asked Jimmy.

"The River of Crocodiles. Bones and body parts are a common sight on the riverbank, often washed ashore by the current." Jimmy, whose stress was mounting throughout the entire conversation, felt it leave him in an instant like air out escaping a punctured balloon. The Wolfpack Cartel, the River of Crocodiles . . . it all sounded like something out of a TV show. It couldn't be real.

Jimmy laughed, "Come on, Juan, stop winding me up. I'm dumb, but I'm not that dumb." He had done a deep-dive into the resort on Google, and found no mention of this Crocodile River. However, this cartel stuff was far more entertaining than listening to Juan explain how his ninth-generation relative had given a blowjob to a well-known Mexican general. Even if it was probably made up for his benefit.

"It's all true, Mr Myers. *El Río Cocodrilo* runs through several towns from the highlands of Jalisco, and it empties into the ocean at Los Piñata."

Jimmy merely smiled. He was convinced affable Juan liked to tell tales to his clients to spice up the trip, and he was okay with that, as Lucy and Max weren't in the vehicle. Otherwise, they would be a bit freaked out by the talk of crocodiles.

"*El Cártel Manada de Lobos* is not to be taken lightly, as their hitmen, known as sicarios, are notorious for their brutality. Their sombreros come in different colours, showing their position in the organization's hierarchy." Juan continued, "Fancy-dancy sombreros are worn by 'capos' who supervise the organization. The big boss doesn't wear one, only his important underlings."

"Juan, you sure know a lot about cartels. How do I know you're not in one?" Jimmy teased. Just then, he noticed Lucy pushing the trolly of provisions towards the vehicle and Max trailing behind, holding a new dinosaur stuffy. Lucy was also carrying a large plastic bottle containing lime green-coloured Imodium in case they got dodgy tummies. Max was pretending to drink the liquid from the closed bottle. Lucy was telling Max not to do that because it was a drink for adults.

Jimmy and Juan clambered out of the car and started moving the contents of the shopping trolley into the spacious sedan. Lucy and Max sat in the back and buckled up. Jimmy had taken the front seat so he wouldn't have to listen to Max's grumpy complaints for the three to four-hour drive. Plus, that way Juan could keep telling his endless supply of tall tales. Lucy was keeping Max entertained, and neither of them were listening. At least, Jimmy hoped they weren't.

The cab driver was all too happy to discuss his personal life and people's run-ins with the *El Cártel Manada de Lobos*, and Jimmy, with nothing better to do on the ride to Los Piñata, was happy to listen. Juan kept on talking, increasingly put-off by Jimmy's flippant attitude towards the cartel. He said he hadn't taken it seriously either until his best friend Alejandro, a local jeweller, suddenly disappeared, along with Alejandro's brother, uncle, and nephew.

"One day, they were here. The next, they were gone." Jimmy, who had previously been slouching, sat up a bit in his seat and looked at Juan. He knew the cartel was just a titillating story. It had to be. But something in Juan's tone was making him doubt his earlier instinct.

"What happened?"

"Alejandro's fine jewellery business was a front for dealings with the cartel, but he vanished after reportedly short-changing them. Soon after, we discovered his snazzy shoes along the shore of *El Río Cocodrilo*. His relatives' shoes were with them." Jimmy waited to see if Juan would smile; he did not.

"Then, a load of half-eaten heads washed up along the river bank. The police claimed they could not identify any heads, but everyone in Los Piñata knew what happened to poor Alejandro and his family." Jimmy turned in his seat, craning his neck to peer back at his wife and son. Max, having exhausted his complaints, was leaning against Lucy and appeared to be asleep. Lucy also had her eyes closed, and if she was awake and listening, she was doing a good job of hiding it. Jimmy hoped neither of them were hearing the morbid conversation happening in the front.

"Wow! I thought Los Piñata was just a sleepy town by the ocean. You make it sound like the wild west."

"Yes, *señor*. But for tourists, it is not so bad. You've just got to remember not to mess with *El Cártel Manada de Lobos* . . . and don't ever owe them money. Don't let them do you any favours, and you'll be fine. You're a gringo, so they won't bother you." Jimmy was sure if what Juan was saying was true, there wasn't any way he or Lucy would get into the cartel's crosshairs.

"Alright then. Thank you for the warning, Juan. Now let's change the subject. My wife and son might overhear, and I don't want to give them anything to worry about." Juan nodded empathetically in agreement, but he simply traded in one upsetting topic for another. Somehow, he landed on the subject of his sexual history, and Jimmy learned much more about the man than he had ever wanted to. He now knew Juan had contracted STDs twice and fathered children with two different women. Juan also revealed he struggled with *hemorrhoids muy malas* and had them treated three times.

His passenger looked baffled.

"Do you know the term *hemorroides muy malas*, or, in English, my bad haemorrhoids?"

"Not personally."

"Well, they got so bad I had to visit the hospital clinic due to excessive bleeding from my ass. Every time I sat in my car, the seat would get soaked in blood."

"Gross," Jimmy muttered, wrinkling his nose in disgust.

"I went to the hospital for them to be 'banded.' That's when they grab the biggest piles and wrap a strong rubber band around them to cut off the blood supply. Then they fall off."

"Fascinating," lied Jimmy, who couldn't unsee the visual Juan was painting for him. Like a child unable to endure a long road trip, he asked Juan if they were nearly at Los Piñata.

"Not quite, señor. Oh, and about my haemorrhoids, I had to get butt-naked at the hospital and lay on my belly. The doctor who walked into the room was like a giant, casting a shadow over everything. I swear he had hands that could easily palm a basketball."

Jimmy stared out the window, dearly wishing he was sitting in the back and playing games with Max.

"He shouted at me to open my legs and relax. But with this huge man yelling at me and my ass hanging out, relaxation was the last thing on my mind. Then this doctor put rubber gloves onto his gigantic hands and tried to stick them up my ass."

Jimmy pulled another face and groaned.

"I know, I know, Mr Myers, I groaned too. Naturally, I tightened up—I mean, who wouldn't? So, I turned around and said to the doctor, 'Hey, amigo! It's not so easy for me to relax. I'm not used to having a huge *hombre* shove hands the size of a watermelon up my *culo*.'"

"*Culo peludo?*" asked Jimmy, remembering the Spanish phrase from his encounter with the immigration officials.

"*¡Sí, es extremadamente peludo!*"

"What does that mean, Juan?"

"My ass is extremely hairy." Juan puffed out his chest—Jimmy let out a weak, strangled laugh. He wanted the story to end very soon, as he was becoming more uncomfortable by the second.

"Well, I just couldn't relax, and two years later, I had the same piles removed by surgery. Oh, that reminds me, I must tell you the story of when I took my first shit—"

"Los Piñata!" Jimmy exclaimed loudly, interrupting Juan as soon as he caught sight of the massive welcome sign.

"Yes," Juan said with a nod and a smile, translating the rest of the Spanish for Jimmy: "Welcome to Los Piñata. Sun, sea, and wonderful company!" Juan reached over and patted him affectionately on his shoulder. He had thoroughly enjoyed oversharing about cartels, his life, medical past, and sexual triumphs with his congenial Canadian passenger.

Ten minutes later, they arrived at the condo, *La Casa Blanca*. One by one the Myers family got out of the vehicle and stretched their arms into the air.

Four

Frozen

IT WAS AN ABSOLUTE delight to wake up at *La Casa Blanca* the next day and experience the beauty of the morning. Jimmy sank into a comfily-cushioned chair, feeling the sun's warmth on his skin as he sat on the deck. He closed his eyes and let out a long, deep sigh, feeling as if a weight had been lifted off his shoulders. The sound of the uprush and backwash of waves crashing upon the shore, in combination with the blue skies and wispy clouds high in the troposphere, contributed to the serene ambience. For the very first time, he felt pure bliss in his new surroundings.

Fishing boats passed at a distance between Los Piñata and Albatross Island. From afar, the island appeared to be an enormous emerald-coloured boulder amid the sea. Jimmy smiled as he thought of his conversation with Juan, and imagined a bask of crocodiles with short legs and long tails marching along the beach, tearing off sunbathers' limbs with their powerful jaws and razor-sharp teeth. It would make a good horror story, he thought, one with a lot of dark humour. Maybe he could write it, and call it something like *Revenge of the Reptiles* or *Massacre at the Beach*. Jimmy had written a book before, about roulette. He could certainly write another. His book wasn't fiction, despite what some people insisted, but so what? He could write a novel; he had all the inspiration in the world right in front of him.

The blackbirds were perched in a neat row along the swimming pool wall, dipping their beaks into the water to drink and preen their feathers. Palm trees swayed along the condo's boundaries, their coconuts ripe and ready to drop onto the property.

Jimmy's attention was drawn to Vincente, the property manager, who was currently cleaning the swimming pool of feathers and other debris. He greeted Vincente with a wave and received one in return. The condo owners, a wealthy family from the Polanco area in Mexico City, employed the friendly worker. His office and living space were in a larger unit adjacent to Jimmy's condo. Vincente helped sort out any issues the guests had to deal with, provided large water containers, and managed the swimming pool area. A handsome and happy-looking man with dazzling white teeth, Vincente's wife lived far away from Los Piñata in a tiny Mexican conurbation on the outskirts of El Cerdo Rosa, renowned for its splendid bacon from its award-winning pigs. Although Vincente's English was limited, foreign guests could communicate with him through a mixture of pidgin English and sign language. On the flip side, the English he had shared with Jimmy via email or text was quite clear, hinting at the use of an effective translation tool.

The one drawback of the condo was the internet could have been better for the guests. Dial-up would have been way faster and much more reliable. However, it was so lovely that this wasn't a dealbreaker by any means. Sure, the condo needed some upgrading, but the guests were still getting what they paid for. The fantastic ocean view alone was worth every dollar of the rent.

Vincente was well-aware that, on occasions, large Mexican contingents descended upon Los Piñata for certain seasonal holidays and festivals, and there could be issues with North American guests if the celebrations were too raucous. The most boisterous festivals were *Semana Santa* and *El Día de los Muertos*, which occurred on Easter and the first week of November. Jimmy assumed Christmas celebrations, or *Celebraciones Navideñas*, would be much quieter and respectful events. In an email, the property manager told Jimmy he didn't usually have foreign guests and Mexicans share accommodations. However, on this occasion, and for a short time, the Myers family would be required to share with a wealthy family from Mexican high society based in Guadalajara. Vincente had no option but to accept the booking due to the visitor's strong connection to the property owner.

As Jimmy sighed again, looking at their tropical paradise, a pelican dive-bombed into the sea to grab a fish or two, sat on the water and ate, and flew away. *Poor fish, you didn't see that curveball coming, did you pal?*

Jimmy could have easily spent the entire day on the deck, taking in the scenery and letting the sun's rays warm him and scour away the previous day's stress, but his family's cash problem loomed over him. He and Lucy had gone through all their luggage, and found no sign of his wallet. The thirty dollars the immigration agents had mocked him so mercilessly for really was, it seemed, all the cash they had, and while lying on the deck was great, they needed more than that if they were going to enjoy the next three months. With the holidays coming up, the few stores on the way to Los Piñata accepted credit cards would likely be closed or low in stock. There was no way around it: cash was king.

Even so, it was with great reluctance Jimmy got up and went with Lucy and Max into town to solve the lack-of-cash conundrum they were facing. He tried his luck in a local phone booth that accepted his credit card, and he insisted on doing the talking. He was relieved to be connected with a friendly guy who introduced himself as Mahmud, who lived in Mogadishu. Knowing he had little time to make pleasant conversation, Jimmy quickly cut to the chase and requested an emergency wire transfer. Strangely, after he said this, Mahmud became extraordinarily agitated and commanded him to calm down and not panic. It sounded like Mahmud was yelling in Somali at his colleagues at the call centre. Jimmy assumed there must be some crisis, as it sounded like a fire had broken out.

"I have called the emergency line. You will be okay."

Jimmy was confused, as he was bound to be okay if the fire was thousands of miles away. The worker became increasingly upset each time Jimmy mentioned the word 'wire.'

"Don't panic, sir, don't panic. They're on their way," Mahmud kept yelling.

"Who's on their way? What's going on?"

"One will arrive soon, sir."

"My money will arrive soon?"

"The fire truck, sir, it is on the way. It is all part of the service, sir."

At last, Jimmy realized what was going on. Due to the combination of his baritone voice and twangy Canadian accent, Mahmud mistakenly assumed he was calling about a *fire*. He knew his client was in Mexico and feared the worst, thinking there had been some catastrophic incident and the phone booth was ablaze. Each time Jimmy clearly enunciated W-I-R-E, the worker started to lose his shit. He had likely told his supervisor the client might be burning to death.

Jimmy ended the call before a fire truck turned up and charged him for putting out a non-existent fire. Cursing, he tapped the bank's emergency number onto the phone's keypad. Although frustrated by the misunderstanding, he composed himself and spoke to another outsourced bank worker from Kinshasa, who introduced herself as Chéckina. The phone line crackled and was of very poor quality.

"Hi, I'm really sorry, but I need some money wired, and I need it right now—"

Lucy was asking him questions at the same time he was talking to Chéckina. He held the phone away from his ear and shushed his wife, "Lucy, I'm talking to someone and it's a bad line."

Jimmy held the phone back to his ear. "Sorry, um . . . anyway, yes, I'd like to request a wire transfer from me or my wife's account." He thought he'd spoken perfectly clearly, so he was surprised when Chéckina responded with a curt "What?" Though he could hear her adequately, there were distracting humming and crackling sounds on the other end.

"My wife Lucy and I are on holiday in Mexico and we need money wired over, lickety-split. I lost my wallet."

Chéckina surprised him and yelled, "Why are you swearing at me? Why are you calling me a shit? What's wrong with you?" Jimmy held the phone away from his ear, looked towards Lucy, and shot her a look of utter confusion. She didn't seem to have heard the woman on the other line, and motioned for him to keep talking. Reluctantly, he reintroduced his burning red ear to the phone, hoping he could still salvage the situation.

"I'm not swearing, I'm not! I was only trying to ask that you transfer money from my or Lucy's account from British Columbia to a Mexican bank near Los Piñata. That's all."

Chéckina snapped. "I will not sit here and be patronized by some metrosexual misogynist who calls women *juicy* and *honey*." This was going from bad to worse, and Jimmy knew he had to salvage it somehow if he was going to get them their money.

"That's not what I'm saying. I said *Lucy's money*—please listen to me!" In his panic, he heard himself raise his voice.

"I am not going to listen to you, snowdrop! You European men are all the same. Colonizers, all of you. You think it is okay to harass and bully me because of your white-boy privilege and entitlement. You sexualize me, yet I am a strong, independent Congolese woman. You don't see me as a person. But I am, and you are disgusting. Absolutely disgusting."

"*Wait!* I'm not European. I am Canadian, for heaven's sake. I just want our money."

The phone line continued to pop, crackle and hiss.

"I will not be your *mate*. Neither will I be forced to engage in a long-distance relationship with you. I will not date you for money." Of all the nutty things Jimmy had heard in this disastrous interaction, this took the cake.

"Whoa!" was all he could say in response.

"I know a scammer when I meet one. Stop calling me mate, juicy and honey—you make me want to throw up."

The buzzing noises on the phone were somehow getting worse, like a swarm of bees poised to assault his ear.

"Listen, spawn of Jeffrey Epstein . . . I am going to make sure you can't scam anyone else. Due to this severe breach in security, I will be freezing all associated accounts and credit cards. Your Mexican scam is not going to fly past me. You are not calling from Canada—and your accent is preposterous!"

"*My* accent is preposterous?" Jimmy's face turned bright vermillion. Chéckina abruptly ended the call. Jimmy was stunned, left staring at the phone in disbelief. He shook his head, left the booth, and approached Lucy with a slouch of defeat.

"Unbelievable. The idiot bank worker froze our accounts and credit cards!"

"Sweetheart, please let me do the talking next time. Sometimes, your accent is quite hard to understand—from a non-Canadian perspective."

Jimmy rolled his eyes, "Whatever!"

With the holiday season fast approaching, Jimmy examined the contents of his nearly-empty belt bag, which only held a few cards and pesos. The vibrant energy of the busy Los Piñata street engulfed them as they tried to make their way through the crowds. He kept shaking his head and cursing as he looked at the sunny blue skies.

"Argh, I can't believe I was stupid enough to get us into this mess."

"Babe, calm down and just let me—"

"Hun, our money situation has become critical." He angrily kicked a tin can into the middle of the road, barely missing a passing truck, "I am calm as fu—"

Lucy covered Max's ears and gave her husband the stink eye.

⟫⟫⟫ ⟪⟪⟪

LATER THAT NIGHT, Los Piñata was buzzing with activity. Every third or fourth store was a restaurant, street vendor, or souvenir shop. Quaint cobbled streets led to the town centre, where a big, whitewashed church was built. Jimmy walked alone, as Lucy and Max opted to stay at the condo. Despite the day's stress, the traditional feel of the town put Jimmy at ease. Even with all the stores that had almost certainly popped up to cater to the tourists, Los Piñata had an undeniable authenticity. With just a few days before Christmas, families were still buying churros, hamburgers, ice cream, and different kinds of snacks. As Jimmy walked by the crêpe store, he found it hard to resist the tempting aroma of freshly made crêpes and waffles. He decided to return to the store after having a beer at Tequila Tommy's, a popular pub a few hundred yards away from the church.

Locals had told Jimmy two gringo bars were popular in town: The Stump Arms, also known as The Jackson's, and Tequila Tommy's. The name of the former was no coincidence; it was to commemorate the Confederate general, who lost an arm during battle. The bar had a conservative vibe and displayed the Star-Spangled Banner, Fleurdelisé, and Battle Flag of the Army of Tennessee. The sign at the entrance, marked with a skull and bones, made Jimmy smirk. It read: *Strictly for meat-eaters; Vegans may be shot!*

Jimmy headed for the more liberal sounding Tequila Tommy's, as The Stump Arms sounded like a bar for war amps and Confederate vets. He saw Tequila Tommy's sign on the bar's outside wall. The doors were open, and music was blasting into the street. Jimmy walked in and was immediately beset by stares. A pale white guy like him stuck out like a sore thumb. An older man with an impressive tan said, "Welcome, Mr Blanco," and held out his hand for a fist-bump. Jimmy, emboldened by the display of friendliness, complied.

The man smiled and asked, "First day here, bud?"

"How did you guess?" Jimmy replied, looking at his own pale arms. The friendly man did as well, and his smile widened.

"Just a wild hunch. Hey Patsy, get this *hombre blanco* a beer on me." The man raised his hand and clicked his fingers at the bar area as he spoke. Jimmy approached several empty barstools on the U-shaped serving counter.

"Thanks, um—" Jimmy began before realizing he hadn't gotten the friendly man's name.

"Name's Tommy," he said. When Jimmy reached the bar and took a seat, the woman behind the counter turned to him.

"New to town, amigo?"

"Yup, I'm Jimmy. You must be Patsy. I've heard lots about you." Lucy's buddies had raved about Patsy's delicious passion fruit and mango margaritas.

"Si, *amigo. ¡Espero que esté todo bien!* I hope that it's all good?"

Jimmy looked around the bar, wondering if Lucy's friends Mac, Mella, and JayBee were there. As he scanned the room, he noticed an attractive blonde lady in her early 50s who had her back to Jimmy and was playing darts.

"No pressure," goaded her playing partner. Immediately after, the blonde lady threw the dart and missed the board entirely. The dart bounced off the whitewashed wall and nearly skewered one of her flip-flops.

"Whoopsie," said her playing partner. "Guess you owe me yet another drink."

Another woman beckoned the blonde lady to come to the bar and join her. She too was middle-aged and gorgeous, with distinctive bright blue glass frames and auburn hair, wavy and shoulder-length, that perfectly framed her face.

"JayBee, give it a rest. We both know darts are for losers and overweight pie-eaters. Come and finish your drink. I'm getting lonely," the woman said. Then she looked at Jimmy, the new arrival at the bar, and her face lit up with a wicked grin.

"And we have some fresh meat . . . I mean, new company!"

"You must be Mella," Jimmy proclaimed, walking up to her with a beer in his left hand and extending his right to shake her hand. "Hi there, I'm Jimmy."

"Oh, halloo Jimmy."

"Are you Lucy's friend?"

"I sure am!"

"I'm JayBee," interrupted the blonde.

"Well, hello, you two. I'm Lucy's partner and Max's dad." Jimmy gave them both a huge hug. As Lucy had warned her husband, Mella was renowned for her big boobs, major potty mouth, and sublime, sarcastic sense of humour, and all three were on display. After the hug broke off, she flashed Jimmy a smile and a wink, and, looking directly into his eyes, said, "Welcome to the quiet and uneventful town of Los Piñata, where eligible men are in short supply, and certain female organs cease to function."

Jimmy looked confused and furrowed his brow, not understanding what Mella had said. She noticed this, and decided to explain as succinctly as possible.

"Welcome to Los Piñata, where vaginas come to die."

***

JIMMY WALKED HOME, his steps slightly unsteady after his first taste of Tequila Tommy's. He kept replaying the memory of his wonderful time with Mella and JayBee, made even better by Tommy's steady stream of free drinks.

He let out a loud burp that echoed through the now-quiet street, sending a few dogs into a barking frenzy. He turned to look at them and saw a red neon sign that read *Sexy Shop*. It was attached to a building with walls painted a brilliant scarlet. Nestled between a used clothing store and a 24-hour emergency medical clinic, the shop seemed slightly out of place. Jimmy chuckled at the thought of customers walking out of the sex shop with bags of outrageous items, setting themselves up for a visit to the clinic next door. Red curtains hung down from the Sexy Shop's door, and even though it was well into the evening, it appeared to be open for business.

Jimmy, being naturally curious, poked his head through the curtains for a quick litmus test. If it seemed too sketchy to enter, he would leave. He was greeted by a warm "*Hola*" from the woman who seemed to own the store. Conservatively, she looked to be about 374 years old. She was skimpily dressed in a non-fetching teddy and held a black leather whip in one of her hands.

"*¿Eres un buen chico o un chico malo?*" she asked, each word dripping with seductive twang. Jimmy laughed nervously.

"I'm sorry, I don't speak Spanish."

Cracking her whip, she enquired, "Señor, are you a good boy or bad boy?" He noticed she worked it with remarkable skill. Jimmy laughed again.

"I'm a very good boy."

She asked another question in Spanish, running her tongue over her lips. They were blood-red with thickly-applied lipstick. Jimmy had no idea what she had said, but he could feel the weight of her words in the awkward silence that followed.

"I'm sorry," he said. She paused for a moment to think before translating the question into English.

"Do you want to hire me?" Jimmy understood this cheeky suggestion loud and clear, and he saw her face light up as she noticed his comprehension.

"I'm good, but thanks for the offer," he demurred, blushing furiously. As red as this place and its proprietor were, he was certain his face was redder.

"Señor gringo, you no want to miss this!" the old dominatrix insisted. She ran her hands up and down her body, from her breasts to her pubic area, put her finger in her mouth and sucked it like a popsicle.

Jimmy's eyes nearly bugged right out of their sockets, and for a moment he was stunned into silence. When he regained his composure, he chuckled and retrieved his mini-Spanish/Mexican phrase book from one of the pockets of his cargo shorts. Afraid she might corner him in the store, Jimmy didn't want to speak the wrong words. He also didn't want to explain to Lucy how he got love bites on his neck from a cougar granny. Thumbing carefully through the pages, he found what he was looking for before the proprietor could say or do anything else.

"*Muchas gracias, pero pasaré esta vez,*" and repeated in English: "Thank you very much, but I will pass this time."

The old dear looked disappointed, pursing her lips in a pout as she wrung the whip handle in a gesture that could have been disappointed or threatening. Jimmy waited for her response; his breath caught in his throat. He wouldn't have put it past himself to say something rude by mistake, and he didn't like how well she used that whip. Finally, however, she broke into a big smile, exposing her one lonely incisor. She gestured there might be something in her shop, apart from her, that the tourist might be interested in. Jimmy smiled back and looked at the shelves full of huge dildos, fantasy role-playing gear, and arousal creams and lubricants. Something caught his eye; he chuckled and said, "*Si, Si,*" pointing in its direction. "Yes, this may come in handy in the coming days."

He made the purchase and thanked the shopkeeper, who pulled him towards her for a kiss. Jimmy avoided her open mouth and long, lizard-like tongue and kissed her two cheeks, Italian style. Then he chastely shook her hand and began to walk away.

"Enjoy yourself tonight, sexy amigo. I am always here if your Sexy Suzy gift disappoints!" The old woman cried out as he reached the curtain doors. Jimmy laughed and went on his way.

FIVE

Love Thy Neighbours

THEY ARRIVED LATE AFTERNOON, leaving the dust from the convoy's black SUVs and Toyota Tacomas hanging heavy in the air behind them. Lucy peeked out the rear kitchen window, and her heart began to race when she saw the massive convoy arriving with trucks loaded with sound equipment and other electronic gear. The number of woofers and subwoofers was lost on her as she watched in awe the crew of men and women unloading a seemingly endless supply of equipment and lighting fixtures.

"Holy guacamole," she said out loud. "These are our quiet and unobtrusive new neighbours?" Lucy dashed to the front of the condo, stepped out onto her first-floor deck, and watched a large team assemble the sound equipment under the shared palapa. Other workers were beavering away, attaching what looked like large smoke boxes and putting up array after array of lights. She expected the best but prepared for the worst, hoping this would be a new, exciting experience for her family.

Jimmy and Max walked along the beach, their feet crunching shells and gathering sand as they searched for bits of sea glass. As he returned to the property with his little lad, he heard laughter and splashing fill the air as people joyfully jumped into the pool. The area around it was jam-packed, and it was clear the sun loungers had all been taken. If this were the new normal, the Myers family would be confined to their condo until their new neighbours returned to Guadalajara.

He looked up, saw the humungous array of speakers, and stopped dead in his tracks with Max at his side. Jimmy stared at the multitude of equipment, slack-jawed. The colossus of a sound system nearly gave him a heart attack. Each woofer and subwoofer looked dangerously unstable, and they were all piled precariously on top of one another. It was a wonder the entire thing didn't come crashing down.

An extraordinarily portly man was tapping the microphone, shouting.

"*Probando, probando, uno, dos, tres!*" His voice was deafening. Jimmy hurried back to the condo, ushering Max along with a hand on his back. When they got back, they saw Lucy looking at the spectacle through the window.

"What the flip is going on?" Jimmy asked her. Lucy laughed, and before she could answer, the DJ—or whoever was holding the mic—spoke again in a booming voice.

"*¡Mi nombre es Pedro Cordoba, primo del magnífico Armardo López!*" Jimmy cringed; his voice was just as loud in the condo as it was outside. It felt like their walls were made of tissue paper.

"Luce, what's the fat guy saying?" Lucy turned to him with a disapproving frown.

"Jimmy, stop it with the pejoratives—that's body shaming!"

"Well, he's hardly Mr Slenderman; he's the size of a fully grown whale!"

Lucy sighed in exasperation, but let the subject drop. "He said his name was Pedro Cordoba, cousin of *the magnificent* Armardo Lopez."

"Holy burrito! Who the flip is Armardo *the Magnificent*?"

"*Bienvenidos a el sonido de la resistencia mexicana ¡Viva la Santísima Virgen!*" the DJ continued. Once again, Jimmy turned to his wife and shrugged, waiting for her to interpret.

"I think he was saying, 'Welcome to the sound of the Mexican Resistance; long live the Blessed Virgin!' He speaks super-fast, and my Spanish is a bit rusty."

"Mexican Resistance? Blessed Virgin?" repeated Jimmy.

"Jimmy, it's coming up to Christmas, so I guess these folks like to party."

"If they're going to party in a public space, they should do it quieter." It frustrated him Lucy was taking this so much better than he was. To him, this whole scene heralded the end, an apocalyptic event that would obliterate their relaxing family vacation.

"I'm sure it won't be as bad as it looks. Vincente said the people renting next to us will be very respectful, and I trust him."

"I don't. Vincente is a liar, liar, pants on fire." Jimmy kept looking from the window at the scene unfolding below him. The thought of taking Max to the pool area could not have been less attractive. Wading through the sea of people to get to a packed pool and occupied sun loungers was not how he wanted to spend his day. It struck him as almost cult-like, this massive gathering of people taking over a space and waiting for their leader, *the magnificent* Armardo, to appear. It seemed so long ago the pool was idyllic and calm, a refuge from the stresses of their trip.

As he watched the scene unfold, Jimmy noticed two distinct characters who appeared to be pointing and organizing the rest of the workers. These were a strange-looking pair. One was a little person wearing a fancy black sombrero, and the other was a veritable giant of a man wearing a gaudy pink sombrero. Both men wore cowboy boots. He didn't know what to make of them, and he didn't ask Lucy. They didn't say anything he could hear, and he doubted his wife knew any more about them than he did.

Later that evening, after the three of them had eaten dinner, they heard orders being shouted in Spanish. It wasn't the DJ this time, but the man in the black sombrero. He was speaking with a great deal of animation, looking out at a vast host of workers. Jimmy saw this from his balcony, where he sat with a beer in his hand. The guy with the pink sombrero looked up and saw him sitting. Jimmy reluctantly waved; the guy didn't respond and looked away.

"Rude," he muttered.

Then, the DJ's booming voice returned. It made the condo shake.

"Oh, it's the fat dude!"

"Pedro Cordoba," replied an indignant Lucy.

"I wonder if he will introduce *Armardo the Magnificent*?"

They all laughed, including Max.

"*Damas y caballeros, buenas noches y bienvenidos,*" Cordoba announced.

"Ladies and gentlemen, good evening and welcome," Lucy repeated. He continued his speech, his words coming out through the skyscraper of amplifiers next to, in front of, and behind him. Then, out of nowhere, the condo was awash in a kaleidoscope of laser lights that danced into the night sky, accompanied by thick clouds of smoke in every hue imaginable. The music started soon after. The sound effects in the background were deafening and dramatic, a cacophony of noises included exploding lasers, blaring air horns, and random sounds such as claps of thunder, jet engines, helicopters, and detonating atomic bombs. The condo trembled violently as the noise raged on, as if a magnitude-eight Richter earthquake was striking the peaceful town of Los Piñata.

Jimmy groaned. He hoped the noise would stop soon, but his hope was in vain. The din lasted all night and went into the morning. What's more, the flimsy curtains were insufficient to keep the strobe lights out. They exploded like starbursts into the bedroom, and no matter how tightly he closed his eyes, the light always managed to reach them. He had no previous experience with epilepsy, but as the night wore on, Jimmy became more and more convinced the pulsating lights were a sign of an impending seizure. He crammed earplugs into his ears and covered his eyes with a blackout mask, but none of it helped; he couldn't get a wink of sleep. He wished he could pour liquid concrete into his ears and over his eyes to escape the light and noise.

BOOM, BOOM, BOOM.

THUD, THUD, THUD.

The sound reverberated through every fibre of Jimmy's being that sleepless night. But as the sun rose, the lasers faded away, and he breathed a sigh of relief. Now there was only one thing keeping him awake, instead of two.

⠿⠿⠿ ⠿⠿⠿

IT WAS MORNING, and the *BOOM, BOOM, BOOM, THUD, THUD, THUD* from Pedro's sound system was still going strong. Max exacerbated the situation by tapping his feet and playing drums on various saucepans and metal dishes.

BANG CLANG, CLANG, CLANG.

Max grabbed more pots and pans, thrashing them with increasing fervour as he replaced his plastic spoon with two spatulas, using them as makeshift drumsticks. Somehow, despite being kept up all night by the noise, he was having great fun. Jimmy was completely baffled.

"I *is* a drummer. I *is* a Mexican shithead!"

"Max! It's '*I am* a Mexican drummer,' and '*I am* a Mexican shithead.' And, remember sweetie, 'shithead' is a bad word," flashing him a strained smile. She showed more patience than Jimmy felt.

"Daddy says 'shithead' a lot," Max protested. He gesticulated wildly as he spoke, and one of the spatula drumsticks flew out of his hand and landed at Lucy's feet.

"Max, for the love of god, just stop!" Jimmy yelled.

"Fhurck," declared Max with a massive smile on his face. "Mother-fhurck-uh."

"Woah! That's unacceptable, Max. Go to your room right now," Jimmy demanded. Lucy picked up his metal spatula-drumstick, again exhibiting the patience of a saint. She still had that pained smile on her face.

"Dadda, leave Max alone. He's saying '*fforch*.' Listen, instead of judging him. He's banging the pans with his . . . *fforch*. That's his Welsh coming out. A fork is *fforch*."

Jimmy was wholly unconvinced. "Lucy, he said mother-effer!"

"Even if he did, your foul language isn't helping. Max lost his *fforch* or fork. It landed at my feet, and he asked his mother to give him back the fork. Maxy used my personal pronoun 'her.' Put it all together—motherforkher."

"Luce, I can't believe you're jumping through this many hoops to keep him out of trouble," scoffed her husband as he rolled his eyes.

"He wouldn't be in trouble if you washed out your ears, dear Dadda." Lucy turned her gaze to her son, still smiling.

"It might help if he learnt just one language," Jimmy responded.

"You're jealous because you can't communicate in English without swearing."

"Not effing true."

Lucy rolled her eyes and continued her Welsh lesson to make her point.

"Maxwell Myers, please put the *fforch* down, and stop banging the '*sosbenni*,' or pans." Her son smirked and gave the pan one last loud *CLANG* before his dad snatched the utensil from his hand.

"That's it. I've effing had it. I'm talking to Vincente about this freaking noise from fatty Cordoba. He's doing my head in!"

"Pedro Cordoba," corrected Lucy, "and that's a good idea."

"I'll ask him to speak to our neighbours. I swear, the penguins in Antarctica can hear Porky Pedro's racket."

"Pedro Cordoba," Lucy reminded him again.

"*Cordoba mochyn tew*," added Max with an impish smile.

"Max! Stop it. Don't call the man a fat pig," snapped his mother.

"Daddy says he is."

"Amen, Max," chortled Jimmy.

"That's it, off to your room." Lucy pointed towards the bedroom door as she spoke, her patience having run its course. Max's smile fell and he sulked away, leaving the adults alone.

"Whatever, Luce, this noise drives us both up the wall. Vincente needs to do the asking, as that's his flipping job; then, there won't be any bad blood between the nutbar Mexicans and us."

"Could you also ask that his Mexican guests leave at least *two* of the twenty-odd sun loungers for the *other* guests that use the pool area, as they have hogged every last one?"

"Word, Luce!" Jimmy applauded enthusiastically. Lucy went to the window and peeped from behind the curtains at the Mexican contingent still dancing to the music, chatting away in the pool with beers and cigarettes in their hands. They were acting like it was a weekend afternoon instead of early morning. Looking around, she immediately noticed there was a red substance covering every inch of the pool and patio area. The vacation rental, once a peaceful haven, now resembled a crime scene out of *Dexter*, complete with Mexicans playfully spraying each other with cans of red mist.

"What are they doing down there by the pool?" she asked, dumbfounded. Jimmy walked towards the large patio window and saw for himself. He was just as shocked.

"What the heck? It looks like a bloodbath."

Even the black and pink sombrero guys had their faces covered in the slimy red substance. The pool was also saturated in red colouring, as was the adjacent hot tub.

"Don't they know there are other people living here?" he muttered as he threw on some clothes before rushing off to find Vincente.

THE PROPERTY MANAGER could often be found in his side annex next to the condo. Jimmy had learned that while the condos were rented, Vincente would stay in his office space, which consisted of a small living area, sofa bed, and kitchenette, with an ensuite bathroom. His office was well-organized, containing filing cabinets and a large-screen television on which he watched his beloved football games. Jimmy tapped on his door, and almost immediately heard the manager's voice ring out.

"*¡Hola!* How can I help you?" Jimmy took that for permission and tentatively opened the door. He saw Vincente there, his eyes glued to the game between rival clubs, Club América and Chivas Guadalajara. Jimmy was sure Vincente would prefer to be disturbed after the game, but he had reached the end of his rope. He didn't waste any time getting to the point of his visit.

"Vincente, for flip's sake . . . the noise from the Mexicans—I mean the other occupants—is driving my family bananas!" Vincente turned from the game to face Jimmy, and he looked baffled. Jimmy helped clarify what 'going bananas' meant by acting like a crazy gorilla eating bananas and throwing away the skins.

"Bananas!" he said. "Loco!" The property manager nodded sympathetically, even though it was clear from the confusion in his eyes he had no idea what his client was going on about. He looked back to the game.

"It simply has to stop. And what's with the *Texas Chainsaw Massacre*-style scene out there, with all the red stuff?" Vincente's eyebrows raised in surprise, but otherwise he gave no response. Jimmy thought of another famous piece of media: *The Twilight Zone*. He felt like he had been placed right into an episode, the lone sane person in a world gone mad. He pounded his fist on Vincente's desk. Again, he managed to draw the man's attention from the TV, but all he did was look bemused. Jimmy continued his tirade.

"To make matters worse, our neighbours' beach towels have claimed every last one of the million sun loungers on the patio. There's not a single one left for us to use." Vincente nodded along with Jimmy's complaint in the way people do when they want to appease someone to get them to stop talking. Suddenly, cheering erupted from the television to distract him once again; Club América had just scored the equalizing goal. Vincente jumped out of his chair, punching the air in jubilation and yelling profanities in Spanish. Jimmy stared at him in disbelief.

"*¡Vamos!*" he shouted. Then he turned back to his tenant. Jimmy stood before him with his arms cross and his lips curved downwards in a disapproving scowl. Perhaps, he thought, staring the property manager down would work better than verbal complaints, which seemed to go unheard.

Vincente, feeling awkward, was now trying to guess what his client wanted him to do; he played back in his mind some of the highlights of their brief interaction. There was one thing he knew for sure: the sooner he could get rid of this client, the sooner he could refocus on the game. His confused expression morphed into a big smile, as if he'd just had a eureka moment, and he said, "Mr Jimmy, I'm sorry you are mad. Can I offer you some bananas?"

Jimmy had flashbacks of speaking to the bank's customer service personnel, and he saw red.

"No, Vincente, the musico is driving me feckingo loco. BOOM-O! BOOM-O! BOOM-O! from fatty PEDRO CORDOB-O!"

"Pedro Cordoba," corrected Vincente, tutting at Jimmy's inappropriate body shaming of Mexico's favourite DJ. "He is good, yes?"

"No! Can you ask them to turn the music down? El volum-a, down-a." Jimmy gestured—pointing his thumb down. This request, too, bewildered Vincente, and it quickly lost his attention as he heard on the screen Club América had just been awarded a penalty. He jumped up in the air, cheering at his team's turn of fortune. Jimmy held his head in his hands and shook it, resembling a heartbroken mourner. Nothing he said in English or Spanglish was reaching Vincente, so he would have to get creative. He reached for the phrasebook that was in his pocket. He was so frustrated he picked one random Spanish phrase and blurted it out.

"Would you like me to kiss you?"

Vincente stood up aggressively and made the 'Halt!' signal with his hand. Jimmy didn't look at the English translation, but whatever he'd said had worked; he now had the property manager's full attention.

"No! Get away from me, or I will call the police," he yelled at Jimmy in Spanish. Now, it was Jimmy's turn to be confused. He looked down at his phrasebook and realized what phrase he'd chosen. Vincente must have thought Jimmy fancied him and wanted to give him a pash.

"No, no. I'm sorry, my mistake," he said, holding up his hands in a 'I come in peace' gesture. Vincente sat back in his chair, looking relieved. The danger of his guest kissing him had dissipated. The two men stared at each other in awkward silence for a moment before Jimmy had another idea.

"May I use this?" he asked, pointing to Vincente's MacBook on his desk. Vincente walked over from the TV and turned the laptop towards his guest. He googled 'English to Spanish translation,' and typed in: *can you ask our neighbours to turn down the volume of the music?* Now, finally, Vincente understood.

He tapped his reply: *Mexicans like to celebrate festivals yearly.*

Jimmy frantically tapped away: *The music is so loud. They have covered the whole place in red dye. They take all twenty loungers, leaving none for us. It's terribly rude. Please tell them to be more respectful of their neighbours. We can't sleep because of the noise. It goes on all night.* Jimmy looked up and waited for Vincente to acknowledge what he had written.

Vincente sat down by the computer and tapped the following in reply: *Sir, Mexicans love to party. They may not like foreigners who demand that they reduce the music volume.*

Jimmy typed back: *I don't care! It's about respect. They are being selfish and unreasonable. We can't take it anymore.* Vincente leaned forward to read it, frowning. Then, he typed a response:

Sir, this may not be as easy as you think.

Jimmy shrugged his shoulders and wrote: *I don't give a rat's ass!*

Vincente looked up from the laptop, shocked, and Jimmy took the opportunity to keep typing:

Go outside. Look at the patio and pool. Everything is covered in red-coloured shit.

Vincente sighed and nodded. He went to the window and immediately exclaimed, "*¡La Noche de Rábanos!*" He came back to the computer and wrote out a message in the translator:

The Night of the Radishes! This celebration will be all over by Christmas Eve, I promise.

Jimmy shook his head: *That's not good enough. Can you ask our neighbours, Mr Armardo the Magnificent and his sombrero-wearing buddies, to turn the music down so his neighbours can sleep at night?*

Vincente asked, "You want music down?" Jimmy punched the air in mock celebration, in much the same way the property manager had when Club América scored. Finally, Vincente understood.

Jimmy nodded. "Yes, Vincente. That's exactly what I want!"

The property manager still looked reluctant, and Jimmy knew he would have to sweeten the deal. He opened his belt bag to give a few peso notes, and realized with dismay it was empty. He did, however, see his late father's cherished membership card for the *Cosmic Intergalactic Agency*, which he had been a member of for years. While living in Langley, near Vancouver, Raymond Myers had gotten really into *Star Wars*, *Star Trek*, and *Battlestar Galactica* role-play battles. The glossy card showed a picture of Jimmy's dad many years ago—he was the spitting image of his father. Momentarily distracted, Jimmy took the card out of his bag and looked it over, memories of his dad flooding back. After a few moments, he noticed the property manager was staring at it with interest.

"Wanna have a look?" he asked. Vincente nodded, and Jimmy handed him the fancy card. His mouth hung open in disbelief as he stared at the ID: Commander Raymond "Skywalker" Myers, CIA., Langley. A motto, in a subscript font under the Commander's details, said: *The Work of a Galactic Nation. The Centre of Intelligent Life: And ye shall know the force, and the force shall set you free (Yolo 8:32).*

Jimmy broke the silence. "Vincente, I'm good for a few bucks when I access some moolah. You can borrow the card if you'd like, but be sure to keep it safe for me—it's irreplaceable. I'll make it worth your while when I'm back on my feet financially."

"C-I-A? I can't believe it," mumbled Vincente in disbelief.

"Yep, he sure loved crossing lightsabres with enemies like Vader and Khan," Jimmy replied with a tinge of sarcasm that the property manager didn't notice. Vincente had a hard time understanding the Canadian's babble. Nevertheless, he felt thankful, considering he might need to call a favour from this CIA agent someday soon.

"*Sí*, I will ask señor Lopez. I hope they no throw me into the *El Río de los Cocodrilos*. I will see what Vincente can do—they no like Colombians. But, I have *this* as you say, for Vincente's insurance!" Vincente waved the shiny card in the air. Jimmy was a tad puzzled why he was so happy to borrow his Dad's *Cosmic Intergalactic Agency* identification card, but if it got him to talk to the neighbours, he wasn't going to question it.

"Whatever floats your boat, Vincente. Just make sure it stays safe."

"Oh, I will." With these assurances, Jimmy couldn't help but be filled with joy. After a sleepless night, the promise of restful quiet nearly brought tears to his eyes, and addled by fatigue and emotion, he leaned into kiss Vincente on the cheek. The property manager went wide-eyed and bolted, leaving him alone in the office.

As Jimmy returned to his condo with renewed hope, drunken laughter filled the air, and he had to dodge the guests' bodies stumbling around in red paint.

Six

The Invitation

THE LOUD *BOOM! BOOM! BOOM!* of their neighbours' Mexican music showed no signs of stopping. It wasn't entirely unbearable—or perhaps Jimmy was just used to it by now—but it was brutal nonetheless. Jimmy dreamed of walking into town and visiting his new favourite spot, Tequila Tommy's, where he could watch hockey while sipping an ice-cold brewski.

Escaping to this tropical paradise was a welcome change from the commercialized Christmas season, but the noise soured everything. Part of the reason they'd taken a vacation was to give Jimmy a quiet environment in which to come up with a new book; there was no way he could get any writing done with the music drowning out his thoughts. He also recognized his financial state was highly problematic, and he couldn't continually sponge off drinks from expatriates and snowbirds. Indeed, it was becoming quite embarrassing. He had to resolve their monetary problems. If relief from the noise wouldn't come, he could at least resolve one of his issues.

Despite prior frustrations and setbacks, Jimmy remained determined to contact his bank, but he needed help to afford a Mexican SIM card for his phone. He considered asking one of the barflies, Mella, Mac, or JayBee, if he could use one of their phones, but he was hesitant to approach them; he didn't know them well enough to be asking for money. Whatever he did, one thing was for sure: when the cash finally came through, Jimmy would buy everyone who'd been kind to them plenty of drinks at the pub.

For now, Lucy was the voice of calm and reason, exhibiting a patience Jimmy envied. He knew that wouldn't last. With time, Lucy's stress levels would escalate until she reached her breaking point; were his wife to lose her calm demeanour, the situation would quickly become catastrophic. As he ruminated on the mounting difficulties of his vacation, gazing at the beautiful cobalt-blue ocean and watching the palm trees sway in the breeze, Jimmy heard footsteps behind him. He turned around to see an unfamiliar Mexican man approaching.

"Hey, my friend, you look troubled," the man said, sidling up to Jimmy with two large glasses of clear liquid. "This will help, I promise." He gave Jimmy one glass, and he took it from the man's outstretched hand. Then, they both raised their respective shot glasses into the air.

"To happier days," toasted Jimmy before chugging back the colourless booze. The dense liquid tasted like a cross between vodka and an excellent whiskey, somehow ice-cold and fiery at the same time. The other man took a small sip and smiled. Jimmy noticed his voice contained barely a hint of an accent. He was a handsome man, with high cheekbones, amber eyes, a neatly trimmed moustache, and a thick grey streak in his professionally sculpted hair. He was quite tall and had an athletic build. He also, Jimmy realized, drank slowly instead of downing his glass in one gulp.

"Was I supposed to drink it slowly?"

"Well," the man replied with a smile, "It is a limited-edition drink and a tequila for savouring, not mixing in a cocktail or taking as a shot. It must be sipped and swirled around, so you can taste the beautiful agave nectar on the roof of your mouth." He looked at his glass and held it up again. "My friend, this will never give you a hangover, no matter how much you drink, because it's high quality."

"I'm sorry, I didn't know." Jimmy looked down sheepishly, feeling foolish in front of this extraordinarily well put together man.

"This Amador 1836 tequila is exquisite. The bottle has been made using 21-carat gold, adding to its beauty and elegance."

"Wow." Jimmy looked at the bottle and read aloud, "1836 . . . 100%, . . . Agave Azul— *Envejecida durante ocho años.*"

"It's made with 100% pure blue agave and has aged for at least eight years," his drinking partner helpfully interpreted.

"Why Amador 1836?" Jimmy asked curiously.

"We celebrate General Juan Amador, our national hero," the man replied, sticking out his chest in pride. "This tequila brand commemorates the famous battle of the Alamo and the courageous Mexican forces that recaptured the fort.

Two hundred Texans died, including the scumbag Davy Crockett." The Davy Crockett comment unsettled Jimmy, but he quickly recovered.

"I'm guessing it's quite expensive?"

Armardo chuckled, "A single bottle costs about three thousand U.S. dollars."

Jimmy let out a gasp. That was more than half of what he'd originally brought for his family's vacation. His drinking partner poured another 1836 into Jimmy's empty glass and motioned for him to try again.

"This time, my friend, just sip and savour." Jimmy did as he was bid. He swished the tequila around in his mouth, pushing it up to the roof with his tongue and letting it linger there before swallowing.

"I haven't drank tequila since my university days. My buddies and I would chug a whole bottle of cheap tequila. I got sick as a dog the last time we did it. This 1836 is nice. Thank you—" Jimmy hesitated, realizing he didn't know the man's name.

"Armardo Angel Lopez, but please call me Armardo. Your name is Jimmy, and your partner is Lucy, correct?"

Jimmy was stunned into silence for several moments. He stared at Armardo, wide-eyed, and his mouth hung slightly open. This kind, sociable man was his neighbour? The one blaring music all through the night and day? He couldn't believe it. Armardo looked at him patiently, waiting for a reply. Once he got over his shock and realized how rude he was being, he nodded.

"Um, yes, that's right."

"And the spirited boy you have with you, the little guy with the potty mouth, is Max, yes?"

Jimmy laughed. "Max is often misheard. His accent is slightly confusing because his mother is Welsh, and I'm Canadian."

"Of course, now I understand."

Jimmy noticed two men standing behind Armardo. He recognized them from the day before. One was the little person with the black sombrero who had been shouting orders at the workers, and the other was the tall, slim man with the pink sombrero. Up close, he looked to be around three feet taller than his companion. Both their faces were painted bright red; combined with their sombreros, they both cut very distinctive figures. The short one had a friendly demeanour, while the tall one was silent and intimidating.

Armardo continued, "So, Jimmy, why the long face? You have such beautiful scenery—the palm trees, the crystal blue ocean, the sandy beach, all at your doorstep. You have a beautiful wife and a spirited bilingual child."

Jimmy was again surprised; he thought he was doing a good job of looking polite and engaged, hiding his stress and anger. Armardo, however, had seen right through him. He did not have the heart or the balls to tell him the truth: the loud, all-night music the Mexicans played drove him up the wall. He also didn't want to share with a stranger he had money issues. However, noticing the blood-red pool area, he plucked up the courage, "Armardo, I'm a curious foreigner. An idiot abroad, you might say. I've spent the majority of my life in Canada. Can I be honest without hurting your feelings?"

"Go ahead," Armardo replied. Armed with his permission, Jimmy felt emboldened, and pointed at the mysterious red substance that covered the patio.

"I've never seen anything like this. This *red stuff* is everywhere—in the pool, sunflowers, sun loungers, and your assistants' faces. Honestly, it looks like a crime scene." Armardo raised his eyebrows, blinked exaggeratedly, and grinned broadly. The result was an expression that resembled mock surprise. Jimmy wasn't sure what to make of this; the tequila was making him feel warm and fuzzy inside.

"And?" Armardo prompted.

"I'm trying to say we're getting freaked out by the red colour sprayed on everything. Is this some mystical Mexican voodoo thing?" Armardo cleared his throat, and looked back to the two men with sombreros.

"Of course, he doesn't know; a visitor to our country would not be privy to our customs." The guy with the black sombrero spoke for the first time.

"Durr! The little gringo wouldn't know any better," letting out a mischievous chuckle.

At being called a 'little gringo' by a guy no taller than an eggcup, a wave of indignation rushed through Jimmy, warming his body like another shot of tequila. Meanwhile, the one with the pink sombrero kept on a perfect poker face. As he looked at the taller man, he noticed he had heterochromia; one of his eyes was hazel, while the other was a strange purple-blue shade. The tall man stared down at him, or rather through him. His gaze was so intense Jimmy felt like the man was staring a hole through his head.

Then, Armardo turned his head back and locked eyes with Jimmy.

"Noche de Rábanos."

Black sombrero repeated, *"Noche de Rábanos."*

Pink sombrero grunted in agreement, then fell silent.

"Noche de Rábanos?" Jimmy asked, furrowing his brow. "Vincente mentioned that before. What does it mean?"

"*La Noche de los Rábanos* is 'the Night of the Radishes.' We celebrate December twenty-third, the night before Christmas Eve. It is a significant and sacred festival," answered black sombrero.

"That's what Vincente told me," Jimmy responded, still not sure what the Night of the Radishes celebrated or why. He was, however, impressed by how proficient their English was. Judging from pink sombrero's silence, he hadn't been sure if he or black sombrero could speak the language at all. Maybe pink sombrero couldn't.

"By the way, both of you speak English amazingly well," he added.

"Thank you," said Armardo with an appreciative nod, who turned to the man wearing the black sombrero. "Jimmy, excuse my rudeness; let me introduce you to Fred."

Fred grinned and nodded at Jimmy. Armardo pointed towards the man with the pink sombrero.

"This is Fred's brother, Raul." Pink sombrero acknowledged Jimmy with a frown. "Fred and Raul Montana, meet Mr Jimmy Myers, who isn't sure about our *Rábanos* event."

Jimmy smiled back at the brothers. However, he still didn't understand why anyone would commemorate a vegetable.

"So, you commemorate a radish?" he asked Armardo, hoping to get more clarity from him. All three men nodded in response, and Fred smirked.

"*Si*, radishes make us very horny; they are like veggie Viagra to us Mexicans!" Fred replied.

Armardo was clearly uncomfortable, "I can assure you radishes have no place in our lovemaking."

"Sorry, boss," Fred chuckled before turning his attention back to the foreigner. "The radish is used for other purposes, not for eating. We use them to make carvings, like the Halloween tradition in North America."

"You guys carve pumpkins; we carve *rábanos*," Armardo added. The comparison to Halloween helped, but Jimmy was still confused. It showed on his face, and Armardo continued explaining.

"*Noche de Rábanos*, or Night of the Radishes, is an annual event in Oaxaca, Mexico. Francisca, my beautiful wife, hails from Oaxaca and is devoutly religious. The Blessed Red Lady is venerated in her home. She was a priestess who turned red after eating too many radishes, and she performed incredible miracles. The local community honours her by cultivating and sculpting enormous radishes. Jimmy, are you interested in learning about Mexican history?"

"Sure," said Jimmy, holding out his empty glass for a refill of tequila.

Armardo filled up his glass once again. "In 1897, the mayor of Oaxaca decided to dedicate radishes to the Red Lady and ran a carving competition for the townsfolk."

"Radish carvings?"

"Yes. Then some farmers discovered that if they heavily fertilized the land and left the radishes in the soil after harvest, they would grow and contort into many shapes and sizes. Every year on December twenty-third, people enter a radish-carving competition, and the winner can earn up to fifteen hundred pesos, which is a lot of money for poor Oaxacan workers."

"So, they carve shapes from these malformed radishes?"

"Exactly, but the radishes wilt in the warmth, and they only retain their shape and form for six to seven hours."

"That's a lot of trouble for so little radish time."

"Yes, but it's more than a carving competition; it's a sacred religious occasion. The Red Lady is also known as the Lady of the Radish, and occasionally appears to the townsfolk to bless them and bestow them with prophecies. In fact, the brothers here were the subject of one of those prophecies."

Jimmy noticed whenever they spoke of the Red Lady, he and the two brothers simultaneously made the sign of the cross. They did this multiple times, almost frantically, as if trying to get as many crosses in before someone started speaking again.

"How is that?" Jimmy inquired. He was still puzzled as to how a radish could become an object of religious significance, but he was more curious about the brothers' prophecy.

"The Red Lady appeared to Ms Guadalupe Montana during her pregnancy with the twins. Guadalupe received a message from the Divine One, revealing she would bear identical twins who would serve as my lifelong protectors. The Red Lady even imparted the precise names of my godsons, Raul and Fred. Wouldn't you agree this is a miracle of our time?"

Jimmy was taking another sip of the 1836 tequila as Armardo finished telling the story, and he almost spit it back out. Jimmy sputtered and coughed as he gulped down the tequila, stifling an instinctive burst of laughter. At first, he thought the other man was joking, but his expression was dead serious, even reverent. He seemed to truly believe what he was saying. Jimmy might have corrected him, but he was enjoying the moment too much and didn't want to risk upsetting Armardo. Choosing not to challenge Armardo's grasp of cellular biology, he cleared his throat, looked at the two wildly dissimilar brothers, and said, "I can see the resemblance. So, how do you tell them apart?"

"Their sombreros, of course. They help our friends and family recognize who is who."

Fred, the short man in the black sombrero, nodded and smiled proudly at Armardo's account. The brother in the pink sombrero continued to glare at Jimmy. His stare was like a death ray, burning into his skull.

Armardo sipped his tequila and continued. "When I married my wife, Francisca, I promised her and her best friend's family I would carry on the Oaxacan tradition of *Noche de Rábanos*. Furthermore, when Guadalupe Montana was carrying the twins and had her miraculous encounter with the Blessed Red Virgin, she envisioned two little wolves fighting off vermin and predators to protect the pack's alpha. This might not seem like much until you consider my surname, Lopez, means son of *Lope*, a Spanish term deriving from the Latin *lupus*, meaning wolf. How cool is that?"

Jimmy, once again, suppressed his desire to laugh out loud. If he were to post this story on social media, he would use the hashtag 'BatShitCrazyFamily.' But he was not afforded the anonymity of the Internet, and had to take the diplomatic route.

"Amazing!" Jimmy injected as much enthusiasm into his voice as he could muster.

Armardo, fortunately, didn't see through his act—he nodded in agreement and continued, "So, this is why there is red all over this area. My family and friends pay homage to the *Rábanos*, the holy vegetable, by colouring everything red."

Jimmy smiled, "Thanks for the explanation. I actually adore the colour red."

"Excellent. We are preparing for our big event and are already planning our carvings. Would you and your family like to join us? We have some spare radishes for you, your beautiful wife, and Max. He could do a carving for the children's competition that my Hector is in," Armardo offered generously as he held out his hand to make the deal. Jimmy took it, and pumped his arm up and down in a vigorous handshake. Armardo's grip was strong.

"Winners in the *Noche de Rábanos* competition typically receive prize money, as I had mentioned. In my competition, the winnings will be much larger than is customary," he added. Jimmy's ears pricked up, especially at the sound of the words 'prize money.'

"How much larger, would you say? Just out of curiosity," he asked, trying not to be too transparent about his desire for cold hard cash. He doubted he had done a very good job. Armardo hadn't yet let go of his hand, and so he was caught in an increasingly-tight handshake

"There will be three categories, and three prizes for each: traditional, new, and a children's competition." It wasn't exactly an answer, but Jimmy decided not to press the issue, not while the other man had his hand in a vice grip. He released his own grip on Armardo, but Armardo didn't let go of Jimmy. Instead, he kept shaking, waving his limp hand around like a wet noodle.

"However, in the adult category, I must warn you. Our tradition is the *Rábanos* loser gets waterboarded by my right-hand man, Raul," he added. At this, Jimmy instinctively jerked his hand back, but Armardo would not let go. He turned to look at the man with the pink sombrero, who gave him a cruel smirk.

"Waterboarded? Seriously, the loser gets *waterboarded*?"

"No room for losers," Armardo declared. "It's a family tradition. Waterboarding helps us grow spiritually." At this, both Fred and Raul chuckled. Jimmy looked around at the three of them, aghast, hoping someone would laugh and tell him it was just a dark joke.

"Spiritually? How does waterboarding help someone to grow spiritually?" he asked. Fred was happy to answer.

"It's obvious, doofus. The loser gets waterboarded using a cloth soaked in holy radish juice."

No one said another word. Sweat was running down Jimmy's back, and not just from the heat. His hand was clammy and throbbed with a dull pain. He remembered Vincente's reluctance to talk to señor Lopez, and his comment about not wanting to end up in *El Río de los Cocodrilos*, and began to fear he had just made a grave mistake. Armardo's grip suddenly felt like a crocodile's razor-sharp teeth on his arm, ripping it off his body to leave stranded on the shoreline. Just as Jimmy felt he couldn't take much more of this quiet tension, Armardo chuckled, breaking the silence.

"Just kidding." With that, he finally let go of Jimmy's hand. He pulled his hand back immediately and let out a weak laugh that quickly petered out. Relief flooded through him, but it was not enough to drive out the fear that had been there only a moment before.

"Good one, Armardo. You really got me," he said, trying to put on his best and brightest smile.

"Fred will drop off our spare radishes and some carving knives to you and your family so you have a chance to win. To answer your earlier question, I have decided to increase the prize to a thousand dollars in each of the adult categories and fifty dollars in the children's competition."

"Wow! That's incredibly generous. I'd hate to take it from you when I win." His smile was real now, as he thought of the security money would buy them. It was less than he had brought originally, but it would keep his family's vacation financed for a little while as he figured out how to get more money wired over. Plus, he could stop mooching drinks off people at Tequila Tommy's.

Armardo raised his hand in a toast, "May the best radish win."

Jimmy added, "May the radish games begin!"

The two men clinked their glasses and took large sips of the expensive tequila. Armardo went on to explain that two celebrities from the area would be the impartial judges, but he had also asked the family priest, Father Dominguez, to attend the celebration and convey blessings from the Red Virgin. Once again, all three men made the sign of the cross. Jimmy followed suit, but felt awkward as he tried to imitate their frantic cross movements. They kept going, looking like they had no intention of stopping, and Jimmy proposed a toast to get them to do anything else with their hands. The hurried crossing motions were stressing him out.

He raised his glass again and toasted the Holy Red Trinity: The Father, The Virgin, and the Holy Radish.

SEVEN

All Quiet on the Western Front

LUCY WAS THE FIRST to notice the quiet. There was no *BOOM, BOOM, THUD, THUD*. Only sweet, sweet silence. She punched the air and did a little jig with Max. Finally, she could hear the ocean waves crashing against the rocks and the sea wall. She could hear birds squawking, dogs barking, and the local cockerels doing their cock-a-doodle-doo-ing. Lucy could finally hear herself think. The first thing that flashed into her mind was that the Mexicans had left. If they did, they didn't clean up after themselves; she could see the patio hadn't been cleaned. The humungous sound system was still present. Red dye, or, as Jimmy explained, radish juice, was everywhere—everywhere except the pool, at least. They had done that much. The water was a clear blue colour once again.

"Honey," Lucy yelled, "I think they've gone!" Jimmy woke up from a deep sleep. He took off his purple eye mask, pulled out his lime green earplugs, and rubbed his eyes.

"What?"

"They're gone! I can't hear them anymore. Listen to the beautiful silence."

He hopped out of bed with his boxer shorts half-mast, baring most of his buttocks. He didn't believe Lucy for one minute, thinking this was one of her little ruses to get him out of bed. Jimmy looked out the window, however, and saw she appeared to be telling the truth. There were no signs of life from his neighbours, and the air was blessedly free of music. *Thank you, Holy Radish*, he thought to himself, a grin breaking out on his face. However, their beach towels were still on every beach chair and bed, and only the pool was free of radish juice.

"It's Sunday, Luce. Maybe they've gone to meet Jesus and repent for all the noise and bother they've caused. If we pray, maybe God will make them disappear like my Burberry wallet."

Although it was still early, around this time Jimmy would typically observe Mexicans working in the pool area, cleaning up the mess and cigarette butts left by his neighbours. Vincente regularly cleaned the pool, testing pH levels like clockwork. The condo, deck, pool, and sandpit seemed abandoned. If Vincente had spoken with Armardo and his noisy group, Jimmy would be grateful enough to kiss him and give him a generous tip. His good mood was helped by the fact he had woken up feeling clear-headed, despite drinking several glasses of Armardo's costly tequila. He had been right; the 1836 tequila didn't cause hangovers.

A surge of adrenaline coursed through Jimmy's veins; discovering what happened relied on locating Vincente, and he felt emboldened to find and thank him. While getting dressed, however, he couldn't help replaying his conversation with the property manager. He also recalled the stories of Juan, the cab driver, complete with details about the Wolfpack Cartel and their flashy sombreros. The little person and the non-verbal giant wore two large ones, one black and one pink, which seemed to line up with Juan's description of the cartel's 'capos.' He hoped they were not Wolfpack Cartel members. But Juan had talked a great deal, and most of what he said was so outlandish—it had to be a load of bollocks! Armardo had been friendly and welcoming—at least, when he wasn't crushing Jimmy's hand and joking about waterboarding. The brothers had been with him, and while the tall one was intimidating, Jimmy couldn't imagine a little person as a cartel member. But they seemed to be his bodyguards, and that was another thing that gave Jimmy pause. Why did he need bodyguards unless he was sketchy? Was Juan full of shit with his stories, or was he telling the truth? Could Armardo be the boss, and these men his sicarios?

Jimmy told Lucy he was going to walk around the complex to chat with Vincente and maybe grab another couple of purified water containers. He said he hoped they were still invited to the Radish Night celebration if the Mexicans hadn't left, as he was eager to win some much-needed moolah. Then finally, he grabbed some beach towels and books to claim a couple of sun loungers for the day, and set off. He skipped down the condo steps to the communal swimming pool area. Once he got there, he stood still, looked from side to side, breathed in the ocean air, and stretched his arms up towards the sky. *Today could be a perfect day*, he thought. He removed the towels on the two closest sun loungers to their condo, replaced them with his, and put two books on the chairs. The Mexicans hogging every sun lounger had pissed him off, especially when most of the chairs remained empty for the entire day. If they weren't there to claim the seats, Jimmy considered them as good as his.

The silence was simply wonderful. There was not a single Mexican, sombrero, Fatty Boom-Boom Cordoba, or Vincente in sight. Maybe the property manager, too, had attended church. Jimmy went to look for him and went directly to his office. The door was wide open, which was unusual, as Vincente often closed the door behind him. Even more unusual, he wasn't there. Whenever he left his office, he'd hang up a sign in Spanish and English that read, 'I'll be back soon.' There was no sign up today.

"Vincente?" Jimmy called out. No response. He noticed a few large, recently printed signs on his desk. Curiosity got the better of him and he went over to read them:

Attention! Guests will not play music in public areas between 9:00 p.m. and 9:00 a.m. By order of Vincente Property Rentals.

Attention! Guests will behave respectfully towards each other. Sun loungers and umbrellas will be shared between the two casas. If the number of guests exceeds the number of sun loungers, a 2-hour limit will be placed on each chair. By order of Vincente Property Rentals.

Jimmy let out a triumphant cry and saluted the signs. Then he pranced around the pool, practising his victory dance moves, before heading towards the large palapa that covered the outdoor kitchen and BBQ area. He continued to walk around the property, looking for posters that Vincente may have put up. Now, he was sure that he had talked to Armardo. Why else would he have printed out those signs?

Being mindful not to walk in front of the 'colossus,' in case it collapsed and he ended up buried alive beneath a sea of subwoofers, Jimmy soon found one another sign. This one was next to the sink and fridge freezer. Then he spotted two more, one stapled by the outdoor washroom and the other by the sandpit area where the inflatable toys were situated. The one that caught his attention, however, was the sign in the food preparation area, which appeared to have been vandalized. It looked like it had been sprayed with a red substance, though he couldn't quite tell whether it was radish juice, paint, or dye.

Jimmy investigated further and found the fridge compartment was crammed with radishes, leaving little room for anything else. This could explain the red spatter marks on the new sign. He searched for a cloth to wipe the sign; whether they vandalized it or not, the loud neighbours had to follow the new regulations. He chuckled at the authority with which the words were written, as if the sign read 'By order of Billy Big Balls Vincente.'

As he cleaned off the sign, it occurred to him how bizarre it was the Mexicans had used the entire fridge to store vegetables rather than beer or meat. Armardo had explained their traditions regarding the Red Virgin, but the fixation on radishes was no less strange for having been explained. What was not strange, however, was the Amador 1836 tequila. Now *that* had been divine. Then, like his thoughts manifested it into reality, Jimmy spotted out of the corner of his eye a bottle of Amador 1836 tequila left on a counter. Knowing that the bottle was best iced, he picked it up. At $3,000 a pop, it blew his mind to think someone would leave it out in the open. If Armardo was annoyed someone had complained to Vincente, putting away his expensive tequila might help ease tensions.

Jimmy admired the bottle. It was a quite fancy, wrought in the shape of a golden pistol. Armardo had bragged actual gold had been used in the design. He couldn't understand most of the writing on the label, but he saw the tequila was 100% Agave Azul, or blue agave, as Armardo had translated for him before. Sure, the drink was super-smooth, and it tasted fruity and floral, but a person had to be a little crazy to pay that kind of money for a bottle of booze.

To Jimmy, Armardo was anachronistic; he seemed like a nice, modern, well-groomed guy. He was generous with his money and friendly to strangers. However, his associates might be feeding people to crocodiles, he venerated the Red Virgin and believed the bullshit prophesies, and he celebrated the death of Davy Crockett at the Alamo. Although he did have good taste in liquor, another point in his favour. Jimmy was considering asking Armardo if he could keep an empty bottle and take it back to Canada as a memento.

Thanks to the property manager, the deafening music and other noises had stopped. Jimmy had an opportunity to make some money on the horizon. Things were now looking up for the Myers clan. The only thing that could make this day better was if he found his wallet or had money miraculously wired from his bank. Jimmy kissed the bottle of 1836 and opened the freezer compartment.

SMASH!

The bottle broke into a million golden shards; tequila and glass were everywhere.

Jimmy had dropped the bottle of expensive liquor onto the concrete patio. He let out a blood-curdling, high-pitched scream as he backed away from the freezer unit. Jimmy couldn't believe the horrific sight that was before him. He lost his footing, stumbled, and fell backwards into the pool. Despite being soaked and submerged, his eyes didn't leave the freezer. Staring back at him was Vincente's head, covered in blood and encased in cling film. One of his bloodshot, brown eyes was still in its socket, but the other was missing; his lips had been removed from his face, making his pearly-white teeth protrude like Mr Ed, the talking horse.

Shocked, Jimmy waded through the pool further and further from the freezer, unable to take his eyes off the grisly sight, until his arms felt the pool's edge behind him. His heart was beating out of his chest.

"What the feck!" he cried out. As his stomach was churning round and round, he desperately tried to process what he was seeing. If his brain was made of gears, there would have been deafening sounds of whirring. There was only one explanation he could think of: Vincente must have told the Mexicans to lower the noise and been decapitated for his troubles. The realization made Jimmy sick, and he threw up in the swimming pool.

He immediately hopped out of the pool, still looking at the head, whose one eye stared at him from inside the freezer. It dawned on him his fingerprints were all over the fridge freezer and the broken bottle. The shards of shattered glass on the patio floor refracted the morning sunshine. It was a crime scene sprinkled with gold.

Lucy had heard the brouhaha down at the pool, as well as Jimmy's cry of terror. She had left the front room and leant over the balcony of their condo to see what had happened. She knew his scream well. Jimmy yelled when watching hockey, losing a game of *Settlers of Catan*, or seeing an ant or a caterpillar. He had a distinctive screech, like an 11-year-old schoolgirl, and she'd had many opportunities to hear it. Looking down, she saw him throw up in the pool and hurry to get away. He looked as pale as a ghost.

"What happened?" she asked. He struggled to get the words out. She saw an inflatable plastic shark in the swimming pool, and recognized it as belonging to Hector, Armardo's son.

"It's okay, sweetheart, it's not a real shark," she teasingly reassured her husband.

"V-v-v-v-Vincente." Jimmy shivered and pointed towards the freezer.

"What about him, hun?"

Jimmy ran up the stairs in his soaking wet clothes.

"He's dead. Vincente is dead!"

"Dead? Are you sure?"

"He's deader than dead."

"Did you take a pulse?"

"A pulse? No, unfortunately, his head's been severed off his shoulders. Shucks, maybe I should have felt his carotid artery?"

"I don't understand; you're not making any sense," she said, walking past Jimmy and heading towards the stairs.

"Stay there. He's dead. His fucking head is in the freezer."

"What's a fucking head?" asked Max, who appeared between his mom's legs.

Lucy lied, "Daddy had said he was *ducking* his head in the pool because he felt sick." With that explanation out of the way, they sent Max to his room. Her freaked-out husband ran into the condo, took off his clothes, grabbed a towel, and dried himself. Lucy saw a man in a state of complete and utter panic. Jimmy was hardly paying attention to anything he was doing; he put on a dry T-shirt back-to-front and his shorts inside out with both pockets hanging out like dog's ears. Lucy's hands were covering her wide-open mouth.

"We-we-we need to find a phone in town. We have to call the police. The reason we couldn't find him is because he was . . . he is . . ."

"Ducking dead," parroted Max, peeking around the bedroom door and helpfully finishing his dad's sentence.

"Max! Stop that right now, and please go to your room." He scowled, hung his head, and complied. Jimmy waited for their son to leave, and leaned towards Lucy and spoke in a hushed tone.

"Vincente, his freaking head was staring at me as I opened the freezer to put away a stupid tequila bottle. It's wrapped up in cling film, one of his eyes is missing, and oh, *his lips are gone!*" He could see Lucy taking this all in, her mind whirring much as his had just a little while ago, trying to come to terms what she was hearing. Jimmy waited, knowing she would need time to collect herself.

"I'm going to see for myself," she said at last.

"No, no, don't do that. When we call the cops, they're going to bring in a forensics team or something to preserve the evidence. Think of all the CSI shit they'll have to do." He watched enough Netflix crime thrillers to know that messing with a crime scene was a big no-no. He just had, of course, but he hadn't known it was a crime scene.

"What do you suggest?"

Jimmy hadn't thought that far, but he did know that he didn't want it to look like he'd tampered with the scene of the crime. "I'll take a picture of the fridge to show to the cops, so they know where to look. Then I'll . . . close the freezer with a stick or something," he blurted out. He spoke without confidence, and it was obvious to Lucy he made this plan up as he said it, but she was in such a state of shock that she made no objections.

"Alright. I just can't believe he's . . . who would do such a thing? The poor man."

"That freaking nut-job dude with the pink sombrero, he's my number one suspect. Luce, lock your door until the cops arrive. Please don't open it for anyone except someone in uniform or me. Shit, I pleaded with Vincente to ask the Mexicans to turn the music down. Now look what happened to him. I should have taken the hit and put up with the din for a few more days; then they would have left, and Vincente would still have a body to go with his head."

"Could it have been the other guy with the black sombrero?"

"No, he'd need a ladder just to reach Vincente's neck. There's no way he could sever his head." The two of them stood in silence for several moments, having a plan of action but too stunned to make good on it. They were in a daze, as if having just woken up from a horrible dream.

"You'd better go, then," said Lucy, the first to recover.

"He even made fresh signs and put them up. He also made some spare ones on his desk. The one by the fridge freezer had blood splatter . . . I thought it had been defaced out of malice. Oh my God, oh my God, oh my God!" Jimmy was clearly still in shock. He spoke as if he hadn't heard her.

"For the love of God, please go to the cops. And please, calm down."

"Calm down? He's dead! His one eye. His lips—"

"Take some deep breaths."

"Stop the psychology bullshit."

"It's my job—it's what I do."

"I've just witnessed a gruesome murder scene on our relaxed Christmas holiday. I have the right to freak the feck out!" He was shaking and hyperventilating. Lucy sighed and pulled her trump card from the therapy pack, holding up her hands and gesturing as she spoke.

"Jimmy, just take a breath . . . and . . . calm . . . the fuck . . . down."

"Calm the fuck down." Both parents whirled towards the bedroom door. Max had echoed Lucy's words, his voice audible even muffled behind the closed door.

"Shush, Max! Stop being such a stickybeak. Daddy's upset, so mummy's trying to calm him down." Afterwards, she went back to the business of calming her husband.

A short time later, Jimmy was feeling more himself. He took a deep breath, just as Lucy had advised, and with that deep breath his composure returned. Or at least, enough of it to go back down and face Vincente's head again.

"Thanks for the session, Dr. Myers," he said, tongue-in-cheek. He returned to the freezer, closed the freezer door with a large pool noodle and from there went to report the murder to the police. Unfortunately, he forgot to take a photo of the crime scene.

EIGHT

The Loco Locals

JIMMY WISHED HE HAD tried to find one of the barfly's apartments. He had jogged to Tequila Tommy's, only to find the bar closed. He groaned. Los Piñata was like a ghost town on Sunday morning. Then, he noticed a local woman was strolling towards him. She crossed the cobbled road to give the pale white man a wide berth, wearing a back-to-front T-shirt and inside-out shorts.

Seeing this crazed and angry-looking gringo banging on the bar door at 8.30 am, she remembered how her alcoholic father had behaved when he was desperate for another drink of grog. She prayed the gringo would bang on the church door, rather than Tequila Tommy's, begging to be saved instead of for another drink.

"Hey, *por favor*, where can I find a phone?" Jimmy called out to her, waving frantically. He ran after the woman, caught up, and stood before her so she could not go further. She avoided eye contact and attempted to move past the demented gringo.

"Sir, I have no liquor. Kindly let me go on my way." She spoke in Spanish, as she didn't speak or understand English.

"Lady, I don't know what you are saying. *Por favor*, how do I contact the *policía*? Please, where is the *Policía Casa*? There's been a murder." To illustrate his point, Jimmy twisted his face into a grotesque expression as he made a throat-slashing motion with his hand, causing the woman to recoil in fear.

"Do you want to contact the police because you have murdered someone?" she asked, worried the crazy-looking gringo might also murder her.

"*Sí*, contact the *policía* . . . where is the po-leece stay-shun?" ensuring to enunciate his words slowly for her. The woman nodded affirmingly.

"I'm glad you're confessing to your crime. I'm sure they will be merciful to you in prison." Jimmy couldn't believe his luck that he had met such a gracious lady; he was finally getting through to her.

"Are you mentally ill, a murderer, plain stupid, or a combination of all of them?" she asked sympathetically. While he still had no idea what she was saying, she did point at her head and make a circle with her finger. He assumed it meant crazy.

"Yes, yes, I believe the killers are *severely* mentally ill," Jimmy answered, making a deranged Hannibal Lecter face. Some manic impulse overtook him, or perhaps it was the adrenaline running through his veins that clouded his judgment, but when he spoke again he tried to imitate Anthony Hopkins's performance as the notorious cannibal, hissing and slurping.

"I killed them for you, *Clarice*." The lady gingerly retreated, keeping a wide berth from him like she had encountered a rabid dog. Reading body language was not a strong point for Jimmy. While he didn't understand her words, he interpreted her nervousness as horror at the story he recounted. This comforted him, for he was certain she would help. She gestured towards the highway as she slowly backed away, and he immediately put his charade skills to use, confirming the direction. He followed the directions with his fingers, mimicking a walking motion as his fingers turned right on the road and took another right towards the highway. He could have cried tears of gratitude. The woman's gentle, soothing smile was infectious, and he smiled with her, deeply moved by her empathy for his plight.

For her part, the local woman suddenly felt sorry for the man's apparent mental illness and moved closer to him, resting her hand on his shoulder.

"Don't worry. I'm happy to send you some of my skirts and fishnet stockings to make jail time easier on you," she suggested. His Spanish had improved since arriving in Los Piñata, if only a little, so he felt confident enough to express his gratitude with a heartfelt "*Muchas gracias.*"

With Jimmy's hand in hers, she smiled and closed her eyes in prayer, commanding Satan to depart from him in the name of Jesus.

"Thank you for praying for me," Jimmy replied with a grateful smile. "Your kindness has left me speechless."

"I'll call the police and tell them you're turning yourself in for murder. I don't want to jump to conclusions, but to be safe, I'll advise them to be cautious around you in case you are a serial killer." *And maybe I'll get some reward money for turning him in. I deserve it, for dealing with this psycho gringo*, she thought to herself after she spoke.

Jimmy stepped aside and let the extremely helpful lady carry on her journey. Although still overwhelmed by what had transpired at the condo, he was thankful the people in this town were so friendly towards foreigners like him.

As she walked away, she turned, waved, smiled, and shouted, "Goodbye, you murderous son of a bitch!"

Jimmy waved back, even blowing her a kiss of gratitude. "You're welcome to visit me and my family any time. We're at the *Casa Blanca*," he yelled after her.

Jimmy scurried towards the highway, and when he reached the main road, he turned right, just as the kind lady had shown. He continued to walk at a brisk pace to the police station. Few cars passed him on the typically busy road, and he saw no pedestrians out and about during the thirty-minute walk. If the streets were empty because everyone was at church, the services here were surely far more interesting than the typical bore-fest ones he'd been to. Though he'd never say it to her face, Jimmy would rather have a root canal without anaesthetic than attend Lucy's church.

He arrived at the official-looking building panting and breathless, his back-to-front shirt drenched in sweat. As he entered the police station, the sound of phones ringing and radios crackling filled the air. Pushing the revolving door, he was surprised to see a uniformed policeman reading a porn magazine behind the plexiglass.

"Hello. *¡Hola!* Does anyone here speak English?"

The cop looked irritated by the disturbance.

"*¿Hablas inglés?*" asked Jimmy.

The cop shook his head and hunched his shoulders.

Jimmy reverted to charades again, as it seemed to do the trick with the helpful lady. He gestured towards his eyes with two fingers to indicate he had witnessed something. He mimicked Marcel Marceau's door-opening imitation and acted like he was shivering, hinting that a freezer might be present. Jimmy pretended to slit his throat with an imaginary knife and fell dramatically to the floor as if succumbing to a spine-chilling death. The climactic moment of his drama, which had up to this point used only bodily movements, hand gestures, and facial expressions, came when he broke the charade's code and dramatically sputtered out, "A man . . . has been . . . murdered!" He made the gasping sounds of a man taking his last breath. When he was done, Jimmy stood triumphantly, proud of his performance. He felt he deserved an Oscar.

The police officer yawned, gave a sympathetic nod, and moved towards the door. Jimmy waited expectantly. Quick as a flash, the cop reached out to Jimmy, grabbed his arm, and slapped a handcuff onto his wrist. He snapped the other cuff on the waiting room's metal seat armrest.

"What are you doing?"

The police officer remained silent and didn't respond. The prisoner was hunched over as the officer searched him, confiscating his driving licence and the meagre amount of peso notes in his pocket before retreating behind the plexiglass window.

"Why did you do this to me? I just came here to report a crime. Someone's been murdered at the condo we are staying at!" Jimmy cried. The police officer gestured to Jimmy to remain calm and with difficulty, said in English, "My boss, the Inspector, no here. He go to church. He here soon."

Groaning in frustration, Jimmy rattled the handcuffs against the chair. Quick as a flash, the officer's demeanour changed.

"Shut up, you murderous psycho-freak!" he yelled in Spanish. The venom in the cop's voice shocked Jimmy into silence. He struggled to grasp why he was being treated so severely, but he hoped help was coming.

He closed his eyes and listened to his breathing, hoping it would calm his racing heart. Jimmy congratulated himself on his miming abilities, despite the predicament he now found himself in. He felt satisfied he had done everything possible to prove a crime had occurred. He took a deep breath, desperately hoping the Inspector was a man of intelligence, faith, and moral values, praying that the Inspector could speak English and swearing he'd take Spanish classes once he returned to Canada.

⤜⤜⤜ ⤛⤛⤛

JIMMY ENDED UP waiting for two hours. During that time, he tried frequently to communicate with the officer behind the plexiglass screen. Using his one free hand, he expressed it was an emergency and tried in many ways to show that a man's head had been cut off. The officer said nothing and remained expressionless, but appeared to jot down a few things in his notebook.

Jimmy was overjoyed when, at last, another man strode into the station. He stood up in his excitement, forgetting he was still cuffed to his seat. He moved too

THE MAN WITH THE PINK SOMBRERO

quickly and yanked so hard against the handcuffs he lost his balance and slipped, falling flat on his bum. Humiliated and sore, Jimmy tentatively stood up to see the man was ignoring him and instead talking to the cop at the front desk.

After their exchange was over, he at last turned to Jimmy and motioned for the scruffy foreigner to come forward. He lifted his handcuffed wrist, hoping to elicit sympathy from the dapper-suited guy.

The man identified himself in English as Inspector Lopez of the Federal Police and head of the serious crime division. Boom—just like that, his prayer was answered; Jimmy was ecstatic he and the Inspector shared a language. The policeman was tall, like Armardo, but leaner and had sharper features. His hair was jet black and heavily oiled, and his smile was a welcome sight for a very stressed and frustrated Jimmy Myers.

"Leading Constable Baños said you've come here to confess a crime?"

"What? Leading Constable Baños? No. I want to make it clear I did not confess to anything. I came here to *report* a crime, and I was handcuffed by the man you referred to as Baños. My two hours of *detainment* have left me feeling quite traumatized."

"Two hours, eighteen minutes, and sixteen seconds have elapsed. Do you struggle with basic counting skills?"

"What?"

"According to Leading Constable Baños, you admitted to slicing the throats of four men from ear to ear." Jimmy was confused. The Inspector had changed the subject, and just like that had changed it right back. Why did it matter exactly how long he'd been here? And how could Baños possibly have misinterpreted his stunning performance? He rolled his eyes in exasperation.

"That's interesting, considering he can't speak or understand English."

"According to Leading Constable Baños, you managed to overcome the language barrier by reenacting the crime, and you threatened him by making a slicing motion across your neck."

"What the—"

"When Leading Constable Baños saw you, he suspected you were the serial killer responsible for the deaths of thirty-two people in Baja, California. We know him as 'The Slash Throat Strangler' or, as we Mexicans refer to him, *El Estrangulador de Garganta Cortada*." Jimmy was shocked, both by this putrid turn of events, and by how a man being referred to as 'Leading Constable' could be such a colossal idiot.

The Inspector's eyes narrowed as he spoke, his suspicion palpable. "Or perhaps you are the one they call *El Decapitador*, who has terrorized the Yucatán Peninsula?"

"You must have a murderer infestation in Mexico if you can rattle off two to accuse me of being right off the bat. I assure you—I am *not* a serial killer. After leaving the crime scene at the White House, I arrived here in a hurry. Leading Officer 'Washroom' didn't understand English, so I gestured and mimed to explain the situation." Jimmy spoke calmly and steadily, albeit with a hint of agitation.

"You are staying here with a woman?"

"Yes, my wife."

"By the way, women aren't exempt from being serial killers. I solved several ghastly murders committed by a beautiful blonde lady. She poisoned her victims with anthrax."

"Was she called 'The Anthrax Assassin' perchance?"

"No, 'The Cupcake Killer.'"

Jimmy chortled, his shoulders shaking with hilarity. "Firstly, I want to clarify that I'm not a woman. Secondly, my cooking skills are so bad that I can barely even make beans on toast, let alone cupcakes laced with the deadliest bacteria on the planet."

"Are you saying you didn't murder anyone?"

"Yes—I am a Canadian! I am on holiday. I am staying in a condo with my wife and son for a few months. This morning, I found a severed head in the poolside freezer while looking for Vincente, our property manager."

"Could your wife be the killer?"

"No, and neither is my four-year-old son."

"Can I ask if you identify as a female?"

"What?"

Inspector Lopez grinned. "If so, it's possible that you desire to be a woman, and your frustration has caused you to feel imprisoned in a man's body, which led you to cut off your property manager's head."

Jimmy sighed. "No, I am a cis-gendered male. Please, can you stop asking me irrelevant questions?"

"What may be *irrelevant* to you may be *vital* to an experienced detective like myself. You have one eye and two ears for that reason."

Jimmy scrunched up his face. "One eye? Don't you mean one mouth?"

"No. 'Cyclops,' the 'Acid Bath Killer,' comes to mind. He had one eye and a large left ear that was five times the size of his head."

"It must have been so hard to track down a one-eyed man with a bulbous ear. Only a real genius could have brought him to justice." Jimmy's voice dripped with sarcasm.

"If you would please rest your mouth and let the professionals do their job," the Inspector replied. He took out his notebook and pen and asked Jimmy more questions about the crime scene. As he answered, Jimmy realized he had forgotten to take pictures of Vincente's head in the freezer and smacked his forehead in frustration, calling himself an idiot.

Inspector Lopez gazed upwards at the ceiling and muttered "Vincente" repeatedly, attempting to recollect the person's identity.

"He was the property manager at the White House," Jimmy explained.

"Oh, the odd-looking Colombian that lives and works at *La Casa Blanca*?"

"Well, he wasn't odd-looking when I talked to him yesterday. He still had two eyes, lips, and a head attached to his body."

"Apart from yourself, are there any other suspects we may want to investigate?"

Jimmy groaned. "Yes, a large extended Mexican family and their servants are also staying at the condo, and I'm sure someone from that group killed him."

"Why would they do this thing, this act of barbaric butchery?"

"Well, they were playing obscenely loud music and hogging all the loungers by the pool, so I asked Vincente to ask they turn the music down and be more respectful of their neighbours. They didn't take it well." At this, the Inspector let out a barking laugh that wracked his entire body. Once he recovered, he entered the waiting area and released Jimmy from the handcuffs. He jotted down additional details in his notebook and took out a business card, which he passed to Jimmy.

"I will send my people to investigate the scene. In the meantime, you are the prime suspect in this investigation. You must not leave Los Piñata. If you attempt to do so, you will immediately be placed under arrest."

Jimmy shook his head in disbelief and muttered, "Whatever!"

Free of his cuffs, he beat a hasty retreat from the police station and started his walk back to the condo. Several emergency response vehicles sped past him on the highway. These included military-like armoured cars and black sedans with sirens blazing. Jimmy was relieved. He reached into his pocket to retrieve the business card the annoying officer gave him. It read:

'Inspector Ramon Lopez, *Detective de Delitos Graves, Unidad de Delitos Federales.*'

As Jimmy looked at the name 'Lopez,' he felt a knot form in his stomach; he hoped and prayed the Inspector wasn't related to any of the Lopez family members staying at the condo. Then his thoughts drifted back to Vincente's head, and his wife and son hunkering down at the very place his head was found. The killer could come after them too. Tired as he was from his walk to the station, he hurried back to the White House as fast as he could.

When he finally reached the condo, Inspector Lopez was in discussion with Armardo and the Montana brothers. He was drinking a small can of beer. Armardo laughed and gave him a congratulatory slap on the back. He was the first to recognize Jimmy had arrived at the scene.

"Hey, what is all this glass piled up on the floor? Is that my expensive tequila?"

Jimmy responded, "I'm sorry about that, but—"

"Señor, why did you make *my brother* come to the casa? The entire task force is here. Their guns were drawn on arrival, and we had to put our hands in the air. It was very humiliating."

Jimmy's fears were confirmed; the Lopezes were related. "It may have been something to do with the severed-off head I discovered this morning," Jimmy pointed to the fridge-freezer unit.

The four Mexican men laughed out loud.

"Look in there if you don't believe me."

Inspector Lopez obliged and opened the door. Inside was a head covered in blood-smeared plastic wrap.

"This?" Inspector Lopez raised his eyebrows and pointed at the head.

"That?" cackled Armardo, also pointing. Jimmy tentatively moved closer to within three feet of the head.

"This supposed severed head is, how do you say, a *rábano*," Inspector Lopez said.

"A what?"

"A radish, or a *rábano*, that Don Armardo had carved himself. He is very skilled with the blade."

"Yes, I can see it *looks like* an exquisite carving, but *where* is Vincente's head? I know the difference between a man's head and a turnip."

"Radish," chirped the little guy with the black sombrero.

Jimmy couldn't believe his eyes; a face had been carved into the radish with one eye missing, and pearly-white teeth had been embedded into the vegetable.

"This is not Vincente!" cried out Jimmy.

"No shit, Sherlock," Fred replied.

"So, you wanted to report the murder of an edible root vegetable?" asked Inspector Lopez.

"Maybe it was *vegicide?*" laughed Fred, who was becoming more annoying by the second.

"My ex-wife used to 'murder' the guacamole, but Mexico doesn't allow me to arrest someone for their terrible cooking," Inspector Lopez added, flashing a wry smile. Everyone laughed except for the bedraggled Canadian, who stared at the freezer in a catatonic state. When he finally spoke, all he could say was, "Vincente's head was right there." He pointed at the freezer hopelessly, as if with the power of his finger he could will the severed head back into existence.

"Señor, your report was not helpful and has caused this family many problems. It's a radish, you moron!" declared Inspector Lopez.

"Why would anyone in their right mind carve a man's ghoulish-looking face onto a radish?"

Inspector Lopez, Armardo, and Fred answered simultaneously, "*Noche de los Rábanos.*"

NINE

The Gringo Quiz Nite

THE HULLABALOO SURROUNDING VINCENTE'S head left Jimmy unsure of how to proceed. He couldn't stop revisiting the memory of first seeing it in the freezer, uncertain if it was indeed a work of art or a grisly murder scene. He was initially confident he discovered Vincente's head—also known as his bonce, noggin, nut, noodle, bone-dome, or cranium. However, after the initial discovery, it had become a vegetable. The more he thought about it, the more convinced he became his mind had been deceiving him.

Lucy, meanwhile, had heard about the 'Quiz Nite' held at the gringo bar and thought it would be nice to throw Jimmy's name into the mix, as a good bit of fun competition might help him to move on from the 'decap-a-radish' incident. When she told him they were attending a 'Quiz Nite' at Tequila Tommy's, he was ecstatic. He paced around the condo fervidly, practising his silly victory celebration much to the amusement of Max, who tried to do the same and ended up falling off the table. He'd have suffered a nasty bump to the head if Lucy hadn't caught him at the last minute.

"Remember, if we win tonight, it's a team effort. Let's not get too eager for victory dances, or we'll be as popular as Putin popping into the Lululemon store in Kyiv." Jimmy ignored his wife. He was busy trying on one of the few button-down Hawaiian shirts he'd brought on holiday if the opportunity arose to compete in any games.

"I might do MJ's intro to 'Thriller' and get the DJ to play the song," he said, already anticipating sweet, sweet victory.

"Daddy's impossible, isn't he?" Lucy sighed, turning to Max. He wasn't listening either; he'd gone back to imitating his dad by running around and flailing his arms.

"Why do we have to be on the same team as your giggling amigas?" Jimmy suddenly asked, turning to Lucy.

"What's your issue with them? They're all very bright, and they hold Masters or PhDs. Each one of them is a strong, intelligent, powerful woman."

"Excuse me?" chortled Jimmy, "PhDs and Masters? Sure, maybe with research topics like, 'Does a coconut have a big willy?' and super-profound quantitative analysis questions like, 'Can six divided by two equal more than twelve?'"

"Enough!" Lucy raised her voice, pulling a face and frowning. "Mella, for example, is a renowned zoologist, a TV celebrity."

"Zoologist? Celebrity? You mean she was a 'consultant' on *Tiger! Tiger!* The Korean reality show where contestants wear body armour and put on tiger costumes saturated with big cat sex-pheromones, and the contestant who lasts the longest while being humped or savaged wins the grand prize?"

"Stop it, Jimmy. They have credentials and qualifications coming out of the yin-yang. You sound a tad insecure about your past academic performances."

Jimmy made tiger-clawing actions, which came with unconvincing sound effects. He chuckled. "I rest my case."

Lucy scoffed, "What about you, the man wants to end world poverty by teaching people how to win at roulette?"

Rather than shame Jimmy, this made him grin proudly.

"*Red's Hot!* never fails, Luce."

"It would help if you were less misogynistic and took us women seriously."

"I'm just kidding, Luce," he lied. "We should see how the night pans out for us." With that, he returned to practising his triumphant dance moves.

"We also have some guys called 'Sober Bob' and 'Deaf Barry' on our team. Bob knows a lot about sports, especially golf and hockey, and Barry is a wealth of knowledge regarding curling, auditory and olfactory processes, and '70s music," Lucy added. Jimmy snorted, barely suppressing his laughter.

"*Deaf* Barry and *Sober* Bob? They sound like a bundle of laughs."

"We also have a married couple who are well-known around the Hollywood scene, so they'll rock at all things movies and docuseries."

"Sounds more promising."

"Their names are Bradley and Marcus."

"Ugh, I hate the name Marcus. It reminds me of that arrogant croupier at the Desert Springs Casino. The only Marcuses I've ever known are dicks."

"Daddy, what's a dick?" asked Max.

"For goodness' sake, watch your language!" Lucy cried out. Jimmy mouthed 'sorry' to her. "Like it or lump it, you're in a team now, so let's use each other's strengths and stop criticizing people, especially my friends," Lucy continued, pulling him out of his reminiscing.

"Yes, Mom," he replied with a petulant scowl on his face.

Once the couple had gotten ready, Jimmy and Lucy had a gin and tonic before walking to Tequila Tommy's. Mac had kindly offered to look after Max so Lucy could enjoy herself.

Mac was the mother figure of the amiga group; her friendly blue eyes sparkled with warmth and compassion, and often a twinkle of mischief. She wore her short, silver hair with pride. Mac was a cat lover who had become so obsessed with rescuing stray felines her friends had spread the rumour that 'Catwoman' was considering cat whisker implants in her cheeks. She wasn't, of course, but her friends teased her about it relentlessly.

Tequila Tommy's was practically overflowing with people. Rectangular tables had been set out with seven or eight seats each. Jimmy fist-pumped everyone at the table and sat down between a guy named Bradley on one side and Bob on the other, with JayBee and Barry next to them. Despite his jovial attitude, Jimmy was a man with a mission—he was laser-focused on victory; losing was not an option. He got extraordinarily loud, too. He possessed a deep booming voice when sober, and after a few beers, it sounded like a foghorn.

He immediately volunteered to be the quiz team leader so he could control the team's submitted answers and keep the group's eyes set on the prize. Mella had already submitted the team's name in advance, and much to his chagrin, she had called them the STDs, or Sexually Transmitted Diseases. He shook his head in disbelief when he saw the team's name on the large card at the centre of the table. He shrugged his shoulders and let out a huge sigh, knowing nothing could be done about it now. The humiliation would be worth it when they won.

Before the quiz began, Jimmy tried getting acquainted with Bradley, who kept turning around and waving at his partner Marcus, who was sitting two yards away at the bar. Bradley spoke without taking a breath, as if the words were coming from a speaker at the back of his throat. Both men were bronzed, fit, wore spray-on shorts, had bleach-blonde hair, and were considered very good-looking.

"Me and Marcus have been together twenty years. We live in LA, but we spend half of the year in Mexico. We just *love* Los Piñata." He gave Marcus another wave, and his husband waved back. Jimmy looked between the two, curious.

"Is Marcus going to be joining us?" he asked.

"Oh no, he's very shy. He didn't want to be part of the 'Quiz Nite'. . . but he loves seeing me compete." Bradley winked and gave a sly smile. If there was a message there, Jimmy didn't pick up on it.

"Why is that?"

"It's a *huge* turn-on for him. When I answer a question correctly . . . well, let's just say his passion knows no bounds," Bradley answered, leaning towards Jimmy and speaking conspiratorially, as if the two of them were sharing a scandalous secret. Jimmy let out an awkward laugh, finished his beer, and burped loudly.

"If the STDs win, he'll cream his pants," Bradley continued. After downing the beer, Jimmy felt a little less uncomfortable. So what if Bradley was oversharing? They were all friends here, and they were going to win. Jimmy would make sure of it.

Jimmy was feeling more comfortable with his team, but when he saw Tequila Tommy, the quiz master, getting ready, he turned his attention to the task at hand. He shushed everyone as Tommy prepared to ask the first question, making sure his team had their pencils and papers ready. He reiterated the answer sheets should be given to him, and he would decide on the final answer.

"I love assertive men," Bradley whispered to Lucy. She grinned and looked over at her now-domineering husband, who was starting to act like a correctional officer. He shushed Bradley again and reminded his 'inmates' not to speak or shout their answers lest the other team hear their responses.

Jimmy shushed loudly, similar to the screech of brakes on a vintage train.

Deaf Barry looked around, confused. Barry was a tall, handsome, sixty-something black man with a narrow build, salt and pepper goatee beard, and clean, super-shiny shaven head.

"What?" Barry asked Jimmy. In response, he raised his finger to his mouth and pointed to Tommy, who was about to read out the first question.

"Marcus and I had a discussion last night—after our lovemaking, of course," said Bradley suddenly. Jimmy was focusing too intently on Tommy's question to shush him.

"TMI," he muttered.

"And I'd love to hear your opinion, as I'm told you're a brilliant and knowledgeable man." Jimmy just pointed at Tommy, not even looking at Bradley. Unperturbed, the other man pushed on.

"What do you think the worst way to die is?" This got Jimmy's attention; he'd been face-to-face with death only a short while ago. Or at least, he thought he had.

"Did you just ask me what the worst way to die is?"

"Yes, what do you think? Marcus and I couldn't agree."

Sober Bob, known for his quick wit and easygoing nature, raised his hand as if in a classroom. Bob, a short, swarthy man around Barry's age, had a warm smile and friendly blue eyes that lit up whenever he spoke.

"No need to raise your hand, sweetheart—we are all ears," chuckled Marcus.

Sober Bob blushed and lowered his hand. Having overheard the question, he responded, "Maybe . . . to be buried alive in your coffin."

"Oh, that's nasty," said Bradley.

"Or being skinned alive . . . like House Bolton did to their enemies on *Game of Thrones*. Mr Myers, what do you think?" asked Marcus from his bar chair. Jimmy was highly irritated; their ill-timed questioning distracted him from the quiz, but he knew if he didn't give them an answer, they'd just keep pressing him, and he wouldn't be able to concentrate on the questions.

"I think being killed by a ladybug has got to be the worst way to die," he responded cryptically.

"No way, ladybugs are harmless," argued Bradley.

"Oh, not true—" Jimmy smirked, "they have a *vicious* bite."

"Shut up!" Marcus exclaimed in astonishment.

"Google it if you don't believe me. Ladybugs can bite through diamonds."

"We aren't allowed to look at our phones," muttered Marcus indignantly.

Bradley mouthed to his partner, "Don't you dare! We'd be thrown out of the quiz,"

"Oh please, God," mumbled Jimmy under his breath.

When Jimmy was finally able to listen, he realized Tommy was already on the third question. Jimmy had missed the first two, distracted by Bradley's inane questions. He hunched over in his seat and cupped his hands over his ears, trying to drown him out and focus on Tommy. Not so easily deterred, however, Bradley nudged him and got his attention again.

"My ex—"

"We're missing questions." Jimmy snapped. He kept trying to focus, but between Tommy's rapid-fire questions and Bradley's insistent prodding in his ribs, he couldn't maintain concentration on any one thing, his concentration pulled in two directions.

"My ex-boyfriend told me a nuclear bomb enema was the most agonizing way to die."

Tequila Tommy bellowed out, "Question Five: What part of the body is used for—"

"I think he was being silly. Jimbo, what do you think? Who in their right mind would want a Uranusimum-235 enema?"

"It's Uranium-235."

"My goodness, Jimmy Myers, you are a clever one. You should enter yourself on a quiz gameshow like *The Wall* or *Jeopardy*. We have connections in LA. Do you want me to connect you to one of the producers up there?"

"Sure, but can we get through this little quiz first?"

"Okay. Okay. Let me tell you what Marcus thinks the worst way to die is, and then we can focus on the game." Jimmy shut his eyes tight as if he could will them both away. He was desperate to join in the quiz, while they didn't seem to care. Bradley beckoned Marcus to sit closely behind them both, and Jimmy knew there was no escape.

"Honey, tell Jimbo here what you think is the worst way to die." Marcus was quick to oblige his husband.

"According to my best friend, who is a nurse at the emergency clinic in Bel-Air, they admitted a guy with a vacuum cleaner attached to his penis and a can of orange flavour pop inserted up his ass."

Jimmy, for all his irritation, couldn't help but laugh.

"He opened the can of pop in his rectum to see if it felt nice."

"No way!"

"*Yes,* way," said Marcus, matter-of-factly.

Then, Bradley butted in. "He didn't die, though. He went on to star in a couple of our reality series. Therefore, that wasn't the *worst way to die*, as the guy lived." After Marcus and Bradley finished their story, quizmaster Tommy asked what the capital city of Uruguay was.

Deaf Barry announced, "Star Ship Enterprise."

JayBee whispered, "Buenos Aires."

Sober Bob shook his head . . . "Spain."

"Lima," said Mella

"No, no. Lima used to sing with that Kajagoogoo band," responded Deaf Barry.

"That was *Limahl*, you numpty," snapped Mella in reply.

"No, no, no," Jimmy's hands shook with frustration. "*Montevideo* is the capital city of Uruguay!" he shouted in a commanding, foghorn voice.

Tequila Tommy's fell silent, save for the faint humming of the neon sign outside. Jimmy's sudden outburst brought all talk to a halt as the other teams simultaneously wrote down Montevideo as their answer.

"You said we don't shout out the answer," voiced an irritated Bob.

"What do you expect me to do? I'm losing my mind here. Barry, do you seriously think the capital city of Uruguay is . . . the Star Ship Enterprise?"

Deaf Barry smiled. "Oh, I thought the question was 'What was the name of the *spaceship* Lieutenant Uhura was in.'"

"You're right about that," said JayBee. "I remember her on Star Trek. She wore that weird wireless earpiece and was the Enterprise's communications officer."

"Yup. Uhura inspired me to make my 'iTrumpet' listening device," added Barry proudly.

Tommy's voice rang out, "Question number eight."

"Alright, I think I should be the new captain. Jimmy's clearly more interested in whatever Bradley's going on about," Barry declared. Jimmy whirled around to face him, but was once again distracted by Bradley, who gently punched his arm.

"Can we not just listen to the quiz questions, Bradley?" Jimmy's tone was desperate, and his eyes were wide and pleading. His position as team captain, and their victory, were on the line. How did Bradley not get that?

Tommy announced, "That's the end of round one. Please hand in your answer sheets, and I'll post the team's scores."

Jimmy threw his hands up in the air in frustration. Round one was officially a bust.

Unfortunately, as the quiz went on, Bradley wouldn't stop talking to Jimmy, Bob, and Marcus. He asked question after question and became more animated as the evening progressed. The entirety of Team STD chimed in with their views on the worst way to die. The common consensus was the more prolonged the death, the worse it was, so they decided that catching syphilis from a leper or dying from a horrible flesh-eating bacterial infection was at the top of the list.

By evening's end, Jimmy Myers did not get an opportunity to do his signature celebration, as the STDs had come last in the quiz. Thankfully, he had enough beers to make him feel happy and content, and the radish head incident was no longer in his thoughts. Marcus and Bradley liked Jimmy and Lucy, as they were easy to talk to, and kept chatting their ears off after the quiz was over. Bradley insisted they go to their pad for more beers and excellent conversation. Jimmy lied and pretended to be interested in doing that in the future.

The couple left Tommy's and walked home hand-in-hand, doubling over in laughter as they reminisced on some of the quiz answers and Bradley's 'interesting' questions.

"Hey Luce? Never, and I do mean *never*, let me sit next to Bradley again," after recovering from another laughing fit. He laughed so hard he brought tears to his eyes, and he wiped them away with his hand.

"I'll see what I can do, but I already invited him and Marcus over, along with my amigas, to our Boxing Day gift exchange."

Jimmy didn't know whether to laugh or cry, so he kept doing both.

TEN

The Bank of Armardo

FOUR-YEAR-OLD MAX MYERS WAS having the time of his life in the condo's swimming pool. He was playing with little Hector Lopez, who was four years older. The two boys were initially hesitant about interacting, as they didn't know each other well. That initial hesitancy didn't last long; for children, it rarely does. They playfully splashed each other and hung out together at the sand pit by the pool. The boys laughed heartily, built sand structures, and dive-bombed into the water.

Max was a competent swimmer for his age. Lucy had insisted on lessons for him, and he seemed more comfortable in the water than on land. The boys couldn't understand each other's words; Max only knew English and Welsh, while Hector only knew Spanish. But with their hands and facial expressions, the children conversed in a language of their own. Despite the challenges, they understood each other through charades—far more effective than Jimmy's attempts at miming at the police station—and kid telepathy. Jimmy was amazed at how easy it was for the children to get along, even when they faced so many barriers.

"It's good to see the two boys having so much fun!" Armardo said, catching Jimmy off-guard.

"So true. They don't seem to have a care in the world."

"Unlike you, perhaps?" pressed Armardo. Jimmy let out a sigh.

"It's a long story."

"And I have all the time in the world. Well, aside from helping with the radish carvings, but that can wait." Armardo's display of sympathy caught Jimmy off-guard. When he found the radish head, he had thought the well-spoken man and his associates were cold-blooded killers, the violent cartel men Juan had warned him about. He couldn't reconcile that with the kindness Armardo had shown him thus far. Even if he was a little intense, he seemed to be just as he presented on the surface: a kind, gregarious man.

"I never apologized for the misunderstanding with Vincente, by the way. I guess I panicked when I saw the radish carving, being in an unfamiliar country and all. Someone filled my head with all sorts of horrible stories, and I let my imagination run wild. I'm sorry for the trouble." Armardo held up his hands in a way that seemed to communicate 'it's all good.'

"Never mind Vincente's radish head. Why not tell me what's going on in yours? You look like the weight of the universe is on your shoulders."

Jimmy sighed again, this one louder and longer than the last, and told his story of what had transpired during the past forty-eight hours: his missing wallet, his inability to connect with a rational human being from his bank, the freezing of his and Lucy's credit cards, the lack of Wi-Fi, no cell phone service, and the 'head' he saw in the freezer.

Armardo listened thoughtfully. He didn't interrupt, only nodded along with Jimmy's sad tale. The only noise he made was the occasional "mm-hm" of commiseration, sounding genuinely invested in the gringo's plight. It was not until Jimmy finished talking that the other man ventured to speak.

"I am a wealthy man, you know. The fact I'm staking over two thousand dollars on a radish-carving competition is proof enough. I'd be happy to help you until you get back on your feet."

"Are you sure? After what I did? I really don't deserve it."

"Of course you do. Look at how our sons are playing. Why should we hold the past against each other, when they do not?" Even as Jimmy kept protesting, he knew how much Armardo's support could mean. They still had almost their whole vacation out in front of them, and he had no idea how long it would take to un-freeze his and Lucy's accounts and get money wired over. The radish-carving contest, if he even won it, would only help temporarily.

"It's not like I don't have any money; I have a healthy bank balance in Canada. The trouble is trying to access it. I've been incredibly fortunate financially, but I ran into some trouble. Lawyers got involved, and though everything's been resolved, it's taken a toll on us. That's part of the reason we came here on holiday, actually. Of course, I tried to get money wired over and that psycho woman called Chéckina froze our accounts—" Jimmy explained, trailing off as his anger at the woman who'd completely misinterpreted him over the phone reignited.

"Ah, lawyers. You know what lawyers and crocodiles have in common?" Armardo asked, grinning in anticipation of the punchline to his joke. Jimmy shook his head.

"They're both cold-blooded reptiles that will cost you an arm and a leg." He and Jimmy had a chuckle at that and then fell silent.

"I guess success went a bit to my head," Jimmy continued. "I wrote a book, hoping to help others out of poverty."

"That's an admirable thing to do."

"Book sales were terrific. Money was pouring in left, right, and centre. Then it all fell apart. I started to receive the odd bad review, got a bit of a backlash from a few liberal academics, which was followed by legal letters. Before I knew it, there was a class-action lawsuit against me." Armardo's grin fell, and he shook his head in sympathy.

"What was the book about?"

"It was a kind of self-help book. The trouble was people didn't read or understand it properly, and some disenchanted folks broke the golden rule of what I was trying to communicate."

"Perhaps your luck will improve now," Armardo said. That he did not explain his comment gave it a cryptic air, and Jimmy raised an eyebrow in surprise.

"Why do you say that?"

"Celebrating the Blessed Red Virgin may bring you good fortune. Trust in her, for she never fails to provide." After providing his explanation, Armardo made several signs of the cross.

Jimmy gazed at Max and Hector playing in the red pool water. It was true; red was Jimmy's colour, and the entire condo complex was covered in radish juice. Red was all over the condo and pool area, the barbecue, and the walls, and it spattered Vincente's "Do not . . . by order of" sign. As he contemplated this, he looked over his shoulder and saw the black and pink sombrero guys sitting there, casting shadows over their boss. Thumbing towards the two odd-looking men, he asked, "Why do those sombrero guys always stand so close to you?"

"Protection; they guard me with their lives."

"Why?" he asked in his surprise. He had thought they were bodyguards, but the way Armardo spoke, it sounded like their bond was something deeper and more enduring. There was the Red Virgin's prophecy, of course, but Jimmy felt there had to be more to it.

"They are sworn by blood. We consider these blood oaths to be highly significant and binding. I trust them more than anything else on this earth."

Jimmy looked again at the two brothers. Both wore their sombreros and cowboy boots and were now sporting spray-on type Speedos, resulting in a look that was utterly ridiculous. Raul wore pink trunks to match his sombrero, and Fred wore black ones. Jimmy didn't want to snigger and ruin his nice conversation with Armardo, but he couldn't help but make a comment.

"Hey guys, you're looking very colour-coordinated this morning!"

Raul stared right through him. Fred smiled and took the comment as a compliment.

"*Si, señor,* we like wearing our budgie smugglers on a hot day."

Jimmy laughed. An old Australian friend used to refer to his Speedo's tight-fit as 'budgie smugglers,' but he hadn't heard that term for a while. Yes, they both looked silly. But at least Fred had a personality, unlike his expressionless twin.

"So, you are worried about the money situation?"

"Yeah, of course. There's a real possibility I won't be able to talk to anyone from our bank to figure out a solution. It's the holiday season," Jimmy lamented.

"You seem like a good guy, Jimmy, an honest guy. I read people well."

"Thanks. I try to be." Jimmy smiled appreciatively.

Armardo turned around towards the brothers and asked one of them to bring them both a cold beer. Fred went to the cooler and grabbed them. As he brought them back, Armardo reaffirmed his desire to help, shushing Jimmy from responding until he had finished what he was trying to say. Jimmy listened, once again overcome with gratitude. This generosity completely floored him, even as it was tempered by the understanding this man could be dangerous.

"What if you can't connect with the bank? The banks here are closed because of the festive season too. So, amigo, I may have a solution," Armardo said as he took his beer from Fred.

The man in the black sombrero offered one to Jimmy, who took it with a nod of thanks. His mind started to race. What was this solution? After all, for all Armardo's generosity, he still suspected he was connected with this Wolfpack Cartel. If so, given he had the sombrero-wearing brothers working for him, he was almost certainly the boss. Jimmy didn't want to be in debt to a person like that—he recalled Juan's warning against owing the cartel favours. But what choice did he have? Juan was himself a teller of tall tales, but even if Armardo was who Jimmy suspected him of being, refusal could be just as dangerous for him as agreement. All he could think of was politely declining, hoping Armardo wouldn't press him on the matter.

"I broke your expensive tequila bottle. I called the cops on your group. I thought one of you might be the new Mexican Ted Bundy. And now you're offering to help me when I haven't done a thing to earn your kindness. It's more than I deserve."

"Nonsense. I will give you enough money to tide you over until the holiday season ends; then, you can go to the bank and arrange a 'fire' transfer."

The two sombrero guys laughed at their boss's witty remark.

"Or rather, a wire transfer. Then you can pay me back in due course."

"No, no."

"Yes, yes, I insist. Saying no to Don Armardo Angel Lopez is not an option." As little as Jimmy liked the idea of relying any further upon his kindness, he was remarkably insistent, and the money would be a huge help. No matter how he couched his refusal, Armardo wasn't going to take it . . . and the last person to defy him ended up with a radish carving of their head in a freezer.

"Thank you. I'll pay it all back. I promise." Armardo held out his hand and Jimmy shook it with reluctance, remembering how uncomfortable their last handshake had been, but he couldn't be standoffish when the other man was going to lend him money.

"Hopefully, it will also cheer you up. You have a long gringo face and a dark gringo cloud hovering above your head," reassured Armardo.

"*Si*, Don Armardo, the gringo sure looks like he had swallowed a wasp," chimed in Fred. Armardo and Raul nodded in agreement.

"Lending you money would be a drop in the ocean for me. I know you'll be good for it when you get your money back from the bank, so please accept my gift. Fred will sort it out for you."

Fred grinned. Armardo was still shaking Jimmy's hand.

"Thank you, really. I can't say it enough times. You've been incredibly generous." Jimmy hoped that by placating him, he would let go. His grip was just as firm as before.

"Think of it as a favour for your family. You care for them very much, and I admire that. To Mexicans, nothing is more important than family. I do this for them too, your wife and son," he said, casting a glance over at Max and Hector. They were still playing in the water, swimming and splashing each other. There were no uncomfortable handshakes there, or suspicions between them.

As he waited for Armardo to let go of his hand, Jimmy had a flashback of Vincente's head, with his lipless white-toothed smile. A shudder went down his spine. When Armardo finally let go, he opened another cooler box beside him and took out an iced-up bottle of 1853 *Especial.* He poured the tequila into two small glasses.

"May I ask, what's so *special* about this tequila?"

"Jimmy, this is the superior version of the tequila we had before, a super-limited edition. This bottle celebrates the execution by beheading of all the Yankees captured at the Alamo. You're Canadian, so you can't possibly be offended." He nodded politely, but the word 'beheading' made him feel nauseous. For a moment, he felt like throwing up in the pool again. The feeling died down quickly, and when Armardo raised his glass in a toast, Jimmy did the same.

"To new friendships. *Salute.*"

"Cheers," responded Jimmy.

Hector and Max continued to play in and by the pool. Slim and elegant Francisca Lopez came out to watch them. Francisca was a petite, forty-seven-year-old woman with an elegance that only comes with age. Her long, glossy, deep-black hair cascaded down her back, perfectly framing her delicate features. Armardo's position in the cartel has afforded her many luxuries, and she did not shirk from taking advantage of them, but she remained grounded and appreciative of the simpler things in life. She looked happy her husband had made peace with the gringo family. She also knew the Blessed Red Virgin would anoint the Lopez family's important celebration later that evening, now her husband and Myers appeared to be friends.

LUCY HAD HEADED out to see her old friends, leaving Jimmy to look after Max. As she left, she saw her son playing happily with Hector, looking like they'd been friends their whole lives. They were being watched by an attractive woman, who Lucy assumed was Armardo's wife. She heard Max call out for his dad to play with them in the water, and he got up from his seat, where he had been talking to Armardo, and obliged.

On her walk into town, relief washed over Lucy. Yes, the condo was a lovely place to stay, beautiful and idyllic. However, her hubby was highly agitated by their neighbours' behaviour, becoming a ball of nerves around them despite his budding friendship with Armardo. She felt the need to get away—from his anxiety, but mostly from the Mexicans and the drama regarding Vincente's radish head. Jimmy was now second-guessing himself about what he had seen. Lucy would love nothing more than for it to have been a big misunderstanding. As she hadn't seen the head, it was easier to believe Jimmy had let his imagination run wild. Still, it was unlike him to sensationalize something like that.

Lucy was a beautiful, diminutive, intelligent woman with a heart of gold. Her greatest strength was finding humour even in the darkest situations while remaining gracious and empathetic. Not only had she become an extremely competent psychologist and a regular visiting lecturer at the university, but she was also an excellent and attentive mother. She had always been the levelheaded, pragmatic one in the relationship; Lucy was the yin to Jimmy's yang.

Lucy would generally support her hubby's ideas, even the nuttier ones. After all, when he returned from the casino with a bag full of winnings back in the day, she had to concede his *Red's Hot!* craziness was genius. He must have had some divine revelation to come up with it. Lucy had read his publication, and the logic and mathematics were somewhat flawed. However, Jimmy's *Red's Hot!* epiphany was undeniably effective, and his sincere desire to become more affluent than the British Royal family could've been a reality if the book wasn't so provocative.

Today, however, would be her day. After all the craziness of their vacation thus far, she deserved it. Lucy was looking forward to seeing her three pals, and as she walked along the beachfront, broke out into a fit of giggles as she thought of their nicknames for each other. The amigas called her 'Juicer' for two reasons. Firstly, she loved Juicy Fruit chewing gum. Secondly, she was renowned for making the best, healthiest juices with her beloved top-of-the-range Kuvings device.

Lucy remembered how angry she was when she discovered Jimmy had experimented with the super-expensive juice extractor once when she was out of the house. She'd banned him from using it ever again. His fig, Vegemite, cherry, and peanut butter juice not only tasted disgusting, but it also ended up being impossible to clean and nearly burned out the device's motor. When she confronted him, Jimmy blamed an intruder. He told a story about an Australian backpacker who broke into people's homes and made himself Vegemite smoothies. Bizarrely, according to his outlandish tale, the Aussie also stole people's left-footed sneakers from shoe racks and cupboards—and just as he said, the family's left-footed shoes were gone. As it turned out, before Lucy arrived home, crafty Jimmy had hidden the family's left-footed shoes to authenticate his tale.

"Luce, the Aussie guy was on Crime Seekers. Apparently, his modus operandi is to break into a home and steal just one shoe from each pair. Detectives suspect him of having one left leg. They're calling him 'Hoppy the Bush Man-garoo.' After breaking in and taking several left shoes and boots, he leaves his calling card: a Vegemite smoothie. Then, apparently, runs off while humming 'Down Under' by Men at Work."

Lucy called his bluff by pretending to call the police and ask for more information on 'Hoppy.' Jimmy listened as she spoke to two imaginary cops, Constable *Shu* and Sergeant *Horne*. When the fake call ended, he 'confessed' Max had busted her Kuvings, and his daddy was only trying to protect him from his mom's wrath. As Max was only two *and* was with Lucy at the time of the juicing "crime," Daddy was busted, and Lucy had to lock her beloved juicer away from her idiot husband. Somehow, recalling the incident only made her love him more, and for a moment she worried about how he and Max were getting on with the Lopez family. It was too late to turn back now; besides, she'd committed to seeing her friends, and that was what she'd do.

When she arrived at Tommy's, her three friends cheered, and Lucy embraced her gang one by one. The four of them found a table and sat down with each other. Lucy had seen her pals at the 'Quiz Nite,' but it was hardly a conducive environment to having a relaxing chat, especially as her hubby was so intense about winning and the rest of the table was talking over each other about the worst way to die. When they sat down, her friends immediately demanded a rundown of her experiences, as they had only heard dribs and drabs from the ex-pat rumour mill.

Lucy shared the drama with them: the missing wallet, the hilarious immigration officers, the arrival of the Mexicans, the incredible noise, Armardo, the strange twins and their sombreros, Vincente, his disappearance, the head, the Night of the Radish, the quirky cop. There was an awful lot to unpack. The amigas listened attentively.

"Chillax now, Juicer, take a deep breath, suck in the sea air, and chug a tequila shot with your margarita," Mac said, pouring salt onto her hand. Lucy laughed, licked her hand, bit into a piece of lime, and downed the fiery liquid. The girls cheered, and Mella ordered another round. Lucy hushed the girls.

"Hey, we're having a celebration tonight. A party."

"What's the occasion?" asked Mac.

"It's the Night of the Radishes."

The girls laughed.

"Or, as the Mexicans say, *Noche de Rábanos.* The Mexicans invited us, and I'd feel a whole lot happier if you guys were to come over and join us."

"Night of the Radish? Like the vegetable? What on earth is that all about?" asked JayBee.

"Some Oaxacan celebration that's a bit like Halloween. Instead of pumpkins, they use radishes, a kind of religious vegetable veneration before Chrimbo Day. Come on, girls, check out our digs, and bring your swimsuits and some booze. It might be fun!"

The rowdy group cheered, toasted *Noche de Rábanos,* and chugged back some more tequila shots.

ELEVEN

The Surprise Visitor

WHEN LUCY RETURNED TO the condo, Max and Jimmy were sleeping on the king-size bed.

"Up! Up! Up!" Lucy clapped her hands, her green eyes sparkling with excitement. "It's time to carve!" she hollered. Jimmy wiped the drool from his mouth, still feeling the effects of the alcohol. The 1853 *Especial* was very, very good, and he'd drank a lot of it. Evidently, it would take a while for it to all get through his system.

"My amigas will be coming over tonight to give us some much-needed moral support for the contest." Jimmy smiled; anything that meant more encouragement for his and Max's radish creations was a good thing in his book. Unfortunately, as his thoughts drifted to his carving, he realized he had no idea what it would be.

"I appreciate it, Luce, but I have no clue what to carve. Other than something that'll knock the judges' socks off and net us the prize money."

"Just be your usual creative self, and you'll be fine," Lucy replied, planting a kiss on his forehead, leaving a bright red waxy lip mark, making Jimmy look like a romantic Hindu.

"Maybe I'll carve a radish of Raul's head. After all, there's nothing but space up there. I can craft a detachable pink sombrero which, when removed, exposes the vast emptiness within his empty skull. It'll highlight his rebel-rousing personality, extraordinary wit, and charm."

"Steady on—he's not done you any harm," said Lucy. As they got out the radishes they'd procured for the competition and prepared to make their masterpieces, Max insisted on sitting next to his daddy so they could carve together. Jimmy, who had gotten a large can of beer, ruffled his son's hair, cracked the can open, and chugged it in three swigs—followed by *BUUUURRRRRPPPP!*

"Jimmy! That's just gross," Lucy shouted disgustedly. Max laughed, stuck out his bum, and farted.

"Max. Stop it!" She scowled at her husband, "See, he copies all your bad habits."

Jimmy answered Lucy with another deep burp. With another laugh, Max tried to fart again, scrunching up his face with effort, *PFFTHWEEP*—but ended up pooping himself instead.

"Oh no. A shart!" chuckled his dad. Max stuck out his bottom lip and looked like he was about to cry, but it turned into a giggle when he realized his dad was amused.

"Since you find it so funny, you can have the honour of changing your dirty child. I guess boys will be boys," smiled Lucy. "I'm glad my girls are coming over this evening to balance the equation."

Letting out an exaggerated groan, Jimmy got to work helping Max out of his dirty pants and underwear, disposing of the runny turd, and getting him cleaned up and into something new. While he did all this, Lucy finished getting the radishes out and preparing the necessary equipment, including the paring knives and red vegetable colouring. When they were done their respective tasks, Jimmy and Max got to work, and soon they got distracted from the carving and started playing with the paint. Dad was painting Max's face red, and Max was painting his dad and everything within ten feet of him

"Daddy's red hot!" shouted Max, flicking radish juice on Jimmy's face.

"Don't you think you're going overboard with the colouring?" Lucy asked her husband. She didn't want to get any paint or radish juice on her clothes.

"It's all washable, Luce. You know Max and I are *all in* for these radish celebrations."

"Are you sure you're not just taking the piss out of the Lopezes? *Noche de Rábanos* is a very sacred occasion for them, you know." Jimmy flashed her a big grin; with so many tequila shots in him he'd lost count, and Armardo having lent them a wad of money, he was in a great mood. It was like a huge weight had been taken off his shoulders, and he could stretch for the first time in what left like forever.

"No, babe, they want us to join them in veneration of the Red Virgin or the Holy Guacamole Mother of the Turnip, and I respect that. You know how I love Mexican mainstream religion," he said sarcastically.

KNOCK! KNOCK! KNOCK!

THUMP! THUMP! THUMP!

Jimmy and Lucy whirled around to face the door, which was being struck with significant force. Then looked at each other for a tense moment before Jimmy went to open it. Inspector Lopez and Leading Constable Baños barged into the condo, not bothering to wait for the door to be opened. Their shoes were squeaky on the tacky, radish-covered floor.

"Welcome . . . I'd invite you in, but you seem to have done that yourselves," Lucy said with mock politeness. Jimmy just stared at them with his mouth open. His face and clothes had been covered entirely with the red radish juice. He was holding a paring knife, dripping with the red, sticky fluid.

"Have I caught you in the act of committing another crime?" Inspector Lopez asked him, staring at the floor and the knife. "If I look in your freezer, will I find Vincente's head?"

Jimmy shook his head, which was thankfully attached to his body.

"I have a search warrant; you must comply, or you'll be arrested, and Max will be taken into the care of our social services."

"What? Are you serious?" asked an astounded Lucy.

"Your husband is my prime suspect in the property manager's disappearance and probable homicide." At this, Jimmy let out a disbelieving laugh.

"You're really still on about that? It was all a misunderstanding, remember?" remarked Lucy.

In response, Inspector Lopez gave his suspect an official-looking document written in Spanish. Lucy grabbed for it, but Lopez snatched it back, pointing to Jimmy.

"Only *he* can read it!"

"But he can't! He only knows a few words of Spanish. I can interpret for him." Her protests did not move Inspector Lopez, who shoved the paper in the direction of her husband.

"Cry me a river!" he snapped.

"How professional," shot back Lucy with indignation. When Jimmy took the document, the Inspector strode forward and threw open the door to their main bedroom. Leading Constable Baños stood by the door, blocking any attempted entry by either Lucy or Jimmy. He put his hand on his gun holster and frowned at the perplexed couple.

Jimmy was dumbfounded, "This is ridiculous!"

"*Esto es illegal,*" shouted Lucy through the guarded doorway. Inspector Lopez did not respond, which only infuriated Jimmy more. Drunk and angry, he laid into the fraudulent Inspector with everything he had.

"Since you can't do your job, let me do it for you. The signs prohibiting loud music Vincente had recently put up were stained with *his* blood. I discovered *his* head in the fridge alongside your brother's casa. After I report the crime to you, any hope of due diligence goes out of the window. What about searching the residence of Armardo or the psycho Kray twins? Don't give up your day job on *South Park*, Officer Barbrady!" As Jimmy berated the Inspector, Lucy worked off her stress by cleaning the countertop of radish juice. The two of them waited for him to come back, and when he finally reappeared at the bedroom door, Jimmy had another barb locked and loaded.

"Welcome back, Inspector Clouseau."

Lopez replied, "Wasn't he the *Pink Panther* detective who was a complete clown and imbecile?"

"You got it, genius." Inspector Lopez scowled at him, and turned to Lucy.

"Mrs Myers, are you cleaning up the crime scene of one of your husband's victims?" Jimmy, wide-eyed with fear and indignation, looked from him to Lucy. Anxious herself, and seeing her wild-looking husband with his face spattered with paint and radish juice, she let out a little laugh.

"Yes, it's a fair cop, Guv! My 'usband brutally murdered two large radishes. Guilty as charged, innit," she said in a Cockney accent. This got a smile out of Jimmy, but Inspector Lopez did not respond. He slowly walked over to the knife station, took the wet knife with his latex-gloved hand, and held it to the light. He smelt the blade, produced an evidence bag, and dropped the knife into it.

"Great, now we can't even carve our radishes."

"Boo-hoo, sulky man-child." Lopez mockingly rubbed his eyes in a crybaby manner.

"Nice and classy," snapped Lucy.

"Mr Myers, be aware I am watching you closely, and we have not found the weapon used in the so-called 'murder.'" He held up the evidence bag containing the red-coloured kitchen knife and examined it closely.

"I need to send this one to the lab for analysis," he said, turning to Leading Constable Baños.

"You haven't found his head or his body yet, either. Good work, Inspector," uttered an exasperated Jimmy. Lopez took out his notebook and made some notes.

Jimmy asked, "What are you scribbling in your little book? I know, you're writing: 'I, Inspector Lopez, confess to being stupider than the man from Jupiter.'"

"Oh, you are a funny guy, eh? We will see how *stupider* I am when you get charged, convicted, and become a good prison wife for one of the cartel's capos."

Lucy grimaced at this remark. "If you're done harassing us and saying disgusting things, *leave*. Both of you."

"Yes, Inspector Bird-brain, leave now," demanded Jimmy, while making squawking noises and flapping his arms like a bird. Lopez shook his head, clearly not understanding his comment. Then, with parting scowls, the two police officers left the condo. Once they were out of earshot, Lucy's angry, defiant looked faded and she turned to Jimmy. Her concern was written plainly in her expression, with her brow furrowed and eyes darting constantly to the door.

"Hun," she said, "You need to watch your mouth. Calling him 'Inspector Clouseau?' 'Bird-brain?' Saying he's 'stupider than Jupiter?'"

Jimmy smiled nervously and squawked.

"Yes, he's annoying and has the IQ of a lemon. I get it, but don't let him get under your radish-red skin." Lucy tried to suppress her laughter, but it was difficult as her husband looked like an enormous red pepper. In desperate need of a drink, she walked over to the fridge, opened the door, retrieved two beers, and popped them open. She gave one to Jimmy and kept the other for herself.

"Our Mexican neighbours will be gone soon, and we can start to enjoy our time here. Thanks to Armardo, we have plenty of funds, our Christmas dinner, and the Yankee Swap to look forward to. Besides, all this may have nothing to do with the Inspector's brother, who, to be fair, has only been kind to us. Whatever he's involved in."

"Yes, Ma'am," Jimmy replied, standing up straight and giving her a salute. Max, the little red pepper, ran out from his room, where he'd hidden while the Inspector and his crony had been poking around, and mimicked the gesture. This time, she couldn't hold her laughter in. Lucy raised her beer and proposed a toast.

"To a night of radish fun and plenty of laughter!"

⫸⫷

THE THREE AMIGAS arrived at the condo with bottles of booze. They wore bright red bikinis, big red earrings, and their lips were covered in glossy red lipstick. All three punched the air at the same time and shouted out, "Radish Power!"

"My goodness," said Jimmy, and started to sing 'Roxanne' by The Police.

"Jimmy's in the party spirit. Come on Juicer, take a page out of your hubby's book and get your glam rags on. It's time to par—tay!" You've got to get into the spirit," encouraged JayBee.

"I only have a red T-shirt and shorts, ladies. I can't compete with how radish-ing you all look."

Mac threw some red spray-on hair dye and big, red earrings in her direction.

"My goodness, Max and Daddy, look at you both; you're like an advert for Crime Scene Central—so much radish blood," Mella commented, looking at father and son.

"Much like you 'red-lighters,' we're both making an effort. We're gonna take the prize money home to Momma!"

Lucy smiled to see her friends and Jimmy getting along. The girls moved over to Max and admired his radish carving, which looked like a character out of his favourite TV show, *PAW Patrol*.

"What are those, Maxy?" asked Mella, pointing at two enormous spheres under the dog's tummy.

Max looked up at her, "Chest-eye-cals."

"Chesticles, sweetie? Do you mean testicles?" giggled Mac.

"Nope. Apparently, Max insists they're called chesticles," said Lucy.

Max looked at Mella, "These are big balls on Rubble's chest. He's got big, big balls—like Daddy."

The girls laughed in unison.

As the sun set on the horizon, a bustle of activity began by the pool patio and under the large palapa. Jimmy's 'favourite' DJ, Pedro Cordoba, started to crank up the music, and a light show began. The workers in the area moved quickly and efficiently, assembling several tables adorned with brightly coloured tablecloths. The smell of sizzling meat filled the air as the barbecues were fired up, and platters of kebabs, beef steak, and vegetables were set out on the prep table, ready to be cooked. Fred Montana was beavering away at his carving, adding the last touches to his radish masterpiece. Armardo and Francisca proudly applauded Hector's carving effort as one of Francisca's maids placed his radish upon a table.

Jimmy smirked and wondered how the Mexicans would react when his carving was announced as the supreme winner. Looking around, he noticed Raul Montana standing upright and attentive in the shade of the palapa. His eyes moved back and forth, surveying the scene, talking into a radio mic on his lapel, likely checking in with the other bodyguards regarding security issues. Occasionally, he would fiddle with the ends of his well-manicured handlebar moustache. He was dressed in a black sequin-lined outfit, and completed his look with his characteristic large pink sombrero and black, pointy cowboy boots. Every time Jimmy looked at Raul Montana, a shudder went down his spine. Whenever Raul met his stare, it felt like daggers were being buried into his eye sockets. His expression was impassive, looking like it had been carved into his face. He didn't seem to be able to smile any more than he was able to speak.

Turning his gaze away from Raul, Jimmy kept watching the frantic activity below. Within a few hours, without a doubt, he would bring home the win. This victory would be for his family, ex-pat friends, and his beloved Canada. He considered inquiring with Pedro Cordoba about playing the 'O Canada' national anthem to rub his success in their faces. He liked the idea; when he won, he would command old Cordoba to crank up the colossus to play the anthem to the max.

He put in his ear pods and found the tune on his 'essentials' playlist. He pressed play, stood up, put his right hand on his chest, and sang with gusto, knowing few would hear him as Cordoba's Latin Bandido Mix continued to shake the foundations of the resort.

"O Canada! Our home and native land! True patriot love in all of us command. With glowing hearts, we see thee rise, The True North, strong and free! From far and wide, O Canada, we stand on guard for thee. God keep our land glorious and free! O Canada, we stand on guard for thee."

TWELVE

In A While 'Lil Red Crocodile

FOR A CARTEL HITMAN, Fred was a genial, happy-go-lucky, and super-resilient guy. Despite his short stature and stubby fingers, he was an artist at heart who relished opportunities to express his artistic side. Although he would have liked to be a world-class pianist, renowned hair stylist, or legendary lead guitarist, his talent was writing deconstructed, revolutionary poetry, and was where he thought his destiny lied. Becoming one of Armardo's trusted sicarios, however, had stymied his hopes and dreams.

Aside from his size, Fred's most distinctive feature, by a country mile, was his thick mop of black hair. His moustache was much bushier than his brother's and almost concealed his cute little nose. Achondroplasia aside, Fred looked like any other Mexican *bandito* portrayed in classic cowboy movies. He was also known as the 'mop-up' guy, as he was entrusted with the cartel's finances. The twins' occupations were listed as 'Environmental Clean-up Professionals' on tax returns. Raul tended to deal with eliminating waste; Fred was at the disposal end of the spectrum. But his primary goal was to ditch his cartel lifestyle and live an artsy-fartsy life surrounded by his crafts and poetry.

Although they shared the same womb, the brothers' personalities were polar opposites. Unlike his stoic, silent brother, Fred was funny, charismatic, and empathetic, with a great sense of humour. Raul was the cutter and throttler of throats and breaker of bones, and Fred cleaned up his brother's messes. He did so reluctantly, and yet proudly wore his battle wounds. He was also an animal lover, while Raul couldn't stand them and thought the world would be better if all animals were put in a gigantic microwave oven and liquidized. There was only one creature Fred despised: the *Crocodylus acutus*, or the American crocodile, found in salty river systems that hung out in the brackish water estuary in *El Río de los Cocodrilos* that ran through Los Piñata. Part of the reason he hated them was because they were Yankee crocodiles, not like the all-Mexican Morelet's crocodile. Mostly, however, his distaste for them stemmed from having to feed them as part of his disposal responsibilities. He would throw the bodies, torsos, and heads of Raul's victims into the river. He didn't make it easy for the wretched reptiles; he dangled the body parts over the river, taunting them before throwing them in. He wore crocodile skin boots to piss them off, as if they could recognize the material and take offence, and his black sombrero was adorned with a band of crocodile teeth and bore a few crock toothmarks in the fabric, which fed his ego.

Fred's hatred for the crocs was mutual; he was certain of this. He vexed them with his taunting, and this act of defiance had proven dangerous on multiple occasions. One early evening, a particularly obnoxious and aggressive crocodile leapt out of the river, deliberately missed the dangled severed arm he was holding onto, and latched its jaws right in the flesh of Fred's right buttock. After receiving many stitches for the wound, he returned to the river a few days later and taunted a similar giant croc, which lunged at him and tore a gash out of his right bicep. Rather than retreat, his injuries only emboldened him, and he constantly thought of ways to return the love to these disgusting creatures.

Fred had, after some strategizing, made a plan to give the crocs a taste of their own medicine. He devised a method for euthanizing them, which would give him more time for his poetry and put a pause in his disposal duties. He didn't think the plan through beyond his mixture, but he didn't care; he was desperate to put an end to his dealings with the reptiles, and was eagerly looking forward to the last meal Mr and Mrs Crocodile ever ate. He ground up a potent mixture of fentanyl, ketamine, pentobarbital, and xylazine, and injected it into a body part with which he would taunt the hungry crocodiles. However, it wasn't as effective as he had hoped. After he'd fed them, some of the crocodiles were seen staggering drunkenly along the river bank. Some would appear on Los Piñata's beach, snapping at the unsuspecting sunbather's legs, while others washed up dead. This provided him very little comfort, as he'd hoped to kill them all. These reports made the cartel suspicious, and they set to keeping track of their precious disposal mechanisms so they weren't killed off. Thus, Fred didn't get another opportunity to finish what he'd started.

Fred was excited for *Noche de Rábanos*, as this was his opportunity to showcase his artistic skills and put his crocodile failure behind him. Fred rated his dexterity with a paring knife as highly as his poetic and pharmacological veterinarian skills. He smirked as he gazed at the giant radishes, their bulbous shapes taking up most of the preparation table. Fred had been brainstorming for days and finally settled on the perfect carving for tonight's radish event.

"*¡Ganadora, cena de cocodrilo ganadora!*" Fred had exclaimed to the servants helping him construct the work of art. This meant, "Winner, winner, crocodile dinner!" Fred sniggered, took a swig of tequila, and went to work on his masterpiece.

⤜⤜⤜ ⤛⤛⤛

PEDRO CORDOBA HAD been yelling since late afternoon. Lights strobed into the evening sky, and an impressive fireworks display exploded into the starry night. The competitors stood behind their radish creations, each more intricate and unique than the last. It was an ostentatious display, and Jimmy felt butterflies in his tummy. The loud music highlighted Armardo's favoured eclectic blend of Mariachi, Norteño and Banda.

Armardo took the microphone from the ebullient DJ and welcomed everyone present, using both Spanish and English. Most of the competitors had managed to keep their carved creations from drooping in the heat by using fans to blow air over heaps of ice. The crowd waited with bated breath as he announced the radish judging would commence at 9 pm. Time was of the essence, as the radishes would decompose within hours.

Three categories were to be judged: traditional, modern or *nuevo*, and a children's category. Jimmy and Max were the only gringo contenders.

Armardo thanked everyone for being good sports and participating in this momentous Oaxaca tradition. Jimmy loved any competition, and this *la noche de los rábanos* was no exception; he was all in.

For this battle, he was bothered that he was at a significant disadvantage, as he had yet to learn what the other sculptures would be like, hadn't been told about any sort of theme or guidelines, and had little time to prepare. However, he wanted to win and wanted to win hard. He imagined climbing to the top of 'colossus,' that terrible multitude of woofers and subwoofers, and doing his trademark victory celebration as a special 'up yours' to these Mexican lunatics.

Jimmy decided to carve a Mickey Mouse and friends radish display, using the white flesh of the radish for the body and the purple-red colouring as an outline. In his carving extravaganza, Mickey was running, and Daffy Duck, Pluto, and Minnie Mouse followed him. He thought his radish looked dope.

"Gosh, Jimmy, that's SOOO good," remarked Mac.

"That's amazing," commented JayBee encouragingly, who walked past and patted him on the back.

He smiled at them and admired his radish creation.

Being her usual direct self, Mella said, "It's not very Christmassy. Can't you carve a little mistletoe into the scene or even a few bits of holly? Or maybe surround Mickey and his gang with snow falling from the sky, possibly using the white flesh of the radish—" Jimmy, who had heard enough, cut her off.

"Listen, Missy Mella-n-cholic, what does Mickey or Disney have to do with Christmas? In fact, what do flipping radishes have to do with Christmas? It's not a celebration of Christmas, anyway. It's to do with the Red Virgin of the Radish," he retorted.

Mella repeatedly blinked at Jimmy, not expecting him to be such a snapdragon.

JayBee replied, "Actually, Christmas has to do with the Virgin Mary, the three kings, and baby Jesus. Yes, it's Chrissy Eve tomorrow." It was as if she hadn't even heard him.

"Oh, I forgot *the angel* Daffy Duck appeared to *the virgin* Minnie Mouse and said, 'Fear not, for a Radish has been born on this day in Los Piñata and will be *the legume* that becomes the saviour of the veggie world!'" Jimmy was shouting now; in his hyper-competitive state, he had a hair-trigger temper and was quick to defend his masterpiece.

"Honey, a radish isn't a legume. It's a root vegetable. Now take a chill pill and stop snapping at folks trying to help you improve your Disney scene," Lucy admonished.

"Agreed, Luce. Jimbo, it would help if you had a few tequila shots to calm you the flip down," laughed JayBee.

"Yeah. So much for trying to be nice. Peace out, dude," said Mac.

"Yep, we were just being helpful," added JayBee. Jimmy glowered at all four of them until they walked away.

"He's a touchy lad, isn't he?" Mella commented to Lucy when they were out of earshot. "Though I'll admit he's got reason to be. Max's *PAW Patrol* 'chesticles' monster could be *the* winner. I've never seen balls *so big* on a dog." She punctuated her point by downing another shot of tequila.

"Or a man," Lucy sniggered, nodding towards Jimmy.

Left to his own thoughts, Jimmy's initial defensiveness faded, giving way to worry. What if Lucy's friends were right? What if there was some Christmas theme he didn't know about, and not sticking to it would cost him points? He couldn't risk that. Bowing to the panic, he quickly and skillfully carved a couple of Christmas tree silhouettes in the foreground of his newly named 'Disney Mexico Wonderland' carving, and added a shining star to make it a tad more festive. All the amigas clapped and cheered as he finally showed off his festive Disney display, and their support emboldened him once again.

All the carvings were displayed on several tables erected under the large palapa. Each participant had to stand behind their creation, which he found rather odd, as he expected a certain amount of anonymity to avoid biased judging.

Jimmy, finally able to see his competition, was astonished by the standard of radish carvings on display. They had given him just one large radish, yet some carvings contained a dozen, some of which were humungous. He stood back and surveyed what he was up against.

First, he saw a radish nativity scene with Joseph, Mary, baby Jesus, a stable, cattle, and three wise men. Each figure was about two to three inches in height. It looked fabulous. The amigas had been right to suggest making his scene more festive.

The second carving that came to his attention was a massive red turkey-like creation. Someone had carved this mutant bird from a gigantic, oversized radish. Jimmy has never seen such a gargantuan radish in all his life. The red turkey was truly a work of art, featuring exquisite feathers in shades of pink and white, and the artist had masterfully carved the radish flesh to resemble complex claws. This entrant had to be a contender. But Jimmy told himself no one cared about a damned Christmas turkey that looked like it had escaped from a radioactive Dinosaur Kingdom.

The third carving of note was of a crocodile with open jaws. Inside its gaping maw was an actual-sized radish head. This head looked very similar to Vincente's bonce. Adding to the morbid scene, the mouth also held a radish arm. This carving sent a shudder down Jimmy's spine. The arm and hand were sticking out of the crocodile's throat, as if it had eaten someone alive who was trying to escape, but the decapitated head was preventing them from exiting the crocodile's mouth. It was as masterful as it was gruesome.

However, Jimmy had complete confidence this horror show would fall flat; it was two days before Christmas, and the carving had nothing to do with the Christmas miracle, the Red Lady, or anything remotely festive. Jimmy, begrudgingly impressed though he was by the craftsmanship of his competition, had supreme confidence in his creation. He looked at his Disney scene with total and utter admiration. Undoubtedly, the judges would favour his artistic radish. After all, everyone loved Disney.

At around 9 pm, as he had promised, Armardo took the microphone and once again spoke in Spanish. He translated to English as follows:

"Ladies and gentlemen, children and sicarios."

Much laughter came from the audience.

"Welcome to *Noche de Rábanos*, the Night of the Radishes."

Everyone applauded and cheered.

"I will first ask the blessed Red Virgin of the Radish to pour her sacred radish spirit upon our most holy meeting tonight. We do this to honour Her presence." Armardo paused and cleared his throat, and recited: "Holy Mother of the Big Red Radish, give us inspiration and wisdom to judge this event, as we want to honour Your Blessed and Holy Red Name. Oh, Red Radishy Mother, when we mortals look at all the competitors' entries tonight, awarding the winning prizes will be extremely challenging. Please guide the judges; we pray in the Blessed Name of The Very Big and tremendously Red Virgin Radish, amen."

"Amen," everyone else at the event exclaimed loudly, including the increasingly intoxicated gringas. Everyone, even Lucy's friends, spent twenty seconds or so making furious signs of the cross over their bodies. Jimmy, meanwhile, nearly lost his shit listening to Armardo's prayer and waiting for the furious crossing that followed it to be over. He managed to maintain his composure; he needed to come through for the win tonight, and mocking the Mexicans' tradition wouldn't help his chances.

Then, everyone chanted, "*Rábanos, Rábanos!*"

Armardo hushed the excited crowd by waving his hands and putting his finger to his mouth.

"Here tonight, we have two extraordinary guests whose intellect and fairness are renowned. Our celebrity judges will assess this competition with total impartiality. Here they are. The dynamic duo, the one and only—"

Jimmy gasped.

"Inspector Ramon Lopez and Leading Constable Baños, from the Federal Police Department."

"Shit! Inspector Goldfish Brain and his dumbass sidekick. How is it fair getting these two knobs to judge the contest?"

"Dadda, what are knobs?" asked Max, who standing beside his dad with his mom on his other side.

"Shush, Max," interrupted Lucy. "Daddy said he lost his key *fobs*." Max nodded and smirked. Even at four years old, he knew Lucy was lying.

Rapturous cheers and hand claps greeted Inspector Lopez. Jimmy faked a clap. Lopez held a pocketbook in one hand and a pen in the other; he bowed and waved, acknowledging his importance amongst those present.

Yep, that notebook will be as blank as the inside of his head, Jimmy thought. To amuse himself further, he envisioned the Inspector's detailed, profoundly complex notes Lopez had made regarding Vincente's disappearance: *Head severed from property manager's body. No other suspects. Jimmy Myers did it!*

Jimmy tried to think positively. Thankfully, he remembered Lucy's breathing techniques to soothe his troubled soul. He slowly and deeply inhaled and exhaled and muttered trendy mantras under his breath. "I am at one with the universe," and "I am a strong, successful, and privileged cis-gendered male."

Inspector Lopez and Leading Constable Baños walked around, surveying the creations. Finally, they arrived at his radish masterpiece. Jimmy gave him a phony smile, lied and said he was pleased to meet him again.

Lopez warmly grinned back. "What category is this?" he asked.

"The modern or *neuvo* one, señor López."

"But it . . ." pointing at the radish, "is so *incredibly* festive, so *fabulously* traditional. Wow! Is this really your first attempt at *Rábanos,* señor Myers?" Jimmy looked flummoxed. He couldn't believe this was the same Inspector Lopez who was determined to put him behind bars.

"Yes, it's my rookie appearance," he answered.

"I am very impressed. Well done!" Leading Constable Baños said nothing, but grunted in approval. He followed after Lopez as the Inspector went to the judge at the following table.

Jimmy was surprised. He felt proud. He felt warm and happy. Inspector Lopez's comments were kind and generous. Maybe he wasn't so bad after all. Maybe he wouldn't let their previous animosity cloud his judgment. Momentarily, Jimmy felt guilty for judging him so harshly.

Inspector Lopez and his fellow adjudicator, Leading Constable Baños, returned to Jimmy's table after another walk-around. He looked again at the Canadian's radish carvings, making notes in his pocketbook and talking to Baños in Spanish.

Lopez asked, "Is this a Christmas scene?"

"*¿Una escena navideña?*" Baños said as he let out a snigger, his lips curling into a smirk.

"Yes," Jimmy responded proudly, but he was confused by the sidekick's reaction.

"In detective school, we were trained in asking the six W's: Who, what, when, where and how?"

"That's four W's and one H," corrected Jimmy helpfully.

"Do you find arithmetic to be problematic? Might dyscalculia be the underlying issue?" Lopez asked.

What the heck is dyscalculia? Memories of his encounter with the cop at the police station resurfaced. *Why is he so fixated on counting?* The Inspector's sudden sarcasm and hostility, completely at odds with his previous warmth, made Jimmy apprehensive. He took a few more moments to inspect the carving, as if he hadn't already done so, and rattled off a series of questions:

"*Why* is Joseph of Arimathea wearing Mickey Mouse ears?"

"*Why* is there snow and mistletoe in a nativity scene?"

"*What* are Pluto and Daffy Duck doing at baby Jesus's birth?"

"*When* was the birth of Christ? Perhaps it was in 1901—the same year Walt Disney was born?"

"*Where* was Bethlehem? The North Pole or south of Jerusalem? I didn't realize Christmas trees were located in Palestine."

"*How* can Mary have a tail coming out of her skirt and big, flappy ears, like Cyclops, the 'acid bath' serial killer?"

The embarrassed Canadian didn't answer. He couldn't answer because all he could think of were the five W's and one H in the barrage of investigative questions. The idiot had contradicted himself yet again. He sighed as he realized Lopez was still abusing his power to make Jimmy feel foolish and humiliated. He clenched his fists and gritted his teeth in anger. The red radish juice hid his face, so Inspector Lopez was none the wiser.

Lopez and Baños guffawed and moved on to the next competitor's table, continuing to make notes of their observations.

THIRTEEN

Poetic Justice

THE AMIGAS WERE KNOCKING back tequila and having fun at the celebration. They were trying to cheer up Jimmy, who was ranting about Inspector Lopez's comments. It took a while, but at last they got a laugh out of him with their insistence that he down a few shots and chill out. He was far from over Lopez and his buffoon sidekick's rudeness, but with good company and good drink around him, he couldn't stew in his anger forever.

Father Dominguez, Armardo's priest, had arrived at the event. He was a tad late, having just finished a late-night service. The priest had volunteered to announce the winners of the competition. The girls pulled Father Dominguez into the middle of the dance floor and started salsa dancing with him. Each of the amigas was laughing hysterically, as was the Holy Father. Mac, a born-again atheist, liked the look on Father Dominguez's face and plucked up the courage to ask him if she could borrow his dog collar. The cleric politely declined and thanked the ladies for the dance; Father Dominguez headed towards Armardo. He walked up a small set of stairs in front of the masses of speakers and lighting systems under the palapa.

Armardo silenced the pulsating music and gave the cleric the microphone. Inspector Lopez presented the priest with a piece of paper containing his final prize ranking. Dominguez explained in both languages Lopez and his sidekick had made three decisions, one for each category, and he'd now read them out.

The first decision was the award for the best *Niños y Niñas* or Children's *Rábanos*. The second decision would be for the *tradicional* or traditional entry winner, and finally, the third award would be for the *nueva* or modern category. An eerie hush filled the complex as the attendees waited to hear the results. The priest tapped the microphone to make sure it worked, and he took his time in doing so. Jimmy's impatience mounted, and he could see people shuffling and hear them muttering; they didn't want to wait, either. Just when he felt he had no more wait in him, Father Dominguez spoke.

"In first place for the children's award is . . . Max Myers, with his entry entitled 'Dog's Bollocks.'"

Lucy jumped up and down in excitement and started to applaud her son, and her applause was joined by raucous cheers from the amigas. Jimmy gave him a quick hug. Max, pleased but looking a little nervous, held Lucy's hand and headed towards Father Dominguez. He gave Max a red thousand pesos note. Again, the amigas erupted into cheers. Jimmy joined them, proud of his son's creative genius.

Father Dominguez tapped the microphone again before announcing the next winner. "Our second *Rábanos* winner for the most *accurate* and *traditional* religious nativity radish goes to . . . Fred Montana, with his thought-provoking entry called 'Crocodile Rock.'"

"What? '*Crocodile Rock*?'" gasped Jimmy. Mindful of little Max, he spluttered, "How the effedy-eff could that be about baby Jesus's birth?"

Wild applause drowned out his irreverent comment. Fred waved at the cheering spectators. He took off his black sombrero and curtsied with a huge grin, and his thick black Fred Flintstone hair fell over the front of his forehead.

"Well done," Father Dominguez said to Fred, giving him a considerable wad of pesos. The short man triumphantly raised his hands full of money, looked towards the Red Lady in the heavens and thanked her for the inspiration of his Christmas scene. Jimmy looked at Fred's twin brother Raul, who was smirking directly at him.

"Finally, in the *nueva* section of the competition . . . drum roll please, Pedro," said the priest. Big Pedro Cordoba played a deafening drum roll sound; it was as if a thousand drums were beating in a tense battle march.

Jimmy had butterflies in his tummy. The anticipation was overwhelming. Would the priest call him out by his first name, or would it be more formal? He didn't care, as he just wanted the win. He didn't see how he couldn't; spiteful as they were, Inspector Lopez and his sidekick had to recognize his skill. In fact, they already had, before reverting to their old ways. If there was any justice in the world, they'd put aside their feud and acknowledge his artistic talent.

The priest hushed the crowd.

"First place, and the generous prize of one thousand U.S. dollars, or eighteen thousand pesos," Gasps from the spectators. "goes to—"

Jimmy Myers, Jimmy thought as he prepared to raise his hands in the air.

"Francisca Lopez, with her entry, 'Psycho Turkupine.'"

"*What the feck*? Psycho-effing-turkupine?" he gasped.

Francisca came up to Father Dominguez, took her money, and raised her hands to the heavens and thanked the Red Lady of the Radish, just as Fred had. Jimmy was beyond shocked. He shook his head and turned to Lucy.

"How could a red and white turkey resembling a terrified porcupine beat my 'Christmas Disney?'" he muttered.

"It is what it is, hun," she said, patting his back in consolation.

"That dumb-as-shit Inspector, Armardo's 'impartial' brother, judges a man-eating crocodile and a Chernobyl-radiated turkey were 'the most festive' and deserved the prize money? Are you effing kidding me?"

Lucy couldn't help but laugh at her husband's comments, as he continued to shake his head in disbelief. He couldn't possibly hide the pain of the loss, but the radish juice did a worthy cover-up job. It hid the red flush to his cheeks that only intensified as he seethed with anger. He knew Armardo's brother and his dumbass assistant had loaded the deck.

Still, he couldn't stay mad forever. Later, with the amigas, Jimmy's competitive edge began to wear off, drowned out by shot after shot of tequila. Though he was no less certain the competition had been rigged against him, he couldn't fault the winner of the *nueva* prize; Crocodile Rock was spectacular. Who would ever have thought Fred Flintstone's doppelgänger would have created such a fabulously macabre carving?

"I have to give it to the guy. He knows how to carve a radish," Jimmy sighed. He punctuated his point by downing another shot. Mella gave him a supportive pat on the shoulder.

"Oh, speak of the devil," she said suddenly, prompting Jimmy to turn around. He saw Fred approaching him, holding a bottle of 1853 in his hand.

"Hey gringo, can I pour us a drink to celebrate me and commiserate with you?"

Jimmy bowed towards the supreme winner, and mimed like he was holding a microphone.

"A round of applause for Fred Montana, who celebrates his winning nativity scene, and a shit load of money." Pointing towards Fred's radish creation, he exclaimed, "Merry Christmas, man-eating reptile." He was putting on the show for the winner's benefit, and it seemed to work. Fred grinned.

"Come on, amigo, drink with me, and tell me how your rendition of Joseph of Arimathea suddenly grew big Mickey Mouse ears?"

After an initial silence, both men laughed.

Fred, emboldened by Jimmy's good humour, opened the cold bottle of tequila, poured the liquid into two large shot glasses, and gave a toast: "To baby Jesus . . . riding on Space Mountain at Disneyland."

Jimmy replied, "To Vincente . . . his head and arms didn't give your baby crocodile indigestion." Jimmy could've sworn he saw a scowl come over Fred's face, but as quickly as it appeared it was gone, replaced with the same gregarious look he had on before. Both men laughed again, clinked glasses, and downed their shots in one gulp.

⇒⇒⇒ ⇐⇐⇐

JIMMY'S HEAD WAS pounding when he woke up. It wasn't Cordoba's blaring music causing the headache; he was utterly hungover. If he'd stuck to the tequila, he might have been fine, but he had some beer and spiced rum as well, the combination of which proved too strong for him. He reached out to touch Lucy, but she wasn't there. So, instead, he pulled open his bedside table drawer and fumbled around until he found a bottle of extra-strength Tylenol. He popped out two pills and put them on his parched tongue before washing them down with a large gulp of water.

He remembered parts of the evening: the girls going topless, the carvings display, the thick-as-shit Inspector Lopez, and his heart-to-heart chat with Fred Montana, the amusing twin. He seemed like a nice enough fellow last night, especially compared to his intimidating brother. But neither of the twins bothered him anywhere near as much as Inspector Plonker.

Lucy was right, as always. Jimmy had to stop judging his neighbours. He had expected Fred to be a dunce, like his silent brother. His first impression of Fred had deceived him; the man was, in fact, something of a paradox. He worked for a wealthy man and walked around with a towering oaf of a brother, but Fred was approachable and intelligent, with an appreciation for the arts. He was specifically interested in poetry, which was the last thing Jimmy would expect from a cartel sicario. He'd suspected as much already, but last night Fred had told him the truth plain. As foggy as his memory was from all the drinking, he remembered the conversation like it was being played on a screen in front of him.

"You must know who I am by now," Fred said, his smile fading. He and Jimmy had been laughing at something, but suddenly, in that moment, his expression turned serious.

"Of course. You're a renowned radish carver," Jimmy replied, not comprehending Fred's meaning.

"One day of the year, sure. But the rest of the time, I'm one of Don Armardo's most trusted sicarios. I make collections for him—rent, taxes, protection money. Surely you don't think he's just an innocent wealthy man?" Now Jimmy understood. Perhaps it was the drink, or his previous suspicions, or both, but he wasn't at all surprised to hear this. It was almost comforting, in fact. Before, he'd wondered if he should be scared of Armardo. He didn't have to wonder anymore.

"Right. I figured. He's with the Wolfpack Cartel," Jimmy said, not feeling scared at all. He was too drunk for that.

"He *is* the Wolfpack Cartel," Fred declared ominously.

"Ooh, scary." Jimmy poured himself another shot of liquid courage.

"It is. And if you knew, why did you take his money? Are you really *that* desperate?"

"Desperate? You were there when I was telling Armardo about my book, right? It made me a lot of money. I just can't get to it right now," Jimmy answered, getting a little indignant in his drunken state. Fred heard the sharpness in his tone and raised his hands in a conciliatory gesture.

"Alright, alright. But you should know the people Don Armardo lends money to are just trading in one problem for another. If you don't pay it back—" Fred jerked his thumb across his neck in a vertical line to illustrate his point. "Well, if you've heard of the cartel, you know what happens. Just make sure pay back his loan with interest, amigo."

"Your bossman didn't mention paying interest on the loan or having my throat cut from ear to ear."

"No," said Fred, his expression still deathly serious. "But it's about paying an important person respect, and Don Armardo doesn't like to be disrespected. After he returns to Guadalajara, he will send me to see you if he hasn't gotten his money back. If he still doesn't get it after that, he will send my brother, and you will end up like my carving." This warning managed to cut through Jimmy's drunken stupor; it made him realize, in a way, nothing else did— he was dealing with real criminals. He stared at Fred and blinked, slack-jawed. He really should have listened to Juan. Fred met his gaze for a little while, unsmiling, and without warning, he burst into laughter.

"I'm just teasing, amigo, but please keep your eyes out for my brother. He doesn't like you. I love him wholeheartedly, but our personalities are very different. If we were not identical twins, you wouldn't be able to tell we were related." Jimmy started to object, but still had enough of a filter not to. It wouldn't do to insult the one member of the Wolfpack Cartel who seemed invested in his well-being. Besides, he was having fun talking to Fred and didn't want to turn their chat into an argument.

"You don't have to worry about that. *Red's Hot!* made me a fabulously wealthy man. At least, for a little while."

"And what is this book again? Something about casinos and the colour red?"

"It's about roulette, so yes, red is involved, but it's more focused on the strategy and psychology of the game. It'll make you filthy rich." Jimmy, under the influence, was more boastful than he might have been otherwise, but it didn't seem to bother Fred. In fact, the man in the black sombrero was leaning closer to him, as if trying to hear some whispered secret.

"Tell you what, amigo. I'm a writer myself. I have a collection of 'deconstructed' poetry. It's revolutionary stuff. If you give me a copy of *Red's Hot!*, I'll give you a copy of my collection." Jimmy was more surprised by this than by the reveal Armardo, Fred, and his brother were in a cartel.

"Poetry? Really?"

"Is that so hard to believe?" Fred asked. The more Jimmy thought about it, it wasn't; given Fred's skill as a carver, it made sense he'd be proficient in other arts as well. Drunk and intrigued, he gave the sicario a nod.

"Alright, you got me interested. Your poems for my roulette system." They shook on it, and Fred looked off wistfully into the distance, towards where the palm trees swayed in the breeze.

"I'd rather be a poet than a sicario, to tell you the truth. It's my dream to live by the ocean, without a care in the world beyond my craft. A life of pure, unbridled passion, far away from any freakin' crocodiles," Fred murmured. He clearly spoke so as not to be overheard, but there was something else in his voice. Even inebriated, Jimmy could tell in his mind Fred was already there.

Despite himself, his heart went out to the cartel man. He didn't want to be surrounded by violence any more than Jimmy did.

"I have connections in the publishing industry. I could help you publish another collection, make a name for yourself. Who knows; if you get big in the U.S., you could become the first little person cartel sicario poet laureate. You might even win a Pulitzer."

"What do you mean, little person?" Jimmy was too drunk to read Fred's tone, and so he ignored the comment and kept talking.

"You know, Natalie Diaz recently became the first Latina poet to win the Pulitzer Prize. Why couldn't Fred Montana also make his country proud? You could even be the next Octavio Paz. He won the 1990 Nobel Prize in Literature, and was crucial in the development of Latin-American literature."

"You seem to know a great deal about poetry and Mexican culture," Fred remarked. Jimmy shrugged.

"I enjoy researching and preparing for quizzes. I guess I know a little about a lot."

"You sure are a weird gringo," Fred replied, chuckling and shaking his head. Jimmy ignored the comment and continued.

"I have an in with *Coastal Life* magazine. If your poetry is as good as you say, I might be able to pull a few strings and get some in there."

Fred frowned and exclaimed, "It's way better than good, amigo."

After that, the conversation drifted to lighter things. Jimmy remembered they clinked their glasses, toasted to weirdness and poetry, and proceeded to down yet another tequila. Although his head was throbbing, he couldn't help laughing to himself. He was looking forward to reading Fred's poetry. How many people could say they'd read literature written by a sicario?

FOURTEEN

Pelican Belican

THE DAY AFTER *RÁBANOS,* the three amigas visited Lucy and Max and helped clean up the mess made during the festivities. Although they had each showered, they couldn't quite get rid of traces of the red radish colouring that stained their hands and feet.

Mella said, "I'm sorry Juicer, we kinda overdid it last night, didn't we?"

Lucy replied, "I'm sure your tits were the first pair of boobies Father Dominguez had ever seen *that* close-up before."

"They," Mella was referring to her boobies, "Just needed to be set free from my bikini top. Call it a type of spiritual deliverance."

"Release the Kraken!" called out Mac.

"At least my boobies weren't bouncing up and down on little Fred's head," cackled Mella, looking at JayBee.

"He didn't mind at all," laughed JayBee.

"Poor Father Dominguez, he'll never be able to unsee those whoppers," added Lucy. She and her friends continued talking as they cleaned the condo, regaling each other with wacky stories from *Rábanos* and commenting on the carvings. Fred's, in particular, had caught their attention.

"The whole thing was crazy. I can't imagine how many radishes he had to go through to make it," Mac added.

"And what was the deal with that head?" Mella added.

"I think it was meant to be Vincente's, the property manager. Jimmy found it in the freezer and thought he'd been decapitated. Of course, now he's missing and that idiot inspector's trying to pin it on Jimmy—" Lucy said, trailing off. It upset her just as much as Jimmy. He had been trying to do the right thing, even if he'd overreacted, and now he was seemingly being punished for it.

"Speaking of Jimmy, it was good to see him loosen up a little. That contest really got his panties in a bunch," Mac chuckled.

"You know how he gets with anything competitive. Plus, losing the vacation money really upset him. He feels awful about it," replied Lucy.

"And a turkey-porcupine hybrid beat him in the radish competition," laughed Mella, less sympathetically.

"None of that stopped him from busting a move with Fred Montana," Mac said, laughing. They all chuckled at that; the two of them had ended the evening dancing together, both drunk as a skunk. Lucy, Mella, Mac, and JayBee had found it so hilarious they joined in, starting a full-on dance party.

"Lucy, your hubby is such a hoot," laughed JayBee.

Mac added, "When your Mexican friends leave, you'll have a much better time, gringa."

That was the end of that, as the amigas' attentions drifted to other topics. They talked about Christmas dinner, The Yankee Swap on Boxing Day, and going to New Year's Eve at Tequila Tommy's. Lucy listened as her friends told her about how eccentric Tommy was, his sexual conquests and outrageous stories, and how bringing in the New Year at Tommy's would be memorable for their visiting friends.

Later, after Lucy and the amigas had finished cleaning, she and Jimmy were back in their room. He had recovered from his hangover and had come out to help them, but now he was lying on the bed with a big glass of water on his bedside table. He was in the middle of listening to a proposal that was bringing back his headache full force.

"I know the Lopez family is . . . eccentric, but Armardo has been nothing but kind to us. He loaned us money and let his son play with Max. I really do think it would be nice to invite them over for Christmas dinner. I can reach out to Francisca," Lucy said, insistent.

"You really want to have Christmas lunch with the bundle of laughs Raul Montana and his uncle, Inspector Dumbass?" Even if Armardo wasn't the head of a cartel, he wouldn't want the Lopez family over. He liked Fred well enough, but Raul unsettled him, he was still upset Francisca's monster turkey was chosen over his Disney holiday scene, and there was no way he was setting foot in a room with Inspector Lopez ever again.

"We *won't* invite the Inspector. I've had enough of him for a lifetime. I was just thinking of having Armardo, his wife, Hector, and the twins."

"You remember who Raul is, right? The silent psycho with the killer smirk?"

"Yes, I remember, but I don't see why inviting him would be so awful. You seem to be getting on so well with his brother, your new bestie. Have you a bromance going on with Freddie Boy?"

"Very funny."

"Anyway, it will make me feel a lot better. It's Christmas, the season of goodwill to all mankind, and *all* includes Raul. They'll probably say no anyway, but please, for my sake, can't we at least ask?"

The second Lucy began to plead, Jimmy knew he couldn't refuse. He smiled and nodded, hoping all the while she was right and the Lopezes would have other plans. "Maybe we can use Francisca's radioactive 'turkupine' as a dessert?"

"Don't be such a sore loser. You seemed okay knocking back shots with the creator of the man-eating Christmas crocodile."

"I'm not a sore loser. I'm sure Francisca *really* needed her husband's prize money." Jimmy rolled his eyes and grimaced.

"Let it go, Jimmy."

"But at least we're not having stupid-balls Inspector come along too." Jimmy then impersonated Inspector Lopez at the judging of the radishes. "Hi, Signor Himmee, I'm from Chee-waa-waa. I don't theenk Bambino Jeeeesus was beeest amigos with Meekey Mooose. Duuun't you knuuuw that eet wasn't snoooowing in Bethleheeeem, you stupido greeengo?"

Lucy giggled at his terrible impersonation. Max clapped and watched with wide eyes, enjoying his dad putting on a show.

"Get that out of your system before we have his family over, okay? And can you get some money from the safe? If we're having company, I have to get some things from the bodega downtown." Jimmy went to the built-in safe containing their passports, credit cards, and the thick wad of cash Fred had dropped off from Armardo before last night's festivities, and entered the code. The safe door popped open. He peered inside and saw a couple of passports, credit cards, two driving licences, and holiday insurance documents. The envelope was missing.

"Luce? Have you moved the envelope with Armardo's dosh from the safe?"

"I haven't been in the safe."

"Oh, for flip's sake!"

"What's the matter?"

"It's gone. The envelope, the money . . . and wait, there's more. My passport is missing!"

Lucy quickly joined Jimmy in the bedroom.

"Are you sure? You did have a lot to drink last night. Maybe you put it somewhere else and forgot," Lucy said as she started to look under the mattress and through the drawers. Jimmy just stared at the safe, unmoving. Lucy didn't find anything, so she searched their suitcases and his discarded red-stained shorts in the washing basket. When she was done, she looked at him helpless and empty-handed.

"That bastard!"

Lucy rebuked him. "Jimmy Myers! Max has ears like Larry Boy from *Veggie Tales*."

"Guess who, apart from your amigas, came into our home yesterday?" As soon as Lucy realized what he was getting at, her eyes went wide.

They both said together, "Inspector Lopez."

"No way, he's a cop. He wouldn't steal." But even as she spoke, she sounded unsure.

"A cop? He's Armardo's brother, who barged into our home and produced this weird 'search warrant' which he didn't let you read when he knew you could understand Spanish." Lucy looked at him but said nothing. He could see she had no objection to give; she knew just as well as he did this was suspicious behaviour. Jimmy, emboldened, kept expounding on his theory.

"He entered our bedroom and had his lackey cop guard the bedroom door, then he came out and left the property el-pronto. He is the prime and only suspect."

Lucy replied, "The safe was locked and had a password, which we created. He couldn't have known it."

"But Vincente knew the master override number. Remember Vincente? Our property manager whose disappearance Lopez is trying to pin on me?" Again, Lucy had no objection.

"What do we do now?" was all she could say. Jimmy sighed, realizing he had to report the theft to the police. That meant making a statement to the person who had probably robbed his safe and taken his passport in the first place. Lopez would, of course, ask if he suspected anyone of the crime. Jimmy would say the prime suspect was the same Federal police officer taking the report. It wouldn't go down very well.

"How much was in there?" Lucy asked after a pause.

"I didn't count it."

"You didn't count it?"

"Lucy, stop being a parrot, repeating everything I say. I took the envelope with the cash and put it straight into the safe. I'd had a few tequilas, so I didn't want to count it when I was slightly inebriated."

"So, how are you—"

"And don't ask me how I will pay back Armardo when I didn't know how much was in the envelope."

"How can you pay off a debt when you don't know how much you owe?"

"I don't know, Captain Obvious."

Jimmy felt sick to his stomach. This must be a supreme setup. However, what he couldn't figure out was whether Inspector Dumbass was working under Armardo's orders, or if this was a solo enterprise. Jimmy was berating himself once again. First, the wallet full of their vacation cash went missing, and now, an unknown amount in an envelope given to him by a cartel overlord had disappeared. And there was more, like one of those 'buy *one,* get *three* free' infomercials he'd seen on TV. The police officer had also taken his passport.

You needed a passport to get out of the country; now, Jimmy was stuck here. Could the situation get any worse? Should Lucy ask Armardo or Francisca how much money Armardo lent them? Maybe Fred was aware and kept some ledger? After all, he was their money man. But asking them would only reveal they'd lost the money in the first place, and if Armardo gave them more, they'd owe him double—and after what Fred had told him the night before, that seemed like a bad idea. Whatever he did, he would have to sit with the Lopez family, make small talk, and try to enjoy their Christmas dinner together, with the debt hanging over his head like the sword of Damocles.

Life sucked.

AFTER HER CONVERSATION with her reluctant husband, Lucy invited the Lopez family for Christmas dinner. Francisca immediately accepted and seemed delighted. Armardo thought it would be lovely, especially after the success of the radish celebration. Fred, the little sicario, spoke on behalf of his brother and accepted the invitation, as he liked Jimmy and thought he was a very funny gringo. Raul was with Fred at the time of the invite, and he stared and said nothing.

A crestfallen Jimmy Myers sat in the deckchair on their patio, beer in hand, outside the bedroom window. The ocean ebbed and flowed, crashing against the seawall. He was fascinated by the pelicans that were divebombing for fish in the rough sea. He thought of the old limerick he recently told Max, written well over a hundred years ago by Dixon Lanier Merritt:

A wonderful bird is the pelican.
His bill can hold more than his belly can.
He can hold in his beak.
Food enough for a week!
But I'll be darned if I know how the hellican?

Once the funny-looking bird spotted the fish, the pelican dropped from the sky, and on impact with the water, it opened its bill, disappeared from view, and emerged with a pouch full of fish. Seeing this in real-time, Jimmy wondered if he was watching his life playing out in Mexico. He was the little fish in a big pond and had been caught by the pelican, and tossed into its gullet and eaten alive. Except in his case, the predator was a wolf, with razor-sharp claws and teeth.

In the living room, Lucy was dancing with Max, playing the '80s classic, 'Hungry Like the Wolf.'

Jimmy thought of the Wolfpack Cartel and Raul Montana. He looked like a hungry wolf, with his curled lips, bared teeth, fixed gaze, and sharp features. Hearing the song, Jimmy hoped he would never be on the receiving end of Raul's hunt. He had to pay back Armardo before he dispatched the pink sombrero to collect payment. Jimmy was more certain than ever he'd seen Vincente's head, but no one, including his wife, truly believed him. Now, he had to be hospitable to these hungry wolves at a time when he'd rather eat his arm than entertain them.

Jimmy let out a big sigh; he knew he had to report his missing passport and money to obtain new travel papers from the consulate. Before the Lopez family arrived for dinner, he would trot to the police station and get that taken care of. Jimmy prayed stupid-balls Ramon Lopez or the Baños fellow had taken a day off. He felt like screaming in frustration.

Deciding to avoid acting out the situation by charades, as that ended up going pear-shaped the last time, he kissed Lucy goodbye and walked briskly to the cop shop. His heart was pumping fast, and thirty minutes later, he arrived at the Federal police station. He walked up the steps and went through the revolving front doors. Much to Jimmy's chagrin, Lopez's sidekick, Baños, was in the front office. Baños immediately recognized the gringo and shouted out to his boss.

"*El gringo, señor Lopez, El gringo idiota!*"

Inspector Lopez quickly appeared behind the screen, and Jimmy's heart sank.

"So, what do we owe this pleasure to, Mr Myers?" Lopez asked in his irritating Chihuahua drawl, a wide grin on his face. Before Jimmy could answer, the Inspector continued.

"Are you reporting another radish murder mystery? Maybe your Mickey Mouse is still trying to catch up with Joseph and Mary in Bethlehem?"

"I'm here to report my money and passport have been stolen," Jimmy replied, ignoring the sarcasm.

"How much has gone missing?"

"Just under USD $50,000." Jimmy vastly exaggerated. Lopez looked visibly shocked, then composed himself.

"When was the last time you saw such a large amount?"

"In our safe."

"So, your passport and a lot of cash escaped your safe? Did they both have legs?" Jimmy didn't answer. He just stared daggers at the sarcastic police officer.

"So, diddums, what do you think happened?" the Inspector asked again.

"My theory is the same moron who 'disappeared' Vincente knew the code to our safe, probably tortured him for it, opened our safe and took the money and the passport."

"Did you take it yourself? After all, you are the prime suspect in Vincente's disappearance. Do you, perhaps, have dissociative identity disorder?"

Jimmy scrunched up his face. It was all he could do to keep from exploding into a furious tirade.

"We have good mental health facilities here. Would you like me to refer you for a stay and receive some nice, electro-convulsive treatment?"

He looked at Lopez with contempt and didn't respond. With how forcefully he was gritting his teeth, he wouldn't be surprised if he chipped one.

Lopez cleared his throat and took out his notebook. "Do you have any suspects?"

Jimmy had pinky-promised himself he wouldn't say what he was about to say. As he walked over to the station, he told himself again and again he would show restraint. Lucy would want him to. However, now that he was staring right at the smug Inspector-slash-cartel man, he couldn't resist.

"How about *you*, Inspector Lopez?"

Lopez raised his eyebrows and grinned.

"The only possible time someone could have removed the passport and money was when *you* and Leading Constable Washrooms visited our home with a phony warrant. Do you remember the deepfake warrant? The document you wouldn't allow my wife to read? So, you waltzed into our bedroom, cracked open the safe, and swiped my passport and cash. Members of the jury, I give you an open and shut case."

"An interesting little theory. Do you want me to arrest and interrogate myself to gain a confession? Perhaps I could even torture myself. I'm sure that would make you very happy."

Yes, please, thought Jimmy.

Inspector Lopez rubbed his chin. "You have read too many Agatha Christie novels. Do you have anyone else who could be a suspect besides me, Inspector Ramon Lopez, the most decorated police officer in Los Piñata?"

"I want my passport back."

"You're lucky I didn't confiscate it in the first place, you being the prime suspect in the disappearance of the poor little Colombian." Jimmy rolled his eyes, turned around, walked through the revolving glass door. He cursed Inspector Lopez under his breath all the way home.

FIFTEEN

Cinio Nadolig

FOR CHRISTMAS DINNER, LUCY made chicken and vegetable stew with a mint and cilantro garnish, rice and beans, and grilled cheese fingers for the kids. Jimmy prepared the dining table and set out wine glasses and cups. He also placed Christmas crackers on each plate, a festive tradition Lucy inherited from her family in Wales.

Max insisted on helping his mom make the food with his newfound friend Hector Lopez, who had joined them. Hector had kindly taken Max under his wing, and they had shared their 'kid-to-kid' language. They were also adapting quickly to each other's mother tongues. Max now spoke more Spanish than his father, and Hector was picking up some English from being around the younger boy, but not enough. Hector had started his own English lessons at his father's insistence, but he still needed help understanding Max's brand of English and Welsh, which was a kind of *PAW Patrol* meets *Peppa Pig* patois. Most excitingly for Hector, Max remembered several spicy expletives, which he was happy to pass on. Lucy hated it when Max cursed, but she thought he'd stop if his dad didn't laugh.

There was adequate kitchen space for Lucy and the boys to work in. They had many spices, bottles of sauces, and other essential ingredients. Most of these were either in the fridge, on the shelf, or in the small pantry area. She gave easy instructions to Max and Hector; she gave the lads a ladle and a spoon and showed them how to stir the stew. She allowed the boys to add certain ingredients to the bubbling mixture and praised them for their contributions. Lucy enjoyed enabling the boys to express their creativity, and they were having fun too. Hector giggled as he stirred the stew. Max chuckled as he slowly added vegetables to the mix. The stew simmered, and the aroma smelt divine. All this occurred under the watchful eye of Momma Bear.

"Yum, yum," Max said, rubbing his tummy.

"Yum, yum," imitated Hector.

Then, there was a knock on the door. Lucy wished and hoped for anyone but Inspector Lopez to arrive. She left the kitchen area, entered the living room, and opened the door.

No one was there.

She walked onto the deck and looked around. Finally, she eyed the base of the door and saw a bottle with a ribbon tied to it. She picked it up. It was ice-cold spiced rum. Lucy looked over the balcony and saw a black sombrero.

"Hey, Fred."

Fred stopped, looked up at Lucy, and waved, "Hey, amiga!"

"What's the bottle of rum for?"

"It's my *Navidad*, or Christmas gift to you both."

"That's so sweet of you." She ran down the stairs and hugged Fred.

"I'm looking forward to celebrating your gringo *Navidad*, Mrs Lucy, and seeing my new friend, Jimmy." Lucy heard the boys laughing heartedly above, and it sounded like they were having fun—which could be good or bad for the stew. She quickly thanked Fred, turned around, and walked up the stairs back to the condo.

Unbeknownst to Lucy, Hector noticed a plastic bottle on the kitchen shelf hidden amongst the spices in her brief absence. The bottle contained a bright green liquid with a child-proof lid. However, it wasn't Hector-proof, and he took off the top and smelt the contents.

"Mmmm," said Hector. "*¡Olor a menta!*" He put the bottle under Max's nose.

"Mmmm, you're right, yum, it's minty."

Hector looked around to see if Mrs Lucy was still out. He smiled, looked at Max, and poured the entire bottle of super-strength Imodium into the stew. Both boys frantically stirred the green liquid into the Christmas meal, hiding their trickery.

"Yum, yum, Rubble's big bum," said Max.

"*Deliciosa!*" sniggered Hector.

Lucy returned and praised them for doing such a great job. She cranked up the Christmas music, grabbed both boys, and put bright red Santa hats on them. She danced around the condo singing along to 'I Wish It Could Be Christmas Everyday,' 'Last Christmas,' and 'Santa Claus is Coming to Town.' Hector and Max were laughing and becoming over-excited. Lucy loved Christmas and looked forward to sharing the occasion with her Mexican neighbours.

When the stew was ready, Lucy garnished it, set it on the table, and waited for her hubby to return from the police station, hoping he would be in a better mood for their Christmas dinner.

⟫⟫ ⟪⟪

THE LOPEZ TRIBE arrived on time. In walked a well-dressed Francisca, followed by Armardo, wearing a very expensive-looking short-sleeved shirt and cargo pants. Fred and Raul trailed in after them, with their distinctive sombreros. Lucy was surprised when they entered the condo, as the brothers immediately doffed their sombreros and placed them on the coat rack. The twins had been wearing their signature hats for so long that seeing them without them was jarring.

Fred had a thick, raven-coloured mop of hair. Raul had a severe buzz cut, which made him look more sinister than ever. Fred, as always, was dressed in black from top to tail. Raul wore a nicely ironed white dress shirt with tight white trousers and brown leather boots with a silver wolf's head on each toe.

"*Nadolig Llawen!*" greeted Lucy.

"Sorry?"

"Merry Christmas!"

"Lucy is showing off her Welsh," Jimmy chucked.

"*Feliz Navidad,*" said three of the four Mexicans. Raul just grunted.

There was a momentary silence before Armardo tried to kick off the conversation with an awkward question.

"How will you guys tell the difference between my identical twin godchildren now that they've taken off their headgear?"

Jimmy looked at seven-foot-tall Raul and then at his four-foot twin brother, and let out a chuckle. He was going to say something sarcastic, but decided on something less controversial.

"I think they have different coloured eyes." Raul gave him a heterochromatic death stare. He immediately regretted his comment; the last thing he wanted was the towering man's attention.

Jimmy changed the subject by thanking Fred for the spiced rum gift.

"Your place is quite lovely. Perfect for a family of three," Francisca exclaimed, looking around, as Jimmy took out his newly-acquired rum bottle from the freezer. He liked his rum, but had never seen this particular brand before.

"ZED-17 Spiced Rum, nice."

That was far from the only alcohol the family had brought. Armardo had a bottle of 1836 El Alamo tequila, a bottle of 1821 Independencia de México red wine, and a bottle of 1970 branded white wine. Raul also unveiled a bottle of Mezcal dated back to 1993.

"Wow! You guys sure like using dates for brand names," Jimmy commented as he took them in. As if sensing he was struggling to not say anything that could set off the guests, Lucy chimed in right after, asking everyone to take a seat at the dining table. Once everyone was seated, she followed up on Jimmy's comment.

"Is there any significance to the dates on the bottles?" she asked. Her hubby had shared with her that the 1836 tequila celebrated the Battle of the Alamo, and she assumed the others had meanings too. Armardo cleared his throat and answered.

"1821 celebrates Mexican Independence. 1970 celebrates the birthday of Joaquín Archivaldo Guzmán Loera."

"El Chapo," added Fred helpfully.

"1993 celebrates Pablo Escobar's death, and ZED-17 celebrates the birth of Luciano Diaz," Armardo finished.

"Diaz is most often referred to by his alias 'ZED-17.' He is a hero of Mexico, and ran an organization called *Los Leones Locos*," explained Fred. He made the sign of the cross three times when he said Diaz's name.

"Wowsa," said Jimmy, looking at Lucy. He didn't understand the Spanish.

"The Crazy Lions," Lucy interpreted.

Fred continued, "Yes, The Crazy Lions. The Yankee-influenced politicians falsely accused Diaz of intimidating gringos and weak government workers throughout Mexico. The dastardly authorities framed him for being a significant part of the violence in our country, including the slaughter of 21,143 migrants in 2013 and the extermination of 43,743 people in 2016."

Lucy gasped.

"They even accused him—" Fred pretended to spit in disdain, "of creating an interrogation method known as *el guiso* or 'the stew,' in which his alleged victims would be placed into a large cooking pot, doused with mung beans, tapioca, spinach, sherry, and gravy granules, and cooked until a confession came forth."

The room went deathly quiet. Lucy and Jimmy stared at the stew, her homemade *el guiso*. Then, something absolutely shocking happened to break the silence. Raul, who was nodding vigorously along with his brother's account, stood up and raised his glass, and made a loud toast.

"Luciano Diaz!"

"A true Mexican hero!" Fred added.

Everyone at the table, including Hector and Max, stood up and followed Raul's lead.

"Luciano Diaz. A true Mexican hero!" they all cried out simultaneously.

They sat back down on their chairs. Jimmy was stunned he had just toasted a notorious freedom fighter-slash-cartel leader who invented a cook-em-alive torture method called '*el guiso*.' He was even more surprised Raul had spoken. He didn't think the tall man could.

"Fred, thank you for that. Now, regarding another, *less painful* and *more tasty* type of stew, please help yourselves," Jimmy said, pointing at Lucy's crock pot. The group smacked their lips and passed the stew around the table. The stew was accompanied with veggies and, Lucy's signature dish, Yorkshire pudding.

The host added, "Lucy has made cheese finger sticks for the boys and plenty of rice, refried beans, tortillas, pico de gallo, and guacamole." He was still trying to unsee images of people cooked alive in gravy granules and rice wine.

Glasses clinked as everyone passed drinks around and tucked into the food. Jimmy had lost his appetite for stew and opted to eat the cheese sticks with Hector and Max. Lucy gave her husband a look, suggesting the cheese sticks were for the young children. He rubbed his tummy and explained to their guests he had to watch calories to maintain his beautiful figure.

"Then don't drink so much booze, sweetheart." Her tone was playful on the surface, but beneath he could tell she thought he was being rude.

"You know, in Mexico, tequila is an aphrodisiac. It also has terrific slimming properties. Drinking tequila is like taking healthy and horny medicine," Fred added.

Raul grunted and continued to scarf down the stew like a man who hadn't eaten in weeks, while Francisca looked uncomfortable with Fred's comments. When she heard Lucy and Jimmy had invited her family for Christmas dinner, her face had lit up with joy. However, Francisca needed help to figure out what the eating celebration was for, as this wouldn't have happened in Mexico. So, she ignored Fred's bawdy remarks and asked the hostess to explain.

"In the United Kingdom, Australia, New Zealand, and parts of Canada, *Cinio Nadolig*—which means Christmas dinner in Welsh—is quite common. It usually includes turkey, gravy, vegetables, roast potatoes, Yorkshire Puddings, and stuffing. My family always served this type of meal on Christmas day."

"Welsh sounds like a very *poetic* language. I think I'd like to learn it. Perhaps I could start by learning to say 'Merry Christmas?'" Fred chimed in.

Lucy obliged. "*Nadolig Llawen.*"

All eyes were on Lucy as they listened intently to her use of the language. She said she would phonetically help Fred learn the saying.

"NAH-DOL-LIG, or *merry* . . . then, CLLH-OW-EN . . . for *Christmas.*" Armardo, who had mastered several languages, tried to repeat after her, getting a feel for Welsh. Even he was having difficulty.

"The two Ls together make the sound 'Clugh,' or 'THLAN,' if you struggle with the back of the throat sounds," Lucy continued.

"Neee-dawl thlan-ooowin," Fred spluttered.

"Well done, Fred, good attempt," encouraged Lucy. Francisca applauded.

"Now, for the two Ls sound, gently place your tongue behind your teeth and blow gently; you should feel air coming out of the sides of your mouth," Lucy instructed. Fred tried and sprayed out spittle on either side of him, which the Mexicans and Max found hilarious. Jimmy was glad none of it landed on the food.

"Enough with learning your super hard weirdo language, Luce. Come on, let's tuck into the food."

"It's hardly weirdo—your Vancouver Island accent is like Captain Jack Sparrow. You know, the pirate from that Johnny Depp movie."

"*Pirates of the Caribbean,*" Jimmy clarified.

"Yes, with the way you roll your r's. Ooooooh, arrrrrrr, I'm a pirrrrate." Before their argument went any further, Armardo broke the cultural tension between the hosts by holding up a Yorkshire pudding on his fork.

"So, what is this?"

"It's a pudding made from a batter of eggs, flour, and milk or water," Lucy said, still giving her sarcastic hubby the stink eye.

"It's a furck!" yelled Max.

The table went deathly quiet. Hector sniggered.

"That's right, Maxy, it's a *fforc*. He's saying fork in Welsh."

Laughter broke the silence.

Armardo tried to pronounce 'Yorkshire,' which made everyone laugh some more—except Raul, who kept staring at Jimmy.

Lucy chimed in. "*Pwdin Swydd Efrog,* or Yorkshire pudding."

"I don't have enough spittle to get that out. If I did, I might drown the entire table," Fred giggled.

The Lopezes nodded in agreement, and even Jimmy had to concede there was no way anyone but Lucy was going to pronounce that word.

"This stew is delicious," Armardo said, again changing the topic back to the food. Francisca nodded vigorously, taking a big spoonful. Lucy smiled proudly.

"Thank you. Also, I meant to ask earlier, but what are your plans after Christmas?" she asked.

"Well, we're going to attend the Boxing Day service at our Church on Sunday, for starters," Francisca answered.

"It's the one day of the week I look forward to. The service at the church here in Los Piñata, for lack of a better word, rocks," Armardo added.

Jimmy imagined Fred and Raul sitting in the pews, washing themselves of their many sins and secretly hating being there. Armardo, a cartel boss, coming for absolution was an even more absurd idea. The ridiculousness of the image gave him courage, and he turned to Raul.

"You like going to church?" Jimmy asked. For him, attending church was like a death of a thousand cuts. He was the complete opposite of Lucy, who loved contemporary church services.

"We all do. It's the most exciting time of the holiday season," Fred chimed in.

Raul, who kept staring at Jimmy, stammered, "I l-l-l-l-love it more than l-l-l-l-life!" Jimmy had no reply. He and Lucy were stunned. This was the second time they had ever heard Raul talk, and when he'd made the strange toast he hadn't spoken with a stutter. It was almost as surprising as his declaration he loved church. Suddenly, Jimmy realized why the hitman chose to be silent.

"Would you like to attend church services with us?" Fred asked, patting his brother on the back.

"We have a very accepting church. It is a mix of Radishers, Catholics, and Protestant denominations," Francisca pointed out. She turned to Armardo for help finding some of the words; while her English was passable, she lacked her husband's mastery of the language.

"Um, no thank you. I'm not the churchgoing type," Jimmy said quickly. He wanted no part of any 'love-fest' church services with the Lopezes and the brothers—well, Raul at least. Fred, he was learning, was all right. Then he winced, as Lucy elbowed him in the ribs under the table and leaned over to whisper something in his ear. He gritted his teeth, forced himself to smile, and asked: "Would you like to come over on Boxing Day evening and experience a *Canadian* custom?"

"Thank you for the invitation; it is very kind. I will let you know after church. Spiritually, it is incredibly taxing. Sometimes I am too exhausted for anything else," Armardo replied.

"Can I come to your Canadian thing?" Fred asked.

"Of course," Lucy replied.

Jimmy hoped their prayers and supplications were so intense they would have to stay home and recuperate until they left for Guadalajara.

⤜⤛ ⤚⤙

LUCY BASKED IN her satisfaction as she gazed at the empty plates and bowls, evidence of a successful meal. The dinner had gone well, and judging by how voraciously they ate, everyone enjoyed the food. The conversation was lively, with Fred, Armardo, and Jimmy doing the heavy lifting and Lucy chiming in when necessary. Francisca did her best to join as well, adding the odd witty remark. Still, as her grasp of English was far more limited than the others, her husband often repeated sentences for her in Spanish. Everybody seemed to be having fun except Raul, who kept staring expressionlessly at Jimmy, making him feel completely uncomfortable. Lucy could see how awkwardly he fidgeted in his seat whenever he looked over at Raul.

After the conversation died down and an awkward silence took over, Jimmy clapped his hands and spoke up. He was being stared at yet again by Raul, and he needed any distraction he could get.

"Who wants a Christmas cracker?"

The guests looked at him, not understanding what he meant. He picked up a cracker, the same type Lucy's family had used for generations, and explained their holiday tradition. The cracker was a cardboard tube wrapped in brightly coloured paper and twisted at both ends. Each person had a cracker in front of them. One person would pick it up on one end, and the person next to them would take hold of the other. Once everyone was holding onto an end of a cracker, they would pull on the count of three, and a novelty or gift would drop onto the table. Max and Hector clapped excitedly after Jimmy finished explaining, eager for the game to begin.

"When I was pregnant with Max, me and Jimmy made Christmas crackers for each other. When I opened mine, a beautiful gold chain fell onto the table. Then—" Lucy began, trailing off to look at Jimmy. His eyes lit up; he knew what was coming next. It was one of the most wonderful surprises of his life. She prompted him to tell the rest.

"When I opened Lucy's, this white, plastic thing fell into my Yorkshire pudding. I pulled it out, absolutely no clue what it was, and I saw the two pink lines. It was a pregnancy test. That's how she told me Max was on the way," he finished, beaming.

Fred let out a snicker, "I'm sure the urine added a nice tang to your dinner, amigo! My ex, Tonya, was so obsessed with Bear Grylls that she drank her own pee. I think she got quite used to the taste." Lucy and Jimmy's smiles fell, their happy memory tainted by Fred's anecdote. Armardo saw their discomfort and acted immediately.

"Fred, that's enough. Don't upset our hosts." Fred flashed them a sheepish grin, and said no more.

Soon, it was time to pull the crackers. Lucy shared one cracker each with Francisca and Fred. Hector shared one with Max, and Jimmy shared two crackers with Raul and Armardo, sitting on either side of him.

Jimmy counted down. "3-2-1, *pull*!"

BANG! CRACK! BANG! CRACK! BANG! BANG!

In the span of less than a second, Armardo, Hector, and Francisca dropped to the floor while Raul and Fred pulled their Belgian-made FM 5.7 guns from their holsters and pointed them at Jimmy and Max. The host's hands shot up in surrender, as did Max's. The boy, not understanding what was happening, laughed out loud.

"D-d-d-don't m-m-move m-m-m-m-mo-f-f-f-fo!" snarled Raul. Jimmy was staring down the barrel of his handgun. His eyes were bugging out of his head. Fred, realizing he was pointing his weapon at the head of a four-year-old, re-holstered his gun. Raul was not so merciful.

"*Put the gun down*! Have you two lost your minds?" Lucy shouted, moving closer to Jimmy as if she could shield him from the bullets.

"Again!" yelled Max. Raul kept his gun up. Jimmy struggled to catch his breath, waiting for someone, anyone, to break the excruciating silence that could at any moment be filled with the sound of gunfire. When no one spoke, he mustered all the composure he had left and tried to talk Raul down.

"Guys, let me explain. There's a type of banger in each cracker. When they're pulled in opposite directions, two strips of chemically impregnated paper react to the friction. So, when you pull the cracker apart, it makes a loud bang."

"Bang!" shouted Max, which caused Raul to shoot out of his seat and shove his gun into Jimmy's forehead. He could feel the cold metal press against his skin, forcing his head back against his chair. At this point, however, Armardo picked himself off the floor, dusted himself down, and helped his wife and Hector to their feet.

"Why didn't you warn us?" he asked with a scowl on his face.

"It was a surprise."

"Well, amigo, it was a surprise that sounded a lot like gunfire. There have been many attempts on the boss's life, so we are trained to respond to any life-threatening situation," Fred explained.

"Pulling a novelty Christmas cracker with the neighbours is life-threatening?" asked Lucy sarcastically. Armardo sighed, turned to Raul, and ordered him to take his gun away from Jimmy's temple. He did so, but his movements were slow and reluctant. He kept staring daggers at his host.

"You'll have to understand this is Mexico, and, like Fred just said, there are people who want to kill my family," Armardo explained. Jimmy felt the indentation Raul's gun had left on his forehead; the red circular mark made him look like he'd just been blessed by a Hindu priest.

"Headline: Gringo family use Christmas crackers as suicide bombs to assassinate dinner guests," he said, rattled and enraged. He didn't have high hopes for the dinner, but so far it had gone even worse than expected. The atmosphere was tense, and as a quiet fell over the room, Jimmy realized his sarcastic comments didn't help. Awkward with silence at the best of times, he spoke again, this time taking a more conciliatory tone.

"Anyway . . . sorry for the confusion. Maybe the gifts in the crackers will make up for it." He indicated the spilt-out contents on the table, and Max and Hector immediately got to work collecting the novelties. Jimmy, desperate to restore the previous pleasant—or rather, less unpleasant—atmosphere, found a folded piece of paper, opened it, and put the makeshift hat on his head.

"These hats represent the three kings who visited baby Jesus, and the novelties symbolize the gifts they presented to Joseph and Mary," hoping an appeal to piety would appease the Lopezes and the brothers. Their only response was to look dubiously at the hats. The tension was so thick you could cut it with a knife. Or put a bullet through its head.

Jimmy encouraged everyone to put on the novelty hats, and said he would read the small pieces of paper that came out of the crackers, which often contained wise words, mottoes, and jokes. They reluctantly put on the paper hats, apart from Raul, who continued to snarl and stare at his adversary. The host picked up a small piece of paper and read the first joke.

"Why was the snowman looking through the carrots?"

No response.

"He was picking his nose!"

Fred laughed. Lucy smiled.

Jimmy awkwardly read the next piece of paper. "This is good for you, Francisca, because of your radish creation: Which side of a turkey has the most feathers?"

Armardo interpreted. Francisca shrugged her shoulders.

"The outside!" Jimmy laughed at the incredibly unfunny joke.

"Okay, this last one's for Raul."

"What do you call twenty rabbits hopping backwards?"

Raul reached for his firearm and stared at Jimmy. Armardo interpreted the joke in Spanish for Hector and his wife.

No one responded.

"A receding hare-line!"

Lucy was the only one to get the pun. She just looked at Jimmy with her eyes narrowed in warning, and he belatedly realized ribbing the man with the hair-trigger temper and a gun at his side was not the best idea.

"So, these are kind of . . . silly jokes?" Fred asked.

"Yes," responded Lucy.

"I think I have a good one."

"Go ahead," said Armardo.

Fred cleared his throat. "Why couldn't Vincente's head go to the Christmas party?" Jimmy's eyes went wide. Lucy was fidgeting visibly, looking like she wanted to hop out of her skin and leave. Fred looked around the room, pausing before delivering the punchline like any good comedian would.

"Because he had NO BODY to go with!" At this, Raul and Armardo laughed hysterically, to the point they started to tear up. Fred was nodding and trying to milk the applause from the boys, who were clapping even though they didn't get Fred's joke. Armardo wiped away tears of laughter and took the paper hat from his head. Suddenly, he clapped his hands and commanded, "Enough!" That got everyone to quiet down, and the room fell dead silent. Even Max and Hector went quiet.

"This meal has been a very *interesting* experience. We don't want to overstay our welcome. Lucy, the food was lovely. Thank you!"

"The stew really was delicious. There was a subtle hint of . . . something. I would love to get the recipe," Francisca added. Lucy thanked her and tried to put on her best smile. Max and Hector looked at each other and sniggered.

The Lopez contingent headed for the door. Fred took a few steps and stopped in his tracks, rotated his body, and locked eyes with Jimmy and smiled, "Amigo, let's meet tonight by the pool for a drink, just you and me. We'll finish off the tequila and rum."

Jimmy looked at Lucy for affirmation. If it was just Fred, he didn't mind going. He had a holstered gun and an off-colour sense of humour. Jimmy didn't mind the former and liked the latter. Well, he minded the gun thing, but since Fred didn't have his brother's itchy trigger finger, he felt safer about spending time with him.

Lucy nodded, "Oh, go on, it's Christmas. The girls might pop over to join me later for a nightcap. I know you'd rather hang out with Fred and share your funny jokes."

"Okay, Luce." She smiled at him, but he could tell she was still angry and shaken after the Christmas cracker incident.

"Hey, maybe Fred could teach you how to quick-draw. Then you could hold a gun to Max's head during the next family gathering," she said with faux good nature. Jimmy gave her a strained smile and told Fred he'd see him down at the poolside in a couple of hours after doing the washing up. Then the Lopez family made a brisk exit, with Hector lingering to say his goodbyes to Max and Lucy. When they were all gone and the door finally closed behind them, Jimmy turned to his wife.

"What the flip just happened?" Lucy just let out a nervous laugh.

"Excuse my French, but they're all batshit crazy, is what happened. If those two nutters had pulled the trigger—" she trailed off. It wasn't lost on Jimmy that the guns had been pointed at her husband and son. He had a 'told you so' locked and loaded but realized now was not the time to fire sarcasm at her. She'd almost lost her family at Christmas dinner. She put on a composed front, but was understandably distraught, and he desperately needed to alleviate the tension.

"Merry effing *Nadolig*!" he said, aware Max was listening. Lucy looked at him, let out another anxious chuckle, and fell into his arms.

SIXTEEN

New Religion & the Non-Yankee Swap

ON SUNDAY MORNING, THE entire town attended the local church, *La Iglesia Evangélica Calvinista de la Santísima Virgen Roja*, otherwise known as The Evangelical Calvinist Church of the Holy Red Virgin, which at first glance contained oxymoronic theologies in its very name. The beauty of the church lay in its mission statement, which emphasized grace for all, harmony and tolerance for many, and peace for the masses.

The streets of Los Piñata were empty, and it seemed like a ghost town. Boxing Day was a special occasion for which everyone turned out. The parishioners were practically thrumming with excitement, and formed roiling, eager crowds. Many congregants ran to get a good pew. The busiest and feistiest Boxing Day service started at 8.30 am, and no one wanted to be late, or get stuck with a seat far in the back.

This once-a-year post-Christmas service was where the common folk—the street vendors, store workers, and housekeepers—rubbed shoulders with professionals: the dentists, doctors, lawyers, whores, and cartel bosses. It was also a sacred time when Armardo, Fred, and Raul could escape the week's torture, murders, disappearances, and crocodiles. The congregation was a strange mixture of evangelical Protestants and radical Radish Catholics. The evangelicals sat on the right-hand side of the central aisle; the Catholics sat on the left-hand side. There was a healthy tension between the two opposing sides of the church.

On this particular Boxing Day, the Protestant pastor, the Very, Very, Very, Very Reverend Larry Pennelli, preached a fiery 'turn or burn' sermon, followed by a message from the much-loved Radish Catholic priest, Father Dominguez. To an outsider, it certainly was entertaining stuff. Pastor Larry went off on a tirade about hell, fire, and brimstone, and the right-hand side of the church shouted things like, "Amen," and "Burn in Hades, radish worshipping shit-eaters," directing their devout fury at the RCs on the left-hand side of the church.

Pastor Larry gave a thumbs up to the righteous believers, then angrily yelled at the fake believers on the left-hand aisle. He accused them of being "scumbags" and "heathens" who were nothing more than "wolves in sheep's clothing." The left-hand side, especially those from the cartel, shrieked and howled like ravenous wolves and gestured to the evangelicals their throats would be cut after the service. Rapturous applause accompanied the end of Pastor Larry's sermon from the Protestants.

The tension built as Father Dominguez approached the pulpit. Wild booing and hissing came from those on the right-hand aisle; excited football-style cheering came from the left-hand Catholic side.

"Dominguez! Dominguez! Dominguez!" the left yelled.

"Heretic! Heretic! Burn the Heretic!" the right shouted.

Dominguez held up his aspergillum, and all went quiet. This very holy device was a perforated metal ball on a handle that held the priest's holy water. The silence that followed its rise was so intense even the slightest sound, like a dropped needle, would seem deafening. With a press of an imperceptibly-small button, the aspergillum turned into a morning star. Dominguez swung the medieval weapon above his head and violently sprayed holy radish water onto the evangelical side of the aisle, as if he was holding a water cannon. The force of impact caused the evangelicals to be thrown from their seats.

Father Dominguez cried, "Satan, get out!" and "Evil spirit of false religion, leave these knuckleheaded infidels in the Red Virgin's name!"

Pandemonium broke out. The left and right sides of the congregation shot out of their seats and launched at each other with raised fists. Both sides threw wild haymakers in a frantic melee of spiritual and physical violence.

"Brothers and sisters, put on your armour and slay the heathens in our midst!" Dominguez yelled to the left side of the church.

The sound of Kevlar body armour being strapped on echoed through the church as members prepared for the service. Others, like those from the Wolfpack Cartel, produced machetes and tomahawks, their versions of the 'Red Sword of the Spirit.' Somehow, all this deadly and dangerous gear made its way into the church, and now outfitted the Catholics as they prepared to wield them against the evil evangelicals on the right-hand side.

As the fighting continued anew, with the weapons and armour adding to the scale of the destruction, the air grew thick with the sound of clashing metal and the acrid smell of smoke. The two religious leaders stood at the altar, overlooking the violence. Calmly and with the utmost sensitivity, Pennelli and Dominguez exhorted all the infidels, pagans, and godless idolaters to come to the altar and be "saved." After this profound call for ecumenical salvation, the two religious leaders instructed both sides of the church to return to their seats, as both pastor and priest held hands at the front of the church, wishing everyone "*Ana Feliz Navidad*!" The clerics gave the benediction simultaneously, and all present repeated it wholeheartedly.

Each congregant agreed a mighty spiritual revival was close to breaking out in Los Piñata. The Very, Very, Very Very Reverend Pennelli and Father Dominguez hugged, then asked the congregation to give alms to the poor, as in religious tradition. People from both sides of the aisle picked up severed fingers, hands, and appendages lying on the marble church floor and held them up, dedicating them to those financially struggling or with missing limbs. Pannelli and Dominguez, their heads in their hands as one, tittered and admonished their righteous flock for mixing 'alms' with 'arms.'

The service was over; both sides of the church embraced, hugged, and hung out, eating cakes, crêpes, and ceviche together. Both clerics shared a spliff and agreed the service had been "da bomb." With arms around each other's shoulders, they spoke in tongues, their conversation peppered with phrases that sounded like, "What tha dilly yo," "For real, cuz," "Word up," and "Wiggity-wack."

The first aid room medical staff were busy suturing cuts and treating congregants for concussions, severed limbs, and other injuries. The atmosphere in the blood-soaked triage area was amiable and light-hearted, just like a church should be on the day after the birth of the Lord.

The church members finally left the church to return to their homes, singing 'Kumbaya,' holding hands, dancing, and waving 'Freedom' flags. The congregants couldn't wait until next year's Boxing Day service.

⤜⤜⤜ ⤛⤛⤛

JIMMY HEARD THE Mexican contingent returning from church. They sounded full of gaiety. Lucy overheard them talking about blood, alms, passion, travelling mercies, spiritual warfare, and Armageddon.

"It must have been a cracking church service," Lucy commented to Jimmy as she peeked from behind the curtains. "Do you regret not going with our neighbours?" she asked, poking the bear.

Jimmy didn't regret *not* going. However, he deeply regretted inviting the Mexicans to the Boxing Day gift exchange that would be held later in the condo's pool area. He remembered explaining the concept to Armardo et al. after they left dinner; Armardo and Raul had joined him and Fred for drinks afterwards, much to Jimmy's chagrin. It had been yet another excruciating experience, as painful as yanking out nose hairs with duct tape.

The gift exchange was just a fun Myers family tradition. Jimmy assured Armardo there would be no surprise Christmas cracker noises or anything that would cause his sicarios to draw their weapons on him or his four-year-old son. He explained that the gift exchange was called a 'Yankee Swap.'

"I hate the Yankees," said Fred unhelpfully. Armardo nodded in agreement, and Fred continued.

"They tried to steal our Alamo. Stupid George Patton with his macho-gringo pistols with ivory handles. How'd that work out for you, Georgie-Boy Patton?"

Jimmy corrected Fred with a sigh, "The Yankees were, in fact, *Texans*, and George Paton was an American general during World War II."

"Well, we still hate him. What with all the 'Yankee Doodle this' and 'Yankee Doodle that.' He sure got himself whooped at the Alamo. I won't shed any tears for that bastard."

"Who, what?"

"Patton." Jimmy honestly didn't know if Fred was trying to bait him or if he genuinely had no idea what he was talking about. He decided to assume the latter and take the higher road.

"Anyway, Yankee Swap is just a fun game. It doesn't have anything to do with Yankees, George Patton, Buzz Aldrin, or anyone from the U.S.," he explained.

"Hate him too," added Fred.

"Who? Why?"

"I always preferred Woody." Jimmy realized Fred was talking about Buzz Lightyear, not Buzz Aldrin, and again he wondered whether he was being deliberately dense.

"Okay," said Jimmy, scratching his head and hoping the Mexican's hatred of all things north of the border would help them decide not to attend the gift exchange.

Armardo frowned, "It sounds amusing, though I'd prefer it if it were called some other name." Just like that, Jimmy's hopes were dashed.

"We can call it an 'Acapulco Swap' if you like," he suggested. Armardo nodded in gratitude.

"That sounds good. Anything does, as long as it doesn't mention Yankees or that stupid astronaut toy Buzz Lightyear," added Fred helpfully.

"Buzz *Aldrin*," corrected Jimmy. "He walked on the moon."

"Over-rated gringo song, if you ask me," said Fred. Jimmy put his hand to his head with an audible slap, rubbing his forehead in exasperation.

"No, not the song by The Police. Buzz Aldrin—the real astronaut, not the toy—walked on the moon with Neil Armstrong on July 16th, 1969." He tried to refocus Fred and explain the premise of the now renamed 'Acapulco Swap.' However, the little sicario wasn't done being random yet.

"I wrote a poem about the Alamo," he blurted out partway through Jimmy's explanation.

"He did," Armardo proudly stated. "It was brilliant; he got an A+ from the teacher."

"With distinction," added Fred.

"Awesome," added Jimmy, condescendingly. He bit his tongue to keep from pointing out the fact that no teacher in their right mind would give the godson of a cartel boss anything less than a perfect grade, no matter how inane their poetry might be. He had been feeling generously towards Fred and his poetry before, but all that goodwill had dried up. Fred was proving to be either an idiot or an asshole, and either way, Jimmy didn't care to read anything he wrote. Using characters like Buzz Lightyear, George Patton, or even The Teletubbies in his wackadoodle 'deconstructed' revolutionary poetry would make it an 'interesting' read, though likely not a good one. But—and it was a big but—no publisher would go anywhere near such a book.

Jimmy tried to deflect the conversation from the Alamo and back to the fun gift exchange, now known as the 'Acapulco Swap.' He explained each person would bring a gift, either used or unused. The gifts were nothing too valuable, and nothing worth above fifty dollars. They should be wrapped up with paper provided by Lucy, or the Mexicans could wrap them themselves. However, they were not to tell anybody else what their gift was. They would draw numbers, and according to the number chosen, the person picked a gift, opened it, and showed everybody what it was. Then, in order of numbers drawn, the next person picked up a present or took number one's gift. If this were to happen, number one would open a second gift for themselves; this continued until all presents were opened. The person who drew number one, the best number to draw, would finally decide what present they would take as their own out of all the presents. After Jimmy finished his careful explanation, Fred yawned.

"Sounds complicated," Armardo noted.

"So, it kinda sucks to be number two?" Fred added.

"Kind of," said Jimmy. "It's supposed to be a *fun* game, not a competitive one. You shouldn't take it too seriously."

"I don't like 'Acapulco Swap' anymore. The game is very sly, and people might be sneaky and steal your present," Fred insisted. Raul frowned and felt for his weapon.

"I think you should call it the 'Colombian Swap,' as all Colombians are sneaky and vegan," he continued.

"Maybe call it the 'Nazi Germany Swap,'" suggested Armardo.

"Or the 'Vietnam War Swap,'" added Fred.

"What about the 'Hindenburg Airship Disaster Swap?'" chimed in Armardo once again.

Jimmy's head was spinning, which led him to suggest a name for the gift exchange in honour of Lucy, who had just made everyone such a fabulous meal. Armardo and Fred agreed. Raul nodded and made an approving grunting sound.

"Now before I say the name, we all have to promise to keep it."

"Pinky promise," said Armardo

"Pinky promise," giggled Fred.

Raul held out his little finger, wiggled it, and made grunting noises.

"Sounds good. What do you have in mind?" quizzed Armardo.

"It's to do with St. Mary's church, a white hazel tree, a whirlpool, and another church near a red cave."

Armardo nodded, "Yes. It sounds peaceful, non-American, and non-Colombian. In other words, perfect."

Jimmy took a deep breath and made the announcement. "It's now called the '*Llanfairpwll . . . gwyngyllgogerychwyrndroblllllantysiliogogogoch*'—"

Fred laughed out aloud. "*Gogo-goch*. What the—"

"Swap," finished Jimmy, interrupting him. "Or, for short, the *Llanfairpwllgwyngyll* Swap."

"Impressive. Are you speaking in tongues?" Armardo asked. He sounded genuinely in awe of Jimmy's deft pronunciation.

"Lucy taught me to say it to amaze her Welsh parents. It's the name of a train station on the Island of Anglesey in North Wales. The only other Welsh words I know are swear words."

"And *Nadolig Llawen*," said Fred proudly.

"Remember your pinky promises. I formally invite you to participate in the 'Llanfairpwllgwyngyll Swap' tonight and for the rest of eternity. And there's no pressure to get gifts, as we came prepared with some extras," Jimmy announced. At this, Armardo and Fred broke into frowns.

"I guess you guys won't be coming then?" he probed, optimistically. He hoped his eagerness didn't come through in his tone.

"We will bring our gifts, thank you," snapped Armardo with his chest puffed out proudly. Jimmy was disappointed. He knew the event would be way more fun without Armardo and his sicario with the pink sombrero hovering over his shoulder, his gun at his side and his trigger finger itching for some action.

Armardo turned to the brother and spoke in Spanish. The only words Jimmy understood in Armardo's diatribe were '*Go-go-gogh*,' 'Yankee,' and 'Buzz Aldrin.' Fred smiled. Raul frowned. Armardo happily announced they would participate in the '*Thlan-fair-pwill-gwin-gill* Swap' after all. Jimmy nodded, stunned that Armardo remembered the name phonetically after just one or two mentions. After that, he got up and left. That gave Jimmy some relief, but unfortunately Raul remained with his brother.

"If the name can be silly, what about the gifts?" Fred asked once his godfather was gone.

"Of course. It's just a fun little Christmas tradition among friends and family. In fact, the funniest gift comes with great kudos, and I've won the kudos award five years running. If you want to take a shot at the champ, you've got your work cut out for you," Jimmy answered. Fred flashed him a wicked grin.

When he told Lucy what had transpired, she was in hysterics, but reminded him Fred might have been pulling his leg, too, as he seemed to be a bit of a wind-up merchant. Lucy also pointed out '*gogogoch*' translated into English as 'cuckoo,' which was an apt name for a game involving these three nutbar Mexicans.

SEVENTEEN

A Sheep in Wolves' Clothing

WHEN THE GIFT SWAP was about to begin, there was a convivial atmosphere around the pool and patio area. Presents had been wrapped and placed in a central pile, ranging from large boxes to small bags. Some of these packages were spectacularly decorated and adorned with pretty bows; others looked like they had been wrapped in the seconds leading up to the Chernobyl disaster. Jimmy had donated two gifts. One was decorated beautifully, the other thrown together using newspaper and duct tape. He loved to trick people into taking the more aesthetically pleasing present.

Jimmy, the gamemaster, rubbed his hands together, and when all the participants had arrived, he reminded them of the gift exchange rules. He had made cards with numbers written on them, and each person was to pick a card blindly from the deck. He looked around at the circle of people present. Lucy, JayBee and Mella, Bradley and Marcus, and Armardo and Francisca were there, as were the brothers. Fred sat next to Jimmy. Raul stood a yard behind Armardo, scanning the motley group with his penetrating eyes. Both brothers were wearing their distinctive sombreros. Mac had kindly volunteered to look after Max, so his parents could have fun at the "Swap."

Jimmy remembered Bradley and Marcus from the 'Quiz Nite' at Tequila Tommy's and he wasn't particularly happy to see them. Marcus, at least, had been somewhat entertaining, but Jimmy disliked Bradley, mainly due to his annoying barrage of absurd questions that ruined his team's chances of winning.

They were in their late forties, and their claim to fame—beyond their successful producing careers—was that they declared themselves to be the gayest couple in all of Mexico. They were well-known in Hollywood circles, having written various screenplays for several blockbuster movies. Their latest on-screen ventures tended to be reality-based series, like the dating show *The Pink Pyramid* and the survival show *Proud, Naked, and Gayfraid*.

Mella loved them both, but had warned Lucy that Bradley could talk a person's ear off. As far as Jimmy was concerned, her warning was too little too late; he'd already been in the eye of Hurricane Bradley once before. Marcus was quieter, but tended to make hilarious and inappropriate sexual innuendoes.

Jimmy saw Armardo was glaring at the couple. He had a sneer etched on his face. As they drank more, their flamboyance increased proportionally. At one point, Marcus reached out and gave Armardo's knee a reassuring squeeze. The cartel boss shot him a murderous stare, and Raul stepped towards his boss. Armardo lifted his hand, holding it in the air like a signal to halt. To Jimmy, it looked like Armardo knew Raul was going to deal with the touchy-feely man cartel style and had given him the order to stop. Raul, ever-obedient, backed off and continued to people-watch.

"Let the games begin!" Jimmy cried, hoping to nip any potential violence in the bud. He held out ten cards, and the participants each took one and turned it over to see their number in the swap. The draw was:

Bradley #1
JayBee #2
Marcus #3
Mella #4
Armardo #5
Francisca #6
Fred #7
Jimmy #8
Lucy #9

As Bradley had drawn the coveted #1 card, he was the first to take a prize. He reached out to a small package and unwrapped it. Bradley squealed as he showed everyone a spa day gift certificate for two, including wraps, a massage, and fish that exfoliated the feet.

The gamemaster, Jimmy Myers, reminded him he would ultimately have the last pick of any prize he wanted. The rest of the participants chose or swapped their gifts.

Bradley clung to his spa day gift certificate.

JayBee was left holding a lipstick and nail varnish set. Marcus, who went next, took Bradley's spa day gift certificate. Bradley called him a slutty cow and reluctantly took a gift and opened it—it was one of Deaf Barry's customized ear trumpets. "Great!" said Bradley, suggestively holding the trumpet to his groin. "Hey, Marcus, do you want to blow my trumpet later when we get home?" Armardo scowled; Francisca blushed. Lucy looked around and rolled her eyes. "You guys! What if Max was around to hear that?" Bradley stuck out his lower lip and mouthed, "Sorry, darling," to Lucy.

Mella pretended she was thrilled to receive a CD of Fred's recited poetry—*Radical Poetry Through the Ages*.

Armardo proudly held onto a bottle of 1958 McJebediah White Walker scotch. Francisca blushed and smiled as this was the gift she had brought to the exchange. She had wrapped it up in Mexican colours of green, white, and red so her husband would choose it if he had the opportunity. Armardo was stoked and gave the stink eye to anyone who dared to take it from him.

Francisca's gift was tangerine-flavoured bath salts, hand crème, and a shower gel set. She took off the cap of the shower gel and smelt the aroma. She was delighted with her gift.

Fred opened his gift and roared with laughter, "How ironic," he chuckled as he held up a pair of green Crocs.

It was Jimmy's turn to choose. He reminded the group their chosen gift might not be theirs to keep forever, as it was subject to being exchanged for another present. He was very tempted to take Armardo's expensive-looking whiskey. However, he remembered he had irritated him at the dinner and had accused him of conspiracy to murder Vincente and thought better of it. The last thing he needed was to give Armardo a reason to feed him to the crocodiles.

"I'll open this bad boy up," he said, picking up a large yet lightweight package. He unwrapped the first layer of paper and laughed as he realized the person donating the gift might be a prankster like himself. There were many more layers beneath. Jimmy's fingers were covered in paper cuts from peeling away the layers, but finally, he reached the cardboard container box.

Bradley cried out, "Oh, the excitement!" Finally, Jimmy opened it up and saw a mug with a T-shirt.

"Take it out," Bradley encouraged.

"You've got to wear it!" squealed Marcus. Jimmy looked at the rainbow-coloured mug, turned it around to read the writing, and laughed when he beheld, written in bold and colourful letters, the words 'Loud, Gay and Proud!'

Jimmy smiled, "Perfecto." He took out the bright crimson-coloured vest, which had been rolled up in the mug. He unfolded it and saw that the front had a fluorescent green donkey logo.

"Nice." Everyone else, however, was roaring with laughter. Jimmy realized they were staring at the back, and he turned the shirt around to see what had gotten everyone so riled up. 'Pinch My Ass—I'll Buy You a Beer' was boldly written on the vest.

Armardo, Francisca, and Raul were the only ones not laughing.

"Guess who bought that one?" asked Marcus.

Bradley pretended to blush, covered his mouth with his hand, put up his arm, and shouted "Guilty as charged."

"It's just what he's always wanted," Lucy said with a smile. When it was her turn, Lucy took Mella's poetry CD, swapping it for her gift: some attractive-looking Mexican artwork. Jimmy groaned at Lucy's decision, as he wanted Fred's CD as much as he wanted to catch Ebola. Besides, the sicario had already promised to give Jimmy his poetry collection. Reading his poems was enough; he didn't need to hear them, too.

The gift exchange had succeeded, and folks were smiling, laughing, and clapping—most of them, anyway. Jimmy told everyone it was finally #1's turn to choose the final present. Bradley could keep his present, not choose a present and keep the one he had received, or be savage and steal any gift from any of the players.

"Go, Bradley, Go!" the amigas chanted. Bradley picked up the ultimate gift. This last present was a large box someone had beautifully decorated and wrapped. Unlike JayBee, who had painstakingly opened her gift to preserve the wrapping paper, Bradley tore his apart. Wrapping paper flew everywhere until he exposed what lay beneath a cardboard box. He looked inside it and burst into laughter. Laughing so hard he could barely breathe, he took out a large plastic package containing what looked like a deflated sheep.

"Can you . . . can you translate?" he asked Lucy between bouts of laughter, handing her the package.

"Hi, I'm Sexy Suzie, your shy or sheepish friend. I am there for you on those long, cold winter nights." Most of the group roared with laughter. Lucy continued to translate what was on the package. "It also says Sexy Suzie 'comes' with four AA batteries, which gives the user a perfect experience."

Mella and JayBee made baa-ing sounds. Bradley took the package back from Lucy and rummaged around inside.

The laughter was now as loud as Pedro Cordoba's sound system.

"Are you going to keep Suzie the Sheep or exchange her for another gift?" Jimmy quizzed Bradley once everyone regained some semblance of composure.

"I can't believe you put *that* in our gift exchange!" Lucy said playfully, giving Jimmy a light swat on the arm. Jimmy smirked proudly, pleased at the reception it got.

"I got it at a local sex shop run by the oldest dominatrix I'd ever seen. I was lucky to get out before she started whipping me."

"We're not exactly swimming in cash up here. Was that really money well-spent?"

"Totally," laughed Jimmy.

Bradley dramatically put his fingers to his lips and pondered his decision. He opened the package, took out the flat white rubber sheep, found the blow hole in the sheep's bum, took deep breaths and blew into it until it inflated to a full-size six-foot inflatable sheep.

He inserted the batteries and pressed a switch labelled *El botón del orgasmo de Suzie.*

Lucy translated: "Suzie's Orgasm Button."

"Baa," said the sheep. "Baa, Baa, Baa, Baaaaaaaaaaaaaaaaaaaaaaa!"

Bradley nodded and said he had come to a decision. He went around the circle of people, pointing his finger at each one, asking them if they wanted Suzie. Hardly anyone made eye contact with him except Armardo, who stared daggers through his eyes. Bradley, showing no fear, asked Armardo if he wanted Suzie's attention for the night. Francisca coughed uncomfortably.

"She seems shy, or a bit sheepish, but super-friendly," chuckled Bradley, trying to get Armardo to smile or at least blink. The cartel boss didn't bite. Then Bradley, clearly unsatisfied with the other man's response, did the unthinkable. He took Armardo's luxury bottle of Scotch and exchanged it for Suzie.

"She will be waiting for you tonight," winked Bradley. The amigas and Marcus laughed out loud, but Jimmy felt a cold shudder go down his spine. None of them understood how much danger they'd put themselves in. Vincente had gone missing after asking Armardo's people to turn down their music; what would he do if deprived of a lovely gift? Jimmy decided to help Armardo out of the bind that he was in, hoping it would placate him.

"Hey Armardo, I'm happy to have Suzy. I'll swap her with my cup and vest." Armardo scowled at Jimmy. Raul walked forward to stand behind his boss. He touched the handle of his firearm. Armardo held up his hand to Raul, took his wife's arm, stood up, and the couple left the group without saying good night. Raul was quick to follow. There was stony silence. Bradley looked affronted at the Lopez's rudeness.

"Hey, amigos and amigas. I wouldn't push it with Armardo. He didn't look too happy," Fred cautioned.

"Oh, he's fine. It's all good fun. Surely he can take a joke?" asked Marcus.

Fred replied, "Amigo, your partner suggested to one of the most powerful people in Mexico he might want to forgo his wife tonight and make love to a blow-up sheep."

"Baa baa, black sheep, have you any wool? Yes, sir, yes sir, three bags full. One for Amardo, one for his dame. And one for little Fred, who lives down the lane," sang Marcus, completely ignoring Fred's comment.

"Baaaaaaaa," most of the group bleated in unison.

EIGHTEEN

The Day of Pranks

AFTER THE CHRISTMAS SHENANIGANS, the Lopez clan took the 'colossus' sound system, several crates of assorted alcoholic beverages, their suitcases, and huge chests of items, and drove away into the sunset in a long procession of Black Sedans and Toyota Tacomas.

It was wonderfully quiet once again. The squeaks, whistles, and croaks of the blackbirds, the cacophonous gulls squawking, the waves crashing, and the palm trees swaying in the breeze were music to their ears—far more pleasing than Cordoba's cacophony. Jimmy and Lucy hugged, overjoyed to have solitude reign over their condo once again. With the Lopez family gone, Jimmy felt like a man reborn.

"To celebrate, why don't we go to Tequila Tommy's? They're having a New Year's Eve celebration," Lucy suggested. The three amigas were going to Tequila Tommy's and had told her Tommy usually made the evening a lot of fun. He was also, as Jimmy had found, very generous with free drinks.

"That'd be great," Jimmy said, letting out a relieved sigh. He was all too happy to enjoy New Years and forget about his plight for one evening. He, Max, and Lucy could celebrate Canadian-style without having guns pointed at their heads or having to change the name of a fun gift exchange to not offend a touchy cartel boss. No more Wolfpack Cartel, no sombreros, no 1835 tequilas, no radishes, no toasts to a cartel mass-murderer, no more porcupine turkeys, and, hopefully, no Inspector Knobhead raiding their safe. Tonight, he and Lucy were determined to have fun. She was looking forward to seeing Jimmy get out of his funk; she wanted to show off her husband, who could be wildly funny when he was in the mood. Hopefully, he would get blasted, stand on the table, rip off his shirt, and do his MJ 'Thriller' dance.

Lucy's only genuine concern was that, since Christmas Day, she hadn't been able to go to the toilet. Jimmy's bowels were fine; however, she hated struggling with constipation, so she started to drink gallons of prune juice. She didn't think for one minute her constipation was due to her four-year-old son and his eight-year-old cartel buddy.

⟫⟫⟫ ⟪⟪⟪

THE SUN WAS setting with beautiful hues of yellows, reds, and oranges. Looking at the explosion of colours in the distant sky, Jimmy thought this was a stunning place to stay, and he was looking forward to the celebration at Tequila Tommy's in a few nights. As he anticipated the night's festivities, he was distracted by a voice from behind him.

"There's the *hombre*!" Jimmy turned around and grinned to see a small man in a large black sombrero.

"How are you, Fred?"

"I'm doing fine, amigo. Armardo has been called back to the big city; he has some business to deal with."

Thank goodness, Jimmy thought. Aloud, he said, "Going so soon? You have five or six more days left of the festivities."

"Yes, but business is business, amigo. However, about festivities, it's just as well we're not here on the 28th."

"Why's that?"

"It's *Dia de los Santos Inocentes*, or 'The Day of the Innocents.'" Jimmy stifled a chuckle. Raul would undoubtedly have to skip that particular celebration.

"It's a day of pranks, a little like your April Fool's Day. The day commemorates when King Herod ordered all baby boys executed in his bid to kill baby Jesus," Fred finished.

Jimmy asked, "So, Herod commanded, 'Kill all the babies!' Then, when his soldiers reported they had done what he had asked, he announced, 'Just kidding?'"

Fred laughed, "I see your point, amigo."

"Seriously, I can't imagine anyone playing pranks on your pink-hatted brother."

"Raul is the biggest prankster. He always pranks back, but if he suspects the culprit isn't a family member, his pranks can get a bit . . . dangerous." Jimmy wasn't even scared by this. It was just par for the course for the psycho-looking sicario.

"Never would've guessed," he muttered.

"Amigo, my brother has cut people's fingers off in the past, then told them, '*Feliz Dia De Los Santos Inocentes!*'" Fred exclaimed. Jimmy frowned. Clearly, their mother had never taught Raul the definition of a prank.

"Just kidding. See how easy it is to prank you," said Fred, breaking into a big grin. Jimmy smiled back, but only briefly. Fred's smile was short-lived as well; his expression became sombre and he walked closer to Jimmy. When he spoke again, it was at a lower register.

"But seriously, pranking Raul is a bad idea. Always has been. You know, when we were young, kids used to tease us. Called us Fred Flintstone and Dino the Dinosaur."

"Which one were you?" Jimmy asked, hoping to lighten the mood. Fred ignored him and continued.

"Raul ate so many green vegetables the kids said it was proof he was a dinosaur. They even spread a rumour his teeth were green due to the pigment in the plants."

"Chlorophyll," Jimmy added helpfully. Fred nodded.

"Then the kids stopped calling him Dino and started calling him Phil. He didn't mind that so much, at least for a little while. Anything was better than being compared to the dinosaur from *The Flintstones*."

"They called him Phil, after Chloro-PHIL. Smart kids," Jimmy chuckled.

"Then, on *Dia De Los Santos Inocentes*, some of our idiot classmates left a gift-wrapped box outside our home. It was addressed to Raul. He didn't get many presents, so he was very excited. He took it inside, tore off the wrapping paper, and found it was a mini-garden with plants and soil. It was just a dumb prank, but Raul went loco."

"What happened to the kids who planted the horticultural gift for your brother?"

"All I can say, amigo, was that two of them disappeared and were never seen again."

"Just because they called him *Phil*?"

"Yup. I didn't realize it at the time, but he had a complex about his teeth. He was convinced the kids were right and they had a greenish hue. It didn't matter that he saw pearly-white gnashers whenever he looked in a mirror. The taunts had got to his head."

"Sounds like you two have always been close." He was becoming increasingly uneasy and wanted to change the subject.

"Yes, of course. We shared the same womb and came from the same egg. That's why we are identical." Jimmy looked away from Fred, worried that if he made prolonged eye contact in the wake of such a ridiculous statement he would burst into laughter. Instead, he took the high ground and said nothing. Fred walked away, only to come back with two glasses and two bottles, one of tequila and one of rum. Fred poured a glass for himself and Jimmy, and the two sat together in silence for a little while, drinking and looking at the sunset.

Fred broke the silence, "You aren't so bad . . . for a gringo."

"For a cartel hitman, you aren't so bad either."

Both men laughed. There was another pause in the conversation, and Jimmy realized, with Armardo gone, now might be a good time to ask Fred about Inspector Lopez. Though he may be one of Armardo's sicarios, Jimmy felt Fred could be trusted to keep this conversation between them.

"Can I ask you something? Something that you could, maybe, keep to yourself?" Fred turned to look at him, mid-sip. He finished his drink and answered.

"What do you mean?"

"I'd prefer Armardo not hear what I'm about to ask."

"I'll do my best, amigo. Don Armardo is my boss, and we're bound by blood, so I can't lie to him. But if he doesn't ask, I don't have to tell," Fred replied, after taking a few moments to deliberate the request. That was good enough for Jimmy; he didn't think he'd get a better answer.

Jimmy explained, "The reason I don't want him knowing is because it's about his brother, the Inspector. He made a house call with a bogus search warrant. He and his lackey search our place, and later that night I found the money Armardo lent us had disappeared, along with my passport." Again, Fred paused before replying. It seemed he was choosing his words carefully.

"What are you saying, amigo?"

"I think Inspector Lopez and his assistant took them. They were the only ones who could have, and I know for a fact I didn't misplace the money or the passport. Plus, the guy's had it out for me since I reported the head I found in the freezer." As soon as Jimmy mentioned the head in the freezer, Fred frowned. Jimmy realized belatedly it was a bad idea to mention it to one of the people who had been involved in putting it there.

"Radish," corrected Fred. Jimmy could have let the matter drop, but he wouldn't let himself be gaslit again. That was Vincente's head, and he knew it.

"That wasn't a radish in that freezer," he insisted. He met Fred's gaze, and the sicario looked away.

"The missing money and passport are very odd. I know nothing about it, I promise. However, are you saying you no longer have Don Armardo's money?"

Jimmy nodded.

"Amigo, you are in shit's creek without a paddle."

"I reported it as missing or stolen to Lopez, who laughed as he took the report. He either did it himself just to be an asshole, or someone gave him the order." Jimmy let out a huge sigh. "Now I need help getting out of Mexico. I don't have the money, and even if I did, there's nothing I can do without my passport. I can't even get my own money wired over now that I don't have proof of identification."

Fred sighed in commiseration and filled his and Jimmy's glasses with tequila. The two men raised them to the air, and both said simultaneously,

"Shit's Creek."

"Without a paddle." They clinked glasses and downed their shots.

"So . . . how do you plan on paying Armardo back?"

Jimmy shook his head. He didn't want to respond, because the only answer he could give was he had no idea. From the sound of things, Fred wasn't able or willing to help him, and so he just sat in silence. Los Piñata didn't seem so beautiful anymore.

Fred winked, "I might have a way to help you make some money."

Jimmy turned to him, eyes wide in surprise, "Really?"

"You might not like it."

"What do you mean?" Jimmy's surprise and relief gave way to suspicion. He didn't like the sound of that.

"If I can get some weed and cocaine and you can help sell it, we can split the profit. That should solve your money problems, at least." Somehow, the idea was both worse and better than Jimmy was expecting. He even considered it for a moment, but just couldn't imagine himself as a drug dealer. Lucy wouldn't be able to imagine it, either.

"Thanks, but no thanks."

"Are you sure, amigo? It's low-risk and makes good money. I collect taxes and do the bookkeeping all by myself, since Raul guards Don Armardo in Guadalajara. That means there's no one to supervise me, and no risk of getting caught. I manage the cartel's money and make my own on the side."

"I'm sure. I'm desperate, but not that desperate." Jimmy said emphatically.

"Your loss. How much money do you owe Don Armardo, anyway?" Fred poured himself another shot and threw it back as Jimmy answered.

"I'm not sure. I didn't get to count it." Suddenly, Fred went into a violent coughing fit, sputtering and spitting up tequila. He sounded like he was going to hack up a lung. Jimmy waited for him to recover.

"*You're not sure*? You're in debt to the head of one of the most dangerous cartels in Mexico and you don't know how much you owe him?"

"I was tipsy when you gave it to me. I was planning on counting the money when I sobered up."

"What kind of stupid gringo reason is that?" Fred wasn't going to let this go, so Jimmy tried to change tack.

"How much time do you think I have before Armardo wants the money repaid?" he asked, a twinge of desperation in his voice.

"Not for a while, unless you piss him off again. Like I said before, first he'll send me, and then he'll send Raul if you're not quick enough paying him back."

"Does he send Raul a lot?"

"On occasion. If people are smart, they see me and know what comes after, and that gets them to pay up. They know better than to mess with my brother. But I don't use force, so some debtors see me as a soft touch and they don't negotiate or pay up. That's when Raul visits them, and it ends in a bloodbath."

"Like the 'Dino' kids?"

"Like the 'Dino' kids," Fred concurred. Jimmy, despite his buzz, was getting antsy. He suspected all this before, but hearing Fred confirm all his fears about Raul made him uneasy. He didn't want the man in the pink sombrero coming after him—or worse, his family. "Any advice you can give me on how to keep that from happening?"

"You know the saying 'pay unto Caesar what is Caesar's?' Do that. If your wife still has her passport, have her get the money—lots of it. If you don't know what you owe, the safest thing to do is pay more than you think you should," Fred replied. It wasn't what Jimmy wanted to hear; he had hoped for some loophole, some clause in the informal cartel-debtor contract that could get him out of this jam. But he thanked Fred for his help all the same. A cartel man helping him get out of paying the cartel had been too much to hope for.

"If you see me in the future, you'll know the boss wants his money repaid. Again, I'm sure it won't be for a while."

"Thanks for being a friend."

"It's not over until the fat lady sings, Mr Myers."

Jimmy sarcastically said, "Hey, that's body shaming, señor." There was no sense in wallowing in despair. If he was going to be in debt for an unknown amount with no recourse but to pay up big-time or risk being fed to the crocodiles, he could at least have fun.

"I disagree. It's a 'reclaiming term' for many fat people so they can take their power back." Fred sniggered as he stuck out his tummy and rubbed it with both hands.

"As if," chuckled Jimmy.

"It's a proverb, bro. It's a bit like 'counting your chickens.' I know these things. I'm more enlightened than you think." With that, Fred poured them both another drink. Both men raised another glass of tequila and made several toasts:

"It's not over until the . . . plus-sized person sings," saluted Jimmy.

"To enlightenment," toasted Fred.

"To chickens," clinking their glasses and laughing as they downed the fiery liquid.

"While we're talking about money, just remember you promised to help me publish my poetry."

"I promised no such thing," Jimmy said solemnly.

"No one likes a liar, amigo. But I'll still read your book, if you read mine."

"Right. I'll get you that copy of *Red's Hot!* and you can give me your revolutionary poetry book. Though, now that Lucy has the CD, we can just listen to you read in your beautiful dulcet tones, the way it was meant to be experienced." Fred laughed, and pushed three thousand pesos into Jimmy's hand, telling him to use it as seed money. Jimmy tried to return it, but Fred was adamant that he accept it, and returned to the Lopez condo before his new friend could give it back.

NINETEEN

The Crazy Canadians

SOBER BOB WAS AN Albertan, an amiable character, and a successful retired businessman who owned a few properties in Los Piñata. Bob loved escaping the harsh Albertan winters and was passionate about playing golf. He was a recovering alcoholic, but couldn't seem to recover from his terrible handicap. He golfed like an inebriated man even though he was now as sober as a judge.

That had not always been the case. Back in the day, when Bob was a boozer, he was a golfer deeply respected by all who played with him. With a handicap that was the envy of most semi-pros, no one doubted he could compete at an elite level. However, his skill came from his drinking, and as the former increased, so did the latter. His downfall came when he was so intoxicated he drove his golf buggy over a dune, lost control, ploughed over the 18th tee, and then directly through the clubhouse restaurant's window. The situation was exacerbated as the portly Premier of Quebec, Pierre Merde-Rasage Douche, was visiting the golf club on vacation.

Bob flew through the windows of the fancy restaurant with his buggy and landed on top of the Premier's dinner table, utterly spoiling his *chateaubriand* steak, the *au pied de cochon*, as well as his *Foie, rein et cervelle d'agneau*, and a side dish of *pouding chômeur*, with a triple portion of St. Catherine's taffy. Adding to the humiliation was the fact the Premier was publicly a staunch vegan, and based his reputation on it. He had infamously fat-shamed several opposition leaders in the government. Monsieur Merde-Rasage Douche claimed the best way for the Québécois to attain independence from the Canadian Federation was to incorporate a strict vegan diet for Quebec's inhabitants. He declared only the Ottawa-loving, lard-assed anglophile losers ate meat.

The press arrived at the scene to discover the two-faced minister had been gorging himself on carnivorous delights at the golf club's five-star restaurant. Bob received minor injuries, mainly from the Premier's half-eaten pig's hoof that had pierced his cheek; he was charged with driving a golfing cart under the influence.

With media coverage from coast to coast, it was big news. To avoid further controversy, the prestigious golf club dropped all charges. To this day, Bob happily maintains the Canadian Federation is still in one piece thanks to him, as Quebec's independence was no longer on the political agenda with the disgrace of the Premier. His bid for independence died soon after his meat-loving ways were outed.

The incident forced Bob to sober up, which messed up Bob's ability to play a respectable round of golf. As he spiralled into a more profound sobriety, the thought of returning to his second love, Russian vodka, became increasingly tempting. He would have done anything to become the skilled golfer he once was.

Seeing that his best friend was in emotional pain, Deaf Barry, an entrepreneur and inventor extraordinaire, worked hard to ameliorate Bob's golfing angst. Barry appeared on the famous TV show *Piranha Tank* to receive funding for the new invention. He pitched his ear-trumpet business concept to five ridiculously wealthy business moguls, and struck a lucrative deal with all five tycoons to NOT produce more of the trendy-sounding 'iTrumpets.' Instead of throwing in the towel, however, Barry invested all he had in his new design to help those suffering from alcohol afflictions, like his best pal Bob. He'd had one of those eureka moments and designed an ingenious gadget he was certain would help make the world a better place.

Barry found that many drunk drivers believed they were much better at controlling their vehicle when they were utterly shit-faced. He had also noticed a trend amongst the drunken revellers at nightclubs and bars: under the influence, they would meet some alluring stranger and have a night of hanky-panky, only to realize the person looked completely different when seen with sober eyes. In addition to a shocking hangover, the one-night-stander might find their lover had a nose the size of the Eiffel Tower or half of their face had been ravaged by leprosy. Worst-case scenario, they might have copped off with a work colleague or even a relative. Barry was certain he could solve both problems—and monetize them.

Barry's invention was a miraculously simple cure-all. The most stupid ideas are often the most genius: the wheel, the paper clip, and the adult diaper. Barry called his invention iBubbles, a non-prescription pair of glasses for sober people that would distort their vision. Donning them was like travelling back into inebriation; the ex-alcoholic, for example, could recreate past visual experiences without falling back into old habits. Hungover lovers could put on the glasses before looking at their sketchy partner first thing in the morning, and all would be well with the world. Muslims, Seventh-Day Adventists, and radical evangelicals could simulate the joys of intoxication; reformed alcoholics could recreate double vision when driving a vehicle. The possibilities were endless. Barry got his iBubbles trending with the hashtag "No Regrets."

He gave his prototype to Bob to try on the golf green. Although he had to ask Barry to help put his ball onto the tee, Bob struck the ball perfectly, and it travelled two hundred and fifty yards straight down the middle of the fairway. Barry's glasses worked a treat, and his friend played the best golf of his life, sober as a judge. Bob promised his pal he'd invest much-needed capital into his new venture. Barry also encouraged him to try them out with any barroom conquests or lend them to some hot and vivacious lady so she wouldn't have to look at his ugly mug while enjoying his delightful company.

All went well for a season. In addition to his much-improved handicap, Bob drove around wearing the iBubbles and swore he was a much better driver with them than without them. However, fortune did not favour the bold, in his case. Lightning did strike twice. Bob became so accustomed to his iBubbles he forgot to remove them. He was at a course near Calgary with his distorting glasses on, driving his buggy with speed. They rendered Bob blind as a bat and he failed to see a vast dune as he approached the 18th hole. He and the buggy flew through the air and crashed through the clubhouse windows. Bob landed on top of a bride's and groom's wedding table, ruining their fancy confection and inflicting injuries that required them to visit the emergency outpatient department at the local hospital. The bride suffered a fractured clavicle; the groom had, unfortunately, ruptured both testicles. The Police turned up and found Bob stone-cold sober, so he evaded charges once again. He was, however, banned from every golf club within the Dominion of Canada apart from a two-hole par three in Nunavut.

Quitting wasn't in Barry's DNA, and he put his genius to work yet again by creating the iBubblesPro. These spectacles were equipped with top-of-the-range motion sensors that set off a siren if too much movement occurred, making them far more effective when worn for things like driving a golf cart. Bob was happy to be Barry's guinea pig. They were like conjoined twins in golf; one couldn't play without the other. The pals found a few golf courses across the border in the USA and started to play again.

Sadly, Bob struggled with the iBubbles Pro when playing golf with his bestie. Deaf Barry's bizarre and unorthodox golf swing involved him running ten yards up to the ball, swirling his golf club around in his right hand while still holding his ear trumpet in the left like a crazed banshee on crystal meth. Upon reaching the tee, Barry would drive the ball straight and true. However, his ludicrous golf swing triggered the iBubblesPro's built-in motion sensors, activating a deafening air horn that ruined other golfers' enjoyment of the game. Bob and Barry received bans from all golf courses in North America. Bob reluctantly decided to doff his friend's glasses for good, choosing to play sober and accept his triple-figure handicap when golfing wherever he could in and around Los Piñata.

⤜⤛⤚ ⤙⤚⤛

THE THREE AMIGAS met after a serendipitous incident occurred at their university campus. A flasher had exposed himself to several students, post-grads, and professors gathering to support women's empowerment outside the Student Union building. Amidst screaming and general pandemonium caused by the allegedly well-endowed miscreant, Mella was first to notice him. She pointed at the flasher's manhood and guffawed. Mac, standing a few feet away from Mella, followed suit. She brought her thumb and forefinger together, half an inch apart, inferring the length of the flasher's manhood was the size of a maggot.

The proud flasher's face immediately turned red. He pulled up his pants and bolted across the campus, disappearing past the waterfall feature and into the college library area.

Lucy, a visiting lecturer, tried to calm down the shocked students and kept her eyes on the two ladies, Mac and Mella, who seemed unperturbed by the incident, as they both were roaring with laughter. Campus security showed up promptly and took statements from the witnesses. They were woefully unprepared for the amigas and their snark.

"What did he look like?" asked the 20-year-old official.

"He? That's a bit judgmental of you," piped up a voice in the crowd of ladies. It was JayBee.

"I agree," said Mac. "How do you know that 'he' was a 'he'?"

"They may have identified as she, or her . . . or as a furry," chimed in JayBee. She made her way over to Mac and Mella, and just like that, the amigas were united for the first time.

The security guy scratched his head. "Okay, okay, what did the flasher look like?"

"His winky was small," Mella giggled.

"I think he was uncut," added Mac helpfully.

"It was more like a little wasp," was JayBee's contribution.

"No, no, the flasher's description. What was he wearing?"

"He didn't have a condom. I think he was bareback," Mac said, turning to JayBee for confirmation. The security guy, by this point, looked extremely flustered and his face was beet-red. He shook his head and tried again.

"What I mean is, what kind of clothes was he wearing?" Lucy overheard and was amused by the three women, so she joined Mac, JayBee, and Mella. They discussed whether the flasher's willy-winky was so tiny it could have been a clitoris.

"After all," reminded Lucy, "It was supposed to be a woman's empowerment event. Maybe she flashed her clitty as a sign of solidarity?"

"Honestly, I hope so. If it was a dude, and his thing was a willy, the poor guy could never satisfy a woman," chortled Mac.

"Maybe an oyster?" suggested Mella.

"Look, ladies, it may have been a joke to some of you, but this matter is grave. Please, let's start at the top of him. What was the colour of his hair?" The young security guy took out his notebook and pen.

"We couldn't see his pubes," Mac joked.

"Brown and curly," said Mella, giving him his first real answer.

"Brown and curly hair," the security man muttered to himself, scribbling it down.

Lucy added, "He was wearing a red university hoody and a white lab coat over it. He had spindly legs, fishnet stockings, and a pair of Blunnies."

"Doesn't have much going for him," remarked Mella

"Apart from his Blundstones," JayBee clarified.

"Have any of you seen this guy around campus before?"

"It looked like the Dean of the Engineering Faculty," said Mac.

"What? Seriously?"

"No, I was just kidding. But if I do see the flasher again, I'll give him a few dollars for making my day. Normally, I would have to go to a freak show to see a dick that small on a man." All the ladies laughed. The security guard gave up at last, leaving to interview some other younger students.

From that moment onwards, the four became friends, and it didn't take long for their relationship to evolve into that of lifelong besties. Lucy loved how they made her laugh, their liberated attitudes, and unabashedly inappropriate language. She often talked about her amigas, and the four of them regularly kept in touch by phone and social media. Although much younger than her friends, Lucy was the 'responsible' one, as the amigas had taken early retirement or had taken advantage of working remotely to improve their work-life balances—resulting in lots of free time and allowing them to relocate to the beautiful Los Piñata coastline.

⟶⟫⟫ ⟪⟪⟵

MELLA O'MAOLDHOMHNAIGH HAD a name that most of the world's population would find difficult to pronounce. Although she has the same salty vocabulary as a psycho football hooligan, her last name meant 'a servant of the Church of Ireland.'

Mella's father had been defrocked from the Catholic priesthood after being caught shagging three female members of the choir in the confessional. Her mother was a pious lady who believed cleanliness was next to godliness and made the family wear plastic bags on their hands and feet inside their home. She knew she was marrying a philandering man with a high sex drive, so, apart from her fertile months when it was time for her to conceive, Mrs O'Maoldhomhnaigh covered herself in Marmite and complained to her husband that she kept shitting herself. That kept the horn-dog at bay.

Mella's hometown family doctor ran a side hustle of selling weed, Percs, Dillies, Demmies, and Oxys to their small community. A physician in Ireland at the time was paid a pittance; he told anyone who would listen within Mella's community he still had to repay his student loan. Folk in the village overlooked his peccadillos and were happy to have a doctor nearby to help them work through their many addiction issues. It didn't take young Mella long to fully embrace the village's drug culture, but her drug-use days also didn't last long; on her eighth birthday, she stopped and never dabbled again.

Despite her humble religious background, in her teens, she joined a cult that worshipped Venus and Aphrodite, the goddesses of debauchery and licentiousness. A strong feminist, she didn't like that one of her goddesses' names rhymed with 'penis,' so she went through a transitional phase of following Ba'al and Asherah—and finally, turned a 180 and fell in love with a televangelist.

When Mella moved to her tertiary education, she studied hard and went on to gain a PhD at university, putting much of her learning experience into her thesis. She was highly regarded in her field, becoming renowned for her work in studying the North American Lynx's mating rituals. It was serendipitous that she met the Hollywood producers, Bradley and Marcus, as they were looking for an expert who could act as a consultant in their new production, *Tiger! Tiger!*

This innovative show was to be filmed in South Korea. Mella, in her talks with the producers, had been transparent and stated that a Lynx was a very different animal from the Bengal tiger.

"Sweetheart, are they both cats?"

"Of course."

"Do they have stripes?"

"Not exactly; they can be a bit stripey, but—"

"Do these dude big cats have todgers?"

"Of course."

"Are they both attracted by pheromones?"

"Yes, but—"

"Have they both been known to attack humans?"

"Yes, but—"

"So, Dr O'ldMacDonaldhadafarm—"

"Dr O'Maoldhomhnaigh, but you can call me Mella."

"Thank the Lord for that, girl."

"You're welcome."

"So, do you want to earn $100,000 and have an all-expenses-paid vacay in the Far East?"

"Totally."

"Then welcome to *Tiger! Tiger!* We now have our very own expert doctor and consultant."

Mella signed on the dotted line, and *Tiger! Tiger!* became a monster hit in Korea and Japan.

The show's premise was that twenty contestants were soaked in a bath of tiger pheromones and the best-selling ladies' perfume, Miss Minxy. They were made to wander around in orange and black striped onesies and a tiger camo Kevlar jacket in a jungle set near the North Korean border.

The last contestant that hadn't been humped or mauled to death collected a staggering one million South Korean won, or thirty-two million Iranian rial. One or two American contestants, while recovering in hospital, complained the prize money wasn't worth the risk of harm, as it was only seven hundred and fifty U.S. bucks.

Bradley countered these claims by saying the prize was 'reasonable,' and they were paying a lot for several tigers to undergo PTSD counselling, a move which PETA and other animal rights groups applauded. As Bradley told a reporter for the *Feline Times*:

"Look honey, not everyone has the bragging rights to say they were shagged half to death by a Bengal tiger. That story will make you the life of the party till the day you die."

Bradley, Marcus, and Mella became friends through their work on the show, and the boys recommended Los Piñata to her. Mella was quick to relocate, and spent most of her winters in the beautiful town with the two Hollywood superstars.

TWENTY

Ring Out the Old, Ring In the New

CANADIANS, AMERICANS, AND THE odd Limey were all in a boisterous mood at Tequila Tommy's for the New Year's Eve celebration. Jimmy, Lucy, and Max joined the three amigas at a reserved table. The place was chockablock, but there was one spare seat beside Jimmy.

"Who's sitting there?" he asked.

"Raul Montana," replied Mac. Jimmy's face turned white. He hadn't had anything to drink yet, but if he had, he was sure he would've thrown it up.

"We've reserved it for Vincente's missing head!" yelled JayBee.

"Funny, not funny," sneered a relieved Jimmy, realizing they were just messing with him. Still, he wasn't out of the woods yet. He hoped beyond hope neither Bradley or Marcus would take the empty chair; he was still scarred by the painful loss they made him suffer during 'Quiz Nite.'

"We always keep a spare chair for Tommy. He usually comes over during the evening to join us." It was Mella who gave him the real answer, and he gave her a grateful nod.

"Yeppers, he sits down with each table, brings a round of drinks on the house, and tells us a story about his past or goes on a rant. Both are hilarious." JayBee added.

"Sounds fun!" Jimmy said as he scoped out the busy bar. He recognized Patsy, the bar manager, renowned for her yummy-scrummy award-winning cocktails. She was incredibly popular with the patrons at Tommy's.

The demographic at Tommy's was split between females and males from their mid-40s up to their 80s; most were snowbirds, folks who escaped the cold winter conditions up north. The rest were ex-pats who had made Mexico their second home.

The girls had ordered jugs of cold beer and tequila shots Jimmy tended to gravitate towards ice-cold beer but conceded that certain tequilas were very pleasant, incredibly smooth, and down easy-peasy lemon-squeezy. Armardo's 1836 tequila was among them, and apart from Fred's company, it was the only thing he missed about the Lopez contingent.

The amigas were getting louder and louder, and Lucy was joining in the fun. Max was doing his own thing on his tablet, playing an interactive *PAW Patrol* game. Seeing his family and all their friends having fun, unrestrained and unburdened by the looming presence of the cartel, Jimmy let out a huge sigh. He was feeling much more relaxed. As the night went on, he had a few drinks and started getting a nice buzz; his voice became louder and louder, as was customary when he chilled out. With every rising decibel of his voice, Lucy was increasingly certain the fun, boisterous Jimmy had entered the building.

Out of the blue, the sound of a chair being pulled back interrupted the conversation, and the amigas erupted in cheers. Jimmy braced himself before turning to look at the person standing next to him.

"Tommy! Tommy! Tommy!" chanted the mildly intoxicated gringas. Tommy raised his hand to acknowledge his adoring fans like a celebrity entering an auditorium and sat beside Jimmy. He had no trouble imagining Tommy as a player back in the day, what with his muscular build, white ponytail, dark-tanned skin, and piercing blue-green eyes. He was relieved the suave Tequila Tommy had joined him, and not the chatterbox Bradley.

Tommy looked towards the bar, raised his arm, and cried out, "Patsy! A round of shots for the table, on me, and give them some of the better stuff." Patsy acknowledged with a nod and a smile.

"Give them Olde Shagger," added Tommy, brashly.

Olde Shagger was his brand. It was amber in colour and had a sketch of Tommy's face printed onto the label. Snowbirds often bought bottles of Olde Shagger tequila to take back to their homes when they left Los Piñata. Giving out freebies and samples was an excellent way of making money for Tommy, who, as well as being quite a character, was also a shrewd businessman.

Patsy left, and soon returned to the table with a few bottles of the potent booze. Jimmy picked up one of the bottles and studied it.

"Looks impressive."

Tommy beamed, "Yup, that's my brand of tequila, named after yours truly," he said with a chuckle, pointing at himself. "Many a lady has given me that nickname in the past."

Mella abruptly stood up and pointed at the T.V. "Tommy, can't you turn that shit off? No one likes that curling crap. It's New Year's Eve, and having *that* on the screen is a vibe killer!"

JayBee added her opinion, shouting, "No one likes it apart from the Manitobans, and everyone knows they're all as weird as shit!"

Everyone within earshot laughed, including most of the Manitobans.

"My Bella Mella, they got here first and put on the TV. You know my policy; first come, first served," chuckled Tommy.

Jimmy looked at the adjacent table of six people, three women and three men. One was using an old-fashioned ear trumpet. Jimmy recognized him as Deaf Barry, the Denzel Washington look-a-like who was culpable for ruining his team's chances at the 'Quiz Nite.' Once Patsy had filled all their glasses with Olde Shagger, Tommy stood up and raised his high in the air.

"A toast!" The whole table stood up with him. Mimicking a *Braveheart* accent, Tommy cried out, "To the wee, miserable Scottish wanker who invented the game of curling!"

"To the miserable Scottish wanker!" they all yelled back and downed the tequila in one gulp.

Deaf Barry turned his hearing trumpet towards Tommy, smiled, and yelled, "What?" Tommy turned to Jimmy and nudged him in the ribs, which seemed to be taking a lot of punishment these days.

"Don't mind Barry; he's deaf as a post. *Bazza* is an inventor who refuses to believe he has hearing issues and won't use hearing aids."

"Oh, so that's his deal," Jimmy said, nodding.

"Barry's loaded too, so he could afford cochlear implants if he wanted, but he's a stubborn git."

"Why does he use a hearing trumpet if it doesn't work?"

"He says it's purely cosmetic. Barry believed his invention would be the next trend to hit the Western world. He's good with his hands and has made thousands of non-functional trumpets in custom colours and designs. Look it up on Amazon—Bazza's iTrumpet. The silly old fart is convinced he'll be the next Stefano Gabbana or Gianni Versace." Both men had a hearty laugh at this. Jimmy smiled, looked at the adjacent table, and gave Barry a big thumbs up.

"Jimmy, can I share two facts with you tonight? If you'd rather I didn't, just tell me. Tequila Tommy never gets offended."

"Sure. What two things?"

"Firstly, I have shagged a hell of a lot of women in my time."

"And secondly?" asked Jimmy, hoping the next fact would be less awkward.

"Secondly," he said, pointing at the TV screen, "I really, *really* don't like curling."

Once again, Mella stood up, gave her boobs a shake, and offered to make another toast. She thrust her empty glass forward and Tommy refilled it with tequila. Mella held up her drink, the liquid sloshing over the edges of the glass.

"A toast—" she cleared her throat before beginning her salute. The guests at the table rose and lifted their glasses in unison. When she spoke again, she tried replicating Tommy's fake Scottish accent.

"Och aye. For auld lang syne—and we agree, curling's a load of shite!"

"Curling is shite!" the group echoed and downed their shots.

Lucy immediately went to cover up Max's ears and saw he wasn't paying the slightest bit of attention. She was relieved he was engrossed in his PAW Patrol game; his favourite Bee-bop-alula headphones were good enough to keep out the salty language.

Tommy nudged Jimmy, "Just look at them," pointing at a group that included Deaf Barry. "The Manitobans over yonder, on that table, transfixed by the so-called 'action.' My question is, excuse my Irish, how the feck do they even call it a sport?"

Jimmy looked up at the screen; it was a mixed doubles match. One player was sliding on his knees, holding onto a sizeable disk-shaped stone by its handle. The guy released the stone and yelled, "Harder, harder," at his two teammates. Lucy heard and playfully covered Jimmy's ears. The two sweepers, each equipped with giant broomsticks, seemed to be trying to reach Australia by pure friction, brushing the ice like crazed banshees.

"I mean," said Tommy, "Anyone in the world can do that. You need absolutely no skill."

"I'm sure it's not that simple," chuckled Jimmy.

"I'm with Jimbo here. It's not easy . . . otherwise, it wouldn't be an Olympic sport," Mac said. She actually liked curling, though she'd never admit it. Tommy, however, was having none of it. He kept talking, drowning her out.

"Simple? I bet you thousands of dollars someone who'd never played in their life could easily win an Olympic medal after just a week or two of practice."

"Come on, Tommy, it's much harder than you think." Lucy interjected, sticking up for Mac.

Tommy guffawed, "Not only would you be able to master the 'sport' after a couple of weeks, but anyone without arms, legs—"

"Or head. Even poor old Vincente could be a champion without his noggin on his shoulders," added Mella.

"Not funny," muttered Jimmy.

Tommy grinned, gave Mella a nod, and continued, "Anyone without head or extremities could become an Olympic champion in a couple of weeks or even days. Besides, my new friends, if you played curling shit-face drunk, you'd still be better than if you played it sober."

"Amen!" cried out Sober Bob enthusiastically.

"Sounds like you're not a fan of curling," Jimmy noted dryly.

Mella interrupted, "It's as skillful as playing 'shove-a-penny' at the fairground."

"Exactly," said a smirking Tommy. "But shoving a penny takes a lot more skill and strength." He raised his hand, flicked his fingers, and flexed his bicep.

Most people guffawed. The Manitobans jeered, and Tommy called Patsy to give all curling lovers a free drink on the house by way of a 'sorry-not-sorry' apology—which caused most people to suddenly become curling fans.

The evening finally ended with karaoke sung totally out of tune as several inebriated gringos performed songs like 'Sweet Caroline' and 'A Town Called Alice.' An intoxicated Jimmy put his fingers in his ears and moaned to Lucy the singing was so awful he'd suffer hearing loss and have to buy one of Deaf Barry's ear trumpets.

When the evening came to an end, and he and Lucy were walking back to the condo with Max on his back, Jimmy conceded to Lucy the evening had been a lot of fun. She beamed, her smile radiant as it hadn't been for several days. Finally, they were both truly and unabashedly happy. The little lad was dead to the world in a deep sleep, soon to be joined by his mom and dad. At last, it finally felt like an actual holiday, and Jimmy and Lucy were both certain things could only get better from this moment forward, regardless of the challenges ahead.

TWENTY-ONE

The Bowels Toll for Armardo the Magnificent

ARMARDO WAS ONE OF two boys born to Loco Moco Lopez, a third-generation Don that headed the Wolfpack Cartel. Armardo had been groomed into a leadership position since his early years. With an IQ in the high 140s, he quickly assimilated everything he had been taught. He could speak English, Italian, and French fluently; his parents insisted this would help the family in business matters.

Señor Loco Moco Lopez was fortunate his firstborn son was blessed with discernment, intellect, wisdom, flair, good looks, and heaps of character. Armardo also had a keen sense of humour and could be friendly, charming, generous, and charitable. In fact, he could have been a celebutante of the highest order if he hadn't been hand-selected by his papa to perform a cartel leader's duties. Under his father's tutelage, Armardo Angel Lopez became a cold-hearted, ruthless, and utterly vengeful member of society.

Siblings often battle each other to get into their father's good books. This was not the case for Armardo and his brother Ramon. Papa Loco Moco dearly loved both of his boys. However, there was only one contender to succeed him as Don. As much as he cared for Ramon, the boy undeniably had the intellectual and emotional intelligence of a gherkin.

The Lopez family fought several cartel wars both within Mexico and outside the country against the Colombians. The Wolfpack Cartel came out on top, cementing Armardo's status as the boss of all bosses, lord of all lords, and king of all kings. His modest and unassuming family motto hung below a gargantuan twenty-foot-high portrait of himself, which read:

I am the big cheese. I am the cream that has risen to the top.
To my enemies: eat shit and die!

Armardo's family was now in a season of peace, yet they had never worked longer hours and their business had never been busier. Vacation opportunities were scarce, but when they took a break, they did it in style. Even though it might be just a few days here or there, they loved and encouraged the celebrated DJ Pedro Cordoba to attend with his sound system and entourage.

Armardo had always wanted to be a family man. He needed a son to pass on his empire and legacy to. He was married to the lovely Francisca, a jewel in his crown who was born and raised in Oaxaca. Francisca, a profoundly religious person, was not actively involved in his businesses or decision-making. She was a homemaker who loved him with all her heart.

The couple had unsuccessfully tried for many years to have children. Francisca suggested a spiritual remedy, which Armardo reluctantly agreed to. They visited her home church in Oaxaca and received blessings from the priest, who made the couple endure ten abstract rituals to satisfy the Blessed Virgin of *La Rábanos* so her favour would fall upon the mother's womb. Through a modern lens, these rituals would appear a tad weird. However, to the average Oaxacan, *La Rábanos* sacraments were powerful and occasionally worked.

After the ninth ritual, however, Armardo had nearly lost his patience. It involved the priest covering his testicles in a mixture of Viagra, cactus glochids, and bison urine. Armardo felt savagely uncomfortable by the third successive day of the prickly fertility ointment. He also felt humiliated by the ceremonial practices.

This last 'prickly' caused him to visit the confessional box to speak to the holy man.

"Father, I am about to sin."

"Child, this is unusual—more often than not, my flock tell me they acknowledge past sinful thoughts and actions, and seek absolution."

"Father, I have a rusty razor blade in my hand."

"Child, I beseech thee to not take your own life—the sin is unforgivable."

"Father, can you remember the name of the game people used to play in the '60s and '70s with two balls that swung back and forth?"

The priest breathed a sigh of relief. "Child, are you thinking about Bocce? Bolas? Ladder Toss?"

"Nope. Clackers."

"Clackers. Oh, I remember. Two balls attached with string. They made an ear-splitting sound, and I had many bruises on my wrist from playing them."

"Father, I have come here today to tell you I will cut off your holy balls with this very rusty razor blade if my wife is not with child in six weeks."

The holy father began to tremble—he knew who he was dealing with. He was thankful Armardo could not see him, sitting in the other booth of the confessional. He would have beheld a shaking, sweating mess of a man, whose nervous perspiration was staining his garments.

"Don Armardo. Sir, please—"

"After I have cut off your wrinkly old balls, I will thread cord through each sack and see if Newton's laws of motion apply to your testicles as they clack, clack, clack against each other."

"Don Armardo, I promise on the Red Lady's honour—the final ritual will be the last one you need to endure."

Armardo Lopez let out a groan in frustration. He really wanted to cut off the holy man's testicles. "One more, for my beloved wife's sake. Then, if Francisca is not with child, your balls will swing like clackers during morning mass six weeks next Sunday."

The freaked-out priest informed Armardo the tenth and final ritual was allegorical to the ten plagues that fell upon Egypt during the time of Moses. He assured the cartel boss this would undoubtedly lead to total success.

Miraculously, after having begrudgingly participated in the tenth and most magical ritual of having covered his entire body in radish juice, pickled herring, and Bovril, followed by having to chug half a pint of fermented ram's epididymides, Armardo's wish was fulfilled. Francisca became pregnant, and nine months later, Hector was born, a spirited boy with a full head of hair and a handsome countenance.

Francisca was also well-aware she'd been blessed due to her close friendship with Guadalupe Montana. The Red Lady had visited her friend before the birth of her identical twins and had accurately predicted both of their names. Francisca and Armardo visited Guadalupe before her water broke and were present when she popped both boys out, having been in labour for just eight minutes. Armardo vowed these 'miracle' twins would be at his side as his Wolfpack Cartel expanded; the rest was history.

Later in their development, Armardo took the Montana twins under his care and guardianship. As his papa Loco Moco had done for him, he insisted the boys learn English, as most of the people they would have to deal with were English-speaking. Interacting with gringos negotiating property deals became much more straightforward, especially for Fred Montana, who helped Armardo with financial negotiations and collected the taxes from the locals.

With both his son and godsons blessed by the Red Virgin, Armardo was confident in the Wolfpack Cartel's future. One sicario was shrewd and well-spoken; the other was deadly and relentless. They helped Armardo to offer those he dealt with both the carrot and the stick, presenting an urbane front with the promise of violent retribution waiting in the wings. And when his son became a man, he would be ready to inherit the Lopez empire and ensure it continued well into the next generation.

⤜⤜⟫ ⟪⤛⤛

MAX, JIMMY, AND Lucy were chilling out at the condo. The weather was almost perfect. Although it had been hot and very sunny, the sea breeze was refreshing, making sitting out in the sun a pleasant experience. As much as Jimmy and Lucy adored Vancouver Island's temperate summer days, it was often damp and cloudy, much like Lucy's beloved Wales, at the same time of year. It was nice to spend the winter under a clear sky and bright sun for a change.

Max was dozing under the palapa. Lucy was reading an enthralling book about the Anglican Church through the eyes of an eighth century Wiccan priestess. Jimmy had a cold beer by his side, and he was lost in thought, gazing out at the horizon. He was puzzled by the Mexican grackles, a type of blackbird. These birds visited the pool area each day before the sun went down. They would land on the pool's edge and dunk in the pool water. They would, annoyingly, bombard the patio, deck, and pool with vast amounts of bird poop.

The freedom these birds had to loosen their bowels regularly reminded Jimmy that Lucy was still struggling with constipation, yet he and Max were as regular as clockwork.

Jimmy's thoughts of poop brought him back to his money troubles. He was, after all, in deep financial shit. He desperately needed a passport and money. Their credit cards had been frozen due to a bizarre act of economic and sexist sabotage by Satan's daughter, Chéckina. He had hundreds of thousands of dollars in various bank accounts at home but no access to any of it, thanks to poor-quality phone lines and his bank's ludicrous policy of using call centres whose employees couldn't understand a single word he said. Jimmy tried to comprehend why his bank would employ workers from non-English-speaking places like Chechnya, Glasgow, East London, and New Zealand.

The grackle's squawk and jet-black plumage also reminded him of Fred Montana. He knew when he saw Fred's black sombrero in the distance, it would mean Armardo was calling in his debt. But as long as it was the black sombrero sent after him and not the pink one, he still had a chance to get the money. He desperately needed to get to Guadalajara or Mexico City, where he could try and get new identity papers to help him with the bank situation. He also needed a plan to flee the country if Pinkie came after him, and that plan had to ensure Lucy and Max would be able to get out before he did.

Jimmy took a big slurp of his beer and sighed. He wished he could be as free as a bird, like the pesky grackles. He'd shit on Raul's gaudy pink sombrero and fly away from his troubles.

⤜⤜⤜ ⤛⤛⤛

IT HAD BEEN ten days since most of the adult Lopez contingent had been able to pass a motion. At first, it wasn't a noticeable issue. Hector seemed the only one that hadn't been affected by constipation. His bowel movements were as regular as a Swiss clock. That wasn't the case for the others, who felt severely bloated, uncomfortable, and bunged up inside. Armardo was quite nauseous, and his tummy was making angry noises. It only made him angrier.

"I'm sure it started after eating the gringos' stew," he told Francisca one day. He had spent another unsuccessful couple of hours sitting on the toilet in one of the many washrooms in his home. He desperately wanted to go, but he couldn't pass a pebble.

Francisca gently rebuked him. "You shouldn't point fingers. Lucy Myers was a wonderful host, and the stew was delicious." Armardo simply grunted, not in agreement but in discomfort. He stalked off towards the nearest washroom, even though he had just been. He needed relief more than he needed anything in his life.

Hector vacated the main bathroom the following morning, humming, whistling, and acting very jolly. He sat down for breakfast with the twins and his mom and dad, having successfully expelled his regular 8 am poop. Armardo did not fail to take notice of this.

"How have your . . . bowels been?" he quizzed the twins. Fred didn't look too uncomfortable, but Raul was a little bit green in the face.

"To be honest, boss, I usually find myself running to the bathroom several times in the morning, but since Christmas day, I have had a normal bathroom experience. I've never felt better," Fred answered.

Raul grunted and frowned. "Not good, boss. I m-m-m-might need to g-g-g-go to see the doctor." Hector looked from his father to the twins. He fidgeted in his seat, uncomfortable with the conversation.

"Can I leave?" he enquired.

"No, Hector, I want you to stay at the table. I want to know why you can poop and the rest of us can't," Armardo replied, his tone harsher than he intended. Hector shrank into his seat as if hoping to make himself so small he couldn't be seen. He looked down into his lap, diligently avoiding eye contact.

"Leave the boy alone. This is hardly appropriate talk for the breakfast table," Francisca objected.

"No, it's very appropriate, seeing as we haven't been able to shit for ten days! My love, please, share *your* gastrointestinal experience with the table. Are you having issues as well?" Armardo's tone grew increasingly hostile. Francisca could tell that her husband was nearing the end of his rope; his kindness and civility were giving way to anger, and he would not be placated until he got what he wanted. With a sigh, she answered his question.

"I struggled initially, but I took some fast-acting suppositories and had been eating lots of fibre, and my bowels are back to normal now."

"So you had bowel issues as well," said Armardo. Francisca nodded.

"Hector? Do you have something you'd like to share with us?" he asked, turning back towards his son. Hector kept his eyes down and looked very uncomfortable. He might not have known exactly what it was he and Max put in the stew, but he was smart enough to figure out there was a reason everyone who ate it was having issues, while he was fine. With how furious his papa was, he was certain a grave punishment awaited him if he fessed up.

Francisca looked kindly at her son. "Hector, your father is asking you to tell the truth. Why can you poop so easily, and the rest of us can't?"

Hector looked up at his dad, started to cry, "He did it!"

"He did what? Who is *he*, and what did *he* do, little Hector?"

Hector did not want to throw his little gringo friend under the bus, but he knew his family already disliked Mr Myers. Otherwise, Raul wouldn't have held a gun to his head. If he blamed Max's dad, no one would doubt him.

"Mr Jimmy did a bad thing, Papa."

"A bad thing?" All eyes were upon little Hector.

"We were cooking the food. Mr Jimmy approached Max and me and told us to stir some green liquid into the stew." Hector paused and narrowed his eyes in mock concentration, as he wanted his father to believe he was retracing the events in his mind. He did quite a good job of selling it. "Mr Myers laughed and said, 'This should teach the BEANER shitheads not to be so shitty.'"

Armardo gasped. "Beaner?"

Raul gulped. "Sh-sh-sh-sh-shitheads?"

Francisca stared daggers at her son, "Hector! Watch your language, or I will get Raul to wash your mouth with soap and caustic soda."

Hector turned an even whiter shade of pale and apologized.

"What was the green liquid? Do you remember?" barked Armardo.

"I can't remember what was written on the bottle's label, papa, but I think the word was spelt: I-M-O-D-I-U-M. It was minty and green."

Armardo took out his phone and googled 'Imodium.' He read: "Imodium contains an active ingredient called Loperamide, which helps treat diarrhoea. This chemical ingredient treats chronic diarrhoea in patients with irritable bowels."

"Hallelujah! *That's* why my tummy started to behave," beamed Fred.

Hector was on a roll, and when he saw his dad's face go a bright puce, he knew his anger was being directed full force at Mr Jimmy and away from him. Emboldened, he embellished his story even more.

"Yes, Papa. Mr Myers kept saying, 'Stir it in, boys,' and waved a carving knife in our faces. I thought he was going to kill us. Papa, I'm afraid of him. I wish Raul would have shot him through his fat gringo head when he tried to kill us all with his sneaky cracker bomb."

Fred immediately leapt to Jimmy's defence. "That's ridiculous. Why would he do that?"

Francisca opened her mouth, about to join Fred in defending their host in Los Piñata, but stopped. Hector's story aligned with Jimmy's own actions. "He was the only one who didn't eat the stew—he ate the children's cheese sticks instead."

Fred continued, "But Mrs Lucy ate the stew. Why would he have targeted his wife?"

"Maybe she drank an antidote afterwards," said Armardo angrily. His eyes looked murderous.

Everyone could tell a tirade was coming on, and stayed quiet until he finished speaking.

"That gringo, he disrespects my family. He complains about our music, breaks a bottle of my expensive tequila, accuses us of murdering that idiot caretaker, and involves the police. Then, after all that, I loan him monies, and he does what? Poison us with Imodium? He brings three slutty women to Our Lady of the Radish's veneration, and they rub their big breasts into Father Dominguez's face!"

"They also bounced them on my head. I've had worse experiences!" Fred couldn't help giggling. "Still, with all due respect, Don Armardo, it is a bit far-fetched he has a vendetta against our family."

Raul stood up from the table. "I am happy to p-p-p-p-punish the gringo, boss!"

Armardo gave him a nod and turned to stare at Fred, unhappy he was defending Jimmy, the degenerate Canadian.

"Fred, I want my money back from that son of a gun. Get it back, with extra interest for my troubles." Fred hesitated for a moment before nodding.

"Since you are so set on protecting this gringo, you'd do well not to fail. If you can't retrieve my money, then I will have to send Raul. I know *he* will restore honour to our family. Do you understand?" Armardo demanded.

Fred nodded.

"Raul, if you have to deal with this gringo moron, bring his head back on a silver platter with a bottle of Imodium wedged in his mouth."

Raul smiled and thanked his boss for the opportunity.

TWENTY-TWO

A New Kid in Town

APART FROM THE FAMILY name and their differences in physical appearance, the Montana twins stuck out like sore thumbs at school. Fred was interested in sports, and Raul wasn't. Due to his height, however, Raul was forced to play basketball for the school team. His teammates would give Raul the basketball, and he'd bounce it a few times before running and slam-dunking it into his own net. He was self-conscious of his stutter and afraid to tell the coach he hated basketball and didn't want to participate.

"Raul, *idiota!* That's the wrong net you just scored in," the coach yelled.

Once again, a teammate would pass the basketball to their tallest player, and Raul would bounce the ball, travel at speed, jump up high and slam the ball into his team's basketball hoop. The coach would put both hands on his head in frustration and command him to take a break and sit with the rest of the team on the bench. Raul would do as he was told, give the coach one of his death stares, and the game would continue. The coach would come over and ask him:

"Why do you do that, doofus?"

Raul would just snarl at him, scaring off the adult man by staring right into his eyes, unblinking.

One day, the coach decided to do something different. He thought if Raul wouldn't cooperate, maybe the other brother would, and so he cornered Fred in the school corridor.

"Hey Fred, what's up with your lunkheaded, pillock-brained brother? He gets picked to play against Santa Anna, our arch-rival, and whenever he gets the ball he dunks it into our basket. Free points for the opposition."

"He doesn't like playing basketball, coach."

"Bullshit! Our team would be unstoppable in our league. He's made for basketball. He's the size of a fully grown giant. How hard is it for the imbecile to score points for his team? Why won't he listen?" The coach looked down at Fred, red-faced with anger. Fred showed no sign of fear; he simply listened and nodded.

"Because he thinks basketball is for pussies," he replied. Raul had never said that, but it amused Fred to cause the coach discomfort. "Why not choose me, coach? I love basketball, and I'm happy to play."

The coach blinked and rubbed his eyes, as if he couldn't see who he was talking to. He stared intently at Fred, who had dwarfism and was the smallest kid in school. It took him several moments to comprehend what this child was asking him.

"Are you utterly bereft of a brain, Fred? My coffee mug is taller than you!"

The coach did not attend school the following day, nor the next. Predictably, he was never seen again. Anyone who dissed the Montana brothers tended to vanish. The Oaxacan community was mindful that the Montana family had connections with the Wolfpack Cartel—disappearances were not reported to the authorities.

The last and most controversial school incident the Montanas were involved in was when the twins attended their district secondary school. A new kid had just come into town. He was muscular, fifteen years of age, and wanted to make a name for himself. His name was Kyle Garcia. He had a Mexican mom who married a blond-haired surfer gringo from San Jose, California. He was a spoiled only child, and Fred envied him for all the trendy clothes he wore to school each day. Infuriatingly, he was not only entitled but talented; he excelled at soccer, baseball, and—to his detriment—running his mouth.

One day, he deliberately bumped into Raul in the school corridor. He turned to look at the tall, thin, weird-looking kid who had just started to wear a pink-coloured sombrero.

"Hey, look where you're going, you tall piece of shit. Kyle Garcia is in the house!"

Fred witnessed the altercation, and his eyes went wide. He knew Kyle was digging his own grave with every word. He came over to his brother, grabbed his arm, and said, "It's just a power move, ignore him."

Raul nodded and carried on his journey towards his next class.

Kyle Garcia, however, was not so easily dissuaded. He wanted to cement his reputation as the school's top dog, and that meant picking fights with other kids, winning, and making them beg for mercy. The tougher-looking the kid, the more impressive he'd seem. So, of course, he was going to go after Raul.

During one recess, some students were playing soccer. Raul and Fred were watching some girls practising netball, and they had their backs turned away from the soccer field. Kyle got hold of the ball, dribbled past a few players, and ran towards Fred and Raul.

He shouted, "Hey, Raul!"

The tall twin turned his head to see who had called his name, and Kyle unleashed a power shot at Raul's head. He saw the soccer ball coming towards him at great velocity and stared at it. He refused to move an inch. The ball struck him full on the face, knocked off his pink sombrero, and bounced back to Kyle.

"Thanks for giving back my ball—donkey face! Shame you've got a bloody nose. Next time, take off that gay pink hat and head the ball back to me, you useless lanky freakshow."

Raul stared back and retrieved a tissue from his jacket to wipe his bloody nose.

Fred sighed. Kyle's fate was sealed.

After school that same day, Kyle was skateboarding his way home. He was enjoying showing off his kick turns and tic-tacs. He pulled off a 180-ollie down some steps, and a broadslide along a railing. He was speeding and turned a corner into an alleyway leading to a skate park adjacent to his parents' luxury family home.

Suddenly, out of the blue, a hand appeared from an alcove along the alleyway and grabbed Kyle's neck. Kyle was lifted a foot off the ground and found himself face-to-face with Raul Montana. His skateboard continued to roll along the passageway. Kyle gasped for air and tried to speak, but all his words were unintelligible. He couldn't breathe, and he kicked his legs uselessly in the air, seeking a surface he could use to push off the bigger boy. He grabbed at Raul's arm and face, but he couldn't get him to loosen his grip even a little.

"Now this str-str-str-string bean is g-g-g-going to teach you a le-le-le-lesson." With each stuttered word, the strangulation was prolonged, and Kyle desperately wanted him to speak normally so he would be released sooner. It didn't occur to him Raul wasn't going to let go until he was dead.

Raul smiled and intensified his vice-like grip as Kyle's eyes began to bug out of their sockets. Seeing the look in his victim's eyes, Raul grinned, showing off his pearly-white teeth, which made him look like a snarling dog. Kyle's face was becoming deathly white. He looked around and saw Fred was with his brother, unsuccessfully attempting to de-escalate the situation.

"Bro, look at you go . . . and one-handed, too! I think he's learned his lesson, so why don't you let the half-Yankee cockroach go? He's never gonna mess with you again."

Kyle couldn't beg for mercy with his words, so he looked into Raul's hazel and purple-blue eyes with a pleading expression. He gasped and spluttered, nodding, agreeing with what Fred had suggested to his brother. However, as Raul's grip intensified, Kyle's eyes started to roll upward, as his spirit was about to depart this earth.

"Whoops-a-d-d-aisy!" said Raul, smirking.

"Bro, he's about to cross the rainbow bridge. It's not too late to—"

"S-s-s-shucks, so s-s-sad, too b-b-bad," stammered Raul as he squeezed Kyle's neck extra tight. Something popped.

"Sounds like his trachea, bro," sighed Fred in wide-eyed wonderment.

"I guess the little Yankee shit has now met his maker." Words ran freely from Raul's mouth, as if his tongue was liberated by the violence and the death of his school nemesis. He finally released his grip. Kyle fell like a ragdoll to the ground. Fred sighed, trying to ignore how fast his heart was pounding.

The brothers retrieved a large crate on wheels from the alley and quickly got to work, stuffing the body inside.

Raul was satisfied. School life would become easier again now Kyle Garcia was no longer 'in the house.'

⤜⟫⟫⟫ ⟪⟪⟪⤛

A VEXED ARMARDO Lopez was pacing back and forth in his study. A whining mosquito buzzed around his head and landed on the face of his cell phone, which he had left on his desk. He gripped a fly swatter tight in one hand, which he desperately wanted to use to kill the wretched insect. He held his walkie-talkie in the other hand, and pressed a button on it.

"Raul, please come and see me. I need you to sort out the gringo problem."

Raul answered and was soon at the door of his master.

"Usually, we wait for Fred to return from a mission before I dispatch you. However, I have a bad feeling in my gut. This gringo is a—" Suddenly, he lashed out with his fly swatter, smacking the bug and the phone until both were a wreck.

"Pest! A shit-eating, stupid-looking, iritating little pest!" Wiping spittle and drool from his lips, Armardo snarled, "I've changed my mind; we're not going to kill him yet. I want the gringo brought to me, ALIVE!"

Raul nodded. His boss was losing his mind, and this mosquito of a gringo was its cause.

"You must deal with that ungrateful insect buzzing around in Los Piñata."

Raul nodded.

"Raul, your brother is under the gringo's spell. We must break up their bromance."

Raul continued to nod.

"Deal with him and bring back my money. We must repay him for poisoning our family."

"Y-y-yes, boss."

"Find him, tie the little shit up like a hog, put a funnel in his mouth, and pour a gallon of his constipation medicine down his throat."

Raul smiled.

"But first, do whatever you must to get me my money. Perhaps take off a finger or two, maybe his dick, whatever you think will serve as the most effective reminder not to fuck with Armardo Angel Lopez!" More spittle flew from Armardo's mouth as he ranted and raved, making himself red in the face.

Raul's brilliant white teeth sparkled. His smile could not get any larger.

"If he hasn't got my money, we'll sell his ass until we get the money back. A nice, white gringo, ladyboy ass can earn back my money in Chihuahua."

Raul left Armardo's study, his orders clear, and donned his pink sombrero. He looked in a mirror to ensure he was wearing it at the perfect angle. Raul rolled the end of his moustache with his finger and thumb and winked at himself. He had his orders, but he knew his boss; once Armardo got back his money, Raul could do whatever he wanted to the gringo. He had no idea why his brother had taken such a liking to this foreigner. Fred would certainly not like being passed over by his boss, but he had failed to comply with a simple order. It seemed that, as good as Fred was with the cartel's money, he had gone soft, and he needed a reminder of who he served and where he stood in the cartel's food chain. Dealing with Jimmy should do the trick.

Concern for his brother quickly gave way to happy thoughts of violence and vengeance. The idea of Jimmy, terrified, selling his rear-end in a dank sex shop in Chihuahua made Raul very happy. With that image to comfort him, he climbed into his SUV, looked at his pearly whites in the rearview mirror, and imagined the gringo was Little Red Riding Hood while he, Raul Montana, was the big, bad wolf.

"Jimmy, you mosquito—*estas tan jodido!*" He smirked and headed out on his long drive to Los Piñata.

⟶⟩⟩⟩ ⟨⟨⟨⟵

JIMMY WAS SITTING on the first-floor deck of the condo, enjoying the sunshine and staring into space, when he heard a familiar accent.

"Amigo!" Fred's big, booming voice rang out. Jimmy yelled down the stairs for Fred to come up and see him. As the sicario came up the stairs, the first thing Jimmy saw of him was his black sombrero. Eventually, the rest of him came into view, and when he reached the top, he walked towards one of the comfy deck chairs, took off his sombrero, and laid it on a table next to his gringo buddy. It looked larger than Fred's entire body.

"Is Mrs Lucy at home?"

"Lucy and Max are visiting her friends." There was a hint of resentment in his voice; she had started spending more time with them and less time with him. Jimmy was a tad sullen and uncommunicative these days, as their money situation weighed on him so heavily.

"Guess what, Mr Jimmy?"

"Armardo sent you."

"You've got it, bro!"

"I thought he would have given me more time," Jimmy confessed, trying to appear nonchalant. But he was feeling nauseous and starting to sweat—and not just because of the hot Mexican sun. He had been hoping Fred was just paying him a social call, but why should he be that lucky? He wasn't any closer to getting the money than he'd been the last time they talked.

"He probably would have, but poisoning his food kind of amped things up a bit."

"Poisoning? What are you talking about?"

Fred sighed and explained to an open-mouthed Jimmy what had transpired in Guadalajara. Mass constipation had hit the household, and Hector's contrite confession laid the blame wholly on him. The icing on the cake of offence was Jimmy referring to the family as 'beaners.'

"The little shit. I didn't put anything in their food. Why would I do that, especially as Lucy ate the stew? Why would I poison my own wife just to mess with them?"

Fred giggled. "Little shit is an interesting expression, amigo. If only they could have done just a *little* shit, as you say. Don Armardo had to see his physician, who gave him a whopper of an enema—"

"Woah!" said Jimmy in disbelief.

"As he also gave a mammoth one to Raul."

Despite the bleak news, he couldn't help but laugh.

"Sorry, Fred, but the thought of your brother having a tube stuck up his ass is something I can't unsee."

"Amigo, they are not happy with you. It is not good for a cis-gendered, heterosexual Latino man, especially the head of the Wolfpack Cartel, to have something put up his *culo peludo*. It's a pride thing."

Jimmy snickered. "I didn't do anything. As if I would do something like that to a guest." He paused, smiled, and looked at Fred. "Did you have to have an enema, too, my little friend?"

Fred chuckled. "No, your poisoned stew was a blessing for me, amigo. Normally, I'm running back and forth to the toilet. I have always had a sensitive stomach. So it actually helped me become more regular with my morning poos."

"Too much information. Anyway, I didn't poison anyone or put anything in the food. That's ridiculous."

"Hector said you did."

"Hector is a lying little bastard."

"Hector was scared, amigo, so he said you ordered Max and him to do the wicked deed, making them stir in a green liquid called 'Imodium' into the stew."

Suddenly, a wave of realization came over Jimmy. He jumped up from his chair and walked inside the condo. He poked around the pantry, looked on a shelf, and eventually discovered a nearly-empty bottle of mint-flavoured Imodium anti-diarrhoea syrup. Jimmy returned to his chair and threw Fred the nearly-empty bottle.

"There's your poison . . . the little buggers!"

"To him, it's an open and shut case, amigo. Do you remember you ate the cheese sticks and refused the enema-causing stew? It does not look too good for you, Jimmy, even from my perspective, and I'm your friend."

"Perhaps if you hadn't mentioned your mass-murdering Mexican folk hero had boiled innocent people alive in his own fancy mung bean stew, I may have had an appetite to eat Lucy's," Jimmy snapped angrily. As soon as it came, however, the fury faded, leaving Jimmy with a dull ache of hopelessness. He was being punished for something he hadn't done, and couldn't see a way out. He doubted he had much longer after Fred's visit until Raul dropped by, and that would be the end of him and his family.

"So, you can see why Armardo is unhappy with you, what with everything else that happened during the holidays, including the embarrassment of being given a blow-up sheep to have sex with on your gift exchange evening."

"Sexy Suzie," Jimmy added helpfully.

"Yes, Sexy Suzie, the inflatable sheep with an orifice in her rear-end that made impressive baa-ing noises." Fred laughed heartily before continuing. "Therefore, he wants his money and 100% interest on top of the principal amount."

"Of course, he does. Did he tell you an actual figure?"

"Nope."

Jimmy shook his head in disbelief. Sure, it was foolish of him not to have counted the money, but how could a debt collector not know what they're owed?

"So you came to collect without having any idea how much? What kind of operation is Armardo running?" Jimmy asked in utter disbelief. Fred didn't answer, acting as if he hadn't even spoken.

"Raul wanted to come and see you immediately. I think his ass was very sore after the enema thing. He *really* hates you now."

"Fred, I have no money."

"I thought you'd say that. The bossman does not want me to fail this mission. If I do, you know what comes next. Don Armardo ordered my brother to bring your head back on a silver platter. But you might not be the only one who ends up dead, amigo. Don Armardo doesn't take kindly to our friendship. If I don't get that money, it could be curtains for me too." Listening to all this, Jimmy was surprised he didn't throw up on the spot. It seemed almost a foregone conclusion now that he was going to die.

"So, what should I do?"

Fred produced a small bottle of cheap tequila from his inside jacket pocket. He ordered Jimmy to get a couple of glasses. Upon returning, Fred poured the warm liquid into several shot glasses.

"Drink," Fred said. The two men chugged the warm liquid.

"Ugh, that was gross."

Fred smirked. "What I'm about to propose to you may be equally gross."

"You asked me before about selling weed, and I gave you a categorical no. How does this change anything?"

"You now have fewer choices, my friend."

"How the hell do I sell weed or coke to people? I don't even know what smoking weed is like!"

"Amigo, we are now in a race against time. Don Armardo might press the pink sombrero nuclear button if he thinks I am stalling. Man, he is pissed."

Jimmy was ashen-faced and speechless. Fred gave his friend time to take all this in before continuing.

"I don't normally sell products; I just collect the money. However, I will stand by you, and we can sell it together. You are an ideas man. Therefore, while I go and obtain the product, you can sit here, gaze at the ocean, and devise a cunning plan. I'll be back before your wife and Max get home. You can share your plan with me, and we will go out tomorrow evening to raise some much-needed moolah. I trust our plan will not fail."

"Our plan? What plan?"

"Weren't you listening? The one you will come up with very quickly."

"Right. One foolproof plan to save both our lives, coming right up," Jimmy muttered. None of this felt real. It was happening too fast, too soon. He was supposed to be on vacation, and now he had to figure out how to sell drugs or end up like Vincente. He wondered if he should tell Lucy; she was typically the more levelheaded one, and she might have a better idea of what to do. However, he quickly dashed that notion. Their relationship was already strained enough by the stress of the trip, and he didn't want to give her anything more to worry about. His mind still whirling with thoughts, Jimmy gave Fred a nod. He didn't have a choice. He had to devise a plan and execute it by tomorrow morning.

Jimmy Myers thought long and hard about the best way to be a drug dealer. He was still relatively wealthy, and his family wouldn't want for anything in the future if Raul got to him—assuming he didn't come for them next. He cursed Inspector Dumbass, whose dishonesty had put him into this ridiculous, horrifying position. As bizarre as it sounded, he had to sell weed so Fred's psycho brother wouldn't behead him.

Jimmy thought of the many programs he had watched on *Crave, HBO, Amazon Prime,* and *Netflix*. Everything he knew about selling drugs, he knew from TV. Surely, something in those shows would help him. He didn't have anything else to turn to. So he thought and thought and thought until he felt like his brain was going to burst out of his skull . . . and suddenly had a eureka moment.

"*Ozark*! Of course." That was how he was going to sell Fred's contraband.

He didn't know of any local church ministers besides Father Dominguez, Armardo's favourite man of power for the hour. However, he knew someone who had been proselytizing the benefits of sobriety: Sober Bob.

He desperately needed to hang out with Bob to get his hands on a few essential items that would help him sell the product. And this meant he'd have to ask Bob if he could tag along with him first thing in the morning to play golf.

TWENTY-THREE

A Round of Golf, the Widow and the Poet

Now WHOLLY SOBER AND having put aside Barry's iBubbles and iBubbles Pro, Bob never used a buggy. Instead, he kept a reasonably trim waistline by walking the golf course and carrying his clubs.

Jimmy happened to know JayBee was a good friend of Bob's, and when he asked her if she could arrange a golf outing with him, she kindly obliged, getting Jimmy into Bob and Deaf Barry's game first thing the next morning at Los Piñata's nine-hole course. When Fred returned to the condo and informed his Canadian pal he had a lot of 'product' to move, Jimmy told the sicario his plan in turn. Fred was gone by the time Lucy and Max arrived back at the condo.

The next day, Jimmy borrowed spare clubs from JayBee and took a taxi to meet his two playing partners at the golf course. They all shook hands and prepared to take their first shots at the par-four first hole. Jimmy teed off with a monstrous, oversized driver. When Bob and Barry saw the massive club, they sniggered at how ridiculous it looked.

Hearing the laughs, he quickly stated, "It's JayBee's. I didn't have much choice in the matter."

He was put off by the schoolboy giggling from his playing partners, and he slightly hooked his shot. The ball still travelled a decent length, however, and landed on the green.

Bob was next to play. His stance looked excellent, like a professional, and his practice swing was immaculate. Jimmy thought the tragically-sober golfer might not be as bad as he'd heard. He placed the ball on the plastic tee and shuffled back. Once he reached his ideal spot, he looked up, looked down, looked up again, and took his swing.

SWOOSH!

He missed the ball completely.

"Shit."

Bob reassumed his position. He shuffled and waggled his bum. He looked up momentarily, looked down at the ball, looked up again, and took a final look at the ball on the tee.

SWOOSH!

Miss.

SWOOSH!

Miss for the third time.

"Shit, shit, shit a brick!" he growled. "This driver pisses me off. It's useless!"

"Want to borrow my wee driver?" asked Jimmy sarcastically.

"Piss off," he sneered, letting out a small chuckle.

Finally, he connected with the ball, which travelled fifteen yards.

"Well done," praised Jimmy, trying to encourage Bob. He remembered being told by JayBee that Bob, when sober, played "like a man with no arms." She was barely exaggerating.

It was Deaf Barry's turn. He was carrying his clubs over one shoulder and a bag of colourful ear trumpets over the other. He placed the ball on the tee and swung at the golf club with arms so stiff he looked like a corpse with rigor mortis. He did everything one shouldn't do when driving the ball, including running up to the tee and waving his golf club around in a circle. His head was up, and he didn't look at the ball at all. Finally, Barry lifted his left leg, connected with the ball, and jumped back after striking it.

PING!

Jimmy was astounded a guy with such an unorthodox golf swing could make such a solid drive. The ball slightly veered to the right of the fairway but was parallel to Jimmy's ball. The two were fifty yards apart.

"Did you see where it went, guys?" Barry asked.

"To the left," Bob replied, followed by gesticulations using his gold club.

Jimmy also pointed to the left.

"What?"

"Left, it went left, near Jimmy's ball."

Barry marched off in the opposite direction towards the right side of the fairway.

"Oh, brother," Jimmy muttered under his breath. Still, he couldn't help but smile at the absurdity of the scene. Meanwhile, Sober Bob took five shots to reach the ball nearest to his. By that time, Barry had gotten out a long net to try and fish his ball out of the water. He had come no closer to finding it. Bob, taking pity on his friend, picked up his ball and rolled it to the centre of the green. He shot Jimmy a conspiratorial wink.

Bob and Jimmy jumped up and down and waved their arms, trying to get Barry's attention. Finally, Barry saw their gesticulations and walked towards his ball. He pulled out his ear trumpet, put it to his ear, and leaned towards Jimmy.

"If you want to be a better player, you should carry one of my trumpets. Makes you look chic, too."

"I'll keep that in mind," Jimmy replied, motioning towards where Bob had put his ball. Barry looked in that direction and saw the small white sphere sitting on the green.

"Hey! That's my ball!" Barry exclaimed. "Guys, why didn't you tell me?"

The nine-hole round of golf was the longest game Jimmy had ever played. He finished a respectable four over par, Barry a solid three over par, and Bob managed one hundred and forty-seven over par.

Bob said, "I love this game, but I'll never understand why I'm so crap now I don't drink."

"Better to be blessed with sobriety than to play well and be drunk as a skunk!" Jimmy replied. This was just the warm-up. Now it was time for him to be the suck-up of the year.

"Sobriety isn't easy, you know. I'm impressed you've stuck with it. Bob, how long have you been sober?"

"Fifty-seven months, eight days—" Bob looked at his watch and added, "*and four hours, forty-six seconds*," he quipped.

"Fabulous!"

"Thanks."

"I'm also thinking of going dry."

"You are?"

"Yeah. I guess there's no way I could get any 12-step information?"

"12 steps? I have a whole boxload of 12-step books."

"Shut up!" exclaimed Jimmy, pretending to be surprised.

"If you're really serious, you could come by my place and grab one."

Bob still seemed dubious, but Jimmy could tell that his fake sincerity was wearing down the recovering alcoholic's defences.

"Of course I'm serious! Honestly, I could do with three or four. You've seen how Lucy and her friends drink; they need the 12-step program as much as I do, maybe more," Jimmy said, lowering his voice and pretending as if he was saying something deeply personal. Sober Bob leaned forward and listened intently. His story was all that more believable for having a kernel of truth. Well, more than a kernel. The amigas were heavy drinkers, and if he was being honest with himself, ever since coming to Mexico, he was too.

Bob's face lit up as if having a eureka moment. "Books are great, but what will really help is going to an AA meeting. You know, Alcoholics Anonymous. There's one in town. I can take you."

Jimmy frowned. That wasn't going to help him, not for his problem. "Truth be told, I'd rather use the books. I'm a bit . . . well, I'm not ready for a group yet," the faux addict said sheepishly.

Bob narrowed his eyes, as if trying to see through his deception. "Well, half my manuals are large NA books, so they might not be all that useful to you."

"NA books?" parroted Jimmy, pretending not to know what the acronym stood for.

"Narcotics Anonymous," replied Bob. Jimmy let out a fake gasp, trying to act as if something truly serendipitous had been said.

"This is amazing. Full disclosure, I also have a secret narcotics habit," Jimmy lied.

"Cocaine?"

"Yep. Ever since the government in British Columbia decided to legalize cocaine, I started to use it, thinking that's what the government wanted. I mean, why else legalize it?"

"Damn liberal pussies!" Bob scoffed in commiseration.

"Then I started gambling because the government also encouraged responsible gambling. So, surprise, surprise, I also have a gambling addiction."

"We, the people, should rise and march on the capital. That is ridiculous!"

"Yup. Of course, they legalized cannabis too, so the government also got me hooked on wacky backy. Bob, I think I'm addicted to legalization."

"What lefty libtards," growled Bob.

"Yep, I just didn't see it coming. I started trying the legalized cocaine, and holy cow, my productivity improved by 1000%. It gave a big boost to my sex drive, too. Before I knew it, I was hooked."

"What about Lucy?"

"Lucy has no idea, although my sniffing drives her insane. One day, she came into my room and caught me with my whole face covered in white powder. She asked me what I was doing. I said I was practising my outfit for Halloween, even though it was still mid-July. I told her I was going as a cocaine addict."

"You did?"

"Yep, and she bought it. She thought I used castor sugar when it was, in fact, high-grade, government-issued, free cocaine." By this point, Bob was nodding vigorously, his expression one of sympathetic outrage. Jimmy's lie had become so ridiculous the other man couldn't possibly doubt it, and it helped that Jimmy had inadvertently played right into his beliefs. A red flush had crept into Bob's cheeks, so angered was he by such a lefty government. He slapped a hand on Jimmy's shoulder, giving it a reassuring squeeze.

"You're on the right track, Jimmy. I'll leave the books outside my casa under the palapa, by the barbecue. Take all you need, my friend."

"Thanks, Bob, you're the best!"

⟫⟫⟫ ⟪⟪⟪

LUCY ANSWERED THE light knock on the door. She swung it open to reveal a pretty lady dressed all in black with raven-coloured hair tied back in a ponytail. The stranger took out her phone and keyed in some text; she showed Lucy a message from Google Translate.

– *I am looking for my husband, Vincente. He cares for this house.*

Lucy took the phone from the lady and typed out a reply.

– *He was working here when we arrived. He disappeared and has not returned.*

– *A man came to my house. He gave me an envelope that contained a lot of money. Do you think my husband will ever return?*

Although Lucy could speak Spanish, she felt awkward answering her questions and kept using the app. It gave her time to think about her answers. Lucy shrugged.

– *What did this man look like?*

– *He was very tall, a Mexican, and wore a distinctive pink hat.*

– *Did you ask what the money was for?*

– The pink hat man said nothing. He turned and walked to his car and drove away.

– All I know is my husband asked Vincente to talk to our neighbours about the loud noise and music. It was driving us crazy.

Lucy did not want to mention Vincente's head; she hadn't seen it, and anyway was still not convinced it wasn't just a radish carving.

– The noise improved the following day. We haven't seen your husband since.

"I'm sorry. *Lo lamento,*" Lucy replied, speaking instead of using the translating app. She gave the woman a hug, which she returned. When they let go, Lucy stepped back and returned to using the app. She asked Vincente's wife if she'd reported her husband was missing.

Vincente's wife shared she had received a call from an Inspector from Los Piñata, who asked many questions. He stated there were some nasty gringos staying at her husband's workplace and he would investigate the matter thoroughly.

"Nasty gringos?" repeated Lucy, too surprised to use the app.

– The Inspector said that only he could be trusted, as he was investigating the incident.

Lucy remembered how Inspector Lopez had barged into their home with a bogus search warrant before Jimmy's passport had disappeared, along with the money they received from Armardo.

– The Inspector said he was part of an elite anti-crime unit. I must trust that he will discover what happened to my husband, the woman commented through the app. She appeared at peace that an elite, professional crime-buster was hot on her husband's tail.

Elite? If that man is 'elite,' then the Earth is flat and the Sun's an alien spaceship, Lucy thought bitterly. However, it wouldn't do to give the poor woman anything else to worry about. She looked into the woman's sad, dark brown eyes and declared, "I sincerely hope you find your husband."

The lady nodded, looking despondent, and it was only when she turned to leave that Lucy realized she hadn't shared her name the entire conversation. By the time Lucy thought to call out and ask her, she was already halfway down the condo's stairs.

Lucy couldn't imagine what it must be like for the poor woman. Her husband had gone missing, and she received a lump of cash from a known psychopathic sicario—though evidently, she had no idea who the 'pink hat man' was. It seemed likely she would never see Vincente again, and Lucy couldn't help but feel the woman knew this. All Vincente did was ask the flipping Mexicans to turn down the music, and now he was gone. Maybe Jimmy had seen Vincente's head in the freezer, after all. Lucy wished she'd gone down with him to check. She could only hope their neighbours wouldn't come back till after her family's vacation ended, because she wanted nothing more to do with that fruit-loop bunch of Mexicans. The only problems were the debt, and Jimmy's bromance with Fred Montana.

⟫⟫⟫ ⟪⟪⟪

LUCY WAS ENTERTAINING Max at the condo while Mac, Mella, and JayBee lounged around in hammocks with the music cranked up.

"I like my reputation as a Barfly, but I'm happy to be a Poolfly too," Mella cackled, sipping her beer. The only one there who seemed at all uneasy was Jimmy. He moved around like a cat on a hot tin roof, unable to keep still. He continued blowing up a large plastic crocodile floaty the amigas had brought for Max and was trying to put on a happy front—it didn't seem to fool anyone. He was too stressed to hide his feelings convincingly. He had to get the money back to Armardo, and then, just maybe, Inspector Silly Balls would accidentally-on-purpose 'find' his passport. He could get his legal cash supply from the bank and enjoy the trip's last three months. Until then, however, he didn't think he could enjoy anything.

A wave rippled across the pool's surface as the enormous air-filled crocodile hit the water. Max abandoned Lucy and his colouring book and eagerly waded into the cool water to get a closer look at the five-foot crocodile.

"He loves it here. Maybe you three should stay," suggested Mella, hopefully.

Lucy and Jimmy looked at each other and both let out a nervous chuckle.

"I'm not a big fan of the neighbours," Jimmy replied.

"You're a fan of one of them. Where is your sketchy little buddy, anyway?" Mella asked, flashing Jimmy a teasing smile.

"He's not a bad bloke. I like him."

"If you two get together with his 'identical' twin brother, everyone would think you were identical triplets," Mac snarked. The girls laughed, but Jimmy and Lucy remained stone-faced. The thought of spending even another second in the company of Raul Montana sent a cold chill through him.

"What exactly do you two talk about? What common interests could you possibly have?" Lucy asked. The three amigas nodded and leaned closer. Clearly, this was a burning question for all four of them.

"Poetry, if you want to know."

Mella spat out her drink.

"Poetry?" repeated Lucy, eyes wide.

"Yes, he's asked me to help him publish his poetry. You know, like the poems on the CD you got in the gift exchange." Jimmy wasn't sure if Lucy had listened to it; he certainly hadn't.

"Since when have you been interested in poetry, never mind helping people publish it?"

"Poetry is for the cultured citizen. It's certainly not for *barflies* who wrote their dissertations on 'Can a duck fall in love,' or 'The Science of Earthworm Cross-dressing.'"

"It's okay, Jimmy. We all see inferiority complex underneath the sarcasm," JayBee scoffed.

"Hey, blondie, I took a minor in creative writing as an undergraduate. I know my Keats from my Byrons."

"Alright, if you're such a fan of Fred's poetry, why don't you recite some? With all your late-night pontificating, you must know all his greatest works by heart," Mac challenged. Jimmy turned red at that, as he'd never read a word of Fred's poetry, but wasn't about to admit defeat.

"It's 'deconstructed' poetry, revolutionary stuff. It's not meant for the hoi polloi."

"Hoi fucking polloi?" Mac jeered, with a smirk on her face.

Mella burst into laughter, "Whatever! I bet his poetry goes a little something like this:

Poor Fred was born smaller
While his bro's ten times t-t-taller.
Pink sombrero's his name
Hitman killing's his game
But Fred wants to be the new Ch-ch-chaucer."

"That's terrible," scoffed Jimmy. "Making fun of someone's speech impediment is not cool."

"Even though he's a psycho-freak?"

"Fair comment," muttered Jimmy. Meanwhile, the girls laughed and applauded Mella's impromptu performance.

"You know, I minored in poetry," JayBee said matter-of-factly, taking another sip of her gin and tonic.

"Good for you," Jimmy declared with as much sarcasm as he could muster.

"This is what I remembered by some dude called Cuthbert Artichoke. He was a famous one-armed poet, circa 19th century, from Yarmouth, Nova Scotia."

"Do I need to cover Max's ears?" asked Lucy. JayBee ignored her friend's question and went straight into the poem:

"I met a lewd nude in Barbuda;
She thought she was crude, but I was cruder.
T'was in her menstrual mood; rubbed her tits in my food.
Then I mucked her, sucked her, and fuc—"

"Alright, that's enough!" interrupted Jimmy. "Max is right there, and that's not poetry; that's verbal diarrhoea, and it's seriously offending my ears. Mock all you want, but Fred is really talented." He remained insistent on defending his friend, whose poetry he'd never read.

"Jimmy would be more believable if he said he and Fred shared a love of mathematics, and they became super-close and bro-bonded over a few beers, polynomials, and other algebraic turn-ons," mocked Mella.

"Then I'd believe they have so much in common," JayBee agreed.

"Exactly, JayBee" added Mac. "Jimmy could've impressed Dr Mella, our resident cat scientist, by sharing with her that he and Fred jerk off to Schrodinger's equation."

"Ugh. Is your mind *ever* not in the gutter?" Jimmy groaned.

When the amigas got together, they played off one another quite brilliantly. They shared a weird, almost twin-like telepathic vibe. Jimmy typically enjoyed it—he was no stranger to crude humour himself—but at this moment, he felt uncomfortable. He genuinely liked Fred, but given who his family was, he felt like he needed a plausible excuse as to why they spent so much time together. Besides, he didn't want Lucy knowing about his plan. He hated not being transparent with his wife, but honesty was even less appealing. He'd gotten her and Max into this mess, and he was going to get them out. Their vacation was already tense enough without giving Lucy another reason to worry. He continued to defend his association with Fred until the amigas changed the subject, worrying all the while about what might happen when it came time to join with Fred and sell drugs to gringos and Mexicans.

TWENTY-FOUR

Raul is on the Hunt

RAUL WAS TAKING THE scenic route to Los Piñata, giving him plenty of time to think about what he would do to the Canadian. The sicario had texted his brother several times, telling him he was on his way to deal with the gringo, via orders from Armardo. He sent a few smiley-face emojis and several head-exploding emojis with the text.

Raul loved emojis. He loved emojis more than words. His clumsiness with words had been an issue all his life, apart from when he spoke to himself or his little brother.

Raul expected a response from his twin, but he never received one. It confirmed Fred was under the gringo's spell; his brother's bond with Jimmy was getting in the way of their relationship. The thought irked Raul, as no one had ever come between him and his identical twin brother, not even his ex, the imbecilic social worker who said 'social construct' every second sentence. She had, however, gotten close, and the strange ideas she put in his brother's head lingered after their breakup. Raul shook his head, thinking about the strange woman who drank her pee to prove how she was at one with the environment.

"The eco-warrior," Raul sniggered to himself, "with her biodegradable silicone boobies."

He was certain his brother had only fallen for Tonya Guacamole for her breasts; he could never resist a good pair. Jimmy had no such allure, which made it even more absurd he should hold so much sway over Fred. However, like with Tonya,

Raul was certain the gringo's power over his brother would not last. Fred had moved on quickly from his ex, and he and Raul soon reestablished their close bond. It would be the same with Jimmy. Once he was dead and gone, Raul would get his brother back.

Don Armardo was pissed off with Fred and had dispatched Raul before his brother could return the cartel's money. The only other time this had ever happened was when a crocodile bit Fred, forcing him to get medical treatment. Fred said the croc had gobbled down the torso he was disposing of, and with it a sack of the Wolfpack's recently collected tax monies.

Raul was all too happy to oblige his godfather. If he wasn't already set on Jimmy's violent and painful death, his constipation would have been the straw that broke the camel's back. Mexicans were proud people and did not want to have enemas forced upon them under any circumstances. However, the pain and discomfort had become too intense for Raul, and he swallowed his pride and underwent a glycerin and bicarbonate enema. The only way he could avenge his ego was to make the gringo suffer as he had, wreaking havoc on his bowels so furiously that he would beg for death. It was no less than he deserved, and it might even be a mercy. There had to be something deeply wrong with Jimmy's brain. After all, no one in their right mind would dare prank the head of the most respected family in Mexico and the most feared sicario in the Americas.

Raul wondered how much pain Jimmy could handle before crying out for mercy. Even though Armardo suggested using Imodium, he would rather place a funnel in Jimmy's mouth, pour liquid Senokot laxative directly down his throat, and give him the shits for a fortnight. Then, he'd cut the man's head off and present it to the Don . . . after he paid off his debt to the cartel, of course. Raul smiled. Thinking about all the ways he could revenge himself upon the gringo was getting him aroused.

Raul pressed the auto-pilot feature of the car, opened the SUV's sunroof, and cranked up the traditional Mexican music that had been playing on Bluetooth. He put his hands above his head like he was on a rollercoaster ride and sang along like he was as free as a bird. There was no one around to hear him, no one to make him nervous and stumble over his words. He sang clearly and perfectly.

Perfect. That's what today was going to be.

⤜⤜⤜   ⤛⤛⤛

LATER THAT DAY, Bob was practising his putting skills. Despite being barely two inches away from the hole, he still managed to miss every shot. With each miss, he cursed his sobriety with increasing vehemence, and this was how Jimmy and Fred found him when they visited his home. He let them pick up as many of his books as they wanted and quickly returned to his putrid putting. They took half a dozen thick AA and NA books back to Fred's hotel room in the town centre.

"This is a great idea, amigo," praised Fred.

"I can't take credit; I got it from watching *Ozark*." Then, he got to work. He opened a book and carefully cut out a massive chunk of text, hollowing it to hold the product they were due to sell. He passed the book to Fred, who demonstrated his cutting skills with a paring knife at the *Noche de Rábanos* competition. Fred tidied up Jimmy's work, and the rectangular hollowed-out section fit snugly in the middle of the book.

Fred placed several small baggies into the hollow, closed the book, and confirmed it looked like a regular AA or NA 12-steps recovery manual. Fred provided baggies containing the 'White Russian' strain of weed for the Alcoholics Anonymous edition. For the Narcotics Anonymous books, he brought cocaine, crystal meth, and speed. The two of them continued this process with their newly-acquired books on sobriety, the irony not at all lost on Jimmy.

Jimmy felt terrible about what he was doing to get himself out of a bad situation, and all the while he looked grim. Fred made jokes to get his friend out of his funk, but Jimmy never gave him anything more than a halfhearted chuckle and went back to his moping. It was clear he was struggling with what he was about to do.

"I know you don't like this, amigo, but what choice do you have? The clients would buy products from other dealers anyway. It's not like we'll be selling weed outside schools."

"I'll need to do a lot of penance to make up for this crap." The prospect of penance was even more sobering to Jimmy; he hated going to church.

"You can do all the penance you want once we're done, but if you don't get the money for Don Armardo, you won't get a chance." Jimmy had no response. He couldn't argue, but he also couldn't deny how awful this whole business made him feel.

"How about we each carry regular, non-doctored books too? Just in case a client really wants to sober up, or some rogue cop decides to encroach on

Wolfpack territory," Fred suggested, trying to get Jimmy out of his head and into the plan.

"Sure," Jimmy replied absentmindedly. Fred could have suggested that Jimmy coat himself in pig's blood and jump butt-naked into *El Río Cocodrilo*, and he would have given the same answer.

"Amigo, if you go into a deal like this, you're not gonna sell anything. Maybe you just need to rehearse. We can practice at Tequila Tommy's and then cross the road to *El Macron*. The locals there will buy anything we sell them."

"And how will we stick together in this club, anyway? If there's tons of people I could lose track of you, and I don't know how to sell drugs on my own," Jimmy blurted out. He couldn't keep his worries down anymore; they were starting to bubble to the surface.

"How would you lose track of me wearing this sombrero?" Fred asked, adjusting his headgear for emphasis.

"Dumbass! You aren't the tallest tree in the forest. It doesn't matter how fancy your sombrero is; I'm gonna have a hard time keeping track of a guy who comes up to my waist in a crowded bar."

"Are you height-shaming me, amigo? If so, you are thinking like a racist, ableist, ageist, misogynist gringo."

"What?"

"Height is just a social construct."

"Height, like any physical property, is not a social construct. You are short, and your brother is tall. The same goes for weight, age, eye colour, and skin colour. End of discussion."

"My ex-girlfriend, Tonya Guacamole, told me heightism is a social construct based upon societal gender norms."

"Tonya . . . *Guacamole*? Was she green with envy of your towering height?"

"She's a social worker and anthropologist. She has more qualifications than you have hair follicles. She said socially speaking, the societal phenomena surrounding height emanate from a deep-rooted humping instinct. Women view shorter men as more likely to have larger dicks, thus providing them with feelings of safety. But *my* height is a moot point, as I'm not short."

"Let me get this straight: women like shorter men because they're supposed to have bigger dicks?"

"Kind of. Anyway, she called out many social constructs."

"Like what?"

"Like the reason men stand up to pee, and women are forced to squat on the toilet. A social construct."

Jimmy shook his head in disbelief. Fred sure knew how to pick them. "Men pee standing up because we have the hardware for it."

Fred just looked at him and smirked.

"Now, can we get back to the matter at hand? Drug dealing. If we get caught, the penalty could well be life imprisonment," Jimmy warned as he cut another rectangle out of the third AA book. Fred, however, wasn't keen to drop the subject of his ex and her inane theories.

"Tonya said societal expectations demand women pee sitting down. Any woman brought up in an equal society would pee standing up too."

"So, in a truly egalitarian society, women would stand up against a tree or a wall, undo their flies to go pee, and the pee would squirt over their trousers, run down their legs, and into their boots? Yep, ha-ha, it's all a social construct."

"Amigo, no offence, but you're an idiot. Why do you think she invented the iPEE?" At this, Jimmy put down his book. He couldn't concentrate on his work and this bizarre conversation at the same time.

"A what? An iPEE? What's an iPEE?" Jimmy asked, praying to the Lord to give him the strength to endure Fred's answer.

"It's a phallic-shaped funnel ladies attached to their coochie. You pee into the device, which travels along the tube and pours out into the receptacle or over a tree, a sink, or a fire hydrant."

"The sink?"

"Yes, my friend, I always use a sink to pee into. My pee is like a water fountain; it creates a beautiful arc in the air, so it's easy for me to point my member towards the sink and have a rapturous piss."

"Fred, I don't want to hear about you and your pee habits."

"My ex-girlfriend, Tonya, used her iPEE all the time."

Jimmy didn't want to hear any more from his friend, but couldn't seem to stop him. If they were going to get back to work, it would be after Fred had said his piece—never mind how many brain cells it cost Jimmy to listen.

"Going on field trips with her was so much fun. We'd stop the car for a washroom break. As all lovers do, we would stand next to each other as we peed, and she would say, 'Freddy, look at my flow!' It was like the iconic scene in *El Titanica*, with Jack DiCaprio and Rose Winslet, standing together, eyes closed at the helm, backs to the wind. Tonya would have the biggest smile on her face as she gushed out through her iPEE device. Amigo, it was like watching a horse urinate. 'I'm Queen of the World!' she'd shout as her pee spray would be blown back into our faces." Jimmy was stunned into slack-jawed silence. He felt like his jaw would disconnect from his face and fall to the floor if he held his mouth open any wider. Fred, however, just kept going.

"The other thing about using the iPEE was Tonya never had to worry about washing her hands afterwards."

"But she'd have to wash her urination device, wouldn't she? *Ew.* Think of the bacteria." Jimmy scrunched up his face.

"Amigo, she was a Bear Grylls fan, so she'd tip the dregs of the iPEE into her mouth and lick the device and her hands until they were spotless."

"If you say another word, I'm going to throw up all over the drugs."

"You can't get sexier than a hairy Eco-warrior Latino chick that drinks her pee to save the planet!"

At this, Jimmy completely gave up. He went back to work, trying his best to drown out Fred's disgusting account of his adventures with Tonya Guacamole. His desire to flee the conversation as soon as possible bolstered his efficacy, and soon he was finished. The converted AA and NA books were now ready, and he and Fred were prepared to sell drugs. For the sicario, breaking the law was an everyday occurrence. For Jimmy, it was a horrifying prospect . . . though not nearly as horrifying as Fred and his piss-obsessed ex.

TWENTY-FIVE

Narcotraficante

JIMMY ASKED FRED TO hand him some of his poetry to read.

"It's not just poetry. It's 'deconstructed' revolutionary poetry."

"Whatever! I need an alibi. The ladies wanted to know what you and I talk about and what we have in common."

"I'm happy to give you some of my writing, but I haven't copyrighted it yet."

Jimmy laughed and told him not to worry about that, as he promised he wouldn't sneakily publish Fred's work and claim all the glory.

The two men continued with this small talk as they approached their destination, carrying the 12-step do-it-yourself drug-selling kits under their arms. As Fred had suggested, some of the books hadn't been carved up in order to add authenticity and plausible deniability. If any of their prospective clients were sincere in their recovery or an undercover cop, he and Jimmy could point them to one of their real copies.

After practising their selling routine at Tommy's, they would cross the road to the Mexican *El Macron* Club. Fred assured Jimmy patrons at both establishments would want some recreational substances to add excitement to the evening, and he buried all his misgivings beneath his desire to protect his family. He was on a mission, and raising money was the first step.

Fred had a different agenda: to help his new buddy out of a bind and mentor him, as he seemed pretty green when it came to selling drugs.

Tequila Tommy's was packed, and rocked to the sound of live music. Jimmy didn't recognize anyone else in the bar, but he had a solid alibi if he bumped into Bob or Barry, so he felt better about the situation. He was ill at ease, but Fred wasted no time in getting started. He went over to someone and struck up a conversation, and Jimmy watched as he gradually entered sales mode. Soon, a book was opened and money was exchanged. When Fred closed the book, the transaction was complete. The customer walked away, satisfied, and Fred looked over his shoulder at Jimmy, giving him a wink and a smile. Then he went off to chase down his next prospective buyer.

Jimmy had butterflies in his stomach, watching as Fred had made another two sales. He tried to hype himself up, thinking of his favourite crime dramas and the gritty intensity of the criminals they depicted. He tried to feel cool and excited rather than scared out of his mind, wondering which of the people at each table was a secret plainclothes police officer. It didn't work. As Fred moved on to his fourth customer, Jimmy realized he just had to go out and do the deed. Thinking about it wasn't helping. So the Canadian approached some young guys sitting at a table. He shook hands with them and tapped his feet to the loud music.

"Hey, homies. I'm just checking to see if you want to try some delicious ganja?" Jimmy importuned, trying unsuccessfully to sound as So-Cal as possible. His arsenal of druggie slang included: "cool," "bro," "dope," "bae," "whassup," "yaas," "dude," "mofo," "fam," and "white-boy." He peppered them throughout his sentences so obsessively that half of what he said was completely unintelligible, but his sales pitch appeared to be working. He negotiated quantity and price, and cracked open one of his books and slipped out some weed, which he exchanged for cash. Then the young guys left, huge grins on their faces, and Jimmy let out a sigh. He felt like he'd been holding his breath for minutes. Still, his success emboldened him, and with newfound courage, he approached two more tables and got a purchase and a refusal. Afterwards he looked around for Fred, worried that he'd lost him, but saw his friend across the bar motioning for him to leave. He followed Fred out onto the cobbled road in front of Tommy's.

"I saw you at work in there. Congratulations, amigo, you've broken your drug dealer cherry. Now let's go to the club and sell the rest of this product," Fred crooned, a wicked smile plastered on his face. He nodded in the direction of a dark maroon-painted building that was directly across the road from Tommy's. Loud, thumping music could be heard from the street, which drowned out the sounds coming from Tequila Tommy's. It wasn't a smoke-free zone like Tommy's, and plumes of thick cigarette and cigar smoke poured out from one of *El Macron's* entrances. Fred had informed him gringos weren't welcome there by the locals, but were encouraged to attend by the bar staff and the hookers. That endorsement didn't make Jimmy feel any better.

"This place looks super sketchy."

"That's why we can sell our merchandise there. The cops stay clear of the joint; it's a cartel-run establishment. *Muchos* beer and tequila get drunk at *El Macron*, and the regulars snort shitloads of cocaine. Besides, the club is super dark inside, perfect for us to ply our trade."

Jimmy saw that Fred was right; there wasn't a single window on the outside of the club. This didn't make him any less anxious. No windows meant more seclusion to sell their drugs, but it also meant no help from the outside. All kinds of horrible things could happen to Jimmy in there, and no one would have any idea.

"Don't worry, amigo. Our main customers won't be psychos. They're construction workers who need help staying awake working long hours, along with the hookers and their clients." With that, Fred made his way across the street, and Jimmy spent several moments psyching himself up before hurrying to catch up with him.

When they reached the front entrance to *El Macron*, Fred commanded him to stand by the entrance to one of the washrooms while he made the rounds along the tables and the dance floor. He'd then direct any weed traffic towards Jimmy. Fred had put all the heavy narcotics into his doctored NA books, for which Jimmy was grateful. He took a deep breath and followed the sicario through the doors and into the smoky environment of the club.

It was incredibly dark inside, and the instant Jimmy breathed in, he inhaled a cloud of smoke and nearly broke out into a coughing fit. Once his eyes adjusted to the lighting, he looked around. Some men were standing at the bar, beer in hand, and others were hanging out with the pretty escort *señoritas*, who were standing with their backs up against the wall and surveying the club for potential clients.

Jimmy found his way to the washrooms, identifiable by the sign *Baños* above the wide entrance, and waited with his AA 12-step recovery books under his arms. He remembered Lopez's sidekick with the same name and smirked despite his discomfort. Oh, the irony.

He couldn't see Fred at all, mainly due to his size. As he scanned the room for his friend, he noticed a young guy approaching him. He tried to look nonchalant as he reached for one of the AA books with drugs inside. The prospective customer asked him something in Spanish. Jimmy smiled back, opened one of the books, and showed the guy several packets of weed. He took out a baggie, and the guy exchanged several hundred pesos for two of the baggies and walked away, stuffing the product into a jean pocket. Jimmy put the cash in his bag, closed the book, and was ready for the next customer.

Twenty minutes passed, and sales were plentiful. The Canadian only had to stand where he was, and make the trade; customer after customer approached to buy his product. His heart was beating so fast he thought it might explode inside of him.

An attractive woman in her thirties approached him and introduced herself as Ella. She looked like an escort, with a skimpy outfit consisting of a tight-fitting crop top and black skirt with boots that had wickedly high heels. Jimmy was astounded she didn't fall over every single step. Ella's face was covered with makeup; she had bright purple lipstick, dark heavy eyeliner, and jet-black mascara. She babbled something in Spanish that Jimmy had no hope of understanding.

"Do you speak English?" he asked.

"I buy weed from you, yes?" she asked in turn. Her English was imperfect, but she knew enough to get what she wanted. Jimmy the Narco-dealer nodded and carefully opened one of his AA books. Once he found the product he looked up at Ella.

"*Cuantas quieres*. How many baggies?"

Ella held up three fingers.

Jimmy gave her three baggies, took her cash, and said, "*Gracias*." His back remained pressed up against the wall.

Suddenly, a firm hand landed on his right shoulder.

He glanced sideways to see who had his shoulder in a death grip. He followed the hand up to the elbow, then to the shoulder, and finally to the vicious grin on Inspector Lopez's face.

INSPECTOR RAMON LOPEZ had a rare evening off work, and decided to take advantage of complementary drinks and escort services at *El Macron*. Ramon casually surveyed the dance floor and the bar area. From his vantage point, he could make out the entrance to the washrooms. He breathed out smoke from his Cuban cigar, which he held up near his face with one hand. He had the other wrapped around the waist of one of *El Macron*'s girls, who was sitting on his knee.

Suddenly, he recognized someone standing by the men's bathroom door. He couldn't place him at first, but soon realized this man was a dead ringer for Jimmy the Gringo. He held a bunch of books under his arms. Ramon would describe his body language as, to use a technical law enforcement term, 'dodgy.' He put his cigar into the cheap foil ashtray and rubbed his eyes in disbelief.

At first, Lopez thought Jimmy might be trying to hook up with one of the many male construction workers who regularly used the bar. Or perhaps he was looking for a pretty señorita to spend the night with. Lopez knew in the dank, smoky atmosphere, he wouldn't be seen by the gringo, but to be safe he used his escort, Ella, as a human shield. He peered over her shoulder, watching and waiting to see what the gringo was up to.

The Inspector was sure Jimmy wasn't on a Jehovah's Witness recruiting drive, but he had no idea what he could be using the books for. However, as he watched people come up to Jimmy briefly and then walk away, he saw the gringo was conducting transactions with them. When people approached him, he would open his book, take something from it, and exchange whatever it was for money. Interesting. Then, a light bulb turned on in Lopez's head; the Inspector couldn't believe his luck. Ramon Lopez despised the gringo. The man's mocking, arrogant attitude enraged him. He treated the Inspector like a dunce, hardly proper conduct towards such a decorated officer of the law.

Ramon grinned, thinking back to when he had taken the Canadian's passport and Armardo's money from the safe. That had been his brother's brilliant idea. Now the gringo was so desperate to raise funds that he could be arrested for a serious drug trafficking offence. Even if he was harmlessly selling candies and raising money for the Girl Guides of Mexico, Ramon would ensure some drugs entered his possession.

The Inspector's eyes gleamed excitedly as he plotted his next move on his mental *let's mess with Jimmy Myers* chessboard. The knight's bold move would take the queen, resulting in a quick checkmate for his nemesis; Sir Ramon would capture Queen Jimmy, and it would be curtains for the little shit. He whispered into the ear of the escort, gave her some simple instructions, and stuffed some peso notes down her skimpy bra. She hopped off his lap and walked towards the gringo, and Ramon followed, sticking to the shadows of *El Macron*.

Lopez then witnessed the transaction between his girl and the gringo, who gave her a package out of the book he had opened.

Smirking, he muttered to himself, "Gotcha, shitball!"

Before Jimmy knew it, Inspector Lopez had him in handcuffs, and he was frog-marched out of *El Macron* to Lopez's bright green Kia Soul. Then the Inspector drove him to the police station.

Jimmy was silent. He thought Lopez's car looked like the type of vehicle Freddo the Frog would drive, but he was too stunned to find his observation funny; he was well and truly shagged.

Upon arriving at the police station, he was immediately booked in, and the custody Sergeant took his fingerprints. The Sergeant spoke to Jimmy in Spanish, his words rolling off his tongue effortlessly.

"I need an English-speaking interpreter," Jimmy said stubbornly, surprised at his own composure. Internally he was screaming; his worst fears had come to pass. But it wasn't over yet. Surely, if he was to be arrested, he at least deserved to understand the charges. And even though he'd been caught red-handed, he had faith Lopez, 'stupider than the man from Jupiter,' would find some way to screw this up. That was Jimmy's only hope.

Lopez, who was waiting in the shadows, carefully watched every move Jimmy made with a self-satisfied smirk on his face. Once the gringo spoke, he was quick to respond.

"You need an interpreter? Then allow me. The Sergeant said you are a little gringo bitch, and you will be sent to prison and become someone's prison wife." Jimmy just rolled his eyes. Lopez was already recycling jokes; he'd heard that one before.

"I want to talk to a lawyer and apply for bail."

"Lucky for you, you only possessed a small amount of marijuana. Another ten grams and you would be arrested for trafficking, which means no bail. Unluckily for you, I'm sure the Sergeant could find the extra ten grams somewhere on your person, if you force us to look. Only a full confession will help you out of the shit you are now in."

"I have nothing to say until I speak with a lawyer," Jimmy insisted.

"Fine. Then you'll be sharing a cell with your new jail husband at a prison in Sinaloa. Your ass will be working overtime there." Lopez laughed out loud, the barking sound filling the air and ringing in Jimmy's ears. He was quickly losing hope there was a way out of this.

Then the custody cop led Jimmy to a windowless room and handcuffed him to the table.

>>>>> <<<<<

IT HAD BEEN a very productive evening for Fred Montana. He didn't like doing the work, and it wasn't as if he was concerned about the local police. He was more concerned about the DEA and the military. Those agencies had been known to work undercover, arresting low-grade dealers to extract confessions that would lead to more senior cartel members ending up in jail.

He worried for his friend, and Fred was loyal to those he liked. He also knew Jimmy would only make a small percentage of what was needed to repay the Don. Fred was confident he could gather enough money from his sales and his personal savings to make up the difference and rescue his pal from Don Armardo's and Inspector Lopez's clutches. The little sicario also believed Jimmy's experience of the stressful life of a drug dealer would provide him with a unique perspective and a valuable life lesson—perhaps one that would make him more sympathetic to Fred's plight. It was a win-win situation. Jimmy would be safe, and Don Armardo wouldn't know Fred had his side hustle and had been putting money aside to escape the cartel life and attend school for poetry sometime in the future.

Fred's plan, however, had gone south without him even realizing. It wasn't until an employee at *El Macron* alerted him the dreaded Inspector Lopez had taken a weedy-looking gringo out of the club in handcuffs, with his weapon drawn and pointed at the gringo's head, that Fred knew Jimmy's *narcotraficante* days were over.

Fred felt sick. Lopez had it in for Jimmy. Don Armardo would be informed, and Raul would be dispatched to clean up Fred's little mess. He believed Inspector Lopez had taken the money and Jimmy's passport from the safe, but wasn't sure if it was a solo act by Lopez or if Don Armardo had asked him to set up his friend. He hadn't heard anything from his brother, but as he was closer with the Don than Fred, it was possible Raul had been told and chose not to tell his brother. He wouldn't be surprised if Raul took poorly to his chumminess with the gringo.

This situation only made Fred more certain he had to escape the cartel life. What happened to Vincente was already weighing on him, as if he'd swallowed a rock. The guilt of it sat heavy in his stomach, along with the horror of everything else he'd done and enabled as Don Armardo's criminal custodian. It was nauseating. Fred was done being the 'mop-up' crew, and he didn't want any more deaths on his conscience, especially Jimmy's. He couldn't afford to let the gringo die. Yes, Jimmy was a friend, but he was also a way out of the cartel; he could be Fred's passport to poetry renown.

Fred couldn't leave his buddy at the mercy of Inspector Lopez, never mind Raul's. But apart from driving back to Guadalajara and begging Don Armardo to intervene, there was only one thing he could do.

TWENTY-SIX

The Interview

DETECTIVE INSPECTOR LOPEZ LOOKED at a pile of paperwork on the desk before him. He was sitting directly across from Jimmy. He could smell the acrid, metallic sourness of the gringo's fear, and he loved it.

"You need to stop farting," he sneered.

"I haven't been farting."

"It's disrespectful to use this room as a flatulence laboratory."

The prisoner looked bewildered.

"This isn't a chemistry experiment. Your farts are pathetic."

Jimmy sighed.

Lopez leaned to one side, lifted his right buttock, and farted. It was loud, and it reeked.

"Mexican-style fart. Nailed it!" he exclaimed, taking a deep whiff. Jimmy gasped; the stench was almost unbearable. It was as if something had died in the Inspector's rectum.

"The moral of the story is . . . if you're going to pass wind, then blow off a good 'un." The Inspector said proudly as Jimmy gagged. Lopez let out a booming laugh; he thought he was being hilarious, and getting to torment the insubordinate gringo put him in good spirits. He looked down at the documents before him, looked up at Jimmy and raised his eyebrows.

"James *Wellington Horacio* Myers."

"Yes."

"What the hell kind of names are Wellington and Horatio?"

"They're my names."

"No shit, Miss Marple."

"My mother was fascinated with legendary English war heroes and hoped I would one day join the armed forces. She thought I'd be famous like my namesakes," Jimmy explained, feeling an urge to defend his name.

"You, Mr Jimmy Wellington Horatio Myers, like the British Empire, are on the precipice of extinction. This interview room may be your very own Alamo."

"I hope not."

"The charges do not bode well for you: drug dealing, dismembering a Mexican citizen, false reporting of a crime, abduction, illegal entry into Mexico."

"Give it a rest. *Dismembering*? *Illegal entry*? Even you have to admit that's absurd." Even as he protested, Jimmy knew it was useless. The man was set on Jimmy's destruction in defiance of logic. If there was a way out, it wouldn't be through appealing to reason.

"You will disappear in our justice system, never to be seen again."

"Like Vicente?" Lopez narrowed his eyes, but did not respond. He continued amping up the pressure as if Jimmy hadn't spoken.

"Drug dealing carries a sentence of life imprisonment here, so to make the time a little easier for yourself, maybe you can write your confession?" Lopez pushed papers towards his prisoner. "Or I can write it for you if you like . . . all you have to do is sign."

"Piss off! You know I didn't do anything to Vincente."

"I can make a deal with the prosecutor for you? Yes?"

"I think I'll take my chances in court."

"You have no chance in court, Mr Horatio Hornblower. I will produce Vincente's head, with your DNA all over it and his DNA on your clothing."

"I never went anywhere near his head. Nice try, Columbo." The Inspector's smile widened, and like a coiled snake lashing out at its prey, he shot out his arm, grabbed Jimmy's hand, and wiped a red, bloody smear on his shirt sleeve.

"Whoopsie! What do you have on your shirt? Vincente's blood?" Jimmy was too stunned to do anything but look at his bloodstained sleeve. There were no lows, it seemed, to which Lopez would not stoop, no abuse of power he would not commit to destroy him.

"Sign the confession, you gringo piece of shit. I'll ensure you only get twenty years in prison, which may be cut to fourteen years with good behaviour."

"No way."

"The alternative is to spend the rest of your life as a prison wife to one of Armardo's jailed capos. You'll look quite dandy in lipstick, eyeliner, and a mini skirt." Lopez looked at Jimmy triumphantly, his smirk exposing teeth that were just begging to be knocked out. If he wasn't handcuffed, Jimmy might have leapt up and slugged him right there. The Inspector's sadistic glee was interrupted, however, when the door to the interrogation room opened and the custody suite Sergeant entered. He looked intensely at Lopez, who fixed him with a contemptuous glare.

"What the hell do you want?"

The Sergeant looked at Jimmy, then back at Lopez, rolled his eyes, and shrugged his shoulders.

A heated conversation ensued in Spanish. Lopez ferociously banged his fist on the desk, pushed back his chair, and shot to his feet. He stalked towards the Sergeant and put his face within inches of the other officer's. He screamed, covering the man's face in spittle. The Sergeant wiped his face, turned around, and left the room. Lopez followed him to the front office.

All the while, Jimmy sat and watched the spectacle in awe. For a brief moment, he loved the Sergeant for causing Lopez to nearly lose his mind.

Having entered the Sergeant's work area, Lopez looked around the empty front office.

"Are you a fool or a halfwit? No, don't answer me. You're both. A dipshit with three stripes. I bet you can't even count to three?"

"No sir." The Sergeant kept jerking his head towards the empty waiting room, indicating they were not alone.

"You can't count to three?"

"Yes sir . . . I mean no sir."

"I will have your stripes for this, you doofus. You can't even count to three."

"Yes, sir."

Lopez held up three fingers and asked the Sergeant how many fingers he held up.

"Three, sir."

"You guessed?"

"No, sir. I can count to three, sir." He, again, motioned with his head, nodding at the empty room in front of him and his boss.

"Do you have Tourette's syndrome?"

"No, sir."

"Then why do you have a tick? You can't count to three and walk around twitching, eye-rolling, and shoulder-shrugging. Why does the academy recruit illiterate, stupid people with dyscalculia and Tourette's who interrupt senior officers when they are about to get a confession from a cold-blooded killer and drug dealer?"

The Sergeant cleared his throat and then pointed beyond the plexiglass counter.

"Sir, please take a look." Lopez walked up to the counter and looked out at the station.

"Lower, sir," the Sergeant said. Lopez obliged. He stood on his tiptoes to gain extra height, and looked down. There, too small to be seen over the counter, was Fred Montana. He smiled and waved at the Inspector.

"Oh great, it's Fred 'Flintstone' Montana!"

"Wow! You sure treat your staff well. Did you tell the Sergeant how *you* managed to get into the police academy *and* what happened after you graduated?"

Lopez went bright red. "What are you doing here? Have you come to see your gringo buddy?"

"I will give your Sergeant one hundred thousand dollars, the entire bail amount. Now, please release the prisoner."

"Have you lost your mind?"

"Nope, I sure haven't. The bail money is courtesy of Don Armardo Angel Lopez."

"I will call him immediately," fumed Lopez, walking over to a phone.

"Yes, yes, go on and call him. But I should warn you, he's in quite a foul mood. If you piss him off any more, he might lose it. And I don't know about you, but I'd rather not be on the receiving end of that particular meltdown," Fred replied. The Inspector's eyes were practically bugging out of his head. His carotid vein was bulging from his neck. Fred sneered at him and continued.

"You know the gringo owes the bossman a shitload of money. The boss insists on settling his account with Mr Myers before turning him over to anyone else."

"But he's been dealing drugs. I caught him red-handed!"

"Yes, and he was working for me and the cartel. Therefore, he was working for Don Armardo, and you, you complete dickhead, arrested him." Lopez, still wide-eyed with shock, took a loud gulp. Beads of sweat were forming on his brow. He knew full well being related to the Don didn't exempt you from the consequences of mucking with his business.

"Let him go immediately, and I won't say anything. Or you can call Don Armardo and face the music." Fred had been placing dollar bills on the counter as he spoke, having to reach above his head to do so. He showed no signs of stopping. The sicario glared at him, making sure to look him right in the eyes.

"You stupid, ignorant, power-abusing sycophant!"

"Sycophant?"

"Yes. Or, if you prefer, a brown-nosing, ball-sucking parasite."

"How dare you, you little turd!" Lopez sounded defiant, but he couldn't bring himself to meet Fred's gaze. He looked between the money on the counter and his junior officer. Fred, meanwhile, was trying his best to catch the Inspector's eye. He said nothing else. He stood in silence, waiting as if he had all the time in the world. It was Lopez, at last, who spoke, and when he did it was to the Sergeant.

"You imbecile! Do you want to prove you can count past three? Count the damn money!"

Half an hour later, after signing the necessary paperwork in triplicate. Jimmy was released. Fred tipped his black sombrero at Inspector Lopez.

"See you later, alligator!" With that, he and his gringo buddy left the station.

Jimmy let out a huge sigh of relief. "I don't know how you did it, but I owe you big-time, Fred. You're a freaking hero."

"Yep, you sure do. But when Don Armardo finds out what just happened, I'm in big caca."

"How did you raise the cash?"

"I used the cartel's money."

"Seriously? One hundred thousand in cartel cash? Aren't they going to miss that?"

"Yes, they will, so we need another plan. Otherwise, amigo, we are both well and truly—how do you say it?—screwed."

⇒⇒⇒ ⇐⇐⇐

A SARCASTIC JIMMY asked, "I guess selling more products is out of the question?"

"Look at you. Mr *Breaking Bad* himself!" Fred exclaimed, sounding more cavalier than he had any right to be in this situation.

"Mr *Breaking Bad*? Yeah, I am . . . because at the end of all this I'll be dead!"

"Not if we pay back the cartel, so get your thinking cap on, amigo. We'll need to pay the bail plus the money owed to Don Armardo, plus whatever the original amount he lent you was, plus double in interest. Since it must be enough for Armardo to call off my brother, we'll probably need even more."

"Oh great, the man with the pink sombrero. No offence to your psycho brother, of course," mocked Jimmy.

"No offence taken. Raul would consider that a compliment," Fred replied.

"Great. Maybe I can flatter him out of killing us." Jimmy was getting on a hot sarcasm streak now.

"As nice as that would be, I think we need another plan. So *think*," said Fred. Now he was starting to sound more urgent.

"I'm trying. Problem is, all I can think of right now is what I want written on my headstone."

Having exited the Police HQ, Fred and Jimmy walked along the highway, turned, and cut through the market area. They headed towards the *Malecon* to sit, look at the ocean, and clear their minds.

The sun was beginning to set; the deep orange, red, and purple hues stretched far across the horizon. Birds continued to chirp. Waves broke in the shallow waters and crashed against the sea wall, and an old fishing boat was returning to port. Some couples walked hand-in-hand on a long stretch of paving. Others took photographs and selfies with their phones. It was very peaceful there. Too peaceful. Jimmy was going to die and the world didn't care.

The two strange-looking friends, a Mexican and a gringo, sat on a wooden chair and waited for inspiration. Fred checked his phone as he waited for a eureka moment, and saw he had messages from Raul. He read them aloud.

"I'm on my way. Boss wants gringo severely dealt with. Angry emoji. Coffin emoji. Skull and bones emoji. Blood transfusion emoji. Head-exploding emoji. Blood dripping from a knife emoji. What is the gringo's last location?"

"That's how he texts?" Jimmy asked. He never thought he'd be killed by a man who overuses emojis.

"He needs to quit with the emojis. He uses *way* too many. Very uncool, bro," Fred commented, as if reading Jimmy's mind. "He discovered them just a few months ago and now he can't control himself."

Jimmy pushed Raul and his emojis out of his mind and kept brainstorming. The sun continued to set. The horizon changed colours constantly against the darkening ocean.

"The sky is on fire tonight. Maybe the Red Virgin is telling us something?" Fred mused.

"What did you just say?" Jimmy asked. He felt like he was close, as if the suggestion of an idea had appeared before him. He had to spot it before it sunk out of sight.

"The sky, look at it. It looks like it's on fire." Jimmy nodded. Then he started to hum a tune and sing a few random lyrics. He was closer now.

"Amigo, your voice sucks. Please don't give up your day job!" Then, at last, Jimmy found what he was looking for. The sign was clear. He stood up and punched the air furiously, like a boxer training with a punching bag.

"YES! YES! Flipping YES!"

Fred just stared at his friend and thought he had finally lost his mind.

"Of course, it's the *only* way!" Jimmy raised two hands triumphantly, like Rocky Balboa's victory celebration against Apollo Creed.

"The universe, or your Red Radish Virgin, has finally spoken to me."

"And what did she say, amigo?"

"Like you said, the sky is on fire. It's time for . . . *Red's Hot!*"

TWENTY-SEVEN

Police Academy

RAMON IGNATIUS LOPEZ WAS the goody-two-shoes of the family, and the least academic of the two Lopez children. Acknowledged as the runt of the small litter, Ramon was an average student with limited sporting prowess. Like his brother, he was made to study languages, but unlike his brother, with his affinity for all things academic, he barely scraped by with a pass in English.

Much to the chagrin of his family, Ramon decided at an early age he wanted to work in law enforcement, having seen old episodes of *Kojak, Columbo*, and *Ironside* on cable TV. Telly Savalas's detective style, in particular, heavily influenced him. He shaved his head and was never seen without a lollypop in his mouth.

Ramon made up for his lack of intelligence with an exceptionally active imagination. He walked around his home taking notes and interviewing family members about their involvement in the cartel, which didn't go down too well with his father. Loco Moco had a heart-to-heart with the lad, having found volumes of journals all entitled 'My 'Lil Evidence Book of Murder, Extortion and Corruption' under Ramon's bed. However, he could see his simpleton son was 'special' and had a soft spot for him. This led him to take a kinder approach than he might have otherwise.

"Son, if you keep a record of our family's dealings, the Yankees may get hold of them and put your father in a Super Max prison in Texas."

"But Papa, I want to make the world a better place."

"And I want to make *Mexico* a better place. I am making it safer for all of us to live in. One day, your big brother Armardo will run our empire, and I'd like you to be fully behind him. After all, we are family."

Ramon took his lollypop from his mouth, ran his hands over his smooth head, and thought for many moments. His father waited patiently before he replied.

"I love Armardo, and I love my Papa. But I want to solve crimes. My school grades are too poor to enter Universidad de Guadalajara to study law and criminology. I don't even think I will pass the police entrance exam."

"Why not kill two birds with one stone?"

"How, Papa?"

"Diversity and inclusion, son. Our country has taken great strides in making our society a fairer and more *inclusive* place to live. One day, there will be a tidal wave of all things liberal, and equity and equality will come upon us. We are on the precipice of a new dawn. One of tolerance, fairness, liberty, justice, and racial parity."

"That sounds wonderful, Papa."

"Wonderful? It's a croc of shit. Those mindless cartel goat-shaggers in Colombia want a piece of our pie. Yes, they will try to muscle into our narcotics and sex trade operations by accusing us of not supporting the body positivity movement. They will judge us for our internalized misogyny, the intersectionality of privilege, discrimination and racism."

Ramon listened intently. His papa used complicated words he did not understand, yet he nodded in agreement.

"The Colombian cartels will point their lefty, cancel culture fingers at us in an attempt to slander our cartel. They accuse us of cultural and male appropriation, with their 'cis' this and 'gender binary' that, highlighting our so-called 'microaggressions.'" As he spoke, Loco Moco was foaming at the mouth, and Ramon's face was getting covered in spittle.

To avoid drowning in his father's saliva, Ramon interrupted his diatribe and asked, "Papa, what do you want me to do?"

The Don walked away without answering his youngest son. Actions, after all, are louder than words. Ramon waited in bewilderment, until a few hours later, Loco Moco Lopez called his son into the front yard. He hurried from his bedroom to meet his father, who was standing in the driveway with a wheelchair by his side.

"Son, this is how you will get through the police entrance exams."

Ramon was thrilled. He climbed into the wheelchair and exclaimed: "I am Police Chief Robert T. Ironside."

"Ramon, the new inclusion and diversity policy of the Federal Police Commission will waive your entry requirements due to their dystopian liberal dogma and ideologies, and you will become the detective you've always wanted to be."

Ramon wheeled around the yard on his new device, and soon after, his father got him a rumpled beige raincoat like his other TV detective hero, Lieutenant Columbo. He was so attached to the wheelchair his mother contracted workers to make the vast staircase in the family home wheelchair accessible.

He entered the police academy in his wheelchair and underperformed in his classes. To make matters worse, he was caught by his roommate out of his chair, exercising in their bedroom. However, his creativity and his roommate's stupidity saved the day. Ramon claimed he had fallen out of his wheelchair and a miracle had happened: he could now use his legs, and was doing squat thrusts, star jumps, and press-ups to celebrate. His roommate, Uriah Baños, believed his story, and they became great friends. Wherever Lopez was assigned, Baños went with him, and they developed a wonderful camaraderie. Ramon's teachers were impressed by his grit and resilience to overcome his disability, so they kept promoting him even before he completed his training and continuously overlooked his poor performance.

After graduating from the academy at a very young age as Chief Commissary, or *Comisario*, the fourth highest-ranking officer in the Federal Police, Ramon started his first position in Guadalajara, much to the chagrin of all the other officers.

The new normal within the Federal Police was to reduce barriers to employment. *Comisario* Lopez took advantage of his employer's generosity and lack of common sense by requesting and receiving a specially equipped police truck that doubled as an armoured assault vehicle with a 360-degree turret—so he could be less hindered going to and from Costco. He also recalled that his wheelchair-bound detective hero, Ironside, had a unique attic floor built in at police HQ, and asked to be granted a similar accommodation. The Secretariat of Security, Fairness and Civilian Protection quickly got to work and made one, costing the taxpayers $117 million.

Although they agreed making Mexico's law enforcement more diverse and accessible was a positive step forward, Ramon's colleagues were aghast at how ineffective he was as the most senior police officer in the city. His fake disability protected him from any consequences, but it could not shield him from his own stupidity. His deception fell apart one day when a reporter from *La Figarola* was walking her dog in González Gallo Park and saw a man hiding his wheelchair in some bushes behind the children's playground. Intrigued, she kept watching him, and saw the man don a ridiculous fake beard and run around the race track several times at breakneck speed, with a uniformed colleague timing him using a stopwatch.

The reporter confronted the two men and realized she was dealing with the new 19-year-old *Comisario*, Ramon Lopez. Ramon tried to explain he was in training for the Paralympics. He furthered the lie by saying non-disabled and disabled competitors were allowed to compete because of the Olympic committee's new inclusion and diversity policy. The reporter, much to his surprise, did not believe him, and sprinted back to the newspaper HQ. The following day, the story ran, and the headline on the front page was:

Lying Chief of Police Involved in Disability Scam.

The reporter disappeared, never to be seen again, and the editor received a hostile and highly threatening call from the *Comisario's* father, the head of the Wolfpack Cartel.

The following paper edition retracted the reporter's story. It printed:

Miracle at the Park by Maria Tortuga: "Severely disabled police officer healed by Rábanos evangelist. Reverend Bonkers met and prayed with the young Police Chief and told him to "get up and run like Forest Gump." After the laying on of hands, Chief Commissary Lopez felt the power of the Red Lady upon himself, threw a stopwatch at eyewitness and heroic fellow officer Uriah Baños, and then sprang from his chair and ran several laps around the athletic track at breakneck speed."

Although the story quietened the public and ended any further investigation, the Federal Police knew they had been caught with their trousers down and subtly demoted Ramon to Inspector, with a caveat he attended detective school in Chihuahua, sans wheelchair. He would also have to accept a posting to the quiet town of Los Piñata once he had perfected his investigative skills, which they were confident would take multiple lifetimes.

Ramon graduated from detective school with an E+. He met his wife-to-be, a Germanic Colombian named Shelley Ardengrupel, when conducting a routine investigation into a cupcake theft at her bakery in Chihuahua. The new Detective Inspector had been seconded to the city to give him some much-needed experience, due to his inability to solve the most straightforward of crimes.

He fell in love with Shelley's big blue eyes, cute ski-sloped nose, and fantastic baking skills, and quickly married her. They remained happily wedded in Chihuahua for a season, until Ramon became conscious something was 'off.' He was becoming unwell. He found it painful to swallow, felt nauseous, and struggled with diarrhoea. His face, neck, arms and hands broke out with painless skin ulcers with an ugly black centre. Unbelievably, his Colombian lover had tried to poison him with her anthrax-laden 'Death-by-Chocolate' torte, to which he was particularly partial. Thankfully, the Inspector survived due to an aggressive course of intravenous antibiotics and antitoxins.

Ramon put one and one together and, realizing Shelley had been lacing cakes and pastries for several years before their meeting, cracked a series of unsolved homicides in the city. Shelley Ardengrupel was known to police as 'The Cupcake Killer,' and she had been at large for several years. Shelley took a plea deal and went to work for Mexico's bioterrorist unit, creating new and innovative ways to kill off rival Colombian cartel members en masse.

Despite the attempt on his life, Ramon and Shelley remained good friends, as he couldn't get enough of her damned cupcakes. Ms Ardengrupel-Lopez shared with her ex-husband she had discovered ways of infecting Colombia's favourite snacks, *Postre de Natas* and *Arepas*, with a hybrid strain of Ebola and Bubonic plague. The Lopez family was overjoyed Shelley had turned her life around and was helping the Wolfpack Cartel to eradicate the Colombians and cement their status as the supreme cartel in the Central and South Americas.

Ramon eventually returned to Los Piñata as lead detective, where he became an integral part of Armardo's cartel empire. He was living the dream and making the world a better place, just as he had proclaimed to his papa Loco Moco back in the day.

~»»> <«««~

ARMARDO HAD RECEIVED a call from his brother, Ramon, who shared the news the gringo had been caught dealing drugs at *El Macron* and arrested, booked and interviewed . . . only for Fred Montana to appear dramatically and bail him out for $100,000. After that, according to Ramon, "the two lovers headed off into the sunset."

Armardo knew it would be difficult for Jimmy to leave Mexico, as he had already arranged for his brother to break into the flimsy safe and take his passport and the money he'd given him. At first, when Ramon told him of the gringo's arrest, he was overjoyed. He had planned on using the gringo for many special favours that could be helpful to him in the future. It didn't matter that the money he 'owed' the cartel was, in fact, stolen under Armardo's orders; lending him money in the first place was just part of a ruse to get him into the cartel's debt without any hope of escape. As soon as Jimmy revealed his money troubles, Armardo realized he would be a promising gringo stooge. He had even hoped the louse would be able to help the cartel to open a new distribution network in British Columbia. Armardo would own him ad infinitum so the arrogant gringo would be, literally and metaphorically, shagged. Even without his arrest, he had the perfect leverage: Jimmy's wife and child were still staying in Los Piñata for a couple of months, and he would never share he had been caught dealing drugs. He was just begging to be blackmailed. Raul would be very disappointed at having to keep him alive a while longer, but after the gringo outlived his usefulness, Armardo would declare open season on Jimmy and let his godson do his thing.

However, when he learned Fred had posted bail, all his happiness evaporated. Armardo clenched his fist, and his face went the colour of an over-ripe radish. He felt the betrayal keenly, and it caused him almost as much suffering as his constipation had. Why did that idiot of a leprechaun get involved? Where did he get the money from? Armardo's mind flooded with visions of Fred and Jimmy drinking Amador 1836 tequila and reciting poetry to each other. His disloyal snake of a godson must have dipped his hands into the Wolfpack's finances.

Armardo had raised the twins as if they were his sons; he could never have imagined this is how he would be repaid. He knew he could trust Raul implicitly. He had entrusted him with his own life on several occasions, and the unflappable sicario had even taken a bullet in the shoulder for him a few years back. Fred had never been that reliable, but Armardo thought he could at least count on him to follow orders and manage the money. He hadn't just crossed a line; he had jumped over it with his size three shoes. Now, it was up to his brother to clear up his mess. Armardo texted Raul to contact him ASAP.

It was late, and Raul lay on his bed, fully clothed, with his pink sombrero on the chair next to the bedside table. Raul hastily obeyed and called his boss, who sounded like he was losing his mind. Their conversation was short and sweet. The Don told him his brother had used the Wolfpack's money to bail the gringo out of jail. Myers needed to be found, severely chastened, and brought before Armardo, face-to-face, so the boss could witness him cry, plead and pray like the little bitch he was. Then they'd put him to work getting back their money.

"Bring them back alive. You can deal with Myers once his debt is paid. As for your brother, I am a man of mercy. We must reprogram his thinking as he's become a gringo."

"W-w-w-what if they r-r-refuse to c-c-come back with me?"

"If the shit hits the fan, do what you must. Take your icebox, and cut off three of Fred's stubby little fingers and Myers's left foot if necessary. That should keep them from running"

"Yes, Boss."

Raul put his phone back into his jacket pocket. Shaking his head, he checked his reliable Belgian-made FN 5.7 and cleaned the mechanism. He also had his trusty machete in his car, along with knuckledusters, zip ties, head bags and a mixed container of Ativan, roofies, and Adderall.

Despite the promise of vengeance, his heart was sad. He hated that the boss would punish Fred. After all, it was all the gringo's fault. He had corrupted his brother, turning him against the family. He was the one who should be punished. Raul imagined Jimmy was one of his pillows that lay on his bed, and he started to punch it, over and over again, roaring and cursing, until the pillow exploded and feathers filled the room.

He looked at his fists covered in feathers. He thought of how good it would feel to see the gringo's blood on his knuckles instead. His anger somewhat sated; he reached over to the chair, grabbed his pink sombrero, placed it back on his head, and headed towards his car.

TWENTY-EIGHT

Red-Hot Plan

LUCY AND MAC WERE hanging out on the outside patio, playing a fun game with Max, when Jimmy suddenly appeared with Fred. She tried to keep a calm front for Max, but she could have cried. He'd been away all night and most of the day, and with the cartel looming over them and the debt to Armardo, her mind went to all sorts of horrible places. To make matters worse, she couldn't go to the police, as they were more likely to hurt Jimmy than help him. All she could do was wait with Max, keep him from asking questions, and hope her husband would return.

"Hello stranger, where have you been?" she asked as Max ran over and gave his dad a hug.

"I was playing *RISK* with Inspector Lopez, Fred, and Tequila Tommy," he answered.

Her eyes narrowed, "Inspector Lopez? Why would you ever play a game with him?" Already, she doubted Jimmy was telling the truth. But he seemed nonchalant, and the words came easily.

"We played for money, which allowed me to own him for once." Jimmy gave Max a kiss on the top of his head, and then went over to Lucy and planted one on her cheek.

"Phew! You smell, dude," she grimaced, pushing him away playfully. "Like a homeless guy just released from the drunk tank."

"That's the Inspector's aftershave. He tried to give me a big kiss to tempt me not to take his fifty bucks, but I resisted . . . so he gave Fred a pash instead," Jimmy said with a wry smile. He then walked into the condo, leaving Fred to regale Lucy with the story of the game they hadn't played. There was just one problem: he'd never heard of *RISK*. He needed another distraction.

"What's a pash?" Fred asked. She had gotten up to follow Jimmy into the condo, and his question stopped her in her tracks.

"A snog, a deep and sloppy kiss," she replied, looking back at Max. They had been playing a game, which the boy had returned to. He had to be watched like a hawk, as he tended to cheat at whatever game he played.

"Huh. Yes, Lopez did do that. He's a funny guy, that Jimmy," Fred said. He didn't know what Jimmy was saying. His buddy had asked him to distract Lucy so he could go into the condo and grab a few essential items without her knowing what he was up to. He was also conscious his pink-hatted brother was on his way, and they both had to disappear sooner rather than later.

"So, Jimmy won the game?" quizzed Lucy.

"He sure did!" Fred lied.

"He always does when he plays with newbies. Did he unbutton his shirt, jump on the table, and shout 'beat you, you losers' with a big, fat smirk on his face?"

"Oh yes, he certainly did that. He got so carried away he undid his zipper and showed Inspector Lopez his pecker, telling him he had the biggest dick in the Americas!"

"What? No way," spluttered Mac.

"Yes, way. His victory celebration went pear-shaped, and he was arrested for indecent exposure and spent the night in jail."

Lucy groaned. "He spent the night in *jail*?"

Fred could see her composure was on the brink of failing and knew his story had gone too far. "Just kidding, ha-ha, he was just irritating Lopez and me. Jimmy only won fifty bucks. You'd have thought he'd won the lottery."

"So, my husband *didn't* expose himself?" At that moment, Jimmy came back outside with a small backpack. She looked back at him, her expression somewhere between a smile and a grimace.

"Your pal is a wind-up merchant. Where are you off to now?"

"Have to dash, Luce. I'm assuming you're okay with me going out again? We promised Raymond—"

"Who's Raymond?"

"Raymond Lopez, AKA Inspector Dumbass, my new cop buddy-not-buddy. We promised him we'd return for a 'double or quits' game of *Poetry for Neanderthals*. Fred is bound to win."

Lucy knew full well her husband had loathed 'Raymond' until yesterday; she still did. Jimmy and Fred's story got more unbelievable the more they told it, but they were already on their way out, and yelling at him to stop seemed like a bad move in front of Max. Besides, he had a smile on his face and seemed more animated than he had in days. Perhaps, despite all odds, he really had turned things around with the Inspector. She sighed, kissed him, and tried to be happy he'd found new friends. The trouble was these new pals had connections to the cartel, but so long as he was safe, she couldn't complain. Well, she could complain about one thing: he really needed to wash.

"Please don't come back smelling any worse than you do now, hon."

Jimmy kissed Max again, pecked Lucy on the cheek, and ran down the stairs to the pool area with Fred trailing in hot pursuit.

"We can't go to my apartment. Raul will head there after he's been to your place. Bob's or Bradley's might work, or better yet, I have another safe house we can use that no one knows about," Fred told him once they were both by the pool. Jimmy nodded and kept hurrying to the car. They could figure the rest out on the way to wherever they were going. He didn't like the idea of Raul showing up to harass Lucy and Max, but they wouldn't be safe anyway until he carried out his plan. The sooner he got the money, and the less Lucy knew, the better.

The two amigos jumped into Fred's black SUV, with its modified seats and pedals so he could drive it without any hindrance. Fred prayed to the Red Virgin that his pal had a cunning plan.

⤜⟫⟫⟫ ⟪⟪⟪⤛

FRED AND JIMMY sped off from the condo, kicking up dust behind them. Both of their stress levels were rising by the minute. Raul Montana was hot on their tails, and Fred knew they had to try to buy some time to delay and confuse his bloodhound of a brother.

"So, you have a plan, amigo?"

"Yup, but you'll have to trust me implicitly."

"Okay, but I've only known you for a few weeks."

"You trusted me enough to put your life on the line, using the cartel's money to get me out of the interview room with Inspector Knobhead Lopez."

Fred grinned, "Oh, 'Raymond,' your new game-playing buddy. That's not even his name. It's Ramon."

"Do I look like I care about that nutbar's name? You pulled me out of the doo-dah, and now I will return the favour and pull you *and* me out of even more doo-dah."

"Doo-dah?"

"You just have to trust me."

"Are you going to tell me your brilliant plan, or what?"

"Yes, I will, but you've got to be all in, or it won't work." Fred, with time against him and nowhere else to turn, nodded vigorously. Internally, however, he dreaded hearing what idea the gringo had cooked up. Typically, if you had a good plan, you didn't ask people to trust you before you even shared it.

"We only have a few hours."

"To do what?"

"For me to explain the plan to you."

"Not if Raul finds us first. He's texted me several times now. I'll have to take out my SIM card and replace it with another one."

Fred was sure Raul wouldn't appear at his secret location, which is where he decided to go. He knew his brother and was aware of how he thought. Firstly, he would visit his original apartment, stay there with the lights turned off, and wait for them to turn up. He'd probably be there until daybreak, then try to close in on them. He'd visit anyone who might know where Jimmy and Fred were. He might even call in some favours from Jimmy's new cop pal, 'Raymond,' to ping his phone.

Jimmy shared if everything went according to plan, they would have a bucket full of cash for Don Armardo. After their cash windfall, he would head to Guadalajara, sort it out with the boss, and get a new passport from the Canadian Consulate. Then, he would return to Los Piñata to pick up Lucy and Max and leave Mexico. That plan involved a lot of risks; Guadalajara was a veritable Wolfpack Cartel fortress. But every second counted against them, so they had to move quickly rather than carefully. There wasn't enough time for both.

Once they arrived at Fred's other place, Jimmy emptied the backpack he'd taken from his apartment onto the bed. He and Fred gazed at the contents that were now lying on his duvet: Max's plastic water pistol, Jimmy's earbuds, two uninflated plastic armbands, a muesli bar, some children's sunscreen, and two colourful booklets. Jimmy picked up the booklets and tossed one at Fred.

"Hey, is this *your* book?"

Jimmy nodded.

"And . . . shit, is that *you* on the front cover?"

Jimmy smiled proudly.

"You look like a Satan-worshipping serial killer," Fred said with a chuckle before going on to read the cover. "*Red's Hot!* Cool, bro, I'm on the run with a Z-list celebrity. Has anyone ever told you this book looks incredibly tacky? Who designed the graphics—Stevie Wonder?" Jimmy's smile fell.

With a mischievous grin, Fred read the booklet cover in a comical Stevie Wonder voice, pretending to play the piano. "Yo! This is a book to inspire and help all the poor people." He lifted his eyes and snorted, "Amigo, this is some crazy shit!"

"Can you just read it and stop taking the piss? Never mind the graphic artwork or my gorgeous photo. Let me coach you and infuse your tiny little brain with the *Red's Hot!* doctrine, and we'll get out of this mess," Jimmy snapped, swiping the book away from Fred.

"So, it's a book about gambling?" Fred's smile gone now. Jimmy was pleased to see he was ready to get serious.

"Not necessarily. Gambling implies there's a chance of losing. If you follow my method to the letter, you're guaranteed money."

"I like the confidence. But it's about roulette, right?"

Jimmy nodded.

"So, it *is* about gambling."

"No, if you just shut up for a moment and listen to me, you can do what I did."

"Which was?"

"You'll walk away from the casino with mega money, an amount beyond your wildest dreams."

"Okay, Mr Red Hot-shot, why do I have to do it when you have the experience?" Jimmy hesitated before responding.

"I swore to Lucy I'd never do it again, and I've still got my integrity." He might be on the run from a psychopathic murderer in a bright pink sombrero, with the Wolfpack Cartel nipping at his heels, but he was doing this for her and Max. He couldn't break the promise he'd made.

"Integrity? Amigo, you left that behind at the station. You're a drug dealer who's lied to his wife already, and you're in debt to the Wolfpack Cartel. Your book says you can walk into the casino with one dollar and walk out with twenty million, and our lives are on the line. Right now, we need the guy who wrote the playbook, not the guy who's never used it," Fred protested. Jimmy grimaced; Fred wasn't entirely wrong. He had lied to Lucy, and though innocent of almost all charges levied against him, he was now technically a criminal. Still, there was a lot about his method the sicario didn't understand, and he wouldn't back down.

"Even if I did break my promise, you really think some pale-faced gringo strutting into a casino isn't going to raise some red flags? I'd stand out from a mile away—look at what I'm wearing!" Fred looked at his friend's attire and almost broke out into a grin. He did look ridiculous with his red 'Pinch My Ass—I'll Buy You a Beer' vest from the gift exchange, light blue cargo shorts and dirt-encrusted Nike flip-flops on sockless feet.

"I can lend you my clothes," Fred said unhelpfully. Jimmy looked at him, blinked a few times, and then pulled a 'you cannot be serious' John McEnroe face.

"Your clothes wouldn't even fit an Action Man or a Ken and Barbie doll."

"Come on, that's hyperbole. My trendy clothes might be tight on you, but I am deceptively broad-chested."

"It has to be you. It's all or nothing." Jimmy insisted.

"Why? I've never played roulette in my life. I've never even set foot in a casino," Fred muttered, looking down at the floor. For the first time, Jimmy realized Fred's objection to his plan might be rooted in self-doubt.

"You can do this. I believe in you. The plan is foolproof. You just need to follow my instructions to the absolute letter, and you'll be fine."

Fred reluctantly nodded.

"This is how it goes down. We drive to the casino. I'll wait for you in the car. You'll wear my EarPods, so you can listen to me or the playlist I've compiled. You walk into the place with your 'I'm a big, tough Wolfpack Cartel sicario, so don't you dare mess with me' vibe."

"And then what?"

"You follow the plan. If you waver even slightly from my instructions, you will fail, epically, and we will both be dead, just like Vincente—if we're lucky."

"Hey, I don't know what happened to the Colombian. Don Armardo doesn't involve me in certain things because he thinks I'm too soft. After all, I write poetry and hate crocodiles."

"But they'd love to eat you, which is exactly what's going to happen if you screw this up."

Fred sighed and threw up his hands in defeat. Then they sat on the queen-size bed and thumbed through the book, as Jimmy explained how his very first time playing roulette would be the game of his life.

Twenty-Nine

Mystery Unravelled

RAUL MONTANA SELDOM DOFFED his pink sombrero, as it was part and parcel of his identity. He had learned not to speak to others too much, as when he did, he would hear himself stammer. Raul didn't have speech issues when talking to himself in the mirror, and he never stammered when singing in the shower or when he was alone with Fred. But while he struggled with verbal communication, he could read nonverbal signs better than anyone. Raul understood body language and could smell people's fear and their lies, although he dearly wished he had his twin brother's confidence. Instead of talking, Raul observed and listened. If a higher diploma were awarded for active listening skills, Raul would have earned it with honours.

He knew who Don Armardo should and shouldn't trust. Jimmy the gringo was in the latter category. How dare he complain to that little cretin, Vincente, about the *noise level*? Vincente's blood was now on the gringo's hands. It was his moronic whinging that had led to the property manager's disappearance.

The little worm from Bogotá had dared to approach his boss and ask him to be more mindful of the casa's rules regarding noise levels. Vincente mentioned he had friends in high places and winked at the boss. When asked who he was referring to, he had the gall to puff out his chest and mention Raymond and the CIA. The boss nearly busted a nut with laughter. He warned Don Armardo he may have to ask his contingent to leave the condo. It was shocking. Did this runt not know who he was speaking to? Suddenly, the little creep with the pearly-white teeth had grown a massive pair of *cojones*.

The boss had paid a lot of money to bring Pedro Cordoba's sound and lighting system from Mexico City, the very same system that had been used for the Miguel Fernandez concert that held 90,000 adoring fans at the Estadio Azteca. Vincente had to learn respect.

The cockroach then dared to print those stupid rules in poster format and place them on the walls under the palapa. Don Armardo had been incensed: "By order *of this*, and by order *of that*; how dare he!"

At first, the boss appeared to listen to Vincente's request. The property manager reminded the cartel boss the Mexicans were sharing the area with the Myers family, the music levels had to be reasonable, he didn't have to use over one hundred woofers and subwoofers, and sarcastically added the music could probably be heard in Melbourne, Australia. Vincente had also gone on and on about the importance of good reviews for the thriving of his business—as if that was Don Armardo's responsibility.

The boss had listened attentively, nodded affirmatively, and then patted Vincente on the shoulder. The boss said, "I'll do anything to comply with a request from a fellow South American brother. Especially one with *friends in high places*. We don't want to upset our Canadian neighbours, eh?" Don Armardo switched his gaze from Vincente to Raul and then back to Vincente. He gave the property manager a sweet smile, lifted his hand, and gave him a bye-bye sign.

Raul had been given the green light to help Vincente learn some much-needed respect, so he put his large hands around Vincente's throat and squeezed with his vice-like grip, then lifted him several inches off the ground. Vincente's legs kicked back and forth like he was on the receiving end of a hangman's noose. The property manager's eyes were bugging out of their sockets, and his face went from bright red to ashen.

Don Armardo came close to Vincente's ear as if he were going to whisper something to him. Instead, he broke into melodic song: "This town ain't big enough for the both of us, and it isn't me that's gonna leave."

Raul tightened his grip, turned his head to the boss, and smiled.

"I l-l-love that s-s-s-song, boss. S-s-sparks. V-v-vintage n-n-nineteen s-s-seventy-four." Vincente spluttered out some unintelligible words, and Don Armardo's smile morphed into a sneer.

"Say hello to your God when you see him; after all, he is your only *friend in a very high place.*"

Vincente made one more desperate gurgling sound, and then his body went limp. The boss stared at it, dangling in Raul's iron grip, and let out a barking laugh.

"However, as you asked nicely, I'll ask my family and associates to reduce the volume," Don Armardo sneered—then he looked over to Raul.

"Get rid of the little shit, but keep his head. Someone might need it to model a radish for *Noche de Rábanos*, so put it in the freezer. Cut off his lips—he talked too much in life; may it not be so in death. Make the miserable little turd look happier, and don't tell your brother. We'll find someone else to do his job; he's no longer cut out for environmental disposals." The boss spoke casually, as if he was asking Raul to take out the garbage.

"Body to the cr-cr-cr-crocodiles again, boss?"

A smile spread across Don Armardo's face as he gave him a thumbs up.

Raul beamed. After the boss left him to do his work on Vincente, he looked at the Colombian's contorted, lifeless face. He always had enjoyed practising his skills with a blade and hacksaw. Obeying his boss's direction, he gladly removed Vincente's lips. Then, Raul carved a friendly, toothy smile on the little worm. Once his work was done, he went to find one of the other sicarios.

The incident had only happened a few weeks ago, but it felt like an eternity. So much had changed between then and now. He wasn't quite sure if he hated Canadians more than Americans, English or the Welsh. As smug as Vincente had been, Jimmy had been even worse. He smiled and laughed and ate his grilled cheese fingers while he and his wife plied the Lopezes, Raul, and his brother with Imodium-laced stew. He spat in the face of the boss's kindness. He had taken Fred. Raul wanted nothing more than to have the gringo in his clutches, turn to his boss, and receive 'the look' that told him he could finally put his hands around the gringo's scrawny neck . . . or worse.

JIMMY AND FRED visited Mella's house to ask her and her pals for a favour: to delay and frustrate Raul for as long as possible. He said they were in a dire situation and needed their help, and asked them not to alarm Lucy. Things were in hand, but they needed an assist with some delay tactics.

JayBee helpfully suggested they drop by and ask the 'boys,' as they were full of mischief and had no fear of creating drama and chaos. She was happy to call Bradley and Marcus to save Jimmy time if they didn't want to help. Jimmy thought back to the Quiz Nite and the gift exchange, and realized they would be the perfect distraction. Hugging the amigas, he thanked them, bid them farewell, and blew them a kiss.

Then the dynamic duo drove to the boys' home. Bradley had been super-annoying with his never-ending barrage of stupid questions. He also ruined Jimmy's chance of winning the 'Quiz Nite' at Tequila Tommy's. That said, Jimmy felt both him and his husband were brave beyond belief. They showed no trepidation at the gift exchange event, taking Armardo's treasured gift from his wife and exchanging it for a blow-up sheep. He was worried at the time, but now knowing how corrupt Armardo was, he was glad the boys had the *cojones* to do the dirty deed.

They turned up at the boys' beautiful, luxury orange home by the ocean, desperate for their help. Pink sombrero would be just one step behind, and that step was getting smaller and smaller by the minute. Jimmy knew he would be asking something incredibly dangerous of the couple, and part of him felt guilty for the position he was about to put them in. But they had offended Armardo once and lived; surely, they could do it again. The cartel might be able to kill a random gringo and get away with it, but offing two Hollywood producers would draw the attention of U.S. law enforcement.

When Jimmy and Fred arrived, the boys embraced the odd couple warmly. Jimmy was direct and to the point, well-aware time was of the essence. Marcus shared that JayBee had given them a quick synopsis of the situation. Jimmy nodded, and the fugitives said they were in a giant pickle and desperately needed their help.

"We love pickles," blurted Marcus.

Jimmy explained the pink sombrero was after both of them, and they were as good as dead unless he was delayed and distracted. Buying them time could help them to make everything right again.

"And how exactly do you think the gayest men in Hollywood are going to stop a hitman?" Marcus asked.

"You guys have the biggest balls we have ever seen," Fred replied, stone-faced. At this, Bradley let out a cry of excitement and clapped his hands.

"When did you see my hubby's super-sized gonads?" Marcus turned radish-red. "Seriously, Marcus, you'll need to buy a wheelbarrow to carry those big balls of yours around if they get any bigger."

"They are what they are," Marcus replied bashfully, looking below his belt. Jimmy's eyes were wide open; Fred guffawed.

"Are we really having this discussion now?" Jimmy asked. It was no use; Marcus and Bradley were in a world of their own.

"It's true, you know. Sometimes, I use them as floatation devices when we swim in the nude." Marcus spoke to Jimmy and Fred. The red in his face was subsiding; his embarrassment hadn't even lasted a minute.

Bradley exaggeratedly nodded and said, "Remember those 'Space hopper' things?"

"People called them 'Hippity Hoppers' in America," pointed out Marcus matter-of-factly.

"All my Marcus would need was to paint his gonads orange, and then we could use his bally-bags to bounce our way around town."

Jimmy coughed and then interrupted before Bradley managed to go even more off-topic. "Alright, that's enough. This was too much information thirty seconds ago. Any other time I'd love to compare your partner's testicles to a giant orange space hopper from the 1970s, but right now we have to move."

"You're right, you're right. So, the pink sombrero is looking for you and Fred?" Bradley asked, getting back on topic. Jimmy nodded.

"His hat's a nice shade of pink, but his personality sure sucks," scoffed Marcus.

"He has a personality?" Bradley asked bitchily.

"Raul is going to visit you and the amigas eventually. When he comes, all we need you to do is keep him here as long as possible," pleaded Fred. His humour had gone and his voice carried an edge of agitation. Fred didn't like people insulting his brother, but now wasn't the time to mention anything. He just had to get the couple on task.

"Can we use handcuffs?" Bradley asked suggestively.

"Sweetie, let's be serious for a minute. They need our help," said Marcus, looking at the friendly fugitives again. "Of course, darlings, we can delay him. We can even point him in the wrong direction."

"Where do you want us to send him to?" Bradley asked, looking a little more serious—but not much.

"Guadalajara," answered Jimmy.

The boys clapped their hands, gave their visitors high-fives and sent them on their way. Before they left, however, Fred gave them a warning. "Remember not to piss him off too much. I know you are Hollywood people, and your notoriety keeps you safe around these parts, but if he sees red, he stops thinking. Then he has no impulse control."

Jimmy pulled his pal towards the doorway.

"On the subject of RED, we had better be off!"

As they climbed back into the car and headed towards the casino, Jimmy felt immense gratitude to these two fearless souls and hoped he would be able to pay back this colossal favour one day.

THIRTY

Red is Hot!

FRED DROVE TOWARDS PUEBLO de Velásquez's oversized, recently-built casino. It was run entirely by the Wolfpack Cartel, as it was an excellent way of laundering vast amounts of money.

Fred took a deep breath and shook his head, "They will lose their shit if this pays off."

"On the other hand, *when* it pays off, we can pay back what we owe and expose flaws in their system. It's a win-win. It should only take thirty to forty-five minutes once you start your *Red's Hot!* assault. Remember, they will have eyes and surveillance cameras on you as soon as you start your winning streak."

"And what if the casino manager contacts Don Armardo?"

Jimmy could tell from how his eyes darted this way and that, and the sweat forming on his brow, that the sicario was still nervous.

"Relax, I've thought of this. After the big win, you strut into the manager's office—and you can do this because you're Fred Montana, sicario and bag man for the Wolfpack Cartel with balls bigger than Marcus'. Once you're in, take out your gun and place it on the manager's forehead—" Jimmy used his two fingers and made his hand resemble a gun, "and tell him, 'This is a message from Armardo Angel Lopez. Tighten up your practice, you imbecile!'"

"Nice and subtle, then?"

"You dump the heavy bag of winning chips in front of him and tell him to open his safe and pay Armardo his winnings. Then you tell him to say nothing until the boss decides his punishment."

"You really think holding a gun to his head is the way to go?"

"It was pretty effective when you and your brother did it to me and my four-year-old son." Then, Jimmy continued to detail the rest of the *Red's Hot!* plan. Fred would get the winnings, deal with the manager, wipe the security tapes, grab the cash, exit the casino and get into the car.

"We'll be out of there before psycho pink sombrero boy arrives at the scene."

"Then what?"

"I guess we'll find a Burger King somewhere."

"BK? I'd much prefer a Signor Froggy."

Jimmy rolled his eyes. "I was being sarcastic, dumbass. I guess we'll cross that bridge when we come to it. We give Armardo half the winnings. I'll get my passport from Inspector Ass-face or go to Guadalajara and get a replacement from the consulate."

"Have you thought about how I explain conspiring with you, the ultimate badass gringo?"

"You can say you did it to expose flaws in the cartel's security process. The casino paid out millions because you used my awesome book. It could happen again. You proved that Armardo's brother, Inspector Shit-for-brains, is a complete dickhead for taking my money and passport. Show them they need someone better in law enforcement. Desperate times call for desperate measures and all that stuff."

Fred still looked doubtful, but nodded. Jimmy was speaking like a seer, as if he already knew for a fact the plan would work as he'd devised it. That confidence was infectious, even when it seemed so ill-advised.

"Whatever happens after, we'll be set for life, each with over twenty million dollars. You can fulfill your dream of being a deconstructed porn star—"

"*Poet.* A deconstructed revolutionary poet."

"Whatever. Half of that will surely sweeten the deal for Armardo."

Fred, however, was less worried about his godfather than his brother. The money might placate Don Armardo, but Raul wouldn't forgive so easily. He would see this as a grave betrayal, and their relationship might be forever damaged.

"As for Raul, maybe take him out for a few beers and buy him some pink lip gloss. It's his favourite colour, right?" Fred's eyes went wide in shock, and Jimmy chuckled.

"Relax, that was just a bit of pre-victory humour. You want to patch things up with your brother? Take care of your parents, help Raul get a girlfriend, pay for him to start up a hobby or something. Show him you still care about the family and give him a purpose that isn't killing innocent people." Jimmy was just rattling off whatever he thought might calm Fred down, and it seemed to work. The sicario nodded and breathed in, trying his best to steel himself. Jimmy gave him a pat on the back and leaned close to his face.

"None of that happens if this goes belly-up. So, what you need to do right now is start feeling *all things red*."

⤳⟫⟫⟩ ⟨⟨⟨⟪⤶

RAUL FINALLY ARRIVED in Los Piñata after sunset and decided to take a quick look for his brother and the gringo at Lucy's condo, then go to Fred's apartment near the centre of town. If he still hadn't found them, he'd scour the local area, asking cartel contacts and some of the gringo's friends. Raul could catch them both—it was just a matter of time. He checked his phone; no text from Fred. Raul, once again, typed a message to his brother: *Where are you?* His frustrated text included several angry face emojis, a machete emoji, a Mexican flag emoji, an Alamo emoji, a blonde girl emoji that looked like General Custer, and two coffin emojis. Man, he loved emojis.

He got no response.

The first thing Raul did was go to the Myers' home. He got out of the car and approached the condo, finding a spot where he could look up at the balcony. He saw the gringo's wife standing there. She was with a friend, one of the three who disgraced herself with Father Dominguez. The foul-mouthed boy, Max, was also by his mother's side. He watched them in silence for a minute before she looked over and saw him.

Raul couldn't tell, but a shiver went down Lucy's spine when she noticed him watching. She turned to her friend and said something, and the woman took the boy and led him inside the condo. Then, Lucy approached the balcony.

"Can I help you?" she asked.

"I'm l-l-loo-loo-looking for my b-b-b-br-br-brother F-F-Fr-Fred. I believe he w-w-w-was with your h-h-hus-hus-husband?"

"So, you're looking for your brother Fred? The guy with the black sombrero?"

Raul nodded.

"And Jimmy?"

Raul nodded again.

"You missed them. They left a few hours ago to play a game of *RISK* with some random guy called Raymond."

"R-r-r-risk? R-r-r-random? R-R-R-R-Raymond?" stammered Raul, who hated words that began with the letter R.

"Yes." Lucy didn't want to disclose that 'Raymond' happened to be Inspector Lopez.

Raul had no idea what Lucy was talking about. They were playing a game of *RISK*. What was this *RISK*? Who was Raymond? The only person called Raymond that Raul had ever known was Ramon Lopez's detective hero, Raymond Burr, from the TV show *Ironside*. Why was he random?

Gringos! They talked gibberish most of the time. But Jimmy and his brother were here a few hours ago, so Raul knew he was catching up with them slowly but surely. His fists clenched into tight balls. He tipped his sombrero towards Lucy, turned, and left the condo.

THIRTY-ONE

The Casino

JIMMY KNEW THE ROULETTE wheels at the Crystal Palace Casino in Pueblo de Velásquez were based on European tables. There was one green number on the roulette table, rather than some of the tables in Mexico that had two or possibly three non-red or black spaces. With that in mind, his book would do the rest. He reacquainted himself with the *Red's Hot!* doctrine and worked through the book, line by line, page by page.

He made a music playlist, including King Crimson, Red Fang, Heatwave, and the song 'Hot, Hot, Hot' by Buster Poindexter. The songs were all about feeling it, and Fred needed to *feel* it! However, for a man whose life was in jeopardy, Fred was being incredibly picky. He tested Jimmy's patience to the max.

"Can't I listen to Pink or Maroon 5?"

"No! They're not *red* enough."

"Oh, how about adding 'You Sexy Thing'? That's gotta be *hot* for sure."

Jimmy punched Fred in the arm; the music from the band Hot Chocolate was oxymoronic. The 'Hot' was excellent, but the 'Chocolate' was a colour that must be avoided at all costs. Even Earth, Wind and Fire were only partially hot, and partials were not 100% *feeling it*. Any diluted red would cause pink or sickly taupe colours.

"Focus, Fred. You can't risk messing it up. Just accept my playlist. Accept anything *full-blown* red and receive good-reds. Focus on red. You have to *feel* it

. . . *feel* the red, double the stake each time you win until you hit the forty-odd million mark! But whatever you do, *do not* think about BAD-red."

"Remind me, amigo, what is bad-red?"

"For the tenth time, bad-red is things like COVID-19-infected blood, Russian red wine, bloodshot eyes, or Salmonella-infested red meat."

"Why the heck would I think about Salmonella?"

"The more you think about that, the more you think about bad-red. Get it all out of your head, my little buddy."

Fred rolled his eyes, "Amigo, dude, I get it, I get it."

"You'd be shocked how easily bad-red can get into your mind, like a worm burrowing into your brain. So, just good-red all the way, baby! Now, how much seed money do you have left?"

"I have ten thousand dollars left of the Wolfpack Cartel's money."

"Perfecto."

The two amigos arrived at PV's casino via the highway. That way, at least Raul would only find them if Fred's car got spotted or someone ratted on them.

When they pulled into the parking lot, Fred asked if he should wear a disguise, like a ski mask or bandanna.

"Okay, you're walking into the casino as a four-foot-high little person wearing a sombrero the size of Saturn's rings. How can anyone disguise you?"

"Who's the little person?"

"Whatever, doesn't matter. Fred, you strut into the casino. You have *cojones* bigger than Marcus's Space Hopper bollocks. You strut up to the roulette table, sit down, and then go all in on red . . . and bring home the forty million bucks." He'd said it before, but he'd say it again, as many times as it took to brainwash Fred into believing in himself and the process. Fred just looked at Jimmy, taking in the pep talk.

"Fred, you are confident. You are one hundred per cent Mexican. You are red hot! *¡Estás al rojo vivo!*"

"*¡Estás al rojo vivo!*" shouted back the excited sicario.

They both exited the vehicle and chest-bumped each other. The height difference made it a bit awkward, but they were so pumped up that neither of them cared.

"If you want less distraction, put your earbuds in. I strongly advise you to listen to the playlist I made for you. Play the songs; they make you feel hotter than a hooker in Amsterdam."

Fred grinned.

"Wear reflective shades when you get to the roulette wheel. Don't ever listen to the croupiers; they are always utter wankers, just like Marcus the croupier was in Palm Springs. Don't even look at their name tag, in case the casino has read my book and has installed countermeasures."

"Countermeasures?"

"Yes, casino *countermeasures*. These include name tag badges and other distractions."

"I don't understand."

"Imagine you're on a roll and feeling red hot. Win after win after win. You are halfway to becoming rich beyond your wildest dreams—then you notice the croupier's name is José Meningitis or Amanda Rotting-Flesh."

"Come on, you really think they'd have names *that* gross?"

"Every single casino is desperate not to lose money, especially forty million dollars. They employ all sorts of countermeasures, and I've seen most of them: distracting name tags, seductive servers with massive tits and skimpy black outfits, complimentary non-red daiquiris. Some casinos use advanced countermeasures that even I have yet to learn about. Just keep your eyes on the prize and put them out of your mind."

"Good advice, amigo. You've thought of everything."

"Remember, your first bet is ten thousand dollars down on red, and after eleven bets, that will be twenty million, four hundred and eighty thousand. On the twelfth and final bet, take a breath, savour the moment, and put the entire twenty million buckaroonies back on red. Command the croupier to spin the wheel and say, 'Hit me, baby, one more time!' BOOM! Winner, winner, chicken dinner. Take the forty million dollars and head to the manager's office. Then, my friend, you know what to do."

RAUL WAS, ONCE again, on the prowl. He stopped his vehicle outside Mella's home. The lights were on, and someone appeared to be playing music. Donning his pink sombrero, he looked into the rearview mirror and went about placing it at the correct angle, adjusting it until he was satisfied. He checked his phone one more time, saw Fred still hadn't replied to his messages, and proceeded to the entry gate of the house.

Mella lived in a compact home with bright green security railings. Thankfully, the front door looked ajar. The gate creaked quite loudly when he opened and then closed it behind him. Then, drawn by the sound, two small and super yappy dogs appeared out of nowhere and started snarling, barking, and growling at him. Raul's flared trouser bottom suffered a bite from a terrier-cross dog with a savage underbite. He tried desperately to shake the dog off by kicking his leg outward. Meanwhile, the other mutt, an angry-looking sausage dog, latched onto Raul's other leg. Both dogs held onto his flapping trouser legs with gusto, growling and snarling. Raul was shaking both legs and, increasingly frustrated, was tempted to reach for his firearm.

"Chewy! Donald! Why are you making so much fuss?" yelled Mella from inside her home. Then, to add icing to the cake, a White Highland Terrier tore out of the house, jumped up at one of Raul's flailing arms, and bit down on his sleeve.

Mella appeared. "Donald, Chewy, Scotty. Let him go!"

The three dogs released their grip immediately, fell to the floor and stared at Raul, growling furiously. When she saw Raul, Mella burst out laughing.

"Come and see this!" she called out. JayBee appeared at the door and joined her friend in riotous laughter.

"They're good judges of character!" JayBee cried between laughing fits.

"Clearly, they're not enamoured by your presence," Mella said, finally addressing Raul. Although all three pooches were highly aggressive and had small dog complexes, they were also incredibly obedient and fell behind Mella immediately. They continued to snarl at the man with the pink sombrero.

Raul dusted his trousers and didn't take his eyes off the angry dogs. He was wary of them, but he was not a man for small talk, and got right down to business.

"I am l-l-l-looking for J-J-J-Jimmy Myers and my b-b-br-br-br—"

"Brother," finished Mella impatiently. Raul hated it when people finished his sentences. He hated this more than gringos and gringas combined, but not as much as Colombians. Or maybe Raul hated Canadians more and Colombians less. Recently, he hated them both so much he couldn't tell. Raul looked up at Mella and nodded. She was intoxicated, as was her friend.

"Look what the cat's dragged in," said JayBee.

"More like the dogs have dragged in," chuckled Mella.

"It's the man with the pink sombrero," JayBee added.

"Are you here to party with us ladies?" Mella asked, grinning.

"N-n-n-n-no, I just w-w-w-w-want—"

"A shag?" asked Mella, sounding hopeful. Raul blushed and declined the offer with a jerky shake of his head. He knew his stutter was getting as bad as it could get, but he had to push on.

"I'm loo-loo-loo-loo-looking fo-fo-fo-for—"

"A blowjob?" giggled JayBee.

"Sorry, but we don't do that kind of thing," smirked Mella.

"With strangers, anyway," JayBee clarified matter-of-factly. At this point, Raul was almost as uncomfortable as he'd been during his bout of constipation. His tanned face was bright red; if it got any brighter, it would be as red as a cranberry.

"J-J-J-J-Jimmy—"

"You want to give *Jimmy* a BJ?" asked JayBee. Raul couldn't tell if she was genuinely misunderstanding or just messing with him. He hated it either way.

"N-n-no, I n-n-n-n-need to f-f-f-f-f—"

"Fondle him?" Mella finished, trying her best not to laugh. Under any other circumstances she would've felt bad for humiliating the poor guy and his speech impediment, but he was a killer chasing her friend's husband. He had it coming.

"Pinky, you don't want to do that. Jimmy's a married man," JayBee advised, looking almost comedically serious.

"F-f-find him," Raul spluttered.

"Oh, you need to *find* Jimmy?"

Mella turned to JayBee, reiterating to her friend that Raul was looking for Jimmy. He nodded. His sombrero went up and down, which caused the dogs to snarl wildly and edge closer to him.

"So, you wanted to find Fred, and you're also looking for Jimmy?" asked JayBee. Raul nodded again.

The dogs inched closer to him each time his pink sombrero moved. They began to bark in unison. He could keep trying to talk, which was becoming impossible with the damned women being so inappropriate. It was like they were conspiring to make his stutter worse. Alternatively, he could make signals with his head, which seemed to incite the dogs into a violent frenzy. If he kept it up, they might even attack him again. *Yappy little rats.*

Mella and JayBee, meanwhile, laughed at seeing a grown-ass sicario terrified of three small dogs.

Mella turned serious for a moment, "I haven't seen the dynamic duo for days. Last I heard, they were looking for some important dude called Raymond."

Raul, realizing they would be no more help than Lucy, turned around and headed for the gate. That was all the cue the three dogs needed. They simultaneously went for Raul's trouser legs. Once again, the snarling pooches bit down on him. He wanted to pick up each one and bite their horrible, scrawny little necks off one by one. He imagined kicking each mongrel like a rugby ball over Mella's fence. The fingers of his gun hand wiggled involuntarily; any other time, he might have whipped out his pistol and blown their heads off.

However, Raul had to find Fred and the gringo, and this mystery guy called Raymond, and he was wasting time. Finally, he shook the dogs off, closed the gate behind him, entered his vehicle, and drove away.

"Strange dude," said Mella. She and JayBee returned to the house with the dogs, satisfied they had frustrated Raul's quest to find Jimmy and Fred.

THIRTY-TWO

All or Nothing!

CRYSTAL PALACE CASINO WAS bustling, as always. It was popular with the rich and famous, tourists, and some of the locals. The casino had a modern hotel attached to it and had courtesy buses running to and from it every hour.

Dressed in black, Fred strutted into the casino with a confident swagger. Initially, he wasn't recognized, as he rarely visited the casino. Transactions between the casino and the cartel typically came directly from the casino to Guadalajara HQ. He made a beeline to the finance desk and exchanged $10,000 for the respective chip values. Fred wasn't unaware the large amount of money he exchanged alerted security. Cameras zoomed in on him. He was quickly recognized as one of the sicario brothers, the little one with the black sombrero—*El gemelo pequeño que lleva el sombrero negro.*

Fred followed Jimmy's instructions to the letter. The *Red's Hot!* music playlist banged out *red hot* music in his earbuds. He visualized he was surrounded by flames under a burning, red-hot sun. Although he was sweating profusely, he reached the roulette table and sat down. A waitress approached him, and Fred ordered a Campari on the rocks. Although he disliked the drink's bitter taste, he wanted to embrace the red, as Jimmy had advised. He tipped his black sombrero at the croupier and adjusted his reflective sunglasses to fit his tiny nose.

Fred placed all his $10,000 worth of chips on the cloth-covered table, pushing them confidently onto the red section of the betting area.

The croupier looked at him, hunched his shoulders, and spun the roulette wheel one way, then added the ball, rolling it in the opposite direction just as Jimmy had said he would. The other players at the table noticed Fred put all his chips on red, and were giving him looks that varied from perplexed to suspicious.

The white ball eventually stopped.

"Number seven, red," the croupier called out in English.

Fred's winnings had been doubled. Once again, he left all the chips on red, chanting his mantra under his breath: *"¡El rojo está en llamas!"* Red, indeed, was on fire!

The ball spun again, landing on red number sixteen this time. The croupier pushed Fred's winnings towards him.

Fred yelled out, "I FEEL red, I FEEL hot. I feel red is *hot, hot, hot!*" Then, with another yell, he exclaimed, *"¡El rojo es más caliente que el sol!"* A couple of foreigners furrowed their brows and stared at him. He then translated, very loudly, "Red is hotter than the sun!"

For the third time in a row, the ball landed on a red-hot number—red twenty-three.

Fred's winnings had gone from $10,000 to $80,000. The croupier forced a smile.

"Señor, would you like to do *roja* again?" he asked.

"Of course. All on red. Hit me, baby, and hit the red again!"

The croupier spun the wheel for the fourth time. Then, he dropped the ball counterclockwise to the wheel. The white ball slipped into a pocket.

"Red, number nineteen. *Rojo, número diecinuevein.* Señor, you are having much luck tonight."

Fred could only faintly hear what the croupier said, as UB40's 'Red, Red Wine' was blaring through his earbuds.

"Leave all the money there. ALL ON RED!" A small crowd had gathered around Fred's table.

As the ball rolled, it created a soft, rhythmic sound. With each sip of his bitter drink, he felt a small glimmer of hope the magic words were about to be spoken.

"Red! Number twenty-five. *¡Rojo! Número veinticinco,*" the croupier announced. The spectators gasped, and then there was an explosion of nois. Fred's face lit up with joy as the ball landed on a red number for the fifth consecutive time. The thought occurred to Fred that a staggering $320,000 in chips were now placed on the cloth-covered betting area. The outside red diamond was obscured by Fred's chips.

"Same again, amigo?" asked the croupier, trying to get Fred's attention. However, the little sicario was jamming out to his playlist, lost in thought and the heat of the moment, but did notice the croupier was waving at him.

"Red all the way, dude!" The other players started putting their money on black, as the little guy with the big black sombrero surely couldn't win with red six times in a row.

However, the ball landed on number three.

"*Número tres rojo*," shouted the excited croupier, "RED AGAIN!"

"Yes, baby!" Fred shouted, punching the air in celebration. "Roxanne . . . you don't have to wear those red shoes tonight. Dive into my panties, and you don't know if you want a bite." He sang the wrong words in reggae style and played air guitar, but to him, it sounded terrific.

The crowd grew and started chanting. "Red, red, red!" They were drawn by this man who seemed to be able to do no wrong at roulette. None of them had ever seen anything like it.

For the seventh time, Fred left all his winnings on red. The ball spun around the roulette wheel, this time nearly stopping on black as it wobbled between black and red on the edge of the pocket. Finally, the ball dropped into the red pocket at the last microsecond.

"*¡Rojo!* Lucky sevens again!"

Fred raised both hands and punched the air.

The more miraculous his success became, the more it drew the eyes of the entire casino. The little man's streak of wins had become the talk of the town, attracting all the patrons to gather around his roulette table and witness the red phenomenon. All the playing spots were filled, but the others eagerly watched history in the making. Everyone had placed their bets:

65% black.

30% red.

5% green.

The crowd was now under Fred's spell as he commanded their attention.

"What's your favourite colour of wine?"

Those gathered around him laughed and shouted. "Red, red wine!"

Fred hummed the UB40 classic as he re-synced his playlist to it again. "Red again, signor croupier!" he shouted for the eighth consecutive time, his voice echoing across the casino. His thoughts drifted towards his Canadian friend Jimmy Myers and his *red* maple leaf flag. The red pocket seemed to call to the ball, drawing it closer until it finally dropped in with a gentle plop.

"Red again! Un-frickin'-believable!" cried a voice from the crowd.

Before his very eyes, Fred saw red dollar signs—over two and a half million dollars! Jimmy Myers was a freaking genius. Maybe, just maybe, his gringo friend could play a pivotal role in solving world poverty. The crazy notion was becoming more and more plausible with every probability-defying win.

⟫⟫⟫ ⟪⟪⟪

WITH EVERY PASSING second, Raul's frustration continued to build. His search was leading him nowhere, and the gringo was sinking his claws deeper and deeper into his brother. Maybe, thought Raul, they would take refuge somewhere that wouldn't necessarily be obvious to him. They wouldn't be expecting a visit from him, not just yet, but Fred at least had to suspect the cartel would soon be after him. Raul knew his way around 'Gringoville,' the Los Piñata area full of foreigners and where Fred collected revenues from the property owners. He constantly drove his brother nuts, talking about gringos. Cogs started to turn in Raul's head.

Maybe the key to finding them was this mystery guy called Raymond. His brother was a wannabe gringo, with his *Emily Dickinson* this and *Walt Whitman* that. Then there was the asshole, *Shakespeare*, an absolute tool, with his baldy hairdo and ridiculous pantaloons. Raul reminisced Fred would misquote Shakespeare's *The Merchant of . . . Tijuana* and tell Raul he wasn't bothered about his cartel wages and benefits: "All that glitters is not wood," he'd often say. How could his brother want to change his cartel career and become a poet when things had gone so well for them both?

Brits were the weirdest of gringos, for sure. Raul thought of Lucy, with her unbelievably difficult Welsh language and her suicide bomb crackers. Maybe they were looking for Raymond *Antrobus*, Fred's modern-day poet hero? Perhaps this Raymond was vacationing in Mexico? As nebulous as it was, if Raul didn't come up with a real lead soon, he would have no choice but to go down the Raymond rabbit hole. Fred was wholly bamboozled by the grinning Canadian, and he needed to bring his brother back to reality.

Raul arrived at what was known as the Orange Casa, an impressive property with beachfront and stunning ocean views. A couple of annoying Americans rented this property for eight months of the year. Deep down, he didn't want to go to the Orange Casa, but it was a place he might find his brother and Jimmy. Maybe they knew who and where Raymond was. The Americans who rented the property were known for their extravagant parties in the area. These were the same Americans that attended the gift exchange and had embarrassed the boss.

This home had a large movie theatre downstairs, where the Americans would show off their Hollywood movies to their pals. Raul knew they had a large cocktail bar under an impressive palapa and a fabulous infinity pool stretched out to the ocean. The Orange Casa was one of the best properties in Los Piñata, and it would have been Don Armardo's first choice for their vacation had it been available.

Raul rang the doorbell. No answer. He then knocked loudly on the door and rang the bell again. Raul prayed the couple didn't own any yappy dogs. He reminded himself to take a container of chili pepper the next time he made any house calls so he could return some 'love' to any four-legged friends present on the property.

He could hear pulsating music, squeals, and laughter from behind the door. He was about to slam his fist against the door a second time when the music suddenly turned off. Raul felt for his pistol, which he had concealed under his jacket. He walked along the front of the house towards a gate leading to the rear of the property. Raul opened the gate that led to the rear yard, swimming pool and barbeque area.

"Hey there!" yelled Bradley.

Marcus beckoned seductively, "Come on in, amigo, with the sexy pink sombrero."

Raul awkwardly put his hand through the gate to unlock the latch. He couldn't quite reach it. Bradley walked over to the gate, unlatched it for him, opened the door, and Raul stepped onto the patio area and walked towards Marcus's oversized loveseat.

"Want to join me?" asked Marcus, patting the cushion next to him on the seat.

Bradley closed the gate. The visitor shook his head as a negative.

"Hey, we know you, don't we?" asked Bradley.

"He was at the Myers' gift exchange thingy on Boxing Day, don't you remember?" Marcus answered before Raul had an opportunity to either nod or grunt.

"Yes, of course, hun. I will never forget a face, especially one as handsome as his. Oh, and that sombrero, I *love* the colour!"

Raul was visibly flustered. His body stiffened as he felt extremely awkward around these two men, anxious to get his answers and escape.

"He didn't play, honey. He was standing behind Mr Lopez and watching with his pretty hazel and bluey purple eyes," Bradley added flirtatiously.

Raul hated speaking, but he knew he had to overcome his fears. The two men made him uncomfortable in his own body, much like a grown man who had just filled his adult diaper at the shopping mall and then realized it had leaked down his leg.

"J-J-J-Jimmy, and Fr-Fr-Fr-Fred?" He lifted his shoulders and opened his arms towards them, raising his eyebrows and shoulders, expressing the universal body language of 'where the heck are they?'

"Oh, are you talking about Jimmy and little Fred?" Bradley asked.

Raul nodded.

"Yes, they have been here."

"Jimmy and Fred. Yes," corroborated Marcus. "We were having a *long* conversation, and we all had a few drinks together. They were obsessed with that Raymond guy."

"W-w-w-w-wh—"

"What were we talking about?" Bradley incorrectly finished off Raul's sentence. "Thank you for asking. You could probably help us conclude our conversational conundrum."

"Your views and opinions would be *so* welcome," Marcus added.

Raul furrowed his brow. His frown lines were very prominent on his forehead. The pink sombrero offered shade most of the time, but the light of the setting sun caught his face, glinting in his heterochromatic eyes and causing him to squint.

"You see, we were having this discussion—"

"A heated discussion," chimed in Marcus.

Raul interrupted. "I w-w-wa-wa-want—"

"You want a drink? Yes, of course. Forgive me for being rude. I'll fetch you a drink now. Why don't you take off your big pink hat and pointy cowboy boots, then sit down and rest your feet? Marcus is amazing at Reiki and giving foot massages," Bradley interrupted, much to Raul's chagrin. Marcus went to the bar area, opened the fridge door, and pulled out a cold Don Miguel beer. He came over and shoved it in Raul's hand without waiting for an answer.

"N-n-n-n-no—"

"Y-y-y-y-yes—" Marcus stammered back at Raul. He didn't intend to mock him; Marcus would often mimic the accent or speech pattern of the person he conversed with; he maintained this improved his screenplay writing and acting skills—he was a multi-talented man and didn't stop at producing. "We insist, Mr Pinky. We'll spill the beans on where Jimmy and your bro went. Marcus and I just need some mediation to stop our constant bickering. I understand you're busy, but could you answer just one question?"

Raul, begrudgingly, took the cold beer and waited for the question, trusting he'd eventually get the information he came for. He considered wrapping his fingers around Marcus's skinny turkey neck and squeezing the life out of him. Besides being extremely annoying, Marcus violated his top rule: stay away from his personal space. Unfortunately, he couldn't murder the guy yet, as the two irritating gringos were popular in Hollywood circles. Celebrity homicides would attract unwanted attention to a little town like Los Piñata. The Wolfpack Cartel would get heat from the DEA, the United States Consulate, the military, and the non-corrupted Federals.

"You see," continued Bradley, "Your opinion will be the final call on our argument, which Jimmy and Fred were also involved in. So, in your expert opinion, what is the worst way to die?"

Thirty-Three

A Horse Called Henry

For the ninth time in a row, much to the croupier's awe and chagrin, the ball fell into the pocket, landing on twenty-seven . . . *red*.

Even Fred gasped.

Chips were piled high in front of him on the table. Jimmy had advised him not to count the amount, but Fred couldn't help himself, so he did. Five million, one hundred and twenty thousand dollars.

The crowd was ecstatic, cheering and applauding rapturously. The spectators were in a party mood; champagne corks popped and their glasses raised as all eyes were on Fred's roulette table. However, the other players kept betting against Fred. They put most bets on black, black numbers, or green.

"Suckers!" Fred cried out. "All of my coin on red. Red, as in red cherries, red Ferraris, and red nipples."

The croupier gave Fred a strange look, shrugged his shoulders and spun the wheel again. The casino employee tried to get into his head. "Señor, are you really sure about this? That is a lot of money. Maybe your luck will soon run out. Do you want to quit now you are ahead?"

Fred remembered Jimmy telling him about a croupier, Marcus, at the casino where he won his fortune. He'd reminded him croupiers were there to help the casino, not the punter. Just as he'd warned, this one was now trying to get him to leave so he could save his employer money. Fred wasn't having it. After winning the forty million dollars, he planned to take pictures of money raining on him and send them to this gormless-looking croupier.

"*¡Vete a la mierda!* Marcus-clone."

The croupier, bemused by this remark but able to parse from the tone that it was an insult, looked offended as he shrugged his shoulders and spun the wheel for the tenth time. Fred chose 'Great Balls of Fire' from his playlist and ordered a strawberry daiquiri from a nearby waitress. The ball slowed, bobbled, bounced and landed into the green pocket.

A momentary eerie silence filled the air.

Then, suddenly, as if springs had propelled it, the resin ball burst out of the green pocket and plopped gently into the pocket beside it.

The croupier gulped, "Thirty-two, red," not bothering with Spanish.

The noise level became unbelievable.

Some random guy behind Fred screamed, "He's reached the ten million mark!" Fred wanted to experience the cheers and rapturous ovation, so he yanked out his earphones and milked the applause. The crowd chanted with the fervour of English football hooligans:

"Fred is Red! Fred is Red! Fred kicked this casino in the head!"

The croupier was sweating. If Fred had thought about it, he might have had a modicum of pity for the croupier. The guy was just doing his job. Unless he stopped winning, the croupier might become part of the compost for the surrounding gardens. It was time to implement casino countermeasures, or 'CCM.' The croupier activated a secret button under the roulette table. This prompted the countermeasures officer to unleash sneaky roulette weaponry from the control centre. The casino did this to avoid a situation where someone wins beyond its ability to pay. The Armed Forces and the cartel specifically designed these psychological tricks. These state-of-the-art countermeasures gave the casino a considerable edge in their war against clients like Fred. They also provided a non-lethal method of screwing up their game.

Immediately, a dozen beautiful models in skimpy aquamarine bikinis arrived at Fred's table. A girl was lying on the table directly before him, caressing a two-foot sex toy. Three well-built men wearing white spandex shorts came to the table. The guys were slick with baby oil and the crotch areas of their spray-on bathing suits had big bulges. Then the casino revealed its *pièce de résistance*: a horse wearing suspenders and provocative cannon-length leather booties was led into the roulette area.

Fred couldn't believe his eyes. "No, no, not *a horse*!"

The models began gyrating together and performing a sexualized routine. One guy slid along the roulette table, and his crotch ended up a few inches from Fred's face. A strobing green laser shone into his eyes. One model removed Fred's sombrero and put her breasts on either side of his short neck. He could also hear the horse seductively whinny, snort, and grunt.

"Whoa!" cried Fred, unsure whether he was talking more to the dancers or the horse. "Get away from me, all of you. Croupier, roll the flipping ball, and do it now!"

Another of the girls started to massage his shoulders.

"Croupier, whatever your name is, spin the damned wheel!"

The croupier grinned. "Señor, I go by the name of Joey. My full name is Joey *Diablos*."

Fred scowled back at him and turned up the volume on Jimmy's playlist, making sure his earbuds were tightly in his ears. Trying his best to ignore the insanity that was going on before his eyes, Fred yelled out, "All on red, Joey!"

Fred vaguely recalled Jimmy had warned him the casino might use countermeasures. The exotic dancer's boobs were bouncing rhythmically to the beat of the music that now rang throughout the casino at full blast. The music was deafening; Pedro Cordoba's colossus sound system had nothing on this. 'Bad Blood' by Taylor Swift had been backmasked with 'Zombie' and 'Highway to Hell,' which boomed so loudly the other punters covered their ears.

Finally, Joey sent the wheel and roulette ball in their respective directions. The well-endowed models stopped what they were doing to watch where the ball would end up landing.

The ball jumped from black to red to black. The ball's centrifugal force lessened over time, and as it slowed down, and the room went silent in anticipation save for the music.

CLUNK, CLUNK, CLUNK.

The ball fell into the red pocket. Five!

Fred felt euphoric. He couldn't hear the noise in the casino as he had cranked his playlist up to the max. He could see people jumping up and down and applauding. He had just one more turn at the wheel.

Then, Fred remembered Jimmy's advice. He snapped his fingers in the direction of a waitress, and ordered a bottle of Bollinger *La Côte aux Enfants Coteaux* 2016. His stubby little fingers counted up the chips, and he gasped, "Twenty million, four hundred and eighty thousand dollars." He gently stroked the horse on his muzzle and whispered in his attentive but twitchy ear, "One more red, and we gallop to home base, amigo!"

⟿⟫⟩ ⟨⟪⟻

BRADLEY AND MARCUS wanted closure. The question needed to be answered, and who better qualified to answer it than a cartel sicario? They were desperate to know what the worst way to die was.

"What about being buried alive? That's a classic horrible death," Marcus suggested.

Raul imagined their deaths, and for a fleeting moment, he grinned.

Bradley told his partner, "Remember that time in our house in Malibu, the one with the huge walk-in closet? We had a power outage, and everything went pitch black. I had a terrible panic attack. I couldn't see anything. It was the scariest moment of my life!"

"Poor little tulip," said Marcus empathically, "All alone in that thirty-foot-by-thirty-foot sarcophagus, you must have been so scared, sweetheart. How long were you in the cupboard for?"

"Oh, about four minutes, but I swear I was running out of air!"

Raul tried to speak, but Bradley quickly continued the conversation, leaving the sicario open-mouthed and in silence.

"Number two on any Google search of the worst ways to die is torture. You never know what's coming next."

"For sure! It's like death by a thousand cuts, and the anticipation might be even worse than the punishment. Have you ever experienced torture?" Marcus asked Raul.

Raul's eyes opened wide, and as he was about to respond, Bradley interjected once again.

"Ooh, ooh, remember Hannah McSmith's wedding?"

"How could I forget?" said Marcus contemptuously.

"Ugh, *that* dress," they grimaced in unison.

"She wore a dead-skin taupe colour. She was such a pretty bitch, but that dress made her one of the ugliest brides I've ever seen." Marcus scrunched his face as he spoke, as if he'd tasted something awful.

Both guys laughed and looking at each other harmonized, "Bridezilla was a killa!"

"Yes, that was pure torture. I swear to God, my eyes started bleeding," Bradley said dramatically.

Raul looked around to see any possible escape route, as he felt any more time spent with these two nincompoops could drive him insane.

Marcus let out a little mock gasp, "*Third* on the list is drowning—it takes one to three minutes to drown. Imagine being in the water, unable to breathe, hands and legs tied, only to be slowly eaten alive by a sea urchin."

"Marcus, darling, that sounds nearly as bad as never losing your virginity."

Both boys giggled.

Raul did not have an opportunity to speak; the couple kept on going back and forth at a breakneck pace. He knew if he tried to speak up and match their speed, he'd stutter over every single syllable.

"Remember that time we were on vacation in Greece, and you'd pooped yourself, so you had a shower, and the washed-away poop ended up blocking the drain?" Marcus said. Bradley nodded, looking completely unashamed. While Raul had an excellent constitution, any talk of poop or vomit made him queasy, and his battle with constipation and curing enema had only exacerbated this reaction. He felt his stomach turn as if he was going to throw up on the spot.

"Now just imagine, theoretically, if due to your poop blocking the shower drain, the sewer water rose and rose, and you suddenly realized the shower door had jammed shut and the handle to turn off the water wasn't moving, trapping you inside as the sewage gets closer and closer to your head."

Bradley continued where Marcus had left off. "Oh my God! What if, with the water level rising, you kept uncontrollably shitting in the same water? Eventually it would reach your mouth, and you'd have to hold your breath. You would know, in that moment, that you'll end up drowning in your own diarrhoea."

Raul's stomach heaved once again. The couple giggled. Marcus saw Raul's discomfort, but he was set on this imagined scenario. Besides, distracting him was their goal, and he'd say they were doing an excellent job.

"Then, suddenly, as you're about to breathe in the fetid water, you see a tetanus-infested corroded razor blade in the shower. Eureka! Now you have a choice: death by drowning in shit—or suicide by lockjaw!"

"Hobson's choice!" Bradley added.

"But then, at the last minute, a miracle happens . . . Mr Strogalopolis, the property manager, comes to your rescue and heroically breaks down the shower door, drags you out, lays you on the shit-covered floor, and gives you CPR.

Unfortunately, you'd only survive long enough to die from the acute amoebic dysentery you caught from all the poopy water you ingested."

That was Raul's limit, and he threw up all over the patio. He aggressively pushed his way past Bradley, wiping his mouth on his sleeve, to reach the gate and freedom from these couple of inbreeds.

"Rude!" snapped Bradley.

"And you still haven't told us your opinion, pinky sombrero guy?" Marcus shouted after him.

Raul was desperate to get away. He violently pulled the gate towards himself, and as he was about to open it, Bradley yelled: "They're on their way to—"

Raul stopped in his tracks, and the pink sombrero on his head swivelled almost 180 degrees as he jerked around to look at the disgusting couple. He waited for Bradley to finish the sentence.

"They are on their way to that godforsaken city—"

Without stuttering, Raul yelled: "Where did those two *idiotas* go to? Tell me, or I swear by The Blessed Radish Virgin's Name, I will shoot both you morons in the head!"

"Look at you go! We've cured your speech thingy!" Marcus hollered, furiously clapping his hands together as if watching a child learn to ride a bike.

Bradley looked shocked at Raul's aggressive outburst. "Temper, temper," he said, seeing Raul's face go from dead-skin to blistering purple. "Pinky, you should visit a doctor. I'm concerned about your blood pressure. I swear the vein on your forehead is throbbing."

Raul, indeed, looked like he was about to blow a gasket.

Marcus muttered to himself, like he was trying to recall something, "They went to Guadalajara to meet up with . . . hmmm . . . if only we could remember the guy's name?"

"D-d-did they g-g-g-go to s-s-see R-R-R-aym-m-m-mond?"

"Oh no, the stutter . . . it's back," they both said, disappointed Raul had not been cured. They nodded empathically at the furious sicario.

Bradley then added, "That's the guy. They mentioned some *unfinished business* they had to attend to."

"W-w-w-was h-h-he th-th-the f-f-f-famous p-p-p-p-poet?"

"Raymond? Sure, honey. He's a famous poet, and he doesn't even know it!" Marcus's quick-witted rhyme earned him a high five from Bradley, and they both burst into laughter.

Raul turned his head back towards the exit, spat on the ground, walked past the gate, and headed to his parked car on the cobbled road. He reached his vehicle, opened the door, and threw his sombrero onto the passenger seat, desperate to drive away from the insanity he'd been subjected to.

Once inside, he looked in the rearview mirror at his face, then touched the big vein pulsating and sticking out on his forehead. He noticed the two idiots were still yelling at him. Enough was enough. Raul put the pedal to the metal, burnt rubber, and took off to find his twin brother, Jimmy the gringo, and Raymond the famous poet.

Raul was still feeling ill, but he bolstered his spirits by telling himself he'd eventually show those two clowns *the* worst death. He thought of ways to utilize their Hollywood connections to make them participate in their very own snuff movie. Yes, the *first thing* he would do to those nauseating miscreants would be cut out their tongues and superglue their lips together to stop them from talking ever again.

Once Raul's vehicle had disappeared, Marcus and Bradley gave each other another high five and jumped up and down excitedly in their front yard. They returned to the Orange Casa, poured themselves glasses of wine, and made a toast.

"To Raymond."

"Raymond!" They clinked their glasses and saluted the heavens.

"Whoever the hell he is!"

Hopefully, they had bought Jimmy and Fred some precious time and sent the non-communicative psycho in the wrong direction.

THIRTY-FOUR

Hit Me Baby One More Time!

ARMARDO RECEIVED A CALL five minutes after Fred entered the Crystal Palace. The shocked manager informed him his godson was in his casino. He was wearing shades and his signature black sombrero. He had cashed in dollars for chips and had a considerable pile in front of him. The concerning thing was he was acting very cocky and on a winning streak. The manager was hesitant to call the big boss, but the little sicario was causing a massive kerfuffle in the establishment.

At first, Armardo couldn't believe it. He demanded proof, so the manager looked at screenshots from the casino monitors and sent one to his phone. Armardo gasped out loud when he saw it. What was that little shit doing? Whose dollars was he using? He cashed in $10,000, according to the manager, having also wasted $100,000 on bailing out the gringo from the police station. It had to be cartel money. If Fred won an absurd amount, he would most likely do a runner. He had been bleating about not enjoying his day job, and was vocal about his aspirations of becoming a famous poet.

"Did he say who he was?" Armardo asked.

"He signed in as Raymond."

"Who the *hell* is Raymond?" he snarled, furrowing his brow in bewilderment.

"I have no idea. Boss, what would you like me to do?"

"Shoot him in the head."

"I can't do that, boss. It would ruin the cloth on the roulette table."

Armardo shook his head in disbelief. *It's so hard to find good help these days.* "Then employ countermeasures if he starts to win too much."

Armardo knew Fred and that damned gringo must have planned for this. Jimmy could be waiting in the renegade's vehicle or somewhere in the casino wearing a disguise. Or maybe the Canadian *was* the real 'Raymond.' Perhaps he was DEA, and used Raymond as his cover name. It was all fitting into place. Fred had betrayed the family because Raymond, aka Jimmy, was blackmailing him. That made far more sense than his godson's sudden change of heart. As dissatisfied as he might have been with his role in the cartel, he knew how important blood ties were. He wouldn't just break them for some silly gringo. As spineless as he was, he'd been raised better than that.

Armardo froze, and a silence fell as he stewed over this latest revelation. The casino manager intermittently made coughing noises, trying to get Armardo's attention without being overly intrusive. To him, the silence was painfully awkward, but the Don didn't care. He eventually disconnected his phone call with the manager and called up Raul. The sicario answered immediately.

"Fred is at the Crystal Palace Casino. That shitball of a brother of yours is double-crossing the Wolfpack Cartel."

Raul asked, "Is he with the g-g-g-gringo?"

"He's with Raymond, which might be the gringo's CIA or DEA cover name. There's no sign of the Canadian cretin at the casino, but I'm sure he's lurking around like a leper with syphilis somewhere in the car park. It's very likely he's blackmailing your brother into working with him."

"I'm on my way B-b-b-boss."

Due to his stutter, Raul took quite some time to tell Armardo he had just joined the main highway and was looking for Raymond, the English poet. He would arrive at the casino in thirty minutes if he put on the after-burners and went flat-out.

Armardo disconnected his phone. He grabbed a nearby stress ball, imagined it was Fred's or Jimmy's head, and squeezed it hard. The ball exploded, and he threw the remains at a nearby wall with great force.

He looked at the picture the manager had sent him. Fred was smirking triumphantly. If he was being blackmailed, he didn't look like it. He looked victorious, taunting, as if he knew Armardo could see him. The indignity of it all was too much. Armardo placed his phone on his desk, with Fred's grinning face looking at him. He opened a drawer, picked up a hammer, and beat the picture until the mass of plastic, metal, glass, and circuit boards no longer resembled a cell phone.

⤗⤗ ⬿⬿

AS HE WAITED for his red champagne, Fred inadvertently glanced at the croupier's name tag. Sure enough, it read 'Joey Diablos.' What a stupid fake name. As Fred tried to wave away the skimpily-clad models, he noticed the one massaging his shoulders had a devil tattoo on her right boob. The other model, bouncing her boobs against his ears, had a big-assed pentagram tattoo that was oozing blood all the way from her ribs to her flimsy panties.

The horse was also now well and truly in Fred's personal space. He was being nudged in the ear by the massive black stallion, and the side of his face was covered in horse saliva. Fred swore he heard the horse tell him his name was Henry and that Henry wanted to hit him up on Instagram and Facebook. Henry was grunting, neighing, and making clacking sounds. The horse was desperate for Fred's attention . . . or a sugar cube.

Strange things started to happen. Fred pictured Joey Diablos turning into the devil, with horns growing from his head and hooves replacing his hands. Fred shook his head from side to side. What was happening to him?

The croupier asked Fred if he wanted to bet on the colour red again. Fred was experiencing a psychedelic euphoria, a kind of dissociative dissonance. In other words, he was having a multicoloured brain fart. He wondered if the models or the horse had covered him in a hallucinogen. The room spun around like a kaleidoscope, a swirl of reds, oranges, yellows, blues, indigos, and violets.

"What is your bet, sir?" asked Joey as his horns grew outwards, twisting into ram-like cornets, and the whites of his eyes turned pitch black.

The waitress arrived with Fred's bottle of French champaign. It was not the champers he'd ordered. It was a sparking Croatian wine that was a strange blackish-red colour. A glass of this unattractively coloured bubbly was poured into a crystal flute that had been placed at his side.

Fred was struggling to communicate. When he tried to send back the fizzy wine, it was like he was speaking in slow motion. His voice became deep and scary, and his heart rate was abnormally high.

"I'm as red as the devil himself. Joey Diablos is my name. Being diabolical is my game," the croupier said before letting out a demoniacal "Ha! Ha! Ha!"

Fred thought long and hard. If this mind fart continued, he felt like he'd suffer a seizure. Something wasn't right in his gut. What did Jimmy say about the devil? Memories were now brighter and sharper; he felt he could *hear* colours. He was developing synesthesia on the spot.

Joey continued. "Are you ready, *señor*? Am I placing this on red or maybe on black? Surely, it's time for another colour."

The crowd started singing Los Bravos's catchy theme tune, 'Black is Black.' Fred began to hear the crowd singing about 'blacks,' and 'greys,' and 'blues.' He felt like he was losing his mind, or else his success had been so unlikely it shattered reality and was sending him spiralling through a twisted alternate dimension. If he'd been more cogent, he might have tried to put the feeling into a poem. The many spectators continued to sing, and Joey the croupier acted like an orchestra conductor, encouraging the crowd to go along with the song's melody. To Fred's horror, Henry the Horse started to sing a football-type chant:

"Bet on black.

Neigh, neigh, neigh.

Give me sugar and plenty of hay."

Fred finally took in what was happening. The countermeasures had made him see *bad*-red and were, successfully, trying to confuse him. Something magnetic was pulling him away from red.

Fred knew he needed to get back in touch with his *red-hot* spirit. Then, like a barrage of missiles fired from a Stalin Organ, images exploded in Fred's mind. He pictured a sirloin ribeye steak, cooked rare, with blood and juices seeping out.

Thank goodness, thought Fred. *Good-red karma is back!* Except as quickly as the appetizing visions manifested in his altered mind, it changed. He noticed the sirloin steak was riddled with maggots and green mould. His thoughts became one continuous, freaky, hallucinogenic, mind-bending trip. Sickly greens and rotting blacks bled into his wonderful reds. The taste of sirloin in his mouth turned putrid, and he gagged.

Joey laughed and cackled like a warlock. "Do you want to stop now, señor? Maybe take your winnings? You must realize that, in the end, roulette is not about strategy but pure luck. Has yours finally run out?"

Fred's doubts became more serious. He was supposed to focus on the number of spins he had to sit through and had forgotten how many times the little shit had called for red. Was it 8, 10, or 457?

Come on, Fred, he said to himself. Jimmy's calming, imaginary voice joined his own: *Buddy, just say red once more, and you're in for a home run.* However, more vivid images then started flooding his mind, dimming his buddy's comforting support:

Red stop signs.

Green and black gangrene.

It was relentless. Fred held his head in his hands. He looked up and scrutinized the sneering croupier, now wearing a light tan shirt and chocolate brown trousers. Fred's red-hot confidence disappeared like an earthquake that swallowed a house. Jimmy had told him to *avoid* brown at all costs, as brown was way worse than either green or bad-red. It was as if Joey, the devilish croupier, had hexed Fred to think all things brown.

Fred suddenly had flashbacks of filling his diaper as a child. It just wouldn't stop.

"WAIT!" he cried out.

Joey Diablos paused, ball in hand. There were audible gasps in the crowd as Fred moved his massive pile of chips from red to black, back to red, and then from red to black again. He was in a quandary.

Fred Montana was experiencing exactly what Jimmy had warned him about, though he was hardly aware of it. If he didn't feel red, red would surely mess him up. The casino must have sprayed him with a noxious substance, as he was fine before the models and horse appeared.

Fred wasn't *feeling* red anymore. On the contrary, he was now feeling wildly messed up. Fred patted the horse and told him, "I can still walk away with over twenty million dollars." Henry snorted and shook his black, shiny mane in disagreement.

Other players at the table changed their bets from red to black and back to red again as they became as confused as Fred was. Whatever toxic psilocybin-LSD-ketamine infused vapour had been released into the casino's atmosphere appeared to be affecting everyone at the roulette table, including the horse, who did a massive green-hued poop on the carpet. The smell was gut-wrenching.

Yes, he could walk away a wealthy man, but the little sicario was strangely beginning to *feel it* again. It was as if the stench had jarred him from his intoxicated stupor. Unexpectedly, a calming peace came upon him when he thought about Henry's black mane.

BLACK had an alluring beauty.

BLACK is associated with kudos and prestige.

BLACK signifies intelligence, opulence, and luxury.

Jimmy did say Fred had to *feel it*, and Fred was *feeling* black in a massive way. Fred smiled, raised his little arms, followed his heart, and ordered a Guinness, a shot of Eristoff vodka, and a Black Widow cocktail from the waitress.

"Joey, you and this casino are cheating bastards. When the waitress returns with my drinks, be ready to spin the wheel. It's time to put all of my chips on . . . BLACK!"

Joey grinned. Fred was *feeling* black, and that seemed to make all the difference. The hex was broken; Joey no longer looked like Satan incarnate. He was just a croupier, dressed in an unfortunate shade of brown, worried about tonight's outcome.

The croupier tossed the ball from hand to hand and spun the wheel around as hard as he could as he waited for Fred to make his final decision. The waitress gave Fred his drinks. He drank the black vodka shot, glugged down the bitter-tasting Guinness, and then chugged back the entire Black Widow, a dark cocktail made of vodka, Kahlúa and activated charcoal. He wiped his blackened lips with the sleeve of his jacket. He was now ready to make one last bet. Even the horse started nodding, then pawing his leg on the ground in anticipation, as if he was about to gallop through the casino.

"Okay. All on *Negra*, or rather . . . *Dubh, Musta, Mávros, Schwarz, Noire.*" Fred was no polyglot, but suddenly a plethora of different languages were flooding through his mind, all of them pointing towards the colour black. He felt euphoric, and could hear arias sung by choirs of dark angels.

"BLACK! BLACK! BLACK!" he commanded Joey—in the cadence of a drill sergeant.

The croupier moved all of Fred's chips onto the black section of the cloth-covered betting area. Joey nodded, then rolled the ball onto the fast-spinning wheel. As it travelled in circles, Fred thought about the colour black, and it gave him some much-needed peace:

The Night's Watch,
Bert the chimney sweep in Mary Poppins,
Hitler's moustache,
Black sapphires.

Fred removed his earphones and heard people whispering:

"He's changed from red to black."

"That's my boy . . . it's got to be black this time."

"That would have been twelve reds in a row!"

He gazed at the thirty-seven coloured pockets—eighteen black, eighteen red and one solitary green. Joey spun the wheel so fast that all the colours merged into one. He stared at it intently and felt as if he was returning to his trippy multicoloured visions. But this time, he was in complete control of his body and mind.

I'm feeling it, Fred thought as he started humming the 'Black Magic Woman.' It occurred to him that since Jimmy had made a playlist for red, he should make one for black. What songs would he include? 'Paint It Black' by The Rolling Stones was a no-brainer, of course, but there had to be others.

Round and round, the white roulette ball spun. He feared it would never stop. But slowly, it began to lose momentum. As it decelerated, it started randomly jumping between colours and numbers. Fred watched as if in slow motion, each second agonizingly stretched out so he could see the ball's every bounce.

#35 black.

#3 red.

#26 black.

#0 green.

#32 red.

The ball looked like it might come to a halt, but it had a bit of life left. It jumped from #32 red and bounced onto #15 black.

Fred smacked his hands to his mouth, stifling a shriek of shock and anticipation. Joey Diablos looked horrified

The white ball's resurrection continued. As if with newfound kinetic energy, it went from the #15 black pocket onto the top lip, which separated #15 black from #19 red. It balanced precariously, oscillating, and for a moment, appeared to be stuck between the two pockets. It seemed no more likely to drop into one than the other.

WIBBLE.

WOBBLE.

WIBBLE.

WOBBLE.

CLUNK.

PLOP.

The wait was over. The white ball had made its decision. There were tangible gasps from the crowd.

#19 red.

Joey, the croupier, called out, "*¡Rojo, diecinueve!* Red nineteen!" His face looked like the cat that had got the cream. With a huge smile, he used his croupier's rake to sweep all twenty million dollars of Fred's chips towards himself. He happily paid out a couple of the winning bets to other players.

Fred sat staring at the roulette table. He was catatonic, as pale as a ghost. A big, black cloud seemed to have descended upon him. He could see nothing else.

THIRTY-FIVE

Pistols at Dawn

HEADING DOWN THE HIGHWAY at breakneck speed, the man with the pink sombrero soon arrived at the casino car park. He parked, got out, and slowly and deliberately strolled up each aisle, looking for his brother's car. Raul had a gut feeling he could quickly locate Fred's vehicle. Hopefully, he would also find the stupid-looking gringo, sitting in his brother's SUV, grinning like a Cheshire cat, expecting his brother to hop back into the car. With some luck, the mystery man, Raymond, would be the final piece to solving the puzzle. Don Armardo thought Raymond and the gringo were one and the same. Raul hoped he was right; that would make this a lot easier. Somehow, the gringo was the puppeteer, pulling his brother's strings like a marionette. Raul longed to be face-to-face with the dummy who had caused his family so much grief. It had crossed his mind a thousand times what he would do to the gringo, this shitball of a guy, before handing him over to his boss . . . and how he would finish the conniving bastard after the Don got what he wanted.

Raul slowly, quietly and methodically walked along line after line full of parked cars, looking attentively into each vehicle as he passed it. Eventually, he approached a familiar dark vehicle. The number plate was different, but it was undoubtedly his twin brother's car. He congratulated himself for his astuteness, although the large *Flintstones* decal on the rear window and the bumper sticker was a bit of a giveaway. It read:

'Idiot! If you can read this, you're too close. My brother is a serial killer.'

He cautiously approached the vehicle from the rear and peered through the front window, which was covered in condensation as, perhaps, the AC had been left running.

Raul pulled an electronic decoder from his jacket pocket and worked on the lock for a few minutes. The lock popped open and he opened the door, stuck his head inside, and looked around the vehicle. He saw four empty Cheetos bags in the car's driving well. An empty packet of extra hot ghost pepper potato chips was on the passenger's seat. He picked up one of the empty bags with the end of his pistol; it was a tell-tale sign his brother had been there. Fred's fingers and moustache were always covered in either orange Cheetos or ghost pepper chip crumbs.

"Gotcha!" he said out loud.

He opened the rear passenger door, took off his pink sombrero and climbed into the back of the SUV, directly behind the driver's seat. The black glass and the condensation of the windows would conceal him completely. Next to where he was crouched, he saw a book titled *Red's Hot!* by Jimmy Myers.

"Gotcha too, you little shithead."

Raul waited, placing his favourite Belgian firearm on his knees. A broad grin crossed his face. He reached for his phone, ensuring it was on mute, and tapped in the following message to his boss: *I am at the casino. I have located Fred's car. No sign of either the gringo or Raymond. I will bring them to you soon. I will let you know when I am on my way. Love you, Raul.*

He pressed send, and then grimaced. He looked over the message again, a red tinge of embarrassment spreading to his cheeks. Belatedly, it occurred to him the 'love you' may have been slightly over the top.

FRED FORCEFULLY PUSHED away the crowd of spectators and moved away from the table. He felt his pistol's holster against his chest; he could feel his heart pounding against it. He'd lost the money, and he had no way to get it back. Sure, he could storm his way into the manager's office and threaten him with a bullet to the brain, but that was a stupid idea, and he was not *that* stupid. The casino would have contacted Armardo, their boss, as soon as he cashed the $10,000 for chips. Violence would just make things worse.

"Idiot," Fred muttered to himself. He was racing against the clock, convinced his brother Raul was sent to track down the two escaping rebels, and he'd set himself back. It now depended on how far away Raul was from the casino when he received the call from Armardo—he had certainly been recognized, and the casino would have alerted the boss. Fred felt he had been playing for around forty-five minutes, so they should still have enough time to escape.

However, the psychedelic substance caused him to lose track of time. Hopefully, his brother would be at least two hours away and travelling towards Guadalajara. He should be, assuming Bradley and Marcus had come through. When the Don called him and turned him around, he was far enough away that Fred and Jimmy would be gone by the time he got here.

He hadn't listened to Jimmy and had walked away with nothing, instead of twenty or forty million bucks. He was anxious about explaining to his buddy what had happened. Jimmy would go apeshit if he knew Fred failed to follow the rules of *Red's Hot!* How could he say that right at the end, he stupidly chose black? The countermeasures were brutal. The sneaky-assed casino used psychedelic poisons; what cheating bastards! Strippers, a black stallion, and an annoying croupier got into Fred's head. He felt like an utter fool. He didn't have any extra space in his head to dwell on what consequences might await if he got caught by his brother. He already felt bad enough.

As he left the casino and headed towards his car, he knew one thing: they had to run for their lives. Armardo would undoubtedly want to have Jimmy slowly tortured. As for himself, he would be punished for sure—probably not as severely, but enough to teach him a lesson. He hoped if he got caught, he wouldn't be made to work as a cocktail waitress in a strip club in Chihuahua for the rest of his life. There's no way Raul would have mercy on him, even though he was his twin brother. But he and Jimmy still had a vehicle, so they could make a run for the border. Jimmy had to convince Lucy to run away with Max as soon as possible, and Fred was sure it would take some persuasion to get him to do so. What had just moments ago been a wonderful dream had morphed into his worst nightmare.

Fred hastily walked to his vehicle. He couldn't see through; Jimmy must have fogged up the windows of the SUV with his gringo breath. He pushed his fob, unlocked the doors, and opened the driver's side. Jimmy might be hiding in the rear seats. Fred dusted off the Cheetos debris off the driver's seat and threw his black sombrero onto the one next to him. He put his key in the ignition and turned it, and the engine revved to life. He was afraid to speak at first, and judging from Jimmy's silence, he was either too scared or too angry to ask what had happened. He idled in the parking lot for several moments before he worked up the courage to break the silence.

"Jimmy, please don't get angry with me. I've done something unforgivable."

Fred's heart raced as he felt the cold, hard metal of a gun barrel pressed against the back of his head.

"Don't move, little brother. I will damned well blow your stupid head off if I have to."

Fred felt sick. "Raul put the gun down; I can explain."

"Quiet, you little shit. Just tell me where your little gringo *culo peludo* is?"

"I don't know, bro."

"Where's Raymond?"

"Who?"

"*Raymond*! Stop protecting that Shakespeare-loving piece of shit."

"Who are you talking about? I don't know any Raymond!"

The click echoed throughout the vehicle as Raul cocked his weapon.

"I'll ask you one more time. The donkey-faced gringo. Where is he?"

Fred began to panic. "He's gone. He abandoned me when we reached the casino."

"Doofus! Why are you here? Why have you disgraced our family? What possessed you to be such a moron?"

"I needed the money. I read Jimmy's book and I was winning, but I messed it all up at the last moment!" Fred said truthfully, his voice quavering with guilt and fear.

Raul sneered. "I have orders to bring the gringo's head back to Don Armardo on a silver platter. How do you feel about that, donkey brain?" He'd had enough of this. He didn't want to kill his brother, but Fred seemed to have been completely suckered. He was playing dumb with Raymond, so he must still be lying to protect Jimmy. He'd made his loyalties clear. He'd chosen the gringo over his family. It didn't matter to Raul that he might have been blackmailed; he was seeing red and not the stupid red from Jimmy's book. His trigger finger itched. A bullet to the head would be a mercy to his traitorous brother.

"Don't you dare move, you lanky turd!"

A fraction of a second later, the barrel of a gun was shoved roughly into the base of Raul's skull, and he froze.

"Drop the gun now, or I will blow your tiny, maggot-infested little brain out of its stupid head. *Hairy-assed*, am I?"

Raul placed his gun on the empty seat next to him.

"Take his gun!" Jimmy commanded. Fred duly obliged, breathing out a huge sigh of relief.

"Thank God you're here!"

"Shut up. Dumbass."

"Dumbass?"

"Yes. You messed it up, didn't you?"

"Well, not exactly."

"Not exactly? Then where are the forty million dollars?"

"Er. . . um."

"Er . . . um isn't an answer."

"I put the twenty million on black."

Raul gasped, and Jimmy poked him again on the back of his head.

"You need to zip your lip, turd face." He turned his attention back to his friend. "You put twenty million on black. Why, oh why, after all I taught you?"

"It was a bad-red vibe thing! It's *your* fault. If you hadn't gone on and on about not thinking about bad-red, I would have been in the clear."

"My fault?"

"These bad-red thoughts burrowed into my mind. The casino brought out all these distractions and I'm pretty sure I got drugged. I was totally brainwashed. My head was a mess, like the Battle of Stalingrad."

"What on earth do you know about Stalingrad?"

"What *don't* I know about it? It was the famous border battle back in 1922 between revolutionary forces and the Yankee scum. Every proud Mexican knows about world history, amigo. The Battle of El Stalingrad."

"You ignoramus, Stalingrad was a battle between Germany and its allies and the Soviet Union in World War Two, fought from 1942 to 1943!"

"Whatever! That's just a social construct."

Jimmy slapped his head with his hand.

"Many thoughts landed in my brain in the casino, like rockets fired from several Stalin's Organs."

"A kat-kat-kat-kat-katyusha r-r-rocket launcher," added Raul helpfully.

"For the last time, you shut your dumbass mouth!" Jimmy shouted at the bigger brother's head. He would have liked to pistol whip Raul. Unfortunately, Max's plastic water pistol would break, and he would immediately lose all his leverage.

"Don't tell me, you utter dickhead . . . you had won about twenty million dollars, and then started to have a few negative thoughts? Why didn't you just walk away, you plonker?"

"I *felt* black. I felt it in an all-consuming, wackadoodle kind of way. I took your advice, felt it, and then thought of all things good-black."

"*Good* black?"

"Black Lives Matter, Black Pudding, Gorillas, Will Smith's beard, and lots and lots of Blackberries. I was sure it would work!"

"Black pudding? Gorillas? The golden rule, you donkey, was that if you're not *feeling it*— 'it' being the colour red—then you leave."

Meanwhile, Raul remained frozen in his seat, with a gun barrel firmly lodged against the back of his head. The gringo kept digging it deeper and deeper into his skull as he became more agitated with Fred. He was fascinated to learn what had transpired, so the thought of taking back control of the situation didn't enter his mind. He was listening to the back-and-forth chatter of the two morons with whom he was sharing a car. Red. Black. Good-red. Bad-red. Feeling it. His fault. Your fault. Stalin's fault. Henry the Horse's fault. Would these two ever shut up and stop bickering? He still couldn't believe he had been outsmarted by the braindead gringo and his thick-headed brother.

Jimmy had seen Raul's silhouette in the vehicle's side mirror, a guy with a sombrero larger than the state of Arkansas, and he was walking towards the SUV. He couldn't leave the car without being seen, so he climbed into the back and covered himself with a blanket behind the fifth and sixth seats. He remembered his son's water pistol was in the baggie and Fred had taken his firearm into the casino to threaten the manager.

Jimmy shoved Raul aggressively in the back of the head, the fake gun pressing deeper against his skin. It would leave a mark, for sure. "I had to wait here, in the back, listening to old stupid-balls talking to himself in Spanish. Miraculously, with *no stutter*. I stayed back here, eavesdropping and enduring his loud, putrid farts and burps."

Fred rolled his eyes. "You had it easy. A huge black horse crapped next to my chair."

"Easy? I was close to running up a white flag of surrender! It was like being in the trenches during World War One, when armies used poison gas against each other."

Sitting erect in the rear passenger seat, Raul looked in the rearview mirror and gave Jimmy one of his death stares. Still, there was nothing he could do with the gun to his head—he couldn't see it was fake—and after some more bickering, Jimmy decided to tie Raul's hands and feet and gag him with some duct tape he'd found in the rear of Fred's SUV. Now Fred's brother was no longer a threat, Jimmy moved into the more comfortable passenger seat adjacent to the hitman.

"Listen, here, pink sombrero. I'm doing this as I am so tired of hearing your effeminate, squeaky voice." Jimmy roughly slapped the super-sticky tape over his adversary's mouth.

"Jimmy, he hasn't said anything!"

"True," agreed Jimmy, who appeared to have a sudden change of heart. He smiled and tore off the duct tape, making Raul squawk in pain as his thick moustache hairs ripped from his top lip.

"Whoopsie."

"Come on amigo, don't be an ass. Sure, he's trying to kill us, but he's still my twin brother," Fred said, looking in the rearview mirror. He saw Jimmy point to the outside of the car, signalling for them to talk where Raul couldn't hear. Fred climbed out onto the tarmac and waited for Jimmy. He came out holding a plastic water gun. Fred's eyes widened in surprise; it took big brass balls to hold up Raul Montana with a fake firearm. But he didn't want to blow Jimmy's ruse, so he said nothing.

"Firstly, what the heck, Fred?"

"Please say nothing else about this red shit. 'What is done, is done,' as Shakespeare wrote in *Romeo and Juliet*."

"*Macbeth*," corrected Jimmy. "Red shit . . . durr . . . if you'd just put the money on the *red shit* number, we'd be driving away with forty million dollars!"

"So, what do we do now? Do you have a plan, amigo? You must have some plan, sitting idle in the back of the vehicle, smelling Raul's flatulence?"

"Oh, do I have to have another plan to save our asses once again? Yes, I do."

Jimmy's plan was straightforward. First of all, the three of them would drive back to Los Piñata. He saw Raul had a decoder that could unlock other cars. Jimmy would take it and use it to get a car of his own while Fred kept his SUV. Then, he would take Lucy and Max somewhere safe. "You and stinky guts drive to Oaxaca, the radish place where your parents live. Your mom will be merciful; she will probably tell you to talk to Armardo's wife about the impossible conundrum I put you in, including taking money from the cartel; blame me for everything."

Fred's jaw dropped.

"Tell them my deep-cover code name is Raymond, and I work for the DEA and CIA. Just be very clear Lucy and Max don't know I'm a CIA asset. Then the cartel will have no reason to hurt them. It's a whopper of a lie, but you've gotta trust me with this."

"Sounds great," Fred groaned sarcastically.

"Once my family's safe, I'll head directly to the consulate in Guadalajara. I'll tell them I've lost my passport and the cartel has a hit out on me. I'm sure they'll get me out of the country."

⤜⤜⤜ ⤛⤛⤛

IT WAS VERY late. Armardo was still pacing around his home like a leper messiah. He grabbed yet another phone from his safe. There had been no update from Raul. Armardo was simmering with rage, playing the scene over and over again of what he would do to the gringo and the little garden gnome. It was as he stewed in these violent thoughts he finally received a text message.

Boss, bad news. They escaped from me. Jimmy had a gun and threatened to kill Fred. The gringo is behind all this chaos. He is CIA or DEA, and 'Raymond' is his code name. Have no fear. I am close to apprehending them again. Have faith in me, your loyal godson, Raul. Twenty emojis followed the message.

Armardo clenched his hands. He knew in his heart Raul would apprehend the two idiots and bring them home to him in Guadalajara. However, Raul's obsessive use of emojis was driving him up the wall. He unclenched his hands, reminding himself that Raul, the man with the pink sombrero, had never failed a mission.

Armardo immediately texted back. *Yes, apprehend them and bring both here to me. I expect to see you first thing in the morning with your brother's fingers on ice and the gringo's head on a silver platter.* He followed this with eight 'coffin' emojis to counter some of the ones Raul had sent him. He thought about what he had just written and remembered an essential addition: *Don't forget to stuff the bottle of Imodium into his mouth. I am now retiring to bed.*

All thoughts of taking Jimmy alive and using him to benefit his business were gone. He was an undercover agent, an existential threat to the cartel. No amount of money was worth his continued existence. The longer he lived, the more chance he had to expose the cartel to whatever organization he worked for. Perhaps he already had. The thought enraged Armardo so deeply he let out a furious cry like a howling wolf. He kept screaming till his voice gave out.

Fred received the return text on Raul's phone. It wasn't exactly comforting, but at least Don Armardo wasn't sending more sicarios after them. Thankfully, he trusted his brother to get the job done.

THIRTY-SIX

Science vs. The Double Whopper

FRED DROVE. JIMMY KEPT his eyes on Raul, who frequently grunted and appeared to be highly agitated. Jimmy smirked and occasionally waved the toy water pistol in his direction.

"Calm down, sombrero boy, or else!" The prisoner grunted and struggled with his bindings. Jimmy pointed the water pistol at him, pulled the trigger, and water spurted out of the nozzle and went directly into Raul's face. He scowled, kept on grunting, and shook the water from his eyes.

"Next time, I'll fill the gun with my urine and squirt that in your face. Would you like that? A nice golden shower?"

"Come on amigo, leave him alone," Fred said, watching the scene unfold in the rearview mirror. Jimmy lowered the gun, but sneered at Raul and leaned in to whisper to him.

"Be thankful your little brother is saving your ass from being drenched in gringo piss. Hell, if he wasn't here to stop me, you'd be getting a chocolate enema."

Raul's eyes were wide, darting around with maniacal rage, but he stopped struggling and remained silent momentarily. With that settled, Jimmy stared out the window, periodically keeping an eye on the deadly sicario. He grew tired of the silence and tried to make conversation with Fred.

"If you stayed with the colour red and hadn't been a dick, what would you have done with the winnings?"

Fred let out a long, pained sigh. "Enough with the sarcasm. Just drop it already."

"I'm serious. I really wanna know." Fred paused for a moment, keeping his eyes on the road, and then answered.

"Like we agreed, I would've given half to the boss and shared the other half with you."

"Okay, but now say you had an imaginary ten to twenty million bucks. What would you do with the rest of the winnings *if you'd have stayed on red*?" Fred looked at him through the rearview mirror and scowled. He did not like having his failure continuously rubbed in his face.

"I'd give half to my brother—"

Jimmy jabbed Raul with the toy gun. "Did you hear that, old smelly guts? You'd have been a pink sombrero-wearing millionaire."

"And I would give Mom and Dad enough money to buy a new house. Then, I would have gone to Stratford-upon-Avon and attended William Shakespeare's school of limericks."

"Oh yeah, William Shakespeare, known for his *limericks*," Jimmy scoffed. Fred continued, ignoring his friend's sarcasm.

"I would publish my book of rhymes and poems and become a famous Mexican poet. Remember, you promised to help me do that?"

"I didn't promise. We might be able to publish the poems, but I'd need to read the book and see your poetry before I committed myself to any such project."

"When you read it, you'll be begging to share it with the world. It's revolutionary, historical stuff. Absolutely world-class. But maybe, being a gringo, you wouldn't understand it."

Jimmy smiled. As much as he liked Fred, he still didn't think there was a chance this little Mexican sicario's poetry was half-decent.

"So, recite one."

"Recite?"

"Yeah. I'll give you honest feedback. Plus, your brother could hear it too."

"Most of my poems are about Mexican people's struggle with the Yankees. That's why they are called revolutionary poems. I *deconstruct* history."

"That figures. Stalingrad being near Puerto Vallarta, in your *deconstructed* mind."

"I know you, Jimmy Myers. You will tell me that my poetry is terrible and worse than William McGonagall. You told me he wrote the worst poems in the world." Jimmy smiled at this, a genuine smile.

"Wow, you've got a good memory." Jimmy had, indeed, once mentioned McGonagall, a Scottish poet, may have been in the Guinness Book of Records as the worst poet ever. He doubted even Fred's poetry could be as bad, but he was struck by the similarity between Fred and McGonagall: they both had scant disregard for other peoples' opinions.

"I won't be too scathing. I promise."

"It's about the Alamo. This is the one my teacher gave me an A+ for, and it is one of Armardo's favourite poems."

Jimmy groaned, thinking, *why are these guys so obsessed with the Alamo?*

Fred smiled, "It's called '36, and it's a corker!"

"Let me be the judge of that."

Fred took a deep breath and shared the poem with Jimmy and his brother:

"On that day in '36, the Warriors of Mexico they did fix, the Yankee scum had taken our fort, with blood, sweat, and tears, we fought. General Custer was found dead in his bed, scalped, butchered, and blood decanted from his head. Custer's wagons he did circle and fight until brave Mexicans broke through with might! On that day in '36—"

Jimmy laughed out loud, interrupting the poet. "Fred, buddy, just a point of fact, *General Custer* was slaughtered at the Battle of Little Bighorn in 1876. He was killed by Crazy Horse, Sitting Bull, Sioux, and Cheyenne Indians. Mexico had nothing to do with it."

"There you go, using your Yankee social constructs again. Did you say Custer wasn't there? Were you there yourself? Can you prove it, eh? You see, we Mexicans see things through a different lens. We deconstruct the Yankee fake news and disinformation narrative," Fred said with a self-satisfied smirk.

Jimmy felt he had to change track. Although they had a lot of time to kill, Fred wasn't the greatest at having historical facts challenged. However, he still wanted to wind him up, as the Canadian couldn't speak any more of the casino debacle. Besides, there was another question Jimmy wanted to ask. It had been burning a hole in the back of his mind since the very first day they met, and he might not ever get another chance. With Raul safely tied up and no batshit insane Armardo to dissuade him, it was the best opportunity he'd ever get.

"Why do you think you and septic tank guts are identical twins?"

"We have twin telepathy. Most 'identicals' have this."

Jimmy laughed. How could Fred not see it? They were fraternal twins, not identical. It was insane his family had let the charade go on for their whole lives. It would be even more insane if they genuinely believed it.

"What are you laughing at? Are you blind? Or is today national 'Let's attack your best Mexican buddy day?'" Fred snapped, angrier than Jimmy had ever heard him. However, he was prepared for Fred's defensiveness.

"If you were both, indeed, identical—"

"Which we are."

"Your dad's sperm would have fertilized a single egg in your mother's womb."

"Eww. Too much information, amigo."

Raul grunted in agreement.

"Simple biology, my friend. Fraternal twins result from mommy Montana releasing *two* eggs from her ovary, and then *two* of your dad's super-swimmers fertilize *each* egg. The fertilized mommy egg splits into two, creating twins with the same genomes. Two sperm, two eggs."

"Your point?"

"Fraternal twins share the same womb, so they can be super-close with each other, but they are also different."

Fred laughed. Raul grunted in a deep-voiced, mocking way.

"Amigo, your absurd argument immediately became moot." Fred then made the L-shaped sign with his right hand. "Jimmy Myers is a LOSER!"

Jimmy's forehead furrowed. "Moot? And why am I a loser?"

"Because we *are* identical. Any idiot can see that, you *loser*. For a smart guy, you sure are stupid."

Raul made a muffled guffaw sound.

Jimmy turned to Raul and waved his water pistol at him. Taking sarcasm from Fred was bad enough; he wouldn't accept *any* from his psycho brother. "If you don't shut your mouth, I will pistol whip you with Max's plastic pistol you *bravely* surrendered to." The Canadian was enjoying giving his prisoner a tough time, but he refused to back down from his argument. Once he'd finished taunting Raul, he turned back to Fred.

"One of you is four feet tall. The other is nearly seven feet tall. One of you has dark brown eyes. The other has heterochromia. One of you is a nice guy. The other is a psychopathic serial killer."

"Less of the serial, please."

Raul grunted in agreement and Jimmy stared daggers at him.

"One of you has a speech impediment. The other hasn't. You couldn't be more different if you tried!"

Like his opponent, Fred refused to budge an inch. He persisted with his discourse, backing it up with 'factual' evidence. "I know my epigenetics. Some hot-looking professor on a YouTube video talked about gene expression, trauma and non-coding DNA. Environmental factors, such as womb position and life experiences after birth, also came into play. However, let's deep-dive into the scientific actualities. Raul and I have the *same* IQ—"

"As a sea anemone," Jimmy muttered under his breath. "Epigenetics? Gene expression? What the fu—"

"We *both* prefer Burger King to McDonald's. Our skin colours are the *same*. We're so identical we even wear different coloured sombreros so people can tell us apart."

Jimmy snorted as he tried to stifle a belly laugh from exploding out of his chest.

"So, your 'scientific' apologetic for being as different as chalk and cheese is that you *both* like Burger King?"

"Yes, it's amazing we *both* love a Double Whopper with bacon and extra everything. The tang of the pickle, the mayo's creaminess, the sweet taste of salsa and two hot slabs of burgery awesomeness, and the salty chewiness of the bacon."

Raul made an "Mmmm" sound in agreement.

"I told you to shut your mouth!" Jimmy snapped, expressing his irritation at Raul and at listening to his brother's nonsensical argument.

"Hey, that's my identical twin brother you're yelling at." Jimmy sighed and turned away from Raul, trying to compose himself with deep breaths. Fred had a sick attachment to his brother; messing with him wouldn't help Jimmy talk him out of his delusion.

"So you really think you're identical twins? I'd be willing to concede the point . . . if, and only if, you admit your dad's sperm had been laced with Strontium-90 and your mom happened to vacation in Chernobyl for a month during conception."

"Sorry amigo, my mother's never set foot outside Oaxaca."

"Anyway, how can you prove you're identical without mentioning Burger King or Tonya Whackamole's radical deconstruction theory?"

"Hah! Gotcha! QED," proclaimed Fred.

"QED?" gasped Jimmy.

"Yes, *quod erat demonstrandum*. QED, you gringo blockhead. The 'proof' lays with the Blessed Virgin of the Radish."

"What has your imaginary goddess have to do with anything non-insane?"

"Easy tiger! She visited my mom and, miraculously, prophesied our names, *and* we would be identical. You can't argue with the Divine!"

"Divine?" Jimmy chuckled. "Assuming she's even real, who's to say she didn't just blurt out two names and then your mom decided to use them? Hardly a miracle."

Fred shook his head in disbelief. "Everyone in the world, *except you*, my friend, believes it."

"Yeah, because psycho Raul and sociopath Armardo disappear everyone who isn't in agreement with your Radish Queen."

"The Blessed Virgin of the Radish," corrected Fred, making the sign of the cross multiple times. Raul tried to do the same, but as he was tied up, it just looked like he was moving his arms back and forth.

"Hey psycho, do *you* really believe this crap?" Jimmy asked Raul. He grunted and shook his head in the affirmative. Jimmy stared at the tied-up brother for a long time. He didn't know what he was expecting. They were completely at odds with reality. No matter how much he tried to mock or reason with them, they remained unabashedly committed to the idea they were identical twins, and he realized there was no point in arguing. He'd gotten the only answer they were ever going to give. Letting out a big sigh, Jimmy sunk down into his seat.

"I love you, buddy," he said, patting Fred on the shoulder.

"I love you too, just as Jesus loved the doubting disciple, Moses. One day, you will believe the miracle, and will give your life to the Radish Queen."

Jimmy turned to Raul and squirted him with the water pistol. "I don't love you—you crazy psycho-freak."

THIRTY-SEVEN

Thrilla in Manilla

EVERY DAY IN MEXICO, many gifted children and teenagers are targets of bullying. Bullies are either envious of other children's success at school, or their status is threatened. The common perception is that bullying is more likely to occur in school than in the workplace.

Inspector Ramon Lopez was a complex individual. He had a low IQ and constantly felt intimidated by those around him. Ramon was the archetypal workplace bully. Whenever his self-worth or position were challenged, intentionally or otherwise, he would revert to insults, ridiculing and shaming his staff both privately and publicly.

Bradley and Marcus should have asked Raul Montana where the worst place to work was instead of asking what the worst way to die was. For many, Chernobyl, Anthrax Island, and Dhaka would be top of the worst places to be sent to. Others would argue that working as a 'groom of the stool' for a chief in a Boko Haram village or being seconded to Selhurst in the Borough of Croydon should take the top spot. For the officers waiting to be posted after graduation from the police academy, Los Piñata was *the worst* place one could possibly be employed.

Inspector Lopez's reputation was legendary in the worst way. His subordinates were afraid to disturb him at home unless it was a genuine emergency, as he had warned them not to.

"My house is your house," he often told his underlings with a snarl. "You're always welcome to call me after hours . . . *if* you have the gall to disturb me when I'm off duty."

In actuality, Lopez turned off his cell phone so he would not be disturbed when not at work. He didn't cherish his sleep though; he would be on dating apps or playing *Minecraft* until early morning.

On the rare occasions an officer worked up the courage to contact him—due to a national emergency that could impact Los Piñata—he went ballistic. His workplace *modus operandi* was to berate the officer for their poor numeracy skills. Lopez terrified subordinates to such an extent the other officers tested each other throughout the week in arithmetic, algebra, trigonometry, and essential calculus, just in case they had to wake the Inspector at home.

Lopez hated maths and was not at all proficient with numbers. So, to negate this and to keep his officers on their feet, he always had questions and answers on cue cards at hand, either in his jacket pocket or on top of the shoe stand by the door on the inside of his house. He pulled them out whenever he felt like his authority was being undermined. His subordinates would either answer the questions or be made to feel fools, thus upholding his position without having to be any good at it.

For example, the President of Mexico once commanded one unfortunate officer to inform the Inspector a national disaster occurred a short distance from Los Piñata. After leaving several voicemails on his turned-off phone, the officer visited Lopez early in the morning.

A bloodshot-eyed and cranky-looking Inspector opened the door to his home, awoken by the knocking on the door.

"Why have you disturbed me?"

"I'm very sorry, sir. It's a *severe* emergency, sir."

"Has the sky fallen in? Are we being attacked by aliens? Did Tutankhamun's mother ask you out on a date?"

"No, sir. However, I must let you know that—"

"You utter imbecile!" Lopez screamed, cutting the poor officer off.

"Yes, sir."

"You admit you are an imbecile?"

"No, sir."

"Okay, what time was it one hundred and seven minutes and twenty seconds ago?"

"Um."

"Um, is not an answer. Can you count, officer?"

"Yes, sir."

"I'll simplify it for you, shit-for-brains. It's now 4 am. What time was it two hours ago?"

"2 am, sir."

"In Manilla?" Lopez added. His lips were frozen in a horrible rictus of a grin. The junior officer's expression was one of pure, barely-hidden fear.

"Um."

"It's 6 pm there, shit-for-brains. Can you tell the time?"

"Yes, sir."

"In Manilla, doofus?"

"Manilla, sir?"

"Yes, Manilla. I was on a dating app two hours ago, talking dirty to a potential Filipino bride. I was on the verge of proposing to her, but she had to get off to feed the chickens."

"Sorry about that, sir but—"

"How dare you wake me up after only two hours of sleep?"

"But sir—"

He held four fingers up within an inch of the officer's eyes. He then put one down, holding up three, and then held up all five. He rapidly and constantly changed the number of fingers to two, then three, then one, then five, then three, and so on.

"How many fingers?"

"I'm not sure, sir. You're moving your fingers too fast."

"You deserve to be punched in the face. Do you want me to do that?"

"No, sir."

"Is your brain working, constable?"

"Yes, sir."

"Then what is nineteen multiplied by eleven—"

The officer smiled at this; finally, a question he could answer, "Two hundred and nine, sir."

"I haven't finished, you dummy! How dare you interrupt me?"

"Sorry, sir," the officer gulped. His proud smile fell immediately.

"As I said, what is nineteen multiplied by eleven—" Lopez paused, looked at a cue card on his shoe stand, and with a wicked smile spat out the rest of the number, "POINT three, two, seven, four?"

"Um."

"How did you get into the police academy if you can't count? I may demote you to the janitor's position. Think you could handle cleaning toilets?"

"Yes, sir, thank you, sir."

"Good. Now get lost, moron!" Lopez slammed the door in the officer's face and returned to bed.

At 9 am, as he was leaving to go to work, Lopez opened the door and found the same officer standing right where he had been five hours ago. He was so terrified he hadn't dared to move.

"You look like shit, constable. Have you no pride? Why do you smell like piss and poop?"

"My adult diaper is leaking, sir."

"My God, man, you are an imbecile."

"Sir, the President of our Republic—"

"Is an imbecile?"

"No, sir."

"Well, I think he is. Armardo, my brother, will run for the top job in a few years and oust that chowderhead from power."

"That would be wonderful, sir."

"Do you know what that will mean for the likes of you?"

"No, sir."

"It will mean the firing squad for being so stupid. I will personally pull the trigger."

"Thank you, sir."

⟫⟫ ⟪⟪

ARMARDO FOUND IT challenging to sleep. He was incredibly restless, and felt the only way to comfort himself was to make sure his phone was always on; that way, if something happened, he'd know immediately. However, while the phone was in sleep mode, his mind still obsessed over missed calls that might be important. What if he dozed off? What if he'd left his phone on silent and didn't hear when Raul tried to get in touch? The thoughts would've haunted him even if he'd taped his phone directly to his ear. He got up from his bed and checked. There were no new messages besides Raul's, saying he was close to finding the fugitives. Armardo wondered how close he was now. Why has there been no update from Raul? The thought of Jimmy and Fred running around his patch, hood, district, and state, creating havoc and chaos, was driving Armardo bonkers.

He knew Raul would also be upset by this, as he was the most competent sicario he'd ever known. Yes, the man with the pink sombrero always got his man. Always. Unless . . . what if something had happened to Raul? What if 'Raymond' and his CIA connections had proven too much for him? Armardo decided Raul needed some help, and even if he didn't, it was better safe than sorry. He called his brother, Inspector Ramon Lopez. The phone connected to his brother's voicemail.

Frustrated, he left Lopez an urgent voice message. "Brother, call me back. A life-or-death situation has arisen. It concerns Jimmy Myers and Fred. This is a matter of *absolute* urgency." He hung up and checked the time. He didn't understand why the chief police officer in Los Piñata was so difficult to contact.

Armardo had heard it was his brother's professional practice to keep his cell phone silent unless it was an emergency. His colleagues knew they had to knock on the door of his home and break any news to him face-to-face. Ramon had told him he'd always greet them with a smile and make them eggs and bacon. His brother's subordinates were super lucky to have a boss like him!

Ramon Lopez woke up from a deep sleep hours later. He called his brother back, having received the message when he checked his phone. Inspector Lopez listened to Armardo's rant about the pesky gringo and his out-of-control godson. Lopez felt proud he had personally designed the countermeasures for the casino. The psychotropic agent released by the models and the horse, his *pièce de résistance*, had worked a treat. He couldn't believe Fred had visited the casino, used Wolfpack money, and then lost twenty million dollars, much to the merriment of the casino's management. Armardo had yet to learn if the pink sombrero was back on their trail.

Using his detective's training and experience, Lopez realized Raul's cell phone must still be working, as his text message to his boss had been made a couple of hours ago.

"Don't worry, brother, I will catch the little shit and bring him back to you myself."

"Myers's wife and son are still staying in the casa in Los Piñata, you know. Perhaps you should bring them in for 'questioning.' If she knows what her husband is up to, the threat of little Max going to Mexican social services might loosen her gringo tongue," Armardo suggested. Lopez nodded; that was a good idea, but he had other plans as well.

After Lopez ended the call, he hopped into the shower and readied himself for the task ahead. Early morning showers always helped him to plan his day.

First, he would order his subordinates to *triangulate* Raul's phone, whatever *triangulate* meant, as they often did on TV. Although despising all things trigonometry, his TV cop heroes usually found out the location or direction of a fugitive by using hi-tech methods. He'd then set up roadblocks to help stop the little turds from going anywhere. To put the icing on the cake, he would even call some local cartel capos and ask them to do unofficial policing for him.

Yes, the net would soon be closing around the little rebel *bandito* and his gringo lover. Inspector Lopez envisioned his success, his smile as broad as the ocean.

THIRTY-EIGHT

Panic at the Casa

UPON ARRIVING AT THE condo in Los Piñata, Fred gave Raul's electronic decoder to Jimmy, who smiled and shook his hand.

"Good luck, amigo."

"Good luck, my crazy friend. I'll be in touch."

Jimmy found a car, used the decoder to open it, and got Fred to hotwire it for him—another thing he picked up from his ex, Tonya, who proclaimed vehicle ownership was also a social construct. He then grabbed his small backpack, containing the booklets, water pistol, and copies of *Red's Hot!* He ran up the condo's stairs, unlocked the front door, and found Lucy in bed, reading one of her mini thriller novels.

"You're here. Praise the Lord!" she jumped off the bed to greet her hubby. He looked wide awake and highly stressed.

He briefly told Lucy the basics of the story. Throughout it all, she was in complete shock, unable to speak or act. However, that state of surprise didn't last long. She trusted him completely, and so she knew they had to leave as soon as possible. She quickly changed into her travel gear and pulled out her suitcase along with Max's *PAW Patrol* case. The little guy could walk his bag into the airport while awake.

Jimmy was travelling lightly. He went through the suitcase he had left behind, searching each zipper pocket. He thought about his missing passport, which needed to be renewed next year. Thankfully, it contained his old address on the back page. Lopez and his cartel buddies wouldn't know their current address in Canada.

He took Max's little case and told Lucy he might need it. He could take one or two pieces of clothes and the bare essentials, but otherwise didn't think it was worth it to waste time looking for things he didn't need.

"Jimmy, you'll look like a donkey walking around with Max's *PAW Patrol* case. Why not just let him carry it?" Lucy said with a hint of a smile. She was surprised at herself; her family was in danger, and here she was making jokes. It hardly seemed appropriate, but it made her feel better. Safer, even. Or maybe that was just the panic talking.

Jimmy just looked at the case, adorned with colourful images of Chase, Rubble, and Sky, and smiled.

"It will also remind me of little Maxy." At this, Lucy's expression fell back into one of shock.

"What do you mean, 'remind me?'" Jimmy said nothing. For a moment, his fear gave way to sadness. She saw it in how he couldn't meet her gaze, looking instead at the *PAW Patrol* case.

"I can't go with you, Luce. You and Max have your passports, but mine's missing."

"B-b-but, you can't stay here. You're in more danger than any of us!" Lucy protested, raising her voice nearly to a shout. Jimmy looked around, wondering if it would wake up Max. He heard no sign of his son and continued.

"I have to, at least for a little while. I need to go to the Canadian Consulate and get a new passport. Then I'll join you both. I promise." He put a hand on her shoulder and planted a gentle kiss on her lips. She was too distressed to reciprocate.

"But... what if you—" She couldn't even get the thought out. She was as afraid to say it as Jimmy was to think it. Neither of them wanted to consider what might happen if he got caught.

"I'll be fine. It'll be a gamble, but that's what I'm best at." He put on a brave face, grinning broadly as he reached into his own backpack and pulled out a copy of *Red's Hot!* For the longest time, Lucy just stared at it. He desperately hoped she'd make the right choice. She couldn't stay with him, and neither could Max. They had to leave as soon as possible. Worrying about his own safety was one thing, but having to fear for the lives of his wife and son on top of that would be too heavy a weight to bear.

"I just hope the Consulate doesn't think you're a paedo," Lucy said at last, indicating the child's bag in his hand. She let out a small chuckle, and Jimmy immediately pulled her into a tight embrace.

"Thank you," he muttered into her shoulder. She hugged him back. She was certain he'd gotten involved in something completely out of his depth, but she'd been just as certain of that back when he was working on *Red's Hot!* He had a way of twisting the odds in his favour. Maybe, just maybe, Jimmy could keep that hot streak alive.

Lucy knew she wouldn't have a chance to say goodbye to the beautiful three amigas, or, as they liked to call themselves, the *Barflies*. She felt guilty; they'd been such a help to her, stepping in to take care of Max while Jimmy was out running for his life. And over the past few weeks, they'd made some of their best memories. Lucy hadn't laughed so much or so hard in years. After she and Max were safe, she'd call them and explain what was happening. They deserved to know.

Once they broke away from each other, Jimmy immediately fell to emptying the *PAW Patrol* bag of all Max Myers's precious possessions: books, swim gear, shorts, and a packet of gummy bears in the inside zipper. As he worked, feeling along the outside of the bag for anything he might have missed, he felt a long, soft leather object. He pulled it out of the pocket, and much to Jimmy's amazement, held the missing dark-charcoal-coloured Burberry wallet. He looked inside, and all their money was there. Although happiness glowed inside him, Jimmy didn't know whether to laugh or cry. It was the one place he hadn't searched. Why would he? How could his wallet possibly have ended up in Max's bag? Still, if he'd looked there, he wouldn't be indebted to Armardo in the first place. It might not have mattered; after all, he'd still found Vincente's head and made the fatal mistake of thinking he could befriend Armardo Lopez. He probably would have gotten tied up in the cartel either way. But a part of him felt just as frustrated with himself as he felt relieved. A wave of emotion washed over him, and he got up and went to give Lucy another kiss. Lucy pulled away, rolling her eyes.

"Not now, Mr Horny. Jiggy with Mr Biggy will have to wait until we're back in Canada!"

"You think I can't keep it in my pants in a life-threatening situation? Give me a little credit, Luce. And, while you're at it, close your *eyes*. I've got an entirely non-sexual *surprise*."

"Nice rhyme. Did you get that from Fred?" Lucy joked, shutting her eyes tight and holding out her hand, into which Jimmy put the black wallet full of brand-new pesos and dollar bills.

"You can look now."

Lucy's large green eyes opened wide, staring at the bulging wallet. She then looked up at Jimmy.

"Where did you find it?"

"Max's bag."

Lucy looked stunned. A smile broke out on her face.

"We didn't look for it there, eh?"

He lifted the wallet up to his nose and smelt the sweet, earthy aroma of the quality leather. "Aah . . . welcome back to Daddy!" Jimmy opened the wallet, gave Lucy half of the money, and kept the other half for himself.

"Fred also gave me some pesos and a few dollars, which is all I had to survive on, but this—" he said, pointing to the wad of cash that was now in Lucy's hand, "should be enough to get you home on any first-class flight."

"Do you think we'll be able to leave on such short notice?"

"The morning flights are at 6 am and 8 am, and the afternoon flights are at 2 pm and 4 pm. I'm sure you can negotiate with any of the airlines. Give the representative a few extra dollars for their trouble."

Lucy gently grabbed the sleeping Max and carried him to the car. Jimmy fixed Max's car seat into the rear, and they placed their bags in the trunk in a hurry. They left a messy condo behind them, along with plenty of pesos for the cleaner if she came—assuming Armardo hadn't fed her to the crocodiles as well. The thought reminded Jimmy of Vincente; he still didn't know what happened to him, though he had his suspicions. It didn't really matter, of course, as whatever had been done to him, Jimmy had seen the end result.

"Poor Vincente. Never should've asked him to talk to Armardo," he muttered. Lucy leaned into him, holding his arm and resting her head on his shoulder. She remembered meeting his wife and felt just as guilty as Jimmy did.

"I bet it was his head I saw in the freezer, and his body had been disposed of in the River of Crocodiles. There's no way Fred had anything to do with it. He even told me they don't use him for the violent stuff."

Lucy looked up at him, "You really believe that?"

"Of course. Sure, he's a sicario and a crappy poet, but he's got a heart of gold. He stole one hundred thousand dollars from his family to pay my bail. He tried to help me pay off my debt. He took a lot of risks for me, and he didn't have to. He's a good person, I think. Just . . . sometimes, people are forced to do things they don't want to do. He's bound to the Lopez family by whatever sick honour system they have, and they're all he's got. He knew what would happen if he betrayed them, and he did it all the same, just to save a gringo he's only known for a few weeks."

"You're lucky to have him as a friend, then," Lucy replied somberly.

"And now he's taking a big risk, going back to his parents to ask for asylum from the cartel," said Jimmy. He hoped Fred would be okay. If he died, Jimmy couldn't shake the feeling it would somehow be his fault.

"He's nothing like his brother, then. Raul came to the condo and asked about you. *Ugh*, what a creep." Jimmy felt his wife shudder at his side, and wrapped an arm around her waist.

"You can say that again."

⤐⤐⤐ ⤐⤐⤐

FRED STILL HAD Raul in the backseat of the SUV. He told his brother he would untie him if he remained calm and respectful. He said it would be a very long journey, between six to ten hours, so it was in Raul's best interest to shut the heck up, as he would play loud gringo music from the radio to drown out any of his complaints and threats. If Raul stayed chill, they could chat it out. Equipped with bottles of water, Pacifica beers, and plenty of snacks, Fred set off on the long journey. He headed towards Oaxaca, in the opposite direction of Armardo's base in Guadalajara.

Fred also reminded his brother the cartel or the cops halted cars travelling on the highway; if this were to happen, he might have to bribe or even shoot his way out of the situation and would need his brother to stay silent or join him at his side. He told Raul he'd sent a misleading text to Armardo from his brother's phone; if they got caught together, it might look like Raul had betrayed him too, and they could both end up dead. He said they should work together, not be at each other's throats. They were twins, inseparable in birth, life, and death.

Raul nodded. "Brother, we are dead already. And even worse, the gringo was right." Speaking with his brother, he didn't stutter over a single word.

"About what?"

"Your poetry sucks." Fred scoffed, looking affronted.

"I love you, bro, but you don't know anything about my poetry, and neither does the gringo."

"I don't know *you*. I thought I did, but all your time running around with the gringo has corrupted your mind. He made you betray the family, and now we are both looking at a death sentence delivered by Don Armardo." Raul's tone was sombre, and he looked down. He had not only failed, but went with Fred and Jimmy in their escape. It didn't matter that he was forced to. The boss would only see the betrayal. He prided himself on always getting his man. So did the boss. But this time, the man got him.

"You have to *feel it*, bro." Fred, on the other hand, spoke with a confidence that struck his brother as entirely inappropriate.

"Feel what?"

"That everything will be okay, and my poetry will become world famous."

"Did you *feel it* when you blew twenty million dollars on the roulette table?" Raul chortled.

"It was just ten *thousand* dollars, so try not to exaggerate."

Raul did not respond. He had heard Fred and the gringo arguing about the twenty million bucks, Joey Diablos, and countermeasures. He didn't know what his brother and the gringo were talking about, but he knew Fred had messed up and lost all their money.

"*Feeling it* is all about being positive, bro. You keep positive feelings in your head, breathe positivity, listen to upbeat music and imagine yourself swimming in a tub of optimism."

Raul rolled his eyes.

"And it will happen, big brother. We will be rich someday, and I will be a famous poet. You'll see. The Black Sombrero who'll be the next poet laureate. Then our parents will live in a newly constructed mega house in Oaxaca."

Raul yawned. Unlike his brother, all he felt was tired and done with this conversation.

"Put duct tape over my ears instead of my mouth if you're going to keep saying stupid things."

Fred just smiled. He was feeling it, despite what his brother said. Somehow, someway, it would all turn out okay. He was an artist, a poet, a man on the run. He'd won twenty million and lost it all. He had the most dangerous sicario in the world by his side, and felt liberated—for the first time in his life. He learned from his mistake in the casino. He was feeling good-red, red-hot.

"You want something smart, bro? Then it's time for a poetry reading. You'll be singing my praises after you hear these gems," Fred said, turning to his brother and flashing him a wide grin with a twinkle in his eye.

Raul let out a groan as Fred began his recitation.

THIRTY-NINE

Crocodile River

WHILE LEAVING TOWN, JIMMY remembered the cab driver's warnings about the River of Crocodiles that flowed through Los Piñata into the ocean. Passing over the small bridge, he slowed the car to gaze at the stagnant, murky green water. Juan had said he'd seen discombobulated crocodiles staggering along Los Piñata's beach, causing panic among vacationers. Jimmy stopped, exited the car and stood on the river's bridge, scanning the plankton-filled river for signs of reptilian life. He no longer found it hard to believe cartel members disposed of their victims' torsos and heads in the river.

Incredibly, he saw a well-camouflaged crocodile lying on a rock, its mouth gaping out wide as if smirking at him.

Lucy's voice broke the silence. "For goodness' sake, get back into the car and let's get out of this crazy town." Jimmy looked back at her as if in a daze, not sure why he'd gotten out in the first place. He should have kept a lead foot on the gas and torn away, but instead he stopped to stare at a river probably full of crocs stuffed on human remains. His time in Los Piñata had changed him. He didn't yet know how to feel about that.

Returning to the vehicle, Jimmy wasted no time in driving away, and he and Lucy whispered to each other on the journey to the airport so Max wouldn't be woken up.

It was early morning when they finally arrived. The international terminal was relatively empty. Jimmy helped Lucy with her baggage, and she still carried a sleeping Max. They manoeuvred their cases and themselves to be first in line. Then they sat down with their bags and cases, and Lucy rocked Max back and forth, kissing him.

"It will be okay, hun," Lucy whispered. She didn't know if she was talking more to Max, Jimmy, or herself, but she looked up at her husband. She saw he was crying silently, tears falling down his cheeks. Still cradling Max with one hand, she reached up with the other to wipe the tears from his face with her fingers. He cupped her hand in his and held it to his face, as if this was the last time they would touch. She was reminded of the fact it very well could be.

"I will see you both in a few days; trust me, Luce. I love you. I love you even more than I love winning at *Catan*."

"Silly arse!" chuckled Lucy. She was glad for the levity, or she might have cried too.

"Tell the little guy his daddy loves him." Jimmy let go of Lucy's hand and leaned down to kiss Max. Then he kissed her one more time and sprinted to his car. Opening the door, he climbed in, took a few deep breaths, and composed himself before driving off to either safety or certain death.

Jimmy cleaned his tear-stained face with a sanitized wipe, started the vehicle, and drove towards Guadalajara. If he steps on the gas, the trip should take four and a half or five hours. He desperately wanted to avoid getting stopped by the police or the cartel, which could result in a deadly reunion with Armardo.

⋙ ⋘

VIVA MEXICO! FRED was enjoying himself singing Mexican revolutionary music at full blast. He had finished his poetry reading, and Raul had been unmoved—Fred just had to admit, as painful as it was, his brother was uncultured and wouldn't know good poetry if Octavio Paz lobbed a collection of his greatest works at his head. Fred cried out, "Viva the Revolution!" and "Patton, you suck!" so loud Raul begged him to stop.

Soon, however, he wanted a bathroom break, so he slowed the car to a standstill. Fred dashed out and relieved himself behind some giant cacti.

"Watch out your itsy-bitsy dick doesn't get itself pricked!" Raul called out to him. "Do you need Tonya's iPEE? You must have a few spares in the back."

Fred chuckled.

On his return to the car, Raul said, "Give me a bottle of water, you fool."

Fred reached over to the cooler box, opened it, and grabbed a water bottle dripping with condensation. Taking off the bottle's lid, he carefully poured water into his brother's parched mouth. Raul gulped it down; he groaned in delight at the sensation of the icy water surging through his dehydrated body.

"Bro, do you want a cold brewski?"

"Brewski? Have you gone completely gringo?"

"If being a gringo was good enough for Will Shakespeare and Raymond Antrobus, then it's good enough for me."

"Aha! So Raymond *is* a poet, not a CIA agent."

Fred just stared blankly at his brother and raised one of his eyebrows. "What are you talking about?"

Raul winked back at him.

"Do you have something in your eye?"

Raul shook his head and made "tsk-tsk" tutting noises. Fred sighed; he had no idea what his brother was on about.

"Do you want a beer or not?"

Raul nodded, cleared his throat and asked, "Have you heard from the boss?"

"After I sent him the text from your phone, I took out the SIM card and lobbed it into a field of cacti." Raul nodded, looking impressed.

"Smart move, for a turkey brain." Fred chuckled and lightly punched his brother in the shoulder.

"So, big bro, are you ready to hear what I've got to say to you? In other words, have you calmed the heck down?"

"Yes, I have, little brother, but it's hard to stay calm when you know the boss and his minions are searching for you, the gringo and me. He will never forgive us both."

"The good thing about us travelling to Oaxaca is that the cartel presence is minimal. The Don won't expect us to travel in that direction."

Raul grunted in semi-agreement.

"He knows the gringo needs a new passport, and the only places to get one are Guadalajara or Mexico City. He'll probably send most of his people there."

"The gringo, for sure, has the highest hurdles to jump. Is he heading back to the lion's den itself? Guadalajara?"

"All I know is he believes in keeping his friends close and his enemies closer," Fred said cryptically.

"You know, he may have the biggest target on his back, but you're the one who caused all this. If you hadn't bailed out the gringo, the boss would have what he wanted. No stupid roulette routine, no 'Raymond' getting the jump on me. We'd still be working together, the way we're supposed to, living out our best lives." Raul had come to terms with the fact he was on the run too; Fred and Jimmy had made him an accomplice in their escape. But he still regretted the way things turned out.

"We are working together, bro. And my best life is not getting bitten by crocodiles or having to deal with the boss's idiot mall-cop brother—living my best life is that of a poet, with you by my side as my bodyguard. Fame and fortune will not be easy for me to deal with alone, dear brother. I need someone to get all the paparazzi off my back and protect me from the powerful individuals my revolutionary poetry will surely piss off." At this, Raul couldn't help but let out a barking laugh. His brother really had drunk the gringo's Kool-Aid.

"We're dead men walking."

Fred disagreed, "I'm not giving up. Maybe we can still both live our best lives and not have our heads placed upon spikes. Momma will take us in, and the Red Lady may well intervene." Raul made the sign of the cross with neck and head movements.

Fred chortled and touched a button on the dashboard. The car's convertible roof disappeared, and a breeze blew through Fred's long, thick, raven-coloured mop of hair. He tapped another switch on his steering wheel, and music blasted out of the speakers.

"You've got to get away—"

Raul smiled, nodded and then joined in singing the chorus with Fred:

"We've got to fly away, woah, woah, woah!"

Forty

Jimmy Myers

JIMMY READ THE SIGNPOST: Guadalajara 20 km. It was a most welcome encouragement for him. He had neither been stopped nor pulled over by the police. He pulled the car over for a few minutes to double-check the handwritten instructions in the seat beside him.

> Continue onto Carr. Guadalajara - Tepic/México 15 S.
> Keep left to continue on Carr. Guadalajara - Tepic/Av.
> Ignacio L. P Vallenquez /Av Vallenquez Eje Poniente/México 15 S.
> Follow signs for Tonala, Tlaquepaque, Guadalajara Centro.
> Use the right two lanes to turn right onto Av. Mariano Otero.
> 1249 Av Mariano Otero, <u>Consulate of Canada.</u>

Jimmy was jamming out to his upbeat vibe music, thinking of classic lines for his new book. How could he not write a new book after everything he'd been through? So far, his working titles were *#SavagePositivity* or *Karma is a Bee-atch*. Both were excellent; only one could be used. He chuckled at the thought and vowed he would write this damned book one day, whatever happened in the next couple of hours.

Eighteen kilometres later, having followed his own directions, he proudly arrived at his objective without the help of Google Maps or anyone else. The pride was made even sweeter by the rush of relief that loosened every muscle in his body. Getting home to Canada with a new travel document was an intoxicating thought.

He drove into a car park near to the entrance of the building. He looked over at Max's little travel case and spoke to the bag as if its owner was present with it.

"Sorry, buddy, I need to take this with me," opening the bright blue *PAW Patrol* cabin case.

Jimmy quickly changed his clothing in the car. He needed to look intelligent and respectable, so he wore his favourite Hawaiian shirt, Lululemon cargo pants, and smart canvas loafers. The dapper-looking Canadian evaluated himself in the rearview mirror, winked, laughed, and commented he was "one handsome hombre." Jimmy then put on his Ray-Ban shades and trilby hat as a final touch. As infuriating as she had been, Chéckina the bank worker was right about one thing: Jimmy was a metrosexual guy, with his designer clothes, eye-whitening drops, and a silver chain around his neck. The only thing that looked off about him was the small *PAW Patrol* bag, but it was essential for the next part of his escape plan.

Jimmy exited the vehicle and stepped onto the hot concrete lot, immediately feeling the sun's heat on his skin as he stretched out his arms. He couldn't lock the car, but he didn't need to. It had served his purpose, and if all went well, he could just leave it there for the police to find and return to the poor person he'd stolen it from. He patted the roof and thanked Fred for the hotwiring lesson. Then he started walking towards the mall, and saw his destination ahead. With the confidence of a man who had injected himself with 100 ml of testosterone, he walked through the doors, tipped his trilby hat to the concierge, and proceeded with swagger. He moved as if he was untouchable, his ice-cool exterior hard enough to deflect bullets

He knew destiny had conspired with serendipity to bring him where he was right this minute. Soon, he'd have his passport and money—plenty of it. He'd return to Canada in a few hours and reunite with his lovely wife and son. Life was good, and his nightmare vacation would be over soon. Jimmy took a seat and waited. It was relatively quiet that morning. He remembered his finishing touch and reached for a cigar in his shirt pocket, tasting the bitterness on his tongue. He lit the cigar by flipping the flashy silver zippo lighter with his other hand and took a few deep puffs. Although he wasn't much of a smoker, this was an extraordinary occasion.

Behind his Ray-Ban reflective glasses, Jimmy closed his eyes and concentrated. He played a movie memory of his time in Mexico, like a cine film flickering away. Looking back at the crazy few weeks, images flashed before his eyes:

From losing the wallet to the noisy Guadalajara contingent. Vincente's head. *Noche de Rábanos* and Fred's festive radish crocodile that had devoured someone's arms and legs. Christmas dinner, laced with Imodium, the Christmas crackers and guns drawn at him and little Max. The bogus search warrant, missing passports and Armardo's honey trap money. Suzie the Sheep. Armardo and Raul's enemas and the 'identical' twins. Sober Bob's crazy round of golf and Deaf Barry's insane inventions. Drug dealing. Friendship with Fred, the affable cartel sicario. Fred's pink sombrero-wearing psychopathic brother. The little guy taking over $100,000 from the cartel, winning $20 million at roulette, only to blow it all on black. Fred's dreadful Alamo-obsessed poetry, as well as his overwhelming kindness and his sense of humour. Lucy's witty and spunky three amigas. Finally, the hilarious yet brave Hollywood husbands, Marcus and Bradley.

Now that's blockbuster material—maybe I'll get Marcus and Bradley to produce it. Tears started rolling down his face again when he thought about Lucy and Max; he loved them very much. But he wasn't sad. All these precious moments had led Jimmy to total peace, and now he was in his perfect place, exactly where he was meant to be.

He finally decided on the title of a new book, settling on *Karma is a Bee-atch* after all. He envisioned how he might make another bucket full of cash, upsetting more academics and know-it-alls. Maybe it was all just luck, or perhaps the plan of God. It could even be the Red Radish Virgin; after all his close shaves this trip, he'd be willing to concede she might be real. Good vibes flooded through him; he was really *feeling it*. Those warm fuzzies were now back in his tummy for the first time in what felt like forever. He was calm yet focused, determined, and confident as he sat at the roulette table at the Casino *Cielo Ardiente* (the Burning Sky Casino), a mere ten-minute walk from the Canadian Consulate.

Just this once, he would try to make the universe right again. Jimmy hated that he would break a promise to Lucy; however, this was life or death, and he was choosing life.

The croupier announced, "Ladies and gentlemen, place your bets."

Jimmy put on his earbuds and shuffled his playlist. The first song he heard was perfect, the '70s classic 'Burning Sky' by Bad Company, the same song that had inspired him to send Fred to the Crystal Palace Casino in the first place. He placed all his chips and money from Max's little blue case on the table.

He peered over his sunglasses at the croupier and looked at his name badge. It read 'Marcus Gonzales.' With a broad smile, he whispered, "You just had to be called Marcus!" Jimmy's heart raced excitedly as he let out his battle cry.

"Marcus, you tool—I'm betting EVERYTHING on RED!"

Prologue

The Book. The Man. The Legend.

RED'S HOT! BY **J.W.H. MYERS** *"How to make a BILLION DOLLARS in the time it takes for a farmer to milk two cows by hand."*

In Jimmy's words, he wrote *Red's Hot!* to help and inspire all the poor people in the world. Jimmy believed he was driven by a sincere effort to reduce global poverty. As an outspoken armchair hockey enthusiast and self-proclaimed genius, Jimmy credited others for his success. For example, Marcus, the croupier at the Palm Springs Casino, made derogatory comments to Jimmy after he'd shared his *Red's Hot!* strategy with him.

Marcus threw no punches when he said, "Mr Myers, you are an idiot!" He followed up with a dire warning: "Your strategy will lead you to financial disaster!" Fortunately, Jimmy's inner voice reminded him Marcus probably had the IQ of watermelon and was also an employee of the casino. Therefore, it was in his best interest to spread roulette misinformation.

Red's Hot! was more than a successful statistical equation to Jimmy. It was an overwhelming feeling, a drive, a desire, almost sexual. Red was not only a colour that amplified Valentine's Day passions or Amsterdam hookers with songs written by Sting—red was indeed a scorching hot hue. There was no turning back for him; it was all or nothing.

According to Lucy, who loved Jimmy to bits, her husband was not someone who was ever lacking in confidence. "Jimmy is, and always will be, a legend in his own eyes." Despite his hubris, Lucy loved him and treasured the confidence he carried when he became excited about a project, concept, or idea.

Walking away from the Palm Springs Casino, rich beyond his wild imagination, Jimmy sent a selfie of himself to Marcus the croupier, literally swimming the backstroke in an inflatable pool of dollar bills. Cognizant of his heart's desire to end world poverty once and for all, he hashtagged well into the night with hashtag 'Be Filthy Rich Tomorrow.' This also included many smiley face and brain-exploding emojis.

Jimmy woke up the next day expecting social media to be one colossal sea of hashtag 'Reds Hot' tweets, retweets, and tags, and he was shocked to find he had been placed in social media prison on multiple platforms due to misinformation breaches.

"It's the damn Illuminati!" he complained to Lucy. "They just don't want me to end world poverty!" Myers hated conspiracy theories; however, he felt the Russian oligarchs and other well-known billionaires who loved the wealth differential between the 'haves' and 'have-nots' were trying to dowse his red-hot revolutionary flames.

Not perturbed by the Illuminati, Jimmy was determined to reach the masses by publishing *Red's Hot!* himself.

He produced, marketed, and distributed *Red's Hot!* in an old-school paperback format, putting his own finances into the project. The strategy was simple. All the unemployed scallywag track-suited Mancunians, impoverished Kentucky elevator attendants, Canadian school janitors, Ethiopian cow farmers, displaced indigenous Aztecs, and Albanian street-sweepers of the world had to do was to read the book and follow Jimmy's profoundly simple directions to the letter. Then, their lives would change beyond belief. Just do exactly as Jimmy had instructed, and *BOOMSHAKALAKA!* Every person on earth could become an instant millionaire.

As Jimmy said: "Anyone can live their best and richest life!"

Yet, people still asked, "Why not black?"

Even Jimmy's best friend, Darunn LeBronco, a dart-playing buddy and ER nurse, was concerned about Jimmy's focus on all things red at the expense of kinder and more inclusive colours like taupes, pastel lavenders, sumptuous sundials, tranquil blues and apricot crushes, which, he felt were all "cheeky, brave, fearless, emasculating yet empowering."

With tongue-in-cheek, Jimmy reminded his friend roulette tables had yet to include Darunn's array of politically correct colours. Until casinos became more alert to their own unconscious biases and lenses of inequality, oppression, and injustice, the stark choice was, unfortunately, that of red, black, or green.

For some, the sudden obsession with the colour red raised societal tensions that demanded greater social inclusion. Jimmy received hostile letters, emails, and odd anonymous death threats from liberal university campuses. Even kindergarten staff and pupils joined the melee of angst against the publication. Social media blew up with aggressive tropes and hashtags like hashtag 'Better Dead Than Red' and hashtag 'Come Back 2 Black.'

The red versus black divide had become a figurative red-hot potato. Red was seen as a racist and non-inclusive colour. In stark contrast, black was seen as a tolerant and multicultural non-colour.

Jimmy couldn't understand people's lack of common sense. He said, "Red is, and always will be, hot. How the Dickens can the colour black ever be hot?" He continued to rant, "Any idiot knows the hotter the matter, the longer the wavelength. Red is associated with longer wavelengths. Even an abattoir worker with an IQ of twenty-three would know hot water faucet handles are marked red, not black!"

However, the red versus black hullabaloo reached new levels of controversy; modern ideologies in certain liberal-run municipalities proposed changing all warning signs from red to black. Some of the 'Danger,' 'Stop,' and 'Halt' road signs were changed to all-black lettering on an all-black background, creating an entirely black alert, which caused not only an increase in income due to traffic violations but also a surge in injuries caused by accidents.

Jimmy was aware there could be further non-political pushback regarding his book. To placate all the "I've lost all my savings . . . and my house . . . and my job . . . and my marriage" cry-babies and whingers, Jimmy added a crystal-clear caveat in the book.

"IF you don't FEEL it, then DON'T follow the process."

As a clear disclaimer, Jimmy also included this wise yet honest warning: "If you don't sense it (red), if you're angry, sad, or just not *feeling it*, then red will mess you up like a mofo!"

To complicate matters, in Myers's book, there were either good or bad reds. *Good-red* included:

- Eating Red Delicious apples.

- Listening to songs like 99 Red Balloons.

- Focusing on the bullseye on a dartboard.

Good-red feelings also included repeating old nursery rhymes as mantras, like: "London's burning, London's burning. Fetch the engines, fetch the engines. Fire, fire. Fire, fire!" *Red's Hot!* couldn't be simpler.

On the other hand, **bad-red** was to be avoided at all costs, like an outbreak of measles. There were obvious bad reds to avoid:

- Being over-aware of red stop signs.

- Looking at red fire hydrants recently peed on by dogs.

Avoiding all things black leading up to (pre-roulette) or when playing roulette was paramount to Jimmy's teachings. For example:

- Never look at a murder of crows.

- Don't listen to Black Sabbath music.

- Don't focus on Dracula's hairline.

According to Myers, *non-red-hot* things would ruin any chance a person had of owning their first $10 million yacht.

Jimmy even published complex statistical concepts like probability axioms, implicit differentiation and improper integration, power series and finite and infinite sets to prove his astuteness and brilliance. He said the mathematics backed up his *Red's Hot!* revelation. It was as simple as solving $x3+y3+z3=k$, the classically easy-to-solve Diophantine equation. However, he certainly didn't expect a goat farmer from Kabul to be too well-versed in calculus, so he further simplified the math by including red-coloured graphs with exponential curves so even the biggest idiot in the world, like Marcus the croupier, could understand his red-centric roulette rationale.

In his book, Jimmy stated a believer, or one of his *red disciples*, could, through twenty simple "red bets" and a mere $20 investment, be guaranteed to win $20,971,520. Jimmy was happy to spoon-feed his readers all they needed to become outrageously wealthy, yet there was growing societal resistance to this pedagogy.

Jimmy went above and beyond, advising people to wear headphones during the process when at the casino and encouraging them to make playlists of red-hot songs, chants, and spicy-hot nursery rhymes. Finally, since Jimmy had become rich beyond his wildest dreams, he had many opportunities to act philanthropically, and by doing so, he made many new friends. Sensibly, he warned incredible wealth came with great responsibility and a profound increase in popularity—and scrutiny.

Myers reminisced that at one point in his meteoric rise to outrageous wealth and social standing, he was voted one of British Columbia's 'best kissers' in the popular *Coastal Life* magazine. Lucy took this achievement with a grain of salt; she concurred although he was an excellent kisser, Jimmy voted for himself 13,467 times in the free phone-in poll.

Unfortunately, Jimmy's rise was stalled by a massive class-action lawsuit from the many ex-devotees and ex-disciples of *Red's Hot!* According to him, those losers didn't *feel it* and lost everything they possessed. Unfortunately, that wasn't an argument that held up well in court. Jimmy settled out-of-court, which bit deeply into his financial pockets and his growing braggadocio.

Serendipity led Jimmy and Lucy to read other articles in *Coastal Life*. They read an interesting article that had been sandwiched between an advert for lawnmowers and his 'How I won the Best Kisser' piece, which, incidentally, included Jimmy's endorsements for certain lip balms, breath fresheners and a cinnamon and red pepper toothpaste. The *Discover Mexico* article encouraged readers to visit Mexico's beautiful shores. It led to a eureka moment for the couple, giving them the courage and inspiration to get away from the pressures of living a ridiculously filthy rich and successful life. Having been caught up in the wake of the *Red's Hot!* controversy, legal actions, and snide remarks made by shelf-fillers in grocery stores, the Myers family headed down to Mexico for a few months to relax, recharge their batteries, and remove themselves from drama. For Jimmy, it was also a chance to come up with a new bestseller.

Jimmy swore to Lucy he would steer away from all things roulette, especially the colour red. Lucy, satisfied with his promise, suggested they go to the little coastal town of Los Piñata, where some of her besties lived, to escape the harsh Canadian winter. The rest, as they say, is history.

Acknowledgements

Sombrero is, obviously, a work of fiction, but my own experiences loosely inspired some of the incidents or situations. Mexico is also one of my favourite countries in the world. You'll find Mexico both beautiful and safe to visit. The people, culture, food, and vibe are all magnificent. The Yankee Swap (Suzy the Sheep), losing wallets, social constructs, revelations from an oversharing cab driver, curling conversations, Love Thy Neighbours and the River of Crocodiles—were actual events that I've managed to totally embellish. Oh, the fun of writing fiction.

I want to extend a colossal thumbs up to my (at the time of writing) 'nearly' son-in-law, Jibbert, who strives to outmatch the family at *Catan, Ticket to Ride* and *Contagion* during our family game nights. He is an exceptional individual who made me laugh with his absurd concept of winning millions at the roulette table through a daring all-on-red tactic.

Each year in Mexico, I have the pleasure of meeting my gringo/gringa buddies, and I want to thank and acknowledge them. These individuals' kind and beautiful personalities were a fount of inspiration for the characters in the story. We thank Bob for allowing my partner in crime and me to reside in his exquisite condominium during our visits and for Jacki and her unique, quirky personality and kindness. Julie's warm-hearted and caring nature as a sister-in-law is truly appreciated. Pammo always makes us laugh with her sarcasm and bluntness. Patty and her excellent staff, who make the best mango and passion fruit margaritas worldwide, deserve a special shout-out. The inspiration for 'My Three-Legged Friend' comes from Bill, Gayle, and their beloved sausage dog TULO—they call these doggies wiener dogs this side of the Pond, but I think that's rude!

I want to thank Jibbert, Shelley, Suzanne, Bill, Sue, and Sian as alpha readers. Thanks to the Beta readers, Tiffany and the talented Oskar, for their terrific feedback. Shout out to Gabe for his help with the editing.

My heartfelt thanks also go to Anja and Gina, who have always believed in me. They encouraged this silly old goat to share his funny stories and insisted that I put pen to paper in the first place.

Finally, to say that the lovely Shelley has been a tower of strength while writing this (and another book) is an understatement. She is beautiful inside and out and makes the best cupcakes and beef barley soup in the world.

About the Author

Denny Darke was born in the UK, raised in Brighton & Hove, and now lives on boujee Vancouver Island in Western Canada. His love of dark humour helped him successfully survive careers as both a police officer and as a child protection social worker. His long-suffering wife describes him as a very silly individual forever practising his terrible impersonations and embarrassing her whenever they are out in public. Denny has four children that have yet to disown him.

Visit Denny's Website for additional content, stories, chat, book signings and news about upcoming releases: WWW.DARKEMATTER.CA

Printed in Great Britain
by Amazon

43417804R00179